James Cooper Allen was born in Liverpool but over the years has lived in Germany, France, Spain and Jersey. When not writing, he likes to spend time pursuing his other passions which include painting and listening to music, be it classical or rock. He is also an avid sports' fan, football and cricket being top of the list. His other main interests are travelling and sampling the local cuisine. Although, if the truth be known, his real claim to fame was when aged sixteen, he hitched a lift through the Mersey Tunnel in the back of Paul McCartney's brand-new Ford classic car.

It doesn't matter what you do or how much you have in life, it is who you have beside you and I am lucky enough to have my wife, Karen.

James Cooper Allen

The Fears That Bind

AUSTIN MACAULEY PUBLISHERS™

LONDON * CAMBRIDGE * NEW YORK * SHARJAH

A CIP catalogue record for this title is available from the British Library.

ISBN 9781398450660 (Paperback)
ISBN 9781398450677 (ePub e-book)

www.austinmacauley.com

First Published 2022
Austin Macauley Publishers Ltd®
1 Canada Square
Canary Wharf
London
E14 5AA

I would like to thank Christine in Spain, Suzanne, Colin Vibert, Willie Mac, Chloe, Pat Pops, Ronnie and all those who gave me encouragement. Without their enthusiastic input I might never have finished the book.

Forgive your enemies, but never forget their faces.
– John F. Kennedy

Be just in all things.
– S. H. A. Lapidus

Prologue
Northern Bosnia, November 1995

In the end, nobody could deny the day had gone well. It might have taken hours of struggling through pot-holed dirt tracks and pissing down rain, but at last they'd reached their objective, a narrow two-lane road that wound its way along the valley floor. Then, to everyone's relief, the downpour had stopped and for the first time in days were able to see a pale blue sky with a scudding of white clouds high above the tall green canopy. The next vital question was the Croatian army or, to be more precise, their exact whereabouts. The swift answer coming by way of a mortar shell landing far away on his right flank. This in itself was worrying, considering there was supposed to be a cease-fire in place. "What do you think, Boss, is it safe?" asked his radio operator.

"Jebi ga! Fuck it and trust no one," he swore. The English earthiness of his outburst giving it a more pleasing sound, but no matter the danger, he still had a decision to make. "Safe or not, we can't hang around here all day. Tell the troops in No. 2 transporter to fan out and make sure the way ahead is clear." From his position on the side of a heavily wooded slope, he heard the sound of twenty machine pistols being cocked and minutes later watched the platoon cautiously disappear down through the tree line.

One last check of his field map confirmed it was the correct road and a thumb's down gesture to his radio operator, the sign for them to begin their own descent. Yet they'd only taken a few steps, when the high-pitched sound of an engine could be heard from further up the valley.

"Wait!" he hissed. "I think there's a car coming."

Heeding his outburst, the soldiers nearest to him halted in mid-stride, their ears listening for whatever was on the other side of the hill. Using his field glasses, he scanned the valley below and once satisfied the troops were within the cover that ran along the road, re-focused on the bend. The vehicle was now close enough for him to hear the pitch and whine of a supercharged engine, its revs constantly changing as the driver moved up and down through the gears, man and machine in perfect harmony. Then, with a practiced ease, he doubled the clutch, gunned the engine and with a press of the accelerator sent it racing around the bend where it hurtled towards them.

The thickness of the trees below made it near impossible to identify its make. Yet within seconds knew that this was no normal car, but a beautiful vintage 'Roadster', with a long blue bonnet, narrow windscreen and huge polished chrome headlights.

Pointing to the speeding vehicle, he gave a 'thumbs up' to the radio operator, the sign for him to inform the troops they should let it pass. Yet before he'd been able to send the message, a short sharp burst of gunfire came echoing up from the valley below and both men were stunned to see the car begin to weave from side to side, as the driver fought to keep control. They then watched opened mouthed, as it made one last desperate swerve and with tyres squealing in protest, clipped the roadside barrier.

This was enough to trigger off a series of somersaults that resulted in it flipping over on its roof and side for what felt like an interminable amount of time. Then in one last tumble, the car had landed with a shuddering crash the right way up, but now facing in the opposite direction from which it had travelled.

Momentarily shocked and thinking in the spectacular confusion they might be under some sort of attack; it took but seconds to realise the gunfire could only have come from his side of the road. Still confused, he ordered everyone to stay undercover and cautiously made his way down through the trees, until he'd reached the tangle of brushwood that ran alongside the barrier.

The valley air felt as if it was suspended; a silent vacuum in which nothing appeared to be moving. In the shifting light, he stepped around the barrier and observed the smouldering wreck that sat a short distance away. The passenger door having been ripped from its hinges, lay somewhere in between the sight still fresh in his eyes, the sound still ringing in his ears, but that wasn't the only object lying in the road. Spread-eagled to one side, he could see the bloodied form of a middle-aged woman, a closer inspection revealing she was grey-haired and dressed in an expensive looking herringbone jacket. In addition, she was wearing a tweed skirt, brogue shoes and pair of thick green woollen tights through which a trickle of blood had begun to seep, with more pooling below a face that stared lifelessly into the distant horizon.

Crouching down, he was about to look for any visible signs of life when the badge pinned to her lapel came into view. A winged staff with serpent entwined said it was the universal sign for a doctor. "Oh no," he whispered. Momentarily taken aback and mystified as to why she should be here, he stepped around her body and shuffled off in the direction of the shattered vehicle. On his unwilling trek, he'd gone but a few paces, when he noticed a coat or bulky item of clothing that looked to have been thrown clear of the car.

It was only then did he glimpse the tiny hand protruding from the corner of what was a travelling shawl and realise the child was being taken somewhere in the dead doctor's car. A lack of movement and past experience said there was no way it might have survived the crash. "Unbelievable," he whispered, wishing to hell there could be some way out of this shit disaster.

Beneath his boots, the crunch of broken glass made it near impossible to approach the car silently, as it sat with a trickle of steam coming from under its sleek bonnet and seconds later saw the crushed Bugatti radiator grille. "Is that a French automobile?" he muttered, still confused as to why such a vehicle would be so deep in the Yugoslav war zone. "Jesus Madonna, what a mess!" he cursed. The roof was half collapsed, both front tyres had blown and its classic windscreen was cracked and shattered. 'A few minutes ago,' he thought, 'and this had been a thing of immense beauty, but sadly was now a smoking wreck!'

With another weary shake of the head, he moved around to the passenger side and stooped to look through the empty square that had once held the door. Drifting from deep within its luxury interior came the unmistakable smell of polished wood and vintage leather. Slumped against the crumpled steering wheel he could see the male driver, who in the cartwheeling catastrophe had stood no chance of survival. "Seat belts weren't an option when this beauty was created," he murmured. A closer look confirmed that he too was middle-aged, had greying hair and like his female companion, wore the same conservative clothing. Reaching inside, he was about to ease the bloodied torso away from the steering wheel as a last check for any signs of life, when he had another shock.

"Fuck no!" On the driver's lapel was the same unmistakeable badge as that worn by the woman and a plastic covered one lay on the passenger seat beside him. "Jesus Madonna! Two doctors?" he gasped in disbelief. "Why would anyone in their right mind take the risk of travelling unescorted through this point of the conflict?" Still angry and unable to understand, he hurled the plastic emblem at the walnut dashboard and cried, "You stupid crazy imbeciles!"

His next unenviable task was in trying to discover how all this had come to pass. Yet only needed to see the six finger-sized bullet holes in the side of the car to confirm his suspicions.

"Who opened fire?" he shouted. "These people are not soldiers and no-one gave the order to shoot!"

A sudden gust of wind rustled through the trees as he waited for an answer, but as the seconds ticked by no one replied. "I want to know who opened fire!" he screamed again, but as before, there was only silence. "Christ," he swore and then saw his second-in-command appearing through the undergrowth.

"We've got company," he whispered, "and I think it's time we got the hell out of here!" The urgency in his voice leaving no room for argument.

"Okay, okay," he replied, yet in his own mind knew this whole situation was shit. The two doctors and the child were dead and like the tragedy strewn across this and many other valley floors, nothing he could do would change it. Life and death, even for these people of good intention, was transient, one minute you're here and the next you're gone! 'Fucking Karma!' he thought bitterly.

"Radio?" he screamed.

"Here boss!" came the reply.

"Tell the drivers to get their arses down here, now!"

He pointed to the car door. "Throw that in the ditch and then clear the road. But first I need four men to help place the lady back in the car, I'll take care of the child myself." Kneeling down, he gathered up the shawl and carried it the short distance to the still smouldering wreck. Once the clumsy-fingered troops had finished arranging the dead woman in the passenger seat, he gently placed the baby on her lap. He then made a quick sign of the cross and turned away.

"Okay, let's move!" he shouted, the troops needing no further encouragement as they began to clamber aboard the waiting transporters. Taking a seat in the rear of the last truck, he watched in silence until they'd rounded a bend and left the disaster behind. A few kilometres further down the road saw them turning off onto a hidden dirt track that would take them into a different sector of the war zone. At almost the same time, the rain began to fall again and a UN peacekeeping patrol slowed to a halt alongside the still smoking Bugatti.

Part One

Liverpool, 2015
Saturday, August Bank Holiday

The seconds were ticking by as the girl finished her text message and pressed the *send* button. "That should do," she said with a smile. A glance at the screen said it was nearly 8.00 pm and worried she might miss the bus into town, decided to cut through the park via the 'hanging gate'. It was from within these same familiar surroundings that she heard a strange rustling sound from behind, but before she could turn to look, a vice-like hand grabbed her around the throat and began to drag her backwards into the bushes.

Gasping for air and desperately trying to break free, it was only then did she realise her assailant must have been hiding just inside the park entrance, but more fear was yet to come. From the corner of her eye she caught the tell-tale glint of a knife, the very sight of it making her rear and buck with a renewed sense of urgency, her shoes flying through the air like two uncontrollable windmills. *No! No!* she screamed inside, whilst attempting to head-butt the face behind.

Then, and without warning, an agonising jolt of pain surged through her body, as the point of the knife made a hole in her dress and the soft skin on her side. Despite the blood beginning to trickle down her thigh, she'd continued to fight like a wild animal until a voice from behind whispered three words, "Silence and kneel!"

The acrid stink of bad breath and stale tobacco filled her nostrils, as he eased the grip around her throat and allowed her to breathe. In another well-practiced move, he grabbed the hair at the back of her head, viciously twisted it into a knot and began to force her face down into the grass. As she fell to her knees, the tears began to flow and she heard him whisper another grim warning, "Remember, silence or more pain."

Moments later and she could feel him using the tip of his knife to split the seam of her dress and when done, part it up over her thighs. Seeing just the faintest glimmer of hope, she closed her eyes and began to pray, 'Oh Jesus, whatever happens, please let me live!'

Then she heard the scream!

Aintree

Carson was about to throw himself on the settee and watch 'Match of the Day 2', when his mobile sprang into life. "Give me a break," he groaned, wondering who'd be calling him at 7.25 am on a Sunday morning. Then gave a louder groan when he saw who it was. "Jacko?"

"Sorry Guv, I know it's your day off, but this is urgent."

"Okay," he grunted. "Fire away."

"Duty Officer at Central has just called. Seems a young male and female have been found dead in Junkies Corner."

"Is that the one in Waytree Park?"

"Yes Guv and directly opposite the Highwater housing Estate."

"So what's the big deal?"

"The boy is black and the girl's white."

Carson sat up. "Christ, you are not serious?"

"That's what they tell me."

It was so long ago Carson couldn't remember the last time he'd been near Junkies Corner, but first things first. "When you say *dead*, Jacko, *how* exactly?"

"Don't have any details yet, but according to the report, it looks as if they've both been stabbed to death."

"So why aren't CID sorting this out?"

"From what I hear they're busy as hell and probably the reason why they called us in."

DCI Nathan Carson ran the 'Merseyside Serious Crime Unit', or the 'S.C.U.' as it was more commonly known. A small elite squad of detectives, whose normal role was to investigate murder or corruption in the highest of places, but this didn't quite fit the bill.

"Pick me up ASAP."

"On my way, Guv, be about twenty minutes."

'Match of the Day 2' and Steven Gerrard's superb winning goal became a forgotten pleasure, as Carson imagined the media circus that was destined to follow. "What a pain," he winced. "This would have been bad enough if it'd involved a couple of crazed 'druggies', but two dead teenagers; one black and the other white? Not a chance."

Collecting him from his apartment in Aintree, Jacko sped along the A247, looking for the main intersection leading to the Highwater area and supposed crime scene.

Waytree Park, Carson remembered, was a throwback to a more genteel time, one when the locals could go for a stroll within its pleasant leafy expanses and long before they erected the tall wire mesh fence. This was a constant reminder that beyond this 'Faux Pas' cage lay the west entrance to the dreaded Highwater housing estate. Local legend said the 'Estate' had once been a pleasant mix of semi-detached houses, long before the tower blocks had begun to sprout from the earth like a cancerous crop. This was the usual *balls up* from the 60s and 70s. The rights and wrongs of those who'd made a fortune in allowing their construction, being a matter for the historians, or in the real world, the 'Court of Human Rights'.

In an attempt to relocate the poor and needy from within the city slums, they'd tried to modernise their lives whether they liked it or not. Thus creating a huge diaspora of people who, over the years, had become either isolated or unemployed, plus the other lazy sods who didn't give a shit. In this neck of the woods, crime and drugs were just an everyday occurrence.

Reaching the park entrance, the uniforms acknowledged Jacko's flash of the headlights by lifting the tape and allowing them to pass between the two granite pillars. Once inside they met a winding path that circumnavigated the park and were pleased to learn there'd once been a bubbling ornate fountain at its narrower end. Like most things of value, this had long since been dug up and replaced with a skateboard area. Despite this gratuitous sop to modern day destruction, a multitude of trees and bushes had still managed to blossom and bloom.

Approaching the crime scene, Carson could see the small car parking area set back beyond the wire fence, more significantly the wire gate that hung open providing an easy access to the park's grassy expanses.

Waytree Crescent

Steffi was surprised to find her son sitting at the kitchen table.

"Hi Kristian, you're up early for a Sunday, everything okay?"

"Yeah, just going for a kick about with Tommo in the park."

'Tommo' was Tom Hart, his friend from next door, and only a major flood or earthquake would stop them from playing football together.

"I don't suppose you've heard anything from your sister?" she asked casually.

"Ma, you know Kelly would never call me," he muttered. "Well, not unless she was about to give me grief." Another moment went by before he looked up. "Besides, I thought she was meeting Anton last night. Wasn't he picking her up by the park?"

"Yes," she replied, "but when I got home from work, she'd already left and normally, I'd have heard from her by now."

They both glanced at the clock on the wall showing 8.30 am.

"She's probably still in bed," he said offhandedly.

"No," his mother replied. "I've already checked."

Kristian suddenly remembered his older sister would have stayed the night at her boyfriend's flat. *Oops, I shouldn't have said that.*

Steffi glanced at the clock again. *I'll give it another half hour*, she thought, but now that Kristian had mentioned the new boyfriend, it made her stop and think. Anton was twenty-four and to some people that might seem a fair difference in age, but thankfully, Kelly was a very mature nineteen-year-old. Besides, it was she who'd insisted that her daughter went on 'the pill', seeing as they didn't need any unplanned additions to the family.

She was about to pop a slice of bread in the toaster when Kristian sat up. "*Wow!* Get this Ma, Tommo has just sent me a text. He's opposite the 'hanging gate' and said the police have blocked off the carpark. According to him, there are ambulances everywhere!" Steffi was more than familiar with the 'hanging gate', having used it many a time to cut across Waytree Park.

Kristian scanned the screen for a moment longer, before replying with his own message. Steffi watched as his fingers raced across the keyboard, his skill and dexterity amazing her, yet for the younger generation, this was their everyday means of communicating with one another. Reaching for the kettle, she was about to pour herself a mug of tea when he whispered. "*Holy moly!*" This time, however, it was slow and through pursed lips.

Now interested, Steffi took a seat and waited.

"Just had a new text from Tommo."

"And?"

"There's a rumour saying two kids have been found dead in the park."

"Good God!" she gasped. "Does it say who?"

"No, but he thinks it happened in Junkies Corner just behind the carpark and everyone's talking about them being *shivved*."

"Bloody knives!" she swore, realising they must have been stabbed to death. "I wonder if they were druggies?" she queried, knowing it wasn't called 'Junkies Corner' for nothing.

Kristian shook his head. "I don't think so, or Tommo would have told me." He then shrugged and apologised, "Sorry Ma, I know you hate knives, especially with you being a nurse."

She stared at him in frustration and thought, *If only you knew*! Some arrivals on the wards were a real nightmare, with many of the injuries caused by gangs fighting with knives. At almost the same moment her own mobile rang; it was her best friend and workmate, as well as her lift to work. "Hi Anita."

"Morning Steffi, I'll be outside your place at nine, okay?"

"Yeah, no problem, although Kristian says something serious has been happening in the park," giving her a quick up date of what she knew. It was Anita's week to do 'the work run' as they called it, with their shift beginning at 10.00 this morning and finishing at 8.00 tonight. Rising from the table, she was about to collect her clean uniform from behind the door, when she stopped and said, "I have to phone Kelly." Going to speed dial, she rang her daughter's number and listened as the call went through its usual functions, but there was no answer. Sitting down, she rang it again, only to receive the same message, *number unavailable.*

"Kristian," she said without looking up from the screen,

"Yes Ma?"

"Ring your sister."

"What?" he gasped.

"Do as I say and ring your bloody sister!" she insisted.

With a mystified shrug, he rang Kelly's number, listened for a minute before replying, "Sorry Ma, it says her phone's switched off."

Steffi looked at the time on her mobile phone and the clock on the wall; both were showing 8.45 am.

Waytree Park

Carson nodded to the young policeman standing guard. "Find out who's in charge, Jacko, while I have a quick look around." The first thing to catch his eye was the two forensics taping off an area that included the wire gate and the hedge beside it. He was still watching them with interest when Jacko returned with a tall uniform in tow. "This is Sergeant Fitzpatrick, Guv, who's the Scene of Crime Officer."

Carson gave a sigh of relief, this SOCO had professional stamped all over him. "It's early, Sergeant, and supposed to be my day off, so a quick lowdown would be greatly appreciated."

Recognising the familiar face of DCI Carson, Fitzpatrick wasted no time in bringing him up to speed. "Just before 7.00 am this morning, an old lady was taking her dog for a walk when it disappeared into the bushes, began barking like mad and refused to come out. Unsure what to do next, the woman followed it through the hedge and discovered the bloodied body of a young girl lying in the grass on the other side. Assuming she'd been murdered, the pensioner began to shout for help and a couple out jogging heard her cries.

The woman was badly shaken, but able to tell them about the dead body. The male jogger decided to look for himself and found the girl just as she'd described. He was about to make his exit, when he spotted another body lying half under the bushes. This, we now know, was the young black kid, who according to the jogger, was literally *covered in blood!* The uniforms arrived on site at 7.05 am, verified who'd made the callout and proceeded to make a recce of the clearing. Having confirmed there were no obvious signs of life, they secured the area and called in the cavalry."

Carson pointed to the bushes within the taped off area. "Am I right in saying our crime scene is behind there?"

"Yes Sir."

"Which is Junkies Corner?"

"That's right."

"It's been years since I was last here, Sergeant, so another quick recap would help."

"The locals gave it that name," said Fitzpatrick, "and it's been here for as long as I can remember. I think it was somewhere for the gardeners to store the fallen leaves in autumn time, but many years since it's been used for that purpose. The normal way in is through a wooden gate situated around the side. There again, you can just as easily push your way through the bushes like the old lady did.

"Anybody hear or see anything?"

"Not as far as I know."

Carson pointed to the other side of the wire fence. "What about the carpark?"

"It's been sealed off since we arrived on site."

"Okay, just make sure that zilch goes in or out unless we say so."

"I'll guarantee nothing moves, Sir."

"Another thing, Sergeant, see if you can organise some sight screens. It feels like the cuffin zoo around here."

Fitzpatrick smiled. "They're already on their way."

Carson nodded toward the bushes. "Okay Jacko, let's go visit the Time Team."

Junkies Corner, he remembered, was around 20 ft. wide and 40 ft. long. On one side was a wooden fence that ran its full length, against which he assumed the gardeners of the past had stored their dead leaves; the 8 ft. tall hedge on the park side planted as a convenient way of hiding the mess behind. Spying a shrivelled condom lying in the grass, he could see why the place was well frequented and would explain the empty beer cans and cigarette ends strewn here and there.

Having donned the regulatory protective gloves and shoe covers, he and Jacko were about to enter the crime scene proper, when he saw one Forensic holding what appeared to be the remote control for a model aircraft. Then to his amazement, watched as a large circular device with four sets of rotor blades took to the air.

"Looks like some kind of camera drone," explained Jacko.

Only to hear Carson mutter, "This is getting more like *Star Wars* every cuffin day."

Ever curious, Jacko sidled alongside the operator and whispered, "I wouldn't get too close to the Estate with that. The kids around here are likely to shoot it down *and* they'll want points for who gets it first!" At the far end of the clearing, they could see a group of Forensics dressed in their usual oversized 'Michelin Man' suits. Two were crouched beside the girl lying in the grass, the others standing over what could only be the boy.

An impatient Carson was waiting for someone to give them the official nod, when a burly Forensic looked up, passed his clipboard to his companion and made his way towards them. Off came his gloves, glasses and finally the head cover of his all in one suit. "Hello Nathan, I've been expecting you."

Carson's face lit up, as he recognised one of the finest forensic pathologists in the country. "Well, I'll be damned, Reece Armstrong, my old mate, how the hell are you?"

"Stressed out to say the least."

"Remember Jacko?"

"Yes, of course I do, how are you, Sergeant Jackson?"

"Very well," he replied.

A smiling Carson was delighted to see his friend. "I thought you were desk-bound these days?"

"I am and supposed to be playing golf in an hour's time, but when I stopped by at the office, this lot came in," waving a hand. "Still, it is holiday time and they're short of staff, so how could I refuse?"

Carson glanced to the 'eyes in the sky'. "Are we on live TV?"

"Digital Topographical Imaging," enthused Reece. "Or DTI to you and me. This is clever stuff, Nathan, because it means we don't miss a thing, especially at an exposed crime scene like this one."

Carson watched the Drone for a second longer and then gave a sigh. "Care to enlighten us?"

The pathologist pointed to the bodies lying in the grass. "As you can see, we've got two dead teenagers; one a white female aged around eighteen or nineteen. The other, a boy of possible West Indian origin and a few years younger."

"How long have they been dead?"

"From the body temperatures and different skin pallor, I'd estimate twelve hours. We had clear skies last night, which meant it was a tad cooler than usual. Taking this into account and judging by the degree of rigor mortis, I'd say around 8.00 pm."

"Do we know how they died?"

"It's early days, but from their visible injuries, I'd say death by wounding."

"Weapon?"

"Some kind of knife, but no sign of it yet."

"Could it be gangland, or maybe drug-related?"

Reece shook his head. "No. The girl was attacked from behind as she came through the gate and then dragged in here."

"Sex attack?"

"Almost certainly."

"What about the boy, Reece, how did he get here?"

"Not sure yet. Maybe he heard a noise and tried to stop it."

"A bad move on his part?"

The pathologist nodded. "Yes, unfortunately for him."

"Both kids, same weapon?" ventured Carson.

"Hard to say at the moment, but it looks that way."

Carson observed the girl lying face down in the grass. She had long natural blonde hair and was wearing a short light blue dress with thin shoulder straps. More noticeable was the tear in the dress that allowed it to be raised up above her tanned thighs, thus exposing her buttocks, which in turn, revealed a light blue thong. "What happened here, Reece?"

"Good question."

"It looks as though it's been deliberately torn in half."

"Too neat for that, Nathan. I'd say the killer used his knife."

"Oh shit, don't tell me this is some kind of mad ritual job."

Reece shrugged. "Can't think of any other explanation at the moment."

Carson began looking for any visible signs of bruising around the girl's rear legs and genitalia. "Was she interfered with sexually?"

"Nothing obvious, but I can't rule it out."

The distinctive aroma of a strong perfume drifted up from the girl's body. "She looks and smells as if she was going out for the night, Reece."

"With that I can agree."

"So where's her handbag and mobile phone?"

"Good question, Nathan, but at the moment there's no sign of them."

"Sex and robbery?" he speculated.

"No way."

"Nevertheless, you reckon she has no handbag or money?"

"None that we can see."

"Surely she *must* have had a mobile, Reece? *Everyone* has a phone these days!"

"We haven't found one yet and until we finish our preliminary investigations, you know we can't move either of the bodies."

Carson acknowledged his predicament with a wry smile before turning his attention to the boy lying under the bush. "What about him? I take it he doesn't have a phone either?"

Reece shook his head and adjusted his glasses. "None that we can see. Although we did find sixty-eight pounds in one trouser pocket and a single Yale key in the other." He then paused for a second. "Oh yes, he had a set of 'Bose' earphones hanging around his neck and a couple of used bus tickets in his hoodie pocket, but just like the girl, no sign of a mobile phone."

Carson's attention was now focused on the boy's blood-stained body. "Sixty-eight quid," he whistled. "That's an awful lot of cabbage for one so young, Reece. Christ man, you couldn't earn that kind of money doing a paper round." He then thought of something else. "Were the bus tickets separate or connected?"

"Connected."

"And both were for the same journey?"

"As far as I can remember, why?"

"I can't see this kid paying twice to make the same trip."

Reece was thoughtful. "You think he wasn't alone on the bus?"

Carson shrugged. "Can't see any other reason, unless he and the girl were travelling together."

"Uh, uh," Reece said with a shake of the head. "The girl was definitely alone when she came through the wire gate."

"Two tickets mean two passengers in my book, Reece, so who's the other one for?"

"You're the detective," he replied with a smile.

A closer scrutiny revealed the usual dress code for the kids of today. Lying half under the bush, he wore a red and white hooded top with 'Liverpool F.C.' emblazoned on the front; dark jeans and a matching pair of red and white trainers. Yet it was hard to ignore the trail of dried blood that began close to the girl's legs and finished somewhere below his midriff. Carson was still pondering the fate of the two victims, when a Forensic searching near the wire fence gave a shout. "I think I've found something, Sir!"

Reece immediately shuffled off in his direction and saw the reason for the call; lying under the lower branches were two mobile phones. To Carson's frustration, instead of answers, this unexpected discovery required lots more detailed examination and procedure. Ten minutes later and Reece returned carrying two mobile phones in separate evidence bags. "I think this is what we've been searching for, gentlemen, but our problems aren't quite over yet, look closer."

Through the clear plastic, Carson could see a pink Samsung mobile in one and a Blackberry in the other, both phones having serious damage to their screens and outer casings.

"Well, that definitely rules out robbery," declared Jacko. "Let's hope the SIM cards are still intact, they should at least help us track down whoever owns them."

Reece scrutinised the mobiles through the transparent bags. "We could be a little late for that Sergeant. It looks to me as if someone has used the concrete fence post to render them completely useless. But if you give us another half hour, we should at least have a better idea of what happened here."

The two detectives left Junkies Corner and headed for the carpark via the hanging gate, where four evidence triangles had been strategically placed on the pavement. "Better be careful, Guv, it looks like 'Lime Street Station' around here."

A quick count said the carpark could accommodate around thirty vehicles and as expected, was fully occupied with a mix of different sized bangers parked in two uneven rows. Some were missing their wheels and rested on bricks, whilst others were without their boot lids and filled with rubbish. To his credit, Sergeant Fitzpatrick had positioned a couple of patrol cars at both ends to ensure nothing could move in or out. "Make sure Forensics check if any of them have been used in the last twelve hours. Oh, and while they're at it, find out who owns them."

"Christ, Guv, there'll be plenty of squeaky arses around the Estate when that happens." he said cheerfully.

Carson nodded and smiled in agreement.

Jacko was about to pass on the message, when he noticed a grey Ford Escort parked nearest the triangles. "Have a look in here, Guv, I reckon you'd need a thermal lance to steal this rusty heap!" Carson peered through the driver-side window and saw a large padlocked device enclosing the gearstick. As an afterthought, he used the back of his hand to feel the bonnet. "I know they'll do a temperature *and* print check on all the cars, but I'd like to know who owns this one in particular."

Leaving Jacko to speak with Forensics, Carson headed in the direction of the uniforms blocking the entrance and for the first time noticed the steadily growing line of hoodies gathering on the grassy bank opposite. As they arrived either singularly, or in a group, it was plain to see how their skin colour would dictate on which side of the entrance they stood. "I take it we haven't had any mothers searching for their missing offspring?"

"Not at the moment, Sir," the taller uniform replied. "Then again, it's early doors for this mob," thumbing to the hoodies. "They don't go to bed until the middle of the night and rarely get up until after midday."

"Okay," he smiled, "but if anything does happen, keep me informed."

"Yes, Sir," they replied as one.

Carson was about to leave the carpark when two TV news wagons screeched to a halt on Park Drive and the crews began setting up their cameras. Following behind, an aging Mercedes soft-top slid to a halt and the familiar shape of Freddy Dickin from the 'Liverpool Evening Post' clambered out. Speaking through the fence, they gave each other a brief nod and sidled out of earshot. Carson, who'd always been happy to let the local press have a head start, gave the reporter a brief summary of events, but as always kept it to the bare bones. "There'll be an official press release later, Freddy, when hopefully we should have some more details."

On their return to Junkies Corner, he and Jacko paused only to let two stretchers pass, each carrying a body bag en-route to the morgue. With the removal of the two dead teenagers, it was now easier to see the crime scene proper and observe the four uniforms doing a fingertip search of the clearing. Once again, both detectives were relieved to see Reece holding up a large evidence bag, with what looked to be a blue leather bag inside.

"We found this under the girl's body."

"Well, that's a stroke of luck."

"Yes, Nathan."

"Do we know if it belongs to her?"

"Not yet, Sergeant. Although we did find some make-up, two sets of door keys and £25 in cash, but nothing that might identify her."

"Cuffin hell," moaned Carson.

"Not so fast, Nathan. Inside a zipped pocket we discovered this." He then produced another bag with a brand-new Apple S6 mobile phone that looked to be completely intact.

"Have you switched it on yet?" asked Carson.

Reece held up the evidence bag, pushed the 'Home' button through the thin plastic and two text messages appeared on screen. The first was timed at 7.58 pm, and said, *Happy birthday, see you soon.* The next at 9.10 pm, but this time asked, *'Where are you?'*

"Is that it?"

"Yes Sergeant, unfortunately, that's all we have."

"Do we know who sent them?"

"Afraid not, the mobile number appears to have been withheld, which usually means it's ex-directory."

"Cuffin iPhones," muttered Carson. "Can we at least switch it on and find out who sent them?"

Reece used a finger to press the home button again and saw *enter passcode* appear on screen. "Not without the correct PIN number."

"So, without the relevant code, we can only assume the phone belongs to the girl?"

"Yes Sergeant, but it shouldn't take long for Forensics to tell us what belongs to whom."

Carson gave a frustrated shake of the head. "How long before we know about the two dead kids?"

"Normally, one my assistants would carry out the autopsy. But seeing as how I've become personally involved, I think it only right I should see it through to the end. Trust me, when we have something positive, you'll be the first person I call."

A troubled Carson was still looking for possible solutions to the murders, when Reece interrupted his thoughts. "I know what you're thinking, Nathan. Whoever did this must have had ice water in his veins, plus the bottle to see it through." He then pointed to the blood-stained grass. "How much time does someone need to murder two teenagers, search for their phones and smash them to pieces?"

"Maybe he thought one of them might have taken a picture, or worse, receive a call with a loud ringing tone that half the Estate might hear."

"Perhaps, but at the moment we just don't know."

"What about the knife, Reece? Do you think he used it to kill both kids?"

"Almost certainly," he replied. "But even though the girl has a wound in her side, there's something really odd in the way she died. Which calls for a more detailed examination."

Carson's brain was still on the merry-go-round as they left Junkies Corner and headed for the carpark. "Jacko, ask the uniforms to find out who owns the Ford Escort and while you're at it, speak to Forensics and see where they are with the heat scans. I want to know if any of the cars have been moved in the last 12 hours."

Jacko nodded and waved to DC Smithson who'd just arrived on the scene. "Smithy, do me a favour and run a check on the Ford Escort."

But before he could take down the details, the taller of the uniforms guarding the entrance spoke up. "Excuse me sir, but I'm sure the 'Gecko' owns that heap."

"If it's the one with the padlocked gearstick, then it definitely belongs to Vinny," agreed his shorter mate.

Jacko was curious. "Are we talking about Vinny the Gecko?"

"Yeah, that's him, and I know he lives around here somewhere."

"But you don't know *where* exactly?" asked Jacko.

"Afraid not Sir, although it has to be pretty close by."

"Do the check and find out."

The smaller of the uniforms hit his Com's button and began to speak rapidly.

Jacko vaguely remembered someone called 'Vinny the Gecko' floating around the City Centre and as a bonus, caught up with the Forensic checking the thermal images of the vehicles. "What's the heat factor on the Ford Escort?"

"Looking at the graph, there's enough of the orange colour to suggest it might have been moved in the last twelve hours."

A delighted Jacko was about to inform Carson of his findings, when he heard a voice from behind. "Excuse me, Sir?"

Jacko saw the shorter of the two uniforms holding up his notebook.

"Name and address of the car's owner. It's Vincent Snodgrass, Flat 32d Daisy Heights, Highwater Estate."

Jacko smiled at the uniform, "And I take it you know this address?"

"Yes, Sir, it's a block of flats close to the west entrance."

Carson gave a nod. "Okay Jacko, take Smithy along and give Vinny the Gecko an early morning call."

Daisy Heights

A real pain in the backside for those living on the Estate was parking; or to be more precise, a severe lack of it. So along with the rest of the 'plebs' who suffered this over-crowded nightmare, Smithy had to double-park in the road. A bigger headache arose when they discovered that due to the lift being out of order, the only means of reaching the fourth floor was via the stairs. A hot sweaty trudge to the upper regions, eventually found them outside Flat 32d, supposedly the home of a forty-two-year-old male Caucasian named Vincent Snodgrass.

Jacko pushed the doorbell a couple of times and counted to ten; another three long ones confirming there was no response from inside. He then gave Smithy the nod to begin knocking on the door and as if by magic, five others nearby cracked open a fraction and a raft of nosey eyeballs scrutinised their every move. "Ever had the feeling you're being watched?" grunted Smithy, whose knuckles were becoming sore. He was about to continue his knocking, when a short roly-poly pensioner dressed in a white kaftan threw open the door. Somewhat stunned by this strange Demi Rousseau-like apparition, it took but seconds for them to notice the straggly beard on the end of his chin and the ill-fitting black wig sat in the middle of his balding head. But it was the angry look that told them he was really pissed off.

"Who are you two?" he snarled.

"We're police officers," replied Jacko.

"Are you now? And here's me thinking you'd come to read the gas meter."

Jacko gave a sigh and carried on regardless. "Excuse me Sir, are you Reginald Snodgrass?" Remembering the flat was registered in that name.

"Who else would I be, *Genghis fucking Khan*?"

Smithy was biting his lip, trying not to laugh as Jacko went down a more diplomatic route. "Sorry to disturb you, Sir, but the person we really want to talk to is Vincent Snodgrass."

Reggie's mouse like eyes quickly turned to slits. "Why, are you going to arrest him?"

Jacko ignored the question and motioned to the darkened passage behind. "We were hoping you might tell us if this *is* where Vincent lives."

Obviously disappointed, Demi turned to the door on his right, which they could only assume was Vinny's bedroom and began hammering away. "Your date's here," he roared with a voice loud enough to wake the building, but on hearing no reply, shook his head in disgust. "It's early, so the lazy bastard will still be lying in bed and scratching his balls!" Using a stubby finger, he pointed to an imaginary spot on the floor below his Kaftan and warned, "Remember boys, no search warrant means no further than here."

"Do you reckon Vinny's old man is into karaoke?" chuckled Smithy, as Demi disappeared through a door and the tinkling sound of *Save your love for me* filled the air.

"If he was two feet taller, he could be the real thing!" laughed Jacko. He was just about to take over banging on the bedroom door, when they heard the sound of a bolt being pulled and watched it open a fraction. The room behind was in near darkness, the only connection with the outside world being the smell of stale cigarette smoke. Then out of nowhere, a face appeared in the gap.

"Vincent Snodgrass?" asked Jacko, one foot in the door to ensure it stayed open.

"Who's there?" came a quavering reply.

"It's the police and we need to speak to you regarding a vehicle that's part of our enquiries."

A second later and a nervous reply was heard from inside. "I'm sorry, officer, but I don't own a vehicle."

Jacko glanced at Smithy, who pushed the door open a touch further and whispered, "Listen mate, if you don't move your arse now, I'll come in and drag you out by your balls!"

Not exactly in the police training manual, thought Jacko, *but who's complaining.* Without further ado, a saggy backside came reversing out and turned to face them. Both detectives recognised Vinny at once. 'Central' gave his age as forty-two and height 5'3", but never mentioned his skinny white legs, hairless head or the fact he was so thin, his vest and shorts just about hung on his body. But in the end it was the face, that face said everything. The *Gecko* was well named, with lidded saucer-like eyes that never stayed still and a reptilian tongue that slid back and forth from the side of his mouth.

I bet he can catch flies with that, thought Smithy.

"I don't know what you want, but it wasn't me," moaned Vinny.

"Take it easy, Tarzan," smiled Jacko, "We're just looking for some information regarding a Ford Escort registered in your name. It's the one in the carpark next to Junkies Corner; you know where that is, don't you?"

"Of course, I do."

"And the car's yours? The one with the fancy padlock on the gearstick?" added Smithy.

"Yeah, it's mine," Vinny admitted, his swivelling non-stop eyes reminding them of watching a tennis match.

"Well considering it's got your prints all over it," said Jacko "We assumed that might be the case, but I'm more interested in the last time it was out on the road."

Vinny licked his lips a couple of times and went back to returning serves. "Couldn't really say, boys," his orbs moving from side to side like a pinball machine. "It's been ages since I tried to start it up."

"How long's ages?" asked Jacko.

Vinny blew out more air. "It must be months. I never really use it much."

"I take it the car's fully insured and does have its MOT?" smiled Smithy.

Vinny's eyeballs stopped mid-flicker as he realised he might be heading into a cul-de-sac, but before he could answer, Jacko cut him short. "Listen, you thieving little shit. A couple of kids were found murdered in Junkies Corner this morning and your heap is closest to where it happened. You say the car never goes anywhere, but we've been all over it like a bad suit and the engine's still warm even as we speak. Are you expecting us to believe that someone broke in here," pointing to his room, "nicked the keys, took it for a spin and then hung them up while you were still snoring in your pit?" Jacko shook his head in disgust "You're so full of crap, I feel like pulling the chain, so move your baggy arse and we'll sort this out down at the station!"

Vinny's eyes suddenly went saucer-shaped. "Whoa, boys!" He cried in desperation. "Okay, okay, I admit I did use the car to drive into town last night, but I don't know anything about any dead kids! Shitting hell man, I was only out for an hour and then came straight home."

"What time was this?"

"I don't know. Sometime around 8.00 pm."

Jacko shook his head. "That's not good enough. We need details."

"Details? What does that mean?"

"It means times, places and anyone who saw you."

"Come on boys, give me a break," he pleaded.

"Okay, let's start with last night," said Jacko "Where were you from 6.00 pm onwards?"

Vinny's rheumy eyes swung toward him and the tennis match was back in play. "I was here until 7.45 pm."

"Are you sure?" asked Smithy.

"Yeah, of course, I had to meet someone in town at 8.30 pm and they rang to see if I was going to be on time."

"We can easily check that out," threatened Jacko. "So tell me what happened next and remember, I want details!"

Vinny's eyes flicked from left to right "I left here around 7.45 pm and headed for the car park, which normally takes about five minutes."

"Go on," prompted Smithy.

"I opened the car, took the padlocked plate off the gearstick and shoved it in the boot where it normally goes."

"Did you see anyone suspicious hanging around?" asked Jacko.

"No," he began and then paused, as if something had occurred to him. "But come to think of it, I did see four girls."

Smithy's spirits lifted. "What four girls?"

"The ones who walked past while I was putting the plate in the boot."

"What did they look like?" asked Jacko.

Vinny squinted as if trying to remember. "There was a blonde bird at the front and I think the other three had dark hair. Oh yeah that's right, one of them was wearing glasses."

"Tell me about the blonde," prompted Jacko. "And remember, I want details."

Vinny gave a shrug. "She had curly hair, skin-tight red jeans and a pair of them tall shoes they wear these days."

"*Shit!*" groaned Jacko.

Smithy came next, "You didn't see a blonde girl wearing a short blue dress?"

Vinny shook his head in the negative.

"Keep talking," said Jacko.

"That was it. They went through the 'hanging gate' because it's the quickest way to get to the bus stop on the main road. No buses run through the Estate after 7.00 pm in the summer, so they would've been looking to catch the 8.15 pm on the main road, as most people do."

"And you're sure this happened before 8.00 pm?" insisted Smithy.

"Of course," Vinny replied confidently.

Jacko gave a sigh of frustration and continued to ask questions. "What about you, what did you do next?"

Vinny went through his well-practiced shrug routine and rolled his eyes again. "I got in the car and headed for town."

"Are you sure you didn't see anyone else in the area, maybe a blonde girl wearing a blue dress, or a black kid in a red and white hoodie?"

Vinny gave a negative shake of his head. "Nope," he said finally.

Jacko rewound, "Okay Tarzan, I want you to take me through all your movements, step by step."

This time, Vinny closed his eyes in concentration. "I drove to the exit and turned onto Park Road," he said confidently, then hesitated.

In a flash, Jacko realised something had registered in those wide rolling eyes. "What is it, Vinny?"

"Oh yeah, of course," he mumbled. "As I turned out onto the main road, I noticed a white transit van waiting to turn into the carpark."

Anton

The annoying sound of a mobile phone woke him from an uncomfortable and much troubled sleep. "Oh wow, what a night," he moaned, his head thumping as if it were about to explode. To make things worse, the other side of his bed showed no signs of having been slept in. Crossing the room, he stumbled into the lounge, hoping to find her asleep on the settee, only to find it empty.

"Where the hell is she?" he whispered, then realised the only change from yesterday was the sight of his guitar lying on the floor. "Oh shit!" he gasped. "How the hell did *that* get there?" With shaking hands, he returned it to its holding frame by the window and spotted his mobile phone on the coffee table and an empty wine bottle lying on the floor. He was about to check his incoming calls, when it suddenly lit up and the name *Zimbal* appeared on screen.

"Nick?" he whispered, eyes closed, head throbbing.

"How're you doing, Anton?"

"Not good. My mouth tastes like a sheep-shearer's armpit and I solemnly swear never to mix champagne and red wine again."

"Jeez that was some night wasn't it? I was absolutely torpedoed in the end!" As well as being one of his best friends, Nick Norton was the drummer in his band, 'The Red Tide'.

"Listen mate, can I call you back when I get some air in my lungs? I am absolutely shagged out!"

"Yeah no sweat, I just called to ask if Kelly turned up last night?"

Anton sounded despondent. "No. I was hoping she'd be here when I got home after the gig, but there's no sign of her."

"Ah that's a real shame, man. I reckon she'd have gone down a storm at the Charity Gala, especially if that Hamilton guy had heard her sing."

"To tell you the truth, I'm not sure what happened, maybe she got cold feet and decided to give it a miss."

"I personally think it's a golden opportunity lost."

"Let's hope there's a next time."

"Okay. Will speak to you later, mate."

Anton finished the call and as he did so, his head cleared and he remembered yesterday.

Nick's father Joe—who did a bit of promoting on the side—had arranged for him and Tom Stewart, the band's lead guitarist to perform at Liverpool Football Club. Their informal 'gig' had asked for 'guitar and vocals' only and taken place in one of the executive suites. As part of the deal, it had been agreed beforehand there was to be no fee, although that didn't matter.

The plus point came later, when they both got to watch Liverpool beat Arsenal two nil with a grandstand view. 'Whew, just breath-taking!' thought

Anton; especially if you were a fan and it had really turned out to be some day. Their performance had gone down brilliantly, after which the partying really had begun!

Especially when Joe told them the Anfield gig was just the precursor to a fantastic daylong series of events. According to him, this whole shebang was destined to culminate in a huge Charity Gala being held at the Adelphi Hotel. Supposedly something to do with 'Football against Poverty' a charity Maxi Hamilton was sponsoring, who Joe reckoned was one of the richest punters in Christendom. 'The Red Tide', he'd told them, were scheduled to appear later on in the show, which to their amazement was being networked by Sky Television. Nick said his dad knew this Hamilton from way back in the 70s, when they'd both been heavily involved in the Liverpool music scene. Yet the biggest surprise came when he and Tom had been packing their instruments away and the man himself appeared through the crowd, everyone recognising him by his height.

He stood 6'4" tall; with greying combed back hair and a lightly tanned face. He was broad of shoulder and looked incredibly fit for his age. Joe had casually let slip that Hamilton was at least fifteen years older than him, which meant he was somewhere in his early seventies. Then with a genial smile, the mogul had shook both their hands and said, "That was super, boys, absolutely super! Joe said you were good and I couldn't agree more. All being well, I'll see you later at the Gala, which should be quite a night, especially with most of the Merseyside footballers being there." Hamilton was about to leave when he paused and looked back.

"And you I take it must be Anton?"

"That's right."

"I thought so," winked the millionaire.

For a second, Anton thought he was about to be sick, but once he'd recovered from his touch of nausea, remembered his mobile was still lying on the table. A quick scroll through the menu said he'd had no missed calls. "Damn!" he growled in frustration. "Stop pissing about and try ringing her number!" Sadly, there was more disappointment to follow as the online voice said, "Sorry, this number is unavailable."

The Gecko

Amongst the many comings and goings in the park, Carson watched an angry Jacko leap from the squad car, open the rear door and begin threatening someone on the back seat. But it needed more than a few finger-pointing gestures to convince a small, skinny-looking object to step out onto the grass. Still annoyed at his reluctance to move his backside, Jacko took hold of one skinny arm and tugged it in the direction of his boss. "Meet Vinny Snodgrass, Guv, who wants to have a chat with you about a certain Ford Escort."

Carson could now understand why he was known as *The Gecko*, the eyes and head having a lot to do with it. There again, the tongue didn't help either. Luckily, Jacko had filled him in on his less than flawless contribution to society as a whole. Vinny he told him was a perennial small time lowlife, who fenced most of the goods stolen by the kids on the Highwater Estate.

It was the same old story; the young toe-rags would burgle some poor unfortunate's house or car, which in turn allowed him to do his *Fagin* routine and give them next to nothing in return. As always, he'd later be heading for the city pubs and bars selling whatever he could, as long as it was portable and valuable. Carson was creased with laughter at Jacko's tale of the Gecko trying to sell a red disabled cell phone in the bar of the 'Big House', a famous pub in Lime Street.

Vinny was at the bar waxing lyrical about how easy it was to use the over large keypad to a couple of drunken mates, when he heard a loud shout of 'Bastard' from behind. Next came a vicious haymaker that'd smashed him on the side of the head and sent him flying across the room. The ex-boxer who'd punched Vinny near senseless, had been at the bar buying a drink, when he realised the red oversized mobile phone, was identical to the one stolen from his grandma's flat two days earlier.

The slugger had instantly recognised it as being hers, because the scumbag trying to sell it, was showing the last number redial, which just happened to be his. Jacko swore that only the intervention of a passing police foot patrol had saved the 'baldy one' from a fate worse than death!

"Keys for the Escort?" asked Carson. Jacko motioned to Smithy, who held them up so he could see. His boss smiled and pointed in Vinny's direction. "I hear Forensics have just about finished in the carpark. Which means you can take *him* through the fence and get him to open up the Escort."

"Okay, Tarzan, time to make an entrance," said Smithy.

But Vinny had decided he wasn't going anywhere. "You must be joking," he cried. "If I go through there, I'll be fucking dead by the morning. And while we're on about it, I don't know anything about any dead kids either. But what's really pissing me off is that *you* know I don't! Okay, it's no big secret that I do a bit of wheeling and dealing with the kids every now and then, but I wouldn't touch them or harm them in any way. Shit man, I don't even know who we're talking about!"

He then turned to Jacko and pleaded, "Listen blondie, I'll tell you anything and I mean anything, but don't make me go through there," pointing beyond the fence.

Looking out, Jacko knew why. Across the road stood a sea of suspicious hoodies, who having used Vinny's services many times would almost certainly have something to hide. He could just imagine their reaction, plus a sudden sharpening of knives, the moment *The Gecko* stepped through the 'hanging gate' accompanied by the police!

Realising there was a genuine fear in his eyes, Jacko made a snap decision. "Smithy, do me a favour mate and slide Tarzan out of sight." Somewhat confused as to why, his colleague ushered Vinny into the rear of the car, where he instantly disappeared down behind the seats. On the other side of the path stood Carson, who was more interested in the Land Rover trundling across the park with a mobile control room in tow.

"How are we doing, Jacko?"

"Okay up to now, Guv. Although Vinny looks about ready to soil his underpants and I reckon it has to be something to do with them out there," pointing to the hoodies. "But how's this for a turn up. He's hinting he'd be willing to trade some info if we keep his beacon-like head out of sight."

Carson frowned. "Do you think he has anything to offer?"

"Not sure yet. There was nothing hidden in his bedroom, so what's the chances of him keeping anything of value in the Ford escort?"

"True, but what about the two dead kids?"

"I don't think he's involved, Guv, although he might know something. His eyes and ears are everywhere, if you'll pardon the pun."

Carson nodded. "Okay, keep his head covered and take him down to headquarters."

Hiding in the rear of the squad car, Vinny was badly in need of a cigarette and the sweat dripping from the tip of his nose reminded him of a leaky tap. Thankfully, the sudden arrival of the two detectives brought a welcome draught of cool air as they opened the front doors and climbed inside.

"How we doing, Tarzan?" asked the blonde one. To which Vinny gave a half grunt in reply.

"Some more detail on the van driver might help," added his partner. Vinny was about to tell him to 'go kiss my arse', then thought better of it. He badly needed to get out of here. Keeping out of sight, he'd spent most of the time trying to fathom out the crazy events of the last few hours, but more importantly, what might happen next. It had taken a while before his brain finally clicked into gear and began working overtime.

Where did those two kids come from? he wondered, realising the two teenagers found in Junkies Corner weren't your usual everyday drunks. Never mind them, who the hell was driving the white Transit van? No one from around the Estate, that's for sure. Although he'd recognise the same scumbag if he turned up naked at New Brighton Outdoor Swimming Baths on a cold December day. It had taken but a fleeting glimpse, but he'd still managed to store the licence number plate and driver's face in his memory banks.

Vinny had always prided himself on the fact he *never ever* forgot a face, which was very handy in his line of business! Thinking back, he remembered the white van signalling to turn into the car park and seeing the red and white wool hat lying on the dashboard. Vinny had always regarded the corner parking spot as his own and was about to tell the driver to piss off and park elsewhere, then changed his mind the moment he'd taken off his sunglasses.

The cold staring eyes had said it all; *pure unadulterated evil* and the thought of meeting him again literally made his hands shake. "If that bastard did murder those two kids," he whispered, "then let's hope these two idiots sitting up front catch him soon." But one thing's for sure, Vinny intended to avoid him like the plague!

Merseyside Police Headquarters
S.C.U.

Jacko's head appeared in the doorway. "The rest of the team are here, Guv."

"Who made it?"

"Stretch, Joanna and Jason Junior."

"Excellent," smiled Carson, as they headed for the Display Boards and what was now the heartbeat of the murder investigation.

"Oh, that reminds me, Guv. I hear they've just installed a new drinks machine in the hallway, supposedly to save us going down to the canteen. Trouble is, everyone who's tried it reckons the coffee tastes more like reconstituted dishwater."

"Thanks for the warning," grunted Carson.

Jacko began the meeting by attaching a rough sketch and two forensic photos to the first of the boards. "Okay people, let's run through what we have so far." The group were gathered around in a small half circle, Carson taking a seat to the side, thus giving him a better chance to observe the 'team', as he liked to call them.

To his left sat Frank Malone, the oldest member of the squad and because he always wore braces, was affectionately known as 'Stretch'. Whereas Carson, out of respect and because of their long association, would only call him Frank. Beside him sat Joanna Beaton who was all smiles when required, but took no flak from anyone and when necessary, wasn't afraid to speak her mind. Jason 'Junior' Horan on the other hand might be a couple of years younger, but was still a hard-nosed copper who really knew his stuff.

What they all had in common was the fact they were Liverpool born and mighty proud to call themselves 'Scousers'. Bringing up the rear were the *outsiders*, as Carson liked to call them. First off was DC Peter *Smithy* Smithson, late of Derby and a major addition to the team. Then Sergeant Sam *Jacko* Jackson, who originally hailed from somewhere North of Watford, but still managed to make his way through the ranks by plying his trade in various parts of the country, the last one being downtown Birmingham.

Yet, as his No. 2 had evolved into everything you would need in a modern-day policeman, intelligent, bright and open-minded. In addition, Jacko was a real wizard with all that weird stuff he termed *technical*, which was surely the byword for this fast and ever-changing world. Carson suppressed a smile, remembering he too was an outsider; having ploughed his own path from Bristol through God knows how many backwaters, until finding his own 'niche' here in Liverpool. There was a time when he thought he'd been shoehorned into some grim northern backwater, then soon discovered the 'Scousers' were a welcoming, riotously funny and intelligent race of people, who had a language all of their own.

Returning to more pressing matters, he watched Jacko point to the sketch of Waytree Park and the surrounding Highwater Housing Estate. "This is an overview of the carpark, the gate in the fence and the exact spot where the bodies were found. The Forensic photos show a young white girl and black boy found dead in Junkies Corner at 6.55 am this morning. The pathologist has since confirmed that both of them died from stab wounds inflicted at around 8.00 pm last night. Another unknown is the identity of the victims or the weapon used in the killings. However, it looks as if the killer has purposefully trashed both their mobile phones in an attempt to silence them or possibly cover his escape."

"Smashing mobiles is definitely a new one on me," growled Malone.

"I agree, Stretch, and it's worrying to think that someone would take the time and trouble to do it, but here's something even more interesting. When the Forensic teams moved the girl, they found a blue handbag lying underneath her and what looks like a brand-new iPhone S6 inside."

"Now that's more like it. Do we know if it belongs to her?"

Jacko shook his head. "Not yet, but Forensics did discover two unidentified text messages were sent to the iPhone, at around the time of the murders."

"Any idea who?"

"Nope."

"Ex-Directory?"

"We're still looking, but has to be."

"Any witnesses?" asked Joanna.

"That depends on what you might classify as a witness. At the moment, we are yet to find anyone who might have come in direct contact with the two victims at the time of their deaths. Although, we do have someone who says he was in the carpark just before 8.00 pm last night. He claims four teenage girls passed through the fence and walked towards the main gates..." his finger tracing an imaginary line across the board. "This, it would appear is normal practice, as it shortens the time taken to reach here!" A knuckle tapping the two squares that represented the granite pillars.

"Beyond this point is the main road and the nearby bus stop which provides a regular service to the City Centre. The four girls, we assume, would be looking to catch the next available bus which was the 8.15 pm. In addition, our man claims to have observed a white Transit van with two ski bars, indicating to turn into the carpark." Jacko paused for a moment to let this sink in. "The problem is, he just happens to go by the name of Vincent Snodgrass, aka Vinny the Gecko."

"You must be joking!" spluttered Stretch. "There's no way The Gecko can be a witness in our murder case; the little shit's as bent as an Arab's dagger!"

Jacko smiled and raised his hands in a gesture of hopelessness. "I know, mate, but at the moment I'm afraid Vinny's all we've got. If there was any other way we could do this, then believe me, I'd be first in the queue."

"And let's not forget everyone, the Gecko is still regarded as a possible murder suspect until cleared from our inquiries," added DCI Carson.

"Where is he now?" asked Joanna.

"Unhappily languishing in the cells down below," grinned Jacko.

Smithy posed a more important question. "What about the two dead teenagers, I take it we still haven't heard from missing persons yet?"

"Nothing at the moment."

"A question, Sarge, if Junkies Corner is so popular, how come no-one found them last night?"

Jacko gave a shrug. "Good question, Jason. According to SOCO Fitzpatrick, the place is well used, mostly by drunks in the daytime. Other than that, it's the lowlifes trying to inject themselves before night closes in. For reasons unknown, it would appear that both the kids went unnoticed."

The team took a minute to absorb this sad fact.

"Okay, let's go with the positives, if that's what they are," urged Jacko. "The Gecko tells us most people catch the bus into town on a regular basis and as all of today's public transport has CCTV, we start there. Smithy, find out what service runs between the park and town. Request any relevant footage from 12.00 pm yesterday and the last bus." He then turned to a severely pissed off Malone. "Stretch, the Gecko insists he saw a Ford Transit on Park Drive with a red and white hat on the dashboard, but swears he didn't recognise the driver."

Jacko indicated to the boards again. "From the sketch, we can see the carpark itself is directly opposite the West side entrance of where he lives. Which I might add, is half full of abandoned cars that the Council chooses to ignore."

"Do you think it's that important?"

"Yes. Me and Smithy spent more than an hour interviewing him and most of his story rings true."

"Hang on, Vinny's a villain, so why mention the van in the first place?"

"Not sure, maybe he didn't mean to and it just slipped out. What we really need to know is how did it get there?"

Joanna spoke again, "That's a tough one, Sarge. The Highwater junction can take you to so many different places."

"No matter," growled Carson. "Whichever way it was going, it had to meet the main roundabout at the M62 Motorway."

"Okay, that has to be our next move," said Jacko. "Stretch, I noticed a petrol station on the main road right opposite the park gates. Check their security cameras for anything unusual. Then contact Traffic and ask them for any CCTV footage of the approach roads and junctions around the Highwater areas for the last twenty-four hours. If the Gecko's telling the truth, then we're looking for a white Transit van with two ski-type roof bars. So, let's put the wheels in motion and see if we can find it."

Within the hour, a whole raft of new information came rolling in as the investigation changed gear and gathered speed.

"Hey Sarge," called an excited Jason. "This beauty has just leapt off the printer." Jacko finished his coffee and reached for the proffered sheet of paper. A copy of a ticket stub from yesterday's football match at Anfield had been found lying amongst a pile of rubbish close to the park gates. And apparently, a fast brush with the required 'Magic Dust' had revealed the prints from the dead boy

41

were all over it. Jason Junior passed a perfect reproduction of a 'Kop' seat ticket into Jacko's eager hands; albeit on a sheet of A4 paper.

"The real thing is worth a fortune on the day," he said with feeling.

"I know," grinned Jacko. "But I'm more interested in who was sat behind the goal in the famous football stand." He then thought of something else. "Have a word with Anfield Security and ask if they can check their CCTV footage from Saturday's game. With a bit of luck, they should be able to zoom in on whoever paid for the ticket."

Next to brighten their day was an excited Smithy, who'd spent an hour fast-forwarding the recent footage from the bus CCTV. "I think I've found them, Sarge!" Jacko and the others gathered around the screen as Smithy did a voice-over of the on-board camera. "They both left the football ground when the game was over and caught the bus at Everton Brow. Their journey home was a pretty uneventful one, until they reached the park, then this happened at precisely 7.40 pm."

The Team watched the two youngsters, who were obviously fooling around, push the stop button and rise from their seats. A moment later and their faces were pressed together as they laughed and waggled their tongues cheekily at the security camera; one of them giving the *finger* to all who might have reason to watch it.

"Is that him on the left?" asked Joanna, her eyes looking to the display board and the photo of the lifeless youngster lying in the grass.

"That's our boy," Jacko said with a touch of sadness. "We can only assume the other bus ticket was for his friend whom, I might add, we have yet to find."

Smithy however hadn't quite finished. "I've also managed to find the four girls who passed Vinny in the carpark and caught the bus into town. They were recorded climbing aboard at 8.16 pm exactly."

Jacko smiled and gave him a pat on the shoulder. "Nice one, mate. Now see if you can organise the footage showing the two boys stepping off the bus at Waytree Park and then the four girls as they boarded the one headed into town. When done, send both of them to all the TV News channels. With a bit of luck, they should be Nationwide within the hour."

Jacko was grabbing a fast coffee with Carson and Joanna in the hallway when his mobile rang. "It's the lab," he informed them. The call was brief, his head nodding this way and that, but ended with a sigh. "Good news and bad news."

"I'll take the bad news first," said Carson.

"The mobiles in the bushes have been well and truly 'mullered'. To add to our woes, it looks as if we will need the iPhone's PIN number to gain proper access."

"As I understand it, these Apple people are very reluctant to share that kind of information," grumbled Carson.

"That's not all, Guv, Forensics believe the Blackberry's been stolen."

"Any good news?" asked Joanna.

"A fingerprint and DNA test has confirmed both the Samsung and iPhone belong to the girl; the Blackberry to the boy."

Carson looked frustrated. "What now?"

"The men in white coats are going to fax us the information regarding the SIM cards, which hopefully should help us identify the people who pay the bills."

"Keep on top of it," muttered Carson. Then his own mobile began to ring. "Hello Reece, how long?" His free hand beckoning for Jacko to stay. "The morgue in an hour? Yes, of course, we'll be there."

The Morgue

The faint odour of chilled formaldehyde hung heavily in the air, as Jacko and Carson stepped into the antiseptic cleanliness of the morgue. Awaiting their arrival and poised between two sheet-covered gurneys, stood Professor Reece Armstrong. "I kid you not, Nathan," he began. "I've been doing this for so long, I regard myself as immune to whatever life throws at me." He then pulled back one of the sheets. "Yet it still saddens me when something like this comes in."

Carson's first reaction was one of deep regret at the fate of the beautiful young girl. In the park she'd at least had a vestige of dignity in that she'd been wearing some clothes. Jacko too, had been expecting the worse, yet the sight of her body and now visible injuries, made him wince. Her once slim neck was so swollen, one might think she was wearing a dark mauve scarf. Next came the puncture hole in her side from the knife wound and as always, the unmistakable suture lines crisscrossing her body; evidence of Armstrong's recent autopsy. "Jesus, what a waste!" he whispered.

The pathologist waited for the two detectives to take in the scene, before removing the cover from the other table. Here lay the body of the boy, who, compared to his female companion and his own investigative autopsy, looked to be devoid of any further major injuries.

"I think this was meant to be an isolated sex attack on the girl," began Reece. He then moved to a position where he could more easily point to the relative injuries. "It looks as if the killer was hiding in the bushes and as she passed through the gate, grabbed her around the throat. This we can tell by the degree of trauma inflicted around her windpipe, plus the severe bruising to the muscle and cartilage," his finger tracing the damaged area. "His next move was to drag her backwards into the clearing, where I think he intended to rape her."

He then pointed to the small blue-black hole above her hip. "This wound, I'd say, was intended as both a warning and means of bringing the girl under control, which obviously it did, until the boy appeared from nowhere and spoiled his fun."

"Do we know how?"

"Not yet, Nathan. That, I'm afraid, is going to require some detective work on your part. It looks to me as if he'd pushed his way through the bushes and stumbled upon the girl as she was being attacked. At the time, she would have been kneeling in the grass, with the killer more or less right behind her. Which is when our young hero has decided to intervene and lash out with his foot. However, it looks as if the blow was of insufficient force to change the situation and in a flash, the killer turned the tables. The boy's forward movement would have taken him a step closer to the killer, who didn't need a second chance. The knife was in his right hand, which he brought around in an arc, stabbing him once in the lower stomach. I'd say the blow alone would have been more than enough to silence him and at the same time upset the killer's plans."

"In what way?"

"It's important to remember that the girl was still alive whilst all this was happening, but instead of being a prize, became a problem that needed resolving quickly. And it's not the fact that he killed her that has me worried; it's the way the bastard did it. Rather than just strangle her or maybe cut her throat, he pulled her upright and placed the knife here," pointing to the small slit beneath her chin. "He then forced the blade up through her epiglottis, soft palate and straight into her lower brain. Thus causing an instant massive subdural haematoma, which is bleeding on the brain in layman terms, and she died within seconds."

Carson had a bad feeling. "Are you are trying to tell me something, Reece?"

"Yes, Nathan. I think whoever did this," pointing to the girl, "cold-bloodedly executed her and knew precisely how to do it!"

"A trained killer?" Carson asked incredulously.

"It's either that or he got *very* lucky! Yet no matter the method, I'm still convinced his original intention was to rape and then strangle her."

"Hang on, I thought you said he might be some kind of hit man?"

"And I still think that's the case, although this is not his normal Modus Operandi." Reece pointed to an X-ray of the girl's throat. "These bruises and the damaged cartilage on her neck muscles show a distinct finger pattern."

Carson wasn't sure what he was looking for, but nodded along anyway.

"These dark patches on the base of her neck are the important ones."

"They look like a couple of large thumb prints."

"That's exactly what they are, Nathan."

"So what does it mean?"

"It tells me that he has incredible strength and can easily asphyxiate most people from behind. It looks to me as if he was desperately trying to avoid making a bloody mess, yet still enjoys every minute of killing his victims."

"Give me the 'Boston Strangler' any time," quipped Jacko.

"Never mind him, what about the boy?" asked Carson.

"Straightforward murder," Reece replied matter-of-factly. "Of course, it doesn't make it any less serious; how could it?"

Jacko stared at the boy's lifeless form. "Why was he lying under the bushes?"

"Because he was desperately trying to escape. The knife had caused no end of damage as it penetrated his stomach muscles, passed through the Linea Albe and practically skewered his colon. The shock alone was enough to kill him, let alone his injuries."

"Poor little bastard," whispered Jacko, as he remembered the trail of dried blood in Junkies Corner.

"Brave little bastard," Reece corrected him. "He should've turned and run for his life!"

"What about the knife that killed them, Reece?"

"Has to be a dagger of some kind; a long-bladed weapon that's lethal when used in the wrong hands."

"Forensics found anything yet?"

"Yes, Nathan, they did some preliminaries a few hours ago, but as always, we'll have to wait for them to call us."

The Remand Cell

With time on his hands, Vinny watched the fly race back and forth across the ceiling looking for a way out, but knew its chances of success was less than zero; the only way out of this place was through the cell door.

"You stupid fucker!" He swore. But in truth, had to admit his own loose tongue was the real reason he was still here in jail. Without thinking, he'd decided to feed the two detectives a few bits of useless information. Especially the part about the four birds in the carpark, knowing one of them would remember him loading the plate in his car.

However, his casual mention of the white Transit van had seriously backfired. For it meant he was now regarded as a material witness and *Robocop* was using *that* and his Ford Escort as an excuse to keep him in custody! Yet, no matter how long and loud he'd protested that this was against his human rights, Blondie had insisted they were just trying to eliminate him from their enquiries. He'd then patted him on the head like child, closed the cell door and assured him he would be out soon.

This wasn't quite what he'd expected, but what really frightened the life out of him was the conversation he'd overheard, as he lay hidden in the back of the squad car. Momentarily forgetting he was there, one of the detectives had casually let slip, the teenager found dead in the park had been wearing a pair of red and white trainers *and* a Liverpool FC hoodie. Vinny's thoughts instantly went back to this morning's chat outside his flat and the moment Robocop had asked him if he'd seen a young black boy hanging around. But it was the mention of the red and white hoodie that had really left him in shock, as he relived Tuesday night, six days earlier.

With the lift still being out of action, Vinny had taken the stairs and practically fell over a young black kid waiting in the entrance hall. The sight of him hanging around in the shadows set his alarm bells ringing, especially as he lived in the south west side of Highwater and the mutually agreed borderline between the black and whites. Yet despite this unofficial demarcation, he stood before him with his face half hidden by a red and white hoodie. Vinny was about to tell him to piss off, when the kid took a small package from his pocket and showed him four shiny discs. "I want to sell these!"

A couple of things had stopped Vinny in his tracks, the first being the sheer quality of what he might easily get rid of on the open market. Secondly, in the kid's haste to impress on him their value, his hood had fallen back and Vinny realised it was someone who he'd dealt with six months earlier.

He'd been in the car park near the 'hanging gate', when two young black kids had approached him carrying a plastic bag. "I want to sell this car CD system," declared the one in the red and white hoodie, whilst offering him the option to look inside. Vinny had always been wary of dealing with the blacks, feeling they were both untrustworthy and unreliable. He didn't in any way regard himself as being racist; he just disliked them.

Although, he did recall someone in the pub asking if he had a CD player on the go, seeing as he was renovating his camper van. So, if whatever was in the bag fitted the bill, it seemed like an opportunity not to be missed and with this in mind, he'd decided to take a look. To his surprise, the kid really was telling the truth, a quick perusal revealing a fairly modern piece of kit; its newness partly due to the fact it had recently been removed from some unlucky fucker's dashboard. Nevertheless, he was still reluctant to get involved, no matter the bargain.

Sensing his lack of interest, the young hoodie had gone even further. "It's going cheap, man!" he cried.

Vinny was about to make his exit when he decided to make a quick offer. "I'll give you twenty quid and that's it," fully expecting it to be rejected out of hand. Yet to his surprise, the kid had hesitated, glanced at his mate and gave a reluctant nod. "Okay mister, but we want cash!"

Vinny could still remember the smile of satisfaction on the punter's face, as he'd handed over £90 in exchange for the stolen CD system.

It was the same situation with the gold coins and Vinny could tell by his attitude that the kid would be more than willing to make another quick trade. Ever watchful of leaving a fingerprint behind, he ripped a corner from the wrapping paper and used it to inspect the discs one by one. 'Hallelujah', he thought gleefully. 'This could be my lucky night!' However, on reaching the last coin, spotted something he didn't like. "Hang on, you little shit, this one's been damaged!"

As their eyes met, Vinny could see the visible hint of guilt showing through. "It's only a scratch!" the kid had insisted, a look of innocent indignation etched on his face.

"I don't care," snarled Vinny. "This so-called scratch means it's not worth the same as the others," the sound of his voice allowing no room for argument.

A frown of uncertainty appeared on the youngster's brow as he began to wrestle within himself and an interminable amount of time seemed to pass before he spoke again. "Okay, how much?"

Vinny had beamed from ear to ear, as he'd headed for the city. The kid might have whined and moaned over the offer, but knew he had no room to manoeuvre. It was either accept the offer of £100 for each of the good coins and £75 for the damaged one, or he could try somewhere else. In hindsight, it had been a calculated risk on Vinny's part, knowing they were worth a damn sight more on the black market at least three times that amount. But the young Michael Jackson lookalike had an air of desperation about him and very limited alternatives.

So the amount was agreed and Vinny had hurried back to his place to collect the money. He'd been wearing a smug smile for the last few days remembering just how easy it was to make a profit on these things. Yet the smirk was wiped *clean off his face the moment the detective had let slip that the kid lying dead in Junkies Corner might be one of the dreaded 'Sharecropper gang'!*

Top Floor, Sharecropper Heights

A double rap sent Noah in the direction of his bedroom door where he found his sister standing in the hallway.

"Have you seen Moses?" she asked.

"Not since Friday."

Sarah looked worried. "We haven't seen or heard a thing from him since yesterday, not even a phone call."

Noah gave a shrug. "It won't be the first time he hasn't come home." His sister was unconvinced. "That might well be, but he at least calls his Momma."

"I can remember checking his room late last night and noticed his bed hadn't been slept in, have you spoken to Benny yet?"

Sarah shook her head as Noah opened the adjacent bedroom door, woke his younger brother and asked him the same question.

"I saw Moses yesterday," Benny replied. "He said he was going to watch Liverpool play Arsenal with Finbar."

In the confusion, Noah had forgotten all about the game.

"How did he sound?"

Benny rubbed an eye with a thumb. "Okay."

"Something's not quite right," muttered Noah. "I spoke to him around 7.45 pm last night, which wasn't long after he'd stepped off the bus. We had a fast chat about a few things and arranged to meet here at 9.00 pm. For some reason, he didn't make it and his phone was dead."

"Maybe it was just like you said; he changed his mind and stayed at Finbar's place; he's done that lots of times before."

"What about his phone being out of action?"

"He might have forgotten to charge it," Benny replied lamely.

Sarah's face wore a worried look. "Best not say anything to Momma for now."

A concerned Noah left the room and went in search of his own mobile phone. Before going to bed at night, he would usually switch it over to flight mode, where one touch of his keypad could disconnect him from the real world and help him get some sleep. Yet when he'd switched it back to normal, a whole raft of messages came piling in. The majority of them were from people wanting drugs, the others rattling on about frantic police activity taking place in Junkies Corner. The most troubling one came from his friend 'Cruz'. *Earlier today, Vinny the Gecko was spotted leaving the Estate in the back of an unmarked police car!*

Noah sat on the bed and wondered what the hell was going down. He then turned to Benny. "Have you got Finbar Otagi's mobile number?"

"I should have it somewhere."

"Give him a call and see if he knows anything."

"Where are you off to?"

"Mind your own business."

Benny grinned. "It wouldn't by chance be that young Asian bird who lives on the second floor?"

Noah smiled back. "No, it's not. I'm off to meet Cruz and see what's happening down in the Park."

S.C.U.

"Got a minute, Guv? I think you should see this."

Carson took a seat in front of the oversized TV, where a motorway scene looked to have been paused on screen. The other team members were patiently awaiting his arrival, which in due course, allowed Stretch Malone to take up the story. "I spoke to a friend of mine in Traffic and had a long chat about the two murdered kids in Waytree Park. He assured me they would do whatever it takes to help and I thought that was it. Until he rang a few minutes ago and told me about some odd footage they'd found amongst Saturday's traffic recordings.

"Except this isn't the Highwater junction; it just so happens that due to the on-going road works in that neck of the woods, all the CCTV cameras are out of action. This is where the M62 intersection meets the A5058 or, as we know it, Queens Drive and timed at 15.55 pm on Saturday afternoon." He then pressed the play button, so as to let them follow the on-screen events whilst continuing with his own background commentary.

"I want you to keep an eye on this vehicle, as it begins to overtake the two container wagons travelling behind each other in the inner lane. If you watch closely, you can see it gather speed until it's more or less alongside both vehicles. But surprise, surprise, the left-hand indicator has begun to flash, meaning it now intends to squeeze into the narrow gap between the two wagons."

"Wow! That's a dodgy move," exclaimed Jason.

"Which is exactly what my mate at Traffic thought," replied Stretch. "And then realised it was a calculated manoeuvre by the driver in the outside lane. There's a range of different security cameras situated on the gantry half a mile ahead, but when he'd managed to squeeze in between the two wagons, the vehicle and its number plates suddenly disappeared from view."

Carson rose from his seat, leant a little closer to the screen and asked, "Is that what I think it is, Frank?"

"Yes Nathan, it's a white Transit van with a two-bar ski–rack."

Park Drive

Noah wasn't interested in Junkies Corner; he was more concerned with Vinny leaving the Estate in the rear of a police car. Which, if true, could give him problems of nightmare proportions. "Any sign of the Gecko yet?"

"Nothing," muttered Cruz. "Although, there are plenty of other rumours flying about, most of them saying there's a 'he and she' lying dead behind the fence." He then pointed to the crime scene opposite. "Forget that shit, there's something more important you should know."

Noah's eyes narrowed as Cruz began his tale. "I was listening to Radio Merseyside this morning and they were babbling on about a burglary that took place at a house in Chillwall."

"Keep talking."

"The report went on to say an old man found injured at the scene, has since died in hospital and the goods stolen from the property are valued at around £4,000. The police have also confirmed they are treating the incident as a murder inquiry and I reckon this has to be your break-in and the missing gold coins."

Noah stood motionless on the grassy bank, his thoughts going back to the fuck-up from a week ago.

Whilst out delivering a pizza to an address in Chillwall, Finbar Otagi had noticed a couple in the house opposite loading two suitcases into a taxi. Assuming they must be off on holiday, he'd rung Noah and suggested their place might be worth a late-night visit. At first everything had looked good when he and Moses had forced a ground floor window and climbed in, only to find the place was full of worthless junk.

Snarling in frustration, he'd flashed his torch at the ceiling, the sign they should move to the floor above. Once there, he'd indicated he was off to search the bedroom on his left, whilst Moses had headed in the direction of a small study. Moments later, he'd heard a muffled cry of joy and saw his brother's torch flashing around outside. Unsure of what was happening, he'd stepped from the room only to see an old man appear from nowhere and grab Moses around the neck. Stunned to find the place was still occupied, he'd caught a fleeting glimpse of the greying head in the dark and instinctively lashed out with his torch, the blow strong enough to send him crashing down the stairs.

Panic-stricken and thinking there might be more people in the house, he'd followed behind Moses and hurdled the body now lying on the bottom step. They'd then raced for the scooter hidden in the bushes and fled the scene. Having always worn gloves as a natural precaution, Noah thought it safe to assume their only connection with the break-in would be the four shiny coins Moses had discovered in the upstairs study. He'd also warned his younger brother that the coins were much too risky to keep.

He however had argued against this, declaring they were real gold, the scrape of a nail file proving his point. The next day had brought more bad news when the local paper had reported the burglary and said an old man was lying badly injured in hospital. Concerned the police might come sniffing around the 'Estate' and alert the 'Family' to their covert *operation, they'd agreed to get rid of the coins ASAP. Unfortunately, in their haste to dispose of them, Moses had insisted the quickest and easiest way would be to use The Gecko and much to his better judgment, he'd agreed!*

"Put the word out," whispered Noah, "and tell the boys to search every inch of the Estate. We have to get rid of Vinny the Gecko before he opens his mouth and sends us all down!"

Sharecropper Heights

Through the open door, Sarah could hear a voice singing along to a tune on the radio. "If I hear *No woman, no cry* one more time," she sighed, "I swear I'll go crazy." Making her way to the kitchen, she found her Momma 'toot a tooting' a pan or plate from one side of the sink to the other. As always, her ample rump would be sashaying from side to side as she washed the dishes in time to the music.

"Hi Momma," she called, a wide grin filling her face.

"Hi honey, how's you this beautiful morning?" came Estelle's warm reply.

"Anytime I hear *Bob Marley and the Wailers* is always a good day for me," Sarah replied with tongue firmly held in cheek. She then took a seat at the table with its faded chequered cover and four worn PVC chairs that over the years had become an integral part of her mother's world. Throughout the ever-changing seasons, you could always find her framed in the kitchen window, happily surveying the world from the west corner of their tenth-floor apartment.

"My, my, this view is just somethin' to die for," she'd gushed nearly every day they'd lived in Sharecropper Heights, and in keeping with this daily ritual, would always choose a station playing Reggae music. The kitchen was plain and unadorned, her only concession to a past life being a poster of Montego Bay in Jamaica, the four corners dried and curling where it hung on the wall. Not so long ago, Noah had sat a portable TV set on the worktop, hoping that with a little more exposure, Estelle's misgivings of the outside world might change. Yet Momma had insisted she didn't really mind the onscreen happenings, just as long as she didn't have to listen to the hassle going on in the world; thereby keeping the volume constantly muted and mostly ignoring the everyday events that flickered by.

"You seen them lazy no good brothers of yours?" she asked as Sarah rose from the table.

"Yes, Momma," she replied. "Noah left the apartment about an hour ago, Benjamin is still in bed and I think Moses slept overnight at his friend's home."

"I'm tinkin' them boys need to sit down and eat together sometime." Estelle laughed in reply.

Sarah was halfway along the passage leading to her bedroom, when she heard her mother's anguished cry. With a sense of confusion, she quickly ran back and found Estelle pointing at the TV with wide frightened eyes. It was the regular afternoon programme from 'Sky News' and as always, minus the sound. Sarah was still somewhat baffled as to her mother's fearful outburst, until she realised the on-screen reporter was standing in front of Waytree Park and pointing in the direction of the 'hanging gate'.

Estelle gave another despairing cry as an image of her son, still wearing his Liverpool FC hoodie, appeared on what could only be a CCTV video. There was no doubting it was Moses, as he and his friend Finbar smiled into the camera, as they were about to leave a bus. In a state of panic, Sarah began to search for the missing TV control so as to hear what was being said. Yet it was the latest 'Breaking News' that really left her open-mouthed. The report said the police were trying to identify the hoodie, who was one of two teenagers found murdered in the park last night.

"Oh my dear Lord, I been hearing about it all day on the radio," Estelle whimpered, her hands shaking wildly. "Except they never give no names; just it was a boy and girl. I can remember them saying it was a couple, but they didn't mention any black people being involved, so I never give it a thought," her voice trailing off as the magnitude of it all hit home like a sledgehammer. "Besides, Moses don't have no girlfriends, he's only fifteen, ain't that right, honey?" Her fearful eyes searching for an answer in Sarah's troubled face!

"Oh, Jesus Momma," she cried, her own eyes fastened to the screen as it changed from one location to another. Then gasped out loud when the camera swung in a slow arc and came to rest on the West entrance of the Highwater Estate.

"No, no, no!" Estelle groaned, the agony spilling from deep inside, as she realised they were trying to put a name to her son in what seemed to be a living nightmare. Within this on-going trauma, the radio had continued to play its usual blend of 'Ska' and 'Reggae' music as Sarah watched the muted screen in disbelief.

"Where's the damn TV control?" she moaned, whilst searching the drawers with tear-filled eyes. Then to her horror, a blinking Benny, who'd been woken by the commotion, burst into the kitchen holding a small machete in his hand. "Wait!" screamed Sarah, hoping against hope her mother hadn't noticed the weapon and instead directed their attention to a new face that'd suddenly appeared on screen.

He was a thin-faced suit with a receding hairline and without doubt a policeman. It was obvious he was fronting some kind of press conference whilst holding a photo of Moses, whose laughing eyes seemed to haunt Sarah's soul.

"We have to call the police," she whispered as the name, DCI Nathan Carson, materialised beneath his muted, earnest features. Throughout all this, Estelle had continued to gaze at the screen with a look of utter incredulity. Then, it was as if a dam had burst, as she gave a stricken lamentation of grief for the death of her beautiful boy.

Noah departed the grassy bank opposite Junkies Corner and headed in the direction of home, his usual fifteen-minute saunter taking less than five. Turning the corner a familiar sight caught his eye; standing in the window of a second-floor flat was the smiling figure of the young Asian girl.

Pausing mid-stride, he watched in fascination as she gave him a wave; pulled up her t-shirt and seconds later closed the curtain. Torn between the need to organise a search for the Gecko and the sight of her pert breasts, his next decision was a no-brainer. Racing up the stairs, he found the front door half open and quietly made his way along the darkened passage in the direction of the girl's bedroom. From the limited light slanting through the curtained window, he was just about able to see her lying naked on the single bed.

Stripping off his clothes, he'd only just begun to feel her breasts and lick her nipples, when a text message lit up his mobile phone. Hesitating for a moment, he knew the girl had heard the 'ping' and urged him to ignore it by moving her feet down onto his buttocks. Then and in quick succession, another six texts came winging in, each with the same distinctive sound recognisable by only him.

Annoyed at this unexpected disruption to his hour of pleasure, he lost all interest in the girl and sat back on his haunches. Only to hear his mobile let out four more factory sounding hoots before falling silent. In one swift movement, he was standing naked by the side of the bed, the light from the screen illuminating his eyes. "What the fuck's going down?" he cursed. The girl on the bed, however, was more disappointed in seeing his erection return to its normal size and watch him don tee shirt, knee-length shorts and trainers, ready to go. He was just about to leave the room, when she sat up, made a whimpering sound and held out a hand pleadingly.

Unsure of what was happening with the text messages, he was heading for the door when she let out an even longer moan and held out both hands. Hearing her pleas he refocused, unzipped a pocket and threw a small folded wrap of paper, which she grasped greedily to her bare breasts. He could see no obvious signs of tracking or puncture marks on her exposed body and assumed she'd cook it up and inhale it later. Outside in the hallway, he'd paused only to let an old lady dressed in a burkha shuffle past as though he didn't exist.

"Shit! Shit!" he whispered, until she'd turned into another room and he was able to leave the flat. The girl and her family were recently arrived Eastern European immigrants, who didn't speak much English and the Council as always, shoved them in the tower blocks. It was an easy solution to an ever-growing problem, but hell man, he didn't care! Although, the last thing he needed was an influx of righteous whiteys, who might interfere with his everyday operations.

That said, the Council could send as many of them ethnics as they wanted. Past experience showing many of them needed a fix of some kind, the girl on the bed with the opalescent eyes evidence enough of that. Outside the flat, he still had to make a decision; lift or stairs? His own home was eight floors above from where he stood; the four siren blasts signalling serious danger, but they'd never before come from Sarah's mobile phone! Instinctively, he felt the scar on his right thigh and still unsure as to which floor the lift might be on, opted for the stairs which he took two at a time.

Noah's rapid ascent had proved to be no problem and he made the tenth floor with almost consummate ease. His mind however, was still overrun with questions, especially the text messages urging him to watch the TV news. In his world people rarely spoke on the phone, this mostly due to police surveillance tactics and possible phone hackers. A simple text message, mixed with the right amount of code usually sufficed, although sometimes they could never tell the whole story. Stepping through the stairwell door, he found Benny waiting for him with a look of despair in his eyes and listened to his tale with a growing sense of outrage and disbelief.

"Motherfucker!" he growled, his eyes ablaze. "I was down there less than an hour ago and no one seemed to know what was going on!"

"Momma says it been on the news all day."

Noah chewed his lip and tried to make some sense of what was happening in his life, but was even more amazed to find a tearful Sarah and his mother staring at a TV that had suddenly acquired sound. He listened to the broadcast for a few minutes and then turned to face them. "I don't know what this is all about," he said shakily. "But no matter what's happened to Moses, we have to call the 'Family' first!"

Bastion

Jacko tapped on the door and hesitated a second before turning the handle. Normally, such a formality would be unheard of, but to everyone's surprise, Carson was having an unscheduled meeting with an unexpected visitor. Chief Superintendent Mark Bastion had arrived unannounced, along with his steel-tipped shoes, peaked cap and regulation amount of scrambled eggs.

"Sorry to disturb you, Sir," Jacko interrupted. "There's been a couple of new developments in the Park Murder Case."

"That's okay, Sergeant," acknowledged Carson. "What are they?"

"A girl rang Central ten minutes ago and said the boy found dead in the park is her younger brother, Moses Sweetman. From what we can gather, she lives on the Highwater Estate and recognised him when 'Sky News' ran the CCTV footage from the bus."

Carson and Bastion's eyes met briefly, the look of relief more than obvious. "What about identifying him? We'll need a positive ID."

Jacko nodded in the affirmative. "Central have confirmed she and her mother are on their way to the station. So, I've organised a viewing in the morgue at 5.30 pm and following an interview, should have some more information."

"Did I hear you say two things, Sergeant?"

Jacko turned to Bastion. "Yes, Sir, the other concerns the mobile phones found at the crime scene. Fingerprints and DNA have now confirmed the Blackberry belongs to Moses Sweetman, but the serial number has been removed, which usually means it's stolen. In addition, we've discovered that the pay-as-you-go SIM card was registered to some fictitious person, who supposedly lives on the Estate."

"Drugs?" prompted Carson.

"Almost certainly," said Jacko.

"And the other two phones?" queried Bastion.

"Unfortunately the SIM card from the damaged Samsung has a crack in the chip, meaning Forensics are unable to download anything stored on it. However, they did find it's just one of three phones registered to a Mrs Steffi Freeland, whom we are told lives in Waytree Crescent. It's a small private housing estate situated a few hundred yards up the road from our murder scene."

The tip of Bastion's nose rose like Concorde on take-off. "And I take it you're just about to visit this Mrs Freeland?"

Jacko checked a sheet of A4. "Door to door have already done that for us, Sir. The house she normally occupies is empty, but a neighbour said Mrs Freeland works as a nurse in Walton Hospital. Which would probably explain why there was no one at home when they called."

"Does she have any family?"

"According to the report, she's divorced, but does have a son and daughter."

"Blonde-haired daughter?" asked Carson.

Jacko nodded slowly. "Yes, Sir and once we're finished here, I'm hoping to speak with her at the hospital."

"What about this mysterious iPhone?" prompted Bastion. "Anything happening there?"

"We're still looking, but like the Blackberry, it too has a pay-as-you-go SIM card. So without having the relevant PIN codes, it's near impossible to access them."

"Which means we still don't know who sent the two text messages?"

"No Sir, they're still there on screen, but with the sender's number being ex-directory, we're just clutching at straws."

"Any idea where it was purchased?"

"Not yet. Although we're hoping it might be one of the phone stores in Liverpool One."

"Excellent," declared Bastion, his fingers checking the gold braid for possible contamination. "Let me know the results from Forensics as soon as you can, Nathan. This mystery Transit van also sounds promising, especially if we can trust this Gecko person."

Jacko shook his head as he heard *Fred Astaire* tip-tapping his way along the passage. "Where did he come from, Guv? The last time I saw him in the flesh was when he was taking the salute at some official ceremony."

Carson sounded just as pissed. "Says he wants to be more 'hands on' with the day-to-day running of the S.C.U."

"I thought Joe Ainscough was in charge our little operation?"

"As far as I know he still is, but he's just a plain old *Super*. Whereas Mark Bastion is a *Chief Super* and therefore has more *Pips* on his shoulder."

"Do you really believe that crap?"

"At the moment, I don't know what or who to believe and I'm still wondering why CID didn't take on this Park murder case?"

"Racial tension? Inner-city riots? Maybe the powers that be were expecting some kind of fallout from the local population."

Carson shook his head. "I hardly think so, seeing as how one of the victims is black and the other is white."

Walton Hospital, Liverpool

Both nurses were in hysterics as they pushed through the swing doors, linked arms and departed 'Men's Surgical'.

"I'm not joking," declared Anita. "When I pulled back the sheets, Mr Walters was definitely pulling his plonker!"

The image of the pensioner playing with his penis had them both in stiches.

"He's nearly eighty-four!" cried Steffi, tears of laughter forming in her eyes.

"And that's the stroke he was on when I caught the randy old devil," chuckled Anita. Turning the corner, they were about to head towards the canteen area, when she saw them from the corner of her eye. He was a tall fair-haired suit chatting with Marianna at Reception: she, the uniformed WPC standing by his side. But Steffi could tell that something was wrong by the way the receptionist had paused mid-conversation and stared straight at her: it was a look that said everything.

The WPC, who Steffi reckoned was younger than she was, was first to move, the suit bringing up the rear reminding her of some tasty actor in a TV movie. Yet there was no doubting the look of concern on both of their faces, or the way he'd begun to nervously straighten his tie.

"Oh dear God no!" came an anguished voice. Steffi was momentarily transfixed, until she realised the cry had come from Anita who was standing beside her. Slowing to a halt, the suit began searching from face to face as if trying to understand. "Mrs Freeland? Mrs Steffi Freeland?" he asked with a puzzled look.

Steffi took a firm hold of Anita's still shaking hand and replied. "Yes, I'm Mrs Freeland. This lady is my daughter's godmother and lifelong babysitter."

"The Park," cried Anita, the tears beginning to run down her cheeks. "Our beautiful baby's dead in the Park!"

All activity in the reception area suddenly came to a halt and an old lady wearing a silk headscarf closed her eyes and began a silent prayer. The policeman, however, was just relieved to discover it was Steffi. "Is this about my daughter?" she mumbled, desperately trying to keep the fear from her voice.

Jacko broke the spell by whispering to the receptionist, "Somewhere private, please?"

"Yes, this way," a clearly affected Marianna replied.

Jacko smiled and motioned to the distraught figure of Anita. "Could you please take care of her friend? We need to talk with Mrs Freeland alone."

Marianna gave a nod, "Of course," she said, whilst gently wrapping her arms around Anita's shoulder.

Jacko closed the door, which thankfully took the babble of the corridor with it. The young WPC instinctively moved towards the now tearful woman, who held out an arm to prevent her from coming any closer. "Please, I'm all right," she sobbed, standing as far from them as the confines of the room would allow.

Jacko was amazed at the similarity of the nurse and the girl in the park. She too was of slim build, had the same classic high cheekbones and rich blonde hair. However, before he could say another word, the distraught nurse decided to ask *him* a question. "What's your name, Mr Policeman?"

"Detective Sergeant Sam Jackson," he replied, surprised at her sudden directness.

"And you want to talk to me about my daughter?" she whispered; her voice almost inaudible.

Jacko nodded; ever mindful of the stress she was under; yet remembering he still had a job to do. "The body of a young girl was discovered early this morning in Waytree Park," he began. "And our enquiries have indicated it might possibly be your daughter Kelly." The woman's eyes closed and she gave a cry of pain when he said her name.

Jacko waited another minute before continuing, "I'm sorry, but I was hoping you might answer a few questions."

"Okay," she whispered.

"Your address is Waytree Crescent?"

She nodded once.

"When was the last time you saw or spoke to your daughter?"

"Yesterday morning, she was in the kitchen at home."

"Did she seem okay? She wasn't agitated, worried or acting different?"

The nurse shook her head. "No, she was her usual happy self."

"Does your daughter have a blue strapless dress?"

This time she hesitated before speaking. "Yes, it's new, she bought it last week."

"Did she have a bag with her?"

She nodded again. "A small matching shoulder one."

"Mobile phone?"

"A pink Samsung," she replied, aware that every plus might be another stab in the heart.

So as not to confuse matters, Jacko thought he'd pursue the mystery iPhone at a later date. "Do you know where she was going last night?"

"Yes, she was on a date with her boyfriend."

"Do you know his name?"

She nodded once. "Yes, his name is Anton Watson, although I've never actually met him in person."

"Do you know where he lives?"

"No, but I think it's somewhere near The Philharmonic Hall in Hope Street."

"How did they meet?"

"In art school."

"Your daughter went, goes to art school?" Jacko quickly corrected himself.

"Yes, she's in the Liverpool College for Arts and Crafts."

"And Anton? Is he in the same college?"

"Yes. I remember her telling Kristian he was a fantastic designer, but an even better guitarist. Apparently, he's in a group called 'The Red Tide' or something like that."

He was about to ask who Kristian was, then remembered 'door to door' confirming the nurse had a teenage son.

Jacko closed his notebook. "I know how difficult this must be for you, Mrs Freeland, but given the information in our possession. We can only assume that the girl in the park is your daughter and under the circumstances, ask if you are able you to make a formal identification."

The tear-stained cheeks gave a wan smile, before turning to face him. "Have you ever lost someone you love, Sergeant?"

Jacko's face suddenly wore a look of guilt; his younger sister and parents were alive and, as far as he knew, all in good health. That said, he'd been a police officer long enough to know that grief came in many guises; an unwelcome late-night visit from a policeman being one of them. As if reading his thoughts, the nurse looked into his eyes and gave an ironic laugh. "How sad is that, Sergeant? My job is to try and preserve life in any way I can. But now you're saying my daughter, who is the most precious thing in the world, might be lying dead in some god-forsaken dump and you want me to look and tell you she's mine!"

Buxton Mews

Parking the car in Hope Street, both detectives were content to finish the journey on foot.

"Well, look at this place," chuckled Smithy. "I'd live here if I could."

"Me too," laughed Jacko, his eyes appreciating the magnificent red-bricked edifice that was Buxton Mews. "There again, you'd need to be a banker just to pay the window cleaners."

A fast stroll around the designated parking area took them past two expensive looking Range Rovers and a selection of different-sized Mercedes: always a good sign as to who might live there. It was pretty much the same vibe when they rang the doorbell.

"Anthony Watson?" asked Jacko. "I'm DS Jackson from the Serious Crimes Unit and this is my colleague, DC Smithson."

Within minutes, both detectives were admiring the plush apartment and running the rule over the confused-looking youngster who'd answered the door.

"Are we okay to sit down?" asked Jacko, his finger pointing to the luxury white leather suite adorning the lounge.

"Yeah, no problem," he shrugged, before adding, "Oh by the way, most people call me Anton."

Jacko waved a hand to indicate he'd heard and took a seat anyway. Looking around, he was trying to imagine how the Victorian room might have been in its heyday. It was plain to see that with the removal of the odd wall, the once ornate expanse had long since been converted into a stylish open plan area, the result being a large modern lounge and kitchen area. Everything had an air of quality, as if no expense had been spared, just like the Gibson guitar that sat comfortably on its stand in the corner. *Now that is serious money!* he mused. *But when you're an aspiring musician, I suppose only the best will do.*

Sitting opposite, a nervous looking Anton began to fiddle with his phone as Jacko weighed him up. *Age? Had to be in his early twenties.* Shoulder-length dark hair with a fringed 'Oasis' look. There again, his shaky hands and bloodshot eyes couldn't hide the fact he was badly hung over.'

"How can I help?" Anton asked politely.

Smithy spoke first, "We're trying to identify a young girl who was found dead early this morning in Waytree Park."

Anton's rheumy eyes opened wide and he visibly began to shake. "Oh Christ!" he whispered, the phone in his hand rotating with a life of its own.

"Is that yours?" asked Jacko.

The youngster's eyes dropped to the phone as if seeing it for the first time. "Yeah, this is my mobile," he mumbled, the sound of uncertainty creeping into his voice.

"Is it ex-directory?"

"No, it's just a normal number."

"Want to give me it?"

Anton did as asked.

Jacko took his own phone and tapped in a number. A moment later and the riff from *Smoke on the Water* filled the quietness of the apartment.

It was the one Anton used as his own personal ringtone. "It's okay," smiled Jacko. "I was just double checking."

"Had any texts lately?" asked Smithy.

"Texts?" stuttered Anton.

"My colleague is asking if you've had any unusual texts in the last few days?"

"Not as I remember.

Jacko showed him a phone number. "Recognise this?"

Anton shrugged as though unable to understand the question. "Sorry?"

"Have you ever seen that number before?"

"I don't think so," he whispered.

"Positive?" Jacko insisted.

The 'Oasis' lookalike stared at the number as though it was some kind of Chinese puzzle, then blinked and looked again. "Hell man, that's Kelly's number."

The two detectives exchanged relieved glances as they realised the significance of this revelation.

"Who's Kelly?" asked Smithy.

"Kelly Freeland, she's my girlfriend."

Jacko came next. "Describe her for me." His bones telling him that 'Liam Gallagher's underpants' had nothing to do with the girl's death. There again, he might hold a lot of answers to many unanswered questions. Anton, however, had begun to realise his own worst fears and was finding it increasingly difficult to make his brain function.

Without thinking, his head fell forward into his hands and he began to cry uncontrollably. "No, no, no!" he wept, the tears falling down his cheeks, the nightmare of his empty bed hitting home. The revelations of the last few minutes had been so devastating his world had simply fallen apart.

Jacko and Smithy waited for him to recover, before he faced them with a bitter smile and red-rimmed eyes.

"Oh Jesus, this is unbelievable," he cried, his brain trying to come to terms with what was happening. He then stood and began flashing through various menus on his phone until found what he was looking for. The volume was just loud enough to hear some female laughter as he turned the screen towards Jacko and Smithy. "This is her, this is Kelly," he agonised, his face still raw with despair.

It was a video of the girl lying dead in the morgue, but here on screen she was beautiful, alive and in vibrant colour. Jacko and Smithy watched in fascination as she smiled and playfully pointed a finger towards the camera, a few laughter-filled seconds later and Kelly was just a memory.

It was only in the following silence, did Jacko realise that he and the girl were sitting in the exact same place on the white settee.

"Where does she live, Anton?"

"Waytree Crescent, it's a small private estate behind Waytree Park, but I've never been there. If I picked her up, it was always near the carpark opposite the big Estate."

"Were you supposed to collect her last night?"

Anton nodded.

"What time was this?"

"8.00 pm."

"And why didn't you?"

"I'd been doing a gig at Anfield in the afternoon and later taking part in a Charity Gala at the Adelphi Hotel. When I got there just after 7.00 pm, I found part of the sound system was faulty. This meant me either coming back here and collecting a replacement amp, or the 'Red Tide' couldn't take part in the show. It also meant I wouldn't have time to collect Kelly as promised. So I rang her, explained the situation and said I wouldn't be able to pick her up.

"She'd laughed and said it wasn't a problem and insisted she could get the next bus into town. We agreed to meet up at the Adelphi Hotel sometime after 9.00 pm, yet for some reason she never arrived. I tried ringing her phone several times throughout the night, but couldn't reach her. I was also hoping that when I got home, she might be here, but there was no sign of her."

"One last question, Anton, did Kelly have a key to the flat?"

"Yes, I gave her my spare one a month ago."

The Viewing

The metal chairs were both narrow and uncomfortable, yet Estelle hardly noticed as she and Sarah sat side by side, their hands clasped together in the anonymity of the Morgue's waiting room. Following another stormy argument in the flat. Noah had, at last, conceded they might contact the police, but only on the condition he spoke to the 'Family' first. This had led to another acrimonious and bitter dispute over priorities, which he'd eventually won by punching the number into his phone. The TV on the worktop had once again resembled a non-stop rollercoaster, as a sea of different images, people and places flashed by like so much painful static.

"Who to trust, whom to believe?" whispered Estelle, her heart breaking with grief. It was no secret that Noah and the 'Family' had been running their illicit drugs operation from the high-rise block for many years and as time went by, knew there was no possible way she could interfere. The past she feared was destined to pursue her no matter where she went, with the dreaded 'Stokers' stalking her every step. A picture on one wall portrayed green trees and blue skies, yet she'd already guessed its true significance. It was there to ease the pain of anyone unfortunate enough to be in her position, because here in the Morgue, there was no joy, only death and sorrow.

The sense of loss was all around, none more so than when the fair-haired Detective had turned his unwanted attention in their direction and in that one moment, Estelle knew that there could be no hope, or return.

The Grosvenor Bar

Some said the music blasting forth from 'The Grosvenor Bar' was loud enough to make Quasimodo wince, but thankfully there was always the safety of the upper lounge. Squeezing his way through the crowds, Carson took to the stairs and found Jacko and Frank relaxing in their favourite booth.

"Been one bloody long day," Malone grunted by way of a greeting.

"Tell me about it," he sighed in reply.

Jacko had a question. "Ever remember a black boy and white girl being found dead like this before, Guv?"

Carson backtracked through his career and notwithstanding there'd been some pretty grim situations, had to admit this was definitely a one-off. In this job there was always the odd challenging problem to overcome, but not some professional killer with a foot long blade running amok. It gave him the chance to blow off steam and relate the events from his earlier press conference. "Superintendent Bastion," he moaned, "is as useful as a one-armed policeman in a traffic jam and I swear that in another life he was a professional Limbo Dancer. Because when it came to dodging questions, he was practically horizontal under the table. Then, to make things worse, some smart arse from The Times began asking if we could handle the riots when they took off!"

Jacko smiled and tried moving the conversation on. "The Home Office say there are no mad 'psychos' on the loose, Guv, and the armed forces are still checking for any 'Rambos' who might have gone AWOL."

"What about the girl's boyfriend?"

"We're still checking him out, but at the moment, his story seems okay."

"Anything unusual in the mothers' statements?"

"Nothing out of the ordinary, both women agreed it was just a normal holiday weekend, until this lot happened."

"Tell me about the Sweetman lady's reaction."

"Pretty much as you'd expect, Guv, both mother and daughter were extremely distraught when they identified the boy at the morgue. Mrs Sweetman began to wail like a banshee when she saw her dead son! At one point, I thought she was going to pull her hair out she was so far gone, but luckily, the daughter was there to calm her down. Yet it was less than a half hour later that they both became more than a little reticent. Talk about 'clam up'; they were so tight-lipped, I thought they'd contracted lockjaw! That said, I suppose it's to be expected, considering they're from Highwater *and* live in Sharecropper Heights!"

"What about getting access to their place? This after all is a murder investigation and we need to check if anyone else in the block might have some kind of grudge against them."

Jacko's eyebrows lifted. "We can try," he replied dubiously. "But as you know, Guv, these people are less than accommodating when it comes to the police; murder or no murder."

"Some things will never change," said Stretch.

"Tell me about Mrs Freeland."

"She's a nurse, been divorced for the last ten years and has, or *had* two children," he corrected himself. "And just like the Sweetman lady, was seriously distressed when she arrived at the morgue."

"Find anything at the girl's home?"

Jacko nodded. "In a lower drawer of her bedroom we found the original box for the iPhone, all of it brand new. Yet, according to the mother, she'd never seen it. The only mobile she knew of was the girl's pink Samsung. There's also some confusion as to where the iPhone came from. Initial feedback from Amazon and the few online companies we managed to contact drew a blank. So our next move is to go searching in the morning. Other than that, it looked like your everyday teenager's bedroom with lots of pictures, posters and personal stuff. The only odd thing was one wardrobe had a connecting door to the mother's bedroom; something to do with it once being a nursery."

"I take it the dead girl had a computer?"

"Yes Guv. Unfortunately, the mother didn't know the password, but her younger brother, Kristian, did. Forensics are about to open it up and take it apart, which hopefully should tell us more about her friends and private life."

"What about the *Gecko*?"

"Still in custody," Jacko replied. "Thought we'd hang on to him and his banger for a while longer, or at least until he's been cleared by Forensics. The trail of bloodstains finished right beside his Escort and the four girls supposedly saw him in the car park at the time of the murders, so Tarzan's not quite out of the woods. Well, not until they've swabbed each and every one of his smelly orifices!"

The thought of someone having to perform this particularly gruesome procedure had them all wincing in disgust.

"Besides, it's not as if he's Mother Teresa!" grinned Stretch. "And his absence from the Highwater area is sure to keep the burglary figures down, well at least, for a few days."

Carson, however, wasn't amused. "If we are to believe Reece Armstrong's take on this, there's a perverted hit man out there, who, after murdering the two kids, casually smashed their phones to pieces and then disappeared into the night!"

"The last thing we need is some lunatic with a long knife!" grunted Stretch Malone.

Part Two

S.C.U.
Bank Holiday Monday

It was 8.00 am and Carson was looking for more answers. "Are we sure there's no connection between the two dead teenagers?"

"Not according to their families, Guv."

Carson turned to Smithy. "What about the girl? Does she have any jealous ex-boyfriends?"

"None that we know of."

"And there are no mad groupies hiding in Anton Watson's wardrobe? If he's some kind a pop singer, then maybe he likes to screw around on the sly."

"There's no evidence of it, Guv, and he appeared to be genuinely cut up when we interviewed him last night."

Smithy raised a hand in agreement.

"Okay Jacko, bring me up to speed."

"Watson insists he last spoke to the girl on Saturday night at 7.35 pm. Says he had a two-minute conversation and told her about his gig at Anfield earlier in the day. Which I might add, was just before a problem arose at The Adelphi Hotel. From then on, he says it all became a bit of a blur, seeing as the only other available piece of kit was back at his place." Jacko turned a page. "According to Watson, he was meant to collect the girl outside Waytree Park at 8.00 pm. But as everyone on stage was beginning to panic, he opted to collect the replacement amp instead. He called again around 7.55 pm giving her a run down on the latest happenings, which is when she said she'd be happy to catch the bus."

"And because of a broken cuffin' amplifier, two young people died!" Carson said in a withering voice. "Have we checked his phone from yesterday?"

"Yeah, Smithy went through it with a fine-tooth comb and all his calls check out, although here's the real confusion, Guv. Anton Watson swears that the pink Samsung was the girl's regular mobile and Mrs Freeland says she never saw her daughter Kelly with an iPhone."

"What do we know about this boyfriend?"

"He's a student originally from Chester and his father's a wealthy businessman. His mother, would you believe, is also part of the local judiciary and sits on the Juvenile Courts. But talk about a small world, Guv. It seems Moses Sweetman and Anton Watson were both at the Liverpool football match yesterday. The guitarist was performing at a private party in the afternoon and then the 'Football against Poverty' bash at the Adelphi Hotel. "The young black kid was watching in the crowd. Oh yes, the boyfriend has also given us permission to check out his mobile phone, computer and Facebook site."

"Okay, what else do we know?"

. "He plays in a local band called 'The Red Tide' and they're pretty damn good! Smithy and I saw them last summer at the 'Dockland Music Festival'. Although, I must admit, I didn't recognise him until he mentioned it last night at his place. Likes to be known as 'Anton' these days, gives him more kudos with the fans. Sadly, the poor sod's still trying to get over the fact that if he'd gone to collect her, as promised, she'd still be alive!"

"Hang on," interrupted Stretch. "If this Anton supposedly left the hotel to collect a piece of kit, could he have sneaked out to Waytree Park?"

"Not unless he was Lewis Hamilton!" smiled Jacko.

Carson finished off his coffee. "Have we heard from Mitch Brennan at 'Drugs'? As I remember it, he's supposed to be the expert on Highwater."

Joanna, who'd been tasked with building up a picture of the Sweetmans, entered the discussion. "I spoke to him earlier, Sir, and it would appear they're not all 'sweetness and light'. When it comes to Sharecropper Heights, Mitch reckons drugs and this family definitely go hand in hand."

"That should be interesting. What about you, Jacko, where to next?"

"Me and Smithy are heading for the Phone Store in Liverpool One. We've just discovered it's open on a Bank Holiday Monday."

"Frank?"

"Still searching for this mystery white transit van."

"Jason?"

"I'll be speaking to the Anfield security boys in a few minutes."

"Then let's get to it!" barked Carson.

An hour later Jacko and Smithy were about to head for the city centre, when Joanna waved a sheet of paper in their direction. "Just received this from 'Drugs' and trust me, it's very interesting."

Maybe it was the way she smiled at them, but something said they should postpone their visit and follow her in the direction of the Carson's office. Stretch Malone, who just happened to be in earshot, swallowed his cup of sludge and fell in behind.

"Had an interesting chat with Brennan from Drugs, Sir, and as promised, he faxed this report over."

"Just enlighten me, Joanna."

"According to Mitch, the Sweetman family have been resident in Sharecropper Heights for the past thirteen years and have a well-documented history of supplying drugs to this particular corner of the Estate. It would seem the eldest son Noah has been pushing this stuff for at least four of them."

"They like to start them young," grinned Stretch.

"Saves going out to work," Smithy added dryly.

Joanna waited for them to finish. "There's more," she said, "and it's not the children; it's the lady herself." Carson raised a hand for silence.

Joanna turned to Jacko. "When you spoke to Mrs Sweetman yesterday, did she mention her late husband?"

"Yeah, I think she said he'd been dead for a few years."

"Can you remember how long exactly?"

Jacko shrugged. "Not without looking at my notes, we're still checking her out; sort of doing due diligence."

Joanna lifted the report. "Well, Mitch Brennan does and according to him, it was just over thirteen years ago!"

Jacko's eyebrows lifted. "So?"

"Sweetman is not her real name," Joanna began. "That's her maiden name and the one she reverted to when she moved out to Highwater. In another life, she was once the common law wife of a West Indian male named Jacob Stoker. Which means that Moses Sweetman, the young boy found murdered in Waytree Park, just happens to be the grandson of 'Eazy Stoker', the notorious Jamaican drugs baron!"

"Whoa, now there is a surprise," declared Smithy.

"We need to hear some more on this, Joanna."

"I've organised for Mitch to be here just after 2.00 pm, Sir."

The Phone Store,
Liverpool One Shopping Precinct

Posing in front of the staff room mirror, Billy Binney took a moment to peak his hair with a touch more gel, before hurrying to take his place on the shop floor. At 9.00 am on the dot, the glass doors opened and an eclectic mix of local and foreign visitors wandered in, as an array of iPhones, tablets and computers, shone before them like electronic jewels. Billy, who'd been closely watching the new arrivals, noticed an ageing Japanese man wandering towards his station with a Nikon long-lens camera most wildlife photographers would kill for.

As he waited in anticipation of a possible mega sale, Mr Achler, his immediate supervisor, abruptly interrupted his reverie. "Morning Binney," he said without lifting his head from an invoice he was scrutinising. At this point, Billy noticed the two 'Gentlemen', as Mr Achler called them, appearing in front of his station.

"This is the trainee who sold the iPhone on Saturday afternoon," said the supervisor, his free hand directing another salesperson to deal with the Japanese tourist. A feeling of doubt began to fill young Billy's lower region, his buoyant mood disappearing as fast as the Mersey tide. *Oh no*, he winced. The sale of that iPhone, with its huge range of extras, had come to more than £700, and was the highlight of his short tenure at the shop. But the two 'suits' were obviously policemen and he was praying the purchase hadn't been made with a stolen credit card!

"Hello Billy," smiled the tall blonde one with the flash tie. "We're looking for some information regarding an S6 iPhone sold by none other than yourself." Billy's relief was almost palpable as he took a deep breath and looked to Mr Achler, who indicated for him to cooperate as best he could.

"According to your boss," began Smithy, "an iPhone with this serial number was purchased here and we need to know who bought it."

Billy's keen eyes raced across the invoice. "The woman in the white dress and sunglasses," he said, whilst looking to his boss for confirmation.

"That's right," Achler agreed. "But the shop was so busy at the time, I just about caught a glimpse of her. Oh and as I remember it, Billy only needed me to okay the sale."

"Tell us about the woman in the white dress," asked Jacko. "We were hoping you might give us a little more detail, height, colour of hair, things like that."

"Oh yeah, sorry," said Billy, his eyes scanning the store. "I'd say she was as tall as her," pointing to a 5'6" blonde viewing a nearby laptop. "Dark-haired like her over there," directing their attention to a lady reading a pamphlet. "And about the same age as me Ma!" he finished with a flourish!

"Just how old is your Ma?" asked Smithy.

"Err, not really sure," replied Billy.

If it hadn't been so serious, Jacko would have laughed out loud. "How long before we get the CCTV footage?" Smithy asked the supervisor, whilst trying to contain himself.

"It should be ready to view in five minutes," replied Achler, who was also trying to suppress a smile.

"How old are you, Billy?" Asked Jacko.

"I was eighteen, six months ago," he replied, trying to appear older than he really was. Jacko in the meantime had decided to do a bit of calculating of his own. If Billy's 'Ma' had married say somewhere in her twenties, that would put the 'woman in the white dress' at around forty, or older. Hopefully, the shop CCTV should tell them more. Jacko pointed to the sales invoice on the counter. "The lady who purchased the iPhone didn't give her name or address, Billy?"

"No. According to her, it was a company credit card so she didn't need to."

Jacko turned to the supervisor. "Have you ever dealt with these 'Sun-Up Limited' people before?"

"Not personally. All I do know is their offices are situated somewhere in the SEL building on the waterfront."

Smithy read through the sales invoice. "Once you completed the sale, Billy, what happened next?"

"The lady asked me to fit a temporary 'pay as you go' chip, gift-wrap the whole package and a girl would come and collect it later." He then remembered something else. "Oh yeah, she even wrote down the girl's name, date of birth and described what she would look like."

The detectives looked at each other in amazement.

"And?" asked Jacko.

Billy closed his eyes and said, "She was a drop dead gorgeous blonde." He then began rummaging through his desk drawer before producing a small sheet of paper containing some handwriting.

Jacko and Smithy read it together on the glass worktop.

'Kelly Freeland, 16-8-96, Waytree Crescent, Highwater'.

Smithy was about to fold the piece of paper and place it in his pocket, when something else caught his eye. "What are these four numbers, Billy?"

The young trainee scanned the page. "Whoops sorry, I forgot all about them; it's the PIN code for the temporary pay-as-you-go card."

"Why didn't you just transfer the information from one phone to the other, Billy?"

"It was nearly closing time on Saturday afternoon and she was in a mad rush. I offered to do the changeover for her, but she insisted she could do it herself in the morning, which would have been yesterday, I suppose."

Realising it was now possible to access the iPhone's memory, Jacko rang the Lab and gave them the temporary PIN code in the hope it might lead them to the 'lady in the white dress.'

S.C.U.
Two Hours Later

"Bad news, Guv. The Lab have just called and said Kelly Freeland used the iPhone to send just the one text at 8.00 pm on Saturday evening. Problem is, the number she sent it to was ex-directory."

Carson scanned the invoice. "Any idea who these people are?"

"Not yet, Guv. Their offices are supposedly on the twentieth floor of the SEL Building, but like everywhere else, they're closed for the Bank Holiday."

SEL Building, Tuesday

Smithy pointed to a name engraved on the highly polished brass plate. "That looks like it there, Sarge."

Jacko scanned down the list of companies until he came to the appropriate place; but was still confused. The search for whoever, or whatever 'Sun-Up' was, had been protracted, to say the least. According to 'Companies House', it was a subsidiary of at least two other global entities and after hours of searching, eventually led them to the celebrated Hotel Artisano. Under normal circumstances, most people would assume the 5-star hotel occupied the whole of the building. However, they'd since been directed to a nondescript rear entrance and were about to board a private lift that would whisk them both to the twenty-first floor.

To Jacko's surprise, on their way up they passed the hotel's famous 'Restaurante Valencia', where he'd only recently attended a friend's wedding reception. Smithy, as usual, had made good use of the mirrored interior to smooth back his hair and eyebrows. In what seemed to be a blink of an eye, the lift doors opened to reveal a glorious blend of glistening stainless steel and polished white marble. "Very nice," murmured Smithy.

Moving along the deserted hallway, they'd progressed no further than the first glass fronted office, when they spotted a 'Sun-Up' logo, which appeared to duplicate the one in the ground floor entrance. Stepping inside, they were about to familiarise themselves with these new and impressive surrounding, when a panelled door opened and a classy looking lady stepped out to greet them. Jacko immediately recognised her as young Billy Binney's imagined 'Ma' on the shop's CCTV.

She was small and petite, but by no means demure, her sculptured face framed in a dark pageboy circle of hair. That said, the close-fitting red and black number encircling her body was definitely meant to send some pulses racing; his colleague's being one of them.

"Goodness, you two look serious!" she smiled. "How can I help?" Her eyes scanning them with the same intensity as the Xerox photocopy machine sat in the corner.

"Morning," said Jacko. "My name is DS Jackson and this is DC Smith and we're trying to obtain some information regarding Sun-Up," his head nodding to the brass nameplate in the passageway.

The lady paused and sat back in her chair, thus giving her just enough time to appreciate who they were. "Sun-Up," she began, "is a musical heritage organisation whose aim is to preserve past musicians' claim to fame. It might be just a casual piece of music they'd written many years ago. Yet it's more about ensuring that if, for example, one of your family had written an earlier version of 'Rocket Man', they might not get any royalties, but at least everybody would know they first gave us the pleasure."

Jacko shifted in his chair and wondered if sometime in the 1950s, his old man might have whistled an early riff of Elton John's classic song as he worked on the railways. *Most unlikely*, he concluded. He was about to continue asking questions, when a tall well-dressed man appeared in the frame of same panelled door to what they realised was an inner office. The secretary smiled, stood and without making it too obvious, proceeded to have a brief, but inaudible chat in his ear. He'd listened attentively, his eyes fixed and unmoving, before nodding in understanding what he was being told, his urbane and charming smile suddenly reappearing as if by magic.

"Good day, gentlemen," he said, a hand reaching out to shake theirs. "My name is Maxi Hamilton and Michaela tells me you're looking for some information regarding one of my companies."

"We'd appreciate it if you have the time," replied Jacko.

"No problem," he smiled, gesturing to his office.

Plush wasn't the word, as they both stepped into another world. Maxi pointed to the comfortable leather chairs arranged opposite his desk and they took in the sheer quality of the glass-fronted room. Jacko was no art buff, but knew the huge Venetian oil scene and two Lowry's hanging within his immediate eye-line, wouldn't have been purchased at St John's Market on a Saturday morning. Though he did notice Smithy was more intent on studying the finer contours of the curvaceous lady who'd remained in the office at Hamilton's request.

"My secretary tells me you need to know more about Sun-Up, so how can I help?" A more than accommodating look filling his tanned face.

"Late Saturday afternoon," began Jacko, "a Sun-up Limited credit card was used to purchase a mobile from the Phone Store in town." Pushing a copy of the invoice across Hamilton's oversized desk.

"Possibly," he replied noncommittedly. "So what's the problem?"

S.C.U. Interview Room

Jacko had heard the term 'Gnome of Zurich' many times, but it wasn't until he met Maxi Hamilton's lawyer, did he imagine what one might look like. Clinton Levi was a short dapper-looking man, with an obvious taste in expensive clothes and even though the summer sun was cracking the city pavements, was dressed in a double-breasted suit that might have kept him warm in the darkest of winters. To add to this, a matching pink silk tie and handkerchief blossomed forth from his frontage like a hanging basket and the two detectives wouldn't have been surprised to find him wearing Spats. In what appeared to be a prearranged move, he and the secretary had arranged themselves on either side of a grim, stony-faced Maxi Hamilton.

A silence fell as Jacko briefly ran through the reason for them all being there. He was about to move on and start the interview proper, when Levi interrupted him, "I wish to state that my client's presence here today is of his own free will *and* that being the case, will agree to answer any questions, but *only* those which we regard as pertinent to the death of his granddaughter. He would also ask for full confidentiality in all that might be spoken today at this meeting and at any future time therein."

Jacko was momentarily perplexed at this lengthy declaration; it had never occurred to him that Hamilton might require some degree of secrecy. "As you can see, Mr Levi," his hand gesturing to the desk, "we only have a couple of writing pads for this interview and your client is *not* under suspicion in any way. We are merely trying to establish the background and circumstances concerning the death of Kelly Freeland."

At this point, Maxi who'd sat unmoving throughout the exchanges lifted a hand. "It's okay, Clinton, and not unlike Sergeant Jackson here, I just want to get to the bottom of this nightmare." He then gave a sigh and shake of his head. "As you know, gentlemen, this morning was a very difficult time for us both," indicating to a tearful Michaela. "But I can assure you that we are now ready to tell you anything that might be of importance."

Jacko nodded in appreciation before continuing. "You said earlier, that you'd only recently become acquainted with your granddaughter and just for the record, can you expand a little more?"

Hamilton concentrated on a place somewhere above Jacko's head before speaking. "I think it best we start with her mother Steffi, who as you now know, is my only daughter. It also concerns a fatal accident that happened many years ago whilst my wife Sandra and I were on holiday in America. I was fortunate enough to survive the incident, but sadly she didn't. Steffi, who was eight at the time, had remained at home in the temporary care of my wife's sister. However, due to the injuries I'd incurred as a result of the accident and the problems in trying to repatriate my wife's body, it was more than a month before I was able to achieve this.

In this interim period and due to the tragic news of her mother's death, my daughter had suffered a complete nervous breakdown. When I finally made it home and tried to see her, she point-blank refused to meet or speak to me. This went on for many years and as there were no real signs of progress, the doctors decided it best to leave things as they were; Steffi would carry on living with Aunt Charlotte and her husband. As time went by I'd always hoped that maybe one day she might come out of it naturally, which in due course she did. It was stressful and took many years of patience, before she'd recovered sufficiently to lead a normal life. Yet since that first fateful day and in all the years that have followed, Steffi has completely erased me from her life and neither she nor her children have spoken to me since."

The silence in the room was almost deafening, with even Smithy's ardent scribbling coming to a halt. Then Maxi took his finger from the 'pause button,' and continued with his tragic tale. "As she grew older, Steffi went through school, graduated from college and from what I could see, became a typical teenager. A few years later she met her then future husband Tom Freeland, an Australian guitarist playing in a local rock band. They lived together for a while, got married, had Kelly and Kristian and then divorced some ten years ago. That was the way of things, until six months ago when she unexpectedly walked into my office."

"Are you saying that you never spoke to or saw your family again in all those years?"

"No Sergeant, that's not what I'm saying. Yes, it's true we didn't actually *speak*, but I did see them many times, even if it was only from afar. And believe it or not, one of my most fervent wishes, is that one day I might receive a Christmas card from them. Although that's not to say that they ever went without, Steffi included. I was always there whenever help was needed, even if they were unaware, it was me who provided it."

Jacko's thoughts went back to his meeting with the nurse and wondered how much tragedy one person could have in their life, especially with her own mother's death when she was a child. "Can you tell me more about Kelly's first appearance in your office?"

Maxi looked to a tearful Michaela, who until then had remained silent and her own thoughts went back the six short months to early February.

The girl had read the business plates a couple of times, and once satisfied, made her way inside.

"Hi, how can I help?" asked Michaela.

"Oh, sorry," she said, looking a little flustered, "this is Steelyard Enterprises, isn't it?"

"It was when I came to work this morning."

"Oh great," the girl enthused. "It's just that I'm looking for someone who's supposed to work here."

She wasn't sure why, but Michaela was instantly attracted to the girl's obvious charisma and the mini conversation gave a moment to observe her in more detail. 'Striking' was a word that immediately sprang to mind: she being a five-foot eight blonde beauty whose clothes were casual, yet very 'Bon chic'.

"Who exactly is it you are looking for?"

"A Mr Max or Maxi Hamilton?" came the reply.

The knock on his door brought Maxi's head up from the article he was reading. "Michaela?"

"There's someone outside who wants to meet you," she whispered, her voice unlike its normal everyday manner. Yet it was the way she said it that suggested he should follow her into the reception area.

"Hello Kelly," he smiled a few seconds later.

"Do you know me?" asked the confused looking girl.

Maxi's smiled widened. "Yes, and I drank lots of champagne on the day you were born."

"Well, how spooky is that," the girl squealed in delight. "And does that mean we might be related?"

Maxi was thoughtful for a moment, before pointing to the lift in the hallway. "If you'd like to follow me to the penthouse above, I have something that should answer all of your questions."

As they left reception, Michaela deducted two points from her own personal scorecard; it was after all her job to remember everything that happened in Maxi Hamilton's life.

"Wow!" gasped Kelly, as she took in the spectacular views afforded by 'La Rondo Penthouse'. Maxi beamed from ear to ear, as she marvelled at his ingenious, yet very expensive feat of engineering. The building below might be rectangular, but the roof above had been raised another twenty feet to create a circular wall of glass that gave 360 degrees of uninterrupted views. As per his strict instructions, each area had been designed to give them maximum exposure to the elements, yet its privacy lay in the unique layer of film contained within the glass. This had helped create a non-reflective mirror effect on all external surfaces, the bedrooms, bathrooms and private areas having been individually sectioned and soundproofed.

The distant seascapes were magnificent, as they reached way beyond the 'Mersey Bar' and out into the Irish Sea. Across the river and as far as the eye could see, the sun and clouds illuminated the skies above the Cheshire countryside, as well as the tall magnificent 'Liver Buildings'.

To Maxi's credit, he'd always assumed that when it came to taste, in either clothes, furnishing or artwork, he would be hard to beat. So took the greatest of pleasure in watching Kelly, as she spent some time wandering around the apartment, looking and touching things with an appropriate sign of appreciation. She then pointed to an oil painting by one of her favourite artists. "Gosh, this can't be a real Velasquez, can it?"

Maxi gave a nod of agreement and held up a cup. "Would you like a drink?"

"Neo coffee?" she asked.

"No problem, any particular flavour?"

"Now I am impressed," she laughed, before joining him at the table.

"How did you find this place, or me for that matter?"

"Google," she replied, as if it were an everyday occurrence. "And this newspaper article," taking a folded piece of paper from her bag.

Maxi's eyes narrowed. "Where did you find this?"

"One of the girls in my class was doing a fashion project from the sixties and seventies. She needed clothes or anything outrageous that might be hanging around in people's wardrobes. I knew Mum had some stuff gathering dust in the garage roof and found this amongst some letters in one of the handbags."

Maxi fingered the edges of the paper, before laying it flat on the table. 'Local businessman and wife, involved in fatal accident in Miami!' shouted the headline. Maxi closed his eyes, his mouth a grim line.

"Are you okay?" whispered Kelly, as she saw the pain on his face.

Maxi caught his breath, before rising from the table and staring out at the distant horizon. "Did you read it?" he asked without ceremony.

"Uh, uh, but other than the name 'Steffi', I haven't got a clue what it's about."

"Did you show it to your mother?"

"Yes, and that's the funny thing. When she first saw it, I could see she was upset. Then seconds later declared it was just a load of rubbish and I should throw it in the bin. Which is when I got suspicious and began to think that maybe, you were a rich uncle."

Maxi gave a half smile. "Now I suppose is as good a time as any to tell you the truth."

A fascinated Kelly watched as he reached for a leather-bound album sat on the shelf, opened it on a well-thumbed page and pointed to a black and white photograph. "This is your mother when she was eight years old and standing beside her is my late wife Sandra, who is also your real maternal grandmother."

"I don't understand," replied a stunned Kelly, "I'd always thought Charlotte was my grandmother?"

Maxi shook his head and smiled. "Well, it's true Charlotte was her name, but she wasn't your grandmother. She was in fact my wife's sister and when she was killed in a fatal accident, was more than happy to become a substitute mother to Steffi."

"When was this?"

"It happened many years ago, but in a way, could have been yesterday."

"Can you at least tell me what this is all about?" she implored.

A troubled Maxi looked out to sea and remembered the past.

"One morning in 1982. Two first class air tickets arrived at our place, special delivery. Accompanying them was a huge bunch of flowers and Toby Blizzard's impassioned plea for us to attend his wedding in Miami."

"Toby Blizzard?"

"Yeah," Maxi smiled resignedly. "He was an American promoter friend of ours, but even though we'd known him for many years, Sandra refused to go. The problem, of course, being your mother, Steffi, who she doted on to the point of distraction."

"You mean she was spoilt rotten?"

"Oh yes, and I was just as bad," he admitted ruefully. "Your mother's unexpected arrival had been an unplanned addition to our lives, but once here, changed it forever. One minute we'd been cruising in the Far East and the next I was doing the school run. Toby's wedding was intended to be a grown-up affair, with most of the guests a part of the East coast music scene. There was no church ceremony, bridesmaids or any of that stuff. Toby was getting wed at the poolside, to some airhead Italian bimbo with a voice that could cut steel.

The brief, as always, was let your hair down and give it plenty. Knowing exactly what lay ahead, there was no way we could take Steffi along and Sandra was loath to be away from her for even a week. I eventually coaxed her around, reminding her of the many times Toby had helped us out in the past, plus the expensive first-class air tickets he'd just sent us. After a while, she reluctantly gave in and called her sister Charlotte, knowing she and her husband would leap at the chance of having Steffi for a week.

"Charlotte and Eddie Mitchell?" Kelly asked in a hushed voice.

Maxi held her stare for a moment and then nodded. "Yes. They'd spent years trying for kids of their own, but sadly for them, it never happened, so the opportunity to look after Steffi was like a dream come true. Our only proviso was that they didn't spoil her any more than we did! It was also agreed that Steffi could stay up until 9 o'clock each night and wait for her mother to call."

Kelly waited patiently as Maxi paused with a faraway look in his eyes, as though searching for an answer in the past. "That was it," he said at last. "Everybody seemed happy with the arrangement and following a tearful goodbye, we packed our bags and left for America." Maxi took his cup to where the coffee machine sat and raised an inquiring eyebrow at Kelly, who shook her head in the negative.

"The days preceding the wedding were a bit of a blur; we weren't exactly youngsters, but we certainly knew how to party and boy, oh boy, did we!" He said with a smile. "Then on the day itself, there was plenty of champagne on offer and God knows what else, as a couple of hundred people began to enjoy themselves. The ceremony itself had lasted just two minutes, as everyone shouted 'I do' and a whole row of champagne corks exploded into the air." Maxi paused once again whilst focusing on the sky beyond the window.

"Then later that night, we were on our way back to the hotel, when some drunken fool crashed into our car. I passed out through loss of blood and woke briefly in some 419 Emergency Unit in downtown Miami. That was before they put me under and rolled me into theatre. I can vaguely remember surfacing two days later in a private room wanting to know where Sandra was, but some detective at my bedside kept giving me the same 'spiel' every time, 'Relax Mr Hamilton, you need to take it easy.'"

85

Maxi looked out to sea again, his eyes fixed on the horizon. "It was two days before one of the doctors told me that Sandra had died at the scene and no amount of attention by the paramedics could bring her back."

Kelly sat with her hands across her mouth, as the tears filled her eyes and her head moved from side to side in disbelief. "How?" she asked haltingly, "I mean, what?" once again unable to finish the sentence.

"What happened next?" he answered for her. "Was the nightmares of all nightmares. Sandra lay dead in some hospital morgue and I had a punctured lung causing enough damage to keep me bedridden for another two weeks. It was 1982 and everyday objects like this," pointing to his mobile phone, "were a thing of the future. What we take for granted in today's world didn't exist back then. There was no Internet nor email, the only other means of communication being the telephone. Beyond that, it was maybe a telegraph, or in my case the British Embassy and for three nights, Steffi had sat waiting for the phone to ring."

Maxi shook his head as he relived events from the past that had been beyond his control. "Sandra and her sister had always been close and regularly chatted on the phone, whereas I'd never really had cause speak with the Mitchells and would only meet them on special occasions. To make things worse, I didn't have Charlotte's telephone number either, but knew they lived somewhere on the outskirts of Liverpool. Christ, it was some mess and all the time I was stuck in some hospital bed."

Maxi rose and moved to the window once again. "A week later and someone from the Embassy appeared in my room and said the driver responsible was languishing in jail. He'd also assured me he'd spoken to Charlotte and everything was okay, but when I eventually made it home, discovered I'd somehow lost my only daughter!"

The Grosvenor Bar
6 Hours Later

Hooky Wilson, the barman, watched the small group of detectives arrive just before 5.00 pm, but was surprised when, instead of alcohol, they ordered a round of soft drinks. This was mostly due to Hamilton's lawyer, Clinton Levi, insisting on absolute confidentiality during the interview, plus Carson's reluctance to place their findings on the Display Boards. However, that didn't stop him from keeping the rest of the team in the loop and an empty 'Grosvenor Bar' was the ideal place to hear of Jacko and Smithy's meeting with the famous tycoon. Just as Jacko had predicted, a look of disbelief was etched on all their faces the moment he'd finished talking.

"So let's see if I've got it right," began Stretch Malone. "This mysterious 'Sun-Up Limited' is actually a part of 'Steelyard Enterprises Limited' and the dead girl's mother is Steffi Freeland, who is also the estranged daughter of Maxi Hamilton?"

Jacko weighed up the question, before nodding in agreement.

"*And* who's supposedly never spoken to him for most of her adult life, because she blames him for the death of her mother?" Jacko thought for a moment before giving another nod.

"*And* that being the case," continued Stretch. "Maxi farms out his only daughter to Aunty Charlotte in the hope that one day they might get back together?" Jacko grunted at the scenario, held a hand up and gave a 'maybe' shake of the head.

"*But* in the meantime and having been sort of adopted by her aunt and uncle. Steffi creates a whole new life for herself, grows up, gets married, has kids of her own and is trundling off into the sunset, when we discover her only daughter murdered in the park?"

Jacko sighed resignedly. "I know it sounds like some tragic novel from *Mills and Boon*, but it's all true. According to Maxi, his granddaughter unexpectedly walked into his offices looking for someone called Hamilton, who she thought might be related to her. He knew exactly who *she* was, but the girl he insists, knew nothing about him. That is, until she came across an old newspaper cutting mentioning how Steffi's mother had been killed in an accident. For obvious reasons, Kelly Freeland had always assumed Charlotte and Eddie Mitchell were her grandparents and her mother had never implied this wasn't the case. But when she'd accidently discovered the article, the girl was intrigued and decided to look for more details. Maxi in turn, saw this as the perfect opportunity to tell Kelly about what really happened some thirty odd years ago in America."

"Yet Maxi says his daughter wasn't with them at the time?"

"No Joanna. According to Hamilton, his wife had always insisted on taking Steffi with them whenever they travelled, but she didn't go on this trip. The American break might have been a short one, but Maxi thought it was a journey too far."

"And her aunt and uncle were happy to look after her?"

"Yes, Hamilton says that was the agreement at the time."

"Hang on Sarge, didn't you just say she *freaked out*?" Jason asked from nowhere.

"I wouldn't say she *freaked out*," Jacko corrected him. "According to Hamilton and due to the difficulty he had in trying to repatriate his wife's body, a whole month went by and it was during this period that Steffi sort of *flipped*, for the want of a better description."

"Nice way to describe it, Sarge, but what you really mean, is one distraught and confused little girl never got to see her mother again?"

Jacko's face took on a look of doubt before reluctantly nodding in the affirmative. "You could be right, Joanna, and the really sad part of it is, he'd agreed Steffi would to be able to speak on the phone to her mother every night. Yet due to her sudden death, it happened only twice and after that silence."

Silence prevailed momentarily as they each contemplated the dilemma from over thirty years ago. "What I can't understand is why Hamilton didn't make more of an effort to speak to the girl himself," said Stretch.

"Because she blamed him for the death of her mother!" Joanna snapped.

The other team members fell silent as she spoke her mind. "Look, you said it yourself, Sarge, Maxi Hamilton admits it was *he* who decided Steffi couldn't go on holiday, so it's no wonder she wouldn't speak to him again!"

Jacko considered her theory. "Maybe you're right, Joanna, and yes, I have to agree that somehow it might well have paved the way for the Mitchells to continue looking after her."

"Which must have seemed like a minor miracle, seeing as how they were childless themselves," she concluded impassively.

"Well hell, man," Malone said quietly "You've just lost your wife and then you lose your only child, life really can be a real pisser sometimes!"

Carson, who'd been listening in silence, decided it was time to get involved. "So, Hamilton insists he was always close at hand whilst supposedly watching from afar?"

"Yes Guv, according to Maxi, he spoke with the Mitchells once a week and followed Steffi's progress religiously. But how's this for a surprise, he gave them the house in Waytree Crescent for free!"

"When was this?"

"Not long after he'd finished building them in the eighties. 'Steelyard Enterprises', it seems, had once started life as a local construction firm Maxi had added to his ever-growing empire. The houses in question were built on private land and therefore had nothing to do with the Council. Maxi says he signed over the deeds to the Mitchells on the proviso they could never sell the house and Steffi would inherit it when they both passed on."

Carson's eyebrows lifted. "I've been curious as to how the dead girl and this Moses kid ended up practically living on each other's doorstep."

"That's not all, Guv, when she married back in 1995, it was Maxi who secretly paid for the wedding. He was also standing at the back of the same church, when both Kelly and Kristian were baptized."

Carson shook his head. "So where does this cuffin iPhone come in all of this?"

"It was a belated birthday present from Maxi to the dead girl. Over the intervening months, he'd become familiar with the pink Samsung and decided it would be nice to surprise Kelly with a new mobile phone. His secretary, what's her name again, Smithy?" Pointedly asking him the question so as to lighten the mood.

"Michaela Stevens," breathed Smithy, as he remembered the body hugging red and black dress moving tantalisingly beyond his fingertips.

"Yeah, that's her," agreed Jacko. "She paid for the iPhone with the company credit card, had it gift wrapped and arranged for the girl to collect it from the Phone Store later that day. She then asked young Billy to fit a temporary 'pay as you go' chip, because he reckoned the one in the girl's Samsung was too old; hence the reason for the two phones when she died. We're now convinced the girl was making her way to the 'Adelphi Football Gala' to show Maxi her birthday present."

Carson was thoughtful. "How was she going to explain the sudden arrival of a shiny new iPhone to her mother?"

"According to Hamilton, Kelly had twice mentioned her intention to tell Steffi about her grandfather's sudden reappearance in her life. Maybe this was the opportunity she'd been waiting for."

"However, Cinderella didn't make it to the ball, did she?" Joanna reflected sadly.

"That's right," agreed Jacko. "Although she did send the one text to her grandfather sometime around 8.00 pm. It took a while, but we've at last managed to work out what happened on Saturday night and it really depends on what side of the Adelphi ballroom you stood." Smithy unfolded a sheet of A4 covered in pencil scrawl. "Here are the edited versions of Anton Watson and Maxi Hamilton's interviews, yet the key to all this is the girl herself. Because, unbeknown to Anton Watson, Kelly had secretly spoken to her grandfather and organised for him to perform at Anfield in the afternoon and with his group later in the evening at the 'Adelphi Football Gala'."

"Which we assume was also being broadcast live on TV."

Smithy nodded. "Yes Stretch, fame in the blink of an eye and so much quicker than *The X Factor*."

"What happened next?"

"The boyfriend wasn't able to collect her from the Park, Guv, so she opted to catch the 8.15 pm bus into town. He'd expected her to arrive sometime around 9.00 pm and when she didn't appear, assumed she must have gotten cold feet and decided to give the gig a miss."

"Hamilton?"

Smithy glanced at his scribbling. "Basically, the same set of circumstances. He'd spent most of the night on the other side of the ballroom chatting with his guests and generally making sure everything was going to plan. They'd received a text from the girl thanking them for her present. When she didn't appear as planned, his secretary sent a text of her own and tried ringing both the mobile phones, but by then it was too late and she was already dead. She'd also suggested speaking to Anton, but Maxi didn't want to make a fuss and thought there might a perfectly reasonable explanation as to why Kelly wasn't at the Gala."

"Ships in the night," quipped Jacko.

"Just a minute," said Stretch. "If his granddaughter was supposedly murdered on Saturday night and it was all over the news by Sunday. Then surely Hamilton must have been able to make some connection, considering she was supposed to be meeting him the night before?"

"He might've done if he'd been here," Smithy conceded. "But he and his secretary boarded his private jet on Sunday morning and left John Lennon Airport at 6.30 am, heading for a series of business meetings in Zurich. They stayed for two days at The Plaza Imperial Hotel and returned early this morning. They tried ringing the girl's phone late on Saturday night and his secretary did the same when they arrived in Zurich on Sunday. However, the Samsung was already junk in the park and they never thought of the iPhone. So they naturally assumed Kelly would call, or visit them on their return and didn't hear or see anything until we turned up in his office this morning."

"Christ man, you had to be there!" Smithy whispered. "You'd think a bomb had just landed; they were so shocked!"

"Which reminds me, Guv, when we first began talking with Hamilton, I could see a photograph on his desk and only later realised it's the same as the one in Kelly Freeland's bedroom. It's a picture of Steffi, Kristian and the dead girl, together on holiday somewhere."

"Okay," said Carson. "Do a hush-hush background check on our millionaire and see if there are any hidden skeletons is his wardrobe. Everyone seems to have heard of Hamilton, but we don't really know much about him."

"Where's the girl's father again?" asked Joanna.

"Tom Freeland?" said Jacko. "According to Maxi, he went back to Australia not long after the divorce, remarried and never returned."

S.C.U.

So as to avoid the usual traffic jams, Carson had left his place just before seven, only to find Jacko waiting in his office with two take-away coffees.

"You're early, wet the bed?" he muttered, whilst sniffing the contents of his cup.

"Nah," laughed Jacko. "Called in at Costa Coffee on the way."

"What a night," groaned Carson. "Didn't sleep a wink."

"Had a long one myself, Guv. Spent most of it checking out Maxi Hamilton's background."

"Find anything interesting?"

Jacko shook his head. "Not really. When it comes to our millionaire, I reckon you'd find more dirt on the Pope's slippers. His life appears to be a never-ending liturgy of all things virtuous and he has to be the last word in modern day altruism."

Carson knew exactly what his No. 2 meant, but wished he wouldn't sound like a cuffin schoolteacher. "A little more detail please," he grumbled, his frustrations growing, along with the ethics lesson.

"In a nutshell, Guv, I can't find anyone who has a bad word to say about him. He sponsors at least fifteen charitable organisations. Has a huge 'Greenpeace' logo on his yacht and runs a global empire that spans most of the world."

"Christ, I hate rich do-gooders," moaned Carson. "And I don't care what you say, but no one can be that clean, not even Maxi Hamilton. What about this SEL place? I can't believe there's nothing murky floating about in there."

Jacko shook his head in the negative. "Just finished speaking with someone at the Fraud Squad, who agrees that although Steelyard Enterprises Ltd might be a *nest of vipers*, there's nothing to support that theory. Hamilton pays his taxes bang on time and is universally regarded as an all-round *good egg*. And as if that's not enough, he has lots of friends in high places and regularly shakes hands with Prime Ministers, both past and present."

Carson looked disappointed. "How far back did you go and I mean years?"

Jacko shrugged. "Early eighties when he first appeared on the scene."

"We've found him, Sarge, and his name is Finbar Otagi," called Smithy.

"Who?" asked Jacko.

"The other kid travelling with Moses Sweetman. Saw his face on the news, realised he had no choice and decided to come forward."

Jacko remembered the two black faces grinning at the CCTV camera a few seconds before they'd alighted the bus.

"Hang on, Smithy, I thought Finbar was an Irish name."

"It is, but his old man's a Kenyan bus driver, who married a bird from County Wicklow and it looks as if she wears the trousers when it comes to choosing Christian names."

Jacko rolled his eyes and shook his head. "What have we got?"

"It's as we first thought. Finbar and Moses went to the football match together, but he swears Sweetman paid for his ticket," placing the offending article on his desk.

Jacko's immediate thoughts echoed Carson's. 'Where does a fifteen-year-old kid come by all this money?

Forensics

Jacko's head appeared around the door. "The Lab's been on the phone, Guv, who say they've found some very interesting results."

Carson closed the report he was reading and reached for his coat. "That was quick, I reckon they must be on 'time and motion' over there."

A short walk later and they were about to enter Forensics when Jacko's mobile began to ring. "Two minutes, Guv, and I'll follow you in." Nothing appeared to have changed since Carson's last visit, the same group of white-coated people doing the same complicated things. But he'd completely forgotten about Simone le Roux, the lady who'd recently taken charge of the department, albeit on a temporary basis. He remembered her being parachuted in from somewhere down South to replace 'Shaky Baker', a much-missed stalwart, who'd sadly hung up his *test tubes* and passed on to the *Great Bunsen Burner in the Sky*.

Professor Reece Armstrong might well be overall *Head Honcho* of the department, but for the next few months, Simone would be calling the shots at Forensics. With her silky soft raven hair and tanned Mediterranean looks, she reminded Carson of Claudia Cardinale, a famous Italian actress he'd lusted after in his youth. Yet according to Reece, had one of the finest forensic minds he'd ever had the pleasure of working with.

"Inspector Carson," she enthused. "So good to see you again."

"It's Nathan, Simone, no need for formalities."

She was about to acknowledge her boss, when Jacko came through the door and a surprised look appeared on her face. "Oh, hello Sam, what are you doing here?"

Jacko seemed just as confused. "I was about to ask you the same question, Professor, and wondering if I'm in the right place."

Carson looked just as mystified, until he remembered this was Jacko's first visit to the Lab since her unexpected arrival in Liverpool.

"I take it you two have met before?"

"Just the once, socially," she replied with a smile.

Carson reflected for a moment. DS Jackson might be Sam to his family, or Samuel when born. But at all other times, was 'Jacko' to his friends and 'Sarge' when on duty. Now some dream in a white coat was turning him goo-eyed and he was as jealous as sin!

Reece, however, was still a very busy man. "Shall we move on to more important things?"

"Yes, of course," said Simone. Donning a pair of horn-rimmed glasses that in a stroke transformed her from glamour to business. "Okay gentlemen, if you'd like to come this way please," the tone of her voice leaving them in no doubt as to whom was in charge. Following behind, her long shapely legs led them in the direction of two illuminated workstations, where the girl's blood-stained clothing lay on one, the boy's on the other.

Simone read briefly from a folder before addressing them. "Toxicology on the girl came up negative, meaning there were no drugs or substances of any kind; not even an aspirin. And would you believe it, our beautiful young victim has never smoked; which most girls of her age tend to do. A close examination of her hands and nails however, have revealed a couple of things. The first being the earth under them was consistent with that of the clearing where she was murdered. The next revealed minute traces of some kind of latex substance. Traces of this same substance were found around her throat and on her wrists; which more or less confirms her assailant was wearing some type of rubber gloves."

"Anything about them that might give us a lead?" interrupted Carson.

Simone shook her head. "Nothing at the moment. But seeing as the girl did break a few nails during the struggle, we can safely assume they were strong and flexible. Sadly, there's no sign of skin tissue to indicate she actually penetrated them and drew blood."

"What about her clothes?" asked Jacko. "Find any rogue DNA?"

Simone shook her head. "We can't find a single trace of her assailant and there's no traces of semen or pubic hair to show she was in any way abused."

"When we first entered the clearing, I noticed a couple of used condoms lying around in the grass, don't suppose they had anything to do with the attack?"

"Sorry Nathan, I'd say it's at least six months since they hit warm flesh."

Carson gave a disappointed grimace and Simone gave a smile of encouragement.

"Let's move on to what we do know," pointing to the girl's dress. "As you can see, there are bloodstains on either side, yet the right one has a small puncture hole in it. This came as a result of the flesh wound on her hip and contains only her DNA. It also confirms Reece's theory that the boy was first to die. How can we know this? Because a detailed examination of the knife entry in his stomach, found minute traces of the girl's DNA and dress material trapped inside, but no sign of brain tissue. However, when she died a few seconds later, the same blade had left minute traces of his DNA and tee-shirt all the way up inside her brain."

It was hard for Carson to forget Reece's theory of her being summarily executed, but he was also curious. "What about the bloodstain on the left side of her dress?"

"That, I'm afraid, is where the killer wiped his blade clean."

Wish I hadn't asked, he thought ruefully.

Simone pointed to the split in the back of the girl's dress. "Now this is interesting."

"In what way?" asked Jacko.

"At first we thought it might have happened as the girl fought off her attacker. But not so." She then ran a finger along the edge of the split. "As first suspected, this is one continuous cut and a close-up view, confirms the killer did it with his knife."

94

"So you do think he did it on purpose?"

"Yes Nathan."

"A question, Simone. Why? It's not as if the dress was too long for him lift it over her thighs."

"This is true, but like Reece, I think this is some kind of routine he likes to go through before he rapes his victims."

"So you agree that it is a ritual he's done before?"

"It certainly looks that way."

"That's all we damn need," grunted Carson.

"What about the weapon?" asked Jacko, "Do we have any more on that?"

Simone reached for a plastic ruler lying on the desk and held it between two manicured index fingers. "This measures twelve inches in length, but I'd safely add another two on the end and judging by the width of the entry holes, say it has to be a long slim razor sharp stiletto of some kind."

"Sounds like something a professional killer might use."

"Put it this way, you wouldn't find it on your dinner table," she replied.

"The bloodstains in the carpark?" asked Carson. "Any more on those?"

Simone clicked a computer mouse and Vinny's Ford Escort appeared on screen. "Seeing as they all belong to Moses Sweetman. We can only assume the killer inadvertently stepped in them seconds before he made his escape. Yet following an extensive examination of Vinny's vehicle, we couldn't find a single trace of blood on the brake pedal, or any of the other controls."

"Which suggests he's been telling the truth all along and there really was a white transit van waiting to occupy his space."

"Under the circumstances, it's hard to disagree."

Carson gave a grunt. "I didn't think it was him anyway."

Jacko nodded towards the boy's clothes. "Anything on them?"

Simone gave a smile. "A lot more than expected."

Jacko spotted the boy's shrivelled 'Massimo' underwear lying in one corner of the station and thought it's sad they hadn't survived the bloodletting.

"Toxicology on Moses Sweetman revealed he was normal in most ways, but does appear to have a small trace of narcotic in his blood."

"In other words, like most of the youngsters on the Estate, he was partial to a *joint,*" grinned Jacko.

"Joint, wacky-backy, who can say?" smiled Simone. "Although there's no evidence to say he was injecting. So maybe he was partial to a whiff of Hashish every now and then."

Carson glanced at Jacko, who shook his head and looked skywards; Moses Sweetman was just fifteen years old.

"Could the narcotic, as you call it, have been a factor when the attack took place?"

"I think not, Nathan, it was a relatively minor trace."

"So he wouldn't have been stoned, or sort of off his head?"

"I doubt it. The blood trace level indicates it was taken maybe a day before the incident. Although I think it's time, we had a more detailed look at the boy.

A close examination of his clothing has revealed nothing untoward, other than his and the girl's bloodstains." She then pointed to a TV screen. "His hands however, are a different matter. They were covered in dried matted blood, so we cleaned them up and did the usual Infrared and U.V. scans. At first glance they appeared to be normal and then we spotted something odd with his right index finger. If you look closely, you can just about see a small crack in his nail, but when we zoomed in, discovered a tiny fragment of gold."

"Gold?"

"Yes, Inspector, but not just your everyday 'gold.' This tiny speck just happens to be a 24-carat version of that most precious of all metals."

"Any idea how it might have gotten there?"

"Uh, uh," she replied with a shake of the head. "The gold on sale in most retail shops is usually 9 or 18 carats. The reason being that it's a much harder, thus making it longer lasting and difficult to damage. But 24 carat is different. This is a pure gold with no additives, a pronounced yellow colour and much softer in texture. These days most 24 carat gold is used in the manufacture of 'Krugerrands' or something equally exotic. So, unless the boy was working part-time in some type of jeweller's workshop, or maybe carving up his grandmother's antique wedding ring, it's difficult to say."

"Does it have anything to do with our murder investigation?" asked Jacko.

Simone gave a shrug. "You tell me, Sergeant."

Carson was still mulling over the gold conundrum, when she reached for an evidence bag lying on a nearby table and gave them a winning smile. "What we have here, gentlemen, is the most welcome news. That's because less than an hour ago, we unexpectedly came across *this* vital piece of evidence found at the crime scene."

In a flash, Carson recognised the contents. "That looks like the arm from a pair of sunglasses."

"That's exactly what it is, Inspector."

"Are you saying the killer was wearing sunglasses?"

"At the moment it's a long shot, but the odds get better by the minute."

"Where did they find it?"

"Fingertip search team found it in the deep grass close to the girl's body."

Carson and Jacko waited expectantly.

"They bagged it, logged it and sent it along with the rest of the clutter from the clearing. However, it was only as they began to sort through them, did they realise it could be of some importance and decided to prioritise it."

"Tell me more," said Carson.

"To everyone's delight it turned out to be a very good call and this, Nathan, is real dynamite!" Flicking the bag with one beautifully manicured finger. "Early tests have shown that there are two latent prints, one on either side of the arm. In addition they've also found some fresh blood in the metal hinge, which I've yet to analyse in more detail."

Carson looked to Reece Armstrong. "Did you know about this?"

"Yes and no. I found out half an hour before you arrived and tests are still ongoing even as we speak."

"Which reminds me, Nathan," said Simone. "I think it's time we took a more positive view of this investigation, because trust me there's plenty more to come. She then led them to a TV monitor, the screen displaying what looked to be a small segment of bloodied bandage.

They were still wondering what it meant, when Simone pointed to a large electron microscope sat on a nearby desk. "Would one of you care to look?"

Carson was more than happy to take up the challenge, but needed a minute to realise he was looking at a section of shoelace taken from the boy's trainers. It needed a further up and down adjustment until he saw the thin splinter trapped within its fibres. The shoelace might be discoloured and blood stained, yet there was no discounting this one tiny shard of black plastic. Staring at the sample for a minute, he was about ready to concede defeat then suddenly made the connection. "Hang on, Reece, is this to do with the kid in the clearing? I remember you saying that he might have kicked out at the killer, so this has to be a part of what happened there! Right?"

Simone answered for him, "Yes Nathan. Before the attack, this tiny splinter was once part of the sunglasses. But now goes a long way in proving that Moses Sweetman did try to save the girl. With some more research, we should also be able to discover how it got there, but more importantly who the fingerprints belong to."

"Could the blood have come from the boy or the girl?" asked Jacko.

"Wrong type," she replied. "Both our victims have Rhesus A and B. Whereas the blood on the hinge is A plus."

"Does that mean the killer could have a cut on his eye?"

"All the evidence points to that."

"Would it be large enough to send him to the nearest A & E?"

"I doubt it, but he might have a fair-sized bruise there."

"Do we know what these are?" asked Carson who was peering at three strange-looking gold symbols on the inner side of the plastic arm.

"Yes, they are Cyrillic letters."

"I went on holiday to Greece once," said Jacko, "and I'm sure they use it there."

Simone gave a smile. "I think you'll find most of the Eastern European countries use Cyrillic in one form or another, especially when it comes to their alphabets."

"Well, that should narrow things down a bit," laughed Jacko.

"We've also done a quick computer check, hoping it might be from some exclusive range, but the first couple of searches came up blank. Until one of them indicated it might possibly have been made somewhere in Yugoslavia."

Carson looked disappointed, but was still interested. "Do we know what they stand for?"

"Yes Nathan, they translate as V.D.O."

"Have you ever heard of them?"

"Afraid not, but I'd hazard a guess it's the maker's name."

"And you think it belongs to the killer?"

"Without a doubt," she said with a confident smile.

"What I want to know is where's the rest of the frame?"

"If it's not in the clearing, Sam, then we have to assume the killer took it with him and judging by how much of the surrounding grass has been flattened, I'd say he was frantically searching for something."

"Which we assume has to be the broken arm?"

Simone gave a nod. "It certainly looks that way."

"Will DTI be able to tell us?" Asked Reece.

Simone raised an eyebrow and smiled. "That's what they're here for."

Situated in one corner of the Lab was the *Digital Topographical Imaging* unit; supposedly the latest thing in computer wizardry.

"Hey Guv, take a look at this," laughed Jacko, who was peering at the live images on the large screen. "I'm sure that's our crime scene."

"I think you could be right," agreed Carson, who was equally surprised at the bird's-eye view of Waytree Park and its surrounding areas.

"Meet Charlie," proclaimed Simone. "Who's our top DTI operator."

"I'm sure we met yesterday in the park," said Jacko, as the drone operator raised a hand in friendly agreement. He then gave a tweak of his computer mouse and in a flash, they were looking down at the wire gate leading into the carpark. Yet, before they'd had time to absorb this wizardry, he'd transported them as though on a magic carpet and saw them standing in the middle of Junkies Corner. A moment later and they were in Park Drive, looking directly into the carpark, with the individual vehicles parked neatly in their rows. And sure enough, there was Vinny's Escort sat in the bay, nearest the gate.

"So this is your Digital Topographical Imaging?" asked Carson, who was closely watching the onscreen display.

"It's a present from our friends across the water," explained Simone; whom they could only assume were the Yanks and not Seaforth Technical College on the other side of the River Mersey. "It works by way of five individual 3D scanner points," she said. "But the camera drone and the one positioned in the clearing are the central ones. The other three are there to record the outlying areas, each taking a multitude of digital images, which are then sent via GPS to this computer. This in turn, assimilates the data received, shows it on the screen here and with the inclusion of the hand-held cameras, which are thermal as well as infrared, we can achieve movie-like quality."

Most of that went over my head, just like the cuffin drone, thought Carson, as everyone continued to praise its virtues.

Simone, however, who'd sensed his reticence to modern technology, gave the operator a nudge. "Show the DCI how this really works." Charlie, who was more than happy to oblige, began by clicking the mouse, which transported them back to the centre of the clearing, the wooden fence with the bushes and surrounding areas appearing onscreen. "Let it run," suggested Simone, closely observing the detective's reaction to yesterday's events.

Carson was only interested with the images on screen. Especially when the two bodies were lifted from their places in the grass and the moment the blue handbag was discovered lying beneath the girl. "We can fast forward lots of this, Nathan," she smiled.

"I know that, but I'm still waiting for the results of the Luminol scans."

"Results?" queried Jacko.

"Am I right in assuming the magic drone can do a basic Luminol check?"

Simone smiled. "Yes, Nathan." Giving an affirmative nod, as Charlie panned out and they watched the crime scene turn a different set of colours!

Luminol, Jacko suddenly remembered, was a chemical agent used to highlight areas where it was near impossible to see things with the naked eye. A quick spray of the stuff reacts to the iron in haemoglobin and an ultraviolet light will reveal any dried blood and urine. It was also hugely important in an open crime scene like this one.

"We can see the smaller bloodstains in the grass from the girl's wounds and the larger more easily identifiable ones are the boys where he tried to crawl away. Even the trail the killer left behind as he made his escape through the carpark. But this particular area is the one we're really interested in," Simone said, pointing to an over-bright corner of the bushes near the fence. "As you're aware, lots of the duller colours mean they're older stains. But not these ones, they're different. And this particular one here," pointing to a large area close to the fence, "is relatively fresh urine or was when we found it on Sunday morning."

"How fresh is fresh?"

"About twelve hours."

"So Simone, what you really saying is the killer had a piss?"

"Yes Nathan," her eyes focusing on the screen. "A long hot one and guess what, the DNA matches the blood on the hinge of the sunglasses."

Carson was impressed, but needed more.

"Charlie do me a favour, pan out so we have an overall view, but include the Highwater entrance, the park and the bus stop on the main road, I want to check out a theory." Instead of the mouse, Charlie used his fingers to race across the keyboard and as if by magic, Carson's request appeared on screen. Everyone watched and waited, as his eyes flicked back and forth.

"The bloody ticket!" he said at last. "I should have known it would be that." Without turning his head, Carson made a request. "Jacko, off the top of your head, run the CCTV evidence by me."

His No. 2 thought for a second before replying. "On Saturday evening at exactly 7.40 pm, Moses Sweetman and another youth step off the bus outside the Park. The security cameras in the Shell petrol station directly opposite shows them passing by at 7.42 pm and headed in the direction of the small cluster of shops further along the road. The same cameras record the deceased making the return journey alone at 7.49 pm and we can only assume he passed through the gates into Waytree Park."

Carson nodded along with Jacko's narrative, pausing only make a request. "Charlie, pinpoint exactly where the sweep team found the football ticket." The technician instantly produced a close up shot of the seat number as it lay in the grass by the fence. "Brilliant!" Carson enthused, whilst still concentrating on the detailed graphics. "Okay, let's assume the boy reached this point here," indicating to the first junction on the Estate.

"That's Beechcroft Drive where the *Gecko* lives," said Jacko.

"I know. Which is why I now want Charlie to calculate the exact distance from the petrol station, by way of the park, to the drive itself. Then I'd like him to estimate how long it might take a five-foot seven person to walk it?"

"Exactly twelve minutes," came his confident reply.

Carson nodded. "I'm now convinced the boy passed his killer. And although I wouldn't trust the skinny little bastard as far as I could throw him, I think the *Gecko's* evidence is the real key. We're talking about five crucial minutes here and all within a few hundred yards." He then pointed to the screen. "Moses Sweetman crosses the road at 7.49 pm, enters the park and takes the time-worn shortcut towards the 'hanging gate'.

"However, who could have predicted the tragic twist of circumstances that were about to unfold before him. On his short journey, he passes the four girls heading for the town bus at around 7.54 pm. But without realising it, drops his most prized possession; the proof he was at Anfield, when Liverpool trounced Arsenal two nil! Seven fateful minutes later and the *Gecko* leaves for town, presenting the killer, who must now be desperate to have a piss, with his newly vacated parking spot next to the 'hanging gate'!" Carson made another request. "Charlie, go back to where the *Gecko's* car is parked and give us an aerial overview."

A moment later and they were all staring down at the top of the Ford Escort. "Focus in on the bloodstain which is nearest to the car."

Charlie began to home in on the pavement. "Okay, hold it there," he said, before asking another question. "Jacko, how long would you say a Ford Transit van is in length?"

"Not sure exactly, about four meters?"

Carson nodded and pointed to the screen. "This bloodstain here ends up somewhere behind the Escort's rear wheel arch. But if we superimposed a transit van in its place, what would we get?"

"Probably the driver's side door, if he reversed in!"

"Do you think the boy and his killer met face to face?"

"Yes Simone, and I'd say it was around the time when he went to relieve himself!" The gathering waited as he gave instructions to the man with the magic fingers. "Okay Charlie, pan out once again, but slow it down this time."

All eyes watched as the DTI graphics magically transformed the landscape into a recognisable view of the crime scene and carpark. "Stop there," Carson instructed. "Now if we're to believe the *Gecko*, it's 8.05 pm and he's already left for town. So we have to assume the girl was still alive when turning the corner into the carpark. At around the same time the killer has finished having a piss and is about to pull up his fly when she comes into view."

Jacko, who'd been following his boss's narrative, could easily see what happened next. "He stepped back into the bushes and waited."

"Yes, Jacko, the bastard knew the girl would pass through the gate and so he waited for her."

Reece was next to comment. "Do you think the boy might have suspected there was something wrong?"

"Who can say?" grunted Carson. "His true objective was the ticket that lay somewhere on a journey he'd already made. And I think you'd have to be a blind man not to see the girl was a real beauty. So who's to say Moses Sweetman hadn't already passed her in the carpark and then sensed something was wrong. Unsuspecting, brave, foolish, Christ knows?" he continued. "But whatever it was, the girl, the ticket, or both? I'm afraid he drew the short straw and in the end, it cost him his cuffin life!"

Brennan

It was easy enough to spot Brennan from Drugs, his close-shaven head and Asian heritage giving him away every time. He also was Liverpool born and bred and renowned for his languid sense of humour. Except today wasn't the time for joking, as he stepped into the S.C.U. looking to find a few familiar faces, Joanna's being one of them.

"Over here, Mitch," she waved as a welcome.

Keeping her company was another recognisable face. "See you're still wearing those loud flashy ties, Sg.?"

"Have to keep my image up," grinned Jacko.

Brennan grinned back. "There's not much chance of you getting run over with one of those around your neck," he chortled.

Joanna interrupted their revelry. "We were hoping you might shed some more light on The Park murder investigation."

Mitch gave a wink and took a large brown envelope from under his arm. "Just finished printing these holiday snaps from Records."

"Use the second display board, mate, and I'll organise the team," instructed Jacko.

Within minutes, the troops were focusing on the newly attached photos. These included a mixture of police mugshots, undercover surveillance snaps and what could only be described as *selfies.*

"Meet the *Families,*" declared Brennan. "And for those unfamiliar with this lot, the Stokers are on top and the Sweetmans below." A wry smile crossed his face. "There was a time when my ex-boss would refer to them as 'The Bible Belt' and if you listen carefully, you'll understand the reason why."

Mitch pointed to a white-haired, bearded man who looked like a benign Abraham Lincoln. "At a glance, this is not who you think he is. This in fact, is the notorious drugs baron, Ezekiel Stoker. He's also a religious fanatic, strict disciplinarian and known to his close friends and family as 'Papa Eazy'. According to Jamaican legend, he landed on these virgin shores sometime in the early seventies, set up shop in the South of Liverpool and has been dealing in death ever since. But he's no fool and runs his drugs operation with a rod of iron. Oh yes, I nearly forgot to mention the most important part. He doesn't drink alcohol, despises thieving of any sort and won't tolerate any of his people breaking the law."

"What about all this death and destruction?" asked Joanna.

Mitch gave a smile. "As Marlon Brando used to say in *The Godfather*, 'It's nothing personal, just business'."

Cue a sea of raised eyebrows as he moved on.

"Next in line is Elijah, the dreadlocked number one son, who trust me is one *vicious* bastard and runs their everyday drugs operations." All eyes were drawn to the cruel pockmarked face, whose stumpy Rastafarian curls looked more like horns sprouting from the top of his head.

"Whoa," exclaimed one WPC. "I wouldn't want to bump into him in the dark."

Mitch grinned. "Trust me, love, neither would I." A ripple of laughter could be heard, as his finger moved on to the next mugshot. "Eazy's other sons are in descending order, Jonah, Adam and Zachariah, each an essential part of the Stoker's drugs outfit. And of course, we mustn't forget the other regular gang members, Zoot, Thread and Tawny."

He then moved on to the lower montage, showing just the one official police mugshot and four normal photographs. "We now come to the Sweetmans and I'll start with him." Indicating to the young male whose arrogant eyes stared unblinkingly ahead. "Eighteen-year-old Noah is the leader of the Sharecropper gang and generally known as the Snake."

Another WPC was about to ask why, when Mitch smiled broadly and pointed to his crotch. "It's all in the genes, my love, and I don't mean denim ones." Amid more laughter, he pointed to the next photo. "Beside him is his younger brother Benjamin, whose normal nom de plume is *Benny the Hatchet.* Next in line is Sarah; sweet sixteen and nothing points to her being mixed up in the drugs trade. Bringing up the rear is fifteen-year-old Moses; one of the two kids found dead in the Park, but when alive still an integral part of the gang."

He finished his summary by pointing to a large smiling woman. "Last, but not least, we have Estelle Sweetman, mother to them all and partner of the late Jacob Stoker. Incidentally, he was Eazy's second son and might have been dead these thirteen years, yet still figures greatly in today's events."

Carson lifted a hand. "In what way?"

Mitch paused. "I suppose it has to be when he was murdered in 2002. Nobody knows who killed him, but shortly after his death, Estelle Sweetman reverted back to her maiden name and moved out to Highwater. If it was her intention to escape the past and look for a new life, it surely didn't last long. According to the social worker who had been keeping an eye on them, everything seemed to be hunky dory. The kids were doing well at school, Estelle had a regular part-time job and then this scumbag came sneaking back into their lives," his finger pointing to Elijah's menacing face.

"It would appear that young Noah was more than happy to reacquaint himself with his long-lost uncle and delighted to sell his drugs. After that, things quickly went downhill and I can still recall reading a report from his then Probation Officer two years ago. It seems Noah was involved in a knife fight with another drug-pusher over some 'territorial boundaries'. The uniforms received a call from A & E, where both had turned up with serious stab wounds.

Noah received a really bad one to his upper thigh, whereas his opponent survived various cuts and slashes, the worst being the six-inch one on his cheek. As normal both kids went before the Junior Assizes and ended up on probation. Yet it seems the biggest loser was Noah, who'd supposedly had the potential to become a top-class footballer. However, following the knife incident, his career disappeared like confetti in the wind. He can still go through the motions and make all the right moves, but his natural speed of foot disappeared along with the confetti."

Jacko was next to pose a question. "Would you say any of this lot were capable of carrying out the murders in the Park; taking into account they're all heavily involved in drugs?"

Brennan wrinkled up his nose and shook his head. "Nah, I don't think so. Most of the gangs these days carry weapons of some kind, be it knives, swords or even guns. But their usual method is to slash and burn, then run like hell! If what you tell me is right, Jacko, then the MO of the Park murders definitely doesn't fit the bill."

Part Three

The Beehive

Amid the usual chatter at the press meeting, Dickin from the Post saw DCI Carson motioning for him to hang back until the other reporters had left the room. He was also hoping that this might be another of his unofficial chats, but was surprised to find it was the man himself who needed some information.

"Hi Freddy, if you're not too busy I was wondering if you might help me out with something."

"No problem, Nathan, what is it?"

"I'm looking for some background stuff on Maxi Hamilton."

A quizzical look came over the reporter's face. "*The Maxi Hamilton?*" he queried.

"You mean there's more than one?"

Freddy was confused, but still happy to help. "What do you want to know?"

"I can't talk about it now and I don't mean the guff that's normally in the papers. I'm more interested in the stuff from the past you never see or hear about."

"When exactly are we talking about?"

"The late sixties and seventies."

The reporter was momentarily stumped. "Hell, there's no way I can help you there, I wasn't even born then."

Carson didn't respond, he simply waited for something a little more positive and Freddy duly obliged. "Give me a minute Nathan, this requires a quick call."

At 6.00 pm precisely, Carson left Church Street and strolled the short distance to 'The Beehive', a famous pub situated in Liverpool One. Threading his way through the crowded bar, he saw Freddy sitting alongside a frail looking man in one corner of the Victorian lounge. However, on nearing the table, realised the white-haired gentleman in question had to be somewhere in his late '80s and could be as old as the pub itself.

"DCI Carson, meet Archie Speed, who was changing the ribbons on his Olivetti typewriter years before the Beatles were famous," grinned Dickin.

Carson laughed along, aware the octogenarian sipping on a half pint of Guinness might have been capable of doing just that and so much more.

"Freddy tells me you're the person I should talk to regarding Maxi Hamilton's early life."

Archie gave a small shrug. "I can tell you only what I know."

"That has to be better than nothing."

The old man narrowed his eyes in thought. "Maximilian Hamilton," he whispered. "Now there's a name to conjure with. Genuine Liverpool lad who lived out in the Speke area when it was less overcrowded. And I'm sure he was a welder in the Cammel Laird Shipyard around the time they were building the

'Polaris' submarines. But all this is on file in the public domain and I can't remember a time it wasn't."

"I know that, but I'm more interested in the Maxi Hamilton that's not on file."

The old man's eyebrows lifted, as though surprised at this straight to the point directness. Carson, however, had sensed Mr Speed was well named and a damn sight sharper than your average tack!

"I first met Maxi back in the early sixties, when I'd moved from the crime desk of The Evening Post and began covering the Liverpool music scene. Drank in all the right places and became friendly with lots of people in the know. I was also one of the first reporters to do an in-depth interview with the 'Fab Four'."

Who Carson could only assume were *The Beatles*. "Frantic, exciting, magical times!" Archie regaled, whilst staring at his Guinness as if it were a crystal ball. "At the time, 'The Mersey Boom' was still in its infancy and lots of the kids were trying to tune their granddad's ukuleles in a vain attempt to play a song," shaking his head at the thought. "Maxi, as I remember, was the bass player in a local group called *The Instrumatics.* and had his eyes set on being the next Paul McCartney; that is, until his accident came along."

Carson waited for this particular tale to unfold. "One day in 1963, some fool dropped a hatch lid cover on the middle finger of his left hand and completely severed the tip! From what I heard, Maxi was fast, but in that split second, not fast enough," he chuckled ruefully. "So, in the blink of an eye, his playing days were over and the group had to find themselves another bass player. But they couldn't just ditch Maxi seeing as how they needed his Bedford van to get them to the gigs and use his dad's telephone to organise their bookings." Archie smiled. "Unless you were *posh*, Inspector, or shared a party line, the red telephone box on the street corner was the only other option."

Carson could imagine the ups and downs of the 'haves and have nots' back in the early sixties, but had to concede it was probably no different from when he was a kid in the seventies.

"To cut a long story short," Archie continued, "*The Instrumatics* were suddenly caught between a rock and a hard place, because without Maxi, they were well and truly snookered. True, they desperately wanted a new bass player, but needed his van even more! So a compromise was reached and they decided to employ a temporary guitarist in the hope his finger might heal. This in turn meant Maxi could keep his involvement in the band by acting as both their *roadie* and unofficial manager."

Archie's voice trailed off as he recalled distant images from the past. "Magic times," he whispered. "But what you also have to remember, Inspector; is that the teenagers of the early sixties had plenty of money to spend and 'The Mersey Sound' was the flame that lit their own personal touch paper. *The Beatles* were suddenly more popular than *Cliff and the Shadows* and *The Cavern Stomp* had replaced *The Twist.* It also meant that as it took off like a runaway train, every coffee bar or youth club became a potential music venue.

"Another important factor were the audiences themselves; who averaged around sixteen and guzzled mostly soft drinks. It also meant that lots of these places didn't need to serve alcohol and not unlike the kids of today, most of them were happy to try something new. And that's when Maxi became heavily involved in the Liverpool drug scene."

Carson's eyes opened wide and Archie smiled, aware he'd caught the detective's attention with this latest revelation.

"Are we still taking about *Maxi Hamilton*, the millionaire property baron?"

"Oh yes, but he had to start somewhere, didn't he?" he said with a knowing tilt of his silver white head.

A stunned Carson fell silent as Archie spoke on, "In a roundabout way, the injury to Maxi's hand was where it all began and the reason he needed to earn some extra cash by acting as a bouncer in the local nightclubs."

"You mean Hamilton once worked as a doorman?"

Archie gave a nod. "In his younger days, Maxi used to be a half-decent heavyweight boxer, which came in handy for keeping any unruly kids in line."

An amazed Carson was now more than interested in the old man's tale from the past.

"As the Music Scene grew, so did the need for some light relief."

"Meaning drugs?"

"Yes Inspector, but I'm not talking about the heavy stuff. First on the scene was the novel stuff like *Purple Hearts* and *Black Bombers;* which were ideal for keeping people awake at the 'all night sessions'. This sort of stuff had its roots in the London clubs, but in next to no time, 'The Cavern' and 'The Twisted Wheel' in Manchester had followed suit. I can still remember one Saturday night reviewing 'Rory Storm and the Hurricanes' at 'The Iron Door' club in Temple Street. The place was jam-packed and if you needed some type of pill to keep you awake, Maxi was the man to speak to.

"There was a time when he had two or three other rock groups on the go, but in the end lost lots of money and that particular venture didn't last long. But come 1967 and as people's hair had begun to grow longer, so did their appetites for something a little more exciting. Every day, normal people began to walk around with flowers in their hair and Maxi would feed their dreams aplenty!" Archie laughed aloud at the thought, but appeared to exclude himself from such foolishness. "He was also involved in quite a few other legitimate businesses; there was the café, a dry cleaner and a trendy clothes shop. But I think the best move he ever made was to reopen 'Goodman's Private Casino' not long after it was gutted by fire."

"Hang on, that place is still going now, but I never knew Hamilton was involved."

"He might not be today, Inspector, but he was back then. As I recall it, the fire had damaged most of the interior, but not the main building. Manny Goodman, who'd originally owned the place, was seventy-nine years old and getting a bit past his sell-by date. To make matters worse, he'd been a bit forgetful with his insurance policies and had no natural heirs."

"You mean he had no family?"

Archie shook his head. "No one living here in Liverpool. His only son was a doctor in the Israeli army and at the time heavily involved in the Egyptian war. So I can only assume he couldn't just drop his scalpel and return home to run a casino. In the end it all got a bit too much for Manny and he sold it for an undisclosed sum."

"What I'd like to know is how can a known drug dealer like Maxi Hamilton take over a casino, even if it was private?"

"Well, that's the thing, Inspector, he didn't. A private company bought the place and completely renovated it. They then put in a new manager and reopened it six months later. Which is when we discovered they'd bought the adjoining building and expanded their operation."

Carson was still open-mouthed. "I can imagine a private casino being the perfect place to launder illicit cash?"

Archie gave a nod. "Possibly, but at the time nobody knew Hamilton was in any way involved."

"What about drugs, was he still pushing them at this time?"

"It's hard to say, seeing as how he never actually sold them on the streets. But what you have to remember is that I'd been moved from the crime desk, so most of my information came from Hector Dooley."

"Hector Dooley?"

"Yes Inspector, he was the one who took over my job and funnily enough, we used to meet in this very pub every Friday for a few drinks. We'd have a chat and he'd keep me up to date with the latest crime scene."

"Is he still around?"

"Afraid not, he broke his pencil about five years ago."

Carson looked puzzled.

"It means he died," added Freddy.

"Can you remember what Hector said about Hamilton?"

Archie took another sip of Guinness. "The last time we spoke was sometime in 1982. He said Maxi had closed down nearly all his street operations so he could concentrate on the casino and go upmarket."

"Upmarket?"

"Hector said he was selling cocaine exclusively to the rich and famous."

"Why the move?"

"More money, less risk."

Carson was still amazed at what he was hearing. "I don't suppose you know anyone who actually bought and paid for this stuff?"

Archie laughed. "Not a chance. Most of his day-to-day operations were run by BB Benson."

"Who's he again?"

"He was Hamilton's second in command, as well as his main enforcer. The word on the street said you didn't mess around with BB Benson. But I know it all came to an end sometime after Maxi's wife was shot dead in America."

Carson sat bolt upright and Archie's face took on a look of surprise.

"I thought she'd died in a car accident?"

"Ah, is that the story?" He smiled. "Maxi always was the clever one."

"Tell me more about America," urged Carson.

"From what I heard, he and his wife were at a wedding in Florida when some lunatic began a turkey shoot. Both were shot, Maxi survived, but she didn't."

"Were they the target?"

"Don't think so. Hector said some others guests were caught up in the fracas and there might have been another fatality. However, once he'd shipped his wife's body home, he literally dropped out of sight."

"What about press coverage? I can't believe there'd be nothing in the papers."

Archie gave a shrug. "Maxi had lots of friends in the right places, even in those days. I can still recall the reaction from the front desk when we were told to go easy; something about the trauma the family were going through."

An even more confused Carson began to clutch at straws concerning present day murder motives. "When Hamilton was running his drugs operation, was there anyone who might of had some kind of grudge against him?"

"That's a good question, Inspector, seeing as there was a lot of friction in the early seventies, especially with everyone looking to gain an edge. Hector had always claimed it was Eazy Stoker and the Jamaican 'Yardies' who'd caused most of the trouble."

"You mean Stoker and Hamilton were once enemies?"

"Oh yes. There'd been many a running battle between the gangs, especially with Eazy encroaching on Maxi's territory and his policy of selling hard drugs."

"What do you mean by hard drugs?"

"Hamilton only ever dealt in marijuana and cocaine. It was common knowledge he would never go near the really hard stuff like heroin. According to Hector, Maxi had always called it the 'death trap'."

Trust Hector to break his cuffing pencil! thought Carson, as Archie carried on talking. "What you also have to remember, Inspector, is the undeniable fact that Hamilton is one very shrewd person, who to my knowledge, has never been convicted of a crime. They say Teflon was a by-product of the atom bomb and I can only imagine that someone must have plastered Maxi's arse with it." He then turned to his friend beside him. "I would also remind you both that I'm telling you this in the strictest of confidence and ask you not to mention my name when discussing this matter with anyone else. One last thing, I suggest you be very careful in how you proceed, because as everyone knows, Maxi Hamilton is not the sort of person you mess about with!"

Carson left 'The Beehive' and made his way through a crowded Church Street wondering if he'd acquired more questions than answers. Who would have thought the dead teenagers in the park were somehow related to these once bitter enemies? And does their obvious hatred of each other have any bearing on why the kids were murdered? The manner and death of Hamilton's wife had also thrown up huge questions for him and the Team, considering his statement when first interviewed. There again, if it really had been a tragic accident and Maxi was just trying to avoid publicity, then he could tell it any which way he cuffing well wanted.

He was thinking of Archie Speed's warning that he and Freddy Dickin might have to be careful when it came to the multi-millionaire. Hamilton's arse might well be plastered with Teflon, but was still a man of huge power and influence, which meant Carson didn't need his own backside in the firing line. He'd also regarded himself as still being on duty in 'The Beehive' and in doing so refused an alcoholic drink, but now he was badly in need of something strong and a confidential chat. Following a quick telephone call, his No. 2 had readily agreed to meet him for a coffee in Carluccio's.

Aware that passionfruit panna cotta was his favourite Italian desert, Jacko wasn't in the least surprised to find his boss halfway through a double helping. But astonished to hear of Maxi Hamilton's early life as a drug dealer.

"Can we believe him?"

"Absolutely," said Carson. "I doubt Archie Speed has ever stepped off the straight and narrow in his whole life. The problem for us though is that he heard it from a fellow reporter who's now dead."

"Are there any other witnesses?"

"None who are alive to tell the tale."

Jacko paused for a second. "Do you think our favourite pathologist might be wrong about the murder motive? Maybe there's someone from the past looking to get even, or possibly settle a score with either Stoker or Hamilton."

"I doubt it. Besides, when was Reece ever wrong about anything?"

"Never," grinned Jacko.

"Maybe we should do a little more digging, Jacko. Speak to Mitch Brennan in the morning and see if he knows anything about this BB Benson. Archie Speed reckons he was Maxi Hamilton's front man and ran most of their operations. If he was really selling drugs to the public, then I imagine he'd be on record somewhere."

"That's assuming he's still alive and kicking, Guv."

"This is true, but it won't do any harm to check."

"What about Hamilton? Considering we have an exact date when his wife was killed, I could get Smithy to search the Evening Post online archives."

"Why not? And while he's at it, get him to speak to someone in the Miami Police Department. They must keep a file on British women who've been shot dead on their shores."

"I'll give him a call now and with a bit of luck, we should know something by late tomorrow morning."

Carson scooped the last of the raspberry cream from his plate and eyed his No. 2's tie. "You look as though you're about to meet someone special, anyone we know?'

Jacko gave a wry smile whilst remembering he'd slipped back to his place for a quick change of kit. "Had a text message from a certain forensic lady who wanted to know if we could meet for a drink. Says something new has turned up concerning the Park Murders."

Carson looked suitably impressed. "Where and when?"

"Jamie's Italian, in ten minutes."

"You could get a job as an expert on Liverpool restaurants."

"It's only a drink, Guv, no food involved."

"I remember my ex-wife spinning me the same line when we first met. She then dished up her homemade apple crumble and trapped me into thirty years of marital servitude!"

The Professor

Jacko left the restaurant remembering yesterday's visit to the Lab and the shock meeting with the lady herself. It was also hard to believe that two weeks earlier, he'd been attending a friend's wedding reception and saw this stunning brunette amongst the other guests. Taking his seat at the table, he found he was sat beside this same knockout dish and the physical attraction was apparent from the moment they'd both said hello. To the irritation of his date for the day, a blonde barnacle, who'd fidgeted alongside him, plus the brooding Professor of something vague, who'd fretted next to her, they'd hit it off immediately; laughing and chatting like old friends.

They'd also been cautious when touching on the exact nature of their employment. He being guarded about his own personal details, she tiptoeing around the type of work she was in.

"Are you a professor like him?" He'd casually inquired, motioning to her companion.

"Not quite, but I hope to be soon."

The wine and her reply had them both giggling in fits of laughter and helped them move on to other subjects; one being a potted history of where she hailed from. Her grandparents, she told him, had been French and before the war ran a private flying club near Cognac. However, the invasion of France had necessitated them fly both their planes north to avoid them being destroyed by the advancing German Army. A week later came the fall of Paris and for the first time had watched a Messerschmitt fighter-plane swooping low over the airfield. It soon became obvious that the whole of the country was about to be occupied and because petrol was in short supply, decided they had no other choice than to make for *Angeleterre*.

So, in one last throw of the dice, her grandparents and some friends had ditched everything they owned and left Dinan Airport literally on a wing and a prayer. A fraught two hours later and with their engines running on fumes, they'd managed to reach the south of England and land in a field. From there they'd been promptly arrested and taken into custody. Both their planes had been confiscated for the war effort and they'd been interrogated for weeks on end. Six months later, her grandfather had enlisted in the Royal Air Force as a 'Free French' airman; fought in the Battle of Britain and somehow managed to live throughout the conflict. When it was all over, they'd returned home, only to find the retreating German army had destroyed everything they'd once owned.

Witnessing first-hand the devastation all around, they realised they had no choice other than return to England, where they might find some work. Grandma had once told her they only intended to stay for twelve months, but ended up living here for thirty years: her grandfather becoming a pilot for a budding local airline. To their delight, he'd also achieved his dream when they'd returned to their beloved Cognac in the early seventies and reopened another flying school.

As she related her tale, Jacko had been fascinated not only by the sound of her voice, but the unusual colour of her eyes and had to smile when she finished her story in her own inimitable way. "What you have to remember, Sam, is that my grandparents time in England didn't exactly go to waste, as they left behind their own legacy, which was my father, Henri, who later married my English mother, Poppy, who in turn produced their own legacy, *me*!" This last statement, which had been uttered with an almost patriotic innocence, left him wondering which side she really favoured: the blue of France or white of England? Jacko recalled that lots of wine and conversation had followed as they expertly skirted around what type of work they were in.

'Professional Etiquette' he liked to call it, whereas some people would say, *don't be so bloody nosey*! Another telling moment came when their legs had accidentally touched under the table, its unexpected intimacy giving them a lightning-type jolt! When the evening had ended, all they could do was give each other perfunctory goodbyes, their hands clasping together for what he assumed was the last time.

The thrill of yesterday's surprise meeting in the Lab hadn't gone unnoticed by Carson, who'd commented, "Nice to see there's a direct link between our two Departments, Simone." His head nodding in the direction of Jacko.

This had given him the chance to slip her a card and whisper, "Speak soon, Professor." Before going in hot pursuit of his boss.

Paula was first to see Jacko as he entered the restaurant. "Oh yes, Simone, I remember him now tall, blonde and chisel-chinned. If it wasn't for the mini tweak of his nose, I reckon he could be a real star."

"Shush," she whispered; yet delighted at her friend's description of the detective. Besides, she liked Jacko's so called 'mini tweak' and thought it gave his face character, good-looking, but not too pretty boy. It was the same with his choice of clothes, casually smart and of course, the regulatory silk coloured tie.

Jacko waved a hand when he saw them. "Hi Professor, not too late, am I?"

"Not at all," replied Simone, motioning to an empty seat. "I don't know if you remember Paula Lotherington? She was on our table at the wedding."

"Of course, I do," he said, whilst reaching to shake her hand.

Paula however, had leant forward and gave him a close-up view of her more than ample cleavage. "So nice to meet you again, Sergeant," her devouring look suggesting he might be on the menu.

"What time's your massage again?" asked Simone, as she watched Paula go through her usual 'vamp routine'.

"No need to make it obvious," she replied with a smile. "I was just about to ask if Sergeant Bergerac did private investigations?"

Jacko looked pained. "Sorry, I'd like to help. But I only take on minor cases and I think *you* might need special services!"

Paula laughed out loud and reached for her bag. "Something tells me you two need to be alone and it's time I made myself scarce." Rising from the table, she purposely adjusted her décolletage and made a slow, seductive exit into the crowded thoroughfare

"Who's she again?" grinned Jacko.

"Paula works in finance and runs a huge operation for some overseas company based in the city. She's also happily married to a good-looking and much sort after interior designer."

"Liverpool and its people never cease to amaze me," chuckled Jacko, whilst ordering another white wine for Simone and Peroni lager for himself. "And talk about a small world, when you said you worked for the Government. I never imagined it being the temporary Head of Forensics!"

Simone gave a shrug and smiled. "Funny thing is, I had no idea you were Sergeant Bergerac."

"Touché!' laughed Jacko, which gave him the opportunity to ask some more questions. "So how long are you here in Liverpool?"

"I'll be off as soon as they find a suitable replacement."

"Where's off?"

"Princeton University in America."

Jacko was both curious and impressed. "What takes you there?"

"An advanced course in how to counteract Cyber Crime."

"Sounds very technical."

"Trust me, it is."

"Will that make you a real professor?"

"Hopefully," smiled Simone.

Jacko looked into her wide hazel eyes. "Your text said something *very* important had turned up."

Simone's reply took him by surprise. "I know the food here is pretty good, but I was wondering if you might settle for a frozen pizza instead?"

Jacko's confused look said everything.

Simone opened her bag and showed him her iPad. "I think you'll find what's on here *very* interesting and in an hour's time I have to make a phone call that could be vital to the Park murder case. But seeing as I live no more than five minutes from here, I was thinking that we could maybe take a walk and you bring me up to date with this Maxi Hamilton business."

Harbourside Apartments

"How's the wine?"

"Deelish!" laughed Jacko. "What's this stuff called again?"

"Fleurie Reserve," she replied, delighted at his obvious enjoyment. On their arrival, she'd opened the bottle of Beaujolais before moving off to the kitchen, her fridge door opening and closing as she arranged the Pizza and an accompanying side salad. Meanwhile, Jacko's quick sneaky-peak look around the luxury dockside apartment soon had him thinking. *Maybe I should get a job in Forensics.* Just as she reappeared and declared, "Pizza's about to go in the oven."

Taking a seat at the table, Simone filled her own glass and switched on her iPad. "Things have really moved on, Sam, and this is the latest find from the crime scene."

Jacko found himself looking at a long thin black plastic zip-tie. "Where did that come from?"

"Forensics found it lying under Vinny's Ford Escort."

"So what's the connection?"

"None really, other than it looks brand new and has minute traces of flux in some of the teeth."

"Flux?"

Simone nodded. "The proper name for it is 'Rosin' and it's widely used in connecting copper pipes."

"As in plumbing?"

"That's its normal use," conceded Simone, "but at the moment it's hard to say if it has anything to do with the Park Murders."

"Maybe it fell from this mystery white Transit van."

"The thought had crossed my mind," conceded Simone, as she quickly moved onto another subject; the broken arm from the sunglasses. "Now this is where it does get interesting," her finger pointing to a split-screen with four photographs. "Showing here are exhibits A, B, C and D," tapping each one in turn.

"Photo *A* highlights the fingerprint found on the inside of the arm. *B* reveals the one on the outside. *C* is a close up of the wheel hinge that we know contains the blood sample. *D* is the plastic splinter found in the lace of the dead boy's trainer and all seemingly connected. That is, until our latest DNA tests show the fingerprints are actually from two different people."

To say Jacko was disappointed was reflected in his sudden outburst. "Damn, I thought everything pointed to just the one suspect?"

"It did."

He then decided to throw a speculative high ball in the air. "What's the chances one of the prints might have been there for much longer?"

"That's what I like about a really smart detective," she grinned. "Judging by its degradation, it would appear the print on the inside is at least a week older. Yet print *B* and the blood in the wheel hinge are recent and almost certainly from the same person *and* their DNA is a near perfect match!"

"Jeez, Simone, that surely has to put him at the scene of the crime."

"Almost certainly, but we've since discovered something else of importance. Fingerprints *A* and *B* might be different, but further investigation has revealed both the DNA profiles are near enough identical."

"Where exactly are we going with this, Professor?"

"What we *now* think, Sam, is that they might be siblings with close family ties."

"You mean like brother and sister?"

Simone scanned the photos on screen. "I'm not sure about sister, but brother would fit the bill perfectly!"

"Twins?"

"Possibly."

"Are these mystery twins anywhere in records?" he asked, his expectations beginning to dissipate with every revelation.

"Afraid not," she replied. "We ran both sets of prints, plus the DNA profiles through the UK database, but they all came up blank."

"And here was I thinking we had a bloody walkover," he groaned.

"My thoughts exactly," she said, appreciating his despair. "Which is why we decided to concentrate on the broken arm and the 'VDO' gold lettering. An initial search has indicated the sunglasses might be from somewhere in Yugoslavia, but didn't say where exactly. Which is why we did the same search through Interpol and sort of got lucky when this appeared on screen."

Jacko saw some type of official police crime sheet and the mugshot of what appeared to be a young David Bowie lookalike in the top left-hand corner. Any other information however, had been overtyped with a continuous line of X's, as if someone had purposefully kept their finger on the key.

"Who or what is it?" he queried, more than a little confused.

"We've been asking the exact same question, Sam, but due to the massive overtype, no one could understand the text beneath. But just like the broken arm from the crime scene, we think it's Cyrillic in origin."

"Anything else?"

"Yes. We've made numerous attempts to obtain more information, but nothing other than this document and mugshot came up. We're now convinced that this is a police chargesheet of some kind, yet no matter how many times we tried to obtain more information, this message would appear on screen."

(Klasifikuju, Nema pristupa dozvoljen)

"Any idea what it means?"

Simone nodded. "Yes Sam, it can mean either *Classified* or *Restricted*, but in essence says 'access denied'."

"Oh no," he groaned. "So where do we go from here?"

"The answer to that question has to be Zelda."

"Zelda? Who the hell's she?"

Simone sipped her wine, gave one of her thoughtful looks and closed her eyes. "Whilst studying at Southampton University in 1995, a tall girl with long auburn hair unexpectedly arrived on Campus. Her name was Zelda Zamarova, who'd recently joined us as an overseas student. She was gangly, shy and spoke very little English. But as luck would have it, ended up rooming with me for the next three years. It was then I discovered that she was a Bosnian Serb, whose family had paid for her to finish her education far away from what had been a long bloody war of attrition. Although when she arrived here, it was just about coming to an end.

"During our time together, Zelda would tell me stories of all the horrors they'd had to endure; how there wasn't a person she knew who hadn't lost a loved one or been injured in some way. As I listened, I would thank the Lord above for my own peaceful upbringing. I discovered that Zelda was a fiery entity; who wanted to study law with the sole ambition of putting the World to right. But within eighteen peaceful months, became a little less stressed out and began to blossom." Simone reached for her iPad and tapped away until a picture of herself and Zelda, both dressed in tennis outfits, appeared on screen. "This is a photo of us taken at the time."

Jacko gave an appreciative whistle. "Phew, I see what you mean by blossomed," seriously impressed by the striking picture on view. Zelda's hair was tied up in a loose knot with the odd random tress falling seductively down over the shoulder of her short-sleeved tennis top. The top was doing its utmost to keep everything place, the tennis skirt helping accentuate her long and never-ending shapely legs. "She reminds me of a wild Russian rock star," he laughed. Causing Simone to smile nostalgically at the thought.

"It's funny, but Zelda could never understand why most of the male spectators would shuffle to her end of the court when she was about to serve and then applaud her every shot!"

They both laughed out loud, thinking of the wide-eyed letches with their uncontrollable mouths dribbling away, every time Zelda had showed off her delicious backside. "She's not the only beauty in the picture!" Jacko observed casually, moving his head side to side in a show of appreciation.

Simone caught his eye briefly and raised her own, as she studied the snapshot from her youth, *Yeah, not bad*, she mused.

"Where's Zelda now?" he asked, interrupting her thoughts.

"Now? She's a highly acclaimed freelance journalist who works out of Sarajevo."

"Where's that again?" asked Jacko, not wanting to appear as if he wore a dunce's hat at geography.

"Sarajevo is the capital of Bosnia and Herzegovina, but at the moment none of that matters." Staring at the photo. "*This* is what really interests us!" Pointing to the mugshot on the chargesheet.

Simone glanced at her watch and took another sip of wine. "We need to go to the study," indicating across the lounge. "Bring your glass along, it could take a while." The apartment, he realised, had originally been two-bedroomed, but one was now a temporary office come study, with a desk and chairs to one side and a large Mac slimline console centred between the units.

They'd only just sat down, when the printer began to spew a pile of A4 sheets. "Just in time," beamed Simone. She then began moving through a variety of websites before finally arriving at Skype. To Jacko's surprise, a large modern office with a panoramic backdrop of city lights suddenly appeared on screen. But what really caught his eye was the striking looking woman sitting behind the polished desk. "*Simone, jesi li to stvarno ti?*" she cried.

"Yes, Zelda it's me."

"*Tako je dobro videti te ponovo!*"

"And it's so good to see you again," Simone laughed in delight. "This is my friend, Sergeant Sam Jackson, the detective I told you about."

It took a moment for him to absorb what was happening, until he realised the teenage Russian rock star from eighteen years ago, was now on screen before him. Jeez! It really was Zelda in all her glory and to say she looked older would do her an injustice. Her hair was the same colour, but with the addition of some blonde highlights had given it an almost exotic feel. With her red lips slightly parted, she gazed unerringly into his eyes with a look that would consume most men.

"A little closer," she said in almost perfect English. Jacko was unsure for whom this was intended, until Simone gave him the slightest of nudges, directing her eyes at the screen and Zelda.

Oh shit, he thought. *She's giving me the once over!*

A moment passed, before she spoke briefly to Simone, in what Jacko assumed was more Bosnian. Simone gave a wide smile, before replying hesitantly, in what sounded like the same language.

"Have you had time to read my latest emails?" Zelda asked, returning to English.

"Not yet, we've only just this minute received them."

"Okay, let's start with the overtyped document," said Zelda.

Jacko placed them on the desk, so he and Simone might study it together.

"My sources in Belgrade have assured me that this is a Serbian chargesheet," she began. "It's a common document that's used countrywide and there could be thousands more in circulation. The normal way of identification is the printed serial number in the top right-hand corner, which regrettably in this case has been typed over."

"Is there any way we can remove the offending X's?" asked Jacko.

"Not without the original paperwork or documents, which we can only assume is still somewhere in Serbia's filing system."

"Is there any way of enlarging this to reveal the information beneath?"

"Possibly Simone, I've asked a friend who's a specialist in this field to study it for us and with a bit of luck should have an answer soon. However, this document has something missing and that is the all-important second page."

Jacko nearly spilt his wine. "Second page?" he spluttered.

"Yes Sergeant," her eyes fixed on his. "What we have here is page one of two. The first details who and what they've been charged with, but the second would almost certainly have shown their fingerprints!"

Jacko was blown away by this information. "Wow, do you have any idea where?"

"I'm afraid not and the fact the document is incomplete suggests such a scenario. Despite this, we think there's been some kind of administrative error and this document was never intended to be in the public domain."

"What about the sunglasses and the Yugoslavian connection?"

Zelda smiled encouragingly. "This item in particular shows great promise and my people are actively pursuing its origin."

Jacko was all smiles at this news, but deflated by what came next. "We have asked many questions, my friends, and at the moment can only wait until we have some answers."

"Okay Zelda, it's been fantastic seeing you again and we'll speak at this time tomorrow evening, *Zbogom.*"

"Goodnight, Simone and when this is all over, maybe you and your Detective Sam can come and visit us." A mischievous glint showing in her eyes as the screen went blank.

"Some more?" asked Simone, indicating to his empty glass.

"Why not, I could do with something to cheer me up," he laughed.

Simone made her way to the wine rack and Jacko relaxed on the settee.

"Food will be ready in two minutes," she called from the kitchen.

The four cheese pizza was consumed in next to no time and in between the odd gulp of wine, Jacko helped in clearing the table. They were returning to the lounge with the intention of delving deeper into the Sarajevo case, when their hands accidentally touched.

It was just like on the day of the wedding, the fleeting sensation of warm skin sending a lightning like spark fizzing between them and within seconds their lips were together, bodies entwined and the tip of her delicious tasting tongue in his mouth. Jacko was still enjoying the richness of her perfume and feel of her body, when she paused, placed a hand on his chest and to his alarm began to ease him away.

He was still searching for the reason why, when she placed a finger on his lips and with a mischievous look in her eyes began to take off his tie. She then let it drop to the floor, and slowly began to unbutton his shirt. With a smile on his face, he stood and awaited the next seductive removal of his clothing. Simone, however, had other ideas, as well as an inquiring look on her face and it didn't take long for him to realise that it was now *his* turn! Slowly and sensuously, they shed each other's clothes, she left with just her high heels and lacy black thong, he naked except for his briefs and an ever-growing erection!

She then kissed him on the lips and using the tips of her fingers, began tracing the outline of his manhood. Her touch alone was enough to make his heart race, but was once again brought back to earth when she pointed to the floor. "No socks," she whispered. Within seconds, both objects were sailing across the room like a couple of *Exorcette* missiles.

Slipping one hand around the curve of her back, feeling the fullness of her breasts, his tongue savouring the taste of a nipple, when she once again eased a space between them. However, this time she used both hands and slowly began to peel off his briefs, which resulted in him springing free in more ways than one! Jacko could see the gleam in her eyes, as she took hold of his erection and as if taking a child by the hand, led him towards the bedroom. "This is known as *The French Connection*," she breathed in his ear, her free hand opening the door. The night had been one of passion and ecstasy, as they sought and reached their own personal heights of satisfaction, the climax coming when they'd both fallen into an exhausted and contented slumber.

Awaking to a bright new day, a still naked Simone slipped from beneath the sheets and swanned off in the direction of the bathroom, giving Jacko more than enough time to enjoy the rear view and call his boss. "Morning Guv."

"You sound cheery."

"Thought I'd give you an update on all the latest developments."

"I take it last night's meeting was a fruitful one?"

Jacko suppressed a grin. "You could say that."

"Fire away."

"According to our Forensics lady, the two DNA samples found on the arm of the sunglasses aren't an exact match. Although she does concede they might in some way be related."

"What does that mean?"

"There's two of them and they're brothers."

"No way," groaned Carson.

"That's not all, Guv. When they were surfing Interpol's database trying to match the fingerprints, it took them to an unknown Serbian website."

"So?"

"We now think it's an official one and access is restricted."

"A bit more detail, Jacko, it's too early for guessing games."

He took a breath and gave his boss a condensed version of Zelda and the Serbian connection.

"This is getting more confusing by the minute, Jacko, better put your underpants on and meet me back at the ranch."

"Be there in an hour, Guv, but first, me and Smithy need to run through the transcript of our interview with Maxi Hamilton."

Steelyard Enterprises Ltd

The hi-speed lift was designed to carry a minimum of six people, however, the 'Three Wise Men' had always arrived within minutes of each other and always alone. Whether this was intended or purely accidental, Michaela couldn't say and after all the years she'd worked at SEL, was still none the wiser.

First through the door was BB Benson, Maxi's long-time friend and close confidante. Who, in much happier times, would have flashed a toothy grin and said, "Hello gorgeous, how's Miss World today?" However, the news of Kelly's death had left him silent and grim, as he gave her a curt nod and passed through the panelled door. Thinking back, Michaela could remember the night when, after a few drinks, Maxi had told her of his friend's multi-coloured history.

"BB's father had been a Brazilian seaman named Benzo Bunafido, who'd arrived in Liverpool circa 1935 aboard a rusting tramp-ship with the sole intention of unloading its cargo and collecting another. Sadly, things hadn't quite gone as intended. The boat had indeed taken on a new load and later departed for warmer climes, but a bleary-eyed Benzo didn't sail with it. He'd arrived back at the quay just in time to see the smoke from its funnel disappearing over the horizon and find his kit bag stowed in the security hut. 'Someone said you might need this, mate,' smiled the policeman, who'd seen it so many times before.

"On discovering he'd literally 'missed the boat', the errant stoker staggered back to the bar he'd recently departed and continued to enjoy all the pleasures Liverpool could offer. Following a short relationship, Benny Benson, as he was now known, had wed one of the barmaids and sired a beautiful baby girl. Within a few years, his family had continued to expand with the arrival of two more siblings, but sadly for Benny, both were female.

"Then, in 1943, he'd at last been rewarded with his one true desire: a son. To celebrate this miracle of childbirth, he'd named him 'Bonaparte' and two weeks later joined the 'Atlantic Convoy' he'd recently been assigned to. However, within days of taking to sea, a German U-boat lurking somewhere off the coast of Greenland had torpedoed his ship, meaning this new-born son never got to meet his father.

"Yet even more troubles lay ahead, when because of his height, the kids had nicknamed him 'Bony Benson', which couldn't have been much fun in the knock-about world of the school playground."

A smiling Maxi told her of the time one bully had tried to pick on BB, without realising the kid with the suntan could punch like Rocky Marciano, but soon discovered his mistake when he woke up with a black eye and sore head. In another stroke of luck, he'd begun to spar with Maxi in the local boxing gym and in a short time, became the best of friends.

Maxi hadn't gone into any further details regarding their friendship, other than to say BB's one desire in life was to play golf every day. Yet Michaela knew that when it came to Maxi's affections, the man with the two explosive fists had more claim to them than she ever would.

Next came Clinton Levi, a short square man, but what he lacked in stature was more than compensated by his natural flamboyance, as he swept into the reception and placed a fingertip kiss on either cheek. "How are you, little one, especially after yesterday's ordeal?"

"I'm alright," Michaela replied with a sad smile. "But it's the manner of Kelly's death that troubles me the most. She was just the most beautiful person to ever walk through the door and now she's gone."

The lawyer's eyes twinkled, as he recalled his own delight at the magical appearance of Kelly in their lives. His next task however, wasn't quite to his choosing. "I'd better go in," he whispered, indicating to the panelled door.

As he disappeared into the office, Michaela reflected on what she knew of the immaculately dressed solicitor. The two men had met socially sometime in the early eighties, when both their daughters had attended the same school. Their business relationship had really blossomed around the time Maxi began looking to buy some properties; Goodman's Casino being top of the list. Aware he might be in need of some expert legal advice; Maxi had hired the lawyer to help guide him through the many pitfalls that lay ahead.

Yet it was Clinton's shrewd suggestion they form a private company and omit Maxi's name from any of the paperwork that had solved the problem. From that moment on, Maxi wouldn't contemplate using anybody else.

The last of the 'Three Wise Men' to pass by her desk was Maxi's financial advisor, Rupert Hawksworth-Jones. A tall thin unremarkable looking man who might easily have passed for someone's ageing uncle, his herringbone jacket and corduroy trousers being more suitable to the local vet. In Michaela's eyes, he'd always been something of a mystery man and she could count the times on one hand when he'd had occasion to visit SEL. Yet there was no doubting that 'Hawkeye', as BB Benson loved to call him, was an important cog in the everyday workings of the Empire and his presence here today was like discovering roses on the moon.

Over the years, Michaela had met him in so many different locations around the world; albeit mostly in five-star hotels and always from afar. Her brief in all of this had been to watch and wait, as he and Maxi would talk for as many hours it might take to set in motion some complex deal. She was also aware that only the death of Maxi's beloved granddaughter would have brought him here today.

Entering the reception area, he gave a downcast shake of his greying head and whispered, "How are you, my dear? These are such sad times we live in," before shuffling in the direction of Maxi's office.

Beyond the panelled door, angry voices were getting louder by the minute and tempers becoming more frayed.

"I'll strangle the bastard with my own two hands," screamed BB Benson, his fingers forming a cage as though reaching for the killer's throat.

Maxi however, had decided on a more pragmatic approach. "Take it easy, BB. I didn't ask you here to wail like an old washer woman. I'm trying to discover if someone might hold a grudge against SEL and we are somehow responsible for Kelly's death." He then turned to Clinton and Hawkeye. "Unless we can find the reason why she was murdered, then all this rhetoric is just a load of bullshit, do you understand!"

Both men nodded, BB included.

"Okay," said Maxi, "let's make a start."

To everyone's surprise, Michaela came into the room pushing a trolley load of files and folders. "May I suggest, gentlemen, that we begin with these?"

They then spent the rest of the day scouring every business deal: be it legitimate or otherwise, that might somehow constitute a reason to kill his granddaughter, but all to no avail. It was way after midnight before Maxi finally conceded defeat and in desperation turned to Clinton. "What do we know about the murder investigation?"

"Only what the police tell us. The news reports say Kelly was murdered in some place called Junkies Corner, by person or persons unknown. There's also speculation a young black kid tried to intervene and died as a consequence."

Maxi was singularly unimpressed. "Is that it?"

"I'm afraid so and seeing as you're *not* regarded as an immediate next-of-kin, you'll just have to live with it."

"What happens if there's a major development, or some new evidence turns up?"

"When it comes to the letter of the law, Maxi, nothing changes. Which means you won't have your usual front row seat in the dress circle. You'll be the same as *Joe Public*; sitting at the back and asking the same old questions. But there's someone else you need to think about and that's Steffi!"

The room suddenly went quiet as they remembered Maxi's only daughter.

"I'm seriously of the opinion that she will be less than delighted to find you're in any way involved," warned Hawkeye. "So my advice is to say nothing and keep out of sight."

"He's right," agreed BB. "Steffi will go absolutely ballistic if she hears you've started to poke your nose in!"

Maxi shrugged, but wasn't ready to give in just yet. "There must be someone who can at least give us an idea of what's happening?"

BB shook his head. "I've spent hours trying to think of someone on the inside, but nobody comes to mind."

"What about the investigating team?" Asked Maxi. "We've already met this Sergeant Jackson and his mate, but what about the rest of them?"

Clinton adjusted the glasses on the end of his nose and began to read from a file. "The man leading the inquiry is DCI Nathan Carson."

"What's his background?"

"Originally from Bristol and like most coppers has worked all over the place. London, Neath in South Wales, Plymouth, you name it and he's been there. He also has an impeccable record as a police officer and ran Liverpool CID for many years, but following a well-deserved promotion, took over at the M.S.C.U."

"Who are they again?"

"*Merseyside Serious Crimes Unit.*"

Maxi gave a nod of approval, but still wasn't satisfied. "I take it this DCI Carson has no hidden fetishes or kinky ways?"

"Likes the odd drink or two in the pub; there again, tell me a copper who doesn't?"

"Family?"

"Divorced. Although his ex-wife still lives in Bristol and he has a daughter who works as a nursery teacher somewhere down south. Other than that, he's a dedicated policeman who's always looking to arrest the right man."

"Not if I get the bastard first," growled BB Benson.

Hawksworth-Jones had listened to what was being said with a look of distaste. He wasn't into violence and all the hurt that came with it, yet having two daughters of his own could relate to the brutal murder of Kelly and the terrible injustice. "May I make a suggestion?" he said quietly. "Instead of looking for someone in the present, perhaps we should turn to the past." The others waited for him to continue. "It's rare that I socialise these days, but a couple of months ago I was at a black-tie dinner and recognised a face on the table opposite that I hadn't seen for more than forty years."

Taff the Mack

A dog-tired Carson was about to shut up shop for the day, when Jacko appeared at his door.

"Spare a minute, Guv? Taff Jenkins is keen to run something by you." Carson waved them in and pointed to the two empty chairs opposite his desk.

'Taff the Mack', as he was generally known, was Alan Jenkins, a giant-sized bushy-eyed Welsh detective in charge of CID.

"Evening Taff, what's on your mind?"

The tall man crossed his legs and shifted in the chair, until he *felt* comfortable. "I was having a word with young Sergeant Jacko here," he began. "Regarding this problem we're investigating, you know the one: burglary gone wrong?"

Carson remembered reading about it a week earlier. "Is this the house in Chillwall with the body at the bottom of the stairs?

"One and the same," he said, in his broad Welsh melodic tones.

"Might as well start from the top, mate, just so we don't miss anything," aware Taff would do just that.

"Well Nathan," he began, "it's all about this Canadian bloke who landed at Heathrow Airport a week ago, decided to stay in London overnight and arrived at the Chillwall address at 7.00 pm the following evening. We know all of this from the neighbour opposite, who was arranging her curtains the moment his taxi arrived." Pausing only to check his notes. "According to the lady, he's a rare, but not unfamiliar figure, being related to a Mr and Mrs Nichol who live there. Apparently, they'd missed his arrival in Liverpool, due to his flight from Montreal being delayed and them being off on a week's holiday to Spain. But it's no big deal seeing he has his own front door key."

"Who's he again?"

"It would seem he's Mrs Nichol's elder brother Hugo and twenty-four hours later she calls the neighbour asking if she might have noticed any sign of movement from across the way. It appears she'd been desperately trying to contact her brother, but to no avail." Taff slowly came up for air, "Well, spookily, the postman arrives and the neighbour sees this as the perfect excuse to visit the Nichols' place. They ring the bell, knock on the door but hear nothing from inside. Searching further, they find the back door unlocked and the Canadian's body lying at the bottom of the stairs, which is when they called the Emergency Services. First to arrive were the paramedics, who discovered there was still some signs of life and proceeded to whisk him off to A & E before the uniforms could get there!"

"Medical report?" asked Carson, who was familiar with the results.

Taff consulted a page. "Multiple contusions and a fractured skull, each injury being consistent with somebody falling down the stairs."

Carson gave the slightest of nods and Taff moved on.

"The neighbour next decides to open a few doors, the first being the lounge, where unsurprisingly it reveals a break-in has taken place. She's about to make another emergency call, when the 'Blues and Twos' arrive on site and conduct a proper search of the premises. A cursory check of the first-floor areas reveals that a bedroom and study had been rifled, but they still have no idea if anything went missing before the Canadian went ski jumping in the dark." Taff gave an exasperated look in Carson's direction. "What do you do, Nathan? The uniforms suddenly find themselves on uncertain ground. Did he fall or was he pushed? Which is why they called us in!"

Carson suppressed a smile. "What happened next?"

"We had to wait for the Nichols to cut short their holiday: fly home and tell us if anything of value had gone missing. As luck would have it, the lady had taken nearly all her jewellery with her and the husband was only worried about his golf clubs. That is, until they remembered the four gold coins her comatose brother had given them as an anniversary present a couple of years back."

"Am I right in saying they were of some significant value?"

"Yes Nathan, and this is one of them!" passing him a photograph.

Carson focused on what appeared to be the front and obverse sides of a gold coin. "Is this it?" he asked. "It looks like a Krugerrand."

"That, Nathan, is the 'Gold Maple Leaf', Canada's equivalent of the exact same coin. They're normally regarded as bullion, meaning you can buy and sell them anywhere, depending on their value at the time it goes to market. There's no serial number, only the year it was minted. That said, it's pure 24 carat gold and virtually untraceable."

"What's it worth?" asked a curious Carson.

Taff squinted an eye, as though pricing up a new suit in a shop window. "A grand maybe? As I said, it depends on the market. This stuff goes up and down all the time."

"Bloody Nora!" exclaimed Carson.

"And that's when I thought about 'Goldfinger'."

"Goldfinger? Who the hell's he?"

"The young kid lying dead in the morgue, of course," grinned Taff. "That's what us boys on the case have named him. It was just too much of a coincidence for all this gold to be floating about and I thought, 'Christ, it's getting like the bloody *Klondike* around here!"

"Hang on, Taff; if, as you say, this is a gold coin, why would young Goldfinger have some of it stuck in his nail?"

"Because if it was him who'd nicked it from the Nichols' place, how would he know for certain that it was a 'real' gold coin; okay, he might think he'd struck lucky, but how could he be sure? Not unless he decided to scrape a corner with something sharp, just to see if it glitters!"

It was now Carson's turn to show signs of interest as he remembered their earlier meeting with Simone at Forensics. "Tell me more."

"As I said earlier, the 'Swab Mob' had done a real thorough job, even checking a small dirt path that runs behind the properties and would you credit it, they came up with these!" Passing Carson two more photos. Only this time they were of both tyre and shoe prints in the dusty ground.

Carson was still scrutinising them when Jacko spoke, "I saw these earlier, Guv, and something about them jogged my memory. So I rang Forensics and they faxed us these."

The photographs were laid out on his desk, allowing him to scan from one to another. There was no mistaking Moses' red and white trainers had the exact same pattern as the footprints in the dust.

"A couple of things have turned this case on its head, Nathan. The Canadian died yesterday and a more detailed autopsy has revealed a very suspicious 'welt' at the base of his skull."

"You mean, someone purposefully sent him down the stairs?"

"Yes Nathan, it looks like he was smashed behind the head with a solid object."

"Which, if true, could make it a murder investigation?"

"Yes, Sergeant Jacko."

Carson ran his eyes over the latest report from the break-in. "So where are we with this lot, Taff?"

"Originally, I had it down as a burglary gone wrong, but now I'm convinced it's robbery with attempted murder."

"Is that why you asked Forensics to take another look at the body?"

Taff nodded. "In light of the new evidence, I thought it best they do a more detailed autopsy on the Canadian. The first was inconclusive, but that's because everyone had assumed it was just an accident. The big surprise came to light when the pathologist dug a bit deeper."

Carson sipped his coffee and waited.

"The weather tends to be a tad colder if you live in the Rocky Mountains and our Trapper had a seriously thick head of hair on his shoulders. But when parted with a scalpel, they discovered a large contusion at the base of his skull. It being consistent with a blow from a blunt instrument; almost certainly a rubber torch of some kind."

"How the hell did they manage to miss that when he first arrived at the hospital?"

"Who can say, Nathan? Maybe it was a busy period and they weren't doing lobotomy inspections."

Carson shook his head. "What happened regarding the other forensic evidence? Especially the footprint in the dust that matches Moses Sweetman's shoe."

"That, I'm afraid, might also be a problem. We did a check on his trainers and found they're one of Nike's top sellers. 'John Lewis' store is of the opinion that there could be a whole army of youngsters in Liverpool wearing them."

"Do you have any suspects in mind?"

"Well, let's just say there's one lying dead in the morgue and the others live on top of a tower block."

"I assume we're talking about the 'Sharecropper gang'?"

Taff nodded again.

"What about this food delivery bit?"

"When the uniforms did a door to door, a family living opposite the burglary remembered ordering a Margarita and chips from a local take-away the night before the break-in."

"Which was when the Nichols were leaving for Spain?"

"That's right, Nathan; in fact it arrived at precisely the same time as their taxi left for the airport."

"And?"

"The delivery boy was none other than Finbar Otagi."

"Who's also known as *The Scout* by the Sharecroppers?"

"That's him."

"Where is he now?"

"Spoke to him an hour ago, but had to let him go. Swears he didn't see the old couple and was busy working on the night of the burglary."

"I'll ask the same question, where does that leave us?"

"Still searching."

Slumping back in his chair, Carson was thoughtful for a second. "What's the chance of us organising an early morning drugs raid and turning the Sweetmans place over? While they're searching for illegal substances, you could be looking for the gold coins."

"Funny you should ask that, Nathan; I was thinking along those same lines and ran the idea past Mitch Brennan."

"And?"

"It's been tried once before, in the past, but failed badly."

"Why?"

"These kids are not stupid and they do have the advantage of living on top of a tower block. It means they can spot anything suspicious before it can get within a mile of them. The last attempt was a carefully planned dawn raid that hit the buffers in the ground floor entrance. When the squads piled into the lifts and pushed the button to take them to the top floor, they suddenly found they'd been switched off.

"Which is not difficult, Nathan, seeing as how the control room is on the roof. Imagine how much fun it must have been for the teams as they stomped their way up twenty flights of stairs like a herd of buffalo, only to find sod all when they got there."

"I assume the Council has changed the lock on the control room door?"

"Twelve times and the metal door twice."

"What else did you find?"

Taff checked his notes again. "We spoke to Mrs Nichol, who shed some light on her brother's background. It would appear he regularly visits Liverpool to have a game of golf and watch his favourite team play football."

"I take it he's originally from here?"

"Yes Nathan, he was born in Scotland Road and emigrated to Canada some forty years ago, but never forgot his roots or football team."

"You look as if you're going to tell me something else."

Taff nodded. "On the day he was found crumpled at the bottom of the stairs, he was supposed to be at Anfield watching the game and then attend the 'Charity Football Gala' at the 'Adelphi Hotel' on Saturday night."

Highwater Estate

Vinny had spent most of the night slagging off the police for keeping him in custody, but once free discovered the only possession allowed him were his flat keys. His Ford Escort they'd smilingly informed him was still being taken apart by Forensics, meaning he had no choice other than hitch a lift or walk. Thinking back, he remembered some smart-arse uniform offering to take him home in a squad car and politely suggested he should *go away in short jerky movements*!

But things really went off a cliff when the Spanish lorry driver dropped him off near the Estate and one of the kids—who usually kept an eye on his car—said two Sharecroppers were asking what time he arrived home. Painfully aware of Saturday night's brutal murders in the park and the problems posed by the crazy Sharecroppers, he thought it safer to keep to the shadows and stay out of sight.

Slipping across Beechcroft Drive, he took refuge behind a tall hedge ducked down and hid in the bushes. Yet the fear of bumping into whoever was asking of his whereabouts, eventually convinced him into inching his way towards the entrance and mercifully, an empty stairwell. But his joy was soon short lived when two of the gang unexpectedly emerged from the shadow of the staircase and he heard the chilling sound of a flick knife being opened.

"Wer' you been, Gecko man, and who you been talking to?" snarled Cruz.

Vinny gave a scream of terror when he realised who it was. "No one. I swear I haven't spoken to anyone!"

Noah's voice came next. "Wer de fuckin' coins, Gecko man," the razor-sharp touch of the blade turning Vinny's eyes to the those of a giant Bull Frog.

"I s-s-sold them!" He wailed in reply.

"Well, dat no fuckin good, Gecko man!" Cruz hissed in his other ear, delighted the Jamaican *Patois* was instilling so much fear into Vinny's skeletal body.

"A young black kid gave me them and I paid him cash," he pleaded in defence. But the sound of another flick-knife brought forth an even louder moan as he felt the ice-cold touch of more steel against his throat.

Noah eased his grip on Vinny's neck a touch and whispered. "Doan give me that crap you rip off, little scumbag. You got de coins hidden somewhere and we wannem now!"

"I haven't got them," Vinny whimpered, before realising he might have said the wrong thing. "But I can get them back," he cried. "I promise I can get them for you tomorrow!"

Noah and Cruz eyed each other in the gloom of the foyer and pondered their next move. They could probably do the world a favour by sticking a blade between Vinny's skinny ribs and dumping him outside in the bushes, but that wouldn't solve the problem of the missing coins. The Gecko had obviously sold them on for a fat profit and Noah needed him alive if he was going to get them back. "Lissen to me, you ugly little shit, you got till tomorrow night to return de coins, or else. But if I hear you been spoutin' your mouth off to the police, I'm gonna find you and cut your throat from ear to ear!" And with that, threw him bodily across the entrance hall.

Stumbling his way up the stairs, Vinny reached the safety of the flat; turned a deaf ear to Demi's usual rants and scrabbled to unlock his bedroom door. Once inside, he tried to light a cigarette with a hand that wouldn't stay still and not for the first time regretted his decision to buy the coins from the crazy knife-wielding lunatics. But it was plain to see that if he didn't visit a certain person, he could end up well and truly dead!

S.C.U.

The early morning sun shining through his office window had Carson feeling just a little more upbeat, but only until a sheepish looking Jacko and Smithy appeared in the doorway. "Just finished going through Hamilton's interview, Guv, and although he mentioned his wife had died in some kind of accident, didn't exactly say how. Meaning, we'd assumed it was some kind of car crash and pursued the more important connection with his murdered granddaughter."

"So what did you find?"

"Smithy spent the morning scanning through the Evening Post Archives and found Hector Dooley's original article from 1982. This was when he'd written about the death of Maxi Hamilton's wife in Florida and confirms much of what Archie Speed told you; the stuff about Sandra *dying in an accident* whilst on holiday."

"What about Hamilton, does he get a mention?"

"Only in the headline that said *Local businessman and his wife involved in fatal accident.* Other than that, there's no mention of a shooting and you'd need a magnifying glass to find it at the bottom of page three. But that's not the real story, Guv, as Smithy is about to tell you."

"I spoke to the Miami Police Department late last night," he began. "Who put me through to a Southern-sounding detective named Chuck Eggerton. I told him all about The Park murder investigation and how we were searching for any links between our dead girl and the '82 Florida wedding' killings. He sounded both sympathetic and sceptical, especially when I'd asked if there was any chance of getting a copy of the original crime report. Chuck gave me the impression that just like us, they were *very busy* and it was all *a long time ago.* Still in spite of this, when I checked my emails this morning, I found he'd sent me a very nice chatty one, plus a copy of a Detective Calvin Carpinsky's original typed report."

Carson went through his usual routine of waiting for Smithy to tell him what he'd found.

"According to Carpinsky, Sandra Hamilton died instantly from a single gunshot wound to the chest, whereas some guy from New York, who was hit in the head died a week later. Maxi, along with two others were also wounded, but managed to survive the shooting that took place at a wedding at the Hotel Panama in downtown Miami. The lone gunman who'd managed to gate crash the wedding, was dressed as one of the waiters and in the confusion escaped in a car waiting for him in the rear parking lot. Carpinsky's report is of the opinion that Mrs Hamilton and the others weren't the intended targets, just very unfortunate casualties. He didn't exactly say so in the report, but hinted that some of the guests with well-known links to the local drugs trade might have been the real targets."

Archie Speed's tale of Hamilton's involvement in the early Liverpool drug scene loomed large in Carson's mind as Smithy spoke on. "Under normal circumstances, the Miami newspapers would have had a field day covering the wedding shootings, but something much bigger was taking place around the same time. It seems a policeman had shot dead a young black kid earlier that day and the locals had begun to riot in protest! We mustn't forget, Sir, that were talking about the eighties and Carpinsky was just telling it as it was, there's none of that PC stuff here."

"What about the hotel shootings?"

"Much to Miami Tourism's relief and seeing as how they didn't need the adverse publicity, it all got lost in the mayhem. So a month after the shootings, a wounded Maxi discharged himself hospital and shipped his wife's body back to the UK, leaving Carpinsky still searching for possible clues to the killings."

"So what's to tell?"

"Two months later, an Everglades Park Ranger was cruising through the swamps in his 'fan boat', when he spotted something glinting in the water; a closer look revealing it to be the chrome tip of a submerged taillight. Within hours the local Highway Patrol had hauled a blue 'Buick Sedan' out of the drink and discovered two dead males stuffed in the boot. A further search had turned up a .34 calibre handgun used in the Hotel Panama shootings and a waiter's jacket with the letters 'HP' embossed on the lapel. To cap it all, both men had been shot in the back of the head."

"Revenge killings?"

"Detective Carpinsky seems to think so, although whoever pulled the trigger was never found."

Carson reflected on Jacko's observation that Maxi Hamilton had all the hallmarks of a modern-day Saint, but with all these historic drugs connections floating to the surface, he might not be as clean as some people think.

Following the daily Site Meeting, Jacko spotted Mitch Brennan waiting at the rear of the room. "Hello mate, sorry to drag you here at such short notice, but the boss want's a word in private if that's okay." The drugs officer nodded and followed him into the office where, to his surprise, he saw Taff the Mack smiling from a chair in the corner. Carson waved for them to take a seat until he'd finished his elongated telephone call and eventually turned to Mitch Brennan.

"What do you know about Maxi Hamilton?" he asked without preamble.

Brennan's face took on a look of surprise as he weighed up the question. "Not a lot, other than he's mega rich."

Carson moved his head as a sign of agreement, then leaned towards him and whispered, "This chat we're having is strictly off the record, okay Mitch?"

Brennan's eyebrows lifted and he gave a half shrug in reply.

Carson paused for a second longer as if weighing up his next move. "It's not very often I go there, but I was having a drink in 'The Beehive' pub last night, when someone whispered that many years ago the man in question was a major drug dealer here in the city."

Brennan's eyes opened wide and his brow rose even higher at this unexpected revelation, but following a moment of contemplation, shrugged his shoulders and met Carson's gaze across the desk. "If true, then it's the first I've heard of it." He then asked a question of his own. "When?"

"Thirty or forty years ago," Carson said casually and Jacko could see the look of relief forming on Brennan's face.

"Ikey Crikey!" he laughed. "I wasn't even in the Force then, in fact if we're talking that long ago, I'm sure I was still in fucking primary school."

Carson sat unmoved at the outburst, but could understand his elation. Whatever happened in the past certainly wasn't on Brennan's watch today. Which meant that if there was any shit flying about, it wouldn't necessarily hit his fan.

"Take it easy, Mitch, we're not looking to lay anything at your door, because if the truth be known, we're not really sure where all this mess is going ourselves." He then scratched what little hair there was on his head and leant back in his chair. "A few days ago, we had a couple of dead kids in the park who were supposedly complete strangers. Next thing, we find the boy's a possible suspect in Taff's murder inquiry. He's also a part of the local drug scene and has known family ties to one of the biggest narcotic dealers in Liverpool. Then, to top all that, the dead girl with the angel face turns out to be the estranged granddaughter of one of the City's major power brokers. *Who,* as I've just mentioned, has a possible drugs link to *his* past. Christ man, it sounds like the script from a cuffin' gangster movie!"

It was now Brennan's turn to relax and lean back in his chair, happy there was nothing he'd purposefully stepped over, instead of warning the public not to step in. He was also aware that when it came to the people and the Press, drug barons could be a real pain in the arse! "Hang on Nathan; if I've got this right, you *still* don't know exactly how far back in time all this so-called drug dealing is supposed to have taken place?"

Carson grimaced; aware he'd been momentarily put on the spot. "My source swears most of it took place sometime between the sixties and early eighties, which I agree is a long time ago. But there has to be some way of finding out if there's any truth in this stuff?"

Brennan shook his head. "I really can't see how, Nathan. I imagine that most of the Drug Squad from around that time would be either dead, or have a touch of Alzheimer's by now."

"What about Hamilton? I'd have thought there'd be a smell of some kind hanging about somewhere."

Mitch shook his head again. "In the twenty plus years I've been in Drugs, I've never heard the slightest whisper or seen anything to suggest otherwise, so where do you go from here?" he asked with another shrug of his shoulders. "I really couldn't say."

"Have you ever heard of someone called BB Benson?"

"Should I?"

"He was supposedly one of Hamilton's top men."

Mitch shook his head. "Sorry, doesn't ring a bell."

A disappointed Carson eyed Jacko across the desk and wondered if the search for skeletons in Maxi's past might have been a complete waste of time.

The Jeweller

The fumes leaking from the broken exhaust filled the air, as the moped wound its way down the narrow alley and came to a halt at the rear of Dong's Thai Restaurant. Parking it alongside six other aging scooters, head chef Chi-son took off his helmet, lit a foul-smelling cigarette and joined the evening shift in the noisy overcrowded kitchen.

Less than ten feet away and hiding in the shelter of an overflowing wheelie bin hovered Vinny. But he wasn't in the least bit bothered with the racket coming from downtown Pattaya, he was more interested in the doorway directly across from where he stood. And even though it looked much the same as every other rear entrance in the alley, its armour-plated door identified it as belonging to the jeweller's shop situated on the main road.

Normally this would be Vinny's usual means of entry, should he quickly need to dispense with the odd trinket or two, however, today was different. In keeping with his regular routine, he'd timed his arrival to coincide with the shop's closing, only to find it already silent and shuttered. With a rising sense of panic, he'd walked up and down the street twice, rang the number a dozen times, each time receiving no reply. He was also worried that his next move might attract the wrong kind of attention, but knew he had no other choice. Using the heel of one shoe, he began a slow metronomic thud on the metal-clad door that echoed up and down the alley. Two minutes later and he was standing in the dimly lit rear passage of the jeweller's shop.

"What the hell are you doing here?" a horrified Herbert Sheldrake cried. "Don't you read the papers or listen to the radio?" His reedy sounding voice rising in volume with each futile question.

"I don't give a shit about the papers!" snarled Vinny. "I just want the coins back!"

"Have you gone mad?" wheezed Sheldrake. "You don't seriously think I'd still have them here? The police are searching for them everywhere *and* whoever killed the owner!"

Vinny was momentarily taken aback with this news. He rarely listened to the radio or read the papers and it had never occurred to him that the coins wouldn't still be here in Sheldrake's shop. However, the crazy old fool was babbling on about a murder that could somehow be connected to him and could only listen in stunned silence as Sheldrake filled him in with the finer details of the Chillwall murder hunt.

It was only then did Vinny realise their true significance in all of this mayhem; the break-in, the dead body lying at the bottom of the stairs and the young black kid trying to sell the stolen coins on the cheap. Worst of all was last night's deadly ambush in the flats. Yet none of this was of any comfort to him; not unless he could find and return the goods to the murderous Sharecroppers.

"Where are the coins now?" he spluttered.

"I've already told you, they're not here. I got rid of them this morning, when I heard about the murder hunt on the radio."

"Got rid of them, how?" asked Vinny with a growing sense of foreboding.

"I gave them to Colly Morrison."

Vinny was left speechless. Morrison was a Manchester jeweller who reputedly owned a secret kiln; and if the price was right would gladly melt down illicit gold. Somewhere on the distant horizon, Vinny could see himself slowly slipping and sliding down that road to fuck knows where.

S.C.U.

"More lukewarm coffee, Guv?"

"Yes, if I have to, but while you're at it, see if you can brighten up my day with some good news."

"No problem. Taff Jenkins has just confirmed he can spare five men to help us out and operations say there are five WPC desk jockeys already in the lift."

"Well, it's a start," muttered Carson, aware they needed the extra staff to take calls and make inquiries.

"To add to that, we've just received this latest photograph from the Anfield Security Team. It's from Saturday's football game and shows Moses Sweetman and his mate Finbar Otagi sitting in the 'Kop End' of the ground."

"Not exactly utopia, but it's getting better."

Jacko held up Otagi's ticket in a see-through evidence bag and retold the story as to how Moses had purchased both tickets for a knock down price of forty pounds each. "Finbar however, is still unable to explain how Moses might have acquired all this money. When the football game ended, they both caught the bus home to Highwater, visited a local newspaper shop and parted thirty minutes later; Finbar, who doesn't live on the Estate going one way and Moses in the opposite direction."

"I'm still listening."

"We've also been able to ID the four girls who crossed the park around the time of the murders."

Jason Junior, who'd interviewed them, took up the story. "They saw the news footage and clearly remember seeing *The Gecko* in the carpark just before 8.00 pm Saturday night. Two are unsure about Moses being in Waytree Park, but the others are positive he passed them heading in the direction of the Estate and coincidently, all the girls were friendly with Kelly Freeland. Apparently, she'd caught the same bus with them lots of times."

"Which means that for the first time in his life Guv, *The Gecko* could be telling the truth, especially when it comes to his tale of the white transit van."

Carson looked to Malone. "Anything new on that, Frank?"

"Afraid not. We lost him somewhere beneath the flyover on Queen's Drive. It's one pissing busy neck of the woods on most days, but Saturday morning in particular was like a mad house. Liverpool and Arsenal were about to do battle in one of the biggest games of the season and the place was full of red and white football scarfs. Traffic are convinced the transit driver was using some kind of device to avoid the roadside recognition cameras."

"What about the murder weapon?"

It was now Jacko's turn to give a negative reply. "Second sweep team scoured every bush and blade of grass in the Park: never found a thing!"

"Door to door?

Jacko felt like a quiz show contestant who didn't know any of the answers. "Most people on the Estate have sussed out that none of their own are in the frame for the murders. Yet they're still reluctant to help, because when it comes to the boys in blue, it's the usual story, nobody saw or heard a thing!"

With his right earlobe about to turn numb, Carson finished his chat with Bastion and headed for more important things, this morning's Site Meeting.

"Okay people," called Jacko, "can we get started please?" A quiet fell across the room as they focused on the top table. "We've just had some good news from Anfield, and although we didn't score the winning goal, we almost certainly hit the bar," the mere mention of football guaranteed to catch everyone's attention.

"But, as you all know, The Park murders happened on the day Liverpool and Arsenal were about to do battle in one of the biggest games of the season. Which meant the city was jam-packed with lots of supporters wearing the same red and white colours. Yet somewhere within this busy confusion, it would seem the Gecko's white 'Ford Transit' has managed to vanish into thin air. But where did it go and what was its ultimate destination? According to Vinny, there was a red and white striped wool hat lying on the dashboard. So do we assume the driver was a potential football supporter? And if so, which side? As I said, both teams play in the same colours, which won't help in identifying who the suspect might be." Jacko nodded towards Smithy and Jason Junior. "With all this in mind, we dispatched a couple of our best men to Anfield so they might investigate further."

Smithy stood and took over proceedings. "We met with their security people so that we might review all of their recordings, as well as Sky TV's coverage of the game." He then used his iPad to switch on the king-size TV screen; which in turn revealed a packed football Stadium. "Having already received the photo of Moses Sweetman and his mate sat in the Kop, we began to do a more thorough search of the CCTV footage. At first everything seemed to be normal, until one of their eagle-eyed security men spotted this person sitting high in the Anfield Road Stand."

The TV screen froze again and all eyes were focused on the bulky looking male with a dark beard. "I think we can all agree that the two main features of this particular punter are the red and white wool hat, but more importantly the wraparound sunglasses." The broken arm in Junkies Corner immediately sprang to mind as Smithy spoke on. "And barring the fact he might be a perfectly innocent spectator, we decided to put him in front of the queue at the checkout. Another plus positive showed that CCTV cameras constantly monitor all of the public areas in the ground. This was a crucial factor, as it meant we were able to follow him as he left the stadium."

Smithy moved the footage on once again. "The match isn't quite over yet, but we can still see him making his exit alongside some other supporters, as they spilled out into the Anfield Road area. In this next scene, you can just make him out as he turns sharp right in the direction of the Millennium Stand and then disappears somewhere along Breck Road."

Smithy gave a wry smile. "At that point, I was about to give up the ghost thinking we'd lost him, until the security man suggested we let the recording move on. Parking around the Anfield he told me was crazy at the best of times, which is why most people leave their vehicles in the side streets and make their way to the ground on foot. Sure enough at 7:29 PM, a white Ford Transit van with a two-bar roof rack appears on screen heading north in the direction of the A5058. This, we think, is quite a significant development because if he'd kept to that one particular route, it would almost certainly have taken him past Waytree Park at around the time of the murders!"

A murmur of appreciation rippled throughout the room. Jacko glanced at Smithy who was about to inform them of the bad news. "We were hoping to get a look at the van's number plates, but it appears the driver has the luck of the Irish. It's 7.40 pm on a warm summer evening and Liverpool have just won a huge game. As you'd expect the streets in the surrounding areas are full of people celebrating. Which is the moment our suspect has decided to join the other vehicles wending their way through the crowds." Smithy gave a reluctant shrug as he carried on. "Unfortunately it stays like this until the Transit van has moved out of range of the cameras."

"I take it we missed him?" muttered a disappointed Stretch.

"I'm afraid so," said an equally frustrated Smithy.

Jacko decided to chip in. "Which still begs the question, who's the bearded guy sitting in the stands behind the goal?"

Smithy came in again. "Anfield normally allows around 3,000 tickets for the away supporters. They also admit there'll be plenty of latecomers looking to buy a ticket outside the ground on match day. Which is exactly what happened here. We've since discovered that a local man named Joe Bernard bought this seat six weeks ago and on the day of the match sold it to an Arsenal supporter. We were hoping he might tell us what the buyer looked and sounded like, but unfortunately since discovered he's taken his grandchildren to Disneyland for two weeks."

"Why does everybody have to be on cuffin' holiday?" groaned Carson.

Jacko shook his head in sympathy. "Time of the year, Guv."

Smithy in the meantime was getting into his stride. "Seeing as how we've missed our Mr Bernard; we decided to do the next best thing and contact the people occupying the seats closest to the suspect. Sadly, those in front and behind were a complete waste of time and we fared no better with the two sat either side of him. Although, they were all agreed he was one big grumpy faced Arsenal supporter, who didn't say a word throughout the game.

"Apparently, he muscled his way to his seat five minutes after kick off and hunched forward as if brooding over their pathetic performance. This same punter didn't say a word or get angry, even when they were all celebrating Liverpool's second goal!"

Jacko didn't need to look and see the reaction from Smithy's last comment; he could feel the heat of many smiles from across the room. "Yet all were agreed that you wouldn't want to pick a fight with him," concluded Smithy.

"Any facial scars or tattoos on his hands?" asked Carson.

Smithy shook his head in the negative. "Nothing they can remember, Sir. Although they do recall a small shiny badge on the front of his woollen hat."

"Do we know what it was?"

"I am afraid not. Most people were side on and couldn't get a good look at it. However, a close-up image from the CCTV showed the letters might be D and S, but no one knows for sure what it means."

"What about selfies?" asked Jacko. "People are forever taking pictures in the crowd with their mobiles."

Joanna held her hand up. "I'm already looking into that, Sarge. Anfield have supplied me with a list of people who were in the upper stands on Saturday afternoon. So I've set up a temporary website where people can email or send me their photographs from the day."

"Excellent idea, when will it start?"

"We'll start working our way through them when the meeting ends."

Jacko knew it was a thankless, but necessary task. Besides, with a bit of luck they might get a real close up of the suspect's face. "Okay, let's bring everybody up to date with Forensics at the ground."

Smithy took over again. "Just before the half-time break, one person saw our suspect leaving his seat to get a drink and the people sat either side concurred with this. Another remembers him finishing the water and dropping the plastic container between his feet. Yet there wasn't a hope in hell of us finding it, seeing as how the ground is swept clean the moment the game has finished."

Jacko smiled; he knew there was more to come.

"However, that doesn't include the actual seats, which as we all know are hinged. The cleaners will make a cursory check to see there's nothing behind each one and that's pretty much it until the next football game. So unless it's been damaged, each one will stay exactly the same way; upright and untouched. Which is why we had the forensic boys to give this one particular seat a good going over and guess what? On the lower surface they discovered a print whose DNA matches the blood on the broken sunglasses found in Junkies Corner." The ecstatic sound of whoops of joy and hi-fives filled the air.

Jacko was reluctant to take away Smithy's moment of glory, but he was also there to keep some kind of order. "Which means," he shouted over the hub-hub, "that the person sitting in the stands at Anfield Football Stadium was almost certainly present at our murder scene in Waytree Park on Saturday night!"

Sharecropper Heights

"This looks like them," whispered Benny.

Noah gave a grunt in reply, he too having spotted the Chrysler Voyager making its way along Sharecropper Avenue. As always, this would have been normal everyday procedure, as they watched and waited for the drugs to be delivered to the tower block. But following Moses's death and the urgent message he'd sent last night, Noah was terrified that today's visit might have an entirely different objective and when done, a much more painful ending. Using a pair of long-range binoculars, they'd scanned the surrounding areas looking for any unusual activity, whilst waiting for the vehicle to turn into an isolated area near the garages.

But to their surprise, saw it pass by without stopping and carry on until it reached the tower block entrance. This unexpected change of routine had left both of them scratching their heads, as they craned their necks and tried to see what was happening ten floors below. An even bigger surprise lay in store, when they saw not only Uncle Eli climbing from the car, but the curly white head of 'Papa Eazy'.

To Noah's knowledge, this was the first time his grandfather had ever set foot on the Estate and a sense of confused panic ensued as they wondered what to do next. "Look!" He shouted, his finger pointing to the lift call sign that suddenly turned red and began its slow upward climb.

Noah knew that this was to be a seminal moment in his life and although the Sharecropper set-up was a key part of the Stoker drugs operation, nothing was ever guaranteed when it came to Papa Eazy. When things weren't just as he wanted, the old man's temper was best avoided! He would also condemn any type of personal gain, especially if it were derived by way of what he termed; 'ill-gotten means.' But what it really meant was they should refrain from doing any shit that might attract the attention of the police, or the outside world! However, the events of the last week had changed Noah's life and, in a few minutes, he would have to face the consequences of his foolish actions.

He took a deep breath as the lift came to a halt and watched the imposing figure of Papa Eazy step through the door. As always, his eyes were alert to his immediate surroundings and even though his clothes had begun to hang a little. With his silver tipped bamboo cane in hand, most people thought he still cut a fine figure. Although this wasn't the first time, they'd had occasion to meet him. For years he and his brothers had been secretly accompanying Uncle Eli to the Stoker house in South Liverpool. It was here their grandfather would make a huge fuss, give them presents and declare they were *the one part of his family he missed more than anything.*

He would make a point of sitting Moses on his knee, tell him stories and tickle him until he was near exhausted. This would make him and Benny as jealous as sin, especially when he'd whisper in Moses's ear how much he reminded him of Jacob, his dead son. There again, being a distant relation did have some benefits, more so when his cousins would say how envious they were of Noah and his brothers for not having to sit through one of Papa Eazy's lengthy bible sermons. Nevertheless, when it came to business there was no such thing as sentiment, each family member having to pull their weight or *toe the line* as Eazy put it.

Still to see him standing here in Sharecropper Heights was an earth-moving moment and Noah who'd listened to Eli's stories of how secretive Papa was, knew only the murder of his favourite grandson or the reasons for it, would bring him here. The two brothers waited nervously as the seconds went by before he waved a hand and motioned for Noah to join him. Standing beside him at the railing, he waited for Papa to speak, but when he did so, his voice sounded like that of a tired old man.

"Tell me how Moses died," he whispered, and a flood of relief swept through Noah. For he suddenly realised that Papa Eazy knew nothing of the missing coins, but more importantly, his own personal involvement in the robbery. And so with a few omissions here and there, gave Eazy a sorrowful account concerning the tragic death of his favourite grandson.

Southport, Liverpool

"I know the damn things are here somewhere," he muttered, his hand searching in the dark for the pull-cord switch, but when turning on the light, suddenly realised his worst fears. "Oh no!" he groaned. "The stupid cow has only discovered my clubs!" A round of golf would usually find him chipping and slicing his way through eighteen holes and having completed any one shot, give the club in question a quick wipe with his trusty towel. But due to his wife suffering from a severe case of OCD, his clubs now shone like new.

Selecting his favourite six-iron from the bag, he turned it over in his hands and was amazed to see his face reflected in the polished steel. "Christ knows how long it took her to get it like this." He shuddered. "And I can just imagine the stick I'll get from the boys in the clubhouse." Yet, no matter how often he explained that *a bit of dirt never hurt anyone,* his words had fallen on deaf ears and the ploy of sneaking them into the pool house obviously hadn't worked either! Fuming at such infantile desecration, he was about to load his clubs into the boot of the car when she suddenly appeared in the doorway holding his mobile phone.

"There's something odd going on here," she called. "*And* I'm sure I've just heard *this* receive one of them horrible text message things," the scorn in her voice reminding him of how much she disapproved of such everyday trivialities. "And, would you believe it, the paper boy has delivered the wrong newspaper," her other hand waving what appeared to be a Daily Express. "I can't imagine what the neighbours would say if they thought we read this rubbish, when they know we only ever take The Telegraph."

Closing his eyes, he gave a silent groan and shook his head in exasperation; forty years of living within the sterile idiosyncrasies that ruled his wife's world were enough to send anyone around the bend. Yet for some reason she had her dander up about his phone and of all things, the bloody paperboy!

"It'll be alright," he said soothingly. "There's probably an easy explanation to all of this." He was about to dismiss it as just another of her eccentricities, when something inside told him otherwise. To his knowledge, this particular mobile phone was still ex-directory and the number known to just a few very important people. It was also inconceivable that anyone could send him a text message, seeing as how he'd never sent one in his life. Although it wasn't just the phone that was troubling him, it was the Daily Express newspaper, its unexpected appearance sending a chill down his spine. "Can I have a look?" he whispered.

His wife immediately sensed something was wrong. "Are you alright?" she asked. "You look as though you've seen a ghost."

Yet his mind was somewhere else. "Of course, I'm alright," he said with a smile. "But now that it's here, I think I'll take the paper into the conservatory and check the rugby results."

Once inside, he placed both items on the table and studied them in silence. Another moment of hesitation went by before he nervously licked his lips and with a sense of 'déjà vu' reached for the phone. The text message said just four words; *TOG wants to talk.* For ten unmoving minutes, he'd stared at it in the hope it might be some kind of joke and then realised he had no choice other than to open the newspaper beside it.

With a powder-dry mouth, he began to leaf through the pages until he came to the Cryptic Crossword. The shock of which left him ashen-faced, as he found it had been completed in the familiar, but long forgotten green pen. A closer scrutiny of the clues revealed a time and date for the rendezvous and with it came the dreaded realisation that not only had the door to his past been prised open, but his life was about to change forever.

Estelle

Estelle was stood at the kitchen sink humming along to a tune on the radio, when she sensed someone or something was standing behind her. One side of her brain said turn around, the other urging her to ignore it and keep looking through the window. Trying her best to stay calm, she continued to wash dishes in the hope it might go away, but in the end couldn't help herself and turned to look into the eyes of Papa Eazy. It had been a long time since she'd last seen him in the flesh and although he wore his usual fancy clothes, he still reminded her of an old yam tree they'd once had in the garden back home in Jamaica.

For many years it had flourished and grown, then one day it'd just shrivelled up and died. Looking at him now, he reminded her of that same old tree, but she didn't think for a minute he was ready to leave this planet. Yet he'd somehow managed to slip into the kitchen so silently she hadn't heard a sound and for some reason had a look on his face that some people might interpret as being sorrowful. But if his presence came as an unwelcome surprise, then the real nightmare was the sneering face of Elijah Stoker standing beside him!

In an instant, Estelle was transported back to when a naïve and excited seventeen-year-old had left Jamaica for the hurly-burly world that was Liverpool. On arrival, she'd been lodging with her Aunty, who'd been a supply teacher at one of the local schools and for the first year, everything had been so good. She'd found herself a regular job, made lots of friends and by chance discovered she could sing. In next to no time, she'd been confident enough to become a backing singer in a small rock group playing in the local clubs and could clearly remember the moment when she first saw Jacob Stoker.

He'd been so different from the usual backside grabbing lechers who normally inherited her world; but there was something much more important, Jacob had always smiled a lot. Estelle knew from the many compliments she received, plus the offers to take her out, that men would never be a problem. She'd also regarded herself as being pretty streetwise when it came to the male species, but Jacob could have been from another planet. He'd breezed into her life like a breath of fresh air, drove a fast car and always had plenty of money to throw around, forever surprising her with flowers and presents.

From the moment he'd first spoken to her, 'she was a goner' as her aunty used to say and within weeks, he was in her heart and she was in his bed. However, she'd been stunned to discover that the 'Stoker family' were well known on the Liverpool drugs scene and in some quarters regarded as major dealers. At first, she'd been freaked out at this news. But Jacob had just smiled and shrugged his shoulders; an unconcerned look on his face, telling her to 'relax baby' a lot of it was just gossip. It was also around this time that he'd introduced her to his family home, but more importantly his luxury flat.

The 'Family', she discovered, lived together in a substantial roomy old house, containing three floors and a basement. Jacob's place, however, was on the top floor and consisted of a large lounge and double bedroom. It also had a newly constructed shower room seeing as most of the other minions had to share a grotty communal bathroom on the first-floor landing. She clearly remembered the nights when they'd go back to his place, with most people asleep and quietly climb the stairs.

After her stay, he'd always been happy to rise early and drop her back at her place. Which is when the trouble with her Aunty had first arisen. The jungle drums had long since begun to send out messages, with a detail even the CIA would have been proud off. Each telling of Estelle's clandestine affair and the subsequent nights she was either late, or didn't come home. As these occasions began to mount up by the week, her Aunty had threatened to write to her parents if she didn't finish with Jacob.

All this righteousness preaching had been like a red-rag to an angry eighteen-year-old; Estelle telling her Aunty in no uncertain terms that she didn't care and would be quite happy to move, assuring her there must be somewhere better to live rather than in a prison! Inevitably, a huge argument had ensued and after much screaming and shouting, Estelle had found herself out on the street. Luckily, she managed to stop a taxi, that took her to the edge of the road where Jacob lived, but no further, "Too dangerous, luv," was the driver's excuse, as she struggled with her case to find the 'Family' home.

Tired and footsore, she eventually reached the tall imposing building; the odd passer-by giving her a sideways glance, but no more. Afraid and uncertain, she climbed the seven or eight stone steps and tried the front door, which to her relief was unlocked. Hiding her suitcase in the shadows of the open staircase and being as quiet as she could, she made her way up to the third floor. On reaching Jacob's room, she tapped on the door and softly called out his name; a furtive try of the handle confirming it was locked.

Then to her horror, the vacuum switch for the stair lighting had timed itself out, leaving her in complete darkness and a state of panic. Her shaking hand had eventually found another nearby switch, which allowed her to make her way back down to the hallway, only to find her suitcase had gone missing!

With no other alternative, she retraced her steps up to Jacob's floor, but any attempt to keep the lights on had been futile, as they would time out automatically and after a couple of minutes, fell asleep on the top step.

She'd been awoken with a jolt, the moment the stair light unexpectedly came on, a spontaneous cry leaving her lips as she stared into a dark menacing face, whose eyes appeared to contract and expand as they closely scanned her. He must have been in his mid-twenties and stood on the half landing, tall enough to see into her frightened eyes, his own never appearing to stay still. In a swift protective movement, Estelle had clasped her arms around her knees and drawn them tightly together, should he be able to see something untoward.

"What you doin here, bitch?" he asked in a slow threatening drawl.

"I'm looking for Jacob," she whispered, the sound of fear obvious in her stuttering words.

"We don' know no fucking Jacob, bitch!" came the same low intimidating snarl as he took a step towards her.

Estelle froze, her body about ready to hyperventilate in fear, when a loud voice came from the shadows of the stairs behind.

"Whatcha' doing up here, Eli? This ain't your floor," it crowed in a slow scornful manner. He immediately stepped back to the half landing and faced a tall well-dressed man, who with his short grey tight curly hair and beard reminded Estelle of Abraham Lincoln.

"Heard a noise, Papa, was just checkin' it out," Eli replied with a shrug.

"Well, I don think we got a problem here, boy," he sneered, a hand moving him aside so could he look directly at Estelle. "Was your name, girl?" He asked. His head tilting from side to side, as though checking over a horse he'd just bought.

"Estelle," she whispered, before adding, "I'm Jacob's new girlfriend," with a hopeful sound to her Jamaican lilt.

Papa's face broke into a broad smile, his eyebrows rising speculatively as he pondered this latest snippet of information. "Well, well, is that true now?" he said motioning for Eli to disappear down the stairs, which he did with his tail well and truly between his legs. "My, I didn't know Jacob was tied up so," he chuckled. He then passed her on the stairs, drew a bunch of keys from his pocket and choosing one carefully, turned the lock to the open position.

A different pair of eyes woke her in the depths of the night, as Jacob tenderly touched her face. "Hey baby?" he whispered, as she stirred and focused on his warm smile. Later as lay together, her naked body clinging to his, he began to expound a little and throw some more light on his extended family. The old man with the white curly hair was his father Ezekiel Stoker, although more commonly known as 'Papa Eazy'.

The broody looking young guy with the eyes and pockmarked face was his half-brother Elijah who, he agreed, didn't smile much. Eli, as he was known, was twenty-four, two years older than him and the son of Papa's first wife Marnie who'd tragically died at childbirth. Eazy had then married Jacob's mother, who'd later sired his two other brothers, Zachary and Jonah, as well as his sisters, Jezebel and Delilah. To add to their ever-growing family, they were also married, had children of their own and together shared the large rambling house, which was divided up into flats, bedsits and single rooms.

Jacob had laughed out loud when she'd mentioned that all the names were from her Bible class back home, assuring her that his father was a seriously religious man when he felt in the mood for it. In addition to this house, he owned lots of properties near to where they live, his own place being just a few doors down the road and the stories about the drugs? Some true, but plenty of bullshit in between. Following a night of intense lovemaking, she'd cautiously related the events of the day before. Her Aunty, the argument, the missing suitcase and hoping against hope he wouldn't throw her out.

Within no time, the errant suitcase was sat in the middle of the room and a more than thoughtful Jacob had advised her not to take up all the room in the large wardrobe. Within a few weeks and to her untold relief, this unexpected arrangement had worked brilliantly! She quickly worked out Jacob's likes and dislikes, adapting and changing to meet his everyday needs, as he slowly begun to accept her into his life. But it also meant her living with the surly Stoker clan and his scary half-brother, who was forever watching her.

Then after a few months, she suddenly became pregnant. Whether it was intentional or otherwise, Estelle couldn't remember. All she knew was that Jacob liked to play with the other children in the house and for one week she'd forgotten to take her pills. At first, she'd been worried about his reaction to this life-changing news, but was delighted when he said, "Wow, fantastic, I'm going to be a father!"

In order to keep Eazy happy, they'd named the baby Noah. However, six months later and to the delight of her husband, she'd once again found herself pregnant. Benjamin, Sarah and Moses had all arrived in quick succession; and then to her utter despair, Jacob was murdered.

Estelle hadn't recognised the weak knock on the door, but was shocked to find Eazy standing alone in the darkness. He shifted nervously for a moment, as though unsure of himself until his lidded eyes met hers. "You need go the hospital right way," he stuttered. "Report say Jacob's been found dead somehow, so they took him there." The fear more than evident in his eyes.

Confused and desperately trying to understand what he was talking about Estelle could only listen in silence as he rambled on. "The police are now cum involved, meaning there's no way 'we' can go," his curly white head motioning to the household behind. "Besides, his momma don' speak much English which leaves only you, seeing as you his woman."

Their eyes met briefly and she could see the wretched look on his face as he shuffled off down the stairs. To her despair, she'd then discovered that Elijah was waiting to drive her to the hospital and on the way, tell her how Jacob had died. According to him 'Zumo', who was one of the other gang members, had been making a collection at one of their regular haunts when he'd returned to the car and found Jacob slumped behind the steering wheel. To make things worse, a police foot patrol had turned the corner a hundred yards away and was heading in his direction.

He'd then climbed inside hoping the car might move, only to find a knife wound in Jacob's chest and the leather bag containing the rest of the drugs and cash missing. A furtive glance had warned of the patrol's progress and urged him to find Jacob's phone and once done, run for the narrow alleyway on the far side of the street. From there he'd called Eli, who'd joined him within half an hour and they both watched as Jacob's body was loaded into the waiting ambulance. But what Elijah had purposely forgot to mention was the frantic conversation between the two men in the alley as the ambulance drove away.

"What the fuck happened?" Eli wailed. "You were supposed to hit him over the head and steal the money, not stab him to death!"

"Tawny said it was an accident," cried Zumo. "He crept up behind the car, leaned in through the window and thought he'd knocked him out with the rubber cosh. But when he'd tried to grab the bag, Jacob suddenly came to, grabbed hold of his arm and tried to pull the mask off his face. In the crazy struggle that followed, Tawny lashed out and stabbed Jacob in the chest!"

"Jesus," whispered Eli, but on reflection realised this wasn't such a bad outcome after all. His younger stepbrother was now dead and therefore, couldn't take over the family business, as Easy had often suggested might happen. It also meant he could use it as an excuse to get rid of Estelle and move into the luxury top floor flat. But first he needed to call his father and regretfully tell him of his beautiful brown-eyed boy's tragic passing!

For Estelle, the next twenty-four hours had been a never-ending nightmare, as the police had asked a hundred questions, most of them concerning Jacob's involvement in drugs. Yet she could in all honesty say that she'd never been party to drug dealing of any kind. It was whilst she'd been waiting in the hospital that a kindly Social Worker had sat beside her. Without thinking, Estelle had poured out her hopes and fears, especially the ones regarding the future of her four children, who were now fatherless. She'd also mentioned that she and Jacob had never married, meaning she was now penniless and reliant on the Stokers to keep them alive.

If Estelle had ever thought about an angel, then she could never in her wildest dreams have imagined how one might appear. Following her discussion with the lady at the hospital, the situation at the Stoker household had rapidly begun to deteriorate; none more so, than in the ever-menacing spectre of Elijah.

Her worst fears had soon turned to reality, when early one morning, she'd been cornered by him and warned. "Listen Bitch, we don't give a shit about you, whether you stay or go." His finger pointing in her face. "The only ones we're interested in are the children, especially Noah, who is one smart kid and I've always regarded him as one of the Stokers. So if you were to somehow disappear," his menacing eyes staring into hers, "then nobody would give a fuck. So if you fancy packing a bag and leaving before anything should happen, then maybe now's the time to go!"

From that moment on, Estelle knew her days were numbered. Aware of what might lie ahead, she began counting the money she'd been able to save in the period before Jacob's death. But more importantly, discover how she and the children might escape the clutches of the Stoker family! A few stressful days later and the miserable life she'd endured in recent weeks disappeared like magic. It began when she heard Elijah's voice being raised in anger and the chatter of the children in the entrance hall suddenly come to a stop.

Hunkering Moses onto her hip, she'd quietly made her way down the stairs and watched what was happening from the side. Standing in the hallway and being towered over by a snarling Elijah, was a petite old lady wearing a grey suit, silver rimmed glasses and holding a folder under her arm. Hovering directly behind was a smallish nervous man, dressed in brown overalls and carrying a battered brief case.

"I don't give a shit who you are, missus, this is private property and you can't come in here!" Eli growled menacingly.

The lady, who was obviously there in some official capacity, looked at Eli as if he were something unpleasant she'd just found on her shoe. "I don't like your attitude, young man, and I dislike your language even more. So if you'd like to move out of my way, I need to talk with whoever owns this property."

Estelle watched wide-eyed from the stairs, as the lady stepped around him as if he didn't exist. She'd also been fearful Eli might lose his temper, until she heard his father's voice ringing out from the doorway and saw him hold up a hand to silence everyone.

"What the hell's goin' on here, an what you want, woman?"

"You are?" asked the lady, her watchful eyes observing him over the rim of her glasses.

Eazy weighed up the problem and went through his usual horse buying routine. "Well now," he growled, "Somtin' tells me you already know that," nodding to the mauve folder under her arm. "So why don' you just tell me who you are, an' the reason you here lady?"

The two protagonists eyed each other, as though assessing their strengths and weaknesses, before she spoke.

"My name is Superintendent Rose Costello from Liverpool District Council and I have reason to believe that there are 'children at risk' living on this property!"

From where she stood on the stairs, Estelle could hear the gears inside Eazy's brain working overtime, as he tried to absorb exactly what that meant. "What the hell you talkin' 'bout, woman, there ain't no risky children living here!" His hand pointing to the small group who'd gathered in the hallway. "Them kids are so damn fit, they's as healthy as a gang of them marathon runners you see on TV!"

"That may well be, Mr Stoker," the lady agreed, whilst purposely mentioning his name for the first time. "However, our report suggests otherwise," her eyes scanning the mauve folder. "According to our information, we believe there is a serious risk of contamination from a dangerous substance within this property and we are here to investigate if that might be the case."

Eazy shook his head in disbelief. "Das bullshit woman, you got no right to cum walkin' in here. This ain't no council house, this here is private property, an' I tink I'm right in believing that you is trespassing on my property, an' that bein so, I suggest you an him," nodding to the man with the briefcase, "had better piss off."

"Nice one, Papa, let's throw the bitch out onto the street!" Elijah called from behind.

Rose Costello, however, looked to be impervious to the vitriol happening around her and instead turned her attention on Estelle and Moses who she saw standing on the stairs. "Nobody is denying that you do have certain rights Mr Stoker, but at the same time so do I and we can do this two ways. The hard way is for you to obfuscate and be obstructive, of which I'm sure you're both capable and fully schooled in. That being the case, it would therefore lead us to believe you may, indeed, have something to hide.

"If this turned out to be true, we can immediately obtain a Court Order, which would allow us to enter this property and proceed to investigate in which wherever direction we might chose and of course, there's no telling what we might find or how much attention that might bring with it." Pausing only to let this last sentence sink in.

"And the other?" Eazy asked sarcastically.

"The other, as you say, is to allow us free access to the third floor, where I'm led to believe, some recent construction work has been taking place where your deceased son and his family lived."

"We still do and I desperately want to leave this place!" Estelle informed her quietly from the stairs.

The Stokers gathered in the hallway were shocked and stared at her as if she was some kind of demon who'd secretly lived amongst them. But Estelle, who was staring pleadingly into the eyes of Rose Costello, suddenly felt a surge of joy. For she knew in an instant that the lady with the silver rimmed glasses had sensed her danger and in her own subtle way was letting her know that she and the children were safe! But it suddenly dawned on Eazy that for once he'd been caught between a crappy rock and a shitty hard place and could only mumble. "Get a move on, woman!"

Estelle's usual climb to the third floor was suddenly cut short, when the man in the brown overalls had halted the small procession on the half-landing, opened his battered briefcase, donned a face mask and a large pair of rubber gloves. Rose Costello had then advised them they could proceed no further, until the Inspector had checked each of the rooms for any possible signs of contamination. Following what seemed to be an interminable amount of time, he reappeared at the top of the stairs carrying a plastic bag with a knot tied in the neck.

"Place is full of it and needs to be isolated!" He shouted through the muffled facemask, whilst giving a negative shake of his head. Within minutes they'd regrouped below awaiting the verdict.

"What is this shit, woman?" Eazy demanded. Superintendent Costello turned to face him. "There's no possible way these people can live in these conditions, not with this amount of asbestos floating about. Which means we have no choice other than to re-house them, even if just temporarily." She next directed her attention to Estelle. "Do you have any clean clothes for yourself and the children?" Estelle nodded in the affirmative, "Excellent, what about money?" Estelle whispered she had £100 hidden inside her bedroom.

The silver-rimmed glasses glinted in the light of the naked bulb and Rose Costello's countenance took on a satisfied look. "More than enough," she declared.

Eazy's face, however, had taken on a different kind of look and it wasn't one of happiness. "What the hell you doin', woman? These people live here!" Pointing to the threadbare carpet beneath his feet.

"Not anymore," Rose smilingly informed him.

Two hectic weeks later and a delighted Estelle found herself living on the tenth floor of Sharecropper Heights.

Back in the real world, Estelle and Eazy eyed each other across the kitchen table with mixed feelings.

"Me and you met a long time ago in very strange circumstances missy," he began. "An' maybe you got reasons to bear me some grudges and cum think of it, you could be right. But I know my son Jacob had his mind set on you first time he saw you, an told me he doan want no one else." He hesitated for a moment as if trying to think of the right words to say. "It took me a little while, but I know you was good for him in the short time he lived, an' I was mighty grieved when he passed on."

A look of sadness momentarily appeared on his face. "I've always regretted the fact I never did find who it was that killed him, but I don't intend to let it happen this time. Through Jacob's seed, you and your children are now my kin, an' that being so, I feel your pain an' sorrow at the death of one so young."

It suddenly occurred to Estelle that Eazy was talking about the murder of her son Moses and he wasn't finished yet.

"In my world, such things can't be left to rest, an' that being the case, somebody got to pay the price. So cum tomorrow I start lookin' for whoever did it." He then finished his rambling sermon with a chilling. "*An eye for an eye,* said the Lord!"

That was the last time she ever saw or spoke to him again.

155

Part Four

Harbourside Apartments

Waiting for the Internet to connect with Sarajevo, reminded Jacko of watching paint dry. That is, until Zelda suddenly appeared on screen. The backdrop of city lights was still there, its glow framing her image like an icon in a church window and he'd be the first to admit that his manhood shifted a fraction when he heard her soft velvet voice from across the void.

"*Zdravo prijatelji moji kako ste?*" she said, which to his relief was expertly translated by Simone.

"Hello Zelda and yes, everything is fine. Although some of us are a little stressed out to say the least," pointedly looking in Jacko's direction.

The ex-Russian rock chick smiled in sympathy and began speaking in English. "I can understand your frustration, but it would appear we have a chain of events that are somehow connected."

This was just the sort of news he'd been hoping for, until Zelda had once again burst his balloon. "When was the last time you checked the Serbian website?"

"Yesterday morning," said Jacko.

Simone nodded in agreement. "Yes, I'm sure that was the last time I saw it."

"Well, it would appear that you must have ruffled a few feathers somewhere, because if you look now, I think you'll find it's been taken down."

"How do you mean, taken down? I thought it was a police website?"

"So did I, but somebody somewhere must have the authority to close it, considering it's not there anymore."

"What about Interpol, I thought this was Euro-wide policing?"

"It is. But it's also worth remembering, Sergeant that we're talking about different countries, where different rules can apply."

"Meaning somebody knows we're looking for information?"

"Yes, Simone and whilst we were searching for the mystery face on the charge sheet, something else became obvious. This photo seemingly portrays a fair-haired person, yet I've been reliably informed that it's just an amateur attempt to dye it blonde."

"So this is not his natural hair colour?"

"Our people think not, Sergeant."

"It would be nice to know what colour it normally is," mused Simone.

"Could he have been a Punk Rocker?" Jacko speculated. "There were lots of them jumping about and spitting at people in the seventies and eighties."

"But not in Yugoslavia!" Zelda replied witheringly.

"I think the Communists would have frowned on that sort of thing when they were running the country," whispered Simone.

Jacko gave a wry smile as Zelda continued, "I have some friends who are experts in these matters and they are convinced the charge sheet originates from the Serbian district of Erdivos, which is situated north west of Belgrade. They're also confident the name of this person is 'Luka' only due to the over-type, the rest of the name is still indiscernible, but they are working on it even as we speak."

"Do they have a date when it might have been issued?"

"Yes Sergeant, they think the charge sheet is from the early nineties. The reason being they changed the typeset and format when it became computerised in May two thousand."

Simone studied her copy of the email. "I wonder how many blonde *Lukas* were living in Erdivos at that particular time?"

"I wouldn't have thought there'd be many, especially with a head like that," chuckled Jacko. "That said, if someone is still concerned after all these years, then maybe we really are on to something!"

"I couldn't agree more, Sergeant."

"I don't suppose we have a date of birth or anything that may tell us how old this Luka was?" asked Simone.

"I'm afraid not," replied Zelda, "but judging by his youthful looks I would guess he's somewhere around nineteen or twenty years of age."

Jacko and Simone were still pondering the face when Zelda spoke again. "Still, all is not doom and gloom, as you English like to say. I've heard there's been an important breakthrough concerning the sunglasses and all being well, I'm hoping to send you some more news tomorrow. *Zbogom* my friends."

"Goodnight," replied Simone.

Jacko took another sip of Fleurie as Zelda's glamorous image melted into the obscurity of a blank screen.

"Fancy a frozen pizza?" Simone asked innocently.

S.C.U.

Stretch Malone's day was filled with so much joy and pain, he wasn't sure whether to laugh or cry. The 'elation' had begun yesterday afternoon, when he'd watched his beloved Everton (the blue-coloured football team in the city) thrash Sunderland 3-0 at a packed Goodison Park. But the 'agony' had raised its head in the middle of the night, when a rogue haemorrhoid had flared up like a mini Vesuvius, the throb from between his buttocks close to making his eyes water. Yet in spite of this painful inconvenience, he'd still managed to waddle penguin like to his desk and as a temporary means of relief, shift from one cheek to the other. He was also about to head for the nearest chemist in search of some suppositories, when something on screen made him forget all about it. "Bingo!" He proclaimed, his hand frantically waving in Jacko's direction "Hey Sarge, come and have a butcher's at this."

Jacko scanned the information on the screen before letting out a whistle of appreciation. "Holy shit!"

"What do you think?"

"I think you should print it ASAP!"

A stab of the keyboard became the next imperative and within minutes both detectives were sitting in Carson's office.

"As you know, Nathan, I've spent so much time looking at daggers, I'm convinced I know more about them than *Marvo the Knife Thrower* in 'Billy Smart's Circus!'

Carson and Jacko wore sympathetic faces, aware that half the kids in the country were tooled up with a weapon of some kind.

"Nevertheless," continued Malone. "I was reviewing my fiftieth different type of blade and just about to cut my own throat, when Latex and zip-ties flitted across the screen. At first it didn't seem like anything of interest; then somewhere in the back of my mind, it rang a bell." Stretch checked his notes before continuing.

"Earlier this year, a small leisure craft was passing under a bridge on the Leeds to Liverpool canal, when a loose tether rope became entangled with something in the water. The family on board, who'd hired the boat for the Easter weekend, had naturally assumed it might be the usual rusty dolls pram or shopping trolley. However, as they struggled to free the rope, the body of a young girl suddenly bobbed to the surface. According to the official report, she'd been zip-tied to an iron gate that was heavy enough to keep her submerged in the murky depths for at least a year."

"What's the connection, Frank?"

"Tenuous to say the least, Nathan. Still, we do know she'd been strangled and *might* possibly have been raped from behind, though the local 'Time Team' found no traces of semen or DNA on the body and clothes. A later check did, however, find some minute traces of a latex substance under her fingernails."

"Go on," prompted Carson.

"I wasn't sure where it might lead, but thought it worth contacting the local CID who'd originally handled the case." Frank held up a file. "This is the information they faxed me less than an hour ago."

Carson made no move to take it from him.

"As I mentioned earlier, the girl's body, which as you'd expect was badly bloated, turned out to be a twenty-year-old who went missing in August 2013. At the time there was the usual mass search and hullaballoo, that eventually fizzled out when nothing came to light."

"You must remember it on the news, Guv?" Jacko interrupted. "The body on the gate, it was a big thing."

Carson, who'd been following every word, nodded. "Yes, I do, but wasn't there something odd about the gate itself, Frank?"

"Yeah, when the girl went missing, so did a two hundred weight cast-iron gate that used to guard the pathway under the bridge. It was assumed, at the time, it had more than likely been nicked for scrap. Only for it to turn up with the girl's body tied to it a couple of years later."

"And they reckoned it was the work of one man?" Carson speculated.

"One very fucking strong man," growled Frank.

"Any trace of the killer?"

"Not a thing. Forensics concluded that strangulation was the probable cause of death and the girl, who appeared to have been abducted a few miles away, was already dead before she hit the water. Although being submerged for that length of time in a slow running canal was enough to bloat her body and later help it float."

Carson was still absorbing the details, when Frank cocked an eyebrow. "Ready for the next one?"

Carson's ears pricked up like a dog at mealtime. "You mean there's more?"

"More from Central Computer," smiled Malone. "And it really is amazing how many fair-haired birds are lying dead out there," waving his hand as if there were one on every street corner. "Around this time, I'd been searching for similar circumstances, or M.O. depending what might appear first, when something caught my eye."

At which point Carson's inners gave a sudden twitch.

"In September 2014, the body of another blonde girl was found partially buried in a densely wooded area in south east Kent. The on-site photos are definitely *not* for the squeamish seeing as she'd been there for at least a year. But how's this for a twist? The 'Time Team' reckon the local wildlife had dug up the body and began snacking on whichever part they could get at, her neck area being the easiest." Malone paused, only to place some more Forensic photos on the desk.

"And as you'd expect, due to her obvious deterioration, no one could say for sure if she'd been strangled or raped. And even though any possible trace of her

162

killer had disappeared as lunch for the foxes, the autopsy concluded that a series of knife wounds might have contributed towards her death."

Jacko, who'd seen most the shots earlier, watched Carson reviewing the carnage on his desk. "You need to read the report, Guv. The body was lying face down in a man-made ditch wearing only a skirt and blouse, but due to the ripped and torn clothes, Forensics were unable to say how they got that way. They did, however, find some minute traces of a Latex type substance under her fingernails."

Carson interest was beginning to grow. "Do we know who she was?"

"Afraid not," said Frank. "They never did discover her ID, although some were of the opinion she might have been an illegal immigrant, but the quality of her clothes suggests otherwise."

"I'm not sure where you're going with this, Frank, but the girl in the canal was strangled and then dumped in the water. Whereas this one might have been stabbed and then buried, nevertheless you reckon there's a connection somewhere?"

Frank placed two more photographs on the desk. One showed a close-up of the girl on the gate; the other highlighting the body in the ditch. "Something about both killings caught my eye, but where's the similarity, Nathan?"

Carson wasn't into solving riddles, preferring to deal only in hard facts, but he and Frank Malone went back a long way. "Both wrists have been secured with black plastic zip ties?" he ventured.

"Close Nathan, but look a little closer."

Carson studied the photograph. "Okay, it's not just one zip tie, there's two joined together!"

Malone and Jacko nodded as one and Carson had to admit the detailed Forensic shots were hard to ignore. The girl on the gate was face down, her wrists and ankles secured to the four corners with the plastic zip ties. The woman in the ditch was also face down, but this time her hands and feet had been secured from behind. Yet in both cases, the skirt was split and a close up showed a single zip tie was too short to go around.

Coincidence or what, he pondered.

"Okay Frank, two dead blonde girls secured with zip-ties, yet seemingly murdered in two very different ways. So what's the connection, if you'll excuse my pun?"

"Somewhere in the past, somebody *fucked up big style*," Frank informed the hastily gathered team. "Thankfully, it wasn't us. But whoever did the background on the 'blonde' in the ditch, made a costly mistake by messing up a tiny, yet vital link. For reasons unknown, they used the term 'Latex' in their report, which is okay, if this were the case. However, Latex is a naturally occurring rubber substance that comes from one particular tree. Whereas the traces found in both the zip-tie murders was in fact Nitrile. An identical man-made material used in many things, but mostly in the manufacture of so-called rubber gloves." Frank pointed to the enlarged photographs on the board. "Due diligence would have revealed that zip-ties similar to these, had not only been used in both crimes, but had a similar type of Nitrile trapped in their plastic teeth."

Joanna's finger interrupted him. "Surely 'The Ditch' Forensic report, would have noted that?"

"Maybe. But this one tiny slip of the pen meant the Manchester 'Time Team' had missed this very important connection as they surfed the 'Data Base' looking for clues. They knew of the similarities between 'The Gate and The Ditch', but obviously thought plastic zip-ties could be found in any amount of crime scenes. They'd also assumed the MO was different and in their wisdom, decided to look elsewhere. We, however, are of the opinion they were too hasty in their conclusions and in doing so overlooked a few other things."

Jacko took over. "While searching for any similarities to the park murders, Stretch and I had an in-depth look at the two zip-tie murders. And it wasn't long before they began to leap off the page, the most obvious one being 'Nitrile'. Yet when you take into account that the three victims were all young blonde girls and factor in a few other methods used in the killings, like rape, strangulation, knife wounds and last of all torn clothes, we thought there was a definite pattern. That said, if anyone were to take each case on the evidence alone, they could be right in thinking they were all different and I'd probably have to agree with them. Nevertheless, all the evidence points to this being the work of one sadistic man, who likes to torment his victims in a variety of ways before killing them."

Frank took over again. "Realising we were in need of more expert help; we had our forensic people check out the file. They've since informed us that the substances found around the throat and under the nails of Kelly Freeland are similar to both the zip-tie murders. They've also made another surprising discovery. Amongst the Nitrile fibres was a minute trace of the something called 'Flux' and whilst sifting through the rubbish in the Waytree carpark, discovered an eight-inch black zip-tie lying beside Vinny's Ford Escort. This too had a tiny fleck of the same substance caught within its plastic teeth."

A room full of expectant eyes waited for him to explain. "There's a simple process required when someone's about to join two pieces of metal pipe together. First off, they have to ensure both joints are clean, they then need to apply a small layer of 'Flux paste' and use a gas blowtorch to melt the solder. Oxidisation in the joint removes any impurities and guarantees the joint won't leak when the pipe is later filled with water."

"Are we talking about plumbing here?" asked Smithy.

Frank gave a half nod. "Possibly, but if we are to believe Vinny's story of how he swapped parking places at the time of the murder, then maybe the killer inadvertently dropped the zip-tie when he was climbing either in or out of the Transit Van!"

As he normally delighted in describing what was happening between the cheeks of his arse, the news of Stretch's swollen 'Haemorrhoid' had swept through the S.C.U. like wildfire. Which would probably explain why the area around the coffee machine was devoid of people when an angry looking Bastion tip-tapped his way along the corridor.

"Your office, Nathan, and bring Sergeant Jackson with you."

Mystified by this unexpected arrival and unsure of what was rattling his cage; the two Detectives exchanged wary glances and fell in behind.

"I've been going over your latest report concerning The Park murders," began Bastion. "And whilst I'd be the first to admit that you've made some major inroads with the investigation, I am more concerned with this particular section," opening the folder and removing a file with a pink post-it note attached. The Detectives were still unsure where all this was leading, until Bastion spoke on.

"I'd like to know why Maxi Hamilton is a possible suspect in his own granddaughter's murder case?"

"I wouldn't say he's a suspect," a surprised Carson replied. "He's just part of our ongoing inquiry."

"Then *why,* might I ask, are you investigating him? "

Carson looked confused. "I take it you've read the interview regarding his wife's death? Or the fact he never once mentioned both he and she had been involved in a shooting incident?"

Jacko chewed his inner lip, knowing the pink sticker did indeed refer to their probing's into the Miami shootings.

Bastion scrutinised the paperwork on his lap. "If I'm correct in reading the details of the Hamilton interview, I have yet to find exactly where in the transcript he was asked that one particular question."

Carson steepled his fingers and tapped them on his lip, as he ran over the contents of Jacko's report. "This is true, Sir, but considering the circumstances, don't you think he would feel obliged to mention his wife had been shot dead, even if it had taken place over thirty years ago?"

"I think you've just hit the nail on the head Nathan. This Miami incident must have been traumatic to say the least and considering the recent tragic death of his only granddaughter, is it not unreasonable to assume Mr Hamilton would be reluctant to shout about it from the rooftops?"

Carson gave a brief shrug of his shoulders. "We're just trying to solve a brutal murder case, Sir. And I'd recently heard a rumour that Hamilton was heavily involved in the drugs trade long before he became super wealthy. The Miami police have also confirmed that there were known dealers; albeit American ones, present at the time of the shooting."

Bastion narrowed his eyes, as if in thought. "Ah, yes, I was just coming to the 'rumour' as you call it and maybe we should tackle that first. I was hoping you might provide us with a little more detail as to where it originated from and by whom?"

Carson shifted in his seat weighing up his options. He then proceeded to give his boss a quick rehash of his meeting with Archie Speed and the old man's recollections of his time as a reporter on the early Liverpool music scene. But more importantly, the ones relating to Hamilton's humble beginnings as a doorman in the nightclubs, his involvement in selling drugs and the supposed whisper of past territorial battles he'd had with Eazy Stoker.

"I can understand why you'd want to find a connection between Stoker and Hamilton, seeing as both have dead grandchildren in Waytree Park. But the Autopsy and Forensics specifically point to it as being a sex attack, not a calculated attempt to kill either of them."

"I appreciate that, Sir, but how strange is it that the two kids are murdered and we find they could be connected by these happenings from the past."

"A couple of questions, Nathan. What time frame are we talking about here? How many years ago? And did your 'source' ever actually buy any of this stuff from Hamilton personally?"

"I'm just about old enough to remember The Beatles as a kid," he admitted, "so it has to be mid-sixties and according to my 'source', as you call him, he didn't touch the stuff."

"So, do we have anyone else who might be able to verify any of this? And I am talking about people who *did* purchase drugs from Hamilton, or possibly saw him and Stoker together."

"Not at the moment, but I think if we dug a little deeper, we just might find somebody."

"I take it you've spoken to Mitch Brennan at Drugs?"

Carson nodded.

"And?"

"He says there's nothing in records to say Hamilton was involved in the sale of any type of drugs."

"Or any other type of criminal offence for that matter. Not even a parking fine as I understand it," concluded Bastion.

"Excuse me, Sir," Jacko chipped in from the side. "What about the shootings in America and the supposed well known drug dealers attending the party?"

Bastion fell silent, once again studying the file on his knees. "If I'm to read the Miami police report on the incident and its eventual findings Sergeant Jackson. They concluded that the Hamiltons *weren't* the intended targets on the day of the wedding, but were simply caught in the crossfire for the want of a better description. I should also think it most unlikely an event of that particular size and nature would be completely devoid of the odd rotten egg, seeing as how drug feuds were routine and those involved would normally carry fire arms!"

Carson glanced at Jacko aware they were indeed on shaky ground but was reluctant to give up the search without any real conclusion. "What if you gave us another couple of days to check some things out, Sir," he pleaded.

"I fail to see how that would change things, besides, I thought we were looking for a professional killer with a long knife?"

"We are, but I'm still finding it hard to ignore the rumour that forty years ago Maxi Hamilton was a major drug dealer and who's to say the killer in the park isn't somehow connected to all of this?"

Bastion's nose ranged laser like on Carson's face. "Do you have something else in mind?"

"I know it's a long shot, Sir, but I was wondering if we might find an older officer who still has all his marbles intact and I don't mean someone who's trying to remember what he ate for breakfast."

"Anyone in particular?"

"Yes Sir, I think Hughie McClellan might be the perfect man for the job. He was, after all, in charge of Drugs around this period"

"You mean 'Ex-Commander' McClellan?"

Carson nodded. "Had a call from Mitch Brennan earlier today. Says he was appearing in the Magistrate's Court yesterday and unexpectedly bumped into his old boss. Mitch said they began chatting about things 'in general' and he'd casually mentioned Maxi Hamilton's name in passing. And that's when McClellan said he'd be more than happy to help with our murder inquiry."

Bastion looked perplexed. "Are you sure you want to get Hughie involved? From my experience, once he's on board, he has this annoying habit of telling everyone what to do."

Carson shrugged. "I don't care about that, Sir and I know he's been out of action for a while, but the only thing I'm interested in at the moment is solving this Waytree Park murder case."

"What about Maxi Hamilton? Other than his charity work, I doubt most people will have even heard of him. But as we all know he does have some very powerful friends. So I don't have to tell you that it's *not* a good career move to start making wild accusations against him, well not unless you can prove them."

Carson and Jacko's eyes met again. "We fully understand that Sir, but we still think it worth pursuing. Even for a few more days."

Bastion exhaled through his cone like nostrils. "If this happens at all Nathan, I want it done on the bloody quiet, understand?"

"Of course, Sir."

"And while we're at it, I'd like to hear more about this Bosnian journalist woman and the mystery Serbian website."

V.D.O.

Having parked his car overnight in the police compound, Jacko decided a brisk walk to work and some fresh air might do him good. As ever, his early morning stroll would see him turning into 'North John Street' and make for the pedestrian thoroughfare that was Lord Street. But on the way would have to pass *Mathew Street*, home of *The Cavern* and of course, the legendary *Beatles!* Pausing for a minute, he found it amazing to think that what had once been some obscure Victorian back-alley, was now a major part of musical history.

Yet Jacko had lived here long enough to know that for some, especially the older and more passionate visitors, their journey would be more like a 'Rites of Passage'. It was no secret that they came from every corner of the planet, as Liverpool's musical tentacles reached back through time, generations and so many distant places. He'd also been admiring the full-sized bronze statue of John Lennon leaning nonchalantly on the corner of Mathew Street when Simone's urgent call sent him hurrying in the direction of headquarters. Skipping the usual overcrowded lifts, he took to the stairs and reached the S.C.U. in less than half the time. A quick wave of the hand was more than enough to greet the Team, as he zeroed in on the fax machine.

"Listen up everyone, there's been a new development in the case," he called "and this little beauty has just come in from Sarajevo." For some, Jacko's exciting news appeared to be no more than a faded photo cutting from an old black and white newspaper. A closer examination however, had revealed a small thin bespectacled man dressed in a dark suit, standing in front of a pair of tall wrought iron gates. "This," he informed them, "is Mr Viktor Dvoric who's about to open his new factory in a town called Kryjac, situated some thirty kms north of Sarajevo, circa May 1985." The Team focused on the picture, happy to put a face to the now familiar gold lettering found on the broken arm in Junkies Corner.

"Viktor it would seem was the owner of a small independent company named V.D.O, who manufactured a range of spectacles and trendy sunglasses, the most popular one being the *T1* or *'Terminator One'* as we now know it. History also tells us that sometime in the early nineties, the Serbian's invaded Bosnia and practically overran the whole country," pausing only to let this piece of information sink in. "I'm now about to read you part of an interview Viktor's sister gave not long after the war was over."

"As the sound of bombing drew closer, the more I began to fear for our lives. Yet Viktor had always assured me that seeing as we were both Serbian born, we shouldn't be in any real danger. He was also convinced that we were of no value to either side."

Jacko took up the story again; "On this occasion, she'd been referring to the period in 1992, when half the Serbian army were practically camped on their doorstep. But it would seem Viktor's optimism was a little ill founded. He'd been alone at the factory early one morning, when a Serbian bombardment blew him, the gates and the rest of the place to kingdom come. According to the local newspaper, Viktor had always been immensely proud of his gates. Yet on that one fateful morning, the *Viktor Dvoric Optika* factory departed this earth in a cloud of bricks and dust."

The Team listened with a sense of intrigue and fascination, as Jacko continued with his story by placing another cutting on the board. "This photograph was also taken around the time of the Kryjac incursion and I'd be interested to see if anything else catches your attention." The picture showed a smiling group of heavily armed soldiers, relaxing on the bonnet and wheel arches of a large troop carrier, "But if you look closely, you can see they were all dressed in dark battle fatigues and wore black wrap-around sunglasses;" a fact that Smithy was more than happy to point out. The Team were still openly discussing this moot point, when Malone posed a question. "How do we know the broken arm discovered at our crime scene is the real deal, Jacko?"

"We don't, Stretch; well, not unless someone turns up with an original pair of T1 sunglasses that we can compare with ours."

"Do we know if anything else survived the shelling?"

Jacko shook his head. "I couldn't say for sure. But there's some anecdotal evidence to say the back of the warehouse might still have been intact."

"I don't suppose they stored the sunglasses in there, did they?"

"That's something we'll never know for sure, but it still doesn't answer my question. How does the broken arm from a pair of V.D.O. sunglasses turn up at our crime scene some twenty-five years after the factory that made them was destroyed? And here's a much more pertinent question. What's the chances one of these soldiers might actually be wearing them?"

The Baltimore Switch

A whole minute went by before anyone realised there was a stranger in their midst, his surprise appearance bringing most of the S.C.U. to a standstill. First out the traps was Jacko, who caught up with him by the main display areas and grabbed hold of his arm as a temporary means of restraint. But to his horror realised he'd just apprehended an angry looking ex-Commander Hughie McClellan. Having never met him in person, he vaguely remembered the *tuft* of ginger hair that sat like a horn in the middle of his forehead; the rest reminding him of a coral island with a ring of ginger curls circling the outer edge. "Oh, sorry Sir," he stuttered; wondering if he might have dropped a major bollock, but to his relief, heard a familiar voice from behind.

"Hughie, my old friend, how are you?"

McClellan looked daggers at Jacko, before replying in a gruff Scots accent. "What's this all about, Nathan? Had a call from Brennan who said you were looking for some *stuff from the past,* but didn't say exactly what."

Carson shook his hand and patted him reassuringly on the arm. "Yes, Hughie, there are a few things I'd like to talk about, but we can do that later in my office."

The Scotsman listened and nodded along like the proverbial sage he was. "Nay problem, I'll do whatever I can to help. But I'm curious to know what's going on here?" His stubby finger pointing towards the Display Boards and Elijah's face in particular, "I can see some very familiar people I've had the unfortunate pleasure of meeting in the past, especially this ugly bastard with the short Afro hairdo!"

Legend had it that Tufty took no prisoners when in charge of the Drugs Unit and judging by today's reaction, it was easy to see why. Nonetheless when it came to the finer points of police diplomacy, the *Scot's drug buster* must have employed an army of 'Bastions' in order to keep him on the straight and narrow. Especially when he was regaling his views on programmes such as BBC's 'Question Time'.

"I can't tell how many times I've tried to get him and his old man stuck behind bars," he snarled. "But some sweet-talking sharp-faced lawyer always guaranteed they'd walk free."

"Sometimes there's no justice when you need it," conceded Carson, whilst ushering him towards his office, where Jason Junior was waiting with a tray of coffees. "Once again Hughie, I'd like to thank you for sparing the time to help us out in this matter. "

"Nay problem, Nathan, all you have to do is ask."

Carson wasn't quite sure which way to begin or how McClellan would react; but thought *what the hell* and pushed on anyway. "What we're really trying to do, Hughie, is ascertain if a certain person was once involved in the supply of drugs here in Liverpool."

"Who and when?"

Instead of answering, Carson scribbled a name and date on a piece of paper and held it up so McClellan could see.

From his side of the desk, Jacko observed the Scot's reaction to the information written on the page and the long thoughtful look on his face. It also gave him a moment to remember that when his boss had first arrived in Liverpool, Tufty's star had already risen high in the sky. From being a lowly drugs officer, he'd rapidly climbed the ladder to success, eventually obtaining the rank of Area Commander, before moving on to the more demanding role of politician.

It was also easy to see the difference in their ages, Carson being reasonably fit and in his early sixties. Whereas Tufty looked to be at least fifteen years his senior. But luckily the Scot had worked in the Merseyside police force for more than forty years, meaning he might be the one person to shed some light on Hamilton's past life. Yet at the moment seemed more interested in the clock on the wall.

Then without warning he rose from his chair and began to speak. "How long have you been in the Force, Nathan?"

"Thirty-five years."

"And would you agree that, although we don't intend to, we're all liable to make some mistakes along the way?"

"I suppose, but it would depend on the mistake."

"I don't mean those minor everyday schoolboy errors. I'm talking about the kind of fuck-ups that are so bad you have to sweep them under the carpet!"

A puzzled Jacko looked at Carson, who appeared to be just as confused.

"Some might say this is apocryphal," began Tufty. "While others of a more practical nature have termed it a tall story. But I personally think you should decide for yourselves whether there's any truth in an under-cover operation known as 'The Baltimore Switch'."

Taking his seat again, he reached for his now cold coffee, took a sip and began to expand further. "Many years ago, a newly promoted drugs officer heard a whisper that something big was about to happen, yet had no idea as to what it might be. This situation continued for six months or more, however, they still had nothing; only that it was supposed to be *huge!* Then out of the blue they had a break. As part of an on-going investigation, the American DEA were about to charge some small time drug-pusher for selling Cocaine around the Baltimore dockland area.

"At the time, it'd looked to be an open and shut case and the scumbag was almost certainly destined to spend a few years breaking rocks. Having realised he was about to eat custodial slop for the next five years, this same 'pusher' has decided to trade in some valuable information he'd come across a few days earlier. It supposedly involved a massive shipment of drugs destined for the UK, or to be more precise Liverpool Docks. In addition, the wee shit said the vessel was called the 'MV Marillion' and was able to give the exact time and date of its arrival."

171

Tufty allowed himself a satisfied smile before continuing, "As you can imagine Nathan, everything this side of the ocean went into overdrive the moment the Yanks had relayed the information. But more so, when our 'cousins' said they'd managed to obtain a copy of the ship's manifest, plus the serial number and colour of the suspect container. Armed with this information, a massive surveillance operation swung into action; all of it centred on the incoming shipment."

A satisfied Tufty allowed himself another sip of coffee before continuing. "Their next move was to bide their time and wait for the ship to complete its journey, which it did bang on schedule. Keeping everything normal, the containers were unloaded onto the dockside, each of them awaiting clearance by Customs. Standing by, in the wings, were the transport firms who as the hours went by, duly signed for their relevant metal boxes and disappeared through the dock gates. Yet nobody had claimed the one container they were interested in and so for the next twenty-four hours, it sat lonely and unwanted in the main storage area. As time went by and darkness set in, the people who'd organised the operation began to wonder if whoever owned the grey container, for there was no ultimate delivery address, might have gotten wind of their intentions and decided to pull the plug."

"Was someone leaking information?" asked Carson.

Tufty shrugged. "Who knows? But it was late the following day, before a wagon turned up with what appeared to be the required paperwork. However, when they heard the driver was alone, decided he was unlikely to be the main man and were hoping he *might* lead them to whoever was. It had also been agreed beforehand, that they should let the container leave the docks and follow it to its ultimate destination. Everyone assuming that with the right amount of surveillance, it would be near impossible for it to disappear when half the Merseyside police force and Customs were pursuing it.

A five-mile drive later and their quarry turned into what they assumed was its final destination; a small trading estate near Garston. The place in question was a hodgepodge of side roads, each fed from a main circular one, but crucially had just the one way in and out. From the vantage point of half a dozen unmarked police vans, they watched the wagon begin a slow crawl around the estate. Yet the alarm bells soon began to ring, when after making one circuit, it set off on another. When done, the driver slowed to a halt, climbed out the cab and begun to scratch his head. This was the signal for the teams to move in, detain the driver and find out what the hell was going on."

Jacko vaguely remembered 'Apocryphal' as meaning 'invented or fictional', but no matter what, this *saga* was getting very interesting, to say the least.

"Yet for some reason no one had made any real effort to collect it," snarled Tufty. "And the people running the operation couldn't understand why," a look of frustration appearing on his face. "The drugs hidden inside a shipment of luxury beds, had an estimated street value of around a million pounds; which even back in the eighties, was a considerable amount of money. Nevertheless and considering it had been a huge amount of drugs to take off the streets, everyone assumed that it must have been a serious blow to someone's everyday drug operations, but that didn't happen either. A week later and following what everyone believed was a hugely successful operation. They began to receive some very disconcerting calls, but not from whom you might have expected. These were angry complaints from the other major Enforcement Agencies situated around the country and they were all asking the same question."

How could 'Liverpool Drugs Unit' not be aware that someone was flooding the land with tons and tons of cheap cocaine? Especially as this was where the stuff had come from in the first place!

Carson sat back in his chair assuming there was more to come and Tufty wasn't about to disappoint. "It was only then did the penny drop and everyone realise that the Baltimore container had been 'one very clever and sophisticated sham'!"

"A sham in what way?" asked Carson.

"The wagon driver couldn't find the warehouse, because there was no such place. At first glance the delivery note had looked to be a bona-fide one used by some of the other large haulage firms, except it was fake and its information fictional. The unsuspecting driver, who just happened to work freelance, had been in the pub one night when someone asked him to collect the container, but he couldn't remember who and they paid him cash in advance."

Another grim smile appeared on his face. "It would now seem that on that same fateful day, two other ships had docked in Liverpool container port. One inbound from Miami, the other an hour later from New Brunswick in Canada."

Jacko and Carson's eyes met at the very mention of Miami. "According to their manifests, both were perfectly legit, for the want of a better description; the Canadian boat delivering specially treated pinewood logs for use in the horticultural industry. However, the one from Miami, would you believe, was carrying a shipload of refrigerated containers, all of which had been unloaded and departed the Docks within the space of six hours."

Carson asked the obvious question, "Was the Baltimore ship some kind of decoy?"

Tufty gave a shrug of his shoulders. "No one could say for sure and it was days before Customs tracked down the other Miami containers, only to find one of them had mysteriously gone missing."

"Which left them with the Baltimore one, filled with luxury bedding and a million pounds worth of drugs hidden inside?"

Tufty wrinkled his eyebrows for a second and then nodded. "Yes Nathan, but it's wrong to say the Liverpool Drugs Unit had missed this sudden surge of stuff on the streets, they simply hadn't realised it had gone nationwide."

"What about the drugs? Did they assume the surge had occurred as a direct result of the missing Miami container?"

McClellan's lip twisted down as he thought about the question and shook his head. "Impossible to say, but what did filter back through 'the grapevine' was someone had managed to flood the country with over twenty-five million pounds worth of drugs at a knock down half price and if true, sacrificed a million pounds in order to achieve it!"

Jacko let out a silent whistle as he did a quick calculation. No matter how you looked at it, twelve million pounds back in the eighties or whenever, had to be somewhere near fifty million in today's dosh.

"What about these so-called *Recipients*, Hughie, were they ever found?"

A fresh wrinkle creased the Scot's brow as he considered Carson's question. "When they eventually went in search of the suspects, they discovered that all their houses had been sold six months earlier and they'd literally vanished into thin air."

A brief impasse materialised as they each considered his reply and it hadn't been Jacko's intention to speak, but it just came out naturally. "So what happened next, Sir?"

McClellan's bushy eyes ran over him as though seeing him for the first time. "What happened next, laddie?" he growled. "I'll tell you what happened next. They called a frigging Press Conference," a look of triumph appearing in his eyes. "Because they still had a container full of drugs supposedly worth a fortune. And that being the case, decided to invite the world's press to watch them unload it in all its glory," a satisfied smile appearing on his ruddy face.

"And was the decoy container enough to keep everyone happy?"

"Yes Nathan. But as expected, the people upstairs had decreed the Miami part of the operation should remain top secret. More so, when considering the unexpected flood of drugs on the streets, which in their infinite wisdom they decided Joe public didn't need to know about."

"It must have been some cover-up, especially when you take into account the amount of people involved in the original operation."

"Needs must, Nathan, needs must! However, that wasn't the only item to be brushed under the carpet. It was quietly rumoured that a file, regarding a certain person went missing from Records and has never been seen again."

It was now the turn of Carson's eyes to narrow, as he suddenly realised what the craggy Scot was inferring. "I can understand the need to tread carefully and avoid breaking any eggshells, my friend, but that can only mean this person must have had someone working for them on the inside?"

Tufty raised both hands and showed his empty palms. "There's no way I can possibly comment on that, seeing as how I wasn't present and most people still insist it was just a rumour."

Carson caught Jacko's eye briefly, both of them recognising who Tufty was talking about when it came to the *Recipient*. But they still had a murder case of their own to solve and there was no doubting the secretive Maxi Hamilton could have some bearing on its outcome.

"Do you think that, if whoever had been leading the Baltimore investigation were still here today, he might want to help put a wrong right?"

The bushy-eyed McClellan regarded him for moment before rising from his chair. "I should think they'd be more than delighted to assist in any way they could."

A smiling Carson decided to keep up the pretence. "Then tell them from me, that any time they should wish to make a visit, the door to the S.C.U. is always open."

"I think they would ask only one favour in return."

Carson gave a gesture of compliance. "Anything special?"

"Get that frigging coffee machine in the hallway sorted!"

Memories

Kristian stood alone in the bedroom and observed his big sister's life as a pastiche of colourful memories. Every wall had been adorned with her most cherished things from both past and present. Pictures taken from magazines, posters of teenage boy bands and the odd group that amazingly he hadn't realised they'd both been fond of. His presence inside her temple, had always been a strictly 'no go area'! And yet he was more than familiar with its inner surroundings.

A multitude of different size photographs were hung here and there, some going back to when she was very young and he knew the exact spot in the corner where his five-year-old face smiled back at him. However, above her bed and now in pride of place, sat the one taken on their recent holiday to Spain. It showed the three of them sat by the hotel poolside, glistening wet in the warm summer sunshine, their faces alight and bright with happiness.

Moving towards the open wardrobe, he paused beside her dressing table and smiled at the amount of girl's stuff neatly arranged on the glass worktop. But what struck him most was the fragrant perfume his mother had recently bought for Kelly's birthday. "Whew, strong stuff that," he winced, before soundlessly passing through the connecting door into the adjacent bedroom. This particular arrangement had been in place for a long time, thus allowing Steffi immediate access should any problems arise when Kelly was a baby.

His sleeping mother lay entwined in the top bedcover, the spent tissues overflowing from the wastebasket that sat below her head and his eyes brimmed over at the futility of it all. "Don't worry, Ma, I'll always be here to take care of you!" he swore, before quickly returning through the gap.

Crossing the bedroom, he paused only to take one last lingering look around. "Bye Kell," he whispered to his bossy and at times *very* opinionated sister. Then, with tears in his eyes, quietly closed the door behind him.

Erdivos

Jacko met a serious-faced Carson holding two lumps of sugar in one hand and a Styrofoam cup of coffee in the other.

"You okay, Guv?"

"Not really, just having a problem with my dick."

"Nothing serious I hope?"

"Nah," he laughed. "It's more about this," patting his middle-age spread. "It's getting so big lately that I can't see my chipolata when I go for a piss!"

Jacko gave a smile of relief as Carson went into more detail. "I was watching one of those health programmes last night and it warned that too much of this stuff is bad for you. So I am seriously thinking of changing to sweeteners."

Jacko looked doubtful. "Not so sure about that, Guv, I saw another of them programmes claiming *they*'re man-made and twice as toxic!"

Carson hesitated and then smiled, before dropping the offending cubes into his cup. "Nice one, Jacko, if it wasn't for *Tate and Lyle's* finest, I'd never be able to drink this garbage." Pointing to the vending machine in the hallway.

He was still mulling over whether to stay fat when a grinning Jacko followed him into the office.

"You look happy, more good news?"

Jacko waved an email. "Just received this from Sarajevo."

Carson waited to hear from the distant place that wasn't on his normal holiday route. Yet couldn't help but be jealous, especially when his No. 2 had casually let slip he'd been chatting with this mystery Bosnian bird in Simone's apartment last night. 'All in the line of ongoing enquiries,' he'd explained innocently.

"I take it this is about the mystery chargesheet?"

Jacko nodded. "As you know, Zelda's people are convinced it's from an area called Erdivos which is somewhere close to Belgrade."

"Am I right in saying the Serbian Police don't know anything about it?"

"Yes Guv, they claim to have no knowledge of the person on the charge sheet and say the whole thing has to be some kind of prank."

"So what's the good news?"

"Zelda asked a Serbian reporter who's a close friend of hers, to head for this Erdivos and make some inquiries at the local police station. But when he'd showed a copy of the document to someone in charge, he was nearly arrested. According to the uniform behind the desk, he said it was Government property and demanded to know where it came from. Luckily, the reporter whose name is Milos, has managed to convince him it was just a joke and not push it any further. Nevertheless, it seems something had made him mighty suspicious, so our 'man in the field' decided to make himself scarce and look elsewhere."

"Meaning there's more to this than meets the eye."

"So it seems, Guv. His next move was to take a cut-down version of the charge sheet to a local bar where he was met with lots of blank faces, especially from some of the leather-clads who frequent the place. But this was only to be expected, seeing as most of them were in their early twenties and the mug-sheet man must be somewhere in his forties. Which is why he then homed in on an aging drunk and began to feed him a few 'sherbets' as a way of loosening his tongue. It wasn't easy, but he still managed to convince him he was searching for a long lost relative and the sight of a crisp '20-dollar American Greenback', had seriously concentrated his thoughts: from what I hear Guv, you can get 25,000 Serbian Dinars on the black market for the same note!" Carson's eyebrows lifted; he couldn't work out if the amount in question was good or bad, but decided to let Jacko move on.

"Which was when we got our first break. The drunk was happy to confirm that the face belongs to someone who used to play pool there and clearly remembered this one night when all hell broke loose in the bar. According to him, a man and woman had been at the wrong end of a brutal assault and blondie was the man responsible. Somebody called the police: who arrived in two squad cars and four uniforms struggled to apprehend him."

Carson was thinking of the face on the charge sheet. "Do we know who he is?"

"The drunk swears the mugshot belongs to a twenty-one-year-old local youth called Luka Tomovic, but because of his hair, was nicknamed Ziggy. However, this is where it gets very interesting. The drunk vaguely remembers him being remanded in custody, until a date was set for him to appear in Court. Yet two weeks later and to everyone's astonishment, Ziggy has managed to escape from jail and disappear."

"How did he manage that?"

"The drunk didn't have a clue."

"Damn! Do we know where this Ziggy lived in Erdivos?"

"I'm afraid not Guv."

"Does the drunk remember the last time he saw him in the flesh?"

"Yeah, around twenty-five years ago, on the day he was arrested."

"Is that it?"

"Not quite Guv, this Milos punter insists there's definitely a scoop to be had, especially if he treads carefully."

"Is he in some kind of danger?"

"Not sure yet, but judging by the excitement in Zelda's voice, I'd say they've found something big in Erdivos."

"But doesn't say what?"

"Not at the moment,"

"So what happens now?"

Jacko glanced at the email. "According to Zelda, 'Milos the intrepid' is heading back there tomorrow looking for more answers."

Caversham Cut Warehouse

One last chime of the Municipal clock confirmed it was midnight; the signal for him to leave the shadows and cross to the other side of the narrow-cobbled street. Many a year had gone by since he'd first visited the warehouse, but tonight would be his third in a week. An unlocked side door allowed him easy entry, to where a vast range of different size boxes and crates filled the dimly lit room. Having been here before, he was aware that the floor above was a near duplicate of the one below and under normal circumstances, reached by a winding concrete slope. But having conceded it would be too difficult a task to negotiate at his age, opted to take the staircase that acted as both a means of access and emergency exit. Yet unlike the dust covered crates stored on the ground floor, here instead was a line of beautiful and rare vintage cars that occupied almost every available parking space. Unfortunately for him, in one corner of these strange ostentatious trappings, sat the now ubiquitous black Range Rover, whose rear passenger door silently swung open. Gazing into its darkened depths, he wished it were possible to turn and walk away. But knew that the time for such actions were long gone and wearily accepting his fate, climbed in and awaited the inevitable question.

"What did you find?"

"The rumours are true; the dead boy in the Park is Eazy Stoker's grandson. But he's not the reason for the attack, Forensics are convinced it was the girl."

"Why her?"

"Sex."

"Are they sure?"

"They don't often get these things wrong,"

"How did she die?"

"I don't have any exact details. But from what I've heard, she was stabbed in the throat with a long thin stiletto knife that has yet to be found."

A moment of heavy breathing followed. "What about the murderer, do they know who did it?"

"No. Although there has been some talk of a professional hit-man."

"Hit-man? What do they mean by that?"

"They think whoever killed the girl and boy, might have been trained in one of the Armed Forces. Forensics, however, are still convinced the attack was sexually motivated."

"What about evidence? Did they find anything?"

"Nothing concrete, other than the broken arm from a pair of sunglasses that appear to have been manufactured in Yugoslavia."

Maxi's breathing returned to normal. "Keep talking."

"There's also mention of a white Transit van being seen near the Park around the time the murders took place."

"Do they know who owns it?"

"Not yet, but some small-time thief swears they swapped parking places. Unfortunately, there's nothing to say if it's a local vehicle."

"What about the Baltimore Switch? Did you tell them about that?"

"Of course, I did," spluttered McClellan. "And the fools swallowed every frigging word of it!"

Maxi had no time for gratuitous swearing, but the Scot's news made him grunt in satisfaction and pose a much more pertinent question. "Are you sure this Carson and Jackson weren't in any way suspicious?"

Tufty began to massage his chin as though in need of a shave. "Why should they? According to you, this is supposed to be some kind of fairy-tale rumour. But what's really worrying me, is if they discover that I'm somehow connected with this shit from all those years ago!"

"Take it easy McClellan, you're acting like a bloody drama queen," chided Maxi. "Besides, what's for them to find?"

"What's to find?" he groaned. "Christ man, if this Baltimore business comes out, I am well and truly ruined! I'll lose everything I've ever worked for; my self-respect, reputation and God knows what else!"

Maxi spoke from the dark as if addressing a child. "Listen McClellan, I'm too long in the tooth to be worried about such things as rumours. All I'm interested in is the here and now." The Scot was about to continue with his moaning when Maxi cut him short. "Never mind all that, did you mention the file? It was crucial you told them about it!"

"Of course, I did!" He exploded, his spittle flying about in the confines of the car. "They practically wet themselves when I let that slip!"

"Excellent," sighed Maxi. "Now stop blabbering like a baby and tell me everything that's happened so far."

McClellan was about to continue moaning and then realised he had no choice other than comply. Maxi sat back, closed his eyes and listened intently to the unfolding story. A few minutes went by before he held up a hand. "How did they know about my involvement with drugs?"

"Carson met some crime reporter named Archie Speed. It seems he worked for The Liverpool Evening Post back in the sixties and was still there when your wife was killed in the eighties."

Archie Speed, smiled Maxi. *I thought he died years ago.* Still, in the bigger picture, none of this mattered. The Miami police had officially logged Sandra's death as an accidental shooting, and no one could prove otherwise. It was also time to put McClellan straight. "If what you say is true, then there's no reason for Carson to be suspicious in wanting you to help him find the killer. It was a huge stroke of luck that they invited you on board, as an advisor and this 'Baltimore' business should have them running around in circles for weeks."

"I just want to go back to being retired," bleated Tufty.

"That, I'm afraid, is no longer possible," warned Maxi. "I want to find whoever who killed my granddaughter and need you on the inside to keep me informed of the investigation's progress. But more than that, I want a copy of the Autopsy."

Tufty's eyes nearly popped out of his head. "You must be frigging joking!" He gasped. "There's no way I can do that. For a start, I wouldn't even know where to find it."

"Bullshit," growled Maxi. "Considering the hundreds of autopsy reports you must have looked at in the past, I would have thought it only natural for someone like yourself to review all the latest evidence and this should help you record it."

From the darkness of the driver's seat, BB Benson turned and offered Tufty a small black object. "This might look like a normal cell phone, but when needed has a high-resolution camera that will automatically take any size of photograph."

Tufty stared at the device like it was the devil incarnate. "You've got to be kidding," he spluttered, "there's no way I can use something like that in Police Headquarters."

BB smiled. "Relax Hughie, there's no tell-tale flash when you press the button. And as long as there's no-one looking over your shoulder, it's impossible to tell if you're just making a regular phone call."

Tufty was still shaking his head in bewilderment when Maxi added. "Remember, we're only interested is the autopsy report. The rest can be done verbally when you return the camera."

"This is frigging madness; how do I explain it if anything does go wrong?"

Maxi's voice softened, "Trust me, my friend, it won't. Besides, who in their right mind would dare question the legendary Hughie McClellan? The very idea would frighten the shit out of anyone should they get too nosey." He then began to chuckle out loud. "One angry look from those bristling bushy eyebrows of yours would be enough to turn anyone to bloody stone!"

Clambering from the car, a furious Tufty began muttering a long line of profanities as he realised he literally had nowhere to go. "Ye frigging wee shite!" he swore at Maxi and as a last gesture of defiance slammed the door shut.

"He sounds pissed," grinned BB.

"Doesn't he just," smiled Maxi.

"Do you think he still has the file?"

Maxi nodded. "Oh yes, I'd be amazed if he got rid of something as important as that."

"Next question, will he try to leak its contents and are you sure this Baltimore Switch business won't come crashing down around our ears? I'd be sick as a pig if the boys in blue came knocking on my door."

"I can't see him doing that. Besides, Tufty knows he'll be the biggest loser if anything from the past comes to light; the rumours alone would ruin him and his so-called reputation."

"Personally, I'd be delighted," growled BB. "I was close to throttling him the first time we met."

"Take it easy," said Maxi. "He might be an obnoxious little shit, but we need him to get a copy of the Autopsy and keep us up to date with the investigation."

181

"I know," sighed BB. "But I'm still amazed at how much we've learned today. Plus the fact that without our help, McClellan would never have made it all the way to the top!"

"Life's full of surprises," smiled Maxi.

"True, but what about our angry wee Scotsman, do we agree he has plenty to think about?"

"He certainly has."

BB shook his head. "Who'd have thought that after all these years, we'd still be going through this same bloody rigmarole?"

Maxi smiled at the bitter irony of it all, "Not me, my friend, and I bet Tufty McClellan didn't either!"

Part Five

Liverpool, January 1981

Hughie would never forget the dark rainy night that changed his life forever. He and young Brady, his partner for the day, had been making their way back to headquarters, when they received a call telling of a major road accident on the motorway south of Kirby Junction. According to the female operator, who was probably sitting somewhere warm and dry, the traffic cops had found a dodgy substance in one of the vehicles and were asking if Drugs could come and check it out.

Hughie gave a weary shake of the head. "How long have we been on duty?"

"Nearly fourteen hours."

"Jesus wept," he groaned whilst reaching for the handset. "Central? This is unit 35 copy."

"Receiving you 35, go ahead,"

"I don't suppose there's anyone else who could take this callout? We are absolutely frigging knackered!"

"Sorry 35, I'd like to help, but you were specifically requested for this job."

Hughie flicked his cigarette end out into the windswept night and snarled. "I'll bet that bastard Mick O'Hara is behind this!"

Brady said nothing, aware this sort of crap could happen at any time, but more so when you were on callout with the ginger-haired Scotsman sat in the passenger seat.

"Okay," said Hughie, "I suppose we'd better go and have a look."

With the rain still falling and the windscreen wipers working overtime, they headed east and met the bumper-to-bumper line of cars waiting to pass the accident up ahead. "Here we go," said Brady, as he switched on the flashing blue light and used the hard shoulder to overtake the traffic. Five minutes later and he'd managed to squeeze his way between the rake of emergency vehicles parked inside the cordon. Reaching behind for their heavy waterproofs, they clambered from the car and spotted a black Volvo with its bonnet crushed beneath the rear end of an empty articulated lorry. A moment later and a 'Traffico' as Tufty liked to call them, splashed his way through the downpour wearing yellow drenched waterproofs and a pair of fogged up glasses. "You are?"

"Drugs," shouted Hughie. "What's the problem?"

The Traffico waved one hand like a conductor and gave them a quick rundown of the situation. "A couple of Chinese punters were bombing along in the pissing down rain and somehow managed to hit another car in the outside lane. How or why?" he said with a shake of his head, "We haven't got a clue. Yet they still managed to cross two lanes of traffic and get stuck up the arse of the wagon that had broken down on the hard shoulder. The rest of them," he said, pointing at the other damaged vehicles, "began to play dodgems with each other!"

He then led them towards the crumpled Volvo whilst continuing with his soggy dissertation; "It looks as if the driver was wearing a seatbelt, whereas the one in the back wasn't. So when they hit the trailer. *Bam!* He flew over the seat, butted his mate in the back of the head and the two of them ended up jammed between the steering wheel and the dashboard. Jesus, what a mess! Both men sustained serious head injuries and Christ knows how many other broken bones."

The two detectives listened to his description of what happened with a morbid sense of fascination and curiosity. "The wagon driver pulled open the rear side door and heard a faint moaning sound coming from inside. Thinking that someone might still be alive, he then ran to the nearest roadside phone half a mile away and rang Emergency Services. Being first on the scene, we were faced with the exact same problem and unsure of what to do next, waited for the ambulances to turn up."

"Where are the two men now?" asked Hughie.

"Well that's the thing," the fogged-up glasses replied, "When we'd managed to free them from the car, both men died within minutes of each other."

Asking if he could take a quick look, the Traffico pointed him in the direction of the waiting Ambulance. Hughie knew it was a long shot, but under the circumstances, thought it was still worth the effort. However, when he'd lifted the red wool blanket, all he found were two Chinese males aged around twenty-five. But as a result of their injuries, might have been sixty-five, even their mothers would have had trouble recognising them. He'd also been hoping he might get lucky with an ID, but in the end had to admit that both men were complete strangers. Pulling his hood over his head, he made his way back to where the two men were still standing in the rain. "Drew a blank," he said.

The Traffico nodded in understanding.

Hughie thought it time to move on. "Tell me about this dodgy substance."

The fogged-up glasses pointed to the crushed car. "We were doing the usual quick check of the interior and spotted something that looked and smelled like Hashish."

"Where about?"

"In the back."

Hughie leaned in with his torch and saw some cigarette papers strewn here and there on the back seat. On the floor lay a plastic bag half full of marijuana and judging by the amount inside, looked to be someone's personal stash. "Okay," he said a few minutes later. "We'll give the car a fast look over and then seal it up. Once you've managed to cut it loose from the wagon, our people will take it away and make sure there's nothing else hidden inside."

The Traffico nodded profusely. "Soon as you can boys, we need to get this place clear ASAP."

Hughie turned to Brady. "Do me a favour mate, inform Central where we are with this lot and then organise the truck."

"Okay," he grunted, before splashing off in the direction of the squad car.

Hughie was still flashing his torch here and there, when he heard a loud rumbling sound from above and saw a dagger of forked lightning illuminate the night sky. Before he'd even had time to think, a torrent of ice-cold rain came crashing down around his ears. In the blink of an eye, the Traffico and everyone around had gone in search of some kind of cover, of which there was practically none. Realising he too was about to get swamped, Hughie slammed shut the rear door of the Volvo and clambered in the front passenger side. The water hammering down on the roof, reminded him of horse's hooves as he pulled back his hood and waited for it to ease.

Through the shattered windscreen, it was just about possible to see the flashing lights from the Emergency vehicles parked nearby, but easier to see the crushed steering wheel and blood-splattered interior. "Shit, I can think of a damn sight better places to be than this," moaned Hughie. "Still seeing as I'm here, I might as well have a quick look around."

Turning on his torch, he opened the glove compartment and began flashing around inside, but other an old newspaper and oily rag, found it empty. The cigarette tray was much the same, a few twisted dead ends, but again no dope. He'd just about finished going through the motions when something caught his eye. At first he wasn't sure what, but the interior of the glove compartment didn't appear to match the rest of the plastic trim. Using his knuckle, he began to tap the upper surface that in some places sounded hollow. He was still feeling around in the dark, when one of his fingers felt the lip of a panel, which he used to push sideways.

Once open, it revealed a small void with just enough room to get his hand in. Using touch only, he began to probe around and seconds later felt a soft plastic package that he knew was either Cocaine or Heroin. Gently easing it out, he placed it on the lid of the glove box and reached in again. This time however, instead of drugs, he found a large leather wallet with two zipped pockets on either side.

The first contained a large wedge of £20 used notes. "Holy frigging Christ," he whispered. "There must be nearly a £1,000 pounds here." But there was more to come. When he opened the other side, the unmistakable glitter of diamonds sparkled before his eyes and there were lots of them! "Double frigging shit, man," he spluttered.

Hughie wasn't sure how long he'd sat there, but the rain outside was still heaving it down and none of the other crews seemed to have moved. At first he'd decided to hand the contraband in then suddenly changed his mind. "Why frigging not," he grinned. "In times of trouble, I could do with a few extra readies." Keeping both items out of sight, he slipped the wallet into one pocket of his waterproof and the cocaine in another. Making good use of the cloth he'd found in the glove compartment, he was then able to give the facia a quick wipe down and once satisfied that everything looked as before, clambered from the car to meet the still pouring rain.

The bedside alarm said it was 2.00 am, but Hughie wasn't thinking about sleep. He was more interested in the money and diamonds he'd found in the wreck and relieved he was now able to pay off his gambling debts. His last foray into the land of the gee-gees had been a major car crash and cost him a frigging fortune. The hot favourite who was supposed to have romped home by a mile, had fallen at the first fence and left him owing the Bookie over a grand. Which was nearly two months' wages.

Although that was the least of his worries, the real one was if Mick O'Hara should hear of his gambling and find he had money problems. The £1,000 in cash might help to wipe the slate clean and allow him to get drunk ten times over. But on reflection realised it wasn't a good situation for anyone to be in, never mind a serving drugs officer.

Zipping open the other pocket, Hughie fished out one of the sparkling diamonds and it held between finger and thumb.

"Ye frigging wee beauty!" he whispered, as a myriad of lights flashed before his eyes. A quick look around the room reminded him that his one-bedroom flat wasn't exactly Fort Knox when it came to security. Unsure of what to do next, he wrapped the wallet inside a pair of shit-stained underpants and shoved them at the bottom of his overflowing laundry basket. *He'd return later and hide them behind the bath panel, so much safer.*

Nevertheless, there was still the small matter of how to get rid of the sparklers. He'd once heard talk of a dodgy Pawnbroker, who asked no questions when it came to knock-off goods, but was so tight, it was like trying to squeeze blood out of a stone. Which meant he'd be lucky to get maybe a fifth of their true value. His mother had always said that beggars can't be choosers and even though it might take a year or two, Hughie was still confident he could drip-feed him the stones one at a time. The kilo of Cocaine was another unexpected bonus and like many of his predecessors, Hughie occasionally liked to sample what they took off the streets. To his delight he found that the odd 'snort' put a contented smile on his face. (But only on weekends and his days off.)

Three days had gone by since the night of the crash and within that period Hughie had no real way of knowing what might happen next. His only option being to wait and see if anyone claimed ownership of the two dead Chinese. But to his relief and considering what was hidden in the dashboard, he never heard a thing. Thinking about it, there was no surprise in finding that neither of the men were carrying ID of any sort, a subsequent fingerprint check revealing nothing.

It was the same story with the Volvo, which he discovered had been stolen from somewhere in Devon a couple of years earlier. Thus leaving him with a big fat zero when it came to his inbox. He'd also imagined a scenario where *the goods* might easily have gone missing sometime before the crash; a *double-cross* taking place earlier in the day. This at least gave him a crumb of comfort as he fretted over his own safety. The last thing he needed, was to be found lying in a ditch with his throat cut, past tales warning that when dealing with the Chinese, anything was possible!

Then on the morning he'd presented Mick with his findings, he had an unexpected surprise. O'Hara appeared to be only half listening as Hughie went through the report, his general demeanour being one of disinterest, as he took a brief look and declared. "Put it out on the airwaves and see if we hear anything. But personally, I reckon we'll just be flogging a dead horse." Those last words having a final and dismissive sound to them.

Yet Hughie knew the real reason for Mick's lack of interest. Under normal circumstances, he'd be looking to make more out of the motorway incident, especially as they'd found some drugs in the car. But it would also entail him giving Hughie some brownie points and that was something he just wasn't prepared to do. If the Chinese had been known criminals, then he'd have had no choice but to go public. However, a couple of unidentifiable Asians meant he had plenty of room to manoeuvre.

"Is that it?" He asked.

O'Hara nodded and muttered, "Yeah, that's it."

Hughie gave a sigh of relief. Due to the torrential rain on the night of the crash, the Press coverage had been minimal to say the least. The Volvo would eventually be scrapped and the Chinese frozen in the Morgue for a year or two, before being buried in an unknown grave. So, to all intents and purposes, it appeared as if this whole incident had never happened and the case was destined to die in the paperwork. He was just about to leave, when the sound of Mick's voice stopped him in his tracks. "Hang on a minute, I need to double check something with you."

"Oh yeah, what's that?"

"After they'd removed the two Chinese punters from the car, did anyone else go near it?"

Hughie shook his head. "No."

"Emergency Services?"

"No."

"What about you?"

"As the senior officer in charge, I made sure everything was as it should be. Then sealed all the car doors to prevent any kind of unauthorised entry."

"What happened next?"

"I waited for the pick-up truck to arrive, oversaw the removal operation and watched it disappear into the night."

"Tell me about the removal operation."

Hughie shrugged. "I broke the seal on the driver's side door so they were able to steer the car backwards onto the wagon."

"And then?"

"I resealed the door and they took the car away."

"So other than this one incident with the pick-up, nobody else went near the car?"

"That's right."

"Which I assume includes you?"

"Yeah," he replied confidently.

"Well, that's not how young Brady remembers it."

A shiver of uncertainty slid down Hughie's spine. "Is that right?" he croaked. "So what does he say?"

"Only that he saw you open the front passenger door and climb inside."

"I must admit that I'm getting a little confused here, Mick, so when exactly did he say this?"

"About an hour ago."

"Well I'll be frigging damned," he said with a laugh. "I'd forgotten all about that."

"Forgotten what, Tufty?"

"The huge downpour that nearly washed me off my feet. It was so heavy that the only way to avoid getting soaked to the skin was to jump in the car."

"So you were in the car?"

"Yeah, yeah, but only for a minute or two."

Mick pointed to the paperwork on his desk. "But you haven't said a word about that in your report and young Brady begs to differ with your version of events. According to him, you were sat in the car for at least ten minutes."

"So what?" He shouted angrily. "The stupid English bastard was probably playing with his dick while I was getting drowned!"

"Is that an official complaint?"

"Of course not," spluttered Hughie. "But I'd like to know what's going on here. Are you accusing me of something?"

"Not yet," said O'Hara.

"Holy shit! What does that mean?"

"It simply means we are trying to eliminate you from our enquiries."

"What?"

Mick tapped the folder on his desk. "Forensics have just finished giving the Volvo a good going over, meaning they've searched every nook and cranny of the vehicle. Their report has concluded that other than the bag of marijuana found in the rear foot well, the car was clean. However, they did find a secret compartment that was empty of drugs, yet still had fresh traces of cocaine inside, which under the circumstances is only to be expected. But what really did surprise them was the lack of fingerprints in this one particular area."

"Why?"

Mick smiled. "As per normal, they dusted the car down from top to bottom looking for prints and found plenty of them belonging to the two dead Chinese. In fact, they were all over the bloody place. And a quick check with our own Internal Records has confirmed yours were also scattered here and there. But then things started to go a bit skew-whiff when it came to the glove compartment."

"In what way?"

"It would appear that someone used an oily rag to wipe any other incriminating prints clean."

Tufty vividly remembered using the rag to do just that. "So?"

"Well, the next question is who? And why?"

"It must have been the driver's mate."

"I don't think so," Mick replied.

"Why not?"

Mick smiled again. "Because according to your report, he was on the back seat rolling a joint at the time of the crash. But in order to assure myself that I hadn't missed anything of importance, I rang Forensics and asked if they'd found any oily type substances on the hands and fingers of the two dead Chinese. And guess what? There was none. In fact both men had shiny manicured nails. Which begs the question, why would they want to wipe clean just the glove compartment and not the rest of the car? After all, there was nothing of value in it. Or was there?"

"Why ask me?"

"Because you were there at the time."

"Are you accusing me of something?" growled McClellan.

"No, not yet," smiled Mick. "But I *can* tell you that Forensics found a partial print on the access panel that slid back and forth in the void."

Hughie began to sweat. This was different. "So why tell me?'

"Probably because it's similar to one of yours."

"What is this shit?" snarled Tufty. "Is it mine or isn't it?"

"Well, that depends on what they find next. Although it doesn't sound too healthy when your official report says you didn't get in the car and one of your own men swears you did."

"It was pissing down rain at the time, maybe he mistook me for someone else."

"Bollocks," smiled Mick.

"I'm being stitched up."

"Double bollocks!"

"There's no way you can prove this shit."

"Wanna bet? "

Tufty could see his boss was really enjoying himself. "Why haven't I been suspended?"

"There's not enough of us in Drugs and we're overrun with work at the moment. Besides, you haven't been found guilty, yet."

"Fuck you O'Hara, I want a transfer out of here!"

"Sorry mate. That will only happen after the D.P.S. have had a look at the evidence *and* if you are still in the force."

Tufty couldn't believe his ears. "You don't mean, the Corruption Squad?"

"Afraid so."

"I want a Union representative, now!"

"Okay, that sounds reasonable. I'll give my brother a call, he's the local Convener for this district, but like everyone else around here, he's a really busy man."

"What if I spoil your fun and disappear?"

"I've already checked and you don't have a passport."

Hughie was stunned, but realised it was true. If he'd ever contemplated taking a holiday in the past, Scotland would always be his preferred destination and therefore meant he'd never been in need of a passport.

But the real killer moment came when a smiling O'Hara pointed to the file on his desk. "I've been waiting eighteen months to catch you in the act, Tufty, and this should prove once and for all, that you're a lazy thieving Jock bastard. It might take while, but I reckon there's enough evidence here to help bomb you out of Liverpool and send you back over the Border where you belong. Now piss off!"

Back at his digs, Tufty reflected on his original decision to ask for a transfer and relocate to Liverpool.

Eighteen painful months had gone by since he'd first heard they were looking for new blood down south and seeing as he was literally going nowhere back in Aberdeen CID, had decided to take a leap of faith and transfer across the void.

At the time it had seemed like a smart career move and hopefully, would help him climb the ladder. But no sooner had he met his new boss in Liverpool, did he realise he'd made one big mistake. Within weeks of his arrival, a campaign of resentment had begun to manifest itself and a snide rumour began doing the rounds. 'This kilted intruder was an ambitious Jock arsehole, who'd stab anyone in the back if he thought he could further his career!'

Hughie had always regarded himself as both ambitious and hardworking, but for some reason these idiots down here assumed he was after their jobs. Still unsure of what was happening, he'd decided to have a quiet confidential chat with Mick O'Hara. But within minutes discovered his new boss was behind the rumours when he'd casually asked him. "When are you leaving, Hughie?"

"Leaving?"

"Yeah, I want to know when are going to piss off back to Scotland?"

A still baffled Hughie replied, "I wasn't thinking of going anywhere."

Mick's half smile said otherwise. "I've just spoken with one of your boss's back in Aberdeen, who claims exactly the same thing. 'Watch your back, pal, McClellan will be looking to step into your shoes!'" Mick's mouth suddenly turned ugly. "I don't like ambitious arseholes in my department," he declared, "but what I hate more than anything, are sneaky Jock ones!"

A stunned Hughie had left the office worried about what might lie ahead, but equally determined he wouldn't go easy. "Fuck you!" he called back in defiance. However, he'd later regretted his outburst on hearing that O'Hara was claiming to be third generation Northern Irish and despised the Scots, or 'sweaty socks' as he called them with a vengeance. Lionel 'The Cake' Brady, one of the more easy-going Detectives in the squad, had ventured it might be religion, but others reckoned it went much deeper. Some said it stemmed from the time when Robert the Bruce had invaded Ireland and stole the very land in Ballymena where Mick's ancestors hailed from.

"Hang on, that shit happened back in the 16th century!" cried Hughie. Yet his pleas had fallen on deaf ears and he still found himself as persona non grata! Within a short space of time, Mick had taken the greatest of pleasure in sending him out on the shittiest of callouts and if there was a plague of some kind, or even worse, pestilential weather, well so much the frigging better! Yet, one of

192

O'Hara's most hated and teeth grinding peccadillo's had been to tell all and sundry, that Hughie's nickname back home in Aberdeen was 'Tufty', a snide reference to his fast-receding hairline.

This particular jibe had been both wounding and embarrassing; as the loss of his hair was something he'd both regretted and missed deeply. It had also been one of the main reasons for his moving south, unfortunately from that day onward; the name 'Tufty' had been branded cattle-like on his arse!

Staring at the wall, Hughie wondered why when filling in the motorway report, he hadn't mentioned the downpour, or him climbing into the car. He was also finding it hard to believe that he'd been so careless as to leave a 'partial' print at the crash scene. Yet his biggest fear was whether Forensics might find another inside the glove compartment and give O'Hara the perfect excuse to search his flat. If they found the diamonds and Cocaine hidden behind the bath panel, then he really was done for. With hindsight, he realised that acquiring the 'goods' had been the easiest part of this business; the real problem now was in how to get rid of them.

Settling his outstanding debts with the cash had also been a piece of cake, but the cocaine and diamonds were not what you'd normally find for sale on the streets of Liverpool and neither were the people who might want to buy them. His original idea of breaking the cache up into separate pieces and passing them off individually wouldn't work either; that would take much too long. For a time he'd been contemplating shipping the sparklers to somewhere like Amsterdam, aware there was a thriving under-world who'd be happy to take them off his hands. Yet in the back of his mind lurked the Asian connection, plus the fact he still didn't know if they might have come from the Dutch City in the first place.

In Hughie eyes the Chinese appeared to be lurking on every corner, just like their frigging curry houses! It was also obvious that his stint here in Liverpool was over and it was time for him to move on, but where to? If Mick O'Hara and the 'D.P.S' were seriously intent on ruining his life, then Hughie would need lots of money and the diamonds looked to be his only real solution. So in order to survive this mess, he needed to pull off some kind of deal that could be done swiftly and leave no possible trace.

He was halfway through his third double Scotch and struggling to find an answer, when the solution came to him in a flash. There was only one man rich enough to handle something as big as this; problem was, Hughie had never seen or met him. Racking his brains, he vaguely recalled a faded newspaper cutting while searching through a dusty drug's file.

The picture from the early sixties, had been taken outside Liverpool's Registry Office and the subject was a tall smiling blonde-haired male with his bride, minutes after they'd been wed. Unfortunately for Tufty, he was reputed to be as cagey as the KGB and rarely appeared in public. Thinking back, he then remembered someone who was supposed to be very close to him, but was just as difficult to find.

The Cosy Corner Café
March 1981

"Your favourite customer has just turned the corner," called Vivian.

"I can see him," replied her sister Mary as she watched BB Benson stroll across Williamson Square on his way to the Cosy Corner Café.

"Morning gorgeous ladies," he laughed, the sound of his voice making Vivian go all doe-eyed.

"Your newspaper is on the table and I'll bring your coffee in a minute," smiled Mary. And as she'd done many times before, wondered where BB really came from. With his olive skin, silky dark hair and moustache, he had more than a touch of Latin American about him. He was also every woman's dream; early thirties, flashing white teeth, beautiful blue eyes, and enough gold to make a statement, but no more. Yet beneath that 6'4" tall easy-going exterior, dwelt one very dangerous man, who'd take the head off your shoulders; plus a damn sight more should the situation arise! Nevertheless, Mary and her sister had no illusions why BB stopped by on his monthly visit. His boss Maxi owned the café, plus a hell of a lot more around here.

It was early, the place was full of customers and Mary was busy wiping some lipstick marks from a glass tumbler, when an unwelcome circle of ginger hair stepped through the door.

"Empty cup and saucer hen," he instructed, his radar-like eyes ranging around the room; missing nothing.

Scruffy bastard, thought Mary, but like everyone else in the city, knew Bonny Prince Charlie was a Drugs officer and this would be the first time he'd ever had reason to visit the Café.

From his table in the corner, BB had been listening to their verbal exchange with interest and in an attempt to obtain more privacy, raised his newspaper a little higher. He'd also been focusing on one particular clue in his cryptic crossword, when the bowl of a teaspoon suddenly appeared at the top of his paper and as he lowered it, the ginger hair, beady eyes and ruddy features of Hughie McClellan appeared in view. Without bothering to ask, he then plonked his empty cup on the table and stubbed his cigarette out in the ashtray. "Well there you are," he scoffed with a lop-sided twist to his mouth.

Placing his newspaper on the seat beside him, BB watched in stony silence as McClellan began to help himself to the fresh coffee and pastries. "Unless you're suffering from a bad case of cataracts my friend, I think you'll find this table is already occupied."

McClellan's lips parted just enough to reveal a set of uneven nicotine-stained teeth. "Listen Pancho Gonzales!" he snarled, aware the insult would wound, just as he'd intended it to. "I'm here to do business and no make idle chat with the likes of you!"

BB had heard McClellan was new to the Liverpool scene and according to some pushers on the streets, took great delight in plaguing the City's different drug factions when going about his job. Yet, if this visit was somehow drug related, it could no way involve Maxi or himself. Their setup reminded him of a multi-layered Russian Doll, or large Spanish onion that had so many skins, it was near impossible to reach its inner core. However, something about his attitude said this was no shakedown. It was also obvious that the man opposite; who was badly in need of a new shirt, wasn't here just to drink his coffee or fill his ashtray with cigarette ends.

"Okay," said BB, giving an imperceptible shrug of his shoulders, as though he was willing to listen. But McClellan had other ideas.

"No, No, Pancho," he mocked. "And you still don't understand do ye? I'm looking to talk with *The Organ Grinder* no the frigging *monkey*!"

Aware that this was neither the time nor place to lose his temper, BB resisted the urge to grab the tuft of ginger hair and use the crockery on the table to rearrange McClellan's untidy features. And on reflection had to admit that it wasn't everyday an unkempt arsehole like the policeman opposite, would appear from nowhere 'looking to talk.' So, after waiting for what he deigned to be a suitable length of time, picked up his newspaper and headed for the counter. "Can I use your phone, gorgeous?" he asked with a smile and Mary's knickers elastic just about held itself together as she lovingly passed him the handset.

Tufty was halfway through his second cup of coffee, when BB returned and dropped the newspaper on the table. "Seek and ye shall find," he whispered. Then, without saying another word, turned on his heel and left.

McClellan drank his free coffee, smoked another Capstan full strength cigarette and studied the finished crossword. "Not my bag, this frigging shit," he muttered, but eventually worked out where the message lay in between the clues.

Caversham Cut Warehouse
Midnight

"Bingo and right on time," quipped BB, as the distinctive shape of McClellan's head appeared in the cold winter gloom. From the warmth of the Range Rover, both men had been awaiting his arrival with some interest.

"Okay now," instructed Maxi. Heeding his wish, BB reached for a switch on the dashboard and turned on the main beam, which in turn illuminated the Scot like a frightened rabbit in the headlights. Blinking blindly in the sudden brightness, McClellan instinctively raised an arm to shield his eyes, before slowly edging his way towards the car. Sitting in the driver's seat, a still fuming BB had the same volcanic expression on his face as the one at today's meeting in the Café.

I wonder if Tufty boy knew just how close he'd come to joining the annals of history, smiled Maxi, having witnessed the big man's capacity for violence on many an occasion.

McClellan though, looked to be more interested in the shiny black Range Rover and who might be inside. Another moment of waiting went by, before the rear passenger door opened to reveal a lone figure seated in the shadows. The look of fear on Tufty's face quickly turned to one of mistrust, especially when Maxi switched on the interior lights and pointed to the empty seat beside him. Still nervous, yet reasonably confident there was no immediate danger to his person, the Scot warily clambered inside.

As expected, there was no welcome or greeting of any kind, just the sound of Maxi's voice. "My friend here tells me you'll only to talk to *The Organ Grinder*."

McClellan hesitated, his mind in turmoil as he remembered who was sat next to him, but on reflection knew there was no going back. "I've got something to sell," he whispered in his clipped Scottish accent, the effort almost draining him.

A stunned Maxi, who'd spent most of the day wondering what this was all about, was completely thrown by this. Notwithstanding it had been Tufty who'd requested the meeting, this situation had never for a minute crossed his mind. Still unsure of what to do next, he broke the impasse by giving the smallest of gestures, a sign for Hughie to continue with his sales pitch.

Taking a deep breath, the Scot reached into one pocket and took out the packet of cocaine. "This is real good shit and I should know!" he growled.

Maxi smiled inwardly at McClellan's lame attempt at the over-sell, his practiced eye guessing the drug's true value by size alone. Yet his eyes were well and truly opened, when McClellan took off his right glove and began to rummage around in the palm of the other. Seconds later and he'd found what he was looking for; a folded piece of toilet paper, that when opened, revealed a single sparkling diamond.

Hell's Bells! thought Maxi, *that has to be absolute top quality*. However, McClellan had really floored him when he whispered in the quiet of the luxury interior, "There's nineteen more of them we fuckers and trust me, they're all exactly the same!"

Goodman's Casino
Two Hours Later

The croupiers had long since cleared away the tables and the last of the high rollers gone in search of pastures new. But in the quiet of Maxi's office, he and BB went over tonight's surprise meeting with Tufty McClellan.

"Is it real?" asked BB.

Maxi twisted the diamond between finger and thumb. "You better believe it! I'd say it's at least two carats in weight, has perfect clarity, is SS1 in colour and worth around a four thousand pounds."

"Wow, so what does he want in exchange?"

"Seventy-five pounds for the cocaine and at least half the current street value of the diamonds. On top of that, he's demanding we pay him in used fifty-pound notes with no questions asked."

BB whistled. "Doesn't want much, does he? Did he say where he got it from?"

Maxi shook his head. "No."

"So what happens now?"

"We pose some questions and do some checking."

"Okay, that sounds logical, but where do we start?"

"Well, considering Hughie works for The Drug Squad, I'd say it has to be there. Which then begs the question, do we have anyone on the inside who can tell us what's going on?"

"If only," sighed BB. "We've got contacts all over the damn place, yet no-one who's in Drugs. Which is only to be expected, seeing as how they've been trying to bang us up in jail for the last twenty years."

Maxi could only smile at the thought.

"I reckon the nearest I can get you is Isabelle. Who, if I'm not wrong, still works as a part-time typist in the administration department. The problem is, it's on the wrong side of the bloody building. Although I'm sure I did hear her say that if you need to know anything important; eat in the Staff Canteen."

Maxi stared at BB with open curiosity. "Where the hell did you find Isabelle in all of this?"

"We met a few years back when I was playing golf in Marbella and she was doing a girls weekend in Fuengirola. It took a bit of persuasion, but I eventually managed to separate her from this crazy crowd she was with and it all spilled forth later that night over a bottle of red wine."

Maxi smiled. "Does she know who you are?"

BB looked thoughtful. "She never really asked back then. But she does now and as long as she doesn't have to rob a bank, it doesn't seem to bother her."

"Is she married?

"Divorced and bored with life."

Maxi sat back and tried to put a face and body to someone named Isabelle, but seeing as there were so many of them, decided it was an almost impossible task. He then decided it was easier to return to the real problem; the single glistening diamond in his hand. "How in hell's name could McClellan get hold of something like this?"

"It has to be the proceeds from some kind of drugs bust."

"Maybe," said Maxi, "but if eighty grand worth of diamonds have gone missing in Drugs, then surely we'd have heard something by now?"

BB gave a nod. "Absolutely, yet as far as I know, nobody's heard a thing."

Maxi held the diamond up to the light. "I don't know what it is, but there's something about this whole business that doesn't ring true."

"Is it a setup?"

"No, I don't think so. Besides Hughie's the policeman, so why would he begin to sweat for no apparent reason? He was so nervous tonight; he could have been a canary trapped inside a cat's paws; which tells me this is no shakedown by the Drug Squad."

BB nodded. "You could be right and now I think about it, why bring the *sparkler* along to the meeting. The Cocaine alone would have been more than enough to tempt us into doing a deal. There again, where the hell would Drugs find them? It's hardly likely they'd be lying around at the bottom of someone's locker in one of the changing rooms."

"If the truth be told, I don't really care," said Maxi. "Because something is telling me to go all the way with this. So let's put the wheels in motion, but use only our best people. Another thing, when we collect the rest of the diamonds, make sure they're clean of any hidden surprises and then make the necessary calls to get them valued."

BB stubbed out his cigarette. "Okay, will do and it might be an idea to set up a secure line of communication. It'll mean we can keep in constant touch with him."

Maxi finished his own cigarette and rose from the desk. "This is a once in a lifetime opportunity that I don't intend to miss out on BB. Without having anything concrete to say otherwise, we can only assume Tufty McClellan has some real problems in his untidy life. See if you can touch base with this *Isabelle in Admin*, who with a bit of luck might be able to throw some light on what's happening around the corner. And thinking about it, when was the last time someone from Drugs fell from the sky and landed in our bloody nest?" A wide grin forming on his face. "Maybe this Jock cuckoo thought he'd laid his golden egg and that was it. However, we're going to clip his wings and ensure our haggis loving, ginger haired buzzard, doesn't fly the coop for a while yet."

On his way home a short time later, Maxi looked up at the fabled 'Liver Birds' perched high in their lofty towers and hoped his own *magic bird,* in the form of one Hughie Tufty McClellan, had just laid a golden egg.

For some reason, Tufty's alarm had failed to go off, meaning he was going to be late for work. In a panic, he'd begun sniffing under his armpits in the hope he might get by without a shower, when his doorbell rang once. All thoughts of hygiene were instantly forgotten, as he donned an un-ironed shirt and padded barefoot along the passage to the communal entrance. Still angry and annoyed at finding an empty street outside, he was about to hobble back to the sanctuary of his flat, when he noticed a yellow label pinned to his mailbox.

Two minutes later and he was cautiously prodding a mid-size Jiffy Bag lying on his kitchen table. This unexpected package bore no stamp to say it might have been posted. Which was highly unlikely, seeing as the Postie had yet to arrive. It was also much too big to pass through the narrow flap, meaning someone other than himself had a key to his mailbox. He then recalled Maxi Hamilton's last words from the shadows of the Range Rover. "Tonight's meeting will be the only one you and I will ever have. But remember that everything comes to those who wait and all we require on your part is a little patience."

Tufty regarded the Jiffy bag with a certain amount of suspicion. This wasn't quite what he'd expected when Hamilton spoke about 'others'. He was also worried whether he might have made a huge mistake by getting involved with the drug baron. Yet they'd both shook hands on the deal and with time running out, knew it was the one thing he didn't have. All of which, convinced him to pick up the bag and discover it wasn't sealed. A quick perusal of its interior revealed a small brass key and P.O. Box label 201 written in green ink. Keeping it company, was another similar inked sheet of paper that read 'Deliver the Goods to the main Post Office' and signed 'TOG'.

Later that morning, a nervous Tufty opened the boot of his car and with the Jiffy bag safely ensconced within a Tesco throwaway, hurried in the direction of the General Post Office. Once inside, his next task was to go in search of the receptacle whose number matched that of the brass key. But a rather pleasant surprise awaited him when he opened box 201. Expecting it to be empty, he instead found a smaller package full of used £20 notes. "Now that's more like it," he muttered, only to find another note inside and as before, written in the same green ink.

Patience is a virtue, as well as maiden in distress, was all it said. Yet no sooner had he made his way out into Bold Street. When an oak panelled door with 'Staff only', opened and as was normal for this time of day, a trolley-load of newly arrived mail passed through. However, its first port of call was always destined to be the Tesco throwaway bag in Box 201.

Goodman's Casino
Two Weeks Later

"What do you mean McClellan's being investigated?"

"Isabelle doesn't know the whole story, but thinks Hughie's in some kind of trouble."

"Who with?"

"The Anti-Corruption mob."

Maxi's jaw dropped. "Christ, if they're involved, then it has to be the diamonds!"

BB shrugged. "Possibly, but there's no mention of anything going missing at Drugs. So maybe it's something to do with his gambling problem."

"What gambling problems?"

"I made a point of greasing a few palms and heard Hughie likes to have a flutter now and then."

Maxi shook his head in exasperation. "How come we don't know about this Scottish policeman with gambling problems? Especially when he works in Drugs."

"Because he's only been in Liverpool for eighteen months and uses a private Bookie on the quiet."

"Who?"

"Henry Spritzo in Smithdown Road."

"Spritzo? He's not private, he just runs a betting shop."

"This is true," said BB. "But he also has a back alley that conveniently leads to his office."

"How many people know about this 'bad habit'?"

"Surprisingly few. Tufty might be a pain in the arse for the druggies on the street, but is a bit of a loner when it comes to his private life."

"Does he have a wife or girlfriend?"

"Not as far as I know."

"Is he the other way inclined?"

"I don't think so."

"What else did you hear?"

"His boss hates the sight of him."

"Who, Mick O'Hara?"

BB nodded. "So the story goes."

Maxi was even more exasperated. "Why does he hate Hughie?"

"Something to do with him being Scottish and moving to Liverpool. Isabelle says O'Hara went absolutely ballistic when the powers that be agreed to the move and overruled his objections. Apparently they decided to sanction it as a kind of symbolic gesture between our two countries."

"Christ BB, you'd think McClellan had been transferred from China, instead of Aberdeen!"

"Isabelle reckons he might have had a better welcome if he had been. There was even talk of them replacing Tufty with a recruit from the Sicilian Cosa Nostra. His boss O'Hara reckoned he'd be able to understand the language better!"

Maxi shook his head in amazement. "So much for Anglo-Scottish relations or what's left of them. But that still doesn't solve our problems, or the fact that Tufty McClellan's job is still on the line, which we can't possibly allow to happen."

BB lit a cigarette, took a sip of Cognac and concentrated on the ornate plasterwork. "As I see it Maxi, the only solution is to get rid of Mick O'Hara or somehow move him out of the way. If he goes, then hopefully it'll take this Tribunal business with him!"

"That's one tall order BB, because I don't think Mick's planning to go anywhere at the moment."

"Isabelle says we've got just over six weeks before the process begins."

The room was silent as they did what they always did; weigh up the pros-and-cons, as well as the plusses and minuses.

"Tell me about this Tribunal and how it works."

BB was thoughtful for a minute. "As far as I know, it involves a mixture of six senior police officers and two local councillors."

Maxi's face lit up. "Do we know anyone who's on it?"

BB concentrated again. "Not on the police side, but Marty Crabbe must be involved, especially as he's part of the new Law and Order Committee."

"Is this the same Councillor Crabbe who loves a back-hander, as well as a snort of *Charlie*?"

"That's our man."

"And is he not about to take charge of the future 'Dockland Project'?"

"One and the same."

"And are we not about to invest in this same project?"

BB smiled in agreement. "It's early days, but Hawkeye thinks that now is a good time to get involved. It might take a while, but we are still guaranteed to make a small fortune when it happens."

Maxi became serious. "It sounds to me, as if Councillor Crabbe could be just the man to help Tufty in his hour of need. And if he is part of this Disciplinary Committee, then hopefully we should be able find out what's going on. But more importantly, see if he can slow down the process."

BB took another drag on his cigarette. "Funny thing is, I've always regarded Crabbe as something that's just crawled out from under a rock. There again, even he must have his uses when boiled in water."

"A spoonful of garlic mayonnaise should help, BB. But first off, I think we'd better get in touch with Tufty and assure him everything is okay. We don't need him losing the plot or bottle for that matter."

"Maybe it's time to take him out of the firing line and send him on holiday."

"Now there's a good idea," grinned Maxi.

It had never occurred to Tufty that he might be in need of a new shirt, but someone obviously did, thus giving an odd twist to the bell ringing routine. The first 'push' had indicated there was a Jiffy bag in his mailbox, whereas the next 'double push' was a whole different ball game. He'd hurried down the hallway in the hope of catching whoever was delivering them; only to find a paper parcel addressed to D. H. McClellan sitting on the hall table.

Hughie's mind immediately went back to the cash in the PO box and thinking there might be more of the same, took it back to his flat. But instead of money was stunned to find a quality brand new pink shirt inside. He was also about to throw it across the room in disgust, when a glance in the mirror had highlighted the frayed collar of the one he was wearing, plus the grey tinge of its weekly laundering.

A further few minutes went by before he decided to open the box and unwrap the cellophane. In times past and when in need of a new shirt, the needle-like pins hidden around the collar and cuffs had always given him grief and this morning's task was proving to be no different. But once free it of its multitude of fastenings saw an embossed card fall from within its folds and land on the table. At first, Hughie had assumed it was just the usual manufacturing label, but on looking closer saw; *Patience is a virtue*, written on the front, and *£20,000* on the back, both in the now familiar green pen.

And herein lay Hughie's dilemma. Having no idea of the diamonds' true value and fearing the Chinese might discover who he was and kill him, he'd decided to sell everything to Maxi Hamilton in the hope he wouldn't get screwed shitless. But if agreed, this looked to be an acceptable amount of money the tycoon was prepared to pay for the goods. So one week later, it was something of a surprise to hear his bell ring three times and discover the next parcel was of much bigger size than those that had gone before.

Ignoring the cellotape securing the package, he ripped it open and found two casual open-necked shirts, albeit the usual pink and blue colour. But his heart really began to beat, when he lifted the top shirt and discovered another Jiffy bag sandwiched in between. "Ye wee beauty," he crowed, "this surely has to be the money!"

Except and as before, disappointingly found two much smaller envelopes inside. The first contained a paper wallet from a local travel agency, and a B.E.A. flight ticket for someone named Mr Angus Mackie.

In addition, there was £100 in cash and a three-day travel itinerary to Jersey. The next had a formal letter of introduction to a private bank in ten days' time, again for this very same person. However, the real jaw-dropper was the well-worn passport issued in the name of this mysterious *Mr Mackie* and when he'd fingered his way to the back page, was amazed to find a serious-faced, ginger-haired photograph of himself inside. Whether he liked it or not, it seemed he wasn't going anywhere other than the frigging Channel Islands!

The Cosy Corner Café

The two sisters were waiting for BB as he strode into the café.

"So what's the problem, gorgeous ladies?"

Mary's angry look directed him to his table at the rear and the reason why she'd rang; beneath a thick halo of cigarette smoke sat McClellan. "Most people are happy with a fag after their meal, but this is getting like the bloody Gas Works!" moaned Viv.

Relieved to see the café was near to closing, BB assured them he would take care of things and headed for the table. "What the hell are you doing here, McClellan? I thought we'd agreed there was to be no further contact unless I said so!"

"I don't give a shit what we agreed. I've been waiting for weeks to get paid and then this stuff turns up," throwing the travel wallet on the table.

BB took out the passport, flipped through the pages and smiled when he came to the photograph. "Oh, I don't know Tufty, I think it's a damn good likeness, especially that haggard look only cold wind and rain can give a Scottish face."

McClellan ignored the taunt and snarled back, "What's with this Jersey crap anyway? I thought we'd agreed a price and I was being paid in used fifty-pound notes!"

"And that's still the case, Hughie. However, there's been a slight hitch and we've decided to invest it for a while; a sort of 'insurance' if you like."

"I don't remember agreeing to that! Where did this shit come from?"

BB lit a cigarette of his own before speaking. "I know it's not quite what we agreed, my friend, but it looks as if we're going to need your services for a few months more. The reason being you could sort of act as our eyes and ears should anyone come snooping in our direction. I can understand your frustration at these unexpected changes, but sorry to say, that's the way it is."

BB was fully expecting Tufty to be spitting blood, but he instead gave him a contemptuous smile. "Mr frigging smart-arse," he sneered. "And the man who thinks he knows everything. Yet your plan to have me playing the ever-reliable snitch isn't going to happen, Pancho. And do you know why? Because in a few weeks' time, I won't even be in the frigging police force!"

BB waited a second before interrupting Tufty's gloating euphoria. "I take it we're talking about the DPS investigation?"

A shocked McClellan looked as if he'd been hit by a train. "You know about that?"

"Yes Hughie, as well as the £2,000 owed to Spritzo the Bookie. So believe me when I say that we know everything about you." BB shook his head and smiled. "You really didn't expect us to shell out all that money and then watch you disappear without a trace? Christ man, people would suss you out in no time and to make matters worse, seriously put our business at risk."

McClellan listened in stony-faced silence, his once confident mirth now a distant memory as BB continued to burst his bubble. "From now on, you don't do or go anywhere, unless we say so. And I'm talking about any meeting or conversation that might take place between us or anyone else, do you 'frigging' understand?"

Tufty didn't need to be told twice and suddenly realised that his dream of leaving Liverpool might not be as easy as he'd hoped. But as if to rub salt into the wound, 'Pancho' had smiled sympathetically and offered him some advice. "You look as though you need a holiday, mate, and as someone who's been to Jersey, I know you'll just love the place. So trust me when I say that everything about the Island is superb; hotels, food, scenery, it just can't be beaten."

McClellan, however, looked as though he'd rather trust a rattlesnake, as BB returned him the travel brochure. "I think you'll find this trip will be a most rewarding experience and believe me when I say, this is all in your best interests." His voice then turned deadly serious. "However, there is one last important piece of advice my friend; remember to take the passport and letter with you when you visit the bank!"

Liverpool Speke Airport
May 1981

The news that The Channel Islands were still part of the UK went a long way in convincing Mick O'Hara that Tufty wasn't about to flee the country. But seeing as he'd never flown before, this journey would also be a pivotal moment in the Scot's life. Nervously waiting at the airport bar, he threw another stiff drink down his neck and stubbed out his umpteenth Capstan cigarette on hearing his BEA flight would be boarding on the hour. Once on board and strapped in his seat, he grabbed hold of the armrests and nervously chain-smoked his way through the clouds as they headed south towards the French coast. Fifty minutes later and he was stepping onto the tarmac at Jersey Airport glad he'd made it, but desperately in need of some fresh air. Collecting his overnight bag, his itinerary said a car would be waiting to meet him, but more importantly reminded him of this afternoon's meeting at the private bank.

"Work or pleasure, sir?" inquired the driver, as the car wound its way through the narrow leafy lanes. When McClellan had muttered "Bit of both," with a monosyllabic grunt, past experience suggested the pasty looking ginger top sat on the back seat, definitely wasn't a chat show host. A short drive later and they'd reached their destination, The Grand Hotel, a classic five-star hotel situated on the Esplanade in St. Helier.

Tufty was aware his weekend stay had been paid for in advance and like others before him, was mightily impressed by the king-size bed and bathroom that would swallow the one in his flat three times over.

"Ye wee shite," he murmured in appreciation; whilst ignoring the expectant look on the baggage porter's face, as he ushered him from the room. Checking the time, he'd paused at reception only to ask Hugo the Concierge, the easiest way to Hill Street and the GKD Private Bank. However, once within the narrow streets, filled to over-flowing with holidaymakers, suddenly realised he should have allowed more time to complete his journey. The itinerary had clearly stipulated the importance of punctuality, yet his watch said there was now the possibility of him being late. However, and with only seconds to spare he'd made it to the bank, where the guard was just about to lock the door for the weekend. Thinking he might be too late, a stab of panic hit Tufty, until he remembered the letter in his pocket. Babbling like a nervous fool, he was about to introduce himself in his own name, when a lightning bolt thought stopped him in his tracks. "Sorry to keep you waiting," he stuttered, "My name is Mr Mackie and I have a 2.30 pm appointment."

The guard's demeanour changed almost at once and he bowed as though Tufty were minor Royalty. "Straight through, Sir," pointing beyond the glass doors. "The Manager, Herr Dunkledorf, is waiting for you in his office."

An hour later and Tufty lay on the king-size bed smoking a Capstan cigarette, his mind rewinding the afternoon's events like it was a roll of film spooling out onto the bedroom floor. The German Manager had welcomed him like he was an old friend, swiftly perused his dodgy new passport and letter of introduction. He'd then chatted on about how good the weather was and generally fidgeted about like a frigging mother hen. A few more tense moments went by as he'd shuffled a pile of document-like papers backwards and forwards across his desk. Then, with a final flourish, produced a leather-bound folder from within a drawer and began to peruse its contents. "Ah yes, here we are Mr Mackie," he smiled. "This is an up-to-date record of your account and of course, we shouldn't forget the safety deposit box."

Tufty could remember Herr Dunkledorf's hawk like eyes watching his every move as he took the folder, scanned the details and in due course, read the bottom line. A smile passed briefly across his face as he saw Hughie's reaction. Five thousand pounds had been deposited in the account on four separate occasions, each amount worth nearly a year's wages.

"I hope everything *is* in order, Sir?"

"Oh Aye," he stuttered. "Everything is just fine and dandy."

"Excellent!" the German gushed. "But before we check the Deposit Box, I need to ask if you want to register a new access code to the account now or later?"

All of which had left Tufty somewhat nonplussed. "Sorry?" he stuttered.

"At the moment, your financial advisor is the only one who has sole access to the account. The reason being it has a special holding clause and can't be used until they give their permission. However, when that time does come, you can then instruct us to change the code to whichever one you wish. This means that in future, others will be able to put money in, but only *you* can take it out."

A combination of his Granny's birthdate and the year he'd graduated from the Greenock Police Academy was enough to do the trick and five minutes later, he'd excitedly followed Dunkledorf into the bank's strong room.

"This is your key," he smiled, "and of course I have mine." Handing him one of two he'd taken from a metal draw He then chose a numbered wall safe, rattled and turned both keys, before proceeding to place an oblong box on the table. "I'll leave you in privacy," he smiled as always and left him alone in the vault.

McClellan picked up the wad of £20 notes from where they lay on the bed beside him and spread them out like a deck of cards. The safety deposit box had contained a further two grand in used readies, which he could only assume was some kind of slush fund. On the positive side, there was no doubting that Maxi Hamilton had kept his side of the bargain, but Tufty still wondered how much it was going to cost him in the long run. His original plan had been to do the deal and once he'd received the money, regretfully inform every one of his dismissal from the police force. This he'd hoped would allow him to disappear from Liverpool altogether, but he'd underestimated the many people Hamilton knew and just how far his tentacles reached.

That said, if it hadn't been for BB Benson's insistence on him travelling to Jersey, he would never have met the German banker and missed the very important and informative chat they'd had as they were leaving the vault.

"Of course, it's a real bank!" The Kraut had insisted with a smile of Teutonic assurance. "And of course, your money is safe with us," pointing to the iron bars and massive concrete walls. But it was only when he'd explained in more detail about the many other financial benefits on offer did Tufty become really interested. First and foremost, was their insistence on a code of absolute secrecy for all its clients; plus the kid-glove handling of their financial affairs. Another was the bank's willingness to transfer his money anywhere in the world.

"Your account has a combination of eight letters and five numerals. Any six of them in the correct order, would be sufficient information for us to send funds to a reciprocal account wherever the client desires." However, the one benefit that really caught Tufty's eye was how the General Kasse Deutsche private bank would invest his money and in turn, pay him interest for doing so.

"How much?" Inquired Tufty.

"Ten percent, per annum, tax free," replied Dunkledorf.

"Ye wee fucker," Tufty whispered in awe, "that's nearly two grand a year!" Armed with this potentially life-changing information and possible new outpost for his future finances. It suddenly occurred to him that it was time to do some of his famed pragmatic thinking. Could Maxi Hamilton really have enough money and influence to clear him of the motorway debacle? *Not with Mick O'Hara running the show*, he decided. Which meant he had no other choice than to play along with whatever might happen from now on. Another major problem concerned this mysterious financial advisor, who held the bank's access codes.

At the moment, there was no way he could disappear from Liverpool without him having direct access to the money he was owed. He lit another Capstan cigarette, began blowing smoke rings in the air above his head and was poking at them with a fistful of twenties, when the bedside phone rang saying his guest was waiting for him downstairs.

The lift doors opened on the ground floor, where Tufty met the usual busy throng of people moving around the foyer. However, he wasn't interested in the other guests; he was looking for one face in particular. Having had no immediate success, he made his way to the reception desk, where to his surprise, he spoke with Hugo, the same Concierge who'd directed him towards the restaurant the night before. He was also about to make a casual inquiry as to the whereabouts of his special guest, when Hugo's well-rehearsed smile interrupted him. "Sorry Sir, she checked out and left for the airport an hour ago. Ordered a taxi, wished us all good day and was gone."

"I take it she didn't leave a message?" asked a downcast Tufty.

Hugo could see the pain in his eyes. "Afraid not, Sir, but might I suggest a bite to eat? It always helps at times like this," his tonsured head nodding toward the restaurant and breakfast. Problem was, Tufty had no appetite for food. His eyes were raw from a lack of sleep and the 'throb' in his crotch didn't help either, as he slipped a hand into his trouser pocket and tenderly massaged his *meat and two veg.* But on reflection decided another cigarette and a pot of strong tea might indeed help ease the pain.

In the restaurant, he sensed there was something almost *déjà vu* like in the air, as Augusto, the Manager, beckoned him towards the table he'd dined at the night before. Taking a seat, a distinguished grey-haired gentleman wearing a pair of large framed glasses stopped to ask. "I hope you and the young lady enjoyed last night?"

Scrolling back, Tufty vaguely remembered his name was Mr Harry and he owned the hotel. His hopes rose briefly when he saw the table had been set for two, but were swiftly dashed when a waiter appeared from nowhere and spirited the spare crockery away, meaning he really *was* going to eat alone. Food itself was out of the question, yet within an hour had managed to consume two pots of strong tea and chain-smoke a whole pack of cigarettes.

Sitting alone, his mind went back twelve hours and the look of envy on Hugo's face when he'd informed him his *guest* was waiting for him at the bar. Curious as to discover who it was, he'd cautiously slipped into the exclusive Victoria's Restaurant wearing the blue open neck shirt. A quick look around revealed the cocktail bar was empty, save for a classy looking mini skirted young lady sat alone on one of the tall stools. He was still searching for his mystery guest, when he saw the dish on the dais waving a hand as though to catch his attention.

Then to his surprise and before he'd had time to think, she'd crooked a finger at him and wound him in as though he were a floundering flatfish. "Hello Hughie," she whispered, her sky-blue eyes never leaving his. "I just love that shirt and think the colour really suits you." As she spoke, the heady scent of her perfume filled his nostrils like the swirling mountain mists of his youth. She was also smoking a thin, black and gold-banded cheroot and exhaling a cool moist like vapour that tasted of her inner being. "Your friends up North thought you might like some company," she whispered again, her cultured voice having just the right amount of intrigue to keep him guessing.

Yet before he could say another word, the 'dream' had turned to the barman, ordered a lager for him and a vodka Spritzer for herself. "You do still drink lager, I hope?" she inquired. But a stunned McClellan was only interested in the black lacy bra and mouth-watering glimpse of voluptuous flesh that left him in a state of speechlessness. To further torment his senses, whilst she and barman were having a chat, she'd casually crossed one leg over the other, thus exposing an exquisitely tanned thigh and as the skirt climbed higher, so did Tufty's blood pressure.

From that moment on, the night became a confused blurred chain of events. He'd been more than delighted to follow her sylph like figure, as she'd wound her way towards their pre-booked table; chose their food and drank what seemed to him like gallons of champagne. Yet no matter how many times he'd asked her name, she would just smile that smile, sip her drink and suggest he might choose one that *he* liked. And the more the bubbly flowed, the more he'd conceded defeat and called her *Hen,* just like they did back home in Aberdeenshire. He'd also been spellbound by her beauty and when she spoke, could only watch her almost perfect lips move: a snake hypnotised by a hungry mongoose. Then to his horror was jolted out his boozy stupor when the late-night Disco had begun and she'd insisted his protesting body should join her on the dance floor.

Lighting another cigarette, Tufty was left cringing at the memory of his infantile attempts to move in time to the *Night Fever* music; both feet glued to the floor, as she'd effortlessly danced around him like one of *Pan's People.* Then mercifully and to his relief, the Disco had finally come to an end and the *Dream* had whispered in her soft cultured plummy voice, *surely it must be time for bed?*

From the minute he'd first laid eyes on her, Hughie had known what she was and who'd sent her, but at the time, didn't give a shit! It was only what happened next that mattered and in a strange way was the one he dreaded the most. Muzzling his ear with the tip of her delicate nose, she'd persuasively suggested they take one more bottle of bubbly back to his room. Once inside, she'd slipped off her short jacket, which in turn had revealed more of the black see through top he'd been transfixed with all evening. Desperately trying to keep his shaking hands busy, he attempted to open the bottle of champagne.

During their meal, he'd been closely watching Augusto open a selection of bubbly bottles. But when confronted with his own, began to struggle badly with the wired foil top. A moment of embarrassed frustration went by, before she took it from him and casually popped the cork. "You pour," she whispered sexily, before making her way to the over-large bathroom. Hughie took off his jacket, tried desperately not to clink the glasses, sat on the corner of the bed and sweated profusely.

Five more nail-biting minutes slipped by before a steamy bathroom door opened and *The Dream* appeared in one of the hotel's luxury white dressing gowns. Then and to his joy and terror, she'd slowly beckoned him towards her. But as she did so, the robe had slipped open to reveal so much more than he could ever have hoped for.

Hughie drew deeply on another lung-bursting cigarette and recalled the mind-blowing moment the dressing gown fell to the floor. He then closed his eyes and remembered every single curve of her exquisite naked body as she'd stepped into the warm bubble bath and in his mind, ran the scene over and over again.

Goodman's Casino
May 1981

The antique glass chronometer chimed 11.30 am and as though orchestrated, the telephone on Maxi's desk rang in unison.

"Morning Amber," he said, whilst cradling the handset to his ear.

The caller's voice was warm and had a soft upper class feel, but sounded more than a little exasperated. "I've told you before, Maxi, the sea makes me sneeze!"

"Just a minute, love," he said by way of interruption. "BB Benson's here and I'm about to put him on speaker," his finger flicking a switch, so they might both share the call. Yet when Amber spoke again, it sounded as if her voice had dropped a whole octave.

"Hi, gorgeous one," she oozed, whilst paraphrasing BB's favourite axiom. "I didn't know you were part of this little venture?" the delight showing in her voice.

"It's been much too long, beautiful one," smiled BB, his teeth glistening white as he recalled one of his favourite ladies.

Maxi who was also listening closely, decided it was time to interrupt this loving tete-a-tete before it got too serious. "How was it darling?"

"A piece of cake depending on your taste, but one night with the odious Tufty is more than enough for me," she groaned. "There again, if you like it short and crusty, then the *Ginger Snap* definitely fits the bill. And I have to say that I've entertained some really rude and ignorant Sheiks in my time but they've all had more charisma and bigger dicks than McClellan."

Maxi smiled. "I have to say it's a rare pleasure hearing from you Amber, even if it's not in the flesh. And although it wasn't much fun, tell us more about your encounter."

"All it took was a chat with the Portuguese guy at reception," she began. "Then a wink and smile at the Italian Restaurant Manager and the scene was set. Tufty appeared at 8.00 pm and reminded me of someone who was wing walking for the first time. He sort of had an air of uncertainty about him, a bit like your first date, or when the hangman's waiting for you by the trapdoor." The idea sending her into fits of laughter. "Sorry Maxi, it was just a crazy thought," she giggled before continuing. "I whispered that his friends up North were hoping he would enjoy his stay; crossed my legs and an hour later, he was buying my favourite bubbly!"

Maxi smiled at the thought. The whole point of this exercise had been to ascertain McClellan's behaviour following his visit to the bank. "Tell us more, Amber darling, we're all ears!"

For a moment her customary worldly like voice revealed a touch of disgust. "I've never met a man who wears chocolate-coloured underpants," she groaned. "And the parchment like feel of his skin literally made my own crawl. And the spiky ginger hairs on his chest and around his cock? Oh wow, that really had me reaching for the sick bag!"

Maxi and BB's gaze met across the desk as they perceived, rather than saw, the shudder of revulsion in her voice. He was also finding it hard to believe how anyone in their right mind, would climb into a bath with a naked McClellan!

"We knew how difficult a task this could be, Amber, which is why we insisted on trebling your normal fee."

"It's just as well you chose a real classy hotel, Maxi," she sighed. "If it hadn't been for the foam bubbles, I'm not sure I could have gone through with any of this or whether Tufty would have even taken a bath. Some people are allergic to hot soapy water and judging from the odour of the Ginger Snap, I'd say it's probably a year since he's dipped his toe!" Giving another squeal of her infectious laughter.

"So Amber, how *did* you get him into the bubbling hot water?" BB asked mischievously.

"There *are* ways and means, as you well know," she admonished. "And I like to think a naked me, plus the offer of something special would be more than enough to entice him."

The thought of an unclad Amber began to run through Maxi's mind, whilst BB was more interested in the special offer, which he'd insisted she must tell him about.

"I discovered a mini-Loofah amongst the usual potions and shampoos in the bathroom and casually told Hughie that it was often used in the Kama Sutra."

Both Maxi and BB fell silent, as they weighed up the possible use of such a thing in Amber's delicate hands. "At first he seemed deliriously happy as I used it to fiddle around under his armpits and other more sensitive places. And he was almost *sent,* when I massaged between his legs under the bubbles whilst whispering a few sexy sounding incantations. However, I really began to worry that the other hotel guests might start to complain as his cries grew louder and louder."

"Why would they get louder?" An intrigued Maxi asked.

"It was a few minutes after I'd promised to give him the ultimate thrill in the Kama Sutra's quest for sexual enlightenment."

In the silence that followed, BB hunched forward while Maxi waited. "Amber?" he prompted.

"His eyes were closed and he seemed to be in ecstasy when I moved it down to his *cock*," pausing as if to recollect the moment. "And then he began to wail like a baby the minute I used it to scrub behind his grotty foreskin!"

Liverpool Drugs Unit
May 1981

In Tufty's book, Monday being the first day of the week, had always been a pain, but today felt different. He'd first noticed it, as he was making his way towards his desk and heard a normally stressed-out Lenny Knoxborough humming a popular tune. Another equally mind-blowing moment took place when Zoe, the only female officer in the squad, who he'd always regarded as one snotty nosed bitch, waved to him saying, "Morning Hughie," as she headed for her own closely guarded empire in the far corner of the office.

Yet the real Coup de Grace was when he spotted Lionel 'The Cake' Brady sitting behind Mick O'Hara's desk munching on a chocolate éclair. He'd spent a minute trying to work out if this was some kind of freaky dream, when Lionel stood and waved him inside. "Have a seat, Hughie," he said in his starch Yorkshire tones, before taking his own behind the double expanse of wood that had once been Mick's domain. "As you can see," indicating about him, "there's been some major changes taking place in the past few days." It was only then did Tufty realise something serious must have happened whilst he'd been weekending in Jersey.

"Mick's had an unfortunate accident," Lionel said by way of explanation and a half shrug of the shoulders.

"Accident?" asked Tufty, trying to take in the deviations from what was normal.

"Yep, managed to electrocute himself in his own back garden," he said in a matter-of-fact manner. "From what we've heard, he was mowing the grass in his bare feet and cut through the supply cable. One minute he was here and the next *Boof!* He was toast!"

Tufty listened in disbelief, as Lionel droned on about the sudden loss of his boss as though it were an everyday occurrence. "But none of that really matters now, seeing as how I was his No. 2 and the Top Brass have asked me to step into the breech." In the glare of the office lights, Tufty came to the conclusion that Lionel was a damn sight older than his ex-boss and predecessor, but it surely wasn't his place to comment one way or the other. One rumour said he'd acquired 'The Cake' nickname, by virtue of his voracious appetite for all things sticky and sweet. Which was all very well, except he was stick thin and had never changed shape in all the years he'd worked within Drugs. Most of his colleagues were of the opinion he visited the Loo more than most of his counterparts, the food passing straight through from one end to the other without touching the sides. Another rumour warned that soft toilet tissue could become scarce when Lionel took to wearing his nosebag.

But there he sat, king-like on his throne, whilst surveying the few subjects still within his realm, seemingly oblivious to the fact that an already undermanned Drugs Squad was now minus another senior officer. Nevertheless, in spite of this setback, the prospects of life without O'Hara, was enough to put a smile on the faces of the most hard-bitten members of the Squad, but for McClellan, was more like a dream come true!

The next turn of the page came a few weeks later, when 'The Cake' once again invited him into his office and said he was the bearer of some good news.

"It would appear that your Misconduct Tribunal has been cancelled." McClellan was momentarily dumbstruck as Lionel's words sank in.

"But Mick said it was all being processed," he flustered.

"It might have been when he was in charge," Lionel smiled genially. "But this comes straight from the top and cancels out any further litigation. And here's some more good news, the final Forensic report from the motorway incident came up negative, meaning you're completely absolved of this business. But there's one more surprise, they've also agreed to my suggestion that I make you my No. 2." Tufty was speechless as Lionel spoke on. "We all know Mick was a real prick when it came to you, but there's still no arguing that you're top of the list when it comes to drug busts."

To further emphasise his change in circumstances, he'd been threading his way through a crowded Church Street, when someone purposely bumped into him. He'd turned with the intention of giving the clumsy fool a verbal lashing, but to his surprise found a smartly dressed professional looking lady offering him a folded newspaper. "I think you dropped this," she said, pushing it into his hands as though she were the injured party.

Tufty was about to protest that it wasn't his, and then realised it was a copy of The Daily Express and in that one single moment of hesitation, the lady was lost in the mass of moving people. Still confused, he turned into Basnett Street, cut across Williamson Square and made his way towards the Cosy Corner Café.

Once through the door, he could see the taller of the two sisters running the rule over him. "Well hello, wee man, what can I get yea," she teased in a mock Scots accent.

McClellan, who was unsure if the lanky cow might be taking the piss, could only mutter, "Strong tea, no sugar," before squeezing his way through to an empty table at the far end. Taking a seat, he waited for the insolent bitch to deliver his drink, before attempting to open the paper. Flicking through the pages, he eventually came to the Cryptic Crossword, and remembering the rigmarole with the Jiffy Bags, saw the familiar green ink. He then spent a further tortuous twenty minutes checking the clues until he discovered the answer he was looking for. The green pen foretold the exact time and place where a large shipment of drugs would be delivered to one of Eazy Stoker's joints.

Goodman's Casino
July 1981

The architect's drawings were spread out across the desk so they might be more easily viewed.

"What's this?" asked BB.

Maxi tapped the plans. "Do you remember Mike Steel?"

"Yes, isn't he the builder who did all the casino renovations?"

"That's him and he's just finished putting the footings in for a twenty-storey building on the waterfront; apparently for some American conglomerate."

"So what's the problem?"

"Interest rates," declared Maxi. "It would appear the people financing the project scrounged the funds on the cheap, but hadn't reckoned with the US government increasing the cost of borrowing money. Which means they can't guarantee the long-term future of the project. Hawkeye is convinced that if Mike doesn't find a backer soon, the whole thing could go tits-up."

BB's smile widened. "And do I assume that you're the 'Knight in shining armour' he's badly in need of?"

"Why not? It's a fantastic project, but more than that, it's a perfectly legitimate way for us to spend money. Hawkeye's intention is to create a new company called 'Steelyard Enterprises Ltd.' The logo will say 'SEL' for short and just for fun, I'll put a fancy Penthouse on top."

"Are you going to live there?"

"That's the plan," laughed Maxi. "The hotel chain doesn't want to buy the building; they just want to lease part of it for the next twenty-five years. Meaning we will always have a steady return on our long-term investment."

"What about Mike Steel?"

"He can earn his own fortune by completing the project. It'll also teach him not to play around with untrustworthy Yanks!"

"What else is on the agenda?"

"Steffi's school holidays begin next week, so we'll be off to sunny Spain for a while. Sandra's desperate to see how the house is coming along."

"Doing up a dump is definitely not my idea of a relaxing holiday," grinned BB.

"You'd be surprised at how much pleasure there can be in renovating a property, especially one as big as ours."

"Hope it turns out as you wanted."

"So do I, but now I come to think about it. I don't suppose you know anything about Mick O'Hara's sudden passing?"

BB looked wounded. "How could you think such a thing? I swear on my sainted mother's grave that both my hands and conscience are clean."

Maxi looked more than sceptical. "Yeah?"

Marbella, Spain
September 1981

As the sun slowly disappeared over the horizon, they lay on padded sun-loungers searching for an unusual type of object whose orbit sent it hurtling past high in the heavenly firmament. This tiny blip was just one of the many low-level radio satellites, whose golden trails became visible as the World turned and time and daylight moved to another Continent. Yet they forever orbited two hundred miles above them in the Earth's lower atmosphere.

"There's one," shouted Maxi, his finger pointing to the star-filled canopy glittering like so many diamonds in the clear night sky.

"I can see it too!" cried Steffi, her young eyes charting the slim filament of light as it whizzed rocket like above her head; but within seconds was gone. "Will there be more?" she asked.

"Yes darling, lots more," Sandra assured her.

"But not tonight, my beautiful young princess," said Maxi, "because it's way past your bedtime." Nodding in agreement, Sandra led her daughter across the still warm terrace in the general direction of sleep. Maxi meanwhile took another swig from his bottle of San Miguel and lay back on the bed, delighted he'd once again been able to entertain young Steffi with this small snippet of astral knowledge. Yet had to admit that he'd learnt all about the satellites from Toby 'The Blast' Blizzard, an American music promoter he'd first met whilst touring the UK with his band fifteen years ago.

With the usual bedtime drama having been overcome, his thoughts returned to the day their taxi had finished bumping its way along the tree covered drive and emerged into the heat of the afternoon sun. It was also Sandra's first view of the completed Spanish Project.

Stepping from the dust covered taxi they'd stood together in the courtyard and admired the riot of different coloured flowers festooning the whitewashed walls of Finca Bougainvillea.

"Oh wow," Sandra whispered. "I really don't know what to say."

"I do Mummy," chirped seven-year-old Steffi. "I think it's just beautiful!" And with that near perfect description, a smiling Maxi had slipped his arm around his wife's waist, more than satisfied with the fruits of their labour. In the past Sandra had often said that life is full of surprises, especially when you're happy doing one thing and then find yourself doing something completely different. And so it was with The Finca. This unexpected, but welcome addition to their lives had materialised two years earlier, mostly due to a casual conversation they'd had at the luxury Marbella Club on Spain's Costa del Sol.

Whenever they holidayed in The Med, Sandra had always preferred to stay in the razzamatazz of Ibiza. But following a glowing report from some returning friends, had decided to test the waters and venture farther South West along its unspoilt Mediterranean shores.

To their surprise, they'd discovered that Marbella and *The Club* were almost jewel-like in their richness beauty and culture. Yet the real plus had been their fortuitous meeting with Kliff and Brigitte van Arnson, two Danish property developers who regularly stayed there. To further cement their friendship, young Steffi had become infatuated with their blonde and in her eyes, almost God-like, nine-year-old son, Roland.

Having discovered they had much in common and enjoyed each other's company they'd often dined together, but only if Steffi was allowed to sit next to her newly discovered Adonis. Although Sandra's favourite moment was when Brigitte had introduced her to The Marbella Club's owner, Prince Alfonso, a real-life piece of Spanish nobility, who'd bowed and kissed her hand with a flourish of ceremonial elegance.

It had also been late one evening, when a sleepy Roland and Steffi had gone their separate ways to be embraced by the 'Arms of Morpheus' that the Danes had spoken of their intentions to invest in the local Spanish property market. But more importantly, the construction phenomena known as the Golden Mile, a luxury development situated on the shores between Marbella and Puerto Banus.

Maxi had listened to the on-going discourse with only a passing interest, but Sandra was not only enthusiastic; she'd been bowled over by the whole idea. "Do you think we could buy something babe?" she'd whispered, as they lay listening to the soft hum of the sweep fan cooling the air above their bed.

Maxi had smiled in the dark. Of one thing he was sure; in the morning he'd be discussing bricks and mortar with Kliff and Sandra and would be scrutinising a range of different property brochures with Brigitte. Then on one hot sunny day, they'd stumbled across the old Finca, or farmhouse in the hills above the old town of Marbella. A quick look around had convinced them it was a wonderful prospect, but reluctantly conceded that there was no way it could be inhabited in its present state; and so began 'The Project'.

Aware of the many problems that might lie lay ahead in such an undertaking, Kliff and Brigitte had insisted they meet Carlota del Reye, a young, yet very talented interior designer whose shop lay situated in one of the winding back streets of Marbella's old town. Once inside its whitewashed entrance, it appeared as though they were in an Aladdin's cave. Every wall was adorned with original woven tapestries, paintings, plus a multitude of interesting artefacts of different shapes and sizes, that might decorate any of her future projects. To their delight, they'd discovered that Carlota wasn't just a pretty face. She was also a brilliant organiser, who knew how to get things done in a mostly male dominated Spanish world. This soon became apparent when Maxi began to point out potential problems that might lie ahead at the Finca.

Carlota had smiled in assurance and declared; "*No hay problema Senor Maxi.*" Before producing a list of reliable Artisans and experts she'd used on her many previous ventures. "I'd recommend Manuel to drill the bore-hole for the new water supply," she declared, pointing to a particular name. "And the firm below have a superb team of builders and carpenters. However, I never use anyone other than Miguel Delgado of Caracas Piscinas if someone's having a swimming pool installed."

Her detailed list was filled near to overflowing with the names of local plumbers, electricians or anyone else she might use to complete the works. Having been emboldened by Carlota's addition to the Finca project, Maxi and Sandra had spent most of their time visiting the local shops and flea markets searching for anything that might somehow embellish their new home.

On the day of completion, they found Carlota waiting in the shade of the entrance wearing a satisfied smile and ready to introduce them to a new Finca Bougainvillea.

No hay probleme might be a well-worn everyday phrase in Spanish life, but was also the work ethic required when you worked for the young designer. Although in retrospect, even she had to admit that it had been no easy task, conjuring up many unforeseen obstacles on the way. Still and in spite of this, she'd been more than adept in combining a superb mixture of the old and new. Her clever ideas transforming the aging farmhouse, from a dusty ramshackle of broken plaster and splintered wood, into a glorious panache of style and colour. She'd also stipulated that all the original features; high wooden beams, whitewashed walls and dark oak-doors, be repaired and retained throughout. But more importantly, insisted the whole house be modernised from top to bottom. The kitchen and bathrooms all had hot and cold running water, plus the luxury of electric ceiling fans and power everywhere. "Trust me this Casa will breathe again," was her favourite saying.

Maxi and Sandra felt they were in seventh heaven, as they stepped into the coolness of the large open lounge and marvelled at the scene before them. The wide wooden staircase leading to the bedrooms had been polished until it was almost new and in pride of place was their beautiful luxurious four-piece antique leather suite they'd discovered in the backstreets of Marbella.

To their delight and amusement, Carlota had also lit a fire in the huge fireplace, even though the afternoon sun was beating down outside. The wide windows bore Carlota's rich decorative drapes; the ones they remembered choosing when back in the studio more than a year before. The bedrooms too were full of surprises, from the large over-sized ornate beds; crisp white linen sheets and hanging lace-woven mosquito nets, to the unusual hand carved wooden furniture and ornate Moroccan wardrobes.

Sandra ran her fingertip along the contours of one particularly delicate relief and whispered. "So much skill and beauty." In another room Maxi was admiring an oil painting, which in another time and place, might pass as a real Master. But the biggest surprise was yet to come and it duly arrived when they'd followed Carlota out onto the newly built stone terrace and saw the fabulous panoramic views before them. Notwithstanding the roofs of Marbella and the sea in the distance were both breath-taking; all were agreed that nothing could surpass the blue sparkling waters of Miguel Delgado's swimming pool!

"I want to go in!" screamed a delighted Steffi, peeling off her tee shirt and shorts, whilst ignoring Sandra's futile demands she wears a proper costume. Maxi meanwhile was more than sympathetic with his daughter's pleas; wondering in which of the many suitcases his own swimming shorts lay.

However, there was one knotty problem. Waiting patiently in the heat of the Andalusia sun stood Paco the gardener and Magdalena his wife, who were so different in appearance, they'd always made Sandra smile. He was of a short squat shape, had a nut-brown face and wore a battered greasy captain's hat with an anchor on the peak. Below was a wide jolly grin that revealed most of his front teeth were missing and in one corner of his mouth hung the most foul-smelling of cigars. Magdalena in turn was the complete opposite. She being tall, gaunt and thin in stature, her greying hair tied up in a bun that had once been as black as the clothes she wore. But the biggest surprise was when they found that both were Spanish pensioners, who apparently came with the estate.

When first viewing the Finca, the agent had given Maxi and Sandra a brief rundown of its history. The property today consisted of the large disused farmhouse and one acre of land with a small olive grove. Yet many years ago and during a period of real prosperity, had more than twenty acres of olive groves, plus two large orange ones. But the previous owner, a lonely widower, had begun to drink and gamble heavily when his wife passed away. In the years that followed, he started to sell them off acre-by-acre, in the hope he might square up his outstanding debts before he died. Sadly his then immediate family couldn't afford to run the estate and so put it up for sale. This in turn, had left behind the ageing couple, whom for the last ten years had lived in the stone cottage situated on the edge of the estate.

It was only after work had begun on the renovations, did Maxi begin to question whether they really needed these two elderly people living on their doorstep. But when Carlota, who knew something of their history, heard this, she'd tested his wisdom by asking, "Where would they live, Senor?"

Maxi and Sandra then had another surprise.

"Besides, Paco and Magdalena aren't married, they're distant cousins."

"But she's wearing a wedding ring," declared Sandra.

"Yes, Senora, this much is true. But she also dresses in black, which in Spain is a characteristic sign of mourning."

They sat in silence as Carlota told her tale.

"Magdalena was originally born in Malaga along the coast, where her family ran a small backstreet tapas bar and when eighteen, married a local boy. All of this happened around the time of the Spanish Civil War, which as everybody knows was a great ugly scar on the history of my beautiful country." Pausing only to let this particular wound sink in.

"With the sound of gunfire filling the streets and the situation slowly worsening, it mattered not who you were or what you did for a living: you had to choose a side. Magdalena's family as I understand it had always been staunch

Republicans and as the war escalated, she and her husband became heavily involved in the fighting"

"You mean they fired guns?"

"Oh yes, Senora Sandra, they actually fired guns and when needed, were experts at throwing homemade petrol bombs. Especially when General Franco's forces surrounded the city."

"Christ," muttered Maxi.

"What happened next?" asked a now fascinated Sandra; shaking her head at Max's blasphemy.

"They lost," Carlota said simply. "Franco was a ruthless man who would delight in purging any possible opposition. The people who'd been fortunate enough to escape the city, literally had to run for their lives. But those who decided to stay and fight, were executed or disappeared forever; just like her father and husband. Franco's soldiers had arrested them both, set fire to the bar and left it as a ruin. Having no other choice, Magdalena and her mother had fled along the coast and hid amongst their distant cousins, which was possible in those days, as most of them lived in fishing villages or mountain farms."

"Did the men survive?"

"No Senor, they both died in prison, but it was more than ten years before she knew of this."

"Hence the dark mourning clothes," Maxi concluded sadly. "What about Paco, where does he come into all this?"

"At the time he was just a young fisherman living in a shack with his wife and child," said Carlota, "but fortunately was related to Magdalena's father and in this country blood really is thicker than water. So they took them both in as part of the family."

"Where's Paco's wife and child now?"

"Died of sickness many years ago, Senor. Which is why he and Magdalena moved onto the farm and began scraping a living cultivating the olive groves; it doesn't pay much, but they at least have a roof over their heads."

"Who paid their wages when the old man died?"

"No-one Senor, they just carried on growing the olives, harvested them, took a small share in return and used the rest to make sure the farm didn't fall into complete disrepair."

Sandra stared defiantly at Maxi across the table. "There's no way we're going to throw them out after that!" she declared, a sound of finality in her voice.

Maxi held up a hand. "No problem, Senora," he said in mock surrender.

"I would suggest you might employ them in the roles they undertook for their previous employer," said Carlota. "Paco was the gardener handyman who also took care of the olive groves and Magdalena was the cook."

"Can she cook?"

"Magdalena has many hidden talents which you might yet enjoy, Senora. I would simply ask that you try them."

Maxi took another bottle of San Miguel beer from the ice bucket and continued to study the stars twinkling above in the night sky. Six sun-filled weeks had flown by since their arrival at Finca Bougainvillea, each one so very different from the other. At first they'd explored the local countryside and dined out in lots of different restaurants. Yet it had been days like today that he'd come to enjoy the most, the ones when they'd decided to stay at home and let Magdalena do the cooking. Their first meal and what they might eat had been achieved more by luck and semantics, seeing as how no one could understand each other. But after hearing the word 'Pescada' being mentioned a few times, had safely assumed they were having fish. And what a 'Pescada' it turned out to be and what a superb meal!

A smiling Paco was given but a few hundred pesetas by Magdalena and dispatched on his noisy moped to purchase whatever might be available in the local fish market. On his return, he'd struggled into the kitchen with what seemed like a still alive Moby Dick strapped to his back; it was so big. Following which Magdalena had sharpened her knife and expertly set about gutting and cleaning its inners, before stuffing it full of a variety of different herbs and fruits. Another notable step in the cooking process had taken place when Paco (with a little help from Carlota) had begun to show off his own culinary skills.

The young interior designer's Spanish upbringing, had reminded her that the elderly couple would only use wood fires when cooking; an electric one being unheard of in their lifetime. So with the wisdom needed in such matters, she'd had the kitchen one completely refurbished, as well having a new modern gas cooker fitted. But to Paco's delight, she'd also ordered an open range to be built on the terrace, one where he could make a fire and slowly grill the fish above its white-hot embers.

The resulting meal was both sumptuous and delicious in its very simplicity, Magdalena filling the dining table with a cross section of seasonal vegetables, both hot and cold.

A young Steffi was also fascinated by the old couple's way of life and delighted when they let her peek into their daily routine. On one of her many visits to the cottage, she'd revealed that the pensioners had supplemented their needs by having a goat and a few chickens. Yet they forever surprised them with their knowledge, expertise and skill, on a simple wood stove or makeshift barbeque.

Maxi had lost count of the times he'd watched a chuckling Paco cook sizzling slabs of steak, spicy chorizo sausages or a whole chicken, on his homemade spit. It was only when each item had been cooked to perfection, would he place them on the table with an immense show of personal pride. Their time at the Finca had lots of other benefits too, the main one being communication. It had taken a while, but as the long hot days went by, they'd slowly begun to grasp the odd word here and there, that over time became shaky sentences in Spanish. None more so than Steffi, whose young mind was free of the grammatical problems Maxi and Sandra forever seemed to encounter and following a week's tuition in Magdalena's kitchen, was 'que pasaring' as though she'd been doing it all her life.

He laughingly recalled one warm evening a month ago, when Kliff and Brigitte van Arnson had been invited for a meal. At its conclusion, Maxi had been watching Magdalena and Paco help to clear away the table and on a whim asked Steffi if she could help him say a few words in Spanish.

"*Nos gusta mucho esto*," he'd said, whilst pointing to the empty plates. Which immediately brought everything to a halt, Paco's mouth opening so wide in astonishment, they were able see his empty gums and remaining teeth on both sides. Magdalena however, looked as though she might cry.

"What did you say?" asked a concerned Sandra as she saw their reaction.

"Daddy has just told them we think their cooking is fantastic!" Which brought lots more appreciative nods and smiles from around the table.

"The days are passing by too quickly," he mused, the sound of Sandra returning to where he lay on the wicker loungers. But to his surprise and instead of joining him, sat side-on with her hands clasped together on her knees.

"Everything okay, babe?" he inquired, sensing something was wrong.

Sandra stared into his eyes. "You do know that there's only one more week before we go home?"

Maxi took a swig of his beer and nodded slowly in response. This was one of those questions that simply couldn't be ignored. Their holidays these days were always arranged around Steffi's summer-break, that sadly was coming to an end. It meant that in seven days' time his young daughter would have to go back to school in Liverpool.

"I just love this place so much, I don't want to leave," she whispered.

Maxi closed his eyes and let out a long sigh. "I know how you feel, babe, it's the same for me too, but we really don't have much choice."

"Why?"

Maxi didn't reply, yet knew exactly where this was leading.

"Finca Bougainvillea is so beautiful, why can't we just move here for good?" she asked.

Maxi's mind was working overtime; he'd been thinking the same thing for weeks. "Steffi and her schooling, of course," he said by way of a lame excuse.

"Well, who'd have thought it?" she laughed. "Because therein lies the problem. Our daughter, in her innocence, keeps on asking some very awkward questions about what you really do for a living; seeing as all her school friends' fathers' apparently have normal jobs. But I can't smile sweetly and say, *It's okay, darling, your father's a major drug dealer,* as though it's an everyday occupation."

Maxi closed his eyes again, this time to blank out the thought. "You don't have to be so derogatory about it, babe. Being a major drug dealer has kept us in pretty good stead for quite a few years."

Sandra moved across, sat next to him on the wicker lounger and touched his face. "I not being derogatory babe, far from it, I'm just worried that if things go wrong. You might have rich clients and friends in high places, but they won't save us if the police come knocking on our door; the last thing I need is you in jail and Steffi finding out the truth of what we've been doing for all these years.

If we could some way get out and move down here, we might be able to forget the past and start again."

Maxi closed his eyes and thought. 'Is it possible to discard a major part of your life, as if it were an old worn-out coat, but more importantly, forget how it had all begun?' Taking another swig of his beer, he could clearly remember the night seventeen years ago, when he'd been lying on Brighton Beach searching for the same passing radio satellites. Yet in a strange quirk of fate was the same night that Toby Blizzard had introduced him to something called 'Hashish'.

In the few short years he'd worked within the music scene, Maxi had dabbled in and sold, many things, 'pills' being one of them. But this one particular 'Smoke' had come as a totally different mind-blowing experience and left him stoned out of his brains. It also reminded him of how six months earlier, a simple slip of the pen had left him nearly penniless, but thanks to his American friend, was now a very rich man.

It had been the snowy winter of 1963 and their destination, the small town of Wigan, about half an hour's drive from Liverpool. It was also from here that someone named Ken, had rung and booked 'The Instrumatics' to star at the opening of his new club. Despite the near blizzard conditions, they'd eventually reached the venue only to find there'd been a major 'balls up'. Ken, an ex-shopkeeper turned 'music entrepreneur', had sadly informed him they'd arrived a day too early for the gig; it seemed the club wouldn't be ready until the next night.

A fuming Maxi had argued, until he was blue in the face, that this was the agreed day, but Ken insisted he must have misheard him and pencilled the wrong date is his diary. It was at this point that he'd taken a closer look at the ex-shopkeeper's try for fame and fortune. In the usual scramble to climb aboard the musical 'gravy train', Ken and his wife had sold their small mini-market and invested everything in an ancient rundown cinema named the 'Gaiety'. It was also plain to see that the place had been closed for at least ten years, probably due to its location in some obscure backstreet and a lack of paying customers.

However, it did have one thing in its favour, there was no upper tier. This had allowed Ken to rip out the first six rows of seats and level the floor, thus giving them the extra room needed to pack the crowds in.

"They'll be queuing down the street," enthused Marge, his wife.

Maxi wasn't so sure, seeing as how it'd taken him ages to find the damn place, but looking around saw something that made him even more suspicious; the drum-kit and amplifiers already set up on stage. "I thought we were opening the show?" he queried, indicating to the line of musical equipment.

Ken followed his stare and gave a laugh. "You are."

"So, whose is the gear on stage?"

"That's just a temporary arrangement," he assured him. "The stuff belongs to some local kids called 'The Jetstream'. It just so happens that they'd been looking for a place to practice and I was curious as to the sound acoustics in the club."

An angry Maxi returned to the van and reluctantly informed the other band members about the 'balls up'. "Does that mean we won't get paid?" asked Dan the drummer, whose normal job was bricklayer.

"Not unless you can come back and play tomorrow night," fumed Maxi. However, on hearing the mutterings of discontent took a five-pound note from his wallet and said, "There's a pub on the corner, go and have a few drinks on me." Instantly mollified, the group had headed for the bar, whilst a curious Maxi returned to the Gaiety. 'The Jetstream', he discovered, weren't 'just a gang of kids', as Ken had inanely described them. They were a superb group of young musicians who included a saxophonist as part of their line-up. And even though they might be a little rough around the edges, 'talented' was the only way to describe them.

From the first opening chord of Chuck Berry's 'Johnny B' Good' to the final crashing cymbals of 'Money', he knew they were different. Yet on reflection realised that the group's chisel-chinned bass player was the real star. In Maxi's eyes, Sebastian Hartwood had everything the teenagers of today were looking for; glossy dark locks, blue eyes and a sexy smile, but more importantly, a voice they would die for.

"Well played," said Maxi, as he watched from the side of the make-do stage.

"Cheers," they replied, glad to know that someone had been listening to their set.

Maxi focused on Sebastian. "I've never heard of you lot, been going long?"

"Just a few months," he replied, "but we're all from the same Grammar School and been friends for years."

In a flash, Maxi was able to see he wasn't dealing with the usual backstreet boys. "Have you played any of the big clubs yet?"

"If only," sighed Sebastian. "We're still trying to get bookings, which is why we're having to rehearse here."

"Who's your manager?" asked Maxi.

"We haven't got one yet," he replied with a shrug. "We're hoping one will come along when the we start to earn some real money."

On a whim Maxi spoke those few fateful words. "How do you fancy playing a gig at The Cavern Club?"

The group stopped in mid-chore. "Do you mean the one in Liverpool where 'The Beatles' always play?" asked Chas the saxophonist.

"Of course," grinned Maxi. "I just happen to know John McNally, the guy who owns the place, and Bob Woolmer, the DJ, is also a good friend of mine."

"Wow, that sounds fantastic, but wouldn't the place be booked up for months in advance?"

"No problem, I'll tell Bob I'm your new manager and ask him to squeeze you in."

As he later drove home through slush filled roads, Maxi was thinking of how Brian Epstein, The Beatles' manager, had turned four leather-clad nobodies into potential superstars and although it was a massive gamble, he was hoping to do the same. The most important thing he decided was image; followed by good looks and lastly talent, providing there was some. But on reflection decided this would be the least of his problems, seeing as how 'The Jetstream' had bundles of the stuff, especially Sebastian the bass player.

Nevertheless, the biggest risk was money and how much he would have to lay out. Sandra had warned about getting in too deep, but Maxi told of the time he'd come across Sebastian tuning a guitar and stopped to listen. Satisfied all was well, he'd begun to strum a few chords and hum along to an unfamiliar tune. Standing alone in the shadows, Maxi had been spellbound by the simple melodic fluidity of the riff and mightily impressed by what he'd heard. "Nice tune, Seb, any lyrics to go with it?"

The bass player gave a shrug. "I've done a few, but it's not quite finished yet."

Maxi was immediately thinking of a hit record when he said, "Keep it up mate, it's always good to have some original music on stage."

Seb smiled enigmatically. "Trust me, I'm working on it."

Following this fruitful encounter, Maxi was convinced he'd discovered a singular 'Lennon and McCartney' and desperately needed to sign him up. His next move involved a lunchtime session at The Cavern where he'd secretly replaced the Instrumatics with The Jetstream much to their angry protestations. He'd then spent many long hours on the phone booking venues and even more time watching them rehearse in private. But his biggest outlay had been the nearly new van and matching suits for each member of the group. The second was a shiny new 'Fender Precision' bass guitar for Seb. (Image was everything).

To his delight, their appearance on the local music scene had been nothing short of sensational. He'd been enjoying the usual screams of 'more', at the end of one particular gig, when Sandra noticed a stranger standing at the back of the crowd. The fact that he was well dressed, in his forties and wore a tie, told Maxi this wasn't your usual fan, but a music scout. There'd been lots of rumours circulating Liverpool that following The Beatles' success, many of the major record companies were hoping to emulate Brian Epstein and sign up their own version of the four mop tops. With this in mind, Maxi had sidled alongside the stranger, whom he noticed was making notes on a pad.

"Pretty good!" he shouted whilst nodding to the group on stage.

"Very good!" he shouted back, his head bobbing along in time to the music.

"Sebastian the bass player has a great voice!" Maxi enthused over the screams.

The scout nodded again and asked, "Are they local?"

"Oh yeah!" lied Maxi, "they're all local boys."

"I don't suppose you know who their manager is?"

As it turned out, the stranger wasn't from one of big the record companies, as they'd hoped, but arguably the next best thing. John Butler worked for some big shot musical entrepreneur who had lots of famous stars in his stable and as luck would have it, was searching for some new blood. But despite the success of The Beatles, loud, brash young rock bands were still something of an unknown in the music industry.

So, the Mogul's easy solution to this ever-growing conundrum was to create a series of travelling rock shows that would tour different parts of the country, but always with a headline act as the main attraction. One might have The Rolling Stones as top of the bill and descend in order of merit, to the hard to read names at the bottom of the poster. There was a time when Maxi thought he was being well and truly shafted by the 'Entrepreneur', but John had assured him that being bottom of the bill didn't necessarily mean The Jetstream were nobodies. "Think of the exposure," he'd insisted "and you never know who might be watching in the audience!"

The Tour itself had been a sell-out and covered most of the Southern counties, their final destination being Brighton Pavilion. Maxi was first to admit that he'd enjoyed every minute of trip, especially as Sandra had tagged along as his roadie. The Jetstream had gone down a bomb, with scores of girls screaming Seb's name as they'd exited the many stage doors along the way. "Not bad," laughed Maxi, as he and Sandra fought their way through a tangle of grasping nubile teenagers.

It was the last night of the Tour and not long after he'd left a still stoned Toby lying on the beach, when he'd staggered back to their hotel and found Sandra having a late-night drink with the rest of the group. "Where's Seb?" he'd asked, seeing no sign of their future star.

"Gone to bed early," replied Bert the organist.

"Which is where we should be," advised Sandra.

"Sounds good to me, babe," smiled a light-headed Maxi, as he staggered off in the direction of the lift. Once inside the bedroom, Sandra had begun to remove her make-up and Maxi unbutton his shirt, when they heard a strange noise.

"Does that sound like someone crying?" asked Sandra.

Maxi cocked an ear, trying to pinpoint exactly where the squeals were coming from and then realised it was coming from Sebastian's room. Curious to know what was happening, he placed his ear against the inter-connecting door. "Listen to this babe, I reckon our superstar has snaffled himself a groupie and decided to throw a shift in!"

"Leave him alone," she hissed. "He's probably earned every minute of it."

"I know," he agreed, "but wouldn't you just love to see old chisel-chin in action." He was about to continue undressing, when on a whim pushed the door handle, which to his surprise turned to the open position. "Hey babe, this door's unlocked. I wonder if the cleaner's forgot about it when she serviced the rooms?"

"It doesn't matter," Sandra hissed again, "just leave him in peace!"

Maxi gave a mischievous grin. "It can't be that big a deal if I have quick peek at how he's doing" and before she could protest any further; opened the door.

Other than the small bedside light, the rest of the room was in darkness, but Maxi's unexpected appearance had illuminated the double bed as though it were a stage. At first he'd thought it was empty. Then saw the naked blonde lying face down across the crumpled sheets and a still panting Sebastian kneeling behind.

He was about to tell him to 'give her one for me', when a weeping teenage boy looked him in the eye.

"Dear Jesus," whispered Maxi, as he took in the unnatural position of Sebastian, who was still on his knees beside the bed. It was also the signal for him to grab his underpants and head for the bathroom, where he slammed the door shut behind him. A fraught twenty minutes later and Maxi had managed to order a late-night taxi and smuggle the still tearful fifteen-year-old out of the hotel. "Take him where he needs to go," he instructed the driver.

Back in their room, Sandra was also near to tears. "Seb told the boy he loved him and said they would go travelling around the world together."

Maxi shook his head in disbelief. He knew plenty of 'shirt-lifters' back home in Liverpool, but none that would affect his life like this. "Where's that half bottle of whiskey, babe? I doubt I'll be going to bed yet."

He slept little in the intervening hours, twisting and turning through the night whilst pondering his future. This was 1964 and the act of buggery was still a criminal offence. So, more in hope than expectation, Maxi had slipped the teenager £20, praying he wouldn't tell anyone what happened in the bedroom, but what about the lecherous Sebastian?

Maxi rose early and tentatively tried the connecting door; which he discovered was now locked. Nervous and unsure of what to do next, he left his room and began knocking on Seb's door in the hotel passage. Hearing no sound, he and Sandra decided to have some coffee downstairs and try again later. On their return, he knocked on a few other doors and had a casual chat with the other band members, who as one declared they hadn't seen him. He was still wondering what to do for the best, when the cleaner's trolley turned the corner.

Maxi and Sandra were still drowning their sorrows when Toby joined them at the hotel bar. "What a goddamn pisser," he growled in his Bronx accent.

"Tell me about it," grunted Maxi.

"How long had he been lying in the bath?"

"Police reckon he cut his wrists sometime around three."

Toby sipped on his Bourbon. "Holy fuck, that's one bad way to go."

"The cleaner nearly collapsed when she saw the blood," whispered a shaky Sandra.

"What happens now?"

Maxi gave a half laugh. "Not a lot, there'll be a formal inquest to confirm he committed suicide and we're left stony-broke. Like some dumb arse fool, I used every penny we had to finance this fiasco, but will need to sell the van and equipment to help pay the bills." He then showed Toby his missing fingertip. "I was also hoping to keep the Fender bass guitar for myself, but need to grow one of these first."

"What about the other group members?" Grinned Toby. "Did they know Sebastian wore red lipstick on the quiet?"

"Oh yeah, but no-one was going to admit it in public were they."

Toby took another sip of his Bourbon and contemplated Maxi's dilemma. "Nothing else in the pipeline?"

"Just a whole load of screaming creditors waiting to be paid."

The American gave a sympathetic smile, before reaching to his shirt pocket and placing a small square of blotting paper on the bar. "Allow me to introduce you to Lysergic Acid Diethylamide, which back in the States, is more commonly known as LSD. It might not look like much, but it sure as hell will blow your mind. I was also hoping you might help me spread it amongst the masses and change our fortunes forever."

Maxi smiled, remembering the clamour to try the mind-bending drug, particularly from those in the music industry. Toby had been spot on when he'd claimed it would make them rich, considering it was just a tiny drop of chemical you placed on your tongue and then swallowed. Sadly, it was also a fad that was soon to become illegal and Maxi was first to admit that the steady flow of Hashish and Cocaine passing through Liverpool docks had ultimately filled their coffers. Yet even now, had to endure the constant stress of trying to outwit the Police and Customs surveillance teams.

Staring at the stars above, he knew he'd be a damn fool not to acknowledge Sandra's cogent concerns. "It's still early days babe, but I do have this idea running around in my head and much as I'd like to, can't really tell you any more about it until Monday."

"Why Monday?"

"BB's coming down for a few days."

Considering he'd been to the Finca on quite a few occasions, a visit from BB Benson was akin to a coming of the Second Messiah. From the moment he'd stepped from Maxi's car, until his tearful departure two days later, the house was filled to the rafters with the sound of raucous laughter.

"Hello gorgeous ladies!" he declared; his arms open wide to gather up the ecstatic youngster as she ran toward him.

"Welcome back, BB." A more than delighted Sandra enthused, as she kissed the side of his face and became enveloped in his wide embrace. Hovering in the background, a toothless Paco and smiling Magdalena were watching the joyous greeting, content the dark handsome 'Hombre' was once again in their midst.

"Como estais mis amigos?" BB asked in near fluent Spanish: his Brazilian roots helping him with the lingo.

"Muy Bien, Senor BB," Magdalena beamed, Paco nodding along before hurrying to collect his suitcase from the car. Sandra and Steffi meanwhile, had linked both his arms ready to give him a personal tour of the finished project.

"Absolutely superb," proclaimed BB. "I never imagined it would turn out like this, everything is just so beautiful."

"Wait until you see the pool." Sandra chuckled wickedly. "That will really make you smile."

The sight of the cool and inviting water had BB looking around. "Where's the bedroom again?" he laughed. "I need to find my swimming trunks!"

An entertaining afternoon was followed by an even better night, as they sat on the terrace and enjoyed the different food arranged on the table. A sudden squeal of, "Oh mummy, not yet please," could be heard and it was only then did they realise it was time for Sandra to lead her still protesting daughter off to bed. Relaxing in the quiet, Maxi was telling BB how much he was looking forward to the new football season; Liverpool's in particular, when he saw Paco approaching the table with his hat in one hand and a wooden box in the other. A few seconds went by before he opened it to reveal two large cigars, each adorned with a gold band.

"Estamos muy contentos de que usted ha venido a vivir aqui, y estos son un pequeno regalo para ti," he said proudly.

Maxi hesitated, unable to understand what was being said, plus the fact he very rarely smoked cigars.

BB saw his confusion and whispered, "Paco's saying he and Magdalena are delighted that you're living here and because of it, has decided to give you a special gift." He then nodded to the box. "They look like good quality cigars to me, Maxi, which I imagine he's saved up all year to buy and if you don't accept them with good grace, you'll insult his pride no end. So take the damn things and do it as if you mean it!"

Rising from the table, Maxi accepted the old man's present with one hand, grasped the other in a firm grip and said, "Muchas Gracias, Senor Paco."

"Su nada Senor Maxi," he replied, gave the slightest of bows, turned and headed in the direction of the stone cottage. Watching his squat shape disappear through the bushes, the two men were in no doubt that the gift of Paco's two favourite cigars had been a damn sight more than nothing!

Returning to the table, Sandra was surprised to see both men smoking cigars. "Hello, someone had a new baby?"

BB waved his cigar in the air. "No, it seems Paco and Magdalena like you a lot."

Maxi did the same. "An early Christmas present from them both."

Sandra smiled at the thought, but something else was troubling her. No matter the time of year, BB's larger-than-life presence was the one they'd always looked forward to, but tonight felt different. So, with the waft of fine cigar smoke drifting in the warm night air she led the way across the terrace and sat beside Maxi on one of the wicker loungers, BB facing them on the other. The evening's discourse might have been a welcome distraction, but obviously there were much more important things to discuss.

"I stopped over in London last night," began BB, "and met with Brandon du Toit," his tone of voice conveying deep concern.

Sandra remembered him as always being smartly dressed, but more importantly; he was Toby Blizzard's right-hand man.

"Brandon had some rather disturbing news concerning the Cocaine trade back in the USA; Miami in particular"

Maxi took a puff on his cigar, "Disturbing?"

BB enjoyed a drag on his own before flicking the ash in the bushes. "Yeah, very disturbing. It's no big secret that most of the Cocaine we buy is sourced through the West Indies, the Dominican Republic being one of the main routes. But it seems there's a swathe of new dealers getting in on the act by bringing the stuff in from other places. This has resulted in a massive over-supply, which Brandon describes as a 'major glut'. To make matters worse, he's convinced the price of the white powder could fall by as much as sixty percent."

Maxi shrugged his shoulders. "How can that be bad for us? The cheaper it is, so much the better."

"If only that were true," sighed BB, a spiral of smoke rising above his head. "But the problem doesn't quite end there. Due to this over-supply, some people are practically giving it away in order to cover their costs and as a consequence, the price has literally hit rock-bottom."

Maxi and Sandra were still waiting for the punch line.

"Then out of nowhere, some smart-arse thinks he's solved the problem by creating something called *Crack Cocaine*."

"What's that?" asked Sandra.

"Everyone's worst nightmare and a major problem for the rest of the trade."

"Spit it out BB and tell us what the hell's going on."

"I don't need to tell you how we normally buy and sell our stuff, Maxi, but when acquired, the raw material is routinely assessed for quality and strength. It's then mixed with a few other harmless powders to bulk it up and reduce the potency. The next stage is to 'cut' and bag it into small portions, which we then sell to whoever wants to buy it, rich or poor. Past experience tells us that most of our clientele take it on a recreational basis by snorting it any way they can. This in turn puts a smile on the faces of Christ knows how many city hi-rollers, rock stars or whoever else might want to buy it. There are also anecdotal tales of some people using it in a more exotic fashion, which I personally haven't had the opportunity to try yet."

Maxi had been listening to BB carefully. "How does this affect us and how we do business?"

"According to Brandon, this Crack shit came about due to a further fall in prices and it doesn't bode well for us because it's different from what we sell."

Maxi stopped smoking his cigar, "How?"

"I'm not sure, but it seems they take the cocaine and put it through some kind of 'cooking' process. This in turn transforms it into a hard crystalline form which can be cut into small squares and makes it cheaper and easier to sell on the streets."

"If it's in hard squares, how do you take this stuff?" asked Sandra.

"Unlike heroin, which you have to turn to liquid and inject, this stuff is literally smoked raw. It's also incredibly addictive and Brandon reckons the hit is so high, you can get hooked on it for life."

Maxi's cigar was still smouldering in his hand, but his mind was elsewhere as he stared into the night. "I assume that's not the only reason why Brandon is giving us this information?"

BB narrowed his eyes through the smoke and gave a nod.

"So tell me the rest of this disturbing news."

"Even though this Crack shit has yet to go mainline, it's made enough of an impact on the Feds and DEF to have them springing into action. The Americans reckon this stuff is so harmful, that in a few years' time, it could turn into a major epidemic. The word on the street says they're setting up a whole new agency to try and counteract its growth. There's even talk of them bringing Shelton Catskill back to Miami."

"Catskill?" Maxi whispered incredulously. "I thought he was in New York doing his hot-shot District Attorney routine."

"He is, but because of the potentially serious nature of this Crack shit, they're begging for him to return and take over running the operation."

"Christ, no wonder Toby's worried," grunted Maxi. "If it hadn't been for his timely move up North, Shelton would have put us all out of business years ago!"

"If this nightmare takes off in America babe, then surely it'll be the same for us in the UK?" And here's another thought, will we have to sell this Crack Cocaine just to stay in the game?"

"Me thinks that troubled times may lie ahead," whispered BB.

"You could well be right," Maxi agreed, "but as the saying goes, *there's more than one way to skin a cat*."

"What do you mean, babe?'

"I have an idea kicking around in my head that still needs a lot of thought, but hopefully I can tell you more about it tomorrow."

Sandra had planned to make tonight's meal a special one by wearing her new black dress, and inviting some of their friends, Carlota and her boyfriend being first on the list. The Van Arnson family, who were always willing to eat at Finca Bougainvillea, arrived early, especially when they heard BB Benson was in town and the swimming pool was available. With the heat of the day beginning to subside and the night slowly creeping in, Maxi played 'Mine Host' by filling their glasses with one of his favourite Rioja red wines, as they awaited the feast that as always, didn't disappoint.

The Cangrejco starter was a delicious mix of fresh crabmeat and sweet red peppers, but the main course, an even bigger surprise. Having lit his fire many hours earlier, Paco was happily basting a young suckling pig on his open-air barbeque, the sound of crackling skin and the sweet smell of pork, making them sniff the air in mouth-watering anticipation. The night as ever had been a huge success from the food and drink, to Maxi's stint at entertaining them with a selection of his outrageously funny stories. BB meanwhile, had played no small part in the proceedings by telling some side-splitting corny jokes and they spent the rest of the evening trying to out-score one another in laughter.

Sandra, as always, had been intrigued by Magdalena's behaviour when serving their handsome guest. Closely watching the old lady as she filled his wine glass with almost loving care, her eyes alight at the sounds of laughter, unable to understand, yet happy just to be a part of it all. Every now and then, BB would make a point of touching her hand, as if to reassure her she wasn't just a servant and a grateful Magdalena would happily make her return to the kitchen. It was only later that Sandra recalled BB having the same effect on most of the women he met, herself included.

The chocolate mousse dessert was consumed in a flash, its swift departure helping turn the conversation in a much more interesting direction, the Spanish property-boom. And although they each had their own personal viewpoint; of one thing they were all agreed; there'd never be a better time to invest and make some serious money.

"Since the death of General Franco, in '75, the tourism industry as a whole, has begun to shake off its chains and expand at a break-neck speed," enthused Carlota. "I know of a least three applications to build new hotels, with many more in the pipe-line." This in turn gave Kliff the chance to expound on his plans to become involved in the 'Golden Mile' and the possible fortunes to be made there. "Sunny with Money!" was his favourite saying.

The evening's chat and discourse had continued along on much the same lines, as they'd all spoke in glowing terms of their life on the Costa del Sol. Eventually, the night came to an end and it was time to say their last goodbyes to their fellow diners as they disappeared into the night. It was also due to the lateness of the hour, that Steffi amazingly had gone to bed of her own accord, thus leaving just Maxi, Sandra and BB sat alone around the table.

"I think that went down well," said a smiling Sandra.

"Fantastic," agreed BB, raising his glass in salute.

Maxi lifted his own. "Superlative night with excellent guests."

"I like to think of them as more than just guests," Sandra said. "I look on them as friends we can trust."

"I couldn't have put it any better myself," added BB. "I've yet to meet nicer people, the staff included!"

Maxi was thoughtful for a moment whilst turning the brandy snifter around in his hands. "Sometime in the near future, there's a possibility that we might be in need of our trustworthy friends."

Sandra instinctively sensed this was something to do with *the idea kicking around in his head* but had no inkling what it might be. Nevertheless she still felt a small ray of hope and asked, "Why?"

"I think it's time we took our leave of the drugs trade."

Sandra's eyes opened wide in surprise, while BB's took on a decidedly confused look. "Wow, that sounds like one major step into the unknown."

"I'm aware of that BB, but in light of all we've heard concerning this Miami business, then maybe now is the time to talk about it."

Leaning closer, three heads came together as Maxi spoke. "In our game, chance will always dictate whether we can stay one step ahead of the Law. Yet you can only have Lady Luck on your side for so long and there's no arguing we've had more than our fair share of it. With this in mind, I am now of the opinion that we should be grateful for everything we've had and call it a day."

BB's eyebrows lifted a fraction as he considered this home-spun philosophy. "I can agree with everything you say Maxi and I don't doubt that only you could make it happen, but you still haven't told me exactly how we're going to do it."

All thoughts of drink were put on hold and the ashtrays were filled to overflowing, as Maxi walked them through his plan to make an exit from what had always been an extremely dangerous, yet very rewarding way of life.

The family were gathered together in the courtyard to say their sad farewells to a departing BB Benson. Maxi smiled in amusement as he waited for the tears to ease, considering they'd all meet again in a few days. "Come on ladies, time for one last kiss and hug; we're running late and I need to get BB to the airport within the hour."

Young Steffi however, had other things on her mind. "Don't forget, Uncle BB, now we have our new telephone line, you can call us any day of the week!"

He and Sandra were also halfway through one lasting bear hug, when Maxi joined them; but not in an affectionate way. "I'm just reminding you both to be very careful in what we say, especially after our little discussion last night and always remember; *Walls have ears, as well as ice cream,*" nodding in the direction of his daughter. Maxi may have said it lightly, but there was still no doubting the seriousness of the subject.

"No sweat," whispered BB, "and until you say otherwise, my lips are sealed."

"There's something else you need to do when you get back to Liverpool," whispered Maxi. "Remember to book a flight to Miami and arrange a meet with Toby. It's vital he and Brandon should know our intentions, especially as we now have Tufty McClellan on board."

BB nodded. "Okay, I'll do it as soon as I get back, but talk about forgetting things; I've just remembered the wedding."

"What wedding?" asked Sandra.

"Toby's!" He declared. "When I met with Brandon a few days ago, he told me that *The Blast* intends to get married sometime next year and you're both invited."

Seaforth Container Docks, Liverpool
April 1982

At first glance, the ships appeared to be no more than three tiny smudges on the horizon, yet continued to grow in size as they ploughed their way towards the world famous 'Mersey Waterway'. Watching from the windswept quay, the two men noting their progress showed no interest in the two trailing behind. They had eyes only for the first of the approaching vessels.

"How long before she gets here?" Asked Hughie.

"It'll be another hour," replied the Customs officer. "Maritime radar estimate her speed at approximately five knots, meaning it should be sometime around 7.30 am before she enters the Main Channel."

Hughie's next question was directed at Brady. "Are you sure everything's in place?"

"Yes Boss, we've got men stationed all over the dock."

A grim smile appeared on his ruddy features. "Remember, we can't afford any balls-up at this stage of the game, there's too much at frigging stake!"

"Everything is just as you ordered, with all traffic arriving and departing the docks being closely monitored."

Hughie nodded before returning his attention to the vessel so near to completing its trans-Atlantic journey. He was also badly in need of a cigarette and with the latest report saying he had time on his hands, went for a walk. To say he had mixed feelings about this whole business or what might lie ahead was an understatement. If his theory was correct, the container ship arriving from Baltimore had to be a major part of Hamilton's mystery plan, but to his irritation, had no idea what. He was only half way through his fourth lung buster and still no nearer the truth, when he heard Brady's voice calling over the wind. "She's a long way off, but it's definitely the 'Cedar Post'!"

Returning to the quay, Hughie adjusted his binoculars and focused on the name, that hopefully would justify the time and money spent on this massive Anglo-American operation. Not far behind in its wake, he could clearly see the second ship supposedly arriving from Canada and just about make out the much smaller vessel on the horizon. "That's a lot of frigging containers," moaned Hughie, as he watched the 'Cedar Post' being tied up in the Basin. "How long until we find the one we want?"

"Depends on where it's stored," replied the Customs officer. "If we're lucky and it's on the upper decks, then maybe two hours. But we'll only know for sure when we get the ship's loading log."

"Christ!" he grumbled. "This business could take forever. What about the officers checking the paperwork? Are they all up to speed?"

"Yes Sir. Once the relevant container has been identified and loaded onto the quay, they'll move it to the main storage area where two Customs men will break open the seal and have a quick look inside. But as agreed, it will be just a cursory inspection."

Hughie gave a grunt of satisfaction, but wasn't quite finished. "This is a critical stage in the operation, especially if any of the dockside workers notice any unusual activity, or even worse, see sniffer dogs!"

"We've kept the dogs away just as you instructed, Sir."

Listening from behind, young Brady thought Tufty was squeezing the lemon a bit too hard and gave the Custom's guy a sly wink of sympathy. But since Lionel the cake's sudden heart attack, and McClellan's rapid promotion as 'Head of Drugs', they'd all had to doff their caps. Then to the relief of everyone involved, the ship's loading log revealed the grey container was stowed somewhere in the upper hold. Which meant it should take but a few hours before it was safely on the quayside.

"I think it best you head for the Maritime control room and keep out of sight," advised the Senior Customs officer. "There's a coffee machine available and we'll be more than happy keep you up to date with the two-way walkie-talkies."

A frustrated Tufty was about to open his second packet of cigarettes in the smoke-filled room, when he remembered the other two newly arrived vessels. One in particular had caught his eye, the 'MV Mercier' that was supposedly inbound from Miami. A further check said it was a compact refrigerated container vessel and similar to the Canadian boat, was tied up in a more secluded part of the Basin. This meant the usual Customs activity would be practically zero in that neck of the woods, seeing as everyone's eyes were focused on the 'Cedar Post.' Tufty in the meantime had other things on his mind. "What about this empty warehouse in Garston, Brady, any idea who owns it?"

His No. 2 shook his head in frustration. "Not yet. We've driven past a few times in the last twenty-four hours, but there's no sign of movement from inside. In fact, we're not even sure if the place is occupied."

Tufty grunted and took another drag on his cigarette. "Best not ask the locals, one of them might smell a rat and warn the others off. Besides, with a bit of luck, the man himself might arrive at the dock and claim the container." Yet in spite of his optimism, it was more than twenty-four hours before the two-way radio squawked its message.

The ear-splitting clang and bang of sledgehammers breaking free the oversized padlock wasn't lost on Hughie's ears or senses. But when they'd finally smashed open the warehouse doors, all they found was lots of dark dank empty air.

"Judging by the cobwebs and dirt in the door tracks, I'd say this place hasn't been used in months, Sir."

Tufty acknowledged the observations of the officer charged with breaking into the warehouse, whilst staring into the vast cavenous interior. "Take the wagon driver in for questioning Brady and while you're at it, check with the other firms around here. Maybe they saw or heard something."

"Highly unlikely, Sir."

"I know," he growled. "But we have to start somewhere. So don't just stand around scratching your arse, go through the frigging motions!" He then turned his attention to the empty warehouse and the darkening sky above. "Looks like there's rain in the air; tell Forensics to move this lot inside and open up the container. They can spend some time dusting it down for prints and see what's really hidden amongst the boxes." Two more tortuous hours went by before Tufty eventually received the report. "Huge amount of Cocaine, Hashish and Barbiturates, all neatly packed within the bedroom furniture, Sir. Actual street-value? Difficult to say, but I reckon it has to be somewhere around a million quid."

A stunned McClellan stared into the rear of the packed container and shook his head. Other than the late-night telephone call and mystery voice that instructed. *Make sure you keep everyone focused on the Cedar Post;* Hughie was completely unaware of what was happening elsewhere. Then suddenly realised that this huge and very expensive cache of drugs was always meant to be discovered. *Who in their right mind would sacrifice this lot,* he mused *and I wonder what the frigging hell is going to happen next?*

The painful answer was to come a week later.

Manchester Airport
May 1982

The bride was a little worse for wear and the plastic Tiara perched on her head was beginning to slip sideways. Yet to her credit, she'd still managed to perform a perfect pirouette in the middle of the airport bar whilst holding a gin and tonic in one hand and a cigarette in the other. This in turn had helped highlight her gold striped tee shirt, gossamer wings and silk sash with the words 'Queen Bee' splashed across the front. Applauding her valiant efforts, sat her half-inebriated entourage, who were all similarly dressed, but had 'Female Drone' emblazoned on theirs.

Three drink-filled tables away swayed the groom whose lager-stained outfit depicted him as a somewhat overweight 'Batman'. Keeping him company in his hour of need, were twenty of his masked acolytes, all of whom were drunk as skunks and dressed as 'Robin', his ever-faithful sidekick.

Yet neither of these celebrity offerings were destined to meet at the altar in a pact of holy-wedlock. She was about to wing her way to Benidorm in Spain and star in the ultimate Hen Party. And unbeknown to her, the beer-bellied Caped Crusader was about to board the same plane and have his Stag-Do in the same hotel. And although both groups were complete strangers, were still more than happy to exchange good-natured banter from across the busy lounge. Curious as to what was taking place, a mystified Maxi ordered a Heineken beer and asked the barman what was going on.

"Some Charter Airline has begun offering cheap flights to Spain, which as you'd expect were snapped up in next to no time. But what they didn't anticipate were two different wedding parties flying to the same place at the same time. "Should be some fun and games on the way," he finished with a smirk.

Listening to their brash noisy antics, Maxi was relieved to hear they wouldn't be keeping him company on his flight to Malaga. A glance in the bar's mirrored glass, revealed a casually dressed, closely shorn person, who adjusted his gold rimmed spectacles, collected his bottle of lager and went in search of some peace and quiet. Once he'd found solitude in a faraway corner, Maxi sipped his drink, smiled and recalled his early morning chat with Sandra and Steffi in Marbella.

The Spanish weather forecast had promised clear blue skies, Finca Bougainvillea was waiting to welcome him home and both girls sounded happy living their new life in the sun. With plenty of time to spare, he sat back, relaxed and let his mind roam over the ups and downs of the past few months. The complex jigsaw puzzle he'd created had been a long time in the planning and decidedly expensive on the pocket. There'd also been one or two occasions when it'd seemed an almost impossible task to accomplish.

However, with the unexpected and fortuitous arrival of Tufty McClellan, all such doubts had been summarily banished. With a renewed sense of confidence, they'd forged ahead with their plans, which in essence was all about Latitudes and Longitudes; the destination of the two wedding parties in the bar being a perfect example. They were going north and he was flying south.

For as long as he could remember, Toby Blizzard had managed to transport his 'Goods' from a range of different places and in many strange guises; but mostly within the ubiquitous shipping container. With this in mind, Maxi had decided that this one last throw on the wheel of fortune, should be no different from their normal tried and trusted method.

The plan had entailed them using the 'Mercier,' a refrigerated container vessel, regularly used in the shipping of fresh Florida produce to the UK. The ship would depart Miami docks at an exact time and date and track its way north, whilst hugging the Eastern-Seaboard on the first part of its journey. On reaching Latitude 30, it would then turn due east and follow a well-ploughed sea-lane across the Atlantic Ocean; it's ultimate destination, Liverpool Container docks five days later. However, in order to achieve this goal, their modus operandi involved secreting the Cocaine deep within one specific fruit-filled container. On a normal drug run, it had always been a case of 'wait and see.' However, this one last shipment was different, its size and value being so much greater than anything that had gone before. But even with Tufty on board, Maxi was loath to risk everything on this one last throw of the dice.

So following many hours of long-distance discussions, he and Toby had decided to create a smokescreen by introducing another container, filled with a much smaller amount of drugs. They'd also agreed to ship the container on a separate vessel, which they'd termed 'the decoy boat.' This, they hoped, would switch any unwanted attention from Miami, to further up the Coast and the port of Baltimore, where 'Cedar Post', the unsuspecting vessel lay. She might be a much larger container ship, but was also destined for England and Liverpool docks.

In order to complete this particular tricky piece of the puzzle, the 'Mercier' needed to depart Miami two days prior and time it's run so as to follow behind in its bigger counterpart's wake. The need for immaculate timing was imperative it also required a close attention to shipping detail, absolute secrecy; and whilst each of these factors had been important pieces of the puzzle, the latter would always be a major problem. "People like to talk," Toby had warned. "And we have to make sure the fuckers don't!"

Another important factor in making the plan work was the Baltimore drug dealer, who at the last minute had decided to spill the beans regarding the dummy container. In return for giving The Feds a raft of detailed information about the Baltimore shipment, the dealer's lawyer had managed to negotiate a sizable reduction in his jail sentence. The slam of the cell door and the turn of the key were unable to wipe the smile off the dealer's face, as he visualised the pot of gold awaiting him when he walked free in eighteen months' time. Each detailed action had been carefully orchestrated in setting the trap, which the police on both sides of the Atlantic had readily walked into.

Still, some jigsaw pieces didn't come cheap and the sacrifice of the Baltimore container, with its one million pounds worth of drugs was testament to all that. Nevertheless, the welcoming sight of twelve large pre-packed cases of Cocaine, hidden deep within the consignment of fresh oranges on the Mercier had been more than enough to compensate their loss.

Maxi stubbed out his cigarette and finished his drink on hearing a loud cheer from The Gotham gang; apparently their plane was ready to board. It was also ironic that his own flight-path would take him over The Channel Islands, the very place where most of the proceeds from the haul now lay. Ten days earlier, a coach-load of golfers carrying their bulky clubs and suitcases, had arrived by ferry looking to spend a few relaxing days at the Grand Hotel in Jersey. Having personally organised the trip, BB Benson took the opportunity to drop in at the GKG Bank in St. Helier, to offload fifteen of the suitcases and have an important and very fruitful meeting with a certain Herr Dunkledorf.

Part Six

Liverpool 2015 Southport

The idea was to park on the driveway and creep up to his bedroom without being seen, but sadly this plan had hit the buffers the moment the study door opened and his angry wife appeared in view. He couldn't remember the last time he'd seen the pink hairnet she wore to bed at night, or the layer of cold cream covering her face and with an accusing finger point him towards his own leather-bound chair. "What's going on, Hughie?"

He was tired and badly in need of sleep, but something in her voice warned him to be careful; Cressie was not one to be ignored when in this mood. He was about to say. 'There's no problem, hen,' when she held up a hand to interrupt him.

"Don't give me that bullshit!" She snapped, one finger tapping the desk like a woodpecker's beak. "Do you think I'm such a fool that I can't see there's something strange happening around here?"

In all the years they'd been together, Tufty couldn't remember a time when his prim and proper wife had ever spoken to him in this tone of voice and she wasn't finished yet. "All this business with the mobile phone and newspapers and who the frigging hell is this 'TOG' person?" Once again, he'd been shocked at her casual use of his favourite swear word, but astonished to find she must have read the text message from Hamilton.

Peering across the room, his weary blood-shot eyes reflected on what sat before him. To say their marriage had been one of convenience could only be stating the obvious; necessity being a more descriptive term of their conjugal bonding. At the time, she'd been in desperate need of money and he, the cloak of everyday respectability.

They'd met at some long forgotten social function and been attracted to each other almost at once. She hailed from Chester, was devoid of good looks and had a face that some unkind people whispered *would stop a clock.* It would also be remiss of him to say she dressed unfashionably and was half way down the road to becoming a permanent spinster. But what she did have in plenty, were lots of chortling, snooty, countryfied horse-loving snobs, she called friends and in whose exalted company she forever seemed to circulate. He on the other hand, was a Jock loner, who when it came to looks, peered into the same unforgiving mirror as she did. However, following his fruitful visit to Jersey; was now quite a rich man, albeit a very secret one. Yet, none of this newfound wealth mattered a jot; not unless he was able to provide a reasonable explanation as to its sudden appearance in his bank account and at the time Cressida had looked to be the perfect answer. Her widowed father, who'd recently passed away, was reputed to be a well-known businessman living within a large luxurious family home and she'd never wanted for anything in her plush pampered life.

Their wedding she'd also insisted should be a large expensive noisy affair with plenty of fuss, which Tufty had reluctantly paid through the nose for. But it was only when they'd returned home from their honeymoon did he learn the real truth; Cressida was well and truly frigging skint! Over the years, her darling daddy had spent all their money, plus her inheritance on wine, women and gambling; and in the recent past, secretly re-mortgaged the house twice! There'd also been talk of another illegitimate sibling appearing out of the woodwork, whilst looking to claim a share of her pittance. But luckily, a bristling Cressida had managed to stand her ground and fight off this greedy unknown marauder.

Still none of this mattered because in a few months' time, the bailiffs were ready to move in and repossess the house, meaning she had no choice other than to sell up and vacate the place. Frantic that her reputation and good name were about to end up in tatters, she'd decided that a now wealthy Hughie would fit the bill nicely. When Cressida's paucity with the truth had eventually come to light, it had been truly hard for Tufty to swallow, even more so when he got to see the full extent of her financial situation. All that guff she'd pumped out about how good her father was, had been just so much hot air and made his Aberdeen blood boil!

Yet, when he thought about it in the cold light of day, had to admit that his bed was already made; they were married and she was going nowhere, which left him no other choice than to bite the bullet and move on. Having said that, their union had proved to be a quite an advantageous one and other than the rare occasion when he'd unsuccessfully tried to 'get his leg over,' things had ticked along nicely. 'Cressie' as she liked to be known, had been more than adept in guiding him throughout his fledgling career. She had never once asked questions about their finances, but was steadfast in how best he might succeed in reaching the top.

"Be a winner!" She'd drummed into him a thousand times; this same dogma being repeated, even when he'd reached the ultimate pinnacle of politician. Over the years, her influence and shrewd advice had been everywhere, even to the point of instructing the TV make-up girl how best to portray his image. "Make sure his oily skin doesn't reflect the light!" She would insist. Yet Tufty had always been more than happy to have a 'glossy trotter', his late grandma's term for his veined and shiny nose.

It was also around this time that he'd first encountered Cressie's dreaded OCD and the strict rules that must be adhered to. If an object or piece of furniture were positioned in one particular spot, then there it would stay 'Ad Infinitum' until she'd stopped polishing it or deemed otherwise. The buttons on his tunic shone like new and the peak of his cap glistened like a beacon in the morning sun.

But his wife's real asset was the many people she knew and her natural ability to socialise. A once taciturn and friendless Tufty suddenly found himself being introduced to some very influential individuals, who Cressie regularly clinked glasses with. Locked doors had opened wide, opportunities appeared from nowhere and just like in the movies, his star began to rise in the sky.

Looking at her crease-lined face across the desk, he had to admit that he would never have gotten to where he is today without her driving input.

"So who is it?" she snapped, bringing him abruptly out of his reverie.

"Maxi Hamilton," he muttered.

"Hamilton the millionaire?" she gasped.

Tufty nodded.

"What does he want?"

"He wants me to find out who killed his granddaughter; one of the two kids murdered last week in Waytree Park."

A puzzled expression appeared on her creamy white face. "I don't get this Hughie, you're not a policeman anymore, you're retired."

"I know that and so does he. But due to him not being an immediate family member, he wants me to get close to the investigation and tell him how it's progressing."

Cressida was still looking confused. "I still don't understand any of this, nonsense, he's her grandfather, so why the hell would he ask you?"

"Hamilton's always had problems with the girl's mother and if I don't help him, he's threatening to expose something from my past."

Cressida's eyes narrowed as she took this in. "What could he possibly know about you that I don't?"

It was an almost cathartic moment as Tufty began spewing forth all that had been hidden away for so many years and without pausing, told her everything.

She never moved a finger or spoke a word, as he took her step by step through his fatal move from Scotland, the goods in the car, Mick O'Hara, the Tribunal, his dealings with Maxi Hamilton, who was also TOG and of course, the bank account in Jersey. But he never once mentioned his encounter with Amber, that was an exquisite experience he would share with no one!

When done, he awaited the fire and brimstone that was surely meant to follow. Yet it never arrived and only then did he realise his wife was deep in thought. Cressida, however, was silent only because she too could remember some of her more liberal friends from the seventies, who in their stupidity, had also played around with drugs. But to discover that the famous Maxi Hamilton— a person who she'd wanted to meet on so many occasions -was somehow involved, well that part of this business was beyond belief!

"When did you say this took place?"

"Thirty-four years ago."

Which, she realised, was just before they married. "When this 'Baltimore Switch', as you call it was over, did you actually receive any more money from Hamilton?"

Tufty shuffled uneasily in his chair and shook his head. "No, nothing from him personally, but £110,000 *was* deposited in the Jersey bank account in the June of the same year and that was the last money I ever received."

Cressida blinked at the amount, but carried on regardless. "So before these latest series of meetings, how long has it been since you last spoke to Hamilton?"

"Thirty-four years."

"Are you telling me that you never met him at any other time, even socially?"

"Strangely enough, no. Although, as part of the deal, I'd always expected him to plague me on a daily basis for inside information on our drug operations. But following 'The Switch,' he simply vanished from sight, rumours saying he'd been holed up somewhere in Spain for a few years. It wasn't until late 1988 that I discovered he hadn't really gone anywhere. There was an article in The Times showing Margaret Thatcher opening a new office block in London and standing amongst the crowd in the background was Maxi Hamilton. I couldn't believe my eyes, but a few discreet phone calls informed me he was expanding all over Europe and one of his company's actually owned the SEL building on the Liverpool Waterfront Development."

"Did the police ever investigate him when he reappeared?"

"Why should they? When it came to covering his tracks, no one did it better than Hamilton. Besides, it was in my own interest not to 'rock the boat' and bring anything from the past to their attention."

'What about the missing file?"

"It's in a safe-deposit box at the bank."

Cressida shook her head. "I'm finding it hard to imagine you never met each other in all that time."

Tufty smiled. "Whether it was planned or otherwise, we would never have appeared at the same function and if by chance this situation came to pass, we would simply have made a point of avoiding each other."

It was now Cressida's turn to shake her head and smile resignedly. "When we first met, you said you'd made lots of money by playing the Stock Market and like a fool I believed every word of it."

"I wasn't telling lies," he insisted. "And I didn't set it up. Some clever clogs working for Hamilton opened an account with a London Stockbroker with the sole intention of helping me move my money around. He'd also bought ten grand's worth of quality shares for me to play about with. The trick was to transfer funds from Jersey into the trading account; play the market for a while; make some money and then move it on into my current bank account in England. All of which was perfectly legal and wouldn't arouse any suspicions. But one thing I can say, hen, over the years we have made a considerable amount of money by wheeling and dealing; hedging being one of my better skills."

"I didn't know you had a secret offshore account in Jersey?"

"I don't any more. Following the 9-11 catastrophe in America, offshore funds and hidden money became associated with terrorism, meaning everybody had to come clean; the legal banks included. Luckily for us and before it got too heavy in the later years, I'd managed to shift everything back to the UK."

Cressida's face wore an unconvinced expression. "I always thought you were a bloody fool when I married you, Hughie McClellan, and tonight you've proved me right," she said derisively. "Nevertheless, I still want to know what you're going to do about this Maxi Hamilton business."

Tufty screwed his face up and took a deep breath. "I'm still not sure what to do."

"Well, I do; get to work tomorrow and find his granddaughter's frigging killer!"

S.C.U.

The ginger hair alone was enough to tell them who was standing in front of the Display Boards.

"How long has he been there, Guv?"

"Joanna reckons he was here at the crack of dawn."

The hackles on Jacko's neck rose like an angry tomcat on heat, as they walked towards him.

"Morning Hughie, everything okay?"

"Aye Nathan," he replied, a look of surprised guilt on his face. "I hope you don't mind me having a wee peek at how the murder inquiry is doing?"

"Of course not, as I said yesterday, we're happy to have you on board." Tufty gave an uneven smile and showed him the ID badge hung around his neck. (Bastion had obviously waved his magic wand and given him the seal of approval.) It guaranteed him access to the S.C.U. whenever he wanted. There was something, however, about the curmudgeonly Scotsman that Jacko didn't like: maybe it was because the ginger so-and-so could never remember his name.

"A few words in private, Nathan?"

Carson's eyebrows lifted in surprise.

"Repel all invaders," Jacko instructed Jason Junior. "We'll be out of reach for at least fifteen minutes."

Tufty nervously fingered a large grey folder before he spoke. "For the past few years, I've been contemplating writing my memoires and calling them 'The Drug Busting Scot'." Pausing for a reaction, of which there was none. "I was also searching amongst a pile of old paperwork and came across some scribbled notes regarding an imaginary incident that supposedly happened in the early eighties." Laying it on the desk. "But when I say 'scribbled', what I really mean is badly written scrawl. A lot of it is practically indecipherable and I can only imagine that whoever did it was frigging drunk at the time. Nevertheless, I've managed to type up some of the finer points so both of you can read it," passing them a copy each.

The typing was poor, to say the least, but both knew that when in the Force, Tufty would have had a full-time secretary to do this stuff for him, even when he was inebriated.

"Most of it refers to the aftermath of a failed drugs operation and the on-going search for those who involved. But as you can see and for obvious reasons, there's no mention of those suspected of being involved."

Jacko and Carson eyed each other across the room; acutely aware the main suspect was Maxi Hamilton.

"The first page relates to the sudden flow of cocaine across the country and the whispers about those who supposedly supplied it." He then spent another minute droning on about the inevitable backlash and repercussions, before

249

continuing. "The authorities were convinced that the culprits had already disappeared to the sandy shores of Iberia and seeing as there was no agreed Extradition Treaty at the time, were able live a life of luxury far from the reaches of justice. It was common knowledge that most of the scumbags were holed up on the northern shores of Costa del Crook, but it seems our wee birds had winged their way much farther south."

Once again, Jacko and Carson's eyes met; this was definitely new territory.

"You can see in the next part, that something important came to light when most of the fuss had blown over. This was in 1984, when a Warrington farmer decided to unlock the doors to whoever had rented his packing shed for the last two years. This unknown person had paid £1000 cash in advance for the said period, but was never seen again. The story goes that the mystery man had been restoring a vintage car and needed somewhere safe to store the valuable spare parts. But when the farmer had cut through the massive padlock with a blow-torch, all he found was a sealed shipping container sat on the back end of an articulated trailer."

Another piece of the puzzle conveniently fell into place and Jacko who'd been trying to read from the typed script, realised it was easier and more entertaining to listen to Tufty's vocal version.

"The container was padlocked shut in the exact same way as the shed, but the farmer who normally sprayed his fields with a lethal mixture of cow dung, thought he could smell something much stronger leaking from within the metal box. His suspicions being aroused, he then decided to get the police involved. When they'd eventually managed to cut it open, all they discovered were boxes upon boxes of decayed oranges.

"The biggest surprise, however, came when a check of the container's serial number had revealed it was one of three unloaded from a boat inbound from Florida two years earlier. Two of the containers had succeeded in arriving at their true destination, a Liverpool Fruit and Vegetable wholesalers, but the other one had literally vanished. That is until they found it festering in the shed and it was too late to do anything about it."

Jacko couldn't help but smile as he listened to McClellan's tale; which appeared to be no different from yesterday's story of the decoy container on Croxteth Trading Estate. There was no denying that the whole setup had been very well thought out and superbly executed.

"Any trace of the Drugs?" asked Carson.

Tufty gave him a knowing look. "What frigging drugs?"

Carson gave a slight tip of his head. "While we're on about missing items, I see you've mentioned the mystery file."

"I was just coming to that," he muttered. "And as I said yesterday, there's nothing to connect the recipient with the drugs trade."

"But there was a file of some kind?"

"Aye, there was a file that went missing from records."

"Do you know what was in it?"

Tufty wrinkled his nose before speaking. "It was mostly background stuff on the early days in Liverpool and the territorial battles between two warring factions."

"Can I assume it involved drugs?"

"What frigging drugs?"

Carson remembered Archie Speed mentioning the street battles. "Do you think the two dead kids might have something to do with the fight for drug territory?"

"Nay way, it's too long ago in my opinion."

"What else was in the file?"

"There was a photograph of a certain person getting married outside Liverpool's Registry Office and lots of other bits and pieces."

"When did the file go missing?"

"Sometime between 82 and 84."

Carson paused. "How can you be so sure?"

"Because someone made a final entry just after The Baltimore Switch took place which was in April 1982. After that, there was no need to look again, well not until the so-called recipient re-appeared some years later, but by that time the file had vanished."

Carson sat back in his chair. "Any idea who might have taken it?"

Tufty shook his head slowly. "You tell me Nathan; this person had lots of friends in high places, even back then."

"Excuse me, Sir, can I ask a question?"

Tufty's head swung reluctantly in Jacko's direction. "What's your name again, laddie?"

"It's DC Sam Jackson and he's my cuffin second in command!" growled Carson.

Tufty could sense the degree of edginess and decided a change of tack might help. "What's your question, Sergeant?"

"It concerns Sandra Hamilton and how much the police really knew about her death."

"They were fully aware she'd been shot dead in America."

"Would this information have also been in the file?"

Tufty nodded. "I believe so."

Jacko's eyes narrowed. "Forgive me, Sir but what I can't understand, is why there was so little publicity for such a high-profile incident."

"Well laddie, that probably depends on how careful you were when doing your homework!"

The Grosvenor Bar

"Cuffin' Spain?" spluttered Carson.

"I can understand you being pissed off, Guv, but when you think about it, Maxi Hamilton didn't tell any lies at the interview."

"Oh yeah?" he growled. "Well, I'd say he was being less than economical with the truth. Especially when he forgot to mention that before his wife was shot dead in America, they were both living in Spain. Plus the fact he'd managed to ship her body back to Marbella and bury it in his own cuffin backyard!"

"Must have cost a bloody fortune in bribes," whistled Jacko.

"And what about him telling the British Consulate in Miami he wanted no adverse publicity," Carson added caustically.

Jacko nodded. "That would probably explain the lack of press coverage in the English newspapers. And it looks as if Joanna was right about the ugly sister kidnapping Hamilton's young daughter."

Jacko's mention of Joanna and the absence of the other Team members had Carson feeling almost guilty; he regarded them more as friends than colleagues. Yet, this clandestine meeting was all about Tufty's surprise involvement in the investigation and the constrictions they now found themselves under. In his wisdom, Bastion had insisted that any information concerning Maxi Hamilton must first pass across his desk before being released into the public domain; the other Team members included.

This official 'straitjacket' had left them with little room to manoeuvre, particularly when it came to telling the Team about Hamilton's shady past life. But there'd been more headaches along the way, especially with Tufty's latest revelations of his long-held vendetta against the former drugs baron.

Jacko meantime was still confused, but for slightly different reasons. Their earlier chat with the ex-policeman turned politician had been an eye opener to say the least and his intimate knowledge of Maxi's past even more so. Yet how could he possibly have known about The Baltimore Switch? Or, against all odds, the fact Hamilton had managed to repatriate his late wife's body to their Estate in Spain and not the UK as first thought.

"Don't you find this whole McClellan business a bit strange, Guv?"

"In what way?"

"To be honest, I'm not really sure myself, but unless Tufty was running a covert surveillance operation throughout 1982 and onwards; I don't see how he could have known that whilst Hamilton lay in a Miami hospital bed. His wife's sister who was supposedly looking after his daughter in Spain, had taken her back to Liverpool with the intention she never returned."

Carson said nothing, but still listened.

"He seems to know all about these events from thirty-three years ago as if he'd read them in this morning's papers."

"Don't forget, Jacko, we are talking about the famous 'Tufty McClellan'. If he says that's what happened, then we have no choice other than believe him."

"Okay, I can swallow that, Guv, but considering he's so famous, why doesn't he just come clean and tell the world about Hamilton's involvement in this Baltimore Switch business?"

"Maybe it's because he's about to publish his memoires. I can just imagine the uproar in the press, if an ex-politician admitted to taking part in the huge cover-up that followed. He'd be selling books for all the wrong cuffin' reasons!"

La Rondo Penthouse

Michaela awoke with a start, her inner senses telling her that something was wrong. Slipping from the between the sheets, she crossed the room, opened the door and stepped out into the hallway. La Rondo at night was a complex mixture of light and shade; a true reflection of everything its creator had hoped it would be. Still unsure as to what had woken her she padded along the corridor until she reached the open lounge area. Once there, she looked up towards the Crow's Nest and gave a sigh of relief when she saw Maxi hunched over the coffee table.

He'd been late in returning to the apartment last night and instead of going back to her place, she'd decided to stay over. She was also about to climb the steps and have a word with him, when she heard a strange noise. For a second she thought Maxi was leaning forward as if to read something on the table. Then realised he was in fact taking in great gulps of air and sobbing like a child. Her first instinct was to go to him and try to help ease the pain in his time of need. But something inside had told her not to. Staying still, she listened in the shadows for a moment longer, before softly retracing her steps to the bedroom. Closing the door as quietly as possible, she crossed the room, slipped beneath the covers and waited for morning.

Maxi's bitter tears had long since dried, as he'd spent the night struggling to understand the reason for his granddaughter's brutal murder. "Why her?" he'd asked a thousand times! "Of all the people in the world, why did it have to be Kelly?"

Michaela rose with the dawn, made her way to the kitchen and began to make some fresh coffee. She was also relieved to see Maxi still sat where she'd left him a few hours ago. The Crow's Nest had always been one of her favourite places. A place where they would sit together and he would point to one particular buoy that spelt danger for anyone foolish enough to pass on its Western bow. A short beep from the machine interrupted her thoughts and carrying two cappuccinos, she climbed the steps and joined him in the early morning light. Standing beside his chair, she closed her eyes and felt the warmth that only a new day would bring. But whilst she was enjoying the sunlight, Maxi reached for a slim folder on the table, and held it up so she might see. But the words he spoke next were both chilling and controlled. *"I swear to God that no matter how long it takes, or how much it costs, I'm going to find this bastard and kill him!"*

Many hours later and a distraught Michaela had continued to sob and weep as she remembered the horrific photographs of Kelly's mutilated body. Plus the all too harrowing details of Professor Reece Armstrong's autopsy report!

Maxi's Office, Steelyard Enterprises Ltd

The overcast skies above the River Mersey were a deep leaden grey, thus reflecting the sombre mood in the room, as they waited for Rupert Hawksworth Jones to finish reading the autopsy report. "Oh dear God," he whispered. "Who in their right mind could do such a thing to that beautiful young girl?"

Having read the same file, a grim-faced Clinton Levi could only shake his head in sympathy. In a chair near the window, a fuming BB Benson stared blankly through the glass, whilst Michaela, who was still trying to forget the brutal manner of Kelly's death, continued to dab at her eyes with a tissue.

Maxi waited a moment before speaking, "As you can see, McClellan has at last begun to provide us with some very important, if not disturbing, information regarding the murders. But the fool's so damn scared of being caught he refuses to write anything down, or meet with us face to face. And unbeknown to us, he dropped the camera and this pay-as-you-go mobile phone,"—holding it up for them to see—"in the downstairs mailbox yesterday morning. To further complicate the situation, he's insisting on speaking with Michaela only, which we hope should be at least once a week."

"Talk about over the top!"

"I couldn't agree more, BB, especially as Tufty's accent is not the easiest to understand. Yet in spite of this, Michaela has still been able jot it down and type it up later. Which we hope should be the start of a short but very fruitful relationship."

A look of relief filled their faces as Maxi spoke on. "Another thing, before reading the report, I'd been struggling to understand what Eazy Stoker's grandson was actually doing in the Park that night. But it seems he lived on the nearby Estate and might have been trying to save Kelly from whoever murdered her."

"Which if true, has to rule out revenge as being a possible motive for the killings."

"Yes, Clinton, and if the boy really was just another innocent victim, then we have no choice other than exclude Eazy Stoker from the list," said Maxi.

"But the report does conclude the attack was premeditated and perpetrated by some lunatic with a knife," growled BB.

"A Serbian lunatic," corrected Clinton.

"I've been giving that some thought Maxi and I was wondering if it's worth asking around the town. If there's a reward on offer, you can always guarantee someone will have seen, or heard something."

"Okay BB, but don't go over the top or we'll have every freak in Liverpool knocking on our door!"

"I'll do the carrot and stick routine by making it just large enough to tempt them out into the open."

Maxi was unsure if this particular tactic would work, but eventually agreed with a nod before continuing. "According to McClellan, someone named Vinny the Gecko witnessed the arrival of a white Transit van in the car park, but more importantly, managed to get a good look at the driver's face."

Rupert spoke for the first time, "Do we know anything about this Vinny person and is he a reliable witness?"

Maxi turned to BB. "Your department, I think."

"Our man's less than lily-white," he began, before giving them a brief run-down on the Gecko's sordid life.

"Judging by his track record, I imagine he'd be a reluctant witness in any kind of police investigation," said Maxi. "Even if it were a major murder inquiry."

"Do you think he knows more than he's told the police?" asked Rupert. "Who can say?" shrugged BB. "But I'm sure he makes a living from knowing other people's secrets."

"Then maybe it's time we invited him around for some tea and a friendly chat."

BB smiled, "Why not? I'll put the wheels in motion."

Maxi turned to Clinton and Rupert. "However, before we go any further gentlemen, I think it only right to warn you that I personally intend to pursue the monster who murdered my granddaughter."

Clinton's eyes narrowed over the top of his pince-nez glasses. "Considering the amount of evidence at their disposal, I should have thought the police were more than capable of such a pursuit."

"Unfortunately, I don't have your blind faith in their ability to achieve this task, no matter what the evidence might be."

"When you say 'pursue', am I to assume this road you intend to take might not be a strictly lawful one?" inquired Rupert.

"At this point in time, I can give no guarantees as to where the road may take me. However, I think you've known me long enough to appreciate that when I start something, I never leave it unfinished." The room was silent for a moment longer as they considered Maxi's declared intention of finding the killer.

"I wouldn't say I had complete trust in the ability of the police to find out who killed Kelly, but do you really think it wise to take the law into your own hands?"

"Yes, I do, Clinton. Because you, more than anyone, can appreciate how unjust it can be. How many times in the past have we read about some scumbag killer being sentenced to life imprisonment and then watch him stroll out into the sunlight six or seven years later free to do it all over again."

"I think each of us here can understand and feel your pain Maxi, but even in these tragic circumstances I would find it difficult to condone such a course of action. We are after all civilised men and this is a murder investigation."

The fact that Hawkeye had spoken on the matter took Michaela completely by surprise. He rarely voiced his opinion on anything other than some project he'd been planning.

Maxi however, was steely in his reply. "This is still a free country and you are perfectly entitled to your view Rupert. But that won't make me change my mind, or stop me from searching for whoever committed this heinous crime. I want real justice for Kelly and I'm going to make it my business to find out who killed her!"

"Then I suppose the only thing left for me to do, is wish you good luck in your endeavours. We've shared many a journey together, but I'm afraid this is one trip you and I won't be making."

"That's perfectly understandable, my friend, and I wouldn't want you to do anything that might in any way damage your reputation. Just forget you ever saw the autopsy file, or had this conversation here today and the same goes for you, Clinton. The last thing I need is for both of you to be caught doing something underhand. It might have been okay forty years ago, when we were all a touch more reckless in our dealings, but should anything untoward happen, I think the skills of both of you will be required to ensure SEL continues to run smoothly."

"Are we expecting something untoward to happen?" asked Michaela.

Maxi smiled and shook his head. "Of course not, it's just a figure of speech."

"I can agree in part with your views on retribution," Clinton began slowly, "but I'm still not sure about taking the law into your own hands."

Maxi reached across the desk and took a forensic close-up photo of Kelly from within the file. "The last time I saw and spoke to my granddaughter, she was a vibrant beautiful young lady who had everything to live for, but now she looks like this." Displaying the image before them. "And I don't give a shit about the law, Clinton; what I want is to kill the bastard who did this!"

The two men fell into a shocked silence as they contemplated the implications of this last statement: until Rupert spoke again. "Is there no other way of resolving this nightmare, Maxi? If you can identify the person responsible for Kelly's death, then God forbid, maybe we can pay someone to take care of it for us."

"You mean using a hired killer?" he replied without taking his eyes from the photograph. "That I'm afraid won't be enough to satisfy my blood lust. Every time I look at her face, I dread to imagine how much utter terror and fear she felt in those last few minutes of her life. It also tells me seek revenge and I want to see the same fear on the face of her killer before he dies."

"And then there were three!" exclaimed BB, as the door closed behind Clinton and Rupert.

"What happens now?" asked Michaela.

"Now? We begin to sift our way through all the information provided by Tufty McClellan. And even though it may look a little disorganised at the moment, there's always the chance the police might have missed some small clue or minor detail."

Merseyside Police Headquarters

Jacko was so engrossed in reading Zelda's text; he hadn't noticed the lift doors open or had seen the two senior officers until they were almost on top of him.

"Everything okay?" asked Carson. "I haven't seen you this happy in weeks."

Jacko's grin told its own tale. "Of course, Sir, it's because I've just received some very interesting news." Holding up his phone.

The Concord shape of Bastion's nose dipped in his direction. "If it's *that* interesting, Sergeant, then maybe you'd like to share the finer details with us."

"According to the text, Zelda Zamarova has landed at John Lennon Airport."

Carson was almost in shock. "The Bosnian Bird's here in Liverpool?" he said in near disbelief.

"Yes Sir, I've just this minute discovered she's here on a flying visit and touched down less than an hour ago."

"Where's she staying?"

"The Hilton on the Waterfront."

"Who's she again?" asked Bastion.

This was dangerous territory for the two detectives. The Superintendent had been hinting he'd pull the plug on the Yugoslavian side of the investigation unless they could produce some new and updated information.

"She's the journalist from Sarajevo who's been providing us with the background on the Serbian connection," Carson added cautiously.

"And I assume her sudden appearance in the city has to be of some significance?"

"I'm not exactly sure why she's here, Sir," replied Jacko. "As I understand it, she was on her way to a conference in Florida, when something happened to make her change her mind and divert through London."

"But you don't know why?"

Jacko hesitated. "There was some mention of a special package she intends to deliver to Liverpool Forensics."

"Do we know its contents?"

"No Sir," Jacko replied truthfully.

"What happens next?" asked Carson.

"I've arranged to meet her in The Hilton foyer this afternoon."

"Alone?" interrupted Bastion.

"No Sir, Simone Le Roux from Forensics will also be present."

"If my memory serves me correctly, this won't be the first time you've managed one of these secret trysts with the good lady?"

Jacko squirmed uncomfortably at the inference. "Hardly secret, Sir and yes, I admit our paths have crossed before, but this will be the first opportunity I'll get to meet Zelda Zamarova in person."

Carson, meanwhile, found he was having another of his jealous spells. "I assume you'll keep me informed of any further developments, Sergeant?"

The Anfield Gang

Libby's Fabulous Fish and Chip Parlour had stood proudly on the same street corner since the turn of the century. But sadly, once the Council's rejuvenation programme had literally *hit the streets*, a lack of paying customers and the necessary income to keep it going had ultimately signed its death knell. For those locals with long memories, the loss of her jovial face and range of tasty deep-fried delights felt more like losing a huge part of their childhood.

On the other hand, for 'Gibbo's Gang' the boarded up and graffiti covered shop was the perfect place to while away the hours and smoke a few joints. In a strange quirk of fate, Gibbo had been in the town centre shopping for a new pair of trainers, when he'd heard about the 'reward'. Thinking it was no more than a rumour, he'd casually let slip that he might know something and forgot all about it, until he received a rather unexpected call.

"Who is it?" asked fifteen-year-old Kevin the Duck.

"Dunno," he replied with a shrug.

"What do they want?" chirped Maggot, Gibbo's thirteen-year-old brother.

"According to them, they want to talk."

"When?"

"Ten minutes from now."

"Where?"

"Here."

"They're outside already," shouted Maggot, a finger pointing to the Range Rover as it slid to a halt on the other side of the street. Peering through the cracks in the window, the gang watched its unexpected arrival with a mix of wide-eyed curiosity and anticipation. But to some of the older members of the gang, the shiny vehicle opposite represented real money and power, as it glistened in the afternoon sun. Seeing no obvious signs of movement from within and unsure as to what might happen next, the gang began to do an involuntary soft-shoe-shuffle on the pavement outside the shop.

Then both front doors opened at once, the driver side revealing a tall immaculately dressed giant whose hair and moustache looked as black as the tarmac below his feet. The other a stocky, yet just as menacing figure who clambered from the passenger side and stood alongside him.

"I'm looking for a Terry Gibson," called the driver.

This came as a complete shock to the hoody in question, even more so when his younger brother shouted. "How does he know your name, Gibbo?"

"Shut up, arsehole!" he snapped, before replying defiantly. "Who wants to know?"

BB turned to Maxi who was watching from the back seat. "The mouthy one at the front is definitely Gibbo and judging by his cocky attitude, has to be the leader."

Everyone's expectations suddenly went up a notch when a different, but just as imposing figure stepped from the car and with the aid of a pair of gold-rimmed sunglasses, took in his shabby surroundings. Unsure of what might happen next, they were all thrilled to see this same stranger smile and say, "Hello boys, my name is Maxi and I assume you must be Gibbo?"

This one simple statement was all that was needed to put the hoodies at ease, yet more importantly give them a chance to claim the £200 reward. According to the rumour, the big guy with the fancy suit and glasses would gladly fill their boots, but only if they had the right answers.

"I've heard you might know something about a certain van," prompted Maxi.

Gibbo who could see his own reflection in the sunglasses nodded once. "Around the corner, two streets away."

"Show me," instructed Maxi.

BB nodded in the direction of the Range Rover, where a shaven-headed Turbo casually parked his rear against the gleaming radiator grill, folded his arms and watched them disappear from view. The young hoody led the way, the rest of the gang following behind like a scene from the Pied Piper. A two-minute walk saw them arrive on the corner of what was a typical suburban street, with a row of two story-terraced houses and street parking on either side. The youngster came to a halt. "It was here," he declared, his finger pointing to where a black Fiat Estate was now parked.

"What make of van?" asked Maxi, his eyes calculating the length of the street.

"White Ford Transit with two ski bars," he replied, the rest of the gang nodding along in agreement.

"Describe what happened and try not to forget anything. The smallest detail might be of importance!"

"Joey was first to notice him on Saturday afternoon," Gibbo began, turning to a face that matched the name. "Yeah," the thirteen-year-old agreed in his singsong Scouse accent. "I can remember seeing him driving up and down the streets. He looked as though he was going to the footy match and needed somewhere to park."

"What happened next?"

"We saw the same van parked here later in the afternoon," replied Gibbo.

Maxi and BB exchanged knowing glances on hearing this little gem. "That's right," chirped Joey. "And I knew straight away that it wasn't from anywhere around here."

"How?" asked BB.

"The disused tax disc holder in the corner of the windscreen said it was from somewhere down south and it sort of smelt different."

"Which is why we decided to turn it over when it got dark," added Gibbo.

Looking around, Maxi could see five boarded up properties at this end of the street, which would ensure a certain amount of privacy, especially with a few lookouts posted. "Keep talking," he ordered. "That was it. When the football game was over, the driver came back." Gibbo replied with a shrug.

"I need more!" Maxi insisted.

Gibbo took a stab at explaining what happened next. "We'd been trying to open the van doors, when one of the boys spotted him heading in our direction on the other side of the street. He sort of ducked out of sight for a second, reappeared, crossed over and began walking towards us."

"What did he look like?"

"The man in black!" Maggot whispered dramatically.

"What he means," Gibbo butted in, "is all his gear was either dark grey or black. Black sunglasses, a short bomber jacket, grey trousers and black boots!"

"What about his face? Did you get a good look at it?"

"No, not really." Gibbo replied lamely. "He looked like the picture of the guy in the Liverpool Echo, but without the red and white hat. This one was wearing a dark beanie and a pair of sunglasses that covered most of his face."

"I remember him having a thick black stubbly chin," declared Joey. "And thought he was a foreigner: you know, a spic or something."

"He didn't speak?"

The two of them shook their heads negatively "Never said a word."

"What happened next?"

"We waited to see what he might do."

"And?" asked Maxi, encouraging them to continue.

"He got close, offered us the keys and we thought that was it. Then this massive long knife suddenly appeared from nowhere."

Maxi caught BB's eye for a second "Why would he pull a knife; did he have a reason?" The gang began to shuffle nervously at this line of questioning, until Gibbo opened his coat and revealed the small dagger hidden inside.

For a second Maxi's attention was focused on the large Band-Aid plaster stuck beneath the hoody's chin, but in the end decided to ignore it.

"Tell me more about the knife."

"It was a long thin fucker; the blade alone must have been at least twelve inches to the tip. He began to move it from side to side, as though warning us not to get too close. His eyes never left us, even when he climbed in and started the engine."

Maxi waited expectantly.

"No one was going to try and jump him, man," the hoodie whined in defence. "He was like fucking Errol Flynn with that sword in his hand!"

"Move on, move on!" urged a frustrated Maxi.

"That was it!" Gibbo cried, whilst hoping it was enough. "I'm not sure if he even blinked. He just opened the van door, climbed in and drove off down the street."

Maxi stepped into the middle of the road, staring to where it met the busy traffic passing by in the distance. "Licence plate, did you get a number?"

A pregnant pause hovered in the air above the scruffy ensemble. "Fucking hell mister," Gibbo whined uncertainly. "We don't read them; we just steal them!"

"Holy hell," Maxi groaned in desperation.

The frustration and disappointment in his voice sent the gang's expectations plummeting like a spent rocket on bonfire night!

"Did anyone get a licence number?" Gibbo pleaded, his voice reaching near comic proportions!

Maxi waited for a reply, his own expectations disappearing as he realised the hoodie couldn't possibly provide all the answers he needed.

"One last question. When he reached the end of the road, which way did he turn?"

The gang began to argue amongst themselves as they tried to remember the exact events of that day. "He turned left onto Breck Road!" they declared as one.

"They're right, they're right!" Gibbo shouted in desperation. "He definitely turned left towards Anfield!"

Maxi and BB's eyes met, both of them realising the implications of this news. If the killer had intended to reach the M62 by taking that route, it also meant him passing Waytree Park and Highwater!

"Pay them, BB," Maxi said quietly and walked away.

Zelda and Milos

An intrigued Jacko met Simone outside John Lewis Store in Liverpool One. "What's going on, Professor?"

"No idea," she replied. "I'm as confused as you are with all this cloak and dagger business."

"Hope springs eternal?"

Simone gave a shrug. "I can only think it's Zelda's way of telling us she's found something to do with the investigation."

Jacko continued to speculate as they cut through Thomas Steer's Way and made for the tall imposing structure known locally as The Hilton on the Docks. "If she did decide to change her plans and deliver it in person, then it has to be something important!"

"Relax," smiled Simone, as she headed for the leather seated reception area. "I'm sure all will be revealed in good time."

Bastion's remark regarding the 'secret trysts' wasn't the only thing playing on Jacko's mind. His brain was also finding it hard to pin-point Zelda's glamorous image on the Skype screen; would she look and sound as sexy in real life? Another conundrum concerned her lower half, which he had to admit, had remained virtually unseen throughout all their conversations. What if she was a short-legged, midget-like famous journalist? Jacko wasn't sure if he was really ready for that.

In the meantime, an unruffled Simone was more like the 'River Mersey' on a calm day, as she casually flicked through the pages of an in-house 'fashion' magazine. He on the other hand had assumed 'the Bird from Bosnia' would be unpacking her bags in one of the penthouse suites and decided to focus on the high-speed lifts whistling up and down between floors. This particular ploy had lasted less than a minute, before Simone's painful poke in the ribs redirected his attention to the statuesque figure standing at the top of the illuminated glass staircase.

"I think our special guest has arrived," she whispered.

A sigh of relief left Jacko's lips. There can only be so many ways in this world to declare your presence and Zelda's stroll down the Hilton glass staircase had to be up there with the best!

An exotic mix of honey spun tawny hair and gold highlights had been casually arranged above her head and other than the odd hanging tress, the rest was held in place by a large bronze needle. He was also wondering if award-winning Bosnian journalists normally wore black tight-fitting leather jackets; complimented by a pair of sprayed on jeans that disappeared into stiletto high ankle boots. The only other splash of colour needed to complete the ensemble came from the bright yellow silk scarf she'd casually draped across her shoulders.

With a few lights and cameras, Jacko reckoned it could have been a scene from a movie shoot. He decided to hold back and watch from afar as Simone crossed the floor to meet her old school friend. The joy of their reunion was plain to see as they hugged and smothered each other in kisses; intermixed with some strange sounding greetings that Jacko might have heard before.

A further minute passed before they linked arms and made their way to where he stood.

"Sergeant Sam," she breathed as only Zelda could, "I've been so looking forward to meeting you."

There'd been lots of Skype visits when he'd had time to appreciate the finer points of the Bird from Bosnia. Yet as she took his hand, the simple act of them touching was quite a surreal moment. He was also close enough to smell her rich perfume and look into those deep penetrating eyes that had held him transfixed on so many occasions. However, the biggest surprise came when she leant towards him, kissed him softly on both cheeks and whispered in those deep sultry tones. "Hope Springs Eternal."

Jacko's head was still abuzz at this strange message and its possible meaning, when Zelda stepped aside to reveal an untidy looking male standing behind her. "Allow me to introduce Milos, my fellow traveller."

Chalk and cheese, would probably describe the difference between the two voyagers; she being the ultimate in glam, he wearing a black tee shirt and crumpled white linen suit that was seriously in need of a steam iron. He was about mid-forties and had blonde wispy thin shoulder length hair parted down the middle, (Jacko's mother used to call it 'curtain hair.') To cap it all, a waxed blonde moustache tried and failed to compliment his creased and dishevelled look.

Yet the name instantly resonated with Jacko, as he realised this had to be the Serbian reporter who'd found the connection with the charge sheet and Erdivos. The other outstanding feature was the trendy black wraparound sunglasses decorating his face.

Why would he be wearing a pair of shades indoors, crossed his mind, until Jacko realised their true significance. *Christ, they weren't just any old sunglasses, they were a pair of Terminators!*

Simone shepherded them all in the direction of the booths adjacent the bar saying, "Something tells me we're going to need a little privacy."

Jacko turned the sunglasses over in his hand. "Where did you find these?"

Zelda smiled broadly before replying in near perfect English. "I was browsing in a second-hand market last Sunday morning and spotted them amongst a pile of junk."

"Sarajevo?"

Zelda nodded.

"How did you recognise them."

"They were in this." Holding up a leather case with the gold letters 'VDO' embossed in the lid.

"*Viktor Dvoric Optika*," Jacko whispered reverently.

Simone was just as surprised. "I never thought in a million years we'd see a pair in such good condition."

"This is not the only gift we bring you," Zelda declared. "Milos has one of his own." It was only then did they notice the white cloth bag hanging over his shoulder and watch in silence as he produced a narrow three-foot long leather case from within.

"I have a feeling my fingerprints are all over this, but I'd be interested to see if there are any others," he whispered. Then, with a knowing smile placed it back in the bag and lay it on the table.

A smiling Zelda wasn't to be outdone in the surprise stakes, as she took the lid from a small decorated box and showed them a miniature Formula 1 racing car.

Jacko's disappointment was more than obvious when he saw the contents. "A toy car?"

"Yes Sergeant, but not just any old car. It's a memory stick and when I plugged it into my computer yesterday morning, found much of its contents had been encrypted." She placed the box in Simone's hand. "Which is why I need you to reveal its inner secrets."

"Couldn't your own people do this?"

Zelda smiled again. "One of the reasons you haven't heard from us has nothing to do with a lack of new information. It is more to do with a lack of trust in the Serbian security services, as well as the airwaves."

"You mean you're still being hacked?" asked a concerned Jacko.

"More like infiltrated!" spat Milos.

"But you don't know who?" asked Simone.

"We have some idea, but are unable to prove it at this moment," replied a grim-faced Zelda. "Which is why we decided to take a different tack, as you call it."

"Over the past few days, some remarkable information has come to light." Smiled Milos. "We were reluctant to send this via the normal channels for fear it might possibly be intercepted or destroyed."

"It's also why we changed our travel plans so we might deliver them in person," added Zelda. She then held up the miniature silver F1 car and split it into two. "I am confident this stick contains all the latest detailed information you need to move on with your investigation. Unfortunately, only half is readable, the rest I'm afraid is encrypted. Still, should you ever need it, I have all the original paperwork safely locked away in Sarajevo, but it should help you kick-start a search for the two suspects."

Jacko looked at Simone. "We need to get this downloaded and translated ASAP."

"I agree," she said with fervour.

"What are you going to do now?"

"We are off sightseeing!" declared Zelda.

"Sightseeing?"

"Of course, Sergeant Sam. When Milos heard I was coming to Liverpool, he immediately changed his itinerary to suit mine."

"Why?"

"He insisted on delivering his present to you in person. However, he's also a big Beatles fan and desperately wants to visit The Cavern in Mathew Street."

"I've always wanted to take a 'Magical Mystery' tour as well," he chortled out loud.

"But that is only one half of the day," Zelda said sweetly. "Tonight, we are going to listen to some real music in your famous Philharmonic Hall."

Jacko's brows lifted in surprise. "Who's playing?"

It was now Zelda's turn to raise her eyebrows. "Vasily Petrenko, of course."

"Are they a group?"

"No Sergeant," she said with a derisive shake of her head. "He just happens to be the Russian conductor of the Royal Liverpool Philharmonic Orchestra."

Jacko winced. *Definitely put your foot in it that time, mate!*

"It's a recital of 'Elgar's Symphony No. 2' which has been sold out for months," she continued as if it were common knowledge. "I was fortunate enough to acquire two tickets on eBay."

This was one musical recital he could gladly miss, thought Jacko; besides, he and Simone had more than enough to keep them occupied.

"When exactly do you leave Liverpool?" asked Simone.

"Wednesday at 8.30 am."

"Can I at least organise dinner for tomorrow tonight?"

Zelda nodded. "But only if we can go to the San Carlos Restaurant. I've heard the food there is excellent."

"And I would like to try a large Tomahawk steak with pasta!" declared Milos.

Jacko gave a smile. "Sounds good to me."

S.C.U.

Stretch Malone's morning had started badly; his piles were still playing him up and to make things worse, he'd only just been informed that the 9.00 am Site Meeting was happening later that day. However, it wasn't just his own routine that was *up the Swanny*. The rest of the Team had been ordered to 'drop what they were doing' and make an appearance. To add to the confusion, he'd heard a whisper that some of the top brass were coming to the party: which if true, meant something major was in the wind.

At precisely 5.00 pm, a tired looking Jacko—who throughout the day had been conspicuous by his absence—arrived back at base with a white cloth bag draped over his shoulder. In his wake, trailed the tall dark tasty bird from Forensics and a strange looking couple whom Stretch had to admit, he'd never seen before, but how to describe them? The moustachioed male, with shoulder length hair and white suit full of creases, could have just climbed out of the washing machine. Whereas the golden-haired blonde; whose perfume had begun to permeate every corner of the S.C.U., reminded him of a statuesque Venus de Milo wearing Pepe jeans. A closer inspection had revealed both were wearing Visitor lanyards and definitely not from these shores.

A buzz of expectation filled the room the moment Carson, Bastion and Hughie McClellan appeared in view; thus confirming something unusual was about to happen. Stretch took his usual front row pew, the rest of the Team crowding around with their pens and pencils at the ready.

Jacko, as always, played the role of ringmaster. "Sorry to keep you waiting," he said by way of apology; his eyes directed more towards the superior officers on his left. "But these last eighteen hours have been a stressful time for both forensics and the two decoders from Liverpool University, whom I might add, have been sweating blood to turn encrypted *gobbledy-gook* into some kind of readable English."

To those slaving away on the front line, Jacko's opening gambit sounded most intriguing, more so when he nodded towards his other guests.

"This lady is the award-winning Bosnian journalist Zelda Zamarova and her Serbian counterpart Milos Grojacic, who as you know, have been helping us solve the Park Murders. And I'm sure you're all familiar with Dr Simone Le Roux from the Lab?"

Some did and some didn't, but thought it best to nod along as Jacko pushed on. "So to bring our two visitors up to speed, I think we should briefly run over what current evidence we have."

Not again, Stretch groaned inwardly.

Jacko, however, was waiting to ambush the disgruntled detective at the pass. "Following which, we intend to unveil some exciting new evidence that our distinguished friends have brought with them."

This time, all heads were raised in interest.

"But first things first. For over a month, we've been trying to make a connection between the two teenagers murdered in Junkies Corner, the broken sunglasses and the white Ford Transit van," began Jacko. "The victims and the tragic circumstances of their deaths we all know about, but the fingerprints and bloodstains? That, I'm afraid is still ongoing. In the meantime, Forensics have confirmed that the prints on the broken arm were fresh at the time of the murders, which suggests the killer or killers took the rest of the frame with them. We've also discovered that the glasses were actually manufactured by a company called Victor Dvoric Optika in Yugoslavia. Sadly, the factory that made them was destroyed during The Bosnian Wars. Meaning it's impossible for us to prove exactly where the broken arm originated from."

Jacko gestured to his guests. "Thankfully, that particular problem was resolved when Zelda found an identical pair back in Sarajevo." Jacko passed Stretch the sunglasses with the V.D.O. lettering. "Try these for size mate, I reckon they should be a good fit."

The Team chuckled out loud, as Malone donned them with a flourish. "I'll be back!" He growled, as if imitating Arnold Schwarzenegger.

Jacko couldn't help grinning along as he continued his story. "We now believe that both pairs of glasses were made by the same factory in Bosnia. But that in itself doesn't prove there's a direct link between the fingerprints found on the broken arm and the person shown here," his finger pointing to the blonde youth staring from the chargesheet. "We were also wondering why he should suddenly appear on some strange classified Serbian website and then vanish from our screens. Smithy has spoken to the police in Erdivos on numerous occasions, who continue to insist they have no record of this person or the charge sheet."

A grumble of discontent was heard at this supposed wanton lack of cooperation.

Jacko, in the meantime, kept the fires burning. "Running out of viable options, we then contacted our two friends, who using their own time and resources, have since found a name for the suspect."

Zelda and Milo acquiesced with a brief smile.

Jacko pointed to the mug shot on the display boards. "I'll begin with him and bear in mind this photo was taken many years ago. We are now convinced this is one Luka Tomovic, a youth who supposedly hailed from Erdivos, a small rural town situated in Northern Serbia. He was also something of a mystery man until Milos visited this place in search of more information." Jacko focused his attention on the team of detectives.

"As you know, we all need a bit of luck in this business and it was definitely a jackpot moment when Milos met the drunk who remembered a huge altercation that took place in 1990 and identified Luka Tomovic as being the main protagonist on the night. This person had been arrested, placed in Police custody and charged with violently assaulting two people in that very same poolroom. But what the drunk couldn't explain was how this Tomovic had managed to escape from jail. He did, however, let slip that the suspect was also known as Ziggy and had later joined the Serbian army."

The Team ran their eyes across the familiar mugshot with renewed interest.

"We've also discovered that he's normally dark-haired and assume he acquired the nickname because of his blonde peroxide hair."

Joanna spent a moment imagining the face with a full head of mousey locks.

"Ziggy Tomovic, it seems, was never heard of again. Well, not until Milos and Zelda began to unearth a few very interesting facts and seeing as most of it is in Cyrillic, I thought it best to let them speak."

The Team were familiar with the usual Boffins and Shrinks, who regularly bored them to death. But this was beyond the norm and a look of genuine surprise crossed their faces, as the honey blonde bombshell and the untidy looking Serbian joined Jacko at the display boards.

Stretch raised his eyebrows and looked quizzically at Joanna, who could only shake her head in amazement and mouth back. 'This is pure theatre!'

Milos meanwhile, began the show by clearing his throat, parting his curtain hair behind his ears and addressing them in clipped English. "Trying to find a connection between this Ziggy person and your murder case, has proved to be an incredibly difficult task," he began. "The obstacles we encountered were many and difficult to overcome. But as Sergeant Sam said, you do need some luck in these matters." Everyone began to giggle as they realised Milos was talking about Jacko and had completely mis-interpreted their sniggers.

"Three days ago, I met some friends for a drink at a regular haunt in down town Belgrade. The bar was a busy crowded place, with a couple of pool tables in the corner and a particularly boisterous group of university students celebrating their end of term. Being in good spirits, they drank lots of beer and played a few games of pool, before eventually moving on elsewhere. However, two things happened prior to them leaving the bar. To record this momentous occasion, they gathered around the pool table and began to take a series of photos on their mobile phones. As they left the bar, my friends and I thought we'd seen the last of them, that is, until one of them came hurrying back. It transpired he'd forgotten the leather case containing his pool cue, which he gratefully collected and disappeared out into the night." Milos paused for effect. "As the student left the bar, I realised I'd witnessed something so important, that it sent me racing back in the direction of Erdivos the very next morning."

The Team suddenly began to focus on Milos' every word.

"My first port of call was the local high school and a chat with the head principal, Mr Tugonic. I said I was searching for Luka Tomovic, my cousin, who'd once lived in the town. He apologised and said he couldn't recollect the name, the reason being he'd only been employed at the school for the last five years. This particular pupil, he said, would almost certainly have been there long before his tenure. He'd also insisted he was very busy with the school exams and could spare me the minimum of time."

Milos came up for air, flicked a rogue tress behind one ear and soldiered on with his tale. "It suddenly occurred to me that he was becoming somewhat suspicious of my intentions, as well as my credibility; meaning I had to think on my feet. 'I don't suppose there are any old school photos hanging around?' I asked him. To which he replied. 'Yes, there are lots of them in the Assembly Hall; which particular year were you looking for?'" Milos' smile reflected his achievement.

"Two minutes later and I'm searching through the school's history screwed to the wall, but sadly didn't find what I was looking for. Then, as I was leaving I noticed the door to the Gymnasium was slightly ajar and thought it might be worth one last look inside."

Right on cue, Jacko took a large black and white photograph from a folder and held it up for all to see. "This is an official photo dated 1986 showing the school's senior football team." The gathering peered long and hard at the photo that was much too far away for them all to see properly.

Milos however, wasn't quite finished. "The person who we're looking for, is sixteen-year-old Luka Tomovic, the tall one who's fourth from the right in the back row."

A ripple of murmuring began to run through the ranks when Jacko held up his hand for quiet and once again pointed at the photograph. "So who is this footballer standing next to him, Milos?"

"That, Sergeant Sam, is his twin brother, Marko Tomovic."

Jacko couldn't help but smile at what came next. The Team's reaction was one of open-mouthed astonishment, as everyone realised the implication of this new development.

"Bloody hell!" exclaimed a flabbergasted Stretch Malone. "That has to be the reason for the matching fingerprint on the sunglasses, there's two of them!"

"Yes Frank, it would now appear that Ziggy has a twin brother," laughed Jacko. "But hold your horses because there's more to come: Milos and Zelda haven't quite finished yet."

The smiling Serbian, who'd been waiting patiently for the commotion to ease, continued with his story. "Leaving Erdivos, I purposely returned to the poolroom where the altercation had taken place; this being conveniently situated on the main road back to Belgrade. It was just before mid-day and other than a young barman cleaning glasses, the place was empty. I ordered a soft drink and in passing mentioned how popular a place it was. It had taken but a minute to discover he was new and had only worked at his job for a few weeks."

Another flick of the hair briefly interrupted Milos' tale. "From our chat it soon became clear that he had a limited knowledge of its former clientele; even less with visitors and strangers. Keeping it casual, I let him know that I'd regularly passed through the town and often stopped by for a game of pool. The blank look on his face confirmed we'd never met before and was the moment I popped the question. 'Do people ever forget their pool cues or leave them behind?' He thought for a second before replying, 'People are always forgetting their bits and pieces, why do you ask?'

"'I was in here playing pool a few years back, but when I went looking for my cue, I couldn't find it anywhere. It wasn't in the boot of the car, which had me thinking that maybe I'd left it behind.'

The young barman looked doubtful, 'As far as I know, any stuff we find usually ends up in the back store.' I gave him a pleading look. 'I don't suppose there's chance I might look around? It was my favourite cue.'

"'If it's got your name on it, mister, then I don't see any reason why you can't take it with you,' he replied."

Milos might be in need of a haircut and his suit badly in need of a dry clean, but he definitely knew how to keep everyone's attention. "The storeroom itself was a large musty place filled with a multitude of objects relating to pool. In one dark corner I noticed a pile of cue cases stood in a line, but having carefully searched through them all, found nothing. That is, until I spotted a dust covered object lying on a shelf next to the boxes of coloured balls."

Other than the odd telephone ringing in the background, the S.C.U. was silent.

"Would you please pass me the case lying on the table, Sergeant?" Jacko gave a nod and handed him the 3 ft. black oblong leather container. Milos held it up for all to see. "This case bears the initials 'L.T.' on the brass nameplate; but twenty-five years ago contained a two-piece 'screw together' pool cue." He then undid the small brass clip and let it fall open. "As you can see, the case has a couple of very noticeable features. Written boldly on the inside of the lid in a red felt pen, we can clearly make out the nickname 'Ziggy' and in this corner the letters 'SGD'. But more importantly, it's missing the two cue sections that would normally fit inside."

Jason Junior began to smile; he'd guessed exactly where this was all leading.

Milos returned the box to Jacko. "I'd be more than happy to continue with this tale, but I think Sergeant Sam here is better qualified to explain the real reason why the case is empty."

Jacko took up the story. "We've been led to believe that in October 1990, Luka Tomovic used his wooden cue to attack two innocent people in the poolroom. Having inflicted some serious injuries on both of them, he was later arrested, charged with the offence and taken into custody. This being true, we have to assume that the arresting police officers would naturally have taken the offending weapon with them as a form of evidence. It would also go a long way in explaining the now empty case."

The Team were scribbling away nicely, until Jacko brought them up short. "Yet, none of this means a damn thing when it comes to our murder inquiry; not unless we can find a link to the fingerprints on the broken sunglasses in Junkies Corner." A frown began to form on a few doubtful foreheads as Jacko's words sunk in, it was now his turn to hold up the cue-case and lift their spirits.

"When our own Swab Mob gave this a thorough going over, they found absolutely zilch! No prints, no DNA, nothing. The reason being that this type of faux leather case isn't disposed to absorbing the oily secretion normally found on the tips of your fingers. But a subsequent search of its interior, did reveal a small zipped pocket hidden within the lid's silk lining. Having been unsuccessful with the exterior, they weren't exactly expecting any miracles; until they discovered this."

Jacko held up the small see-through evidence bag, and a room full of eyes zoomed in on the red plastic Kraft knife inside. "Now I'm not a big pool fan, but I do know you should always chalk your cue before taking each shot. And allowing for general wear and tear, would naturally assume that whenever Ziggy needed to change the tip on his cue, this sharp-edged piece of kit would be the perfect tool for the job. Barring the fact that the last time he did it was around twenty-five years ago; he conveniently left behind a perfectly preserved thumbprint which we've since discovered matches the DNA beneath the seat at Anfield and the broken sunglasses found at our murder scene!"

A loud cheer of approval filled the room as they whooped and gave high-fives.

Jacko held up a hand to calm things down. "That's only the first part, people; there's still lots more to come. So go check your phones, grab a coffee and I'll see you back here in five minutes!"

The S.C.U. erupted in a babble of animated chatter, as fifteen detectives reconnected to the outside world and tried to absorb all they'd seen and heard.

Minutes before the designated deadline, the Team were already waiting for Milos to 'flick open the curtains' and tell them more. But to everyone's surprise, he suddenly turned another corner. "I think we can all agree that Liverpool is well renowned for its long history of fabulous music and talented football teams. And that being the case, do I assume you all like the game?"

"Absolutely," replied Jacko. "I'd say it's everyone's favourite sport."

Milos smiled and held up a hand in apology. "So sorry, Sergeant Sam, I didn't mean to insult your enthusiasm for such pleasurable things, I assure you that I too am a big fan." He then turned their attention to the cue-case, the three letters written in red felt pen and the photograph of the bearded suspect sitting in the Anfield Road stand, but more importantly the blurred image of the badge on his woollen hat. "I would imagine that unless you came from a certain city and supported a certain football club, you would never know that SGD, actually stands for 'Delje Sever'." Two rows of silent blank faces confirmed his observation. "What if I said, Ultras?"

Taff the Mack raised a hand. "Aren't they a gang of crazy football fanatics?"

Milos nodded. "But not just any old football fanatics, this lot are from Red Star Belgrade." He then smiled and said, "Bear with me please, whilst I expand a little and tell you of a football match that took place in May 1990." The Team hung on to his every word.

"At the time, Serbia's 'Red Star Belgrade' were playing an away game at Dinamo Zagreb's Stadio Maksimir in Croatia, in what was considered a Battle Royale between two bitter rivals. The match was only halfway through, when twenty 'Red Star' supporters, who were also known as the 'Delje Sever' or 'Ultras', began to fight with the home crowd. This small incident rapidly escalated into a huge riot of epic proportions and tragic consequences. Those with long memories might recall the press photos of a Croatian footballer named Bobin, fighting with the police during the Maksimir Riot."

"I remember that!" exclaimed Stretch Malone. "Instead of the ball, he tried to kick a policeman in the head."

"And he later played for 'Inter Milan' in Italy," another voice called from the rear.

Milos smiled along in agreement, but to everyone's surprise, suddenly went off on a different tangent. "Has anyone here heard of Zeljko Raznatovic?"

"I wouldn't know how to spell it," quipped one detective in a flash of wit.

Milos gave another wry smile and waited for the laughter to subside before asking another question. "What about Arkan?"

Jacko was trying to place exactly who this was, when the distinctive nasal sound of Bastion's voice came from the side. "Wasn't he a soldier involved in the Bosnian Wars?"

A smile and nod of the 'curtain hair' acknowledged the correct answer. Then Zelda whispered, "Maybe we should give them some more information."

The Serb was thoughtful for a second, before nodding and continuing with his tale. "Prior to the pitch battle at Maksimir, Arkan, who was reputed to have instigated the riot, had been virtually unknown. But within months had gone on to form his own private army and because of his ruthless methods, became the scourge of both Bosnia and Croatia. He was also a close friend of Ziggy Tomovic, who'd fought alongside him at the riot and I can tell from some faces that you're wondering what this has to do with our murder investigation?"

A few confused heads nodded here and there.

Once again Milos pointed to the group of soldiers draped over the troop carrier; each proudly wearing their sunglasses and black uniforms. "This particular unit almost certainly belongs to Arkan's Tigers and the photograph is a vital clue as to where Ziggy Tomovic may have disappeared to."

Jacko had viewed the photo many a time, but couldn't help looking again as Milos spoke on. "It's the sunglasses that tell us where and when it was taken."

The Team paused in their scribbling.

"The war began in 1990, but this has to be in late 1992 when the V.D.O. factory had been destroyed by the advancing Arkan's Tigers. It was also around this time that the sunglasses became a regular part of their dress code."

"Why go to war with your neighbours?" asked one curious detective.

"That's a very good question, Sir, however, I'm afraid there are no easy answers. I suppose the simplest analogy being the Serbians were unhappy with the possible break-up of Yugoslavia. They, after all, had always acted like big brother when it came to controlling the other regions. Whereas Slovenia, Croatia, Bosnia, etc., all desired their own independence."

A look on their faces said more information was needed and Milo decided a short history lesson might help them understand. "When the Second World War ended in 1945, the victorious Russians had replaced the defeated Germans in occupying most of Eastern Europe. Yet soon discovered that some of the Baltic countries had always disagreed with one another, especially in Yugoslavia where Croatia and Serbia were openly hostile in their relations. As if to deepen the wound, this unholy alliance was later controlled from Belgrade by one Marshall Broz Titov, a staunch communist puppet leader.

"The other satellite Republics including Bosnia, suddenly found they had no other choice than to follow suit and do his bidding. But when Gorbachev and perestroika came to power in Russia, the Berlin Wall fell meaning Communism with all its restraints, more or less disappeared with him." Milos waited for this information to sink in. "However, instead of being a blessing, the Marshall's death had, in fact, solved nothing and for the next ten years, a bitter squabble ensued as they'd argued exactly how this division might take place."

Having heard Simone's stories from day one, Jacko was well clued up with the Bosnian Conflict, but saw no reason why the Team shouldn't learn too.

"The first to break the chains were the Slovakians in the 10 Day War," said Milos. "Next were the Croatians in 1991, but it needed a huge amount of destruction and the deaths of many innocent people before they were able to achieve this."

It hadn't gone amiss amongst the detectives that Serbia appeared to be mainly responsible for much of this death and destruction. Milos, however, appeared to be completely oblivious to this fact as he expanded further.

"Following the riot and their defeat in Slovakia, a period of great unrest began to sweep Serbia and it was amidst this uncertainty, that Arkan and twenty other Belgrade Ultras were able to form the 'Serb Volunteer Guard'. This took place on 11 October 1990 and was at first what you might term a home guard. But by 1991, had grown into a fully-fledged army called Arkan's Tigers; with its own headquarters and training camp based in a place called Erdut."

"I remember them on Telly!" declared Stretch. "The guy in charge used to have a real live baby tiger as his mascot."

Milos nodded in agreement. "The camp was also close to where the Tomovic brothers had once lived and is represented by the initials found inside the lid of Ziggy's cue-case."

Milos studied the room. "Luka Tomovic had been a devoted member of the Ultras, who escaped from jail and joined The Serb Guard in 1991. We think his brother followed in his footsteps a few months later, where he too rapidly rose through the ranks."

"How does this involve the fingerprints and the charge sheet?" Joanna enquired.

"Patience good lady, all will be revealed."

Joanna took the hint and asked another question. "Okay, tell us more about these Tomovic brothers."

"They were born twins, but not identical. Marko came first and Luka arrived soon after, making him the younger of the siblings. As to their early life, we have no further information other than the incident with Luka in the pool bar. Anything else come from witnesses and incidents in the duration of the wars."

Smithy was curious. "I'd like to know more about this Arkan."

Milos paused as though considering his reply. "In some parts of my country, Zeljko Raznatovic or Arkan as he became known, is still revered as a war hero and patriot."

"To the rest of the world he was the Devil Incarnate!" Interrupted a scornful Zelda. "No one man created as much death and destruction as he did and I hope his soul burns in the fires of hell!"

The Team were stunned at her bitter outburst, yet even more surprised to hear Milos carry on unabashed. "We have evidence the Tomovic brothers were greatly admired by The Tigers' hierarchy. Marko attaining the rank of Lieutenant, which in turn led to him commanding his own squadron of troops."

Stretch Malone interrupted their discussion. "Hang on a minute Milos, if this Arkan is supposedly burning in the fires of hell, does that mean he is no longer with us?"

"Yes, he was assassinated in 2001."

"Where?"

"He was sitting with his bodyguard in the lobby of the Belgrade Hilton when someone shot him dead."

"Why?"

"Because of the war. Arkan had become a very rich and powerful man with many friends in high places. But unfortunately for him, knew lots of secrets, much more than some people would have liked. It was assumed he was killed to keep his mouth shut."

Joanna's finger went up again. "I'd still like to know what this has got to do with our murder investigation?"

Milos glanced at Jacko before speaking. "It's been widely rumoured that both the Tomovic brothers are dead."

The room fell into a stunned silence before erupting in a clamour of questioning voices; from the corner of his eye, Jacko could see an equally shocked Carson.

"Hang on a minute!" He shouted over the babble. "Let Milos finish; there's more to this than meets the eye."

The room began to quieten at the sound of Jacko's command; which allowed Milos to continue with his startling revelation.

"When I heard about the connection between Arkan and the Tomovic brothers, I thought it might be worth doing a little research of my own. The obvious place being the Bosnian War and I'm not talking about the one in Kosovo; that came many years later."

Wow, thought Jacko, *this really is a history lesson.*

"During my research, I stumbled across an article written by an English journalist named Kathleen Gallagher, who'd been scathing about Arkan and his cruel ruthless escapades. In her piece she wrote that not long after the war, he and some of his officers had been accused of various war crimes committed during their time in Bosnia. However, because he was so feted and admired in my country, there was a reluctance to put him on trial and seek justice." Milos paused again. "I was young man at the time, yet I can still remember the adulation we felt for this man; and to this day some people still cherish his memory and put flowers on his grave."

The S.C.U. was silent.

"But that doesn't mean all of his henchmen got away lightly; some are being tried for their crimes even as we speak. This English lady was also meticulous in detailing exactly who did what and where it happened. In one particular article, she mentions a massacre perpetrated by a Lieutenant Marko Tomovic sometime in 1993. In it she states that due to his death, he was never brought to justice."

As expected, the room erupted in another explosion of chatter.

In the noisy confusion, Jacko caught his boss's eye and gave him a brief nod and a reassuring thumbs up.

"Okay, okay," he shouted again. "We're not finished yet and as I keep telling you, there's more to come!"

Milos as ever seemed unmoved by all this and smiled serenely at the commotion happening around him.

"Keep it down!" Jacko called. "Milos is about to finish his story."

Once again, an expert flick of the hair over his left ear and the Serb was ready to continue. "I had no idea where to go next; Bosnian war crimes aren't exactly my forte. But fortunately, my esteemed colleague here does."

Standing within touching distance, Jacko was able to smell her perfume and see a wave of male eyes observe every man's idea of perfection. Honey blonde, late thirties and a body to die for. But it wasn't just the way Zelda looked; it was the sound of her voice that sent a tingle down their spines. "Good evening, gentlemen," she said in those warm sultry tones he knew so well.

"We are very happy and privileged to be here today. And hope that our information might not only help in solving your crime, but bring two vicious fugitives to justice."

Joanna and the two other female detectives present in the room felt somewhat left out at Zelda's obvious attempt at male bonding, but grudgingly conceded they had no choice other than to listen in.

"I too, am familiar with the English journalist that Milos talks about, who at the time of the Bosnian war, was freelancing for CNN news. I can also remember her scathing articles regarding the atrocities carried out against the Bosniaks, who were mostly of Muslim descent." Her eyes swept the room and her voice suddenly turned icy. "Not one person in my country escaped the pain, tragedy or heartache, caused by that damn war!"

The room fell silent as she let this sink in. A second later and she continued as if nothing had happened. "I spoke with Kathleen just a few days ago and asked her for any information regarding Marko Tomovic; especially on how he'd died. She said she'd been disgusted at the lack of evidence available at the time and was convinced that no one in officialdom wanted to talk about it. However, she did give me the name of her confidential contact at the Yugoslavian War Crimes Commission." Zelda, like Milos, paused for effect.

"It was now my turn to be surprised, seeing as how I'd met this same person at a Human Rights Convention on two separate occasions. I gave him a call, explained my problem and asked if he could be of assistance. He was his usual courteous self and listened with great interest. He then said that if possible, he would be more than happy to help, but only if his name was never mentioned as a source of information. Yet, to my surprise, he clearly remembered the Tomovic business and Kathleen's interest in Arkan. It had been a long time ago and he wasn't sure if there was anything of relevance he might find. We chatted a little more about trivial matters and then said our goodbyes. His final words were 'don't raise your hopes too high'." Zelda took a breath of air before continuing. "I heard nothing more until two days ago, when a small parcel containing a miniature racing car was delivered to my office."

Jacko's hand reached into the cloth bag and produced the item.

Stretch was wondering if he did magic tricks at kid's parties.

"I had no idea where it came from," continued Zelda. "But looking closer discovered it was a memory stick and in an instant realised it was somehow connected to our inquiry." She then gave a shake of her head. "You can imagine my disappointment when I found most of the information had been encrypted!"

Smithy, who adored the older woman, looked distraught at her plight. "Which is why Milos and I decided to travel here and deliver our findings to you in person."

"Could your unknown postman be the person from The War Crimes Commission?" asked Joanna.

Zelda gave a shrug. "Maybe, but the important thing is we've managed to decode the information on the stick."

Bastion peered at Carson in confusion. "I assume you know where we're we going with this Nathan?"

"Sergeant Jackson gave me a brief run down on the phone earlier this morning, Sir. As I understood it, they were still trying to translate the information."

Jacko faced the Team wearing a confident smile. "I've said many times that you need a certain amount of luck in this business. But it does make life easier when our killers get a little careless and make mistakes: Ziggy's missing leather cue-case being an obvious one." Holding up the miniature-racing car, he split it in two, so the Team might see for themselves. "Whoever sent this, must have known what was on it, but needed some real Forensic expertise from the outside world. So, with the help our own people, we've managed to decode the information and turn it into something we can all understand." Snapping it back together, he held it between two fingers and placed his other hand on the green folder. "Everything: the encrypted paperwork, notes and photographs, are all contained in this file. But more importantly, some small vital clues, the first we think, succinctly hidden in this sentence." The room was silent as Jacko read from a sheet of A4. *Beware of hidden dangers and look for Caduceus.* "Who's he?" asked Jason Junior.

Jacko smiled at the youngster's sudden outburst. "We're not talking about a real person here. *Caduceus* is a symbolic sign widely used by doctors in the medical profession. But it looks in a roundabout way, that someone is telling us to be careful and watch our step." Jacko's next item was a black and white snapshot of two bearded and heavily armed men, which he placed alongside Ziggy on the display boards. "Other than the school football team, we now think this is the only known photograph of Marko Tomovic, who's the soldier standing on the left."

"Who's the other one?" asked Smithy.

"We've been reliably informed that the other soldier is his second in command, Henki Topovic."

Stretch Malone was disappointed that Ziggy hadn't been one of them; it would have been nice to compare it with the school photograph. He was still thinking it over as Jacko spoke on. "This picture and the sworn testimony that came with it, was more than enough to condemn Lieutenant Marko Tomovic of a spate of war crimes. To those that don't know, the Bosnian War came to an end in 1995 and a year later the Yugoslav authorities began to name all those responsible for their crimes. Tomovic as you can imagine, would have been very high on their list. Yet when the order went out to apprehend him in 1997, something very strange happened. It was rescinded almost immediately, when it was discovered that in the very last days of the war, he and his platoon had been mysteriously wiped out on the border between Bosnia and Croatia. But what never came to light was exactly, how, when or where!"

Zelda leant across and whispered something to Jacko, who acknowledged what she was saying before reaching into the file again. "Kathleen Gallagher had long questioned exactly what happened to Marko Tomovic and his men," Jacko said pointedly. "But so did the person who sent Zelda the memory stick. And thanks to them, we now have enough information to theorise what did happen in those last frantic days."

Even Stretch was impressed.

"I'm going to begin with another picture, taken many years ago," said Jacko.

Like the picture of the soldiers wearing sunglasses, it was also a black and white, but this time portrayed a smiling middle-aged couple dressed in ski clothing.

"Anybody recognise them?" he asked offhandedly.

A dozen doubtful heads scanned the picture looking for possible clues. "I thought not," he conceded, "because this was taken more than thirty years ago and you'd have to be of a certain age to remember them." Again there was no response. "Okay," he said. "What if I told you they're two doctors'?

Five different hands rose as one, the first being Nathan Carson's. "Weren't they the Swedish couple killed in the Bosnian War? I remember there being a huge outcry at the time!"

Jacko didn't need to look. "That's right, Sir and even though I was in school at the time, I can still recall seeing it on all the news channels."

Stretch moved closer to the picture. "Come to think of it, I can remember them too."

"This was Olaf and Lottie Lundeberg," began Jacko. "A couple of retired doctors who'd been experts in their own particular fields; he being a renowned surgeon, she a top urologist. They were also known as philanthropists; meaning they liked to *help* other people." A few nodding heads justifying his brief explanation.

"Towards the end of the war, which would be around 1995, the Lundebergs were stationed in Northern Bosnia, acting as Independent Observers with the UN Peacekeeping Forces. However, before Olaf and his wife would put a foot in Yugoslavia, it had been agreed by all the relevant parties, that it could only be in what was regarded as a Safe Zone. In addition, he'd also insisted on taking his vintage Bugatti Roadster with him as a means of transport." Jacko fixed another photograph to the board.

"This snap shows the doctors and their car a week before they made the trip." It was obvious that the earlier shot of them with snowflakes falling on their fur clad upturned faces, had been taken in a soft focus Sixties style camera shoot. "Dr Lundeberg might have been an eminent surgeon with a love of vintage cars," continued Jacko, "but was even more famous for his dislike of authority and red tape."

"You mean he was a loose cannon?"

"Yes Smithy, something along those lines. To be fair, they were also renowned for getting their hands dirty by mucking in at the local hospitals. Yet on this one particular day in November, they left the town in which they were based, with the intention of transporting a young baby girl to a nearby hospital; that supposedly had superior facilities. Which is where our tale really begins," stressed Jacko.

"When the Lundebergs decided to drive to the next town, they did so without the knowledge of this Norwegian Major." A stern-faced soldier appearing from within the folder. "He was the officer responsible for their safety and well-being. As I understand it, a Safe Zone, was just a loose term for a constantly changing situation during any given conflict. There again, it was only Safe if everybody kept to a strict protocol and didn't go pissing about in the countryside.

But for some reason, the Lundebergs had decided to break ranks, do their own thing and head for the hills, or in this case, the narrow valley road that ran between the two towns. An interval of approximately twenty minutes passed, between the time the two doctors left the compound and when the Major went in pursuit of them." Jacko produced two more pictures. "This is the mess he found ten minutes later."

The bullet-riddled car was first to appear on the display board, the fading black and white picture good enough to reveal the smoking disaster that was once the vintage Bugatti. "I personally think this photo of the passenger side, missing door and mannequin-like bodies arranged inside the car's interior is the most disturbing one." Jacko could feel their revulsion, just as he had when first shown the photographs. "The Bugatti had been attacked on the narrow mountain road, the three occupants were dead and the perpetrators long gone."

A silence filled the room as the Team focused on the picture.

"Yet this is where the story gets really interesting. It seems Major Lars Knutfeld's hobby was wildlife photography and at the time of this incident, happened to have a camera in his patrol wagon. He was also deeply upset with the death of these three innocent people and determined to do something about it. So in a flash of inspiration, the Major set an unusual precedent in wartime incidents. He ordered that no one should touch or go near the stricken car and as all good snappers do, began to take as detailed a series of photos, as he was able. He then had the bodies carefully removed from the car and taken to a local hospital. Within hours, a team of army engineers had arrived on scene, sealed the wrecked Bugatti and transported it back to the UN compound where he'd been based. Once there, it lay untouched until the war came to an end in 1995."

Jacko paused in his narrative, the normally vocal Malone silent and attentive.

"We now pick up the story in late 1996 and the arrival of a top French Forensic Team, who'd been tasked with giving the Bugatti a thorough going over. And what did they find after a week of detailed searching? Nothing!" He then pointed to the picture of the stricken car. "The spent bullets found in the bodywork were all standard Serbian issue; which was of no real help, seeing as in any war, it was common practice for both sides to use whatever weapon came to hand."

Jacko posed a simple question. "So who pulled the trigger and who was responsible for their deaths? At this stage of the investigation there was no way the French could be certain, as many things had baffled and intrigued them. Like us, they were familiar with the photographs of the bodies in the car, yet couldn't understand how they got there. In his report the Major said the three casualties were in those positions when he arrived on the crash scene. Further proof was the original report from the hospital. Olaf had a shattered sternum from the impact of the crushed steering wheel. The multiple contusions found on Lottie and the child, a result of them being thrown from the car.

"All of which suggested their injuries had been consistent with a serious road accident. So who took the time and trouble to pick the woman and baby off the tarmac and place them back in the car?" Jacko shook his head. "Mysterious and very confusing to say the least." He then produced the last few papers left in the file. "This has been a long shift, people, but I can assure you that we're nearly there." Some were relieved, whilst others were happy to carry on watching Zelda and enjoy the experience.

Jacko, as always, had moved on. "Considering the difficulty of their circumstances, we have to thank our French counterparts for doing such a thorough job and a special thanks has to go to the Major in trying to keep everything intact. They'd also been delighted to find the Bugatti was still in one piece; and amazed to find Lars had even taken the effort to recover the door from the ditch." He then leafed through the paperwork and attached another faded picture to the board. "When they began to dust down the car in the warehouse, the French found something of extreme importance. As expected, there were lots of unknown dabs on the car's outer surfaces, but inside was different. This, after all, wasn't just a vintage Bugatti Roadster; this was Olaf Lundeberg's pride and joy. People might pass, touch it in admiration and maybe leave the odd smudge here and there. But no one had ever sat inside its polished gleaming interior: well no one except the good doctor and his wife."

Jacko held up one final picture. "To their eternal credit, our garlic-loving French counterparts took great care in cataloguing exactly what they'd discovered inside the car. A thorough search of its interior revealing just two sets of prints; one belonging to Olaf, the other to his wife Lottie. And as you'd expect, they were all in the usual places; door handles, gearstick etc. They then came across one other unusual piece of evidence." Jacko moved the photo from left to right so all could see. "This small plastic square was found amongst the debris on the Bugatti's walnut dashboard. However, a closer look shows two snakes twisted around a vertical staff; the traditional sign of Hermes the healer, as well as Caduceus, the international sign for a doctor."

The Team shifted in their seats, their sense of the unexpected almost tangible as they listened to the story. "In one corner of the plastic square, they found an unknown thumb print, that according to the French has to be circa 1995." Jacko then surprised them by producing another photograph. "What we have here is *thumbprint B* from the broken arm of the sunglasses found at our murder scene, and guess what? They are both a perfect match!"

Stretch Malone's mouth dropped open like a dodgy drawbridge. "Well, I'll go to the foot of our bloody stairs!" he gasped in astonishment.

Amidst more whoops, a smiling Jacko was waiting to continue with his tale. "In the aftermath of any war, chaos and confusion will always reign supreme. Meaning any attempt by our French colleagues at trying to make an ID of the thumbprint became a near impossible task; bearing in mind the sinners who where responsible went running for the hills. Files were shredded and cover-ups became the norm as people of genuine repute began to hide their faces, as well as their involvement. So it's no surprise that the 'Frogs' found nothing of interest as they pissed about in the dark looking for answers."

Jacko wasn't sure; but he thought a brief look of sympathy might have flitted across Stretch's face as he spoke on. "In the absence of them finding any further incriminating evidence, we can only assume this whole incident was shoved to the back of a filing cabinet and forgotten about. That is, until Zelda set the ball rolling and someone delivered the package to her office." Inside the room, the detectives listened in silence as Jacko summed up.

"For years, Kathleen Gallagher had insisted Marko Tomovic and his men were responsible for the death of the two doctors, but could never prove it. According to the only evidence available at the time, he and his platoon were killed near the Bosnian border just before the end of the war." He held up the miniature racing-car again. "However, if that's true, then it in no way explains what we have here: the blood splattered bodies found around the country, or the two murdered teenagers in Junkies Corner. Furthermore, it doesn't tell us why fresh fingerprint 'A' on one side of the sunglasses is an identical match to that of Luka Tomovic; and who wouldn't bet that the 'Caduceus' one belongs to his older brother Marko?"

Jacko paused to let this sink in. "I am now convinced that we have a sadistic serial killer on the loose and as the evidence begins to grow, find it hard to dismiss the thought that maybe the brothers aren't dead after all. Which again begs the question: Was there some kind of cover-up? And if so, where are they now?"

"Brilliant work!" declared Carson. "I had no idea that was about to happen and it definitely throws a new light on the case."

"I fully agree," said an equally impressed Bastion.

Jacko was still basking in their mutual praise when he heard McClellan's gruff voice from behind. "A question, Sergeant, are you saying this Milos chappie is a real Serbian?"

"Yes Sir, he was born in Belgrade."

McClellan's lip turned downwards. "Judging by the way he's slagging off his country, he doesn't sound very patriotic to me."

"There are many ways of looking at patriotism," Jacko replied. "But I think Milos' view became slightly skewed when his favourite Aunt was killed during the early part of the war."

"How was that?" asked McClellan.

"Not unlike like Victor Dvoric, his aunt was Serbian born, and when young, married a Bosnian. She'd also lived in Sarajevo for most of her adult life and according to Milos was out shopping in a crowded market place one Saturday morning, when a Serbian mortar shell landed no more than four feet away."

"War, unfortunately, has many casualties," muttered Hughie.

Jacko nodded. "This is true, Sir, but not during a ceasefire."

Yugoslavia Circa 1990

Part Seven

Yugoslavia, November 1995

Something was missing, its absence loud enough to wake him in the dark. Throwing off his sleeping roll, he propped himself up on one elbow and listened. It was the lack of a certain sound that had brought him from sleep. Not the banging crashing type, but the incessant drumming of water on the canvas above his head. Clambering to his feet, he pulled back the flaps and beheld a welcoming sea of white.

"Well, who'd have believed it," he grinned. "The rain has stopped falling and the snows have arrived early."

Leaping from the rear of the transporter, his landing was cushioned not by the usual ankle-deep water, but a heap of soft crystalline white snowflakes. Looking around the camp, he reckoned that although its duration must have been short, was still heavy enough to cover the trees and vegetation with a satisfying layer of freshly fallen snow. He could also remember times like this, when he would take his two young sons tobogganing; the sound of their excited laughter filling the crisp winter air. 'And it won't be long before we'll be doing the same!' He growled at the silence.

A sudden rumbling sound from deep within his lower stomach said nature was calling and he'd better get a move on. Above him in the night sky, a scant few threads of orange were beginning to penetrate the deep cloud cover, their glow more than enough to light the way. As always, his destination would be the narrow gap between the rocks and the few steps that led to the plateau. A glance behind revealed the tell-tale path of his footprints, as he purposely trod into the virgin flakes ahead.

Reaching his destination, he leant his rifle against a nearby twisted tree, cleared the snow away with his boot and eased down his khaki fatigues. His dirty, unwashed shorts were next to shuffle past his knees, which in turn revealed a pair of hairy buttocks, whose tender white skin flinched as they met the ice-cold wind. Taking hold of one branch, he glimpsed behind and once satisfied all was well, eased his bare backside down above the hole in the rocky ground. He then closed his eyes and gave a smile on hearing a long noisy fart exiting his rear end, its sound and smell foretelling the relief he was about to enjoy. With the wind whistling around his knees, he enjoyed a few moments of bliss as he emptied his bowels into the void below.

However, when he opened them again, another a pair of boots had unexpectedly appeared before him and as he looked up, the Berretta opened fire. The silencer on the gun had guaranteed the 9mm slug would travel the ten feet to its target, unheralded and unheard. The only sound, a splat as the projectile formed a perfect circle in the middle of his Adam's apple, thus causing him to choke as the bullet cut off his air supply. Gagging on a mixture of blood and mucus, he struggled to stand upright, only to find he was comically restricted by his own underwear. Another pull of the trigger created the exact same result, the circle this time appearing in the middle of his forehead, its destructive path exiting from the back of his skull with an explosive surge of bone and brain tissue. This alone was more than enough to send him staggering backwards over the edge of the plateau and into the gloom beyond.

Within seconds, the faint sound of a body could be heard crashing down through the trees and bushes thirty metres below. In the beckoning morning light, a gloved hand reached for the rifle stood against the stump and threw it javelin-like into the void. As it plummeted out of sight, the skies darkened and the winter snow began to fall again.

The Bosnia and Croatia Border
Three Weeks Earlier

The constant slap-slap of the windscreen wipers was having an almost hypnotic effect on Marko's senses, as the transporter ploughed on through the rainstorm. Reaching into his pocket, he flipped a couple of Lucky Strikes into his mouth and used the Zippo to light them both.

"*Hvala vam*," thank you, grunted Rado as he took a welcome drag on the cigarette. But as he watched the driver struggle to keep the bouncing truck on the uneven track, Marko was having a few nightmares of his own.

Who'd have thought it would come to this, he whispered. After five long years of bloodshed, the word *defeat* was now staring them in the face. With it, came the realisation that their best-laid plans hadn't quite gone the way they'd expected. Their mission as always, had been to preserve the status quo by bonding the Republics together as before; one united Yugoslavia! However, it had unexpectedly ground to a halt, when they'd reached the outskirts of the Bosnian capital, Sarajevo and the war had changed in both purpose and direction. This was mostly due to a few thousand Bosniak reserves and civilians, daring to defy the combined might of both 'The Tiger' and the Serbian armies. It was also an ache in Marko's gut that would last for many a year to come. The stalemate had not only succeeded in stopping their juggernaut, it had lasted longer than the Siege of Stalingrad! In the five long years that constituted the deadlock, the Bosniaks had been able to regroup, make secret alliances and re-arm their forces. Which in turn gave the Western Allies an opportunity to poke in their own unwanted sanctimonious noses, as they'd cried foul, in a fight where no quarter had been given and if the truth be known, none was expected!

As history will tell, following the impasse at Sarajevo, Bosnia began to fracture like a giant broken mirror, the cracks spreading like a virus to the many other Provinces. This meant the glue of their unity had begun to dissolve, as friend and foe had inexplicably begun to fight with one another. It also meant the war was now being fought on many different fronts. Within this confusion, Marko's platoon had been directed northwards, where he found himself patrolling the lower regions of Croatia, looking to intercept insurgent forces that were forever trying to cross the border into Bosnia. His unit consisted of three rapid response transporters, plus sixty battle-hardened men and their equipment, who when needed, would travel from place to place. He, as always, would be in the lead truck, Ziggy in the middle and Henki at the rear. Over time they became known as, *Noćni sat* or Night Watch, forever in demand, as the airwaves sang with a multitude of possible sightings.

A sudden lurch of the truck brought him back to the present, its uncomfortable jolt reminding him of the stream of painful stories that forever fell on their ears. Yet the loss of *Banja Luka* and *Sanski Most,* a couple of tactical strongholds they'd held since the outbreak of the war, plus the news the Americans had recently decimated most of their forces with long-range ballistic missiles was a bitter pill to swallow. It also meant that the Serbian forces were inexorably being pushed backwards in the direction of their own borders. As if to confirm this bad news, Marko had recently received his own orders to cease all hostilities and make a formal retreat. This devastating blow to their pride had left his men seething with rage, the roaring bulk of Ziggy, spitting fire at the very thought of taking a backward step.

Nevertheless, as Commanding Officer, Marko was left with no other choice than to obey. To make things worse, this sudden change of superiority in the power struggle had resulted in a raft of unknown dangers. The main one being he wasn't sure where the enemy was, or if they too had laid down their arms in the ceasefire! More problems arose, when communications of any kind became virtually non-existent, as no-one back at headquarters seemed to know what was happening.

His father had always urged him to, *trust a Croat only as far as you can throw him* and with this in mind, Marko had called the troops together and asked for their views on the situation. To a man, they'd been loud and voluble in resisting the idea of capitulation, or worse, the thought of being taken prisoner. Taking into account they were many miles from home, the men agreed to load the trucks with extra food and fuel and make a run for it.

In the early light of dawn ten days later, they found themselves on a narrow dirt road that cut through a heavily forested area. Marko knew from past experience, that with luck, its leafy path should take them northeast and homewards. Yet, without having some reliable information as to the exact whereabouts of the opposition forces, could only do what they'd been doing for the past few weeks; keep a lookout for any potential danger. Fatigue, plus the constant movement from inside the truck had caused him to doze off momentarily, when he was suddenly jolted wide-awake as Rado slammed on the brakes and screamed, "Jebiga!"

This resulted in the following trucks slewing to a halt as they'd desperately tried to avoid crashing into each other. Seething with anger, Marko was about to give the driver some grief, when he saw the reason for his sudden outburst. Through the falling rain and less than a hundred metres ahead, he could see the tip of a camouflaged M10 gun barrel slowly emerging from between the trees. But to his horror, saw the body of a Russian built T55 tank; wearing full Croatian insignia appearing beneath it. Both men stared transfixed at the nightmare unfolding before them. The smoke from the cigarettes added another layer of nicotine to already yellow stained fingers, as the monster trundled snail-like across the track on its journey into the undergrowth opposite.

But the spell was instantly broken when the passenger door of the transporter opened and a rain-soaked Henki appeared on the running board. "What the hell's going on?" he spluttered.

Marko grabbed his collar, pulled him further into the cab and pointed through the windscreen. "There!" he whispered.

Henki's face drained of colour as he realised the danger they were in. "Oh shit," he groaned, the sight of the tank filling him with untold fear. "And there's no way we can turn around," he croaked.

Hearing the terror his voice, Marko punched him in the shoulder and shook his neck as if he were a turkey. "Fuck that crap!" he shouted. "We have to do something now!"

Henki immediately began to refocus at the sound of his Boss's voice; the need for survival overcoming his initial fears, as he took in the dangers ahead. "Do you think they know about the ceasefire?"

"I don't know. Maybe."

"Will they let us pass?"

Marko had been wondering the same thing, but knew in his heart that this would never be. "No way," he growled. There was always the risk they might meet some kind of problem on their journey, but not a T55 Croatian tank.

"Okay, okay," said Henki, his eyes now firmly fixed on the problem that lay before them. "As I see it, we have two choices. We can either abandon the trucks and make for the woods, *or* try and squeeze our way past the tank," his hand pointing to the narrow gap to one side.

Marko quickly grasped what his No. 2 was suggesting. The track where they'd halted was arrow straight for at least half a kilometre behind, which would probably explain why the T55 was moving to a new position and covering its approach. But the bushes on that side of the track were sparse, so if they could somehow slip by, it would be difficult for it to turn and pursue them. There again, if they got it wrong, the tank's long gun would happily use them as target practice! The three men watched in silence, each praying it would continue its journey into the trees. Through the still pouring rain, Marko could see the turret hatch was still firmly closed; thus giving them hope the tank's occupants might have missed them. But knew the game was up the moment its huge clanking metal tracks slowed to a halt.

"I think they've seen us!" cried Henki.

Marko pushed him out of the cab. "Go, go, go!" he shouted and looking behind could see the hulking shape of Ziggy hanging from the middle transporter. "Move!" he bawled, his arm desperately waving for him to inform the others of their imminent danger. Luckily for Henki, his own problems were soon solved when he decided against the rear wagon and scrambled aboard Ziggy's.

Without being told, Rado slammed the engine into gear and let out the clutch, the threat of the tank making the sweat on his forehead look like greased goose pimples. Beside him in the passenger seat Marko was peering through the windscreen searching for any signs of movement ahead. For those sitting in the rear of the wagon, however, it was a case of hanging on to anything at hand, as they made a desperate race for safety.

As the three trucks ploughed on through the pouring rain, it suddenly occurred to Marko that because it was half way into the trees opposite, the T55 might have created a problem with its own manoeuvrability. There was just enough room for them to squeeze by, which meant it was severely limited in how far it could traverse its gun barrel; especially in their direction. The tank's top hatch was still closed, the turret gun unmanned and its forward-facing cannons virtually unusable.

It was only when they'd squeezed by and neared the bend up ahead, did he think there was a 50-50 chance of them outrunning the monster. Then came a huge boom from behind. Despite the deafening roar of its engine or the fact he was in the lead truck, Marko still felt the impact of the explosion and saw a razor-sharp piece of shrapnel clip his wing mirror as it flew by. *So much for the ceasefire*, he thought. Fearing the worst, he pushed open the cab door and was just in time to see a tall water lashed tree come crashing down behind the last truck, its size blocking off any immediate pursuit.

Giving a yelp of joy, he slapped his driver on the shoulder and made a silent prayer to whichever of the holy saints had come to their rescue. They'd travelled less than half a kilometre further along the track, when Rado pointed to the wing-mirror and brought Marko's attention to the frantically waving hands in the trucks behind. Skidding to a halt, he was swiftly out of the cab and with a sigh of relief saw the troops from the middle transporter spilling out seemingly unscathed.

However, it wasn't long before he realised that the gods might not have been so benevolent as he'd first hoped. On reaching the last vehicle, he could see the floor was now a sea of red, as they dropped the tailgate and lifted the stricken bodies out onto the side of the road. A blood-soaked Henki was like a man possessed, as he shouted instructions and helped move the badly injured from the rear of the truck.

A shocked Marko stood aghast, before he too had entered the fray, his own hands becoming crimson in a desperate effort to save his men. It was as they worked together, did his No. 2 give him the bad news. The 'tank', he said, had managed to lose off just the one shell, which could only be a *Russian 15kg high explosive fragmentation* type. There was no doubting it had been heading in their direction, but luckily had been thwarted by the tree. Henki reckoned the missile must have clipped the side with enough force to detonate it and tear out a large section of the trunk. This in turn had caused it to topple lumberjack style across the track and block the way.

The problem was, its destructive path didn't quite end with the fall of the tree. Within a few hundred metres, a shower of razor-sharp steel had cut butter-like through anything unfortunate to be in its deadly arc. The troops sat in the rear of the truck ideally placed to be first on the menu! The canvas cover looked more like a vegetable colander, as a hail of deadly shrapnel had penetrated it flimsiness with almost consummate ease, killing four of his men instantly and mortally wounding at least six more.

Henki, who was using the wet grass to wipe the blood from his hands, faced him with weary eyes. "If we don't get refuge from this shit, Marko, we'll have more dead bodies to worry about."

"What do you suggest?" he murmured, his gaze looking beyond the fallen tree and the threat of a possible pursuit by the tank.

"*The Ridge!*" Henki replied firmly.

The Ridge

Marko sat in the shadows pondering what to do next, or to be more precise, what the opposition forces would allow him to do. He'd had no contact with higher command for weeks, as they'd struggled to reach the safety of their own lines and Serbia. Their arduous retreat had always threatened to conjure up some kind of disaster; but the unexpected detour and the untimely death of the two doctors, was one he hadn't anticipated or desired.

Lighting another *Lucky Strike*, he sucked in a lungful of smoke and let out a long narrow stream from between his lips, his brain trying to make some sense of the last few days. Following their deadly encounter with the Croatian tank and in order to reach a crucial section of a winding valley road. They'd had to make a diversion from their pre-planned route.

This meant them cutting across country so they might more easily reach the hidden turnoff leading to The Ridge. However, even though this short piece of tarmac might look innocent enough, it could still be packed with danger. The obvious one being, that without knowing the enemies' movements, they'd be out in the open and subject to further attack. He remembered thinking their detour had been progressing without any further incident, until this strange blue vintage car had come hurtling around the bend and sped towards them.

A second later and a short burst of gunfire had rent the air, leaving the Bugatti and its three occupants strewn across the valley road below. At the time, he'd been unconcerned about the passengers, assuming they would be just the usual local civilians. He'd been more upset with them trashing such a beautiful car. Yet his walk along the tarmac and a closer inspection of the bodies had proven to be a nightmare one, more so when he'd discovered their true identities. In his eyes, the dead and wounded were a statistic both sides would have to live with; and then move on. But this one incident had been so very different from anything he'd encountered before.

Four of his men may lie buried on the Ridge, but in truth, were casualties of a war they'd freely chosen to pursue. Whereas, the death of the two doctors had been an unmitigated disaster, the circumstances of their passing shaking him to his very core, whilst questioning his long-felt sense of what was right and wrong. In his eyes, they'd fought a different type of battle, which in its own way had represented life itself, the dead child being the very evidence of their beliefs.

Closing his eyes, he knew that if he could somehow turn back the clock, he would be down on bended knee begging for forgiveness and asking them to help save his own men. For it grieved him greatly, to think any actions of his own might have resulted in their deaths. In the days following the fatal encounter, he'd often thought of the crash rail running alongside the road and wondered what might have happened if it hadn't been there. Would he have made a more determined effort to push the two doctors and their beautiful car into the ditch and in doing so hide them from sight, as well as mind?

He liked to think not.

The deluge outside had eased to become a light downpour, as he flicked his cigarette end into a nearby puddle and heard the hiss as it went out. The next sound, however, was the one he feared most. It was the one that grew louder as the Fighter Jet passed overhead. "Jesus, that's low," he whispered, the throb and roar of its engines making the wooden walls shake and tremble. "Why in hell's name would you fly a plane in this weather, especially when it's nearly dark?" It was only when thankfully, it had receded into the distance, did he reflect on Henki's shrewd suggestion they should make the diversion and shelter here.

He could clearly remember the day when one of their patrols had come across the place they'd named *The Ridge*. It was remote, lay way up in the hills and could be reached only by a winding narrow track. Yet had many benefits, one of them being the nearby fresh mountain stream and the deep ravine that would ensure the security of their rear flank. In addition, the small hunting lodge was the perfect place to tend to the wounded, but more importantly bury their dead. In summertime the tall trees had come as a welcome relief from the blazing sun, as they'd camped on the forest floor.

Yet winter was nearly upon them: the sudden drop in temperature bringing all manner of problems and uncertainty. To add to their woes, it was near impossible to predict which way the weather might turn; one day dry, the next freezing cold torrential rain.

In the rear of the middle truck, Henki was going through the daily routine of cleaning his machine pistol, when he saw a light moving through the trees. Thinking it might be the enemy. He was about to alert the other troops close by and then realised it wasn't a Croatian torch, but the hooded headlights of a camouflaged staff car. Yet despite the deep water filled potholes strewn here and there, the vehicle had swept into camp and ploughed through them as if they didn't exist.

Peering through the canvas flaps, a suspicious Henki watched it splash to a halt in front of the hut and saw the hatchet shaped face of Colonel Petrovic; dressed in his trademark leather trench coat, step out to meet the rain. His demeanour as always was that of an arrogant self-important arsehole, who'd paused only to look around and order his driver to retrieve the two suitcases stowed in the car boot.

Henki's spirits had lifted at the sight of such an important person, his unexpected arrival, hopefully bringing them a vestige of good news. Yet in the back of his mind was more worried as to why this same leather-clad officer (whom nobody liked) would deem it necessary to visit their remote camp, considering the many dangers involved.

Inside the hut, one room was doubling as both a billet and temporary headquarters, the other filled to overflowing with the walking wounded. Marko, however, was more focused on the choice of quality American cigarettes contained in one suitcase and the bottles of Johnnie Walker Black Label in the other. Past experience had told him that Petrovic's unexpected appearance wasn't some kind of social visit. It was, at times like this, when he'd been known to casually pass on his bad news as if it were a live hand grenade with the pin removed. He'd also made no effort to take a seat or remove his coat, all of which suggested he was just passing through.

Marko took a pack of Lucky Strikes from the suitcase. "Some might think it a dangerous exercise to be driving about the countryside at this time of the night, Colonel, considering there are bloodthirsty Croats lurking everywhere."

Petrovic gave a nonchalant shrug of his shoulders and a dismissive flick of one hand. "My personal safety is of no importance Lieutenant," he replied. "The purpose of my visit is twofold. Firstly, I've been instructed to pass on these gifts and convey a special greeting from someone who greatly admires the Tomovic brothers and hopes that all is well."

It was no secret within the Tiger Fraternity that he and Ziggy were close friends with Arkan. But having not met for a while, Marko could only assume this was his way of touching base. He was also aware that this leather-clad officer made no claims to being General Rommel when it came to the war effort: even less so when on the battlefield. Rumour said that he only wore the long coat to hide his stick-thin legs, yet basked in the fame of being known as *The Fixer,* who over the years had become one of Arkan's most trusted aids. "Tell him that for the moment we are well, but for how long, who can say?"

Petrovic gave a sardonic smile. "I think that sentiment could apply to all of us Lieutenant. However, that's not the only reason I'm here."

Leaving what little comfort there was in the truck, Henki was alarmed to see Petrovic exiting the camp with a squeal of tyres and shower of wet dirt. To add to the confusion, a concerned looking Marko was framed in the doorway watching this same noisy departure. Spying his No. 2 standing in the rain, he gave a curt nod; the sign he should follow him inside. Shaking the water off his parka, Henki took a seat, leant his machine pistol against the chair and met a serious looking Marko who offered him a Lucky Strike cigarette.

Outside in the pissing down rain, Corporal Sorovac, the trooper responsible for their overall safety was making one last tour of the camp when he noticed one of the shutters on the hut hanging ajar. Aware that security was paramount in these matters, he decided to investigate, but as his hand reached out to close it, heard two familiar voices coming from inside. Realising he'd inadvertently become party to their conversation, he decided to stop and listen.

"I see Petrovic's still wasting the tread on his tyres," growled Henki.

"You know what he's like, doesn't hang about if he can help it," Marko grunted in reply.

"To what did we owe the pleasure?" His head motioning in the direction of the now absent Colonel.

"We've been given new orders. He says it's important we break camp at dawn and leave here as soon as we can."

"Why?"

"The Colonel thinks the ceasefire is just about holding, but doesn't mean a thing, especially when it comes to the Croatians. In his opinion, they're going to be crawling all over this place within the next twenty-four hours."

Henki was silent for a moment. "What about the road ahead, is it clear?"

"It will be until late morning, which is why he's taking it tonight."

"What happens when we leave?"

"We rendezvous with another column heading north, whom he assures me has a fully functional surgical unit. Petrovic says if we can make the Unzini Crossroads by 7.00 am tomorrow morning, they'll be happy to take our wounded men with them, which has to be good news."

Henki gave a smile of relief and a nod of satisfaction. "Thank Christ for that, I reckon a few more days of this shit and it won't be just their war wounds that will kill them."

Marko gave the briefest of smiles before the dark clouds returned. "True, but there is some bad news. Petrovic said that once the wounded have been taken care of, we've been ordered to disappear."

Henki eyed him warily. "What does that mean?"

"It means that it's all over for you, me and the platoon."

For the past few years, the fight for a United Yugoslavia had bonded both their paths in one direction. They'd also become close friends and comrades who'd fought many a bloody battle together. Yet this wasn't quite what he'd been expecting to hear. "What the hell's going on, Marko?"

"*Smo najebali!* We're fucked, my friend!"

The air within the hut began to thicken with cigarette smoke as Marko spoke on. "It looks as if we have some real problems ahead. The first concerns the two doctors who died in the valley a few days ago. Petrovic says they weren't just some everyday village quacks."

"Judging by their expensive looking clothes and car they were driving; I should think that was more than obvious."

Marko took another drag on his cigarette before speaking. "It's not only that, apparently they were both famous for some kind of medical work they did. And seeing as how we don't get to hear much news from the outside world, we wouldn't know that it's gone crazy to find whoever killed them."

Henki's eyes narrowed. "That has to be the reason for all this low-level flying by the Allied Jets; the bastards are looking for us!"

Marko nodded slowly. "And if it wasn't for the torrential rain, they'd probably have found us by now."

Henki remembered the weather as being a double-edged sword in the hours following the car crash. In the periods when the skies were clear, the roar of the planes above had them shaking in their boots, then came the flipside which was when the rains returned. "They must have been some mighty important people for them to waste so much fuel on air searches!"

Marko grimaced before speaking. "Petrovic says one newspaper has offered a $10,000 dollar reward to anyone who can identify their killers, dead or alive!"

"Holy Madonna," Henki whispered. "That's like having a fucking bounty on your head and it won't take long before everyone knows we were involved. Hell man, we'll be lucky to last five minutes with that kind of money being offered and it's all because of that lunatic brother of yours!"

A stunned silence fell as they glared at one another across the table; close enough to smell each other's stale sweat. "This is all Ziggy's fault!" Henki snarled.

Marko gave no response, other than the bright glow from his cigarette and the stream of smoke that left his lips.

"Come on man, everyone knows Ziggy pulled the trigger!" Henki insisted, his voice becoming more strident in the confines of the hut.

"He says it was an accident!"

"Give me a break, do you really believe that shit?"

"How do you know it wasn't?" Marko snarled, his own indignation beginning to rise by the second. "Ziggy insists there was no order to hold fire and swears it was just an instinctive reaction to shoot. Especially when the tank nearly wiped us out during a fucking ceasefire!"

The flickering gaslight briefly outlined Henki's greasy face, before it lapsed back into the shadows, any further illumination coming from the glow of his cigarette. "I don't care what you say, Marko, but the Croats don't drive vintage Bugatti automobiles!"

"Ziggy swears to God it was just an accident."

"What? You might believe that bullshit, but I don't. In fact I think he's mentally unstable and downright dangerous!"

"Yeah? But he's still my younger brother!" he snarled back.

Henki stared into the face of his friend. "That same crappy excuse just won't wash anymore, because you and I know Ziggy is losing it. If what Petrovic says is only half true, then that has to make him a risk to us all!"

"Remember the war, Henki? People do risky things when there's a war on!"

"Oh shit! Is that his excuse? Then maybe he can explain why those three innocent people are lying dead in the road. Hell man, no matter how you look at it, we could never justify it as an accident, especially with two of them being doctors!"

"Only we know that! None of the other men were close enough to see their badges and I removed the lady's one just before they placed her in the car."

Henki was still unconvinced as Marko's voice took on a more sympathetic tone. "What does it matter my friend? There are no witnesses to say we were in any way involved, so it's all in the past and what's done is done. I never wanted it to turn out the way it did and Petrovic only assumed it might be us, because we had to be somewhere near The Ridge when it happened. He's also advising us to play dumb and say nothing. But I wish that was the only piece of bad news, because there's something else you should know." He then took a photograph from his tunic pocket and placed it on the table. "Petrovic gave me this."

Henki stared at a grainy black and white shot of two armed soldiers who looked to be in conversation with one another. Both were dressed in battle fatigues and in what looked to be some kind of farmyard. However, a closer inspection revealed it was a picture of himself and Marko, but to his surprise realised one of the machine pistols was the same as the gun leaning against his chair.

"I've had enough riddles for one day, Marko, so what the hell does *this* mean?"

"Remember the back end of '93, when we discovered all those people murdered in a hamlet called Jovicza?"

"How can anyone forget that sadistic bloody mess!"

Marko paused for a second before giving another grim smile. "Petrovic reckons that someone from a nearby village took this photograph on the day it happened. Problem is, the same person claims you and I were responsible for the massacre!"

Still standing in the rain, Corporal Sorovac was astonished at this jaw-dropping piece of news. His thoughts racing back to the same hamlet and the small part he'd played on that day so long ago.

It seemed a lifetime since they'd been 200 kms north west of Sarajevo, fighting the Bosniak forces on the outskirts of a strategically important town named Lobogran. In what had begun as a minor skirmish, quickly turned into a major battle, as both sides fought for superiority in a densely wooded area. In another unexpected move, a small unit of Bosniaks had succeeded in infiltrating behind their lines and killed more than forty of their own unsuspecting troops.

A further eight-hour fire fight had ensued, involving many more unwanted casualties and fatalities. In the confusion and uncertainty that followed, Arkan had ordered Marko's platoon to break away from the main conflict, so they might pursue and destroy the insurgents.

One such call had reported a contact near to Jovicza, a small hamlet some 30 kms from their then position, but close enough to be considered a threat. Two of the transporters were despatched to search the area, yet no one had ever been able to explain why Ziggy and Henki's units had somehow overlapped and searched the same hamlet, all within a six-hour period.

'Jovicza Hamlet', as Sorovac remembered, was no more than twenty houses clustered together on some dusty back road going nowhere, typical farm people. At the time, he'd been in Henki's truck when they'd entered the village a few hours after Ziggy's had already passed through—he later claiming they didn't see the bodies of the men and boys lined up behind a wall; all executed.

A search of the surrounding dwellings had revealed all were empty, that is, until they'd come across a large farmhouse situated on the edge of the hamlet. A couple of guard dogs lay bloodied in the driveway, the wooden gate swinging back and forth in the breeze. From a distance they were able to make out what looked to be a horse lying on its side in the straw of the paddock, the splintered gunshot remains of its wooden rails strewn all around. Nearing the house, they heard a strange buzzing sound that grew in volume with every step they took—first impressions being of a large fan that hummed beyond the half open door.

Leading the way as always, Henki had used the barrel of his machine pistol to ease it open, later describing it as a sight from hell! Inside he'd found a shuttered kitchen area with a long wooden table that ran down the centre. Lying face down on its worn surface, he was able to see the bodies of twelve women and four young girls, one no older than six. They lay side-by-side and were bound by their wrists to secure them to the table. A closer look said a sharp knife had been used to open their clothes from behind in one single continuous cut, thus allowing them to be peeled apart, exposing their naked bodies.

All of them had been sexually abused, the bloodletting evident from a range of sadistic knife injuries on each of their pathetic corpses. The noise he told him came from the clouds of flies swarming over their mutilated bodies. It was all he could do to stop himself from retching violently as he pulled the door shut and staggered out into the courtyard. In all of this, Henki had said it wasn't their task to bury them. Family or surviving friends would arrive soon enough for that! As he lay awake later that night, Sorova regretted his own stupid curiosity and complete disregard of orders.

For when Henki had gone to the truck and used the radio to speak with Marko, he'd opened the kitchen door and stepped inside. His own lasting images were of the crumpled threadbare carpet lying beside the cooking stove, which having been cast aside, revealed the trap door to a small cramped storage area beneath the kitchen floor. He could only imagine the fear and terror as the women had hid, each aware of the fate that awaited them should they be discovered.

Yet in his mind's eye, amongst the more unforgettable images, had been the tell-tale puncture holes below their jawlines and he vividly recalled the small rivulets of blood that trickled from the wound like a crimson scar, each of them pooling on the table where they'd slowly began to congeal. Within this Bacchanalian feast, the flies had gathered in their hundreds and dined like kings, as the forlorn bodies lay almost sacrificial like on the wooden surface of the table.

It was only much later did it occur to Sorovac that most of the dead women and children in the room were fair or blonde-haired.

The sound of Henki's indignant cry brought him back to the present. "I don't believe this shit, Marko! This photo must have been taken hours after we arrived at the hamlet, so how did Petrovic come by it?"

"I haven't a clue, but he insists this war is coming to an end and the photo could spell real trouble for us both. According to him, most of the top brass are ready to desert a sinking ship even as we speak."

Henki's face wore a look of confusion. "I still don't get what this means and why should it spell trouble for us? We didn't kill any of the villagers; they were already dead when we got there!"

Marko lit another cigarette and nervously rubbed the stubble on his chin. "I know that, my friend, but try convincing some arsehole who doesn't want to listen. Petrovic says there's a rumour flying about that the Allies are setting up a War Crimes Tribunal to investigate certain atrocities. He thinks Jovicza Hamlet is almost certain to be on their list, as well as the two Doctors."

A still confused Henki was searching for answers through the haze of smoke, when Marko changed his tone of voice and spoke quietly. "Nobody expected anything like this to happen, but Belgrade must be quaking in their boots should it make the National headlines. So Petrovic has been ordered to take care of the problem and ensure it doesn't present the *Powers that be* in a bad light."

Henki was under no illusion as to the danger in which he suddenly found himself. Rumour had it, that a bullet in the back of the head and a shallow grave was Petrovic's normal way of taking care of things.

"That wasn't the only reason for his coming here tonight," Marko said hesitantly. "The Colonel says there's talk of the Tigers disbanding in the near future and should that happen, means we can simply disappear and go back to our normal lives. He's also recommending we take the main road and forget the forest track. If we're careful, we should be able to make the Unzini Crossing without risk, but the Colonel insists we mustn't forget there's still a war on."

"You don't need to remind me there's a fucking war on!" Henki snarled. "I've been knee deep in this crap since day one! And unlike some people, I'm happy to admit that I'm no lily-white when it comes to my share of killing, but I've at least managed to keep it out on the battlefield!"

"Ziggy's a good soldier!" Marko seethed through clenched teeth.

"Aren't we all," cried Henki, his voice having just enough sarcasm to ram home the point. "And who knows, Marko? Under different circumstances, your brother might even have been decorated for bravery!"

Leaning closer to the window, Sorovac heard Henki whisper.

"I don't care what you say, killing people has become some kind of blood sport that Ziggy seems to relish. Christ, you can see it in his eyes!" He then shook his head in bemusement. "Funny thing, I can still remember the day we joined as volunteers. Naïve, full of patriotic dreams that were alive with fervour *and* the hope for a greater Serbia! Now, I'm not so sure where the hell we are, or what the future holds!"

"He's a damn good soldier!" cried Marko.

"Maybe, but in my eyes he's still a cold-blooded fucking killer!"

A seething Marko could just about contain his anger as Henki spoke on, "What about this massacre at Jovicza Hamlet, eh? We all know Ziggy was there when it happened!"

"Piss off, Henki!" he spat. "My brother swears the villagers were dead long before he arrived and nothing could be done to save them. You were there when we close questioned him *and* his patrol! They all swore that the enemy forces had been there first, perpetrated the massacre and then moved on. He still swears to this day that they went in pursuit of them."

"Ziggy can say what he wants," snarled Henki. "But I didn't believe any of that crap then and I don't now!"

"He's still a first-class soldier and you know it, but talking of bravery; what about the time in the cornfields and the dozens of lives he saved, yours included!"

Henki ground his cigarette out in the dirt floor and cursed inwardly. He didn't need to be reminded of such things!

He remembered it as being a bleak stretch of open farmland, with a few forested hills overlooking what were now empty cornfields. In the near distance sat an innocuous looking village that a narrow track wound its way towards. The setting sun had warned daylight would be gone soon and because the transporter might present a much bigger target, they'd decided to approach the village on foot. They were less than half way across, when the whirr of a high velocity missile whistled past Henki's ear, its path close enough to part the hairs on the side of his head. He'd been lucky, but the soldier next to him wasn't. He'd departed this world in a huge explosion of blood and brains!

"Sniper!" He screamed, as forty bodies hit the dirt, all praying not to be next. There'd been no sound, other than the whisper of the bullet to suggest from where it might have come from. Meaning the gunman was some distance away and using a silencer. "Ziggy?" he shouted.

"Over here," came a muffled reply from the scrub of bushes on the other side of the track.

"Direction?" he asked desperately.

"On your right, but a long way off. He's either on the high ground or in a tree. Which means we're in shit-street if we try to move."

"Okay, we'll have to wait, it'll be dark soon," he replied, but Henki's greatest fear was that as well as a silencer, the sniper might have a night scope. He was about to order everyone to stay still, when the young radio operator reached out for the set that'd fallen in the dirt beside him. Then could only watch in horror as another missile ripped through his neck and exited the other side with an even bigger spray of blood and muscle.

"Stay still, you arseholes, or the bastard will kill us all!" screamed Ziggy. The squawking radio lay where it had fallen; within arm's length, but no one dared to move or recover it!

From past experience, Henki knew that although the sniper would be enjoying every minute of tormenting them, he wouldn't dare waste a bullet unless he had a clear kill shot. Which meant they had no choice other than to stay motionless and wait for dark. As the sun slowly disappeared and gloom began to descend, he could hear the odd prayer as they lay in the dirt and waited for the sanctity of darkness. Four hours later and one by one, they'd managed to belly crawl back to where the transporters and a couple of nervous drivers were waiting. No one felt like sleeping that night and it was only when the last of the soldiers had crawled back to the safety of the trucks, did they realise Ziggy hadn't returned with them.

An urgent check came next, as they scrambled around in the dark and looked to find him, but he seemed to have vanished without a trace. The threat of the sniper meant they were unable to use any form of lighting, so they reluctantly decided to wait for morning. Dawn eventually broke across an uncertain sky and Marko was nursing his first hot coffee of the day, when he heard the call from the forward lookout. Someone or something was coming towards them.

The troops swiftly fanned out as the morning mist swirled across the expanse of farmland, at times exposing the distant hillside and occasionally the short steeple of the village church. Through a sudden break in the mist, Henki saw someone walking towards them, who didn't appear to be in any particular hurry. Then seconds later heard a joyful shout from up ahead.

"It's Ziggy," the voice roared.

This was followed by a huge crescendo of cheering from the rest of the men, as they recognised the tall figure striding towards them. Using his glasses, Henki ranged in on the unmistakable face of the missing soldier, who with his machine pistol slung across his chest, looked to be carrying a rifle wrapped in sackcloth on his right shoulder. Yet that wasn't the only thing he was carrying. Hanging by the hair in his left hand, he saw what could only be the head of the sniper as it dripped blood and swung pendulum-like in the pale morning light.

In the dark of the hut, the hissing of the gas lamp was the only other sound in the room, as Henki rose and made for the door. In the limited light, Marko could see the strained look on his face, as he adjusted the gun on his shoulder and hesitated for a moment. Then, as if unsure what to do next, turned to face him. "It's true the sniper might have been the enemy, but I don't suppose it's ever occurred to you that the cornfield was just another excuse for Ziggy to kill someone?"

Marko had expected a reply of some sort, but not this. Neither was Henki's next steely edged statement. "If this shit concerning the two doctors or the hamlet at Jovicza ever comes to light, then Ziggy can go fuck himself. Because there's no way I'm taking the rap for any of it. Which means that if a Court asks me what really happened, then I won't hesitate to tell the truth!" He then spat in the dirt and walked out into the night.

Marko rose from behind the table, just in time to see him climbing in the back of the truck where he normally slept.

With Henki's threat of divine retribution still ringing in his ears and Petrovic's warning the enemy were practically on their doorstep, a stressed-out Marko headed for the drink-filled suitcase. Twisting the top from a bottle of Black Label, he filled his metal cup to the brim, threw himself on the camp bed and wondered what to do next. If the Colonel was only half right, they might all be living on borrowed time, especially with the constant roar of the spotter planes overhead.

"The bastards must be a lot further north than we thought," he snarled. And what of the Bugatti car and two doctors? Did he dare tell the troops of the huge reward on offer for whoever was responsible for their deaths? Out in the real world, any normal person would take Henki's stand and deny any involvement and who could blame them? No matter, it still didn't change the situation they now found themselves in. The two doctors were history and Petrovic had a car capable of propelling him to safety, whilst they were still stranded here in the hills! His only other relief tonight had been the onset of darkness, plus the pissing down rain. Which thankfully meant it had been too late to assemble the troops and tell them of the plan to leave in the morning.

Another blessing was the absence of Ziggy, who'd gone hunting for rabbits along the ridge and missed the Colonel's visit. It went without saying he'd been more than happy to avoid what might have been an explosive confrontation with his brother. So along with the rest of the troops, it would be dawn before he discovered what was really going down. Sipping his whisky, he could hear the gas lamp hissing away above his head, which reminded him that it might be the only sound keeping him company tonight.

I wonder how life would have been if I'd had a sister instead of a brother? he mused out loud, before conceding it was a stupid and pointless exercise. Ziggy was a part of the here and now and nothing was ever going to change that.

Marko could recall his father telling him of the day they were born and how he'd been first to come kicking and screaming into the world. Yet nobody had anticipated his mother might be having a second child; seeing as how the midwife had never hinted at such a scenario. A few minutes later and a clutch of surprised faces had watched in shock, as Luka had landed on the table beside him. It took a long time for his mother to come to terms with his unexpected arrival, but only until he'd caught some kind of disease at the age of six. In a flash her whole attitude had changed, she becoming almost frantic for his future safety and constantly reminded Marko of his new responsibilities: r*emember, he's your younger brother and if in trouble, then it's up to you to take care of him, whatever the problem may be!*

Marko shook his head at the thought and muttered, "Having a twin brother can be a real pain in the arse at times."

His mind was drawn back to the present, the Colonel's explosive news and the implications it might have for them all. *If this damn conflict is going to end, then the sooner the better*, he thought. Yet who could have foreseen such a long-drawn-out war of attrition or contemplated the great losses on both sides. Many of the troops were unhappy at the suffering of so many women and children in the fighting. In some parts of Northern Bosnia, they'd found themselves at war with fellow Serbs, who'd lived there all their lives and justly regarded themselves as patriots! At times, it really had been difficult to choose or favour a side.

To add to this, there was Henki's gripe concerning the sins supposedly committed by Ziggy. In the early years of the war there'd been many a story of atrocities being perpetrated by both sides; some true, others not so. But with no real evidence to say his brother was responsible, Marko had dismissed Jovicza Hamlet as just one small isolated incident amongst many others. However, the death of the two doctors in the valley had smacked of pure stupidity on his part;

Ziggy insisting it was just an accident. Yet had to admit he'd overlooked his knee-jerk actions too many times, always assuming that with the passing of time, it might all be forgotten.

"Let's hope there's an easy way out of the mess," he muttered, whilst remembering the Colonel's last words. "Make it to Erdut and we'll review the situation from there." Which could only mean that if needed, help would be at hand. He was also beginning to feel the effects of the whisky as it crept quietly through his inner being, its warmth slowly easing the tensions and making him think of better times.

'Red Star Belgrade and loud music,' Marko smiled. 'I can't remember a time when it had been any different. When Luka was younger, football had always come first, and yet he could still remember the day someone gave him a copy of David Bowie's album, 'Aladdin Sane'. Their sainted mother, who'd always hated loud music being the first to suffer from the sound of 'Jean Jeanie' blasting forth from his bedroom. Then came the time he'd dyed his hair ash blonde and transformed himself into a Serbian version of his hero 'Bowie'. From that day forth, Luka would always be known as Ziggy!

It was also around this time that they'd begun to discover the delights and mysteries of the opposite sex, as well as the many problems they seemed to bring. Even now, Marko swore his younger brother's psychological problems were all woman related. Especially this one bitch named Tatiana Mestovic, whose unwelcome presence had begun to permeate their lives in the early part of 1990.

She was a sassy-faced, busty blonde, adorned with long muscular legs that she loved to spread apart and let Ziggy work his eager fingers in between. He in turn, had played his part by giving her a seriously good screwing for six months thereafter. But why she should set her sights on his brother, whom she would normally pass by in the street without giving the time of day, was anyone's guess. Yet Tatiana had always liked her men to be big and brash. So it came as no surprise to find their coming together had coincided with the renowned Red Star football riot.

Following which Ziggy had joined the SDG or Serbian Volunteer Guard and months later, been promoted to one of Arkan's right-hand men. From that day on, it had given him licence to strut around with an insufferable air of self-importance. Marko had always suspected his brother's newly found status was the real attraction for the bitch Tatiana.

Problem was, 'Super Tits', as he called her, was blessed with a very short attention span. So it came as no surprise to find she'd become bored with her David Bowie clone and turned her attention to pastures new. Marko didn't need to see the writing on the wall, the night Ziggy had stomped into his bedroom above the workshop and began head-butting the wardrobe doors and walls. Their obligatory wrestling match had soon followed, as he'd thrown his younger brother around the room and struggled in his efforts to subdue him, then discovered Super Tits had launched him into the long grass. Yet the most annoying part of this crazy situation was one week earlier and prior to her unwelcome news, he himself had become entangled in this whole crazy mess.

Following a night out on the town, he was in desperate need of a piss, but on opening the bathroom door, found Super Tits sitting naked on the toilet with a tress of blonde hair caught between her teeth. As if that wasn't bad enough, she was squeezing both her nipples and had her legs wide-open so as to display all she had to offer. In the back of his mind, Marko remembered passing Ziggy's half open bedroom door and hearing a snoring sound that suggested his brother had fallen short in fulfilling his rutting obligations.

Before he could move, Tatiana was on her knees and pulling his shorts down around his ankles. She'd then proceeded to give such a detailed demonstration of touch, style and dexterity with her fingers and tongue; she might easily have been playing 'The Magic Flute'. Another roustabout of sweat filled action had soon followed, as she'd clung to the towel rail and between Marko's arse slapping thrusts, declared that she loved being fucked from behind!

Somewhere between the moans and groans, only he had noticed the bathroom door open a fraction and see the tall silent figure of Ziggy watching their live performance. Their eyes had met briefly, yet was still long enough for him to see the hurt inside, before he'd turned and walked away. In the days following the bathroom incident, life at home had been tense to say the least, as they'd both purposely avoided each other's company. Then, and without warning, 'Super Tits' had delivered her bombshell news about terminating their relationship.

Overnight, Ziggy's loathing and hatred for Tatiana (who he blamed solely for his humiliation) had begun to mutate into a smouldering quest for vengeance. He'd then spent the next few weeks stewing over 'The Whore' as she was now known. It finally came to a head when he'd decided to get drunk by visiting every bar in town: his last port of call being the local poolroom. Making his way through the crowded smoke-filled room, he was headed in the direction of the bar, when the distinctive, guttural whining sound of 'The Whore' could be heard high above the music.

Unable to stand the noise, he'd sat with his hands on his ears for a while, before stumbling and pushing aside two people who were playing a game of pool. Over in one corner of the bar, sat Tatiana with her arms draped seductively over the neck of Big Leather Ludo, one of his most reviled and detested ex-schoolmates.

A fuming Ziggy had staggered back to the bar and stewed for a while longer, before deciding to challenge 'Leather Face' to a one-off game of pool. Yet in his haste, forgot that his opponent had been top dog on the table for the last few years. The contest was close and could have gone either way, but Ludo's guile and experience had won the day. As he'd potted the winning black ball, Tatiana let out a loud squeal of delight! Ziggy said later that he might have walked away, but for the smug smiles on both their faces.

Which was probably the reason he'd broken the pool cue on the side of Ludo's head and used the grip end to beat the shit out of him. He'd also agreed *that it was only the thickness of Tatiana's panty hose and the swift intervention of six other pool players that had prevented him from shoving the pointed end up her rectum whilst screaming, "If you like it from behind so much, bitch, try this for size!"*

Two hours later and he was jacked up in the local jail, charged with GBH and reliably informed it could easily become attempted murder. From then on, he'd languished in a cell for weeks as Marko had frantically tried to free him. Except it wasn't just Tatiana's 'super tits' that'd changed their lives forever; and Marko could clearly remember the moment it did.

It was the night he'd been explaining to the police Sergeant lounging behind the charge desk, that he was trying to organise a lawyer and needed just five minutes to go over some important details with Ziggy. The fat lazy scumbag with the unwashed uniform had pretended he was busy and ignored him as though he were invisible. But Marko could see he was reading a girly magazine under the shelf and was deliberately moving his head from side to side in a negative pendulum like movement. Fuming with frustration, he'd cursed the arrogant lump of shit and was about to concede he was done for. When a car, with its brakes hitting metal, screeched to a halt outside the station. In a flash, the Sergeant's flaccid face bore a look of annoyance, as he shifted the service revolver on his hip and went to see who was making all the noise.

As Marko looked on, three immaculately dressed soldiers, each attired in full dress uniform, had emerged from inside the large camouflaged Mercedes saloon and strolled nonchalantly into the entrance hall. The angry Sergeant was about to give them grief, when the middle soldier, who unlike the others had real silver flashes on his epaulets, held up a gloved hand to silence him. He had a slight oval face, thin aquiline nose and piercing penetrating eyes. "I've come here to collect one of my men," he said to no one in particular.

"Excuse me?" the confused policeman asked, whilst trying to make sense of what was happening within his own personal domain.

"My name is Commander Zeljko Raznatovic and it would appear you have Luka Tomovic, one of my top men, in custody; I am here to collect him."

The Sergeant placed his hands on his hips in an act of disobedient insolence. "I don't give a shit who you are, Corporal, but no one goes anywhere without the proper authority!"

"Are you Serbian and a patriot?" the shiny silver epaulets asked, his eyes searching for some kind of activity in the room behind.

"Sorry comrade, I don't know what the fuck you're talking about!" the Sergeant replied with a hint of sarcasm.

"Serbia is now at war with Croatia and I've been informed that you have Tomovic, my officer, incarcerated here. I'm not in the least bit interested in what you think or do, but if you don't release him at once. I'll order my men to take you outside and have you shot for treason and that applies to anyone else who refuses my orders!"

The Sergeant's face took on a stunned look of disbelief, then one of defiance, as he absorbed this threat to his constitutional power. Yet before he could utter what was almost certain to be another oath of defiance, Marko spoke.

"I recommend you should listen to him, Sergeant. This is Arkan, leader of The Serbian Volunteer Guard and I can assure you that he does indeed have great powers of authority; especially those of life and death."

The name registered almost immediately with the police Sergeant and with it came a small vestige of doubt. Following their embarrassing defeat in Slovenia, the country was rife with talk of retribution against Croatia, or any of the other countries willing to try and break free and the name 'Arkan' was on everyone's lips. The Sergeant searched the faces opposite and nervously licked his lips, before turning snail like on his heels and heading for the cells. A few moments of waiting went by, before he and two other policemen appeared with a still handcuffed Ziggy between them.

"We'll need a signature!" the Sergeant pleaded, whilst holding out an official looking form. Arkan directed a hand casually to the soldier on his left, who stepped forward, shouldered his machine pistol and flipped through the two-page document.

"Not sure if I like this fingerprint business," he grunted.

The aquiline nose gazed at the second page. "Get rid of it," he muttered. "But let Fatso keep the top sheet; just make it a little harder to understand."

The soldier smiled knowingly, sat behind a nearby desk, and moments later, the continuous 'clack, clack' of an electric typewriter could be heard. Once finished, he'd scribbled something undecipherable in the required box and watched as Marko and Ziggy, affectionately head butted each other and thumped their chests like Viking Berserkers. "This is my older brother!" Ziggy declared, before proudly slapping him on the shoulder with a force designed to dent steel.

One month later and Marko had also joined the Serbian Volunteer Guard.

Marko lit another Lucky Strike, reached for the gas lantern and turned it off. The whisky had left a warm glow inside, but as he fell asleep fully clothed, was aware that tonight's events might just be the beginning of his problems.

Hearing the sound of angry voices, Marko instinctively knew something was wrong. Stubbing out his cigarette, he hefted the kit bag over his shoulder and stepped outside the hut, but instead of pouring rain, was surprised to find everything covered in snow. Through the drifting flakes he could see two figures slipping and sliding into view. One was Ziggy, the other Sorovac, who followed puppy-like alongside, both their hands pointing here and there in what appeared to be futile gestures.

"Henki's gone missing!" Ziggy said bluntly.

"Missing?" asked a confused Marko. "What the hell does that mean?" The bearded face swung in the direction of Sorovac, who had the look of someone who didn't want to be there, but reluctantly took up the story.

"It was just before first light, when he poked his head into my tent and said we were breaking camp in an hour. We haven't been able to find him since."

"Which is when I first heard about this leaving order," growled Ziggy. Marko waved a hand in dismissal. "Never mind that shit, I'll explain all about it later. I'm more interested in finding Henki."

"Well that's the problem, Boss, we've found his gear, but can't find *him!*"

Before he could reply, two troopers began to gather his camp bed and personal belongings, which along with the wounded, would be loaded onto the middle truck.

"Where did you find Henki's gear?" snarled Marko, who was obviously annoyed at this news. A nervous Sorovac pointed to the trucks stationed under the trees on the other side of the camp. He didn't like it when Marko was angry, past experience telling him his Boss *did not* suffer fools gladly. The buzz of excitement at their imminent departure was plain to see, as the soldiers began piling the Platoon's gear aboard the three troop carriers.

Yet there was no doubting the rucksack gathering snow on the truck's rear tailgate belonged to his second in command. The bedroll on top being exactly where he'd left it, before he supposedly went walkabout. Marko looked around in exasperation. "This is not the *Guca Trumpet Festival*, with a cast of thousands!" He spat at them. "It's an empty fucking forest, so someone *must* have seen him somewhere!"

"One of the guards saw him heading for the plateau just before dawn and assumed he was going for a crap," Sorovac added lamely.

Marko looked beyond the trees. "We need to find him," he muttered half-heartedly, conscious there wasn't time for these crazy diversions, as he remembered Petrovic's words.

It's important you reach the Unzini Crossroads before 7.00 am this morning. A column of troops with medical facilities will be moving eastwards and happy to help.

Their short walk took them in the direction of the plateau, but Marko didn't need a compass, he'd made the same trip on numerous occasions. As if to prove him right, one of the guards suddenly appeared in view whilst buckling up his belt. He was also about to give him an earful for moving about in the open, but decided against it. The spotter planes couldn't fly overhead in these snowy conditions. Pushing on, he led the way to the rocky escarpment that jutted out sharply and formed part of what they'd since named *The Ridge*. Directly below and running left to right, was a steep ravine filled with a mass of tall trees and overgrown brush.

The plateau itself, they'd termed *God's Latrine*, because when first searching the area, one of Henki's men had come close to meeting his maker. The story went that his leg had suddenly disappeared beneath him and he'd only just managed to reach out and grasp a branch of a tree that grew nearby. But when clearing the snow, discovered a large hole in the ground and realised he could see the top of trees some thirty metres below. Not being geologists, they could only assume that a section of the cliff must have broken away sometime in the Ice Age and fallen into the depths below. Whatever the reason, its timely departure had left a near perfect circle in the now snow-covered plateau.

As with every trooper, personal ablutions were an everyday nightmare and when the urge came calling, you did it *when* and *where* you could. Anecdotal tales told of youngsters returning from the battlefield with soggy and foul smelling rear-ends. But if on the odd occasion it was possible to make camp for a few nights proper, then latrine ditches could be dug and everyone would know literally which place to aim for.

Unfortunately, the one-night forest stopovers were the real killer; especially in winter when the ground was so hard it was difficult to hammer in a tent peg. This, as always, would leave them with no option other than to make do with what they could find. For obvious reasons, nobody wanted to stray too far from camp, which in turn forever threw up major problems, especially when they doing their thing. Many a time the guards would chuckle and smile, on hearing a nearby groan from beyond the trees, knowing some unlucky fucker had trodden in someone else's pile. Not much fun, but at times unavoidable with sixty arses on the go.

Marko stood near the edge of the hole, peering down into the temporary sewage drain and couldn't resist a smile. Compared to the overpowering stench of the latrine ditches, this was pure luxury. He'd used it himself on many an occasion, his last visit being yesterday morning. Its very simplicity was also its greatest attraction. Drop your kit grab a branch and Mother Nature travelled back to where it came from; no smell and no mess.

He gingerly moved the few feet past the hole to the edge of the plateau, the snow and ice making it a very dangerous and tricky manoeuvre; one mistake here and it was *a long way down.*

"Do you think he might have slipped and fallen?" asked Ziggy from a safe distance.

"If he did, we can only assume he must have been sleep-walking!" Marko retorted, finding it difficult to imagine anyone would contemplate going anywhere near a one-way ticket to oblivion.

"Are we going to search down below for him?" asked Sorovac.

Marko gave him a look that suggested he might send him head first down the latrine as well! To reach the bottom of the cliff-face would involve many hours of hard work, plus the use of ropes, it being the only practical means of reaching the lower areas. Besides, there was always the danger of a Croat patrol seeing them. However, if Henki had somehow managed to end up down below, he didn't think there was much he could do for him and who would volunteer to abseil into hell! He checked his watch and turned to Ziggy. "Take half the men and make a two-minute 360-degree search of the camp. If there's no sign of him, then we have to move on."

In the first, Rado transporter impatiently drummed his fingers on the steering wheel, ready to drop the clutch and head off. Standing in the snow, Marko watched the last of the troops clamber into the rear of the other two transporters, their departure heralded by a final slam of the tailgates. The Platoon's banter suddenly quietened, as they waited for him to give the signal. This would be a significant moment for them all, as it meant they'd be leaving *The Ridge* for the last time, never to return.

His decision to break camp hadn't been an easy one either. Especially when a thorough search had failed to find his second in command. There'd been one small spark of hope, when he'd heard the sentry's tale of seeing his No. 2 making his way towards *God's Latrine*. Marko fully expecting to see him to stroll back into camp, wearing a perplexed look on his face and wondering what the fuss was about. He'd even considered asking for a few volunteers, so they might search down below the trees. Normally the boys would be jostling like Spartans in an effort to get their arses to the front of the queue; especially as they knew it was Henki they were searching for.

Yet when such a hazardous task had been suggested, the sound was that of shuffling feet and a row of reluctant blank faces. Only then did it dawn on him, that for all the battles and near misses they'd endured over the years, Henki Topovic, his long-time sidekick and brave countryman, might truly have met an unenviable end lying in his own shit thirty metres below in *God's Latrine.*

With this sad thought in mind, Marko took one last look at the snow trodden grass where they'd been camped for the last ten days. Yet more importantly, the four freshly dug graves that lay beyond the trees, each one denoting the sudden and violent passing of some of his closest friends. From the middle transporter, Ziggy waved a hand, the sign to say all was well with the walking wounded and Marko gave the signal to leave. The engines of the three massive trucks fired into life as one and a relieved Rado led the way, as they moved off down the narrow dirt track.

In the rear of the last troop carrier, Sorovac was feeling sick to his stomach. His mother had always warned that his curiosity would be his downfall and in this case, feared she could be right. Except his problems weren't symptomatic of him leaving this cold god-forsaken place. They were the result of him being in the wrong place and hearing a conversation he wished he hadn't. He clearly remembered Colonel Petrovic's worrying news and following his departure, Henki and Marko arguing about Ziggy and the trouble he brought to their lives. Their heated discussion might have been short, but turned into a bitter one, ceasing only when Henki had said his piece and stormed off into the night.

Standing alone in the dark, Sorovac had waited until he'd climbed into the rear of the transporter, before moving off in the direction of his own tent. Then froze stiff, when someone had unexpectedly stepped out of the shadows. To his horror, the flicker of a cigarette lighter briefly illuminated a shadowed face and it was only then did he realise Ziggy must have been listening to the same argument! Watching from the rear of the last truck, the snow reminded Sorovac of a picturesque greeting card he might receive at Christmas time and if things had been different, given him good reason to smile. Yet the bitter altercation between his two commanding officers and the sudden appearance of Ziggy, who'd manifested himself like some kind of spectre, had only served to unnerve him badly. To make things worse, there was the still unexplained and mystery disappearance of Henki Topovic. He'd also slept badly, his thoughts harking back to the two doctors and the massacre at the hamlet, but more importantly, the other troops who'd been present that day.

The middle truck had always been regarded as Ziggy's own personal territory, filled only with the men who'd fought alongside him over the years. Sorovac had no opinion whether they should be a part of the Serbian cause; it simply wasn't his place to judge. Although he'd always felt there was something evil and foreboding about the vicious mix of failed guerrillas, ex-paratroopers and Greek mountain partisans, as they strutted around in their black uniforms and wraparound sunglasses. And yet throughout all of this, a proud Arkan would parade before the world's media holding a gun in one hand and a live tiger cub in the other.

The convoy had slowed to halt where the dirt track met the valley road, when to Sorovac's surprise, a smiling Ziggy appeared from nowhere and vaulted over the tailgate. "Pomerite guzice, *move your arses!*" He growled, the soldiers quickly shuffling along the bench so he might sit opposite. Then, with a wide grin, took a pack of Lucky Strikes from his parka and leant across to offer Sorovac one. It might have been a small gesture, yet still made him very wary. Ziggy's normal attitude was to treat him like shit and the half smile wasn't reflected in his cold flinty eyes.

Taking the cigarette, he once again remembered the rancorous dispute between Marko and Henki and was then dumbstruck when a smirking Ziggy leant forward and whispered, "Shit weather last night eh? Definitely no place to be standing about in the rain!"

An ice-cold fear swept through Sorovac, as he stared into the ruthless eyes which had all but confirmed Henki's tragic fate and, if true, might decide his own. The smile was growing wider by the minute, as Ziggy used his Zippo to light Sorovac's trembling cigarette. However, before he'd reached the tip, an unexpected roaring sound came from nowhere and the world suddenly turned bright red!

Marko could feel an excruciating stab of pain in his back and seconds later, realised someone was struggling through the snow with him draped over their shoulder. Another jolt raked his body as he hit the ground with an agonising thud, the force enough to make him nearly pass out. His head momentarily swam with a tide of nausea, as he closed his eyes and waited for it to pass. Opening them again, he focused on Ziggy, whose still smoking uniform was covered in a thick black residue that stood out against the white of the snow.

As if that wasn't bad enough, his face was scraped down one side and his beard so badly singed, he looked as if someone had attacked him with a blowtorch. "The bastards were waiting for us!" he snarled, one hand scooping up a handful of snow, which he used to wipe away the blood from a deep cut on Marko's forehead.

"I know," he gasped, "I saw the Harrier Jet at the last second." His eyes narrowed as he remembered the convoy rounding the bend and seeing the glittering outline of the aircraft, as it hovered five metres above the field like a giant silver bird of prey, the snow swirling around due to the downward thrust of its engines. Then before they'd had time to think, a single surface to air missile bore down on them, its unerring smoke trail carrying death as its calling card and everything went blank.

From where he lay, Marko was able to see the smoke and flames rising like a funeral pyre above the burning trucks below. "Did anyone else survive?" he whispered through gritted teeth.

Ziggy shrugged and shook his head. "Five maybe, but the rest? All gone." He then sat him upright. "I need to look at that shoulder of yours brother." Zipping open his parka, he loosened Marko's tunic, began probing around the area of his collarbone and as he did so, explained how they'd both survived. "Rado, who like the others didn't make it, swerved the lead truck into a tree seconds before the missile struck. Although that didn't stop it from hitting the middle one and exploding like a fireball, literally incinerating everything on either side. Only six of us managed to survive the carnage and we did so by the skin of our teeth.

We were like corks stuck in a fizzy drinks bottle. The moment your truck slewed off the road, you were thrown from the cab and landed in the deep snow in a ditch. The same went for me, Sorovac and the other four sitting in the rear of the last truck. No one heard a sound. Well not until everything turned red and we finished up lying in the middle of the road choking back the fumes and smoke."

Marko was puzzled. "How come you ended up in the last truck?"

"More room," he said bluntly. A further few moments of exploratory probing went on, before he asked, "Are you okay?"

Marko nodded slowly in the affirmative.

"Good. Give me a second, I need to check that your arm's not broken." He then moved it to a more horizontal position, grasped his wrist in a vice-like grip and gave it a vicious twist.

It was all Marko could do to stop himself from crying out, as he heard the distinctive 'click' from his shoulder and saw the satisfied look appear on Ziggy's face. "Just as I thought," he said smugly. "It was just dislocated."

"What do we do now?" grumbled Marko, his shoulder still throbbing from the pain of relocation.

"We don't have much time, but I need to go back and check on the other men. While I'm there I'll see if there's anything we can salvage, otherwise there's no way we'll survive." He was about to close Marko's tunic, when he paused as if something had occurred to him. Then without further explanation, reached for the set of dog tags hanging around his brother's neck,

"What are you doing!" snarled Marko, in defence of the one thing all soldiers shared alike: the positive proof of their identity.

For a moment, Ziggy's blackened face took on a more menacing look, before he relaxed and placed a hand on Marko's still throbbing shoulder.

"Trust me, brother," he whispered. His grizzled head giving a continuous nod, as he lifted the tags from around his neck and shook them like a minor trophy. He then removed his own and made his way downwards to the carnage that lay on the road below.

The three transporters were still well alight, the dense smoke and flames clouding the sky above. The attack by the Harrier had turned them into a kind of monumental funeral pyre, the heat enough to melt the snow around in a huge circle. Keeping his distance, Ziggy skirted the first truck, but having no luck, moved on until he came to the middle one. Shielding his face, he could see both cab doors had been blown off and the driver: whose body resembled a piece of charcoal, hanging out sideways.

Keeping his winter gloves on as a means of protection, he edged closer and pulled the still smoking figure; who he was sure had once been Igor head first out onto the tarmac. Taking the knife from his boot, he began to pick at what was left of the smoking tunic, the smell of burning flesh stronger than the acrid smoke filling the air. Within minutes, he'd found what he was looking for: the blackened metal dog tags still hanging around his all, but missing neck. The intense heat could still be felt through his gloves, as he used the knife to ease them off and flick them hissing into the snow.

His last act was to replace them with Marko's and go hunting for another victim: who in death would gain a new identity. Somewhere in the back of his mind he remembered the other surviving soldiers, all of whom were badly in need of help. Moving away from the carnage, he saw one of them had managed to sit up and was holding his head in his hands, but compared to the others looked to be reasonably intact.

Sorovac's ears were still ringing from the sound of the explosion and his body felt as though it had been run over by one of the trucks. But the first thing he saw when he managed to open his soot-filled eyes, were a pair of boots standing in the snow. Hoping it might be help of some kind; he raised his blistered face from between his knees and found he was looking into the smiling face of Ziggy.

Marko gave a grimace of pain and tried to sit up, alarmed at the sound of the single gunshot that rang out above the crackle of the burning trucks. A few minutes later and he watched Ziggy scrambling back to his position on the hillside whilst carrying a charred rucksack over his shoulder. "I heard a shot!" Marko said apprehensively.

"It's okay, brother, one of the troops was so far gone, he begged me to put him out of his misery."

Marko lay back in the snow. "Who was it?"

Ziggy hesitated a moment before replying, "Corporal Sorovac, but like his dead compatriot, I doubt he'll be in need of these." Taking the two sets of dog tags from his tunic pocket, he placed one around Marko's neck and tucked it out of sight. "However, they'll definitely come in handy if we decide to disappear for a while."

"What about the other survivors? You said there were four of them."

"There are, but three are in such a bad way, there's no way they can be moved. So it's all down to whoever finds them first. With a bit of luck and it's the NATO forces, then they should be okay." He hesitated again. "If not and the Partisans arrive, then I imagine they'll all go the same way as Sorovac."

An anguished Marko was staring down at the smoking remains of what had been his proud platoon, as Ziggy finished strapping his arm in place. "Can you walk? We have to get out of here before some unwelcome fuckers come looking."

Marko took a deep breath and nodded. "Where to?" he gasped, his shoulder still in agony.

Ziggy pointed eastwards. "Serbia is that way.

Part Eight

Liverpool, 2015

'San Carlos' was no ordinary restaurant, its lavish interior being one of pure Neapolitan flamboyance. With its stylish décor, superb food and Italian waiters who served up every dish with a smile, it really was hard to beat. And it seemed that Zelda, who'd supposedly found it on TripAdvisor, simply adored Tuscan style cooking.

Having been there twice before, Jacko was well aware of its popularity and thought it wise to reserve one of its more secluded tables for this one special occasion. As a precaution and to ensure they wouldn't get lost in the busy streets, he'd also arranged for Simone to collect Zelda and Milos from their hotel and take them to the restaurant by taxi. The evening's first real 'wow' moment came, when the two ladies stepped from the rear of the cab.

Simone as usual, had opted for a simple figure hugging black cocktail dress that complimented her long shapely legs. Whereas Zelda had chosen to wear a pair of skin-tight silk trousers and matching fitted blouse. Under normal circumstances, this would have been perfectly acceptable. Except *The Bosnian Bird* never did things by half, as the Bolero-style open-necked frontage brought a huge in-take of breath from the two security men guarding the doors. This blatant show of cleavage instantly reminded Jacko of 'The Cresta Run', as it disappeared tantalisingly between the lower folds of her blouse. And judging by the commotion, most of the hot-blooded waiters were dreaming of sliding head first down the same flesh filled slope.

Milos unfortunately, was left to take care of the taxi fare.

"Always helps to make an entrance," grinned Jacko, as the two beauties threaded their way through a jostle of male admirers.

"Trust me, it happens all time when you're out with Zelda," chuckled Simone.

'Bees around a hive' immediately sprung to mind, as they settled themselves around the table. "What would you like to drink ladies?" asked Jacko.

"Seeing as it's such a special night, I think we should have lots of champagne," declared Zelda, her sultry voice having the hot-blooded Italian waiters frantically waving their drinks menu in her direction. Jacko gave a sigh, ordered a lager for himself and wondered if he could put the rest on expenses.

He awoke the next morning, nursing a cracker of a hangover that could only be assuaged by the warm sensuous feel of Simone lying beside him, plus the memory of last night's carnal pleasure. A few hours later and they were both having a long tearful goodbye at John Lennon Airport, as Zelda and Milos sadly departed Liverpool and headed for London.

Back at the S.C.U. the sound of ringing phones and a busy squad doing what they're supposed to be do, had helped put a more positive spin on things. That is until the distant sound of metal tips warned that *Fred Astaire* was about to make an entrance. Jacko could tell by the look on Bastion's face and curt nod in the direction of Carson's office, that all was not well.

"I've been thinking about this Bosnian business, Nathan, and I'm still not convinced we have a case."

Jacko's eyebrows lifted in surprise and his boss immediately took up the fight. "You were there at last night's meeting, Sir; I thought the evidence was pretty damn convincing to say the least."

Bastion's face looked doubtful. "I congratulate you on what you've achieved thus far, but I'm still not convinced it will hold up in a Court of Law."

Jacko and Carson were both stunned as he laid out his argument for the defence. "As I see it, there's nothing to connect the Tomovic brothers with our investigation. Yes, we have the fingerprints and blood on the broken sunglasses, but that's all."

"What about the evidence in the cue-case?" asked Carson. "I thought that was pretty damn convincing."

"I agree, but only if you can prove the fingerprint on the Kraft knife and the face on the Serbian chargesheet are from the same person. It's the same with the two doctors and the fingerprint found in their car. There's nothing to say, or prove it once belonged to Marko Tomovic. And I am right in saying that the reward of $10,000 dollars was never paid out, because those responsible for their deaths are yet to be found?"

Jacko and Carson sat in silence as Bastion continued to sink their ship. "The memory stick and its contents are convincing enough, but still circumstantial in what it's trying to say. A good lawyer would have it thrown out before you got started."

Bastion turned to Jacko. "One last point, Sergeant, as I see it all the evidence claims the Tomovic brothers were killed in 1995, which was around the time the war ended and I don't see anything to disprove that scenario."

"We think they're still alive, Sir."

"I need more than that Sergeant, I need proof!"

"Zelda and Milos are convinced they survived the war and so do we."

"It's *me* you need to convince," growled Bastion.

Jacko backtracked. "During the meal at San Carlos, Milos was telling me all about this Arkan guy and how powerful he'd been throughout the war. He was also reputed to be loyal to his men; especially those in need of help. As I understand it, Ziggy Tomovic wasn't just any old recruit; he'd been there since day one; the Riot at Maksimir and the forming of the Tigers. Marko Tomovic was also one of his best officers, so why wouldn't he help them if he had the chance?"

Bastion looked at the ceiling and polished the tip of his nose. "Arkan, as we all know, was assassinated in 2001 and that being the case, have to assume the two brothers were also killed in action twenty years ago. Which leads me to believe that we don't have a viable suspect or DNA sample, to say either of them are part of our murder investigation."

Carson gave a shrug. "That I'm afraid, is the only positive thing we have at the moment, Sir."

"Assuming it's not enough, what do you intend to do next?"

"What we always do sir, investigate further."

"Enlighten me."

Carson looked in Jacko's direction; who took over the conversation. "Before this war business came to light, I didn't have a clue about Bosnia and neither did any of the other Team members. That said, we're all of the opinion that there are far too many overlapping details for it to be purely co-incidental. Which I might add, our two Journalists are more than happy to agree with us."

Bastion had to supress a smile as he rose from his chair and made for the door, he was about take his leave when something occurred to him.

"A question, Sergeant, do we know *where* the Tomovic brothers died?"

"Not exactly, somewhere on the border between Northern Bosnia and Serbia."

"How?"

"It was supposed to be some kind of attack."

"Who identified them?"

"I'm not sure, probably whoever found them."

"Even if it was a small convoy, Sergeant, I'd imagine there must have been a lot of casualties."

Jacko gave a non-committal shrug.

"Do you have a date?"

"Not an exact one, Sir. Although Sarajevo is convinced it happened sometime in early November 1995, not long after the two Swedish doctors died."

Bastion was thoughtful. "Before I joined the Metropolitan Force, Sergeant, I was stationed with the Military Police in Northern Ireland, which would be around 1995. My stint there had just about come to an end and I was looking forward to being posted to a cushy job overseas, as part of the UN peacekeeping force in Yugoslavia. However, my aspirations were soon dashed when a ceasefire was declared and an absolute no fly-zone came into being. Which, as I remember, brought a complete halt to all hostilities, so I believe if there had been some kind of attack, it has to be on record somewhere. Therefore, if you need an answer, I suggest you search the Internet, or even better, speak to the Ministry of Defence."

The two detectives were savouring a couple of chocolate-covered cappuccinos, as they mingled amongst the crowds in Lime Street Station "Imagine our machine churning these out every morning," Smithy said wistfully.

"Dream on!" laughed Jacko, his eyes checking the departure times on the electronic timetable. "If the scoreboard's right, we need platform No. 2 to catch the London train." Today's outing to the 'Big Smoke' had come as a direct result of Bastion suggesting they contact the MOD and Jacko having a chat with a Whitehall desk-jockey named Stephen Millar. At first, their discussion had been relaxed and amicable, until he'd touched on the subject of the two Serbian soldiers and the unusual circumstances concerning their demise.

Unfortunately, it was at this point, Stephen regretfully informed him that the matter was *Classified.*

A further discussion revealed he was more than happy to fax Jacko all those parts made public, but sadly, anything else would require a verbal exchange, or to put it plainly; *a talk in private.*

Having no other choice, it was finally agreed that a short visit to London might, indeed, be helpful with their on-going investigation; hence their journey south. Taking a seat in their first class carriage, Jacko recalled Carson's indignant. "I don't care how much it costs; my men are going in cuffin style!"

He'd also been hoping for a little peace and quiet, but both their mobiles had continued to ring non-stop all the way. There again, three hours of comfort with a hi-speed country view, gave him the chance to relax and answer some of Smithy's questions.

"Where did you eat after the Site Meeting?"

"San Carlos Restaurant in North John St."

"Very nice! I can just imagine the reaction of those Italian waiters when Zelda turned up."

Jacko smiled, as he recalled the stunning cleavage defying outfit. "Yes, you could say she helped put the rest of the ladies in the shade."

"That Milos guy was also something else Sarge and his white suit put me in mind of the man from the Kentucky Fried Chicken adverts."

Jacko laughed at the thought. "I think the blonde hair and moustache definitely helped give that impression. Although the crumpled suit had to be the real clincher."

Surprisingly, their train had arrived bang on time and a black cab took them in the direction of Whitehall. Where lots of annoying security checks had been added to their day, before the *chap on the end of the phone* appeared in person.

"Sorry about the delay," began an owlish looking Stephen Millar. "One never seems to know where the times goes."

Judging by his University-striped tie and corduroy suit, Jacko was convinced Stephen didn't have a Walther PK pistol slung under his arm, or might be taking part in a covert mission later that night. There again, times were tough and everyone had to take whatever was on offer these days. A couple more obligatory introductions were next in line, as they got to know each other and the meeting moved on to more serious matters.

"I've read through all your faxes concerning the murder investigation and still find it surprising that it should bring you here today," smiled Stephen.

"That's brilliant, which means you must have made the connection with our case and the Tomovic brothers?"

"I have indeed," replied the determined looking Ministry man, "and happy to help in any way possible."

"In that case, can you tell us exactly how and where they died?" Asked Smithy.

Stephen acted as though he hadn't heard the question. "As I say, gentlemen, we're here to help in any way possible."

"Then you must know about Operation Deliberate Force, which was created to help the Coalition forces destroy most of the Serbians' ability to fight?"

"Yes Sergeant, I am familiar with that part of the Bosnian Offensive."

"And the ceasefire?"

"Yes," he agreed, realising the two detectives had been doing some research on the subject. "There was a halt in the fighting and a strict no fly-zone introduced to all non-military aircraft."

Jacko decided to take the bull by the horns. "I have to remind you that this is a major murder inquiry and ask if you have any evidence to show that Marko Tomovic and his platoon were killed in early November 1995?"

Stephen rested his shiny elbows on the desk and placed his hands under his chin. "I imagine there were lots of minor incursions during the cease fire."

"Would you describe this incident as a minor incursion?"

Stephen began scratching his earlobe whilst contemplating Jacko's question. "Sorry, I can only tell you what I'm able."

"What about the two Swedish doctors and the fingerprint on the dashboard?"

"French Forensic found nothing to link the Tomovic brothers to that one particular incident, fingerprints included."

Jacko realised he was being stonewalled and tried another tack. "We've been reliably informed that the Yugoslavian War Crimes Commission found evidence of a major incursion in which Lieutenant Tomovic died. Which we understand, is the real reason they called off the search."

Stephen's attitude and demeanour changed to a more official one as he listened to Jacko's plea for information. "As I said, Sergeant, some parts of this particular episode have been made public, whilst others haven't. But I'm more than happy to tell you what I can."

"Can I take notes?" asked Jacko.

The owl nodded, reached for a file and began to speak. "Everything concerning the death of the two Swedish Doctors was made public. However, this particular report is *Strictly Classified* and has never seen the light of day. It tells of an isolated incident that happened in early November 1995, involving a Serbian mobile unit that had been attempting to find a way back behind its own lines. Unfortunately what happened next is a little 'blurred', for the want of a better description. According to the official report, three Serbian transporters were attacked and destroyed by local Partisans who lived in the nearby mountains. It also states that there were no known survivors."

Without looking up, Stephen reached for another file. "What I have here is the sworn testimony of one Lars Knutfeld. He was a Major in the Norwegian Army and the man responsible for the day to day safety of the two doctors during their short stay in Bosnia: which I'm afraid is also Classified."

Jacko blew out air in exasperation. "We know all about the Major's role and what took place, so why should this part be classified?"

"Because Knutfeld never made an official statement," said Stephen. "However, due to the seriousness of your investigation and considering what might be at stake, I am prepared to pass on certain verbal information, but only in the strictest of confidence!"

Fred Astaire tip-tapped his way into Carson's office and took a seat.

"The whole thing was a cover-up," Jacko said bluntly.

Bastion looked puzzled. "How do you mean? I thought the Government were more than happy to help."

"And so they were: but only on one condition. The MOD has insisted we can't publicise any part containing Major Knutfeld's testimony."

"Why?"

"Because of the Official Secrets Act."

"I think a little more detail would be helpful, Sergeant."

Jacko paused for a second. "There's a sanitised version of what happened to the 'Two Doctors' contained in this official file, but what it doesn't have, is Major Lars Knutfeld's personal account of the cover-up."

A tap on the door interrupted his flow, as Jason Junior appeared with three coffees. "Sugar's on the tray," he whispered, before swiftly disappearing from view. Jacko shook his head and continued his tale. "I'd imagine anyone old enough to remember the killing of the Swedish doctors, and considering the outcry, must recall the huge manhunt that followed. But until yesterday had no idea how difficult that'd been. The area was of a steep mountainous type, with heavily wooded scree slopes all around. The search parties had scoured the nearby hills for nigh on ten days, with everyone feeling as if they were looking for a needle in a haystack.

So after a week of frustration, they took a welcome break and requested an air search. Problem was, nobody had thought about the approaching winter weather. Meaning the planes were only able to take off when the skies were clear, which wasn't very often. So, as each futile day went by, the teams on the ground found nothing. Then on the ninth day, it was agreed by all that they should call off the air search, at least until the heavy rains had eased."

Jacko scanned his notes again. "On the tenth day, Major Knutfeld awoke to find it had snowed overnight and received a call telling of a serious incursion that had taken place not far from where the two doctors died. Seeing as how this had happened on his patch, the Major decided to investigate and says the narrow road was snowbound as he made his way towards the scene."

Jacko wore an apologetic smile and showed them the empty file. "As you can see Sir, the Major's testimony comes in *verbal* form only and I will now try to explain why. As Knutfeld's patrol neared the incident, the air appeared to be filled with the acrid smell of burning rubber and what he thought was human flesh. A couple of kilometres further on and they met a roadblock manned by a troop of no nonsense Bosnian soldiers. The Major was about to pass through the barricade, when half a dozen guns had blocked his path. But luckily, had arrived just in time to watch the last of three burnt out transporters being shoved into a nearby ravine; by what he assumed was a locally sourced JCB. He'd then spent ten more futile minutes arguing with the guards, before an officer in charge had let him pass through, but not his Bosnian interpreter."

Jacko checked his notes again. "According to Knutfeld, a heated discussion then took place as he tried to ascertain exactly what'd happened. The Bosnian officer spoke very little English, but instead used his hands to demonstrate how a fighter jet had flown in and carried out the attack. The Major thought this very unlikely, seeing as how the terrain appeared much too dangerous for low-level flying.

Yet the Bosnian officer was adamant it had been perpetrated by one of the Coalition fighter jets. Knutfeld asked if there were any survivors of the attack, to which he'd nodded and pointed to the other side of the road. Lying in the snow, he found five badly burnt men, all of whom appeared to be alive, but only just. There were more surprises in store, when the Bosnian officer informed him that the soldier furthest away, was in fact dead. To confirm this, he'd pointed to the unexplained bullet hole in the middle of his forehead. Major Knutfeld was mightily concerned by this turn of events and asked how this had happened. The officer said he had no idea and swore it had nothing to do with his own unit.

Knutfeld's next enquiry was about the rest of the men from the convoy. A few minutes later and he was led to a sheltered copse in which a large ditch had been dug, presumably by the same digger machine. A closer inspection had revealed that this newly excavated hole was filled to overflowing with a pile of still smouldering bodies. When he'd asked about identification, the officer had shown him a small leather bag filled with their dog tags. He'd then asked what would happen to the four surviving, yet badly injured Serbian soldiers. The Bosnian had insisted they were in very good hands; his immediate Superior having just called to confirm an ambulance was on the way. The Major had politely inquired if he could take some photographs of the scene, this request being firmly rebuffed with the barrel of a loaded gun.

"The Major's statement officially comes to an end, when he and his patrol had left the scene and begun their return to base. Although according to his detailed account, they'd travelled less than half a kilometre when they heard four gunshots ringing out from the rear. At the time, he'd contemplated turning around, but in the end thought better of it."

"Do you think it was the four soldiers who'd survived the air strike?" asked Bastion.

Jacko shrugged. "We don't know for sure, Sir, but the story doesn't quite end there."

"You mean the cover-up?"

"Yes, Sir."

Bastion steepled his fingers and waited.

"When this particular incident occurred, the war was more or less over and the ceasefire holding up. It was within this same period, that all the warring factions had unilaterally agreed to lay down their arms. There's no real evidence to prove otherwise, Sir, but the man for the Ministry speculates that Lieutenant

Tomovic's unit were attempting to avoid surrender by sneaking their way back into Serbia. In order to achieve this dangerous feat, it meant them using the forest back roads and for reasons unknown, had incurred casualties of their own along the way. He was also of the opinion they were responsible for the death of the two doctors. That being the reason they spent the next ten days hiding in the hills."

"Which obviously wasn't long enough," said Bastion.

"That's right, Sir. In an ironic twist of fate, it would appear Tomovic and his men met their own Nemesis on that same snowbound valley road."

"And I assume you're about to tell me how?"

"Correction Sir, I'm only repeating the MOD's theoretical version of what might have taken place."

Bastion's brow furrowed as Jacko continued, "During 'Operation Deliberate Force', over four hundred different Coalition aircraft were employed to destroy the Serbian's ability to wage war; many of them being fighter planes. When the Serbs eventually capitulated and the terms of peace agreed, the only aircraft allowed in the no-fly zone were the American ones, the others returning to their relative airbases and countries. Unfortunately, for the people on the ground trying to discover who'd killed the doctors, the jets became a real nightmare.

For a start they were useless for low-level surveillance and their engines so loud; half of Bosnia could hear them coming. To make things worse, they could only fly in good weather. So, on 9 November, it was decided to call off the air search because of the atrocious flying conditions. Unbeknown to everyone, on the tenth day, a Royal Naval Sea-Harrier was en-route to its Carrier anchored out in the Adriatic Sea. This was one of three aircraft that had been part of the original campaign. The first having been shot down by the Serbs a few months earlier, the other having safely returned to its base.

"Except nobody knew that a third Harrier had been grounded for weeks, this due to a computer glitch that was eventually resolved. It was only days later did they discover that the gremlins plaguing the jets' control systems hadn't quite been cured. When it landed on the mother ship later that same day, they found one of its Sidewinder Guided Missiles had mysteriously gone missing from under the left wing."

Bastion began to polish the tip of his nose using a finger and thumb, a sure sign he was mulling things over. "Fantastic aircraft the Harrier Jet!" He declared. "I can remember them from the Falklands War. It had two directional thrusters, which allowed it to hover and land like a helicopter. It also meant they were able to get to the most unlikely of places; rocky land, sandy beaches and even narrow tree filled ravines."

A moment passed before he turned to Carson and Jacko.

"So gentlemen, what are we to believe? Did the Harrier spot the three transporters and take them out? And if true, is the MOD in a roundabout way, hinting that the pilot didn't report 'the kill', seeing as how he'd just violated the ceasefire? Another thing, if we assume the Serbian convoy didn't open fire first, could the pilot's actions have violated the strict rules of the Geneva Convention?"

Jacko spoke first. "I think whoever was flying the plane had a split second to make a choice, Sir; did he hold fire and let them get away with murder? Or just press the trigger and take a chance with whatever came next."

Bastion's eyes narrowed. "I can just imagine the frantic discussions that went on between the different factions of the Coalition. The last thing they needed was a major incident like this, especially with the tinderbox atmosphere at the time."

"That's right, Sir, one spark could have set the whole war in motion again."

"So I assume they needed to blame someone for the ambush, the obvious choice being the local Partisans, whom we're told, had executed the four wounded Serbian soldiers in cold blood."

"That seems to be the gist of it, Sir."

"Amen to that, Sergeant, but I'd now like to turn our attention back to the present and see where this leaves our investigation."

"There was something else, Sir."

Bastion's fingers were heading for his nose, when they stopped in mid-air.

"Stephen Millar said Marko Tomovic's platoon were generally referred to as 'The Night Shift', and their role was to move from one major incident to the next. A rapid response unit that travelled in three transporters; twenty men assigned to each vehicle. When they first came upon the burnt out convoy, the Bosnians found forty-eight charred corpses, all of whom had apparently died as a result of the fire. The Norwegian Major arrived on the scene later that morning and saw the four men who'd managed to survive the attack, plus the one with the unexplained bullet hole in his forehead. That amounted to fifty three soldiers, yet there was still another twist in the tale."

Jacko checked his notes again. "In the summer of 1996, the French had just finished checking out the Bugatti, when someone stumbled across an old hunting lodge situated high on The Ridge. But it was only after they'd discovered some recently dug graves, did anyone realise that this was where Tomovic and his men had hidden for ten days. French Forensics combed the area with a fine toothcomb and eventually exhumed the bodies of four soldiers, all of whom had died as a result of their wounds. From what I hear, identification had been a piece of cake, seeing as they'd all been buried wearing their army dog tags. It also confirmed they'd belonged to *The Night Shift*. That made it fifty seven bodies so far, Sir."

Bastion, who was quite capable of counting, said nothing.

"Following a further search of the forest and ravine, they found another soldier, who at first appeared to have died from severe head injuries; the result of his fall from the cliffs above. However, an Autopsy had later revealed that this was far from the truth. The soldier had in fact been shot twice, once in the head and another in the throat by a handgun that wasn't standard Serbian issue."

"What are you saying, Sergeant?"

"They never gave a reason why, but according to Stephen Millar, the French thought he'd been summarily executed."

"I take it this dead soldier was an important find?"

"Yes Sir, the dog-tags around his neck identified him as being one Henki Topovic. He was Marko Tomovic's second in command and like him, wanted for war crimes. Apparently, the 'Yugoslavian War Tribunal' had been looking to indict both of them, for a brutal massacre that had taken place in a village somewhere in Northern Bosnia a few years earlier."

"But Marko Tomovic it seems was already dead before the order was issued?"

"Yes Sir, it was only later in the same year did the incident with the partisans come to light, plus the bag containing the identity tags. Amongst them were two belonging to the Tomovic brothers, bringing the total to fifty eight men."

"Which suggests two Serbian soldiers are still missing," said Bastion.

"That's right sir, it would appear that two men have never been properly accounted for."

"Yet rather than admit they were responsible for this whole debacle, the Ministry of Defence decided to cover it up?"

"So it seems Sir, but Stephen Millar did mention something else that I thought was interesting. The French think Henki Topovic was shot dead whilst having a crap."

Bastion and Carson looked puzzled.

"When his body was discovered lying at the bottom of the Ravine, his combat trousers and shorts were down around his ankles."

They crossed Hardman Street hand in hand and took the narrow alley which led to 'The Buyers Club'.

"Hello, this is different," said Simone, "Don't think I've been here before."

"If you like triple cooked chips and delicious fresh chilli octopus, then this is the place to be," smiled Jacko as they took a seat in the crowded restaurant.

Without asking, he ordered a bottle of Rioja and explained the reason for them having an early dinner. "Bastion is threatening to pull the plug on the Serbian connection."

"No way!" gasped Simone. "That's just plain crazy."

"Tell me about it," groaned Jacko. "But at least the MOD's dodgy dossier and the latest stuff concerning the Swedish doctors has him backpedalling for a while."

"Well, that's something."

"He's also questioning whether it's worth the time and money."

Simone shook her head in disbelief. "What about all the evidence we found?"

"As far as he's concerned, the Tomovic brothers died twenty years ago in a Bosnian ambush and unless we can prove otherwise, the rest is just circumstantial."

"What about the fingerprints?"

"Same story; no body or DNA means no further."

A look of frustration crossed her face. "This is pure madness; Sarajevo are convinced there's something strange going on and so do I. How can Bastion be so bloody dismissive?"

"Because he's the man who tells everyone what to do."

"What happens now?"

Jacko shrugged. "We ignore him and carry on."

Simone's eyes opened wide. "Seriously?"

"As you say, there's something weird going on. So with a little help from our Yugoslavian friends, I intend to find out what."

"How are you going to do that?'

"Ask Zelda and Milos to find more about who shot Henki Topovic, but more importantly, how he ended up at the bottom of the ravine."

"The French are convinced he was executed, especially with him having one bullet through the head and another in his throat."

"Talking of bullets in the head," said Jacko. "Who's the soldier lying in the snow with one smack bang in the middle of his? Major Knutfeld reckoned he'd been dead for a few hours and was convinced the Bosnians didn't do it. On top of that, there was no gun lying around to suggest it might have been suicide. So who shot him?"

"Perhaps the Bosnian Sergeant found it beside the body and kept it as some kind of souvenir."

Jacko looked doubtful. "Maybe, but I'm finding it hard to believe that some badly burnt person could hold a gun to his forehead and then pull the trigger."

"So do I," agreed Simone. "The easiest way is through the side of the skull, or under the chin: which means you don't get to see the weapon when you say your last goodbyes."

Jacko fiddled with his glass in frustration. "I'm not convinced these two Tomovic bastards are dead. In fact every time I think about them, the more I'm sure they're still alive and kicking; or worse, killing their way around the country! Speak to Sarajevo before this all gets washed down the pan. Tell them that any information relating to the bodies is vital to our cause. If Bastion does intend to scrap this part of the inquiry, then God knows where we'll end up."

"I'll speak to Zelda as soon as I can," said Simone.

Part Nine

London 2014

The newsagent was busy at the best of times, the Bengali shopkeeper loathe to let anyone hold up the queue of people. "Hey mate," he shouted. "You've forgotten your paper, as well as your effing change!"

Marko, however, was only interested in the grey Pork-Pie hat passing by on the other side of the street. Ignoring the Indian's noisy protestations, he left the shop and went in pursuit of whoever was beneath it. Worried it might somehow vanish in the jostle of Fleet Street; he gave a sigh of relief when he saw the hat turning into a side alley. Re-doubling his efforts, he picked up speed and hurried down the narrow thoroughfare, slowing only when he'd reached the corner and saw the person wearing it waiting for a pedestrian crossing to turn green. Staying calm and keeping out of direct eye-line, he strolled along the pavement until he was stood beside him.

"Tino?" he whispered.

The hat turned to face him, the shock and surprise enough for him reach for his inside pocket.

"*To cam ja, Mapko Tomabnh!* It's me, Marko Tomovic!" he hissed in fluent Serbian, his own hand grabbing the wrist in order to avoid what might become a fatal misunderstanding. The lined face was no more than a few inches from his own, the eyes ranging over him as they fought to understand what was happening. Another moment of uncertainty went by, before the first sign of recognition began to penetrate his brain.

"Holy fuck!" he whispered. "You're supposed to be dead!"

"*Zvanico!* Officially!" Marko whispered in Serbian. Keeping it casual and smiling like an old friend, he placed one arm around Tino's shoulders and began to shepherd him in the direction of The Stag's Head, a pub conveniently situated on the other side of the street. "I think a drink might be in order," he whispered again in the mother tongue.

Like Marko, Valentino Karavak, had once been a Lieutenant in The Serbian Volunteer Guard and when younger, possessed a wiry body, dark sallow skin and a booming laugh that was part of his everyday make-up. Today however, this same individual had changed radically in both hair colour and girth. His skin just about surviving the passage of time, the loud voice no more than a refined chortle. Another notable difference was his fondness for Irish cider, as Marko watched him pour a bottle of Magners over the lumps of ice piled high in his pint glass.

"What are you doing here in London?" he whispered.

"I was about to ask you the same question," Tino replied with feeling. "It must be nearly twenty years since I heard your platoon had been wiped out on the border near Vukovar. Except you're clearly still alive and roaming the streets of London, which tells me that's a load of bullshit." It suddenly dawned on

Marko that if he hadn't seen Tino's hat outside the newsagent's, both of them would have gone their own separate ways and been none the wiser. But seeing as how he'd been foolish enough to initiate this meeting, obviously had some explaining of his own to do. He began by telling the story of the disastrous encounter with the tank, the death of his men and a slightly more antiseptic version of their fatal meeting with the two Swedish doctors.

"Was that you?" Tino asked in astonishment.

"It was just an unfortunate accident," Marko insisted. "One of the troops fired a warning shot and I couldn't believe it when the driver lost control and crashed the car."

Tino drank some more of his cider, belched loudly and shook his head. "No matter, man, you definitely whipped up a storm when that shit made the news!"

Marko gave a shrug. "The whole thing was just a stupid misunderstanding and as you know, we can't always wind back the clock when something goes wrong."

"What happened next?"

"Petrovic appeared on the scene."

Tino was open-mouthed. "Do you mean 'The Fixer'?"

"One and the same," replied Marko. "He arrived unannounced in the camp where we'd been holed up in the hills. To quote his exact words: *I have some bad news. The conflict in Bosnia may be over, but the Allies are convening a War Crimes Tribunal, and you could figure high on their list!* Apparently he had someone close enough to the Committee to hear these things before they went public. His source said we'd be charged with an incident that took place at some village in 1993 and the doctors a few years later!"

Tino was philosophical. "A lot of people died during the war, Marko, many getting killed every week, but the two doctors? Hell man, they were different!"

Marko nodded grimly. "At the time we didn't have a clue who they were, or hear about the reward being offered."

"I know quite a few people who would have been happy to claim it," Tino smiled through narrowed eyes.

Marko paused for a second, wondering if the man across the table might be one of them. "It was the the Colonel who said no one knew of our involvement and advised us to keep quiet until the whole thing had blown over. My original plan had been to offload our wounded and head for home. That is, until we ran into a Harrier Jet!" He then told the story of the devastating missile attack without sparing any of the finer details.

Tino was reflective for a moment. "Funny, I can remember the exact day we heard 'The Night Watch' had been taken out. We were clearing out Erdut barracks at the time. The war was over and it was a case of burning anything that might be incriminating. Shit man, we were really depressed when we heard there'd been no survivors."

Marko shrugged. "As you can see, they didn't quite get it right."

"I take it you and Ziggy were the only ones to make it out alive?"

Marko looked a little guilty. "Not exactly, when the missile hit, a few of the men sitting in the last truck were lucky enough to be thrown clear, but the seriousness of their injuries ruled out any chance of us moving them. Even now, I still can't believe that we were the only ones able to walk away from the attack. Then realised we had no choice other than leave the injured behind."

"Was Henki Topovic amongst them?"

Marko shook his head and decided not to mention his mystery disappearance on The Ridge. Yet did remember that before the war, he and Tino had been close friends. "I'm sure Henki was sitting in the middle one of the burnt-out cabs."

"Do we know what happened to the other survivors?" Tino asked casually.

"I'd always hoped that the UN forces would reach them first, but never did discover if any of them got out alive."

Tino used a finger to tap the ice melting in his glass. "Shit things can happen in war, but amazingly it seems you and Ziggy have lived to tell the tale."

Marko wasn't sure if Tino's voice bore a slight accusing tone, but he carried on regardless. "We didn't need a fortune teller to say how lucky we'd been; considering I'd just lost a whole platoon of good men in the space of a few minutes."

Tino was thoughtful. "How is your brother, I take it he's still alive and well?"

"He's fine," Marko replied, the question rekindling memories of another time.

"Is he still doing that crazy Beatles song? *Happiness is a warm gun!*" chuckled Tino. "I can remember him singing it every time he cleaned his weapon!"

"He doesn't own a gun these days."

"What about that extra-long knife of his? Does he still keep it hidden in his boot?"

Marko didn't answer.

Tino nodded in understanding. "Football? I remember him being a big Partisan Belgrade fan when he was younger. It must be hard for him after being away all this time."

"Ziggy's had to suffer just like the rest of us," smiled Marko. "These days he's an Arsenal supporter and is more interested in fishing."

"No way?" laughed Tino.

"Yeah, he bought himself an old camper van and likes to disappear for a few days. Says he prefers the peace and quiet of sitting on the river bank."

Tino belched again and his stomach began to rumble. "I find that hard to believe, but more importantly, need something to eat."

"Me too, let's go grab some food and I'll tell you the rest."

It soon became obvious that Irish cider wasn't the only passion in Tino's life; Indian food was another and the spicier the better! His lack of table manners was also plain to see, as he wiped his plate clean with a piece of Naan Bread and belched fiery Chicken-Tikka across the table. Much to the discomfort of those unfortunate enough to be within smelling distance. Another concern was the reason he'd continued to ask some very awkward questions. "So how did you and Ziggy get to safety?"

"We kept to the forests and ate off the land, but luckily, didn't have to struggle all the way."

"How come?"

"On the fifth day, we met a Serbian scout patrol who took us back to their camp and cleaned the shit off us. Problem was, within twenty four hours, Colonel Petrovic had made another of his surprise appearances, along with some more bad news."

Tino belched again. "He really is one amazing man."

"He said that following the death of the two doctors, the Allies were still scouring the countryside looking for those responsible. To make things worse, he'd warned that it was now impossible to get anywhere near the barracks at Erdut. I gave him a detailed breakdown of how we'd survived the air attack; swapped dog tags with two of the dead men and escaped into the forest. This he said, threw a different light on proceedings and spent the rest of the day making telephone calls.

"In less than a week, Ziggy and I had been issued with new identities and smuggled to some obscure town near the Hungarian border. To complete the makeover and as a means of disguise, I'd been advised to grow a bushy moustache and wear glasses. Ziggy in turn had opted for a crew cut and Goatee beard. Petrovic as always, had kept on drip-feeding the news that our platoon had been wiped out somewhere in Northern Bosnia."

"The Colonel doesn't fuck about, does he?"

"Even so, he'd assured us that the charade would only be for a few months; or until things had quietened down. In the end we rotted away in that godforsaken town for six years. In fact things got so bad, Ziggy took to fishing in his spare time."

Tino picked at another piece chicken. "Remember, it might have been a damn sight worse, if the War Crimes Commission had caught up with you."

Marko said nothing other than stare at the table.

"I'd always known you had friends in high places. But still don't understand why they would spend so much time and money in trying to shield you from the authorities."

Marko shrugged. "Everyone knows Ziggy and Arkan were close friends."

"What happened next?"

"The stories of people being exposed as possible war criminals and taken into custody were beginning to fill the local papers. We were just a couple of strangers in a strange town and I'd break out in a cold sweat if someone asked my name. Though the panic really did set in when we heard about the undercover snatch teams arresting possible suspects: Colonel Gulag being the most important one. He was shot dead by a British SAS unit who were fully operational in Serbia. According to the reports, they'd tried to arrest him outside his home. When he refused, they cut him down like a dog!"

"English bastards!" Snarled Tino.

"Yet the first of the really bad news came in the summer of 2000, when Petrovic told us both of our parents were dead. The last time I'd spoken to them was in 1990, the year I joined the Tigers." Marko hesitated and his eyes briefly misted over. "The Colonel said they'd both died in a fire at our family home some six months earlier. At the time, we'd already been declared dead; killed in action, which meant there'd be no natural heirs to the family estate. Within weeks of both our parents passing, everything had been swiftly disposed of by our loving nearest and dearest."

"Fucking vultures," growled Tino.

"Petrovic as ever, was consistent with bringing us the bad news. His next visit was in 2001 when he asked if we'd heard about Arkan's assassination. We said yes, of course, it had been headlining the papers and TV channels everywhere. The news of his death had left us devastated, Ziggy in particular taking it very badly and that's when he suggested we move to Poland."

The half chewed piece of chicken was still in Tino's mouth as it fell open. "Poland?"

Marko smiled. "According to Petrovic, when Arkan was alive money wasn't a problem, but now he was dead, our gravy train had finally run out of steam. He'd also said that with the death of our parents and loss of home, we had no real family ties and this was an opportunity not to be missed."

"Poland's still a long fucking way from Serbia, so why go there?"

"Two reasons; if we stayed, there was always the chance someone might recognise our faces and turn us in. The other was an English politician named Dr David Owens. He was the one insisting that those responsible for war crimes should be brought to justice. Petrovic was simply advising us on where best to disappear. Serbia, he'd insisted was now rife with shitfaced traitors ready to turn you in for a pittance. So in the end, it was the offer of some real employment from a Polish sympathiser that finally convinced us to give it a try."

Tino was curious. "What employment?"

"From the day we left school, my brother and I had always worked in my father's small central heating firm."

Tino was still confused.

Marko put him out of his misery. "In England, they're known as plumbers."

A knowing smirk appeared on Tino's face as Marko continued with his tale. "Considering we'd spent three long years living next to its border, Ziggy and I were surprised to find ourselves taking a train ride across Hungary in the direction of Poland. Even now, I'm convinced that Colonel Petrovic had paid for everything. I went first class, supposedly as a Sales Rep, for a large tool firm, whilst Ziggy ended up in the rear coach playing his guitar. The only time we actually saw each other was when we had to stop and change trains."

"I take it there was no problem in travelling?" asked Tino.

"None whatsoever," replied Marko. "Our papers and disguises were perfect and it looked as if the wheel of fortune had finally begun to turn in our favour. Our new Polish benefactor, Pieter, had always been a staunch supporter of the Serbians during the war. Petrovic had also convinced him that although we were responsible for the death of the two doctors, the whole thing had been an unfortunate accident. He'd told him that the outcry from the press was the main reason we'd taken flight. Being a true patriot, Pieter had believed every word and was happy to provide us with both work and shelter." Marko took a sip from his beer before continuing.

"It took a while, but we soon began to settle down and appreciate the finer points of Polish life. So much so, that we lived there for eleven years and I married his eldest daughter Katrina. Although, the birth of my son Grigor has to be the most memorable moment of my time there."

"Smart move," Tino said appreciatively.

"It was at our wedding that I first met Katrina's elder brother Jan. He'd just spent two years doing a compulsory stint in the Polish army and another working here in England. Though before call up, was employed full time in the family business. He never said so, but I think his absence from the workforce was why his father had decided to employ us."

"Surely he must have had other reasons?"

Marko nodded. "Pieter could remember a time when the German armies had torn his own country apart and knew how we'd fought to keep ours united."

"Sounds like a good man to have on your side."

"Although our life seemed safe and secure, there was always a chance someone might inform on us. After all we were still a couple of fugitive Serbs hiding in Poland and in 2012 things began to go badly wrong."

Tino looked confused again. "In what way?"

"We were living in the south of Poland near the city of Krakow at the time, when we heard a young blonde girl had been strangled nearby. We didn't think anything of it, until they linked it to another blonde girl, who was strangled in 2009. Then came a worrying rumour the police were proposing to check everyone's passports as part of their ongoing investigation, which made us very nervous. To make matters worse, Ziggy came home one day, insisting someone had recognised him in the local supermarket."

"Who was it?" asked Tino.

"No idea, I never got to see the person, but Ziggy swore it had happened. Which is when we'd begun to talk with Jan about moving to England."

Tino sipped his cider, belched loudly and listened intently.

"Jan convinced us that the UK really was the land of milk and honey. He'd then used the same argument to persuade his father he could earn twice the money doing the same amount of work, tax-free!

Although Ziggy and I weren't interested in his fanciful stories of fame and fortune, we wanted to know more about the land where people could walk the streets free from the clutches of the 'Secret Police' or without having to carry a passport or ID card."

Tino's jowls relaxed into a thin smile; recalling the sense of freedom he too had experienced when first arriving in the UK. The police carried no weapons and always smiled at him whenever he passed them by on the street. "Judging by this surprise meeting, I assume you've already taken the plunge and relocated here?"

Marko nodded. "In January 2013, Poland and the UK were already fully-fledged members of the European Union's Open Borders Policy. Unfortunately, Serbia and some other countries were still exempt from the treaty. Which meant we would need to acquire a couple of fake Polish passports to get past the UK border control. At the time we'd thought this might be near impossible, but when Pieter heard of our dilemma, instantly came to our rescue. He knew someone in Warsaw who could do just that. However, it would cost a lot of money: it eventually came to 500 Euros each."

"Cheap at the price," smiled Tino.

"In a planned move, Jan, Katrina and my son, left for England six months earlier and once there, rented a large house in Walthamstow. A few weeks later, Ziggy and I drove to the Eurostar terminal in France and joined a train full of hopefuls looking to start a new life in England."

"No problems getting past immigration?" grinned Tino.

Marko smiled at the thought. "When we told them we'd come to work, they welcomed us with open arms."

"And I assume everything has since gone to plan?"

"Sometimes yes, sometimes no."

Tino waited for him to continue.

"Jan's knowledge of how to play the system when it came to work and earning money was vitally important. He'd also explained that England was no different from anywhere else in the world. People might be righteous about their everyday affairs, yet happy to pay cash if it would save them money."

"You mean 'working on the black'?"

Marko shrugged. "I've heard it called many things, but that's near enough. We began by doing small repair jobs or late-night emergency callouts and in next to no time, our reputation had grown, as well as our list of wealthy clients. Nevertheless, we still had to be careful of the authorities and even though we kept on doing the more lucrative stuff, I thought it best to let Jan do the legitimate plumbing work. This arrangement had served us well, until six months ago, when we had the misfortune of meeting 'The Alderman'."

"Who the fuck's he?" asked Tino.

"I can still remember asking the same stupid question," muttered Marko. "Then someone in the know gave us the rundown. Alderman Archibald Troughton, to give him his full name, was some sort of country squire who lived on a large wooded estate in Bedfordshire. We never did discover who, but the Alderman said someone had recommended us and he needed some work done at his home.

"Sadly, Troughton Hall turned out to be an ancient crumbling pile of shit from the 17th century. A quick look at the corroded plumbing and heating systems said it might have been installed around the same time. I'd warned Troughton the hall was a mess and far too big a job for us to handle. It needed a complete refit, plus a couple of specialised high-pressure boilers and would take most of the summer to do the work. He wasn't in the least discouraged by my refusal and insisted we could sort something out.

"Apparently, he had a place in London, where he and his wife could dwell whilst the necessary work was being undertaken. He was also willing to pay cash in hand on a weekly basis and like a fool I took the bait, as well as the job. Following which, we spent the next four tortuous months replacing the crumbling plumbing and heating systems in the Main House and East Wing. The biggest nightmare involved buying the two new boilers and circulating pumps, all of which were *very* expensive!"

"How expensive?" asked Tino.

"Close to £28,000," growled Marko. "And it wasn't long after we suddenly found ourselves being shunted up shit alley. In the beginning the Alderman was as good as his word. He'd arrive on site at the end of each week; inspect the job for progress and pay the agreed amount of cash in hand. But as I said earlier, the equipment needed for the boiler room was special and could only be supplied by one particular Plumb Centre. I'd warned Troughton beforehand that our credit was limited to the end of the month and he would need to pay on time.

He'd insisted we should go ahead and finish the work; assuring us he would be there with the cash as usual. Then a few days into the boiler project, I received a text from him saying his sister had died in an accident in France and he needed to fly there immediately. Assuming it was a genuine tragedy, we'd innocently carried on fitting out the plant-room with the hope of having it up and running by the time he returned.

However, the Alderman failed to make contact or appear on site for the next three weeks and when he did, wasn't quite what we'd expected. Arriving at The Hall early one morning, we found his Bentley Continental parked in the courtyard. Assuming he must have arrived home sometime the night before, we let ourselves in and headed for the plant-room. Our normal routine was to rustle up some fresh coffee before starting work. At precisely 7.00 am the new hot water boiler roared into life, but to our surprise, the heating boiler beside it fired up as well. We were still wondering what was going on, when we heard these loud screams drifting in through the open door. All thoughts of boilers were dismissed, as Ziggy and I raced along the passage towards The Great Hall. I can still remember the shock of seeing this demented woman screaming like crazy. She was holding her hands pleadingly to the roof and other than a thick layer of black sludge that covered her from head to foot, was completely naked. Unable to see through the shit in her eyes, she was stumbling about like a blind woman. I can still remember the rusty water spewing forth from the radiators covering everything with a thick coat of slime. Realising what had happened, I made for the cupboard below the staircase and slammed closed the heating valve. As one, the fountains slowly subsided to a trickle, but in its wake left behind a scene of pure devastation."

"Who was the woman covered in shit?" Asked Tino.

"At first we weren't really sure, but the tits hanging down to her knees said it was The Alderman's wife; apparently, she was just about to have an early morning bath when all hell broke loose."

Tino shook his head as if to dismiss the thought. "That's too much fucking information, man."

Marko smiled grimly. "The only piece of luck was when the maid arrived with some towels and helped wipe the muck from her eyes. Within minutes, the man himself made an appearance and we couldn't help but notice his newly acquired suntan. Even now I can remember thinking about the supposed untimely death of his sister and whether she just happened to live near the beach in Biarritz. His bronzed face certainly pointed him being that far south."

"I take it this Alderman guy was pissed off with all the mess?"

Marko gave a curt nod. "However, rather than worrying about his wife, he seemed to be more interested in the damage done by the water and demanded to know what was going on. I began by reminding him of the heating valve in the cupboard, when he cut me short. 'I know nothing about valves and the like,' he shouted. 'I just want to know who's responsible for ruining my house!'

"It was at this point I sensed something was wrong. Six weeks earlier, I'd spent the best part of an hour explaining what would happen when we reached the cupboard under the stairs. This, I told him, was to be the cut-off point between the Great Hall and the West Wing. I'd also gone to great lengths to explain what might happen if someone accidentally opened the valve and sent the pressurised water flowing through the ageing pipework; the radiator valves would pop like fucking champagne corks!

"Before I'd had a chance to remind him of our conversation, Ziggy grabbed him by the throat, frog-marched him towards the cupboard and pointed inside. 'When we left here last night,' he snarled. 'That valve was tightly closed, but it looks as if some arsehole has decided to play games and I don't fucking like that!' 'Okay Ziggy, you can let him go!' I shouted and to my relief, watched him relax his grip. Unfortunately, the attack on The Alderman had turned out to be a real bad move on his part, as well as the catalyst of what was about to come.

"'You stupid Polish oaf!' he gasped. 'You could have bloody-well killed me!' 'Sorry about that,' I said. 'He's just a little upset at the mess.' The Alderman, however, was having none of my attempts to smooth things over. It was obvious that only he could have opened the valve and caused the pipes to burst, but the little shit saw this as the perfect excuse for not paying his bill and began screaming he was going to call the police. I was still trying to convince him it had just been a rush of blood, when he shouted to his wife, 'Did you see that, darling? That monster has just tried to strangle me!'

"I found it hard to believe his wife could see or hear anything considering the state she was in, but the wily fucker wasn't finished yet. 'I've had enough of you cowboy plumbers coming over here and stealing the bread from our mouths,' he shouted. 'And just look at what you've done to my beautiful home!'"

Marko paused in his narrative and focused on Tino across the table. "I swear to Christ I could have strangled him myself, but there was no way I could let that happen. For nearly eighteen months, we'd kept our noses clean and stayed out of trouble, but Troughton was threatening to spoil all of that."

"I can only imagine what Ziggy was thinking," Tino said in a deadpan voice.

Marko smiled. "Probably the same as me. But this is England, and you can't go around killing people just because they won't pay their bills."

Tino pulled a face and shook his head. "So how did you sort it out?"

"I didn't. In the end we had to walk away."

"What the hell does that mean?"

"Just that," replied Marko. "I think the bastard had always intended to screw us from day one. That said, he's nobody's fool and was always prepared to splash out the cash so as to keep the job moving along. It was only later did we realised he'd been biding his time and waiting for the opportunity to create an argument, the valve in the cupboard fitting the bill perfectly. Looking back, I don't think he realised just how much damage it would cause to his home or that his wife might get covered in slimy sludge. He'd assumed it would be a minor flood that could easily be sorted with some new carpets and a decorator. I can still remember the look of delight on his face when he saw the extent of the carnage."

"How could Troughton be sure you'd give in so easily?" asked Tino.

"The ground rules had already been thrashed out at our first meeting; nothing official, strictly cash in hand. He'd guessed we had no insurance to cover any unforeseen accidents, but more importantly, knew we were working illegally. This more than anything, would preclude the arrival of the authorities on site."

"What about all the money he'd owed you?" asked Tino.

"I assume it's still in his wallet."

"How much was it again?"

"When we included the new radiators, it came to £39,000."

"Hell man, that's a lot of money to walk away from," muttered Tino.

"His last words were. 'Sue me'."

"What happened next?"

"We went bust. Troughton refused to pay-up and warned us about removing any materials or trying to sabotage the job. To make matters worse, we had to settle the bill at the Plumb Centre or they'd have taken us to court. This would have meant more snooping into our background and possible exposure to the police. So, we had no other choice than to use our savings and keep everyone happy. Nonetheless, Troughton hadn't quite finished in grinding us into the dirt, especially when he began to spread the word we were untrustworthy. Within days people were ringing to cancel jobs already in the pipeline. As luck would have it, I've just managed to get us some temporary work with a big plumbing outfit, but that job finishes in a few weeks' time. So after all these years of trying to make a life, we're back to square one."

"I can understand why you hate the bastard!" snarled Tino.

Marko speared a piece of Lamb Bhuna from the plate and twisted it in his hand. "I just wish this was one of the Alderman's balls. It would give me the greatest of pleasure in slicing it to pieces with him still attached to it!"

Tino guffawed loudly before turning serious. "If you and your brother are interested, I might have some work for you, but it's definitely not plumbing!"

Marko stood in the dark and listened to the soft sound of Grigor's breathing. Something he'd been doing from the day he was born, each moment giving him a feeling of immense pride. The arrival of his son had been a most welcome addition to his life and as he turned to leave, resisted the urge to tenderly touch his face. Slipping out of the room, he moved along the passage until he came to another door on which he didn't need to knock. It'd opened almost at once, to reveal a bare chested Ziggy fitting a new reel to one of his many fishing rods.

Marko rarely ventured beyond the threshold of Ziggy's room; his view normally confined to a brief look over his shoulder; today being no different. In the limited light, he could see some clothes lying on the bed; an illuminated computer sat in one corner and a Chinese take-away calendar hanging slightly askew on the wall above it. "Something important has happened and I need to speak to you downstairs." The tone of Marko's voice suggested he should stop what he was doing and be quick about it.

"Two minutes," he replied.

Discussions of any importance were always undertaken in the kitchen and in most cases late at night. Yet Ziggy was surprised to find Jan sat at the table nursing a bottle of Budweiser; it would appear his brother-in-law was going to be party to this latest news. Marko opened the fridge, took out two more bottles of lager and passed one to Ziggy. This in itself was unusual, seeing as his brother rarely drank alcohol.

"Do you remember Tino Karavak?" he asked offhandedly.

"Of course, I do." Ziggy replied automatically. "He was an officer in the Tigers, why do you ask?"

Marko flipped the lid off his bottle, took a swig and waited a second before answering. "I met him today."

Ziggy was genuinely shocked. "Where?"

"Here in London. I was in the city checking out some stuff, when he passed me by on the street."

"What's he doing in London?" asked an astonished Ziggy.

"He posed the same question to me when we were having a few drinks in a pub."

Ziggy was now wide-eyed. "You went for a drink with Tino?"

Marko nodded. "Not just a drink, we went for something to eat and while there, had a long chat. As you can imagine, he was absolutely blown away by the fact we were both alive and living here in the UK. Like everyone else, he thought we'd been killed in the Bosnian ambush." He then proceeded to give Ziggy a rundown of how the day had unfolded and all that had been said.

"Why the hell did you mention the two doctors?" he asked incredulously.

Marko could see the worried look on his brother's face. "Take it easy. Tino's one of us and I had no trouble in convincing him it was an unfortunate accident."

Ziggy seemed somewhat mollified by this bland explanation, but obviously in need of more answers. "You still haven't told me what he's doing in England."

"I was just about to do that, when the steam started to come out your ears."

Ziggy eyeballed him across the table, took a swig of beer and sat back with a shrug. "Okay, I'm listening."

Marko shook a weary head and continued with his story. "Tino's been here for the last three years setting up a big operation and he wants you and me to become a part of it."

"In what way?"

Marko chose his words carefully. "He wants us to become delivery men."

Ziggy mulled over the reply whilst rubbing the top of the beer bottle with a fingertip. "What the fuck does that mean?"

"Just what I said. He needs people he can trust to deliver some very expensive goods around the country."

Ziggy's eyes narrowed and he pursed his lips as though thinking. "What kind of goods are we talking about?"

"Mostly cocaine," replied Marko. "Although that might vary; it just depends on who wants what in the way of drugs."

Ziggy's eyes never flickered. "Why us?"

"Tino's been having some problems in getting his stuff safely delivered to their desired destination. Twice in the last year a different gang has managed to intercept his couriers, beat the shit out of them and steal the drugs. Tino has always manage to find out who the gangs are, but by then it's too late."

"Sounds like dangerous work," murmured Ziggy. "So what's in it for us?"

"We get a small percentage for delivering the goods safely. If the value is £100,000, then we're guaranteed £1,000 in cash, no questions asked. Although Tino said most of the orders are way above that amount."

Jan's voice broke in. "Wish I could do that. I'd make more in a week delivering drugs, than a whole month of fitting bathroom sinks."

Marko smiled and shook his head. "Sorry my friend, there's no way you can be part of the delivery team. Tino prefers to use only people he knows and trusts. Besides, we'll need you for other things, the most important one is keeping the plumbing side going."

A look of puzzlement crossed Ziggy's face. "Why?"

"I don't intend to get rid of it just yet; in fact if Tino agrees, I hope to expand it even more."

This, Ziggy thought, was the difference between them. Marko was always the one to conjure up some plan or strategy to solve a problem and he'd obviously been doing his homework today.

"Tino accepts that their security could do with tightening up," said Marko. "He's also first to admit that anyone delivering expensive parcels into the lion's den, is always likely to be a target; especially if it's the same fancy Limo the gangs have seen before. Which is why I intend to provide him with something completely different."

Ziggy swigged his beer in anticipation.

"I think we should make this whole operation a little harder for them to spot and I'm not just talking about the gangs. I mean anyone who might have reason to stop us and ask questions."

"Are we talking about the police?" asked Ziggy.

Marko nodded and reached for an A4 writing pad lying on the table. He then drew two identical squares on the pad and added four circles, one to each corner. "These represent the two second hand vehicles I intend to buy. Each will be kitted out with enough tools and gear to convince any nosey fucker that they're just what they appear to be; plumber's work vans."

He then drew a small circle to represent the steering wheel and a bigger one at the rear end, before giving it a tap with his pencil. "This is where they normally stow the spare wheel, but I intend to extend the area and convert it into a large airtight compartment in the floor of the van. It'll mean we can safely transport the goods to their destination."

"Where do we get the money to buy these vans?" asked a still wary Ziggy.

Marko smiled. "Tino's so delighted to have us on board, he's prepared to give us what we want in the way of funds."

"Will he be supplying the vans?"

"Uh, uh." Marko replied in the negative. "That's a job for Jan. He can search on-line for the right vehicles. Provided they're roadworthy and fit the bill, we'll pay cash there and then."

"Anything is better than fitting toilets," muttered Ziggy. "So when do we start?"

"It won't be until we've completed the plumbing job we're working on, which I estimate should take another week."

The prospect of crawling around on a cold bathroom floor for seven more days did nothing to lighten Ziggy's mood. Marko however, hadn't quite finished. "I was watching a spy movie on TV last week. It was one where the good guy was being pursued by a carload of baddies. To avoid being caught, he kept using a device to swap the licence plates. I was thinking that if possible, we might do the exact same thing."

Ziggy seemed to like the idea, but had other issues. "If these gangs, as you say, are 'tooled up' and dangerous, then surely we're going to need some protection of our own?"

"Tino reckons there'll be plenty of weapons to choose from."

"I'm happy with my Berretta," smiled Ziggy. "When you include the silencer, it's a superb weapon."

"I bet you didn't know that I was a top marksman in the Army, do you think Tino would reconsider me?"

Marko turned to his brother-in-law. "Sorry, my friend, we'll need you to carry on with the plumbing side of things. Plus it's a perfectly good reason for the vans being parked in the garage."

Jan finished his beer and gave a reluctant shake of the head. "Oh well, looks as if I'm back fitting hand basins and toilets."

Marko smiled in sympathy. "I know it's not much fun, but until we make some real money, we're not finished with the plumbing business yet."

"Yeah, but if this all goes as planned, I intend to hang up my spanners for good," grinned Ziggy.

Part Ten

Walthamstow, London
2015

The calendar hanging on the bedroom wall was a New Year's gift from the 'Happy Wok' takeaway. Although Ziggy wasn't thinking of fried chicken noodles, he was more interested in what was on the other side. Flipping it over, he added another tick to the nineteen already there, each a record of the days since his disastrous journey up North. More troubling was the nightmare of the broken sunglasses and the still missing arm.

In keeping with this daily ritual, he reached for the leather case hidden in his bedside drawer; aware it'd once belonged to his brother. There'd been a time when he'd had one of his own, but for the life of him, couldn't remember where, or how he'd lost it. Yet could clearly remember the day he'd found Marko's lying on the dashboard of the van, plus the memory of being kicked in the face by the black kid and the indignity of scrambling around in the grass searching for the broken arm.'

"What a bitch!" he snarled, angrily shoving the case back in the drawer. Thankfully, his daily trawl through the news channels, especially the Liverpool ones had proved to be more encouraging; the investigation team had said they were still no nearer in discovering who was responsible for the Park Murders. Which, if anything, was one small crumb of comfort.

He'd also come to the conclusion that life really was a matter of ifs and maybes. If Marko hadn't had to go away, then maybe he wouldn't have had to travel to Manchester and, later that day, go to the football match in Liverpool.

In the bigger picture, it had been a relatively small amount of heroin; less than a syringe full, but still required safe delivery to a drugs cartel, working out of Moss Side. They'd been questioning the quality of an earlier batch and were demanding a sample to justify them placing a new order. Under normal circumstances, this would be unheard of, but seeing as how the deal was estimated to be around two million pounds, Tino had grudgingly agreed.

In a strange quirk of fate, it'd happened the same week that Marko was leaving for a family wedding in Poland; his wife's younger sister was getting married to her long-time beau. Ziggy as ever had no real interest in family nuptials; he was just glad to miss the big occasion. So after much deliberation and seeing as there was no actual money involved, his brother had reluctantly agreed to him making the delivery alone.

The package had been safely delivered and as agreed, he'd departed Moss Side by a completely different route from that when arriving. One strict rule stipulated that once an operation had successfully been completed, especially when wearing the false number plates. The Transit van should be returned to the garage in Walthamstow, steam cleaned from top to bottom and kept out of site. This particular stipulation had never really bothered Ziggy, seeing as he would normally use the campervan as his own means of transport, more so when he had the urge to go Fishing. Yet on that one fateful day and seeing as how he had plenty of time on his hands, he'd unwisely let his love of football cloud his judgement and drove to Liverpool.

His ultimate destination was Anfield Football Stadium, the venue where Arsenal, his now favourite team were destined to play later that day. On arrival, he'd gone through the usual hassle of searching for a parking place and finding one not far from the ground, checked the van was secure before moving off on foot. Within minutes, he'd bumped into a small band of Arsenal supporters who like him, were making their way towards the ground. Slowing for a second, he'd let them press on ahead, before swapping the grey Beanie hat for his favourite red and white wool one. Then, and in what was a time held ritual, had lovingly kissed the brass SDG badge pinned to the front.

With less than five minutes before kick-off, he was badly in need of a ticket and as chance would have it, spotted a hand waving one in the air. Problem was, the seat wasn't exactly where he wanted to be. This was in the upper tier and sat mostly amongst the Liverpool supporters, but the roar from inside the ground said the players were already on the pitch and he needed to move his arse! A few extra minutes of haggling were required, before he'd successfully bargained the tout down from £100 to £50.

The match itself had been both expensive and disappointing. His team had lost 2-0 and in a pique of disgust, he'd left before the game finished. On his return to where the van was parked, everything had appeared to be normal. That is, until he spotted the hooded hyenas trying to force open the driver's side window. Eyeing his unexpected arrival, a lookout had shouted a warning to the gang, who as one turned to face him, the leader lounging against the van with a smug smile on his face.

Realising he had no other choice, he stooped down behind a parked car, took the knife from his boot and slipped it up his sleeve. He then held both hands up as a sign of surrender and began jangling the van keys at the end of his fingers. Thinking it was going to be a walkover, the smiling hoodie opened his coat to reveal a small knife sewn inside. This Ziggy assumed was his way of saying 'don't mess with me' and confidently reached to take the proffered keys.

In a flash, the smirk was replaced with one of fear, as he grabbed him around the neck and using the razor-sharp tip of the blade, made a 2" incision beneath his chin. "Oh shit," the hoodie moaned, as he felt the warm blood trickling down his neck. "Please don't kill me, Mister!" he cried in fear.

Angry and aware he didn't need any more of this crazy hassle, Ziggy waved the blade menacingly at the other hoodies, who as one took an involuntary step backwards. Climbing into the van, he started the engine and headed off in the general direction of the football ground. Seconds before he'd turned the corner to meet the traffic in Breck Road, a quick glance in his wing-mirrors showed the hoodies gathered together in the middle of the street.

With the benefit of hindsight and plenty of soul searching, it was easy to see where he'd made so many mistakes. His first was in choosing the Park to stop and have a piss and in doing so meet the ugly dwarf leaving the carpark. The other was in killing the leggy blonde girl who'd turned the corner and walked through the gate. Now that was one major fuck-up!

On the other hand, there was a plus side. It'd given him the greatest of pleasure in silencing the young black kid who'd kicked him in the face and smashed his brother's sunglasses! And although this might have happened weeks ago, he could still remember seeing his guts splattered all over the grass and hear him crying for his Momma.

O kavda radost! 'Oh what joy!'

Part Eleven

S.C.U.

Jacko entered Carson's office grinning like a Cheshire cat.

"With a face like that, I can only assume its good news."

"You better believe it, Guv."

"Take a pew and spread the word."

"Joanna's had a result with the photos taken on the day of the football game."

"Mobile phones?"

"Social media," smiled Jacko.

Carson had never been into websites and the like, but was still willing to try anything that might produce results. "What have we got?

"She's just received an email from a couple living in Carlisle, who say they visited Anfield on the day of the murders. It seems the wife had organised the day-trip as a birthday present for her husband, who's a big Reds fan. According to Joanna, the couple arrived late Saturday morning and did the usual Grand Tour, which included the trophy room, changing rooms and main stands. They were also lucky enough to witness Liverpool beat Arsenal two-nil. The lady said it was just before 7:30 pm, when they left the ground in readiness for their journey home, which is near a three-hour hoof up north. Feeling tired, they both went straight to bed and knew nothing of the Park murders until they saw it on the news the next day."

Carson watched as Jacko fired up his iPad. "It was only when the lady saw Joanna's televised plea for any photographs taken on the day of the game, did she check her own. Having no means of sending us the originals, the lady suggested Joanna visit her Facebook page, where she'd recently posted a selection of photographs. Have a look at this, Guv," pointing to one picture in particular. "From this angle, you can see where the couple left the stadium and crossed the road to where 'The Park' pub is situated.

"Like most Liverpool supporters, they'd had a fantastic day out and as you do, decided to celebrate a memorable occasion with one last photo, except both of them wanted to be in the same picture. Having no answer, they solved the problem by asking another supporter if he would take it for them."

Carson focused on the smiling middle-aged couple standing on the crowded pavement. Directly behind and in pride of place, loomed the tall imposing structure that was Anfield Football Stadium. Looking closer, it was obvious that whoever had taken this much-cherished snapshot was definitely no David Bailey when it came to composition. In one half of the frame, he'd just about caught the smiling twosome, but in the other was something that made him blink twice.

Temporarily marooned within the throngs of people leaving the ground, sat the rear end of a white Ford Transit van. In what looked to be a huge stroke of luck, the crowds had parted for just a split second; Time enough to record the license plate in near perfect detail. A smile crossed Carson's face, as he remembered the grainy footage of the same mystery Transit van on the M62 motorway. "Before today, Jacko, I wasn't sure if we'd been going around in circles like a dog chasing his tail. Now I'm convinced we're going to get this bastard."

Sitting opposite, his No. 2 was the proverbial nodding dog.

Reggie

It'd been three days since 'Noah the Snake' had threatened to cut his throat, but having already missed the deadline by twelve hours and petrified he might slit his jugular instead, Vinny knew it was time to go A.W.O.L. Having been in this situation more than once, his normal procedure, would be to head for the supermarket and stock up with lots of essentials. These being mostly food and cigarettes, but in the frantic mad rush had forgotten all about them.

So it came as no surprise to find him rifling through every coat and trouser pocket he possessed, but was still unable to find a single shred of tobacco. Breaking into a cold sweat, it suddenly occurred to him the only other solution was a cigarette paper and the used stubs piled high in the ashtray.

It was the same problem with food and although he'd tried to eke out his pot-noodles and pizzas, the last of his Pepperoni Specials had long since vanished down his throat. Worse was yet to come, when he found his old man had taken the greatest of pleasure in padlocking shut the one cupboard containing food, which left him rummaging through the waste bin in the middle of the night. "Beam me up, Scotty," he whispered to the TV showing a repeat of *Star Trek*, his favourite programme. Having spent most of the day chewing his nails down to the quick and still in desperate need of a cigarette, it suddenly occurred to him that he had no other choice.

Leaving the safety of his bedroom, he crept along the hallway, wiped one sweaty hand on the side of his shorts, took a deep breath and reached for the door handle. It had been many moons since he'd last ventured into the lounge, but this wasn't quite as he remembered it. Over the years, his crazy father had turned the place into a shrine dedicated to Demi Roussos, the Greek folk singer. Looking around he could see lots of different size pictures and statues dotted around the room. On one wall was a full-size poster of the bearded one on stage and in full flow, but what really opened his eyes was the sight of his old man ironing a kaftan wearing just his underpants and vest.

This lunacy had first begun when Reggie was half-cut at a karaoke night and decided to get up and give a song. Sadly for those listening in the crowd, his old man had had a few drinks too many and nearly swallowed his false teeth in the process. Amidst the howls of laughter and many congratulatory pats on the back, Reggie had completely misinterpreted their smiles and thought he could sing. Following which, he'd decided to grow a beard and call himself Demi-God in honour of his long departed hero.

That said, some things definitely hadn't changed.

"What do you want?" he snarled.

"I need help," stuttered Vinny.

"Piss off!"

"I'm not joking," he pleaded. "I need help."

Reggie paused in his ironing. "What kind of help?"

"I'm starving and need something to eat."

Remembering the sound of his son creeping around in the dark, he'd suspected that this might be the case and was beginning to enjoy his plight. "Try the shop on the main road, I'm sure it's open all day."

"I can't do that."

"Why?"

Vinny wrestled with himself before answering, "Someone's trying to kill me!"

A smile appeared on his father's face. "They obviously haven't succeeded yet, which is a shame, seeing as how I've been thinking about it for years."

"This is no fucking joke!" spat a desperate Vinny.

Reggie hung his finished kaftan on a nearby rail. "Who's joking?"

"I don't want a lot and I'll definitely make it worth your while!"

Reggie's eyes turned to slits; this was new territory in their relationship, plus an avenue he wouldn't mind exploring. "Who's trying to kill you?"

Vinny hesitated. "Does it matter?"

"Not really, but I'm still curious as to who and why."

"A gang of black kids who live on the other side of the Estate."

"That's who, but you haven't told me why."

Vinny's internal wrestle began again. "I took some stuff off them and sold it on."

"Ah and I take it you ripped them off, as you normally do?"

"It wasn't like that," protested Vinny. "I had no idea the stolen gear involved some dead Canadian fucker."

"I heard about that on the radio," muttered Reggie. "They were talking about a burglary in Chillwall and someone found murdered at the bottom of the stairs."

"I don't know anything about a murder," cried Vinny. "I was just helping them get rid of the gear!"

Reggie's face looked doubtful. "Instead of going shopping for food, I think you should talk to the police."

"You know I can't do that," spluttered Vinny. "The last time I was in Court, the Judge said he'd send me down for seven years if he ever saw me again!"

Reggie smiled. "I know you've been in jail before, but it's amazing how quik the time flies."

"Sod that crap, all I want are some frozen pizzas and four hundred cigarettes!"

Reggie gave a shrug. "That's going to cost a few quid in cash."

Vinny took a wad of money from his shorts and counted off some notes. "Here's £200 pounds."

Reggie shook his head. "Sorry son, it's going to cost you at least twice that."

"You horrible robbing bastard!" screamed Vinny.

The Ambush

The Range Rover slowed to a near walking pace, giving Twixy Hartley and Lefty Bannerman more than enough time to slip from the rear and melt into the bushes alongside the tower block. Standing in the shadows, they waited until the tail-lights had disappeared around the bend, before cautiously approaching the entrance. A rusty door hinge was just about to announce their presence, when a loud wail of terror split the night sky. Realising it could only have come from inside the hall. Lefty tapped a finger against his lips, the sign for them to be careful, but seconds later said, "Go! Go! Go!" when another howl of fear was followed by a series of anguished screams.

Unsure of what was happening, they burst into the lift area and discovered two knife wielding hoodies threatening someone pinned against the wall. "Were de fucking coins, Gecko man!" The taller one shouted.

"I haven't got them," the victim cried and it suddenly dawned on Lefty that the person being badly manhandled was none other than Vinny Snodgrass. "Hold him still so I can cut his face!" The smaller hoodie grunted, as they struggled to keep his body in one place. Vinny on the other hand had no intention of letting them do any such thing, as he jerked his head back and forth as though he was having some kind of manic fit.

"Okay boys that's enough fun for one night!" Bannerman shouted forcefully. Alarmed on hearing a stranger's voice, both teenagers spun around as one, their knives extended like a couple of musketeers on guard. They'd been so engrossed in intimidating their victim they hadn't notice the two immaculately dressed figures standing behind them. Vinnie in the meantime had slumped to the floor like a sack of coal, as the hoodies took in the white shirts, Tuxedos and bow ties.

"Well, would you just look at these two oversized clowns," laughed Noah.

"It's the fucking Men in Black!" Cruz cried derisively.

Bannerman gave a shrug. "I've already told you, boys, we don't want any trouble."

"Then what the fuck do you want, Gorilla man?" sneered Noah.

Twixy smiled. "We want him," flicking a finger in Vinny's direction.

"Piss off, whitey, he's ours not yours," spat Cruz; the point of his blade moving from one Tuxedo to the other.

Twixy sighed. "Come on boys, we're just trying to give you some friendly advice."

"And there's no need to bring colour into the conversation," added Bannerman.

"Don't give me that crap, whitey, and if you come near me, I'll cut you and your mate to fucking pieces!"

Lefty shook his head in disgust and turned to Twixy. "Don't you just hate people who swear?"

"Nothing worse," he replied. "It's a sure sign of a bad upbringing."

As he spoke, the second hoodie noticed Vinnie trying to crawl away and without moving his blade, used one leg to trap him against the wall. "He's ours," he whispered viciously.

Twixy gave a smile of regret. "Not any more, my friend, and I'd advise you to move your foot and let him go, or you might be in need a permanent crutch."

"A baldy muscle-bound arsehole like you don't scare me," sneered Cruz.

"It's not me you need to worry about dickhead, it's *him*." pointing to the massive bulk of Bannerman. "And believe me, when he does get upset, things can become real messy and *very* painful."

From the defiant look in their eyes, Twixy knew the two hoodies were yet to be convinced of the potential danger they were in. He'd also been hoping that they'd see the light and refrain from doing something stupid.   But the taller one, who was obviously in charge, had continued to keep Vinnie pinned to the floor with his knee and hold the knife against his jugular vein.

"It appears to me, Mr Gorilla man, that we're both in serious need of this same shit-faced object, which means I'm not giving him up without some kind of deal."

Twixy gave a reluctant sigh and shake of the head. "Let me tell you something, Tonto. Less than an hour ago, we were at a local dinner boxing match enjoying some great food and drink. And I know it's hard to believe, but some of the talented young amateurs in the ring were black and probably no older than you are. Although there was one particular fight that stood out from the rest." He glanced to Bannerman. "Remember that last bout?"

"The one between the black and white kids?"

"That's the one. Two angry young lions who fought each other to a standstill and guess what boys? When it was all over and we were on our feet applauding them, these two young gladiators began hugging each other."

"Who won?" Cruz asked stupidly.

"No one won anything," snarled Twixy. "Other than a feeling of dignity and respect between two very proud young fighters!"

Bannerman spoke next, "Which is why we wouldn't think of doing a deal with you two cowardly scumbags."

"But there are ways and means to sort this out." Twixy smiled wickedly. "The simplest and easiest way is for you to drop the blades and disappear to your side of the Estate. Or, we'll take them off you and break every bone in your hand, one by one. Either way, it's your choice."

Noah, who'd fought many a tough battle to defend his territory, bristled at the snide inference of cowardice, but at the same time was no fool and could see that this was one confrontation he wasn't going to win. In spite of the fact the two bruisers looking like something from a B movie, they both had an air of unruffled deadly malice about them. He was in no doubt that if need be, they'd happily break all of their fingers, one by one. Snapping closed his knife; he held it up in the palm of his hand to show it was harmless. "This is our only means of defence in a shit tough world out there," indicating beyond the walls. "And for this one time only, I'm happy to trade him," giving Vinnie a kick in the ribs. "As long as we can keep them."

Twixy watched the other hoodie reluctantly snap his closed and pondered what to do next. Should he act as judge and juror by stripping these two scumbags of their weapons, or just turn a blind eye and let things be. In the end, he decided on the latter and pointed towards the doors. "Scram, dickheads, and don't let me see your faces again."

The taller of the Hoodies was about to leave, when he suddenly lashed out at Vinnie with his boot. "We no finished wid you yet, Gecko Bumboclaat!" He threatened in a vicious sounding Jamaican patois.

The two tuxedo-suited gorillas towered above Vinny, as he lay crumpled by the lift doors nursing a set of sore ribs and a deep slash on his cheek. "What do you want?" he whimpered.

"We don't want anything, *Gecko man,* but a good friend of mine is dying to have a chat with you in private."

S.C.U.

Carson and Taff were at the coffee machine discussing the Sharecropper's involvement in the Chillwall break-in when a couple of glum-looking detectives turned the corner.

"Just a sec, Taff, something tells me I'm about to be disappointed."

"Just heard from London, Guv and it's not good news."

"How bad is not good?"

Jacko held up an email. "This is from the officer who led the early-morning raid on the plumbing firm in Walthamstow who, would you believe, do have a white Ford Transit van with two ski bars. However, there's a slight technical hitch, seeing as how it's been out of action for more than six weeks."

Carson gave a wince and whispered, "I don't believe this!"

Jacko shrugged and chewed his lip in sympathy.

"Tell me the rest."

"The owner of the firm said the van was in need of a new clutch, hence the reason for it being laid up in a local garage. When the plods went to check it out, they found it gathering dust and minus half its engine."

"So there's no possibility of it being in Liverpool Bank Holiday weekend."

"Not according to the boys from The Met."

"What about licence plates?"

"With the two-bar ski rack, it's a near perfect match for the one spotted outside Anfield, but all similarity ends there. The plumber's vans have the firm's logo plastered all over them, whereas ours is just a dull white runabout."

Carson closed his eyes as if to shut out the pain. "What about the people who work there? Do any of them fit the ID profile?"

"Afraid not, Guv. They all have concrete alibis for the weekend."

Carson shook his head. "I don't believe this rhubarb. One minute people are going to jail and now you're telling me this could be some kind of hoax."

"I don't think it's a hoax, Guv, I reckon it's a clever scam."

"Or someone taking great care not to be caught on camera," added Taff.

"I agree, Guv. Why else would the van driver be taking to the back streets, when it's much easier to use the main roads?"

"Why indeed?" mused Carson.

"And why have a set of false licence plates?" asked Smithy."

Taff was thoughtful. "Remember the scam with the stolen 'Rollers', Nathan?"

"Vaguely."

"Anybody want to tell me?" asked Jacko.

"It was around ten years ago," began Taff. "Some flash boys from the South had been travelling to the northern provinces looking to steal top quality motors, mostly for the Arab market. They would arrive in one car and spend the next few days checking out the local mansions and footballer driveways. As always, they'd be on the lookout for the latest Maserati or Rolls Royce that some lazy fool had forgotten to garage for the night.

"Once they'd chosen their target or targets, it was no problem for them to bypass the car's security system and flee the scene. But to circumvent the possibility of some local Bobby raising the alarm, they fitted false magnetic number plates to the vehicles so they would easily pass any road checks." Taff smiled at the thought. "Must have made a fortune over the years."

"So what happened to them?" asked Smithy.

"They got sloppy on one occasion and couldn't understand why a massive road block was waiting for them at Watford Junction. Well, only until somebody pointed out that one of the magnetic plates had fallen off the stolen E Type."

"Tut, tut, tut," chuckled Carson.

Smithy looked doubtful. "I'm still baffled as to why they would use magnetic plates."

"Do you play golf, son?"

"I have a go, Taff."

"Using the plates is similar to a 'risk and reward' shot, but instead of a birdie, we're talking huge sums of money. I'd imagine these people needed to move around the country unhindered and a set of 'dodgy plates', as you call them, would go a long way in achieving that."

"What happens if they have a crash or get stopped in a road-check?"

"Blag your way out, or go to jail," he smiled.

"Surely we're looking at a different scenario here, Taff?"

"Almost certainly, young Jacko, but the intention is still the same— deception."

"Which means they're either people smugglers or drug dealers."

"I doubt anyone would go to a football match with a van load of illegal immigrants, Nathan."

"Which can only leave drugs," said Jacko.

"Hang on, what if the driver had already done the deal and went to Anfield later that day?" asked Smithy.

"Good thinking, Batman, this guy always does the unexpected and would probably explain why he took a different route out of the city. That said, I've been having a think about the 'Roller' scam and the false licence plates, Nathan."

"In what way, Taff?"

"As I remember it, the whole shebang had been a one-hit wonder and not very sophisticated at that." The others waited expectantly as he sipped his coffee. "The purpose of this exercise was to get the stolen vehicles from A to B as quickly as possible and the magnetic plates helped them to achieve just that. Once the cars had been shipped overseas, they were then free to use the plates on their next job. But if you're going to shift wagon loads of drugs or contraband around the country on a long-term basis, I'd imagine it would need a lot more careful planning."

"As well as being completely legitimate."

"Spot on young Jacko, but more than anything, they had to find a duplicate van that more or less matched their own."

"Which I assume would need to be properly maintained, roadworthy and have no outstanding parking fines, eh Taff?"

"You're getting there, my son."

"And sail past any ANPR road-side cameras with flying colours? "

"Just like the Transit van they use at Worthing and Sons," smiled Taffy.

"What about MOT and insurance?" Asked Smithy.

"You can get anything you want these days boyo, just as long as you're prepared pay for it."

Smithy was still doubtful. "So where do we start looking for these people?"

"Where else but London," declared Carson. "Someone must have had contact with this plumbing firm or maybe even worked for them."

Jacko was thoughtful. "According to the CID down South, there was no match with the 'Identikit' picture; but we are talking about present day employees. What if this scam has been going for a few years and the people have already moved on?"

"Ask them to do another check on this 'Worthing' outfit," said Carson. "Tell them we need a list of the company's previous employees, young and old and while they're at it find out if anyone has worked as either self-employed or a sub-contractor on any of their jobs."

The Pianist

Vinny reckoned his journey must have taken around twenty minutes, but had no idea where to. Lying in the boot of the car, he'd spent most of the time praying things couldn't get any worse. Then the lid opened and the two Tuxedoes appeared before his terrified blinking eyes.

"Move it, Gecko man," Gorilla No. 1 grunted. "And remember to keep that hanky glued to your face," his earlier warning of *no claret on the carpet* proving to be a positive one. Ever fearful of more repercussions, Vinny held the blood soaked square against his cheek as though it were part of him. Clambering from the confines of the Range Rover, he'd began to massage one knee as an excuse to take a look around, but this ploy had lasted less than a second, before the shovel-sized hand of Gorilla No. 2 gripped the back of his neck and marched him onwards.

"No peeking, Gecko man!" he whispered.

Notwithstanding his nose was practically scraping the floor, Vinny was still able to flick his eyes left and right and see a range of packages stacked from floor to ceiling. *A warehouse maybe?* he speculated. He was also trying to work out exactly where he was, when the tinkling sound of a piano could be heard from somewhere to his right. Without warning, the Gorilla's vice-like grip tightened and swerved him in the direction of the music and a rather surreal sight.

In one spacious corner stood a white grand piano, whose silk cover had been folded back to reveal the keyboard only. Another surprise was the dinner-suited person playing a familiar, if slightly disjointed melody using one finger on each hand. Vinny didn't know him, but recognised the tune as *Chopsticks,* something he'd learned at junior school. At first glance, this Liberace look-alike appeared to be of the same build as the other two monkeys, but any other comparison ended right there. They were both shaven headed muscle, whereas he was a dark haired smooth looking giant, whose voice had a ring of real authority.

"Vinny my friend!" he boomed. "I've been so looking forward to making your acquaintance."

The vice-like grip on the Gecko's neck never eased, as he stared bleakly into the face of this newfound musical maestro.

"Take a seat!" he declared; Vinny's backside landing with a painful thump on the metal chair that suddenly appeared below it. Then and in what looked to be a theatrical flourish, Liberace lowered the lid and smiled in the most disarming way. "Do you like music?" he inquired, as though they might be discussing the weather. For a second Vinny was lost for words; the only song he might confidently hum was the theme tune from *Star Trek*. The piano man, however, had no intention of letting him exercise his vocal chords, he'd already changed key.

"I find music can be so relaxing, especially when you're trying to find the answer to a thorny problem and my friends here have assured me you're the very person I should talk to."

Vinny, who still didn't have a clue what was happening, began to sweat like the proverbial 'rapist' he wasn't.

"Doesn't say much, does he?" growled Gorilla No. 1.

"He's just shy," smiled Liberace. "He'll be okay when he gets to know us."

"I could help loosen his tongue," grunted Gorilla No. 2.

"I doubt we need to go that far," smiled the pianist.

No. 1 Gorilla gave Vinny's neck another painful squeeze. "If we don't do something soon, we could be here all night."

The pianist smiled again; his teeth as white as the ivory keys beneath the lid. "Relax boys, I'm sure our Gecko friend will be more than happy to accommodate us." Vinny, in the meantime, was hoping the damp patch appearing around his crotch was just sweat.

"What do you want?" he croaked in fear.

Liberace suddenly burst out laughing. "Goodness gracious, boys, I forgot to ask him that all important question!"

Carluccio's

The crowds in Church Street gave a rousing cheer at the street clown's declaration that: "Liverpool is now the most entertaining city in the whole wide world!"

Jacko, who'd heard it all before, turned into Whitechapel and spotted Carson drinking coffee under Carluccio's awning.

"You look as if you've got indigestion, which can only mean there's a problem with the Transit van."

Jacko took a seat and nodded. "That and a couple of missing Poles."

"So, what have we got?"

"The usual 'Snakes and Ladders'."

Carson smothered his cappuccino with a double dose of chocolate shavings. "Start with the vertical, it'll improve the froth on my coffee no end."

Jacko ordered a latte of his own, and began his tale. "As requested, Walthamstow CID revisited this Worthing's plumbing firm looking to find anyone who'd worked for them in the past five years."

His boss nodded and added a touch more chocolate.

"They reminded them that this was a major murder inquiry concerning two teenagers who'd been brutally slaughtered in Liverpool. Then added that any deliberate withholding of information could have serious consequences. This it seems was enough to frighten the life out of him and do the trick."

"Which I assume is when we climbed our first ladder?"

"Yes Guv. Mr Worthing apologised profusely for his lack of oversight and insisted he'd been focusing only on his present day employees. He then took a closer look at the Identikit image and remembered a big Polish guy who just might fit the bill."

"And I take it we're now about to slide down a slippery snake?"

Jacko nodded. "He doesn't know his real name or where he lived."

Carson took another sip of coffee. "What name *did* he know him by?

"Plain old Pete the Pole."

"That's original, any more ladders?"

"Possibly."

"Let's hope it's a cuffin' tall one."

Jacko smiled. "It would appear this mystery Pole rang about a year ago looking for work. He said he was a top plumber capable of undertaking any job, but there was a catch; he'd only work for cash in hand."

"Which, of course, was 'On the Black'."

"That's right, Guv, nothing official, but for Mr Worthing, who'd been under severe pressure at the time, this was an unexpected godsend. According to him, the firm had taken on too much work and were struggling to make the completion dates: a block of unfinished luxury flats being top of the list. So like many of these small-time outfits, he had no qualms with using tradesmen on the sly. Which really meant he could get the work done cheaply and pay none of the usual taxes."

"And the reason he forgot to mention it in the first place."

Jacko laughed. "Right on Guv."

"I take it this 'Pete the Pole' wasn't alone when doing this work?"

Jacko smiled. "According to Worthing, he and another big punter named Pauli; who apparently didn't say much, would turn up at 6.00 am and graft non-stop until 8.00 pm in the evening. He said it went on like that for the next few months, until they'd finished the job."

"Did he pay them cash every time?"

"Yes Guv, he'd check their work for any problems (apparently, there were few) and meet this Pete in Waitrose's car park on a Friday night, albeit with the usual brown envelope."

"Something tells me I'm about to slide down another snake."

"When the project finished, they packed up their tools and vanished."

"Does he remember what kind of car they drove?"

"No, but thinks it might have been a black Vauxhall Astra."

"What about contact numbers? They must have talked to each other."

"A 'pay as you go' mobile phone that's been dead for a long time."

"Any more 'Ladders' to climb?"

Jacko's face turned serious. "I'm not sure yet, but a month after the Poles disappeared, Mr Worthing visited his local Plumb Centre to collect some copper pipes. While he was being served, the assistant asked if he was still using those *two fake Poles*. This completely threw the boss, who couldn't understand who he meant. That is, until the guy behind the counter explained that 'Pieter and Pauli' were in fact a couple of Serbians."

Bastion looked up from the report. "So tell me again, Sergeant, how did the assistant know the two men weren't really Polish nationals."

"By their accents, Sir, and because he's from Krakow in Southern Poland."

"Yet, he swears this Pieter and Pauli were trying to pass themselves off as two of his fellow countrymen?"

"That's how it sounded to him, Sir."

"Did he ever have a real in-depth conversation with them?"

"Not according to his statement. Apparently, they didn't say much, other than turn up every now then and collect some materials for the job."

"And they had regular use of the firm's Transit van?"

Jacko nodded. "Mr Worthing has confirmed that if, or when, the Dodgy Poles ran out of materials, they could use one of the firm's vehicles to visit the Plumb Centre. But here's the oddest thing. The assistant can clearly remember another time when a small grey Fiat van arrived with Pieter the Pole sat in the passenger seat."

"And?"

"The young guy driving the van was a genuine Polish national who he'd never seen before."

"Did he have a name?"

"He's not really sure, Sir, but thinks it might have been Jan."

"What about signatures, did they sign for anything?"

Jacko shrugged. "If they did, it most certainly wouldn't be around today. Such things are normally thrown in the waste bin."

Bastian switched his attention to Carson. "It would appear this strange Serbian website and mystery crime sheet might have something to do with our murder case after all."

"Especially in light of these latest revelations," agreed Carson.

"What about these people in Sarajevo Sergeant, have we heard any more from them?"

Harbourside Apartments

The silk dressing gown rustled softly on the carpet as Simone crossed the room and sat in front of the mirror. "Have we heard any more from Immigration?"

"Nothing so far. It would appear Serbian Nationals are few and far between in the UK."

"Which makes sense, seeing as how they're not part of the European Union."

Jacko shrugged. "True, but since the year 2000 and the introduction of open border policy, half of Europe have been free to stroll across our boarders. The Serbians, however, require official visas, which I was hoping might make it easier for us find them."

Simone brushed her hair as she spoke. "A half-decent up-to-date photo would help more."

"I agree, Professor, but it would appear these two mystery 'Poles' know how to cover their tracks, as well as their mistakes."

"What about the sunglasses in Junkies Corner? They got it wrong there."

"Touché," grinned Jacko. "I'd forgotten all about them."

"And what about the plumbing assistant who swore they spoke near perfect Polish, or good enough to fool someone having a casual chat with them."

"Like an Immigration Officer checking your passport?"

Simone nodded. "I'm also wondering if they've had language lessons?"

"Possibly and come to think of it, what about the two blonde girls murdered in Poland? Maybe the brothers lived nearby and if so, stayed long enough to pick up the language and speak it fluently?"

Simone grimaced. "If that's the case, I doubt we'll ever find them."

Jacko's face wore a pained expression as he contemplated sifting through the thousands of Poles living in the UK. "As I said, it's only a theory."

"Ah, but did you know that other than Hungary, most of the nearby countries speak a type of Slavic that's understood by them all?"

This time he was really impressed. "I knew you were clever, Professor, but didn't realise you were an expert on Eastern Bloc languages."

Simone smiled smugly. "I'm not. It just so happens that I bumped into Eleanora, our Czech interpreter this afternoon and she brought me up to speed."

"So, are you saying these two Serbs could be living here and masquerading as Poles?"

"Hm, hm, especially if they had enough time to practice and perfect the lingo."

S.C.U.

Stretch Malone waltzed into Carson's office as if he were a contestant on *Strictly Come Dancing*, but instead of the usual glitzy female partner, he was humming a tune and holding a large purple file at arm's length.

"Nice footwork mate, try not to wear a hole in the carpet," advised Jacko.

"My missus has been trying to get me on the dance floor for years," grinned Stretch. "And I've been doing the side-step ever since."

"Well if I was you, I wouldn't give up your day job," laughed Carson. Stretch held the folder protectively against his chest and gave a smile. "You two may mock and titter; but trust me that will all change once you've cast your eyes over this!"

Within minutes the Team had put everything on hold and gathered in front of the display boards. Where, to Jacko's annoyance, Tufty McClellan unexpectedly appeared from nowhere.

Stretch held up the purple file for all to see. "As you all know, I've been searching for any females who are young, blonde, raped from behind and been savagely murdered in the process. And if you thought it was bad enough here, well it seems they're having the same problems elsewhere;" a map of Europe suddenly appearing on the oversized screen. "But at the moment, we're only interested in these three countries: Serbia, Hungary and Poland; plus this report I've just received from the Serbian police."

The room fell silent.

"Around ten years ago, a couple of old timers were out hunting in a place whose name I can't pronounce, but am reliably informed is somewhere in northern Serbia. A few days into their trip and they came across what any man with a hunting rifle has dreamed of, a large stag grazing in a heavily wooded area. Thinking its antlers would make a welcome addition to his study wall, one of them has decided to bring it down. Taking careful aim, he then tried for what is known as the classic shoulder shot, missed the target and the bullet or so he thought, whistled off into fresh air."

Stretch smiled. "Having been spared the meat slab, the Stag instantly took to its heels and disappeared into the bushes, but as it did so, both men were convinced they'd heard the sound of breaking glass. Now intrigued, a closer inspection of the overgrowth revealed it wasn't quite as natural as they'd first thought. It was in fact man made and cleverly designed to conceal. They then began to push deeper and deeper, until one of them spotted a glint from within.

"Ten minutes later and they'd managed to uncover a car with a bullet hole, smack bang in the middle of its shattered windscreen." Stretch paused. "It's important to remember that these guys were a couple of experienced woodsmen, who realised that due to the mass of winding shoots and creepers, the car must have been there for some time. An even bigger surprise came, when they found the badly decomposed body of a blonde girl lying face down on the backseat. Unsure of what to do next, the two men headed for the nearest town and summoned the local police. Who within minutes of arriving at the scene, confirmed the woman had been murdered, but no trace of the killer was ever found."

Opening the folder, Stretch passed Carson the first Forensic photograph. "This shows the scene not long after they'd cut away the undergrowth covering the car's exterior. As you can see, it must have been there long enough for the stuff to find its way inside the engine cover. The next shot gives a more detailed view of the body on the backseat."

Carson passed the photos to Jacko, who began to fix them to the display boards as Stretch continued to reveal his findings. "The first thing to hit you is this close-up of the familiar black cable tie securing her wrists from behind. And of course, the almost identical means of slitting open the victim's clothes from the rear, albeit with the usual razor sharp knife."

"It's the exact same MO as the blonde woman in the ditch," said Smithy.

Malone nodded. "True, although the injuries to this one are much worse. According to the report, the girl had been raped from behind and brutally tortured with the knife. To add to that, she had so many holes, her body resembled a Swiss cheese. Mercifully, the killer ended her misery in much the same way as Kelly Freeland; an upward thrust of the knife into her brain."

The room was silent as it took in the agonising implications of the girl's death.

"Bastard!" Joanna muttered through gritted teeth.

Stretch nodded in sympathy before moving on. "Which leads us to three more European victims with the same type of MO. In 1998, a young blonde girl was found close to the Serbian/Hungarian border. She'd been strangled and later buried in a shallow ditch."

Malone tapped the screen. "Then in 2009, which is eleven years later, the same thing happened in Southern Poland near Krakow. Three years after that and we think the killer needed another fix, because in 2012, a third blonde girl was murdered in much the same way. Incidentally, all the killings took place within a hundred mile radius and all were close to a river or canal."

"I take it they didn't find any suspects?" asked Smithy.

"Nope. Although to give them credit, the police did do an extensive check of the local population."

"But they didn't find who did it?" persisted Smithy.

Malone lifted his eyes and shook his head. "If they had, we wouldn't be sat here today asking the same bloody questions!"

"Do you think he could be an angler or fisherman?" Prompted Joanna.

"The thought had crossed my mind, but whoever carried out the killings, was smart enough to move the bodies to another location and then hide them. In the case of the Serbian girl, he'd used her car to travel north and hide her deep into the forest. Although he did make one major blunder in closing all the vehicles windows to the outside world. If he'd have left even one open a fraction, the creatures of the night would have been more than happy to help dispose of the body. As it turns out, she was pretty much intact when they found her, which brings us to the real mind-blowing part of the story."

The Team waited.

"We are now convinced this young lady is in fact, the first of our serial killer's victims. Who according to her mother, left for work one summer morning never to be seen again. Well, not until the two hunters inadvertently stumbled upon her last resting place in the forest. But here comes the real twist in the tale. The victim is one Tatiana Mestovic, a twenty-six-year-old blonde girl who lived in the small rural town of Erdivos. Tatiana had few claims to fame, other than being Ziggy Tomovic's ex-girlfriend who, we're led to believe, jilted him some time in 1990. So, it comes as no surprise to find she's the mystery blonde viciously attacked by him in The Cue Bar that very same year. Yet the real cherry on the cake is the date she and her car went missing. It was early August 1996!"

"That's impossible!" declared Joanna. "Ziggy and Marko Tomovic were supposed to have been killed in November 1995. That's at least ten months before the girl disappeared!"

"So, what do you think Sir, revenge killing?"

Bastion nodded slowly. "It looks that way Nathan and judging by the MO, would explain why the girls were all strangled and stabbed to death in the same way."

"The Serbian police rang earlier and confirmed the Tomovic brothers regularly hunted in the area where the girl was found," added Jacko.

"Meaning they knew the place like the back of their hands?"

"Yes Sir."

"So, assuming this Ziggy did join Arkan's army in 1990, it's easy to understand why he had to wait until the war was over, sneak back to Erdivos. Then kidnap Tatiana Mestovic and torture her to death in the forest."

"Trouble is Sir, he didn't just stop there, the bastard kept on killing his way across half of Europe."

Bastion nodded to the map on the TV screen. "I can see what Frank Malone meant by a pattern, especially with the forest being so close to the Hungarian border."

Carson tapped the purple folder. "I'm now convinced that both the Tomovic brothers survived the Bosnian air attack and then went into hiding. How exactly? I'm not sure, but they must have moved from place to place, before eventually ending up in Poland. Sadly for us, the UK was next on the list."

"All very commendable," growled Bastion. "But where the hell are they now?"

S.E.L.

BB Benson flopped into the leather armchair and loosened his bowtie. "Christ Maxi, it's been years since we've had to put the 'frighteners' on anyone!"

"Who did you send?"

"Twixy Hartley and Lefty Bannerman; who else?"

Maxi gave a grunt of satisfaction. "Those two would frighten the devil himself."

"Well, it definitely worked with the Gecko. Although there was a time when I thought we'd have to send out for nappies."

"How is he?"

"Shaken, scared and a little cut up."

Maxi's brow furrowed. "What is it with these black kids, are they really trying to kill him?"

"To be perfectly honest, I'm not sure. His usual routine is buying and selling stolen goods, theirs is peddling drugs. "

"So what happened in the tower block?"

"According to Twixy, two of the 'Rasta' boys were about to turn Vinny into chopped salami, when they arrived in the nick of time and saved his bacon. It would appear the Gecko had decided to do some late-night shopping when they ambushed him in the entrance."

"What kind of shopping?"

"He was carrying two plastic bags; one packed with Piazzas, the other full of cigarettes."

Maxi shook his head. "What about this white Transit van? Did he talk?"

BB nodded. "He was a bit reluctant at first. Kept on moaning that he didn't know what we were talking about. Then Twixy began to massage his neck muscles and it really is surprising what it can do for the memory."

"The van driver? Did he see his face?"

"Oh yes."

"And he'd recognise him again?"

"With his eyes closed."

"Excellent!"

"I have to admit the Gecko's not an ideal witness Maxi and I wouldn't want him as my best man, but he is a start."

"Where is he now?"

"The boys dropped him off outside the Estate and warned him not to go missing, or speak to anyone else."

Maxi was thoughtful. "I've never trusted the Yardies in the past and I don't now. So it might be an idea to keep close tabs on Vinny, just in case they try again. And while you're at it, see if you can find out what's going down and warn them to stay away. Or at least until we've finished with him."

"I'll put the word out."

Maxi's features hardened and his eyes glazed over. "That's the easy part BB, our next problem is trying to find the killer!"

A tap on the door interrupted their conversation. "Tufty McClellan has just phoned in his latest report," said Michaela, "he spoke so quickly, I didn't have time to call you on the intercom."

While disappointed at missing the call, both men were still mightily relieved. A whole week had flown by since they'd last heard from the Scot and they were concerned he might renege on his side of the bargain. Michaela however hadn't quite finished. "Don't celebrate just yet. His accent maybe a nightmare and the cheap mobile phone doesn't help either, but with the aid of some shorthand, I managed to get it all down."

Maxi smiled as he received a copy of the transcript. "Good work Michaela."

"Any chance this gorgeous efficient secretary might conjure up some late-night coffee?" Smiled BB. "We're sure to need it while we plough our way through this."

"Once you start reading I think you'll need something a lot stronger than coffee," she advised. On her return, Michaela made a point of placing a large Brandy decanter and three glasses on the coffee table.

An angry looking BB filled his glass and took a sip. "Listen to this, if it hadn't been for the bullet through the windscreen, they might never have found the car hidden in the bushes."

"Or the body of the girl on the back seat," added Maxi.

"Ruthless bastard!" snarled BB.

Michaela read from her own copy. "According to McClellan, the Serbian police are convinced Tatiana Mestovic was the first of his victims. The others happening over a period of ten years and spread across most of Europe."

"My beautiful Kelly being one of them," whispered Maxi.

"This is interesting," said BB. "The S.C.U. reckon the white Transit van spotted near Waytree Park, was using some kind of fake licence plates. Christ and here's me thinking that scam went out with the Ark!"

"Which reminds me, apologise to young Bimmo and his gang. I gave them a hard time for not remembering the van's licence number."

"I wouldn't lose any sleep over it, Maxi. They're just delighted with the reward, especially when they said it came from somewhere down south. But listen to this. The investigation team reckon a couple of Serbians are delivering drugs around the country and using a Polish plumbing business as a way of covering their tracks."

"Wish they'd given us their mobile numbers," growled Maxi. "It would be nice to knock on their door and say hello."

BB finished his brandy. "Better start making some phone calls, with a bit of luck someone might know who this mysterious Pieter and Pauli are."

Milos

Jacko answered Simone's call. "What's wrong, Professor?"

"I've just had an email from Zelda. It says she has some bad news and needs to talk with us."

"Okay, where do you want to meet?"

"Make it my place at 7.00 pm, it'll be easier with the Skype connection."

"No problem, see you there."

Despite the fact she'd departed Liverpool less than a fortnight ago, Jacko was still looking forward to seeing the glamorous Zelda, but not the tearful eyes.

"*Zdravo moji prijatelji*," she whispered.

"Hello Zelda," replied Simone. "Are you okay? You seem a little upset."

Her thin smile suddenly became a grim line. "Milos is dead," she said haltingly.

"Dead?"

"Yes, Simone, according to the police, he committed suicide."

"How?" asked an astonished Jacko.

"They say he ran a hosepipe pipe from his car's exhaust and gassed himself."

"Oh my god!" gasped Simone.

"But you don't think it was suicide?"

"No Sergeant, my friend would never do such a thing, he was much too strong willed for something like that."

"Do you suspect foul play?" asked a stunned Simone.

"There can be no other explanation, little one."

"What about enemies? Did he have many?"

"Everyone has enemies, Sergeant, especially when you're an investigative journalist."

"Jeez, he really must have upset someone if they killed him!"

Zelda was close to tears. "*Izvini.* Sorry, I think this is all my fault and has something to do with the search for Petrovic."

"Petrovic?"

"Yes, he was one Arkan's right-hand men."

A puzzled Jacko began to backtrack. "Hang on, Zelda, this Arkan I do remember, but it might be easier to start at the beginning and tell us what this is all about."

An apologetic smile filled her face. "It all began when my contact in the Government asked Milos if he might help him find this Petrovic person."

"Is he the one who sent you the memory-stick?"

Zelda nodded resignedly.

"Can you at least tell us who he is?"

"His name is Tudor Topovic."

Simone screwed her eyes up. "Is he related to Henki Topovic?"

"Yes little one, the body found at the bottom of the ravine was his younger brother."

"And does this have anything to do with his death?"

Zelda nodded. "When Tudor heard his brother had been accused of war crimes, he was devastated. More so when the French said he'd been executed at close range with a handgun. This alone made him suspicious, but went a long way in confirming his younger brother didn't die from his war wounds."

Jacko shook his head. "This story gets more confusing by the minute. So who the hell is this Petrovic? And why would he want to kill Milos?"

"Many years ago he was known as 'The Fixer', one of Arkan's most trusted aids. His role was to remove any traces of the past and present; beginning with their dental records. Tudor is convinced he helped the Tomovic brothers flee Serbia and escape justice."

"Why would he do that?"

"Orders from above Sergeant."

"He sounds very efficient," said Simone.

"Yes, but also makes mistakes. In his haste to erase their existence, he forgot about the school photographs and mystery charge sheet on the website."

"He must have had a bloody heart-attack when Junkies Corner cropped up!"

"I agree Sergeant, but by the time he'd taken down the website, the alarm bells had already started to ring."

"What about Erdivos?" asked Simone.

"Discovering where the two brothers lived was all down to Milos."

"Plus the fact they'd joined Arkan's Tigers?"

"Yes Sergeant, Milos was a fantastic reporter and so very good at doing his job."

"You said he was helping Tudor, but haven't said why this Petrovic would want to kill him."

Zelda hesitated, produced a small hanky from her sleeve and dabbed at her nose. "Today, Petrovic runs a multi-million pound drugs ring out of the lower Balkans."

Jacko backtracked again. "Are you saying Milos was investigating him?"

"So I am led to believe."

"That still doesn't explain why he would want to kill him."

"When we first met at the Convention, Tudor was astonished to hear the Tomovic brothers might still be alive, more so, when I told him about your murder investigation and the trail of dead women. As you can imagine, he was desperate to discover how Henki had ended up executed at the bottom of a ravine."

"I take it he went in search of the truth?"

"Correction Sergeant, he met Milos and they decided to join forces; Tudor searching for evidence in the archives, my Serbian friend doing the leg work."

Simone asked the obvious question. "What did they find?"

"A still ticking time-bomb!"

Jacko was one step ahead. "Was it something to do with the cover-up?" Zelda nodded. "Tudor's job at the War Crimes Commission gave him unrestricted access to all areas. He knew the walk-in safe had been specifically designed to contain the most secret of information, which meant he could sift through a whole multitude of files and statements without interruption. It was whilst he was searching through one section did he discover exactly what he was looking for; a large sealed folder with 'Strictly Classified' on the front.

"A quick look through its contents confirmed his suspicions; there'd been a major cover-up of the ambush in the mountains which revealed the connection between Marko Tomovic's platoon and the death of the two doctors. However, the biggest surprise came when he discovered a British fighter plane had been responsible for the attack on the convoy."

Jacko remembered his meeting with Stephen Miller at the MOD. "Which violated the terms of the general cease fire?"

"Yes Sergeant."

"Why didn't he make his findings public?"

"Although he'd discovered this highly classified information, it was near impossible for him to prove any of it. Yes, the release of the files might have caused a major diplomatic row, but in no way prove his brother's innocence. The French Forensic team had discovered the fingerprints in the Doctor's car, but had no idea who they belonged to and at the time neither did we. So when Tudor heard I'd become involved in the English murder investigation, he loaded everything onto the memory-stick and sent it to me."

"Which I assume was the Caduceus clue," said Simone.

Zelda nodded slowly.

"What about the fingerprints in Junkies Corner? Did he know they matched?"

"Yes Sergeant, I personally gave him that information, so he was well aware of the hunt for the Tomovic brothers."

"Crikey, I'd forgotten all about Ziggy the psychopath!"

"There was something else in the file," added Zelda. "It was the Major's handwritten account of what happened on the day of the ambush. Reading on, Tudor discovered that the Bosnians had allowed the Norwegian to take one photograph of the soldier with the bullet hole in his forehead, but looking closer suspected something was wrong. Pulling a few strings of his own, he was then able to obtain a copy of his brother's Autopsy and a ballistics friend said all three bullets might have come from the same handgun. Another surprise, were the dog tags draped around the neck of the soldier lying by the side of the road. They identified him as one Luka Tomovic!"

Jacko was open-mouthed. "You must be joking! Why didn't he tell us?"

"Tudor was worried you might assume Ziggy was dead and call off the search."

Simone shook her head. "That's just crazy and I still don't understand where Petrovic fits in all of this."

"The war was over," began Zelda. "People on both sides had begun to count the living as well as the dead. So it didn't go unnoticed when a couple of stragglers named Sorovac and Demetrius fell into a Serbian field camp looking for shelter. Both claimed to have been separated from their unit, were badly injured and in need of food and drink. Having no reason to doubt their story, the officer in charge duly noted their presence and gave them all the help they could. Yet within hours of their arrival, a staff car containing one Colonel Petrovic had rolled into camp, pulled rank and spirited them away."

"So who were they?" asked Jacko.

"Well, they weren't who they claimed to be. From an early Tigers' press photo, Milos had identified a short, grey-haired Corporal Sorovac as being the Camp's Adjutant and we think the other was a Serbian recruit named Boris."

"I take it these two mystery stragglers didn't look anything like them?"

"No Sergeant, they were completely different in both hair colour and build."

"Poor old Sorovac," groaned Simone. "He must have survived the air attack, only for Ziggy to shoot him in the head and step into his boots."

"Personally, I'm more interested in what Milos did find out," muttered Jacko. "It has to be something really big if this Petrovic guy decided to kill him."

"We can only assume he must have gotten too close to the truth. Shortly after Arkan was assassinated in 2001, Petrovic went solo and began importing his own drugs into Serbia. Within a few short years and with the help of some very greedy politicians, he'd created an empire of his own. The last we heard from Milos, was when he rang Tudor to say he could name all of the corrupt officials involved. There was one other thing, he'd discovered that both the Tomovic brothers are still alive and hiding in England."

"Jeez, I don't suppose he said where?"

"I'm afraid not, Sergeant, but we're hoping that you might find them for us."

As the screen went dead, a troubled Jacko turned to Simone. "I'm finding it hard to believe that the man in the white suit won't be able to tuck into another Tomahawk Steak at the San Carlos restaurant."

Simone smiled and whispered, "Let's have a glass of wine and drink to his memory. I think Milos would have liked that."

S.E.L.

The glass door opened and a smiling BB Benson entered the reception area. "Hello gorgeous secretary," he grinned. "I swear that every time I see your face, the more beautiful you look."

Michaela laughed at the over-the-top compliment. "I can't remember how many times I've heard that line and according to you, I should adorn the front page of Vogue magazine every week."

"Every day, gorgeous one!" he declared with a knowing wink.

"Maxi's waiting for you inside," she laughed, indicating the panelled door.

"Is it me, or do I feel there's something in the air?"

"If there is, I'm sure he'll tell you all about it, Amigo."

"Coffee con leche?"

"Si, on its way, Senor."

Once inside, BB found a thoughtful Maxi gazing out at the panoramic view that was the Mersey Waterfront.

"I take it your visit to Manchester was a satisfying one, seeing as how Liverpool were 2-1 winners?"

"That wasn't the only result of the day," smiled Maxi. "Before the game, I was having a drink in hospitality, when an ugly face pushed past and nearly spilt my wine. Do you remember Jughead Johnson?"

"Of course," replied BB. "I'll never forget that circular shaped head and sticky-out ears, but amazed to hear he's still alive."

Maxi laughed out loud. "Someone once told me that because Melvin wasn't exactly endowed with good looks, he'd been nicknamed Jughead. Yet despite all these disadvantages, he still managed to get hitched to a very tasty woman and raise a large family; who I might say, he's immensely proud of."

"I know he was quite an age back then, so how old is he now?"

"It'll be his eighty-fifth birthday this year."

"Hell Maxi, where do you find these eighty-year-olds? First we have Archie Speed crawling out of the woodwork and then Jughead Johnson raises his ugly head."

"As it turns out, BB, our meeting was fortuitous in more ways than one. Melvin, to give him his real name, is a serious Manchester United fan, who just happens to have his own private box in the Main Stand. Where I might add, he insisted we join him in watching the game."

The *we* BB assumed, could only be Michaela, who like Maxi was an avid Liverpool FC supporter.

"Melvin wasn't exactly overjoyed with the result, although even he had to admit we were the better team on the day."

"I'd imagine the last thing he wanted, was to bump into you two at the football match," laughed BB.

"He was a bit miffed for the want of a better word, but by the time we'd consumed a few beers and got to talk about days gone by, the game was the furthest thing on our minds."

BB was serious for a minute. "I can remember Jughead as being the first to take a slice of the Baltimore Switch back in '82. Although I thought he'd be retired from the drugs game by now."

Maxi nodded. "He packed it in years ago, however, the Johnson empire hasn't disappeared just yet. His two sons took over the reins and been running it ever since."

Both men turned to see Michaela entering the room with a coffee laden tray and as there was no big secret of their close relationship, Maxi invited her to join the discussion. "Melvin and I had a few drinks and rambled on for a while about the good times, plus the many hair-raising scrapes we'd had over the years. A few large brandies later and the conversation moved on to our families and their children." Maxi paused for a moment. "How's this for a surprise, Melvin knew nothing about Sandra's death in America."

BB wasn't sure where this was heading, but knew his coffee would have to wait until Maxi got there.

"During our chat, I told him about Kelly's murder, the Transit van and the bastard with the long knife. When Melvin, who's a real family man heard some of the grim details, he was absolutely appalled! The thing is, BB, I'd forgotten all about our conversation until he rang the office a couple of hours ago."

Michaela took up the story. "Someone called just after nine saying he wanted to pass an important message on to Maxi Hamilton. If I hadn't been to Manchester on the day, I might not have realised what it was all about. But luckily, I recognised the voice and managed to record it." Maxi pressed a button on the desk console. "Have a listen, BB."

The voice on the tape sounded old, yet familiar. "I'm sure I don't need to tell you who this is, but I had a word with a relative of mine regarding the chat we had on Saturday. It was the one about a certain mystery van and you know what. It's a bit of a long shot and something that happened a few months ago, yet still might be of interest to you. Today, at twelve, you'll get a call from a person who was actively involved at the time and I'm hoping for your family's sake, it might be of some help. So, all the best and good luck mate. Oh, and before I forget, the code is C9."

BB Benson checked his watch. "Well, at least I can finish my coffee before he calls."

A swift ten-minute period passed before the private line on Maxi's desk rang. He let it ring twice more before switching it over to speaker. "Hello?"

"Who's that?" the voice asked.

"C9, who's this?"

"Hi, my name's Chalky and Melvin gave me this number to call."

"Okay, my friend. I think it's safe to say we're both on the same wavelength and assume our mutual friend has explained the background for this chat?"

"He didn't give any details, other than to tell you what I know."

381

"Okay, that's all we ask, Chalky."

"Six months ago, a shipment of goods destined for our place was turned over by a gang wielding lots of knives and baseball bats. It took a while, but eventually we'd sussed out who they were and took the greatest of pleasure in cracking a dozen skulls of theirs. Thing was, the amount stolen was so big it gave us major problems in satisfying our clients. To make matters worse, our regular supplier said it would take a week before they could replenish the stocks, which in essence meant we were in shit-street. Our nearest competitors were unwilling to sell us any gear, just delighted to see us out of action for a while."

Maxi and BB smiled across the desk, remembering a time when they'd been in the exact same position: *Stuff your fellow man and make hay while you can.*

"We then heard about this mob from down south." Chalky continued, "and I'm still trying to remember who told us about them. Although I do know they were a real pain in the arse to get hold of."

"In what way?" asked Maxi.

"They wouldn't come near unless you'd used them before, or someone could guarantee you were working in the drugs game full time."

"They sound to me like people who don't take chances."

"That was only the half of it," Chalky said exasperatedly. "They had all kind of stipulations before they'd even think about doing business. Any deal had to be a minimum of 100 grand and on this particular occasion, paid in used Euros."

BB Benson raised his eyebrows. "Wow," he mouthed.

"Next came the time and place for the rendezvous, which had to be agreed two days in advance. We assumed they might be checking the place out before they'd complete the deal."

Maxi interrupted him, "Did you see anyone suspicious hanging about?"

"Never saw a thing until they turned up on the day. Oh yes, another surprise was their delivery fee."

"Delivery fee?"

"Yeah, if you agreed to do business with this mob, it included a 1% delivery fee."

"Who the hell were they, Securicor?"

"Thinking about it, I suppose you'd say that's exactly what they were; a really smooth professional outfit, even though there were only two of them. They turned up in a white Transit van an hour later than the agreed time. We were well and truly pissed off at the delay, seeing as they'd been so insistent on punctuality. But it was only when they'd done the deal and gone, did we realise they'd probably spent the time watching for anything unusual on our part."

"Very careful people indeed," repeated Maxi. "Although I'm curious to hear about these so-called 'professionals', Chalky."

"We met them in an empty parking lot on our territory. The van drove in slowly and we could see them checking if the number plates on our cars were the correct ones. Another stipulation said there could be only four of our people present when we did the deal."

Maxi sat back and tried to re-enact the scene in his mind.

"It drove on for a bit, came to a halt and began to reverse back until the rear doors were just a few yards from where we stood. Then to everyone's surprise, these two large heavies climb out. The easiest way to describe them is either ex-SAS, or a couple of military punters who'd been doing combat for most of their lives. The look was reflected in the type of army kit they wore. Beanie hats, short bomber jackets, fatigue type trousers with an array of pockets on the side and the usual elasticated bottoms with boots. The other distinguishing features were the dark wrap-around sunglasses, stubbly beards and colour of their clothing, which was mostly a drab grey."

Maxi had to ask the question. "Were they English?"

"Looking at them, I would say definitely not. Although you couldn't tell from their accents, because they never spoke a word other than to ask for the password."

"Password?"

"Oh yeah, there was lots of pissing about with this mob and nothing would happen unless you knew the passwords. Mine would you believe was Dr Jekyll, and theirs Mr Hyde."

"Very novel," smiled Maxi. "So who exactly are these people?"

"They're called 'Connexion' and spelt it with an x. The next surprise came when they opened the rear doors and revealed the interior. Expecting an empty space, we were amazed to find it was a proper plumber's van filled to the brim with every conceivable piece of equipment. It had shelves on both sides containing lots of different size plastic bends and copper fittings. They even had an old portable bending machine suspended from the roof with some straps. The hard-nose who did most of the grunting appeared to be in charge, but trying to get him to talk was a complete non-starter.

"Besides the word 'Connexion', the only other one he spoke was Cash. Which obviously was payment for the goods. A fast check amongst the wads assured him that no 'Monopoly Money' had inadvertently been mixed in with the wads of Euros in the briefcase. Next thing, his dumb mate has moved some boxes at the rear of the van and produced a portable screwdriver from a cubbyhole. He then began to unscrew a large plate in the floor, where we assumed the spare wheel was kept.

"As before, we were surprised to see a large watertight compartment packed solid with the cocaine we'd ordered. No other words were spoken as we checked for quality, and once satisfied, transferred the goods between the two vehicles; the whole operation taking a couple of minutes to complete."

"I need to ask a question, Chalky."

"No problem."

"Did you see any kind of weapons throughout this operation?"

"I personally didn't see a thing, but with both their jackets zipped half open, you had to assume they were carrying a gun of some kind."

"What about your mate?"

"I remember him saying he'd been watching the dumb one tightening a lace that had come loose in one of his calf-length boots. At first he'd thought nothing of it, until he noticed the leather sleeve attached to the left boot and spotted the ivory handle of a long lethal-looking knife hidden inside."

Waytree Crescent

The sweet aroma of frying onions filled the air as Kristian walked into the kitchen. "Mmm, something smells good, Ma."

"Your favourite food," she laughed. "Sausage and mash with lots of onion gravy."

"Nice one," he grinned, "I could do with something to warm me up."

"How did the match go?"

"We won four nil and Tommo scored all four goals."

"Well done him, he should turn professional when he's older."

Kristian gave a wink. "Trust me Ma, there's a whole horde of football scouts waiting to sign him up."

"How old is he now?"

"He'll be seventeen in two months' time."

"Which will be a month ahead of you, right?"

"Give a day or two," he replied, then sensed the sadness in her voice; birthdays always reminded his mother of Kelly. "Have I got time for a shower?" he asked, hoping to swerve the conversation in a different direction.

"If your quick," she replied, only to stop him short as he reached the door. "Kristian."

"Yes Ma?"

"I need to ask you something."

Uh, uh, he thought. *I don't like the sound of this.* "What is it, Ma?"

"Did you know about this SEL place that Kelly used to visit?"

Kristian began to shuffle; he and his sister had very few secrets, meaning he couldn't just tell blatant lies. "Yes Ma, she often spoke of her visits to Grandad's offices."

Steffi was momentarily stunned at his casual mention of the paternal term. "And did you... have you ever visited it?"

Kristian, who now found himself on rocky ground tried to keep his voice normal. "Yes Ma, I've been three or four times since Kelly's death."

Steffi blinked in disbelief and stuttered, "You have? When?"

Kristian took a deep breath. "The first was around three weeks ago when one of our afternoon classes was cancelled; something to do with the teacher being ill. This meant we had nothing to do. So I thought I'd catch a bus into town and see for myself."

"How? Why would you?"

"Because I was curious, Ma, and it's not what you think. The only reason Kelly swore me to secrecy was in the hope that someday we would all be a family again. She even told me the truth about how Collette and Eddie Mitchell are not our real grandparents."

The onions cooking on the stove began to turn a dark brown colour as Steffi listened in bemused silence.

"So when Kelly died, I thought I'd find out if what she'd said was true."

A shocked Steffi was too scared to ask what happened next.

Kristian however, had decided to say his piece regardless of the consequences. "I didn't know what I'd find when I got there, although I must admit, it's not what I expected."

"Did you speak to him?" she interrupted, not daring to mention her father's name.

"Who, grandad? Of course I did and I was just knocked-out at how fantastic a person he is. He gave me a personal tour of the offices and introduced me to all his friends. He then showed me around his fabulous penthouse called 'El Rondo'. We later talked about the past and he let me look through an album full of family photographs. It was only then did I find out what had happened to our real grandmother, who died when you were just a young girl. There's something else you should know, Ma, he was absolutely devastated at the death of Kelly and swears he's going to find whoever did it."

"He seems to have charmed you, just like he does to everyone who meets him," sneered Steffi.

Kristian gave a shrug. "I don't know what else to say, Ma. Other than granddad loves us and desperately wants to try and make things up in any way he can."

Steffi's voice turned caustic. "Did he tell you to say that?"

Kristian's eyes hardened. "No Ma, he didn't tell me to say anything of the sort and although you might regard me as just a kid, I'm old enough to see some truth in everything he said."

Steffi turned back to the stove and began to stir the pan as a way of salvaging the food, but more importantly, disguise her anger. "Go and shower," she spat. "I don't want to hear any more about it!"

"Okay Ma," he said, and then had a thought. "Oh yes, there was something else. Uncle BB sends his love and is still waiting for you to call him on the phone."

S.C.U.

The Team were waiting for the usual tap on the desk as Jacko called the Site Meeting to order. "Okay people," he said. "We've had a couple of new developments in The Park murder case, one of which fills me with great sadness. It would appear Milos, the man with the shoulder length hair and crumpled white suit is no longer with us. According to the official police report, the Serbians say he committed suicide by gassing himself in his car."

An audible groan of "*No way,*" was heard around the room; they'd all been genuinely impressed with the quirky journalist's revelations. "Nevertheless," continued Jacko, "his close friend Zelda Zamarova swears he was murdered and this is all some kind of cover-up. She's also claiming he must have been drugged in order to stop him from revealing what he knew. Yet no matter the reason, his untimely death has introduced a new and let's call him 'shady character' to the investigation, who goes by the name of Colonel Petrovic."

Jacko focused on the Team. "A few days ago, I had a long conversation with the people in Sarajevo, who filled me in on this Petrovic. Apparently, he runs a huge narcotics ring from the lower Balkan area and doesn't take prisoners should you cross him. Despite this danger, Milos had discovered the identity of the politician backing Petrovic, plus the fact he'd recently extended his operations into the UK. All of which might explain why our blonde friend is not with us anymore."

More irate mumblings were heard from those sat before him.

"Now you might ask what has this to do with our case? Well, it just so happens that this Colonel Petrovic was once Arkan's right-hand man and helped the Tomovic brothers disappear after the war. There's a rumour he helped cover up any official record of their existence, starting with the mystery chargesheet and their dental records."

"How did he manage that?" asked Stretch.

"He set fire to the local dental practice, which oddly enough, was the one the brothers used regularly."

"Is that it?"

"No, there was something else."

Jacko produced two more photographs and attached them to the boards.

"When in Erdivos, Milos spent a few days trying to discover where the brothers lived, but never succeeded. Yet there's a simple explanation why." He pointed to the first photograph. "What we have here, is a fairly modern two storey house constructed sometime in 2002. It just so happens that this has replaced the original building that once stood here and is shown in the next photo." Jacko pointed to the second picture. "If you look closely, you can just make out the faded lettering painted on the brick wall that says 'Tomovicevi Inzenjeri.'

"This I've been told translates as 'Tomovic Heating Engineers' and is the original home of Luka and Marko Tomovic. Who, before they joined Arkan's Tigers, had helped fit central heating systems in schools and public buildings in the surrounding areas. But not I hasten to add, undertake any other type of plumbing work. That came much later, when they moved to Poland and then the UK." Jacko faced the Team. "But the real reason why the Tomovic's house and workshops aren't here anymore, is because in the year 2000, someone lobbed a couple of incendiary devices through the downstairs windows and set the place on fire. Which was bad enough under any circumstances, except on this occasion both their parents were upstairs asleep in bed!"

Part Twelve

Liverpool Landing Stage

A combination of heavy hawsers and calloused hands helped secure the ferryboat to the gently swaying pontoon. Next to hit the boards was the clanking wooden footbridge and a shipload of day-trippers departed its salt washed decks. Waiting to take their place was a fresh batch of people, all destined to make the same journey. Hovering at the rear stood an impatient Jacko, who'd spent most of the morning scanning the crowds for a half recognisable face. Just before daybreak, an unknown text had landed on his phone requesting an urgent meet on board 'The Royal Iris', ferry at 3.00 pm this afternoon. To add to the uncertainty, the mystery sender had hinted they'd be willing to trade some information regarding the Chillwall Break-in, but didn't say why.

The ropes were loosed; the footbridge raised and with the sound of its engines rumbling down below, the boat took off in the direction of New Brighton; a holiday resort situated on the other side of the Mersey Estuary.

This, for Jacko, was a first. He'd watched the ferries ploughing their way up and down the river many times, but never thought of taking a trip. Yet now he was here, found some of the views quite spectacular; the 'Liver Buildings' being head and shoulders above anything else in sight. With the familiar sound of *Ferry across the Mersey* playing through the ship's speakers he loosened his tie, relaxed and began to enjoy the whole experience. However, his reverie was soon interrupted when a hooded figure appeared at the rail beside him.

"Vinny?" he groaned. "I should have known it was you."

For a second there was no reply, then heard him whisper: "Someone's trying to kill me!"

"Now that's a shame," grinned Jacko.

Vinny's hands began to shake. "I mean it, man, someone's trying to kill me!"

Jacko's smile widened. "Well, I don't know what to say, Tarzan, although I did hear you were never popular at school."

"Fuck that shit!" he spat. "I need police protection, now!"

Time to play stupid games, thought Jacko. "Listen mate, that sort of stuff costs a lot of time and money to set up."

Vinny's twisting nicotine-stained hands seemed to have a life of their own. "Listen, I swear I can give you some very valuable information, provided you help me escape these evil bastards!"

Jacko sounded doubtful. "We could maybe sort something out, but only if the info is worth it."

"I know who did the Chillwall break-in!" He hissed.

"I'm all ears, Tarzan, but hear nothing new."

Vinny took a deep breath and whispered, "It was Moses Sweetman and his brother, 'The Snake'."

Taff Jenkins will be a happy man, thought Jacko, but he needed more than just words. "How do you know?"

"They sold me the gold coins."

"Nice one mate. Where are they now?"

Vinny hesitated and Jacko could tell there was a different kind of struggle taking place beneath the hood.

"I haven't got them anymore; I sold them on."

"Okay, that shouldn't be a problem. Just tell us who to and we'll go and get them."

"I can't do that either," he muttered. "When the buyer heard the police were involved, the fool had them melted down!"

Jacko nearly burst out laughing. "Well that's most unfortunate and won't give you any brownie points when I'm asking my boss for any special favours."

Vinny sounded even more desperate. "If you don't help me man, that Sharecropper mob will cut me to pieces!"

"Ah, so that what this is all about?" smiled Jacko. "Noah doesn't know the coins have already been melted down?"

The silence from beneath the hood told its own tale.

Jacko donned a sympathetic look. "This tale gets worse by the minute mate, but without the coins, or reliable witnesses I don't see how we can help."

Vinny's hands began to shake uncontrollably as he whispered. "I swear the Snake and his brother broke into the house in Chillwall and stole the coins. And I know it was him who pushed the Canadian down the stairs!"

"Did he tell you that?"

Vinny looked stricken. "Of course he fucking didn't, but I'd bet my life he did!"

Jacko watched the green Cheshire countryside slipping by and felt the warm afternoon breeze rustling his hair, but couldn't see a solution to the problem. "Let me tell you how it is my friend. Moses Sweetman is dead in his grave; the coins are long gone and 'The Snake' would rather slit his own throat than admit he was there on the night. Which means you're telling us nothing that we don't already know."

"Okay, okay," he whispered desperately. "But I do have something else to tell you and believe me, this is real big shit!"

The Pier Head

In a million to one chance, someone spotted Vinny alighting a bus at 'The Pier Head' and buying a ticket for the local ferry ride. Which in itself wasn't a crime, except everyone knew Vinny didn't look the seafaring type. This came as a huge relief to those watching the Estate, seeing as how in one of his 'Houdini' moments, the Gecko had managed to escape without being seen. However, things hadn't quite gone to plan. The message had arrived five minutes too late, the ferryboat was already mid-channel and Twixy Hartley couldn't say for sure if Vinny was meeting anyone on board. That said, he wasn't overly concerned, seeing as there were no 'stops on the daytrip and whoever went, had to come back.

Confident that all was well at sea, Twixy sauntered off to buy a frothy coffee and some of his favourite chocolate bars, returning just in time to see the vessel complete its journey. In a timeless routine, the ferry was tethered to the pontoon and the footbridge lowered, ready to unload its next batch of human cargo. Anticipating the usual rush for the ramp and aware his next move would need perfect timing, Twixy squeezed his considerable bulk between two similar-sized spectators and took out his mobile phone.

Switching it over to video mode, he focused first on the Birkenhead shore and then slowly panned around so as to capture the passengers as they left the boat. In the usual manic scramble, he'd nearly missed Vinny's scruffy Nike top in the crowd, but his baggy shorts and spindly legs were more than enough to confirm his presence. Assuming this particular mad dash for the exit was now over and unable to recognise anyone else of interest, Twixy decided it was time to quit.

However, ten frantic seconds later and he was all fingers and thumbs as he desperately tried to continue with his recording.

The Grosvenor Bar

Taff the Mack had a finger in each ear as he stumbled into the first floor lounge and cried. "Christ, it sounds as if someone's strangling a cat down there!"

Carson and Jacko chuckled at his obvious discomfort. "Sorry mate, we forgot Wednesday is Karaoke Night in the bar."

"More like torture night if you ask me."

Hooky Wilson, along with a freshly drawn pint of Tetley's bitter, appeared from behind the bar and placed it on the table. "Long time no see Taff."

"And it's years since I've had the pleasure of being deafened!"

Hooky shook his head in disgust. "Elvis would turn in his grave if he heard that bleeding racket!"

The three detectives smiled in agreement and waited until he was safely out of hearing range. "This is all very cloak and dagger," muttered Taff. "What's going on?"

Jacko leaned a little closer and kept his voice down. "We think someone's been leaking information about the murder inquiry."

"Are we talking about *your* murder inquiry?"

Jacko gave a nod. "But that's not all, we think yours might be involved as well."

The Welshman's eyebrows lifted. "The Chillwall murder hunt might be in all the papers, but there are no hidden secrets anywhere."

"We know that Taff and so does half of Liverpool, but we're not talking about secrets, we think someone in the S.C.U. has been passing information on to a third party."

The Welshman shifted uneasily in his seat. "Any idea who?"

Carson glanced at Jacko, who chose his words carefully. "There is someone, although I think I should tell you about my boat trip with Vinny the Gecko first."

A surprised Taff sat back and supped his drink.

"I've just today discovered that following the Chillwall break-in, Vinny the Gecko bought the gold coins from Moses Sweetman and sold them on to Sheldrake the jeweller. Who, when he heard there was a dead body involved, threw a wobbler and so as to avoid any chance of them being traced back to him, had the coins melted down by another jeweller."

"Sounds like a game I played as a kid. It was called 'pass the parcel'."

"This is more than a kid's game Taff. Moses 'Goldfinger', as you call him, ended up being murdered in the park and his older brother Noah, is threatening to slit Vinny's throat if he doesn't return the coins."

"Which he can't possibly do, especially if they've already been melted down?"

"That's right. There again he swears 'The Snake' was in the house when the Canadian went headfirst down the stairs."

"Was he?"

"Probably, but Vinny's just praying we'll arrest 'The Snake' for murder and save him from the bacon slicer."

"Will he testify? That should be enough to put Noah behind bars."

"Not a hope," declared Jacko.

Taff was thoughtful. "So what does he want?"

"He's looking for a safe house and all year round protection from the Sharecropper gang."

"You must be bloody kidding!"

"My thoughts exactly, but when I explained the situation in more detail, his hands began to shake like a tambourine player and I swear he was on the verge of tears."

"If you ask me, the conniving little shit should be on the stage," sneered Taff.

"Maybe, there again if it wasn't for him, we'd never have discovered there's a mole hidden somewhere amongst us."

"What, more cloak and dagger?"

"No Taff, this is the real thing and it comes straight from Vinny's lips." Carson, who'd sat quietly throughout, spoke just three words. "Have a listen."

Jacko dropped his voice and moved closer to the table. "One night last week, Vinny got careless and nearly ended up on the meat slab. From what he told me, Noah and one of his gang were waiting in the tower block, ready to re-arrange his face with their flick-knives. A huge struggle took place in which Vinny fought like Mike Tyson to save his angel-like features. Then, just when he thought all was lost, a couple of dinner-suited gorillas appear out of nowhere, kick both Sharecroppers into touch and kidnap Vinny in the process."

Taff looked dumbfounded.

"A few minutes later and our hero finds himself in the boot of a flash Range Rover, being transported to places unknown. His final destination he thinks was some kind of storage depot with an automatic roller door. Once inside, he's introduced to another tuxedo-wearing gorilla, who, for some reason likes to play *Chopsticks* on the piano. However, this particular Liberace isn't interested in Vinny's taste in music; he wants to question him about the Waytree Park murders! Problem is, some items were never made public; one being Vincent Snodgrass's real name. Plus the fact he happens to be our only reliable witness. Liberace then asked if Vinny could remember who was driving the white van. Which is strange, seeing as it was never mentioned in the papers. Yet the question that really had me going was the one about the red and white wool hat lying on the van's dashboard."

"Now that, I definitely would have remembered as being in the news," declared Taff.

Jacko gave a thin smile. "I had a quick look through all the Press Briefings and the only time it gets a mention is when Ziggy is spotted at the football match.

Which means that only someone with direct access to our inner circle, would know about this vital piece of evidence."

The Welshman shook his head in disbelief. "Do you have any idea who?"

Carson spoke instead of Jacko. "A question Taff. Have you ever heard of a secret undercover operation called *The Baltimore Switch?*"

The Albert Dock

A mere stone's throw away from where Vinny had stepped off the ferry, Maxi and Michaela were having lunch at 'Gusto,' one of his favourite restaurants on the Albert Dock. An added bonus was a quayside table and the chance to enjoy the view across the celebrated square of water. "I just love these surroundings," enthused Maxi. "Because no matter what your taste in architecture, you just have to agree that the beauty and magnificence of the past is still here for all to see."

"I'll drink to that," smiled Michaela. "And it's amazing to think that not so long ago, this place was full of people toiling away and trying to make a living."

Maxi refilled her wine glass. "Yes, I can imagine a time when there would have been hundreds of ships unloading everything from exotic silks to coal. That said, I have no quarrel with the museums and restaurants that have replaced them, or the yachts and boats for that matter. What's more important, is the fact this superb piece of Victorian engineering has managed to survive the test of time, as well as the Blitz."

Michaela was well acquainted with Maxi's tale of how fortunate Liverpool had been when the war ended. Especially when the government of the day, had begun pouring pots of money into the southern cities in an effort to rebuild them. Which meant most of the northern areas, (Liverpool especially) had received a mere pittance, if anything at all. Yet in an ironic twist of fate, some had completely ignored their heritage and bulldozed most of it into the ground. Having been one of those starved of outside monetary aid. Maxi's beloved city had somehow managed to stave off the greedy developers and preserve a multitude of beautiful sandstone and red-bricked buildings, much to the envy of its more foolish contemporaries. Michaela was just about to endorse this sentiment with a toast, when BB Benson joined them at the table.

"Any food left? I am absolutely famished!"

Maxi waved to the waiter and ordered BB's favourite pasta dish; a chilli laden Penne Arrabiata. "I wasn't expecting you today, I thought you were playing golf in Uzbekistan, or somewhere."

BB took a gulp of wine and grinned. "They only fly there late on Monday nights and always via Tiger Moth Airlines."

Maxi gave a mock sympathetic look. "So what does bring you here?"

"The food and a very interesting whisper I heard this morning."

Maxi could tell from the tone of BB's voice that this was important.

"I was playing a game of one-handed golf with 'Fraz the Taz', when he informed me of some very interesting news"

Maxi wasn't sure what to ask next, but opted for golf and Fraz the Taz.

"His first name is Freddy and he's from Trinidad in the West Indies."

"And he plays golf with one hand?"

"Not exactly," smiled BB. "But sometime back in the '70s, Freddy discovered he had a real talent for playing golf and was looking to turn professional. However and unfortunately for him, the fashions at the time and the fickle-hand of fate decided otherwise."

Michaela flicked a glance at Maxi who raised a confused eyebrow.

"Freddy was generally known as Fraz the Taz, because his Afro hairstyle resembled an over-inflated beach ball glued to his head."

"What does Fraz the Taz mean, BB?"

"I've no idea, Michaela, I can only assume its West Indian slang for the size of his head, but apparently it was a real hindrance when trying to swing his golf club."

"You mean it got in the way?" chuckled an astonished Maxi.

"So the story goes," confirmed BB. "But the Fraz wasn't just a golfer, he was reputed to be a real Stud and the women just adored his beach-ball hair-do. So much so, he refused to have it chopped, or reduced in any way.

"Which meant he wasn't going to be an earlier version of Tiger Woods?"

"You got it Maxi, the Fraz was never destined to win The Open championship, or any other trophy for that matter. Still, that wasn't the only reason he didn't make it to the top. It would seem our man liked to mainline."

"What? Do you mean injected drugs?"

"Yes Michaela, he was addicted to Heroin for many years, which didn't really help when trying to swing a club straight. There again, he's been clean for a long time and because of his talent, has managed to make a lot of money over the years."

"Playing one-handed golf?" ventured Michaela.

BB nodded. "One rainy day, he was playing with some friends and demonstrated just how good a golfer he was by smashing his tee shot miles down the fairway one handed."

"Which I assume is something special?"

Maxi grinned at Michaela's innocence, whilst marvelling at the golfing feat.

"Most players use both hands to hit their Tee shot around two hundred yards or more," explained BB. "Whereas Fraz can easily pass that just by swinging the club in his right hand."

"What's the point?" asked Michaela.

"Someone always thinks they're going to beat him."

"And this Fraz obviously knows they won't?"

"That's right, one guy bet £1,000 he could hit his ball twenty yards further."

"I take it he lost?" finished Michaela.

"He certainly did," sighed BB. "Even now, he's forever in demand and chooses each opponent with great care. The more skilful type always have shorter odds, whereas your average hacker gets much longer ones. There again, he's no fool and they all get to win sometime."

"And I assume you're still trying to beat him?" prompted Maxi.

"Been trying to pass the pain for years and still haven't managed it yet."

"How much today?"

"Twenty pounds a shot, but fortunately for my wallet, this morning's session was limited to just nine holes."

"Should have gone to Uzbekistan, it would have been cheaper," smiled Michaela.

BB was about to reply when a plate of steaming pasta arrived and Maxi changed the subject. "Enough of golf, what about this interesting news?"

BB ate a welcoming mouthful before continuing. "The Fraz's beach-ball hair and heroin addiction may be long gone, but he still likes to snort a few lines of '*Charlie*' now and then. And seeing as how his stash was getting low, he'd arranged to have a top up from his usual supplier. But guess what? Eli Stoker turned up instead."

"Elijah?" whispered Maxi.

"One and the same," replied BB. "It would appear that most of the West Indians still buy their Cocaine from the Stoker mob."

"Jesus, I can't believe that vicious bastard is still going!"

"Hasn't gone away according to the Fraz, who I might add, agrees he's one first class scumbag!"

"What did he want?"

BB swallowed a spoon-full of pasta and took another glug of wine. "Elijah didn't want anything, other than to say his father is offering £20,000 to anyone who can point him in the direction of *the man with the knife*."

Maxi let out a low whistle. "You're not serious?"

"It's not the sort of thing the Fraz would make up."

"I never thought Eazy would be that desperate to find his grandson's killer."

"If we're to believe our golfer, I'd say he was deadly serious."

Maxi shook his head. "Who'd have thought he'd be out there searching for the same Serbian as we are?"

"There is a difference," corrected BB. "Eazy Stoker doesn't have a clue who the killer is, whereas we do."

Maxi watched the ripples on the water. "I'd always assumed he'd be upset at the loss of one so young, but never thought he'd pay for information."

BB sat back. "I've been giving this business some serious thought Maxi and one of your favourite quotes springs to mind: *never look a gift horse in the mouth*."

"Tell me what's brewing in that twisted Brazilian mind of yours?"

"I strongly recommend that you and Eazy get together and join forces."

"You must be joking!" gasped Maxi.

"If only that were true and before you dismiss it out of hand, listen to what I have to say."

"Okay, but this had better be good."

BB took a sip of water. "According to Tufty McClellan, there's a psychopathic Serbian who's been slaying his way across Europe for the last twenty years. His preferred victims are always young blondes that he likes to torture, rape and then kill. But the bastard came severely unstuck on the night he decided to murder Kelly, because he didn't anticipate the arrival of young Moses Sweetman on the scene."

"This sounds like something I've already read," grunted Maxi.

BB smiled. "I know, but with the help of McClellan, we've since been able to obtain a copy of the autopsy and have a good idea of who killed them. And his latest missive concerning the two brothers sounds pretty convincing, especially the part that says they might be Serbian ex-army and involved in the drugs trade. That said, when you spread it out like a jigsaw puzzle, I think lots of the pieces could be classed as circumstantial."

Michaela's mouth opened in surprise. "Are you saying it's not them?"

"Not at all, gorgeous. What I am saying is that some of the more important pieces are still missing."

The tone of Maxi's voice became a little more conciliatory. "I'm still listening BB."

"It's the same old dance Maxi; the police can't arrest the Tomovic brothers because they haven't got a clue where they are, but as I said earlier, we just might." The laughter and chatter from the other diners on the quayside was forgotten, as Maxi and Michaela focused on BB Benson. "Cast your mind back to our recent telephone conversation with Chalky Johnson and his tale of the two delivery men from the London based drugs outfit."

"The two bruisers with the van full of plumbing gear?"

"Yes Maxi, although we're not talking about 'Laurel and Hardy' here. They're a couple of gun carrying heavies, who transport huge amount of drugs around the country *and* repair leaking taps as a side line. Nonetheless, when it comes to matching Tufty McClellan's police profiles? You have to admit they do tick every box."

"And don't forget the knife hidden in his calf boot," added Michaela.

"Don't worry, gorgeous, whoever owns the *knife,* has a great deal to answer for!"

Maxi's interest slowly began to grow as BB spoke on.

"It's also important to remember that our own £200 reward wasn't without some success. Especially when Bimmo said he'd been face to face with Ziggy. He might be a lanky arrogant shit of a kid, but I can still remember the look of fear on his face and see the scar under his chin. I'm also of the opinion that if his gang hadn't been watching, young Bimmo was just inches away from having his throat cut!"

"So what happens next?" asked Maxi.

BB paused. "I still think there's more than enough evidence to warrant a very expensive bullet."

"Are we talking about a professional hitman?"

BB gave a shrug. "Why not, a telescopic sight and a single pull of the trigger would solve all our problems."

"Yes, but it wouldn't give me the satisfaction of looking this Ziggy in the eye, or hear him plead for his life!"

The table fell quiet as they remembered Maxi's sworn intention to kill him personally.

"Does it matter how he dies? This way you'll at least have avenged Kelly's death."

"I know that Michaela, but the autopsy report still keeps me awake at night."

"I had a feeling you wouldn't take the easy way out," grunted BB. "Which is why I think we should join forces with Eazy Stoker."

"Why the hell should I do that?"

"If we're not going to pay someone to kill this bastard, then the only other logical alternative is to do it ourselves."

Maxi smiled for the first time. "Now you're talking my kind of language."

"Maybe, but we have to be realistic in how we're going to do this. I can't see us getting tooled up like the A Team and heading off down south ready to blow these people away. The obvious reason being we don't use guns and this 'Connexion' mob do!"

Maxi looked unconvinced. "If we take our time, plan it carefully and take the right amount of men, I don't see why we can't pull it off."

"Wouldn't it be easier to invite them here?" asked BB.

"Where?

"Liverpool."

A look of stunned surprise crossed Maxi's face. "You're not serious?"

"You'd better believe it folks and Eazy Stoker's the perfect way of enticing them here."

"How?" Asked Michaela.

It was now BB's turn to be serious. "In my opinion, going to London is akin to entering the lion's den. The Manchester boys have already met them and swear the two Serbians are real professionals. They're more suspicious than a couple of Meerkats and trust no one into the bargain. However, if we offer to buy a substantial amount of drugs from Connexion, they'd have to deliver them here, where we could take care of them at our leisure. The only problem is, in order to get this stuff, you'll need street cred, which we don't have, but Eazy Stoker does."

"You're not suggesting I go into business with him?"

"I wouldn't say business, let's just call it a temporary arrangement."

"I'd rather run him over!" snarled Maxi.

"You might get the chance to do that later, but at the moment he's our best bet."

"Do you think Eazy would want to get involved with a plot to kill someone?"

BB gave a confident nod. "Yes Michaela, this is like an offer you can't refuse and I think he'll jump at it when he hears what's in it for him." He was about to continue talking when his phone gave a Ping.

"Sounds like an incoming message," said Michaela.

BB used a finger to swipe open his phone. "It's from Twixy Hartley and he rarely sends video messages, so it has to be something important."

Maxi was curious. "Where is he?"

"On the quay outside the Pier Head Terminal. We had a text message saying the Gecko was acting strange and thought it best to have Twixy check him out. Looking at this, he obviously must have found something." BB held his phone so they might all see, before pressing the play button. The on screen camera panned slowly from left to right; and other than the chatter and laughter of the people on the quay, there was no commentary. It reminded Michaela of an amateur recording where no one had real a clue of what was happening. Then to her surprise, the tip of Twixy's stubby finger appeared on screen and pointed to a grey-hooded figure hustling his way up the ramp and the Terminal exit.

"Who's that?" asked Maxi.

"That without doubt is Vinny the Gecko," said BB.

"He seems to be in a hurry."

"Yes Michaela, Vinny never hangs around if he can help it."

Twixy's video panned back and forth, all the time concentrating on the slowly dwindling passengers climbing the ramp. Then it unexpectedly went blank.

"Did you recognise anyone?" asked BB.

"No one I knew," replied Michaela.

"All strangers to me," agreed Maxi.

A confused BB was about to pocket his phone, when they heard another Ping and watched the video spring back into life. This time however, they didn't need sound, the footage alone was enough. As the next batch of passengers rushed to board the ferry, a lone figure stepped past them and began to make his way up the exit ramp.

Michaela peered at the screen. "If I'm not mistaken, that looks like DS Jackson from the Merseyside Serious Crimes Unit."

"He might be wearing a different coloured tie, but that's definitely him," agreed Maxi.

"Well, well if I was a betting man, I'd say Vinny the Gecko has turned *Bandit*."

"It looks a distinct possibility BB; why else would he take a boat ride with a Detective Sergeant?"

"What does it mean?" asked Michaela.

Maxi was thoughtful before replying. "It means Vinny is a pain in the arse and we need to be careful in how we proceed. This was the last thing I thought he would do."

"I wouldn't worry about it just yet," said BB.

"Why not?"

"I'm sure he has no idea where we met the other night."

"Excellent, but maybe we should take him off the streets for a while, sort of save him from himself."

"Not a bad idea Maxi, I'm all in favour of a good cause, especially if it has our best interests at heart."

"Have the boys pick him up ASAP and take him back to the warehouse at Caversham Cut. Tell them to put a camp bed and portable TV in the small storeroom. He can use the toilet and sink to keep himself clean."

"More like a fire hose," grinned BB.

"Will anyone miss him?" asked a concerned Michaela.

"I doubt it," smiled Maxi. "People like Vinny go missing every day, but in light of what's happened this afternoon, it looks as if I might have to meet with Eazy Stoker after all."

"If the police get any closer, we may not get another chance." BB reminded him.

"How are you going to do this?"

"We'll use Fraz the Taz as a go-between."

"Okay. Just try and make the meeting as short as possible," growled Max.

The Meet

The blue Chrysler Voyager turned down the cobbled side street and came to a halt outside the drab nondescript building occupying most of the block. A single toot on the horn was signal enough for the roller door to open; the interior lights revealing a lone figure standing deep in the shadows.

"Well, shit, man," chortled Elijah. "Don't that appear to be one ugly fucking face from the past?"

Perched on the back seat, Eazy used his cane to steady himself and peer at the lone figure of BB Benson, who looked to be the sole welcoming committee. "Maybe, boy. There again, I could tink of a few better people I'd like to meet."

"Looks like he's in charge of traffic management as well Papa."

Craning his neck, Eazy realised what'd caught his elder son's attention.

BB was pointing to the winding concrete slope that led to the floor above.

"Well let's not keep them waiting boy, drive on!"

The familiar looking access ramp had all but confirmed Eazy's earlier suspicions. Many years ago, this had once been a two-story car park he might have used when visiting this part of town. But the bricked up windows and lack of daylight had effectively transformed it to what it was now: a vast private storage area. Heeding his father's warning, Elijah kept a wary eye on BB Benson as he followed him up the steep slope to the next level. However, as they crested the rise, an unexpected scene unfolded before them. Waiting to greet them was an immaculately dressed Maxi Hamilton, who by using his hands, was guiding them to an exact parking position and once satisfied, gave a sign to cut the engine.

"Shit man, this fucker appears to land aircraft as well," laughed Elijah. Realising they'd just performed some kind of carefully orchestrated routine, a nervous Eazy tapped him on the shoulder. "See what's going on out there, boy, and make sure there are no hidden surprises!" Elijah tentatively opened the driver side door and took in the shapes and shadows around him. "There's lots of expensive cars parked around, Papa, and I can see Maxi Hamilton standing next to a table with two empty chairs." He then paused. "Looks to me as if he's on his own, but maybe wants you to join him." A short sharp tap on the window told its tale; Elijah reached for the handle and opened the rear door.

"Stay here," Eazy muttered gruffly.

Elijah waited in frustrated silence as his father made his way towards Hamilton, who'd already taken a seat at the table. To Maxi, the very sight of an aging Stoker, with his fancy silver topped-cane, was nothing short of anathema and the thought of having to do business with him was even worse. If it hadn't been for the tragic death of Kelly, he would never have contemplated such a scenario. But as BB Benson pointed out, in order to make their plan work, they needed to get Stoker on board. Looking back, it had been more than thirty years since he and the Jamaican had ceased battling for the streets of Liverpool and Maxi didn't need a calendar to remember the sweltering August of 1969 and the night they first met.

He and BB had been drinking in 'The Bear's Paw', a popular, but long since departed watering hole, just off Lord Street. When they heard one of the Stoker gang had been caught selling drugs in a nearby alley. Downing their drinks, they'd raced for the lane in question, where the angry shouting from up ahead, had all but confirmed a major disturbance was taking place. Muscling his way past the few people present, Maxi was stunned to see the dreadlocked head of Eazy Stoker and one of his cohorts, thrusting and waving their knives from within the doorway they'd been backed into.

In what was an act of arrogant stupidity, they'd been chancing their arm by selling drugs on his 'Patch' when four of his men had spotted them. Yet it was obvious the Jamaicans had no intentions of giving in without a fight and even though they were all unarmed, Maxi's men kept lashing out with their feet in the hope they might kick one of the blades free. Despite the screaming and shouting filling the night air, it still needed the familiar sound of Maxi's voice, to silence the noisy threats.

"Okay boys, back off!" yelled.

The sweating foursome immediately stepped back a few paces, whilst ensuring there was no possible means of escape for the trespassers.

Maxi stepped to the front and pointed a finger. "I've warned you bastards before about selling that shit on my territory!"

The wiry young Jamaican looked to be completely unfazed by this loud declaration of sovereignty. "Well who da fuck are you, big man?" he sneered in his Kingstown accent. "I tink this here territory belongs to whoever want to use it." These words stunning those crowded in the narrow alley, the arrogant reply sounding more like a declaration of war.

"Relax," whispered BB from the side. "Me and the boys are ready take care of this;" the appearance of four baseball bats confirming his short, but violent solution to the problem.

Maxi held him back. "That's okay, it's better if I take care of this personally."

The Jamaican's eyes lit up at the prospect of fighting this tall arrogant Scouse Colonialist. "Step forward arsehole!" He sneered in a scornful voice. "You ever hear dat saying 'the bigger they come, da harder they fall'?"

Ignoring the noisy hyperbole, BB stepped forward and held up the familiar shaped bat for all to see. "Remember this people of the night, one sign of a knife or weapon of any kind and I'll beat the both of you to a pulp!"

The warning wasn't lost on Eazy, who nonchalantly showed BB the flick-knife, before passing it to his frightened accomplice cowering behind him in the doorway.

"I doan need a blade to take care of dis here fucker!" he grinned. Unable to predict what might happen next, BB swiftly organised the boys into a semi-circle by using their arms and baseball bats.

At the same time, it gave Maxi a moment to assess the situation. The 'Rastafarian' was at least four inches shorter than he was, but of a strong athletic build. The clinging tee shirt was obviously there to show off his wiry upper muscled body and he moved easily on the balls of his feet. None of this was lost on Maxi, as he took off his coat, flexed his shoulders and faced his opponent. Unlike the strict confines of a boxing ring, there were no hard and fast rules when it came to a street fight. A quiet descended on the alley as the men of two different cultures stalked each other, both searching for an opening shot. Expecting the usual grab and grapple and having faced this situation many times before, Maxi opted to keep his hands loosely by his side. But to his surprise, the Jamaican suddenly spun like a ballet-dancer on the ball of his right foot and caught him on the side of the head with an extremely painful kick. "Watch his feet!" Screamed BB Benson.

'Bit late for that' thought Maxi, his ears ringing from the unexpected blow.

"He must be into that Martial Arts shit." BB warned again.

Yet before Maxi could think, Easy had adjusted his stance and in a move that nearly swept him off his feet, delivered an enormously painful kick to his right calf. A quick shimmy later and he'd only just had time to fend off one that was en-route to his testicles.

'Jesus Christ!' thought Maxi, 'If you don't do something soon, this curly-haired fucker will kick you up and down the street!'

A desperate cry of "Move your arse!" Came from BB Benson who was thinking along the same lines. Yet instead of being on the offensive, Maxi was more concerned in warding off a series of swift and potentially hurtful kicks. All of which, were intended to bring him to his knees. Eazy in the meantime, was having a ball. "Try one of these Honky Man!" he whooped, the agonising blow to Maxi's left thigh followed by a high derisive laugh.

To the people watching, BB Benson included, there appeared to be only one winner. But Bob Marley's double suddenly became a bit too smart for his own good and in an act of pure showmanship, decided to go for the head again. Dancing from foot to foot like some flock-haired Mohamed Ali. He feinted to his left and brought his right leg around in a wide arc, with the intention of catching the side of Maxi's head. But instead of fending it off as he'd done before, Maxi dipped his shoulder at the last second and whipped in a devastating left hook to Eazy's lower ribs. The sound of breaking bone was clearly audible, this followed by an agonising scream of pain and a desperate intake of breath. The contest however, wasn't quite over. As Easy writhed and clutched his shattered side, Maxi finished him off with a tremendous right hand that broke his nose in two places and knocked him out cold.

"What took you so long?" asked BB.

"The bastard wouldn't stand still and I'll have to sit down for a week!"

The hatred and images from the past were so vivid, they might have happened yesterday. Yet, here in the present, Maxi's initial reaction was one of immense satisfaction as he looked into the face of the aging Jamaican. *Well, I sure don't look as bad as he does*, he said to himself, the very sight giving him so much pleasure. With the passing of time, Eazy's smooth nut-brown skin had slowly mutated into a morass of wrinkles and creases. His beloved dreadlocks, no more than a curly white perm, the Bob Marley beard having gone much the same way. But the one feature that gave Maxi so much joy was the sight of his flattened nose and sound of laboured breathing. *The ravages of time and a perfect right-hand punch can do much to shape a man's future*, he thought with satisfaction.

Eazy's thin reedy voice brought him back to the problems of the present. "Fraz the Taz tells me you want to talk Big man; says it's mighty important."

Time to move on Maxi thought reluctantly, his attention returning to the task ahead. "Yes, it's very important!" He emphasised.

The Jamaican stared at him with obvious distaste. "What you want man?"

"I've heard a rumour you're offering £20,000 to find whoever killed Moses Sweetman."

"So?" he asked suspiciously.

"I just happen to know who did it."

"What is this shit? You looking to collect the reward?"

"No, but I want you to help me find the person who murdered him!"

"Why the fuck would I want to help you?"

"Because Moses Sweetman wasn't the only one who died in the park that night. A young blonde girl was murdered alongside him. Her name is Kelly Freeland and she was my granddaughter."

A look of surprised comprehension was more than evident as Eazy pondered this latest revelation. "Well ain't that something?" he chuckled. "I had no idea you two were related." A few seconds later, and he was back to his usual self. "Like any man who's had a tragic loss, you got my condolences, but what da fuck do you want from me?"

"I want you to help me find the killer and blow him away."

Eazy's wrinkled brow furrowed even more as he tried to understand. "What?"

"I've been reliably informed that you're a Bible man and one of your favourite sayings is, *an eye for an eye.* Now I'm not so sure about *a tooth for a tooth,* but I reckon this might be the perfect opportunity for you to level the score."

Eazy was stunned. "You serious?"

"Absolutely." Maxi replied in a clear emotionless voice.

The creased face took on another degree of doubt as Maxi pushed home his advantage. "What's wrong 'big time'? Don't tell me you're scared?"

Eazy's eyes flew open. "I ain't scared of no man!" He snarled in anger.

"That's what I thought," Maxi replied by way of placating him. "BB and I were hoping that maybe you might want to avenge your grandson's death. And if all goes as planned, will guarantee you a fitting reward when it's over."

The Jamaican's eyes studied his two most despised adversaries from the past. But seeing as he'd always regarded himself as a practical man, saw no reason why he should cut off his nose to spite his face. A wave of the cane and Elijah was stood beside him. "Looks like Hamilton's got misery just like da rest of us boy. Seems the blonde girl in Junkies Corner belonged to him. But dat ain't the only thing, if we decide to help him, he says he gonna make us rich!"

"Only if you agree to come on board," insisted Maxi.

Eazy spent the next minute whispering with his son; who gave a shrug of uncertainty. "Okay Mr Big time, let's hear what you got to say."

Maxi unfolded a piece of paper and placed it on the table. "Ever heard of these?"

"Connexion?" Eazy said doubtfully.

Elijah was peering over his shoulder. "I heard of them Papa, they work out of the south, but we ain't ever put any business their way."

Maxi fixed his gaze on the wrinkled face. "We've been reliably informed that the killer is a Serbian named Luka Tomovic and goes by the nickname Ziggy. But he's not alone, he has a twin brother called Marko and they both work for this Connexion mob in London. Their job is to ensure the drugs reach their intended buyer and then return to base with the right amount of money."

Elijah pointed to the sheet. "I heard something about these two guys Papa."

Maxi gave a curt nod. "But what you might not have heard, is they're a couple of ex-soldiers who fought their way throughout the Bosnian Wars and have a reputation of being highly trained killers."

"You trying to scare us?" asked Eazy.

"No," replied Maxi. "Just letting you know all the dangers involved."

"You tell da tale man and we be da judge of that."

Maxi gave a grim smile. "There's something else you should know. When he was in the army, this Luka was known as 'Ziggy the knife.' Probably because of the long dagger hidden in his calf-boot. But he's no shrinking violet when it comes to spilling blood. The same bastard is reputed to have murdered at least ten innocent women since he left Serbia."

"Fucker sure gets about," quipped an impressed Elijah.

"There could be more," said Maxi. "But the police haven't found their bodies yet."

"This makes him some kind of serial killer?"

Maxi considered Eazy's question. "Almost certainly."

"Does his brother take part in all this killing?"

"We're not sure, but there is some evidence to put him at the Park murders."

Eazy's eyes narrowed. "These 'sources' of yours, seem real close to what's goin on in this here investigation."

Maxi's voice was emotionless. "If I'm going to kill someone, I like to be sure it's the right person."

Eazy was just as impassive. "What you going to do about his kin?"

"Under the circumstances, I'd say we have no choice other than to kill him too."

The Jamaican's look of surprise said everything, but before he could speak, Maxi hammered home his point. "There's no way we can let the other brother survive! If he were here at the time, then he'd be an eyewitness to his brother's death and almost certainly want revenge. But if we can terminate both of them at once, I reckon we'll be doing the world a favour, as well as guaranteeing there's no possible comeback."

Eazy fingered his curly beard and looked unconvinced. "What about this Connexion mob?"

"They're the least of our problems; I'll tell you all about that later."

The Jamaican was thoughtful again. "When you tinkin' about doin this?"

"As soon as possible."

A look of concern crossed his face. "What's the rush, man?"

"Every day that passes makes it so much harder," said Maxi. "We've been reliably informed that the police are searching high and low for these Tomovic brothers, but luckily for us haven't found them yet."

BB Benson added his own thoughts. "There's nothing to say that could change anytime soon."

"This is true," said Maxi. "And if the law manages to get to them first, the Serbians are likely to get a rap on the knuckles and a short prison sentence."

"Meaning, we'll never get the chance to kill the bastards!" growled BB.

Eazy looked to be having second thoughts. "This whole thing's happenin' a shade too quick for my liking. These fuckers may be Serbian, but I still ain't sure about killin' them both in cold blood."

Maxi reached for the briefcase next to his chair and took out two of the autopsy photographs. "Hopefully, these might help change your mind."

"Holy fuckin shit Papa, that's young Moses!" spluttered Elijah.

The shock tactics seemed to have worked on the son, but it was important they have the same effect on the man himself and Maxi had purposely chosen the most disturbing photos to show Eazy. "Once upon a time these two young beautiful people were our grandchildren," said Maxi. "But that was before this Serbian killer came into our lives."

Eazy spent a few seconds letting his eyes run over the photographs, the face of a now dead Moses reminding him of Joshua, his favourite son. "Okay," he said at last, "let me hear how we're gonna do this."

Maxi repositioned the briefcase so the Jamaican could see the rest of its contents. "I want you to order £500,000 of cocaine from these 'Connexion' people and this is the money to pay for it."

The Stokers were used to handling large sums of money, but the sight of so much ready cash was still an eye-opener. "Why don't *you* call them?" questioned Elijah.

"'Cause they don' have any street cred," replied his father.

"That's right," said Maxi. "These people are a suspicious breed and only supply to regular drug dealers like yourselves. If we rang them out of the blue, they'd probably think we're the police."

"But we've never needed to use them in the past Papa, and everyone knows we have our own people," protested Elijah.

"Which is why you're going to tell them you've been let down by your supplier in Jamaica," said Maxi. "Just act real upset and say a large shipment intended for the UK has been intercepted by Customs. Tell them that things are getting real bad and you only have enough to last a few days. For all that, it's important you act normal and haggle about the price. The whole point is to sound as though you want to do a deal, but don't want to get ripped off."

"One thing's for sure boys, they'll do their homework and check you out." BB said with a smile. "But as we all know, it's virtually impossible to tell what's happening in the West Indian drug trade."

"Say this all goes to plan, where will they deliver these goods?" asked Elijah.

"Right here," replied an uncompromising Maxi.

"Back in the late '60s, I remember this as bein a car park," said Eazy.

Maxi nodded. "That's exactly what it was, until I decided to replace it with an office block. Problem is, someone forgot to mention the new Metro Line was about to pass underneath and the Council refused to give me planning permission. So I bricked up the windows and used it for my own personal storage."

"I take it nobody knows the place is yours?"

"Absolutely no one," said Maxi. "It's been passed through so many different companies, it's virtually impossible to say who owns it."

Eazy appeared to accept his word of assurance. "And I take it this where you intend to kill these Serbian brothers?"

"Why not? It's safe, secure and soundproof."

"You yet to tell us how you gonna do this man."

"Allow me to demonstrate."

The Jamaicans were surprised to see Maxi step between the 'Range Rover' and the 'Chrysler.' "From what we've been told, the brothers have a set procedure when delivering the goods. First off, they'll do a visual check on their surroundings and once satisfied, proceed with the deal." Maxi indicated to both vehicles. "The distance between the two cars is an important factor and the reason we made you park in that exact spot."

Satisfied his earlier suspicions had been confirmed, Eazy was curious to hear what came next.

"It's our intention to have just three people meet them, BB, Eazy and myself."

"What about me?" complained Elijah.

Maxi looked him up and down. "I'm worried you might make them nervous and a little jumpy. It's important they don't smell a rat, or become suspicious in any way. So, I'm hoping a reception party of three respectable old men will pass muster."

Sensing Elijah was about to protest again, Eazy raised a hand, thus making his argumentative son fall silent. "Keep on talkin, 'big man', we still listening."

"We know the Tomovic brothers move the drugs around the country in a white Ford Transit van, but this is not your normal works banger. The rear has been kitted out as a plumber's mobile workshop and from what I hear, is a perfect place to hide the drugs from prying eyes." Maxi moved to the Range Rover and opened the rear hatch. "I think it's important that when the Serbians arrive, the money is already here and on display for all to see."

BB Benson made a point of shifting the money-laden briefcase from the table to the carpeted boot of the luxury car. Maxi flipped open the lid and took out a £10,000 wedge of notes. "This we hope will put the brothers at ease, but it's also important we stay cool and give the impression it's just another business transaction. We've all been here before and know exactly how it works; check the goods are genuine, swap the money for the drugs and complete the deal."

"That's all very well 'Big man', but I don' hear no mention of how you gonna kill these two Serbians."

"I was just coming to that," smiled Maxi.

In a pre-arranged manoeuvre, BB Benson moved alongside him at the table.

"Considering the circumstances," Maxi began. "We could be justified in carrying some weapons of our own and there's no doubting our two killers would expect us to do just that. But I'm trying to create an atmosphere of equal trust and with the help of a simple ruse, hope to achieve just that." As one, they held open both their suit jackets to reveal nothing other than the bright silk inner linings. "As you can see we're unarmed and I'm hoping our two Serbian friends will be thinking the exact same thing."

In another well-rehearsed move, both men let go and at the same time reached behind to their lower backs. In the blink of an eye the Jamaicans were staring into the business end of two shiny Glock pistols and without saying another word, Maxi and BB pulled the triggers.

Eazy's hands instinctively went up to protect his face, while Elijah half turned his body, but there'd been no smoke or sound, just the distinctive click of two empty firing mechanisms.

"Always expect the unexpected," advised Maxi. "And trust no one."

A much shaken Eazy was desperately trying to keep his bowels under control, but in hindsight could see merit in the plan. "Clever shit," he murmured in anger.

Maxi held up the weapons and turned them from side to side. "Both guns are brand new and completely untraceable. The serial numbers, or anything else that might reveal their true source, has been removed with a laser." He then demonstrated how to release the empty magazine and load it with a fresh one. "If needed, the guns have enough fire power to stop a charging Rhinoceros, but from around ten feet? I think one shot should do the trick."

"What happens next?"

"When done, we load the two bodies into the Transit van."

"I'm assuming you ain't forgot about this Connexion mob?" asked a shaken Eazy.

"Not at all," replied Maxi. "But it's important to remember the brothers like to keep to a set routine. They're not always punctual and at times like to create an air of uncertainty by keeping people in suspense. Which is why we wait thirty minutes before Elijah rings London demanding to know where the shipment is."

"What? You want me to speak with this mob, even though you've just killed two of their best men?"

Maxi stared at Elijah's pockmarked face. "That's exactly what I want you to do. We know that when the brothers have completed a deal, they automatically call head office to say all went well. But on this occasion, you're going to frighten the shit out of them by complaining that shipment has yet to arrive. I can guarantee that within minutes, both of their mobile phones will have incoming calls."

"I get it," smiled Easy. "Because unless the brothers have called in earlier, this 'Connexion' mob will have no idea where they really are."

Maxi gave him the briefest of nods. "We've been reliably informed that the Tomovics only call in when they've concluded a deal. Which is why when done, we move the van to a piece of barren wasteland a few hundred yards down the road. It's dark, there's no CCTV and no immediate habitation, but that won't stop an anonymous caller from ringing the police to say he's just heard loud gunfire. Within minutes, you can bet an 'SO18' armed response unit will race to the scene, surround the Transit van and force their way in."

"However," grinned BB, "All they will find are two dead bodies."

"But not just any dead bodies," added Maxi. "Waiting to greet them will be the much sought after and recently deceased; Marko and Ziggy Tomovic!"

"There's something else," smiled BB, "We're hoping a cheeky little ruse of ours will not only confuse the police, but Forensics as well." The two Jamaicans watched closely as he took a small transparent plastic bag full of loose earth from the rear of the car and held it up to the light. "This dirt has come directly from the same empty wasteland, and when we place the two dead brothers in the rear of van, intend to pack a small amount of it into the soles of their boots. With a bit of luck, this should help convince the police that the brothers had mistakenly driven past the warehouse and rendezvoused at the wrong spot. Where, sad to say, someone else was waiting to ambush them and they met their untimely fate."

"But more importantly, means they didn't make it here," smiled Eazy.

BB smiled as though he'd just finished doing a magic trick. "So, when the news hits the headlines the next day, we'll all be in the clear."

"What happens to the money and drugs?" asked Elijah.

"If you help me kill the person who murdered my granddaughter, you can keep the lot," declared Maxi.

S.C.U.

"Got a problem, Guv, Vinny's gone missing."

"Where?"

Jacko shook his head. "Dunno, but I've been trying to get hold of him for three days now and there's no reply from his phone."

"So how do you know he's missing?"

"Front desk just called. His old man has been in and reported him as AWOL, says he's really worried."

"Who? Reggie Snodgrass?"

Jacko gave a half smirk. "One and the same."

Carson shook a bemused head. "I thought he hated his son?"

"That was the impression he gave me and Smithy, but maybe he's had a change of heart and brought him back into the fold."

"What do you think?"

"Don't know, Guv, his old man's a freak at the best of times, but I'm hoping the Sharecroppers haven't got hold of him. Vinny swears Noah the Snake is ready to cut his throat if they think he's spoken to us."

"What about the two tuxedoed gorillas and Liberace, do we know who they are?"

"We're still looking for a warehouse with an automatic door, but that's one tiny needle in a giant haystack."

"Cuffin' hell," groaned Carson. "I've spent half the morning convincing Bastion it's worth putting Vinny in a safe house and then he goes missing."

"Did you mention the 'Mole' and possible leaking of information?"

"No way," he said with a shake of the head. "The only time I'll mention that is if we catch McClellan carrying a load of files through the door."

"I imagine he's done that already," smiled Jacko.

"Yeah? Well I'm not admitting to anything unless it's dropped right here on my desk. Imagine the hassle if we've got it wrong. Jesus, we'd all be out of a job within a week!"

"Don't you think it strange, Guv? The fact that someone like Vinny gets kidnapped and questioned by these mysterious people? It's not as if he could just make this stuff up."

"I'd imagine Vinny tells more lies than the Chancellor of the Exchequer, more so when his neck is on the line!"

"I can agree with that Guv, but it doesn't change the fact that he's still the only one to have seen the killer *and* the Transit van on the night of the murders."

Carson nodded. "This is true, but the real question is, can we trust him and where is he now?"

The Auction

Michaela pressed the key hidden under her desk and released the lock on the reception door. A confused BB Benson stepped inside. "Hello gorgeous, what's with all this security business?"

Michaela pointed a finger towards Maxi's office and whispered, "He's chatting with Antonio in New York and doesn't want any interruptions."

BB had never met the man personally, but knew Antonio de Morres was Maxi's personal buyer of art in America; especially at all the major auction houses.

"What's he's after, a new masterpiece?"

Michaela nodded solemnly. "It would appear there's a new Degas on the market and he's eager to get his hands on it."

"How much are we looking at?"

"Begin at twelve million dollars."

"Wow!" laughed BB. "It must be some painting."

"French ballerinas are quite popular at the moment."

"Who's bidding?'

"Most of the international art galleries, two Russian oligarchs and half the USA."

"Well they'll just have to wait, gorgeous, because I need to speak to Maxi straight away. There's been a new development with the Stoker mob."

"You could be too late, BB, I think the bidding has already started." Slipping through the office door, BB padded silently across the deep pile carpet and took a seat opposite Maxi. Who whilst having a two-way conversation with Antonio via the satellite link, was more interested in watching the *live* auction on the giant TV screen. BB waited until there was a pause in the proceedings before diving in. "Just to let you know the Jamaicans have been in touch and why all the fuss over this painting?"

Maxi gave a wave of acknowledgement and a short explanation.

"In the mid-1870s, Edgar Degas began a series of ballerina paintings, many of which made him famous. However, in today's overpriced market, you couldn't buy one for less than £30 million pounds. So, when someone claims to have found a canvas painted by him five years earlier, the art world sits up and takes notice."

"Will it bring top dollar at the auction?" asked an impressed BB.

"Not necessarily. Most art experts were happy to give the picture the green light. Some however, are not so sure and doubt its true authenticity. But crucially, there's no paper trail to say when or where it was bought and sold. Without this vital evidence, it affects its true provenance, thus making it a risky buy. So we'll have to see how the bidding goes and take it from there."

This last statement was intended for BB to watch, listen and learn, as the Auction got under way.

"Can we open at five million dollars?" inquired the man with gavel. Maxi spoke in a low voice. "Antonio? Hold your fire and wait until I tell you."

"Yes, Senor Hamilton," came his obedient reply.

The man with the gavel spoke again. *"Seeing as there are no takers, shall we say four million dollars?"*

To BB's surprise, instead of a rush to buy, the price swiftly fell below one million and considering all the hype involved, no one seemed interested in buying it anyway.

Then a hand was raised.

"I have a bid for one and a half million dollars," shouted the Auctioneer. His head swung to the left and he pointed to another bidder. *"Two million dollars over here."* The value of the painting slowly began to grow by half a million increments, until it came to an impasse at thirteen million dollars. Another bid was made, but this offer was for a measly quarter of a million dollars.

"They're getting nervous Antonio."

"I agree Senor Hamilton," came the voice from New York.

Three more bids took its value to fourteen million dollars and another pause in the bidding. *"Do I have any more offers?"* Cried the Auctioneer, his hand ready slam down the Gavel.

"Okay Antonio."

The Auctioneer peered over his glasses and pointed straight ahead. *"We have a new bidder who are now offering sixteen million dollars!"*

A buzz of activity hit the room as the people and TV cameras looked to see who the bidder might be. The man with the Gavel however, was only interested in completing the sale. *"Do we have any offers above sixteen million dollars?"*

The looks of doubt and negative shaking of heads were all he required.

"Sold to telephone buyer 234!" He declared.

"Good work Antonio," grinned a satisfied Maxi. "Have it sent to my apartment in New York. I intend to be there sometime next week."

"My pleasure Senor Hamilton," came an equally satisfied voice.

BB shook his head. "Considering the painting's supposed to have no provenance, why pay two million more?"

Maxi gave a smile, "I needed to stop the bidding from continuing any further."

BB still looked confused. "Why?"

"I don't employ Antonio just for his good looks," said Maxi "Have a look at these Daguerreotype prints he sent me earlier today."

BB perused the pictures. "Judging by their style of dress, I'd say they were a large Victorian family having their photograph taken."

"Right period, but wrong country BB. They're actually French and this is Edgar Degas' immediate family. We're pretty confident the photo dates from around 1873, because it was taken just before his father died. However, this wasn't the only shock to hit them. Not long after his death, the family were

415

appalled to discover his brother Rene had accumulated a huge pile of business debts. Worse was yet to come, when he found that he and the family we're responsible for most of them. Having no other option, he resorted to selling their home, along with lots of his treasured paintings." Maxi produced another print. "This is a newly discovered photo of Edgar's father, posing in his study just a few months before he passed away."

BB took the print as well as the proffered magnifying glass.

"What's hanging on the wall next to the fireplace?" asked Maxi.

"It's a little blurred," said BB. "But it looks like a young ballerina in a tutu skirt holding a flower."

"Yes, my friend and it's almost certainly the same as the painting in New York."

"If it's got no real provenance, how can you tell?"

"Because at the time, Edgar was trying to solve the family's debt problems in any way he could; in some cases literally with the shake of a hand and an exchange of a canvas. Antonio can find no record or bill of sale for this particular painting, but is convinced it's a prequel to Edgar's later ballerina works."

"And just as valuable?" asked BB.

"It should double in value the moment we release the Daguerreotype prints."

"Wow," whispered BB. "How to make money."

"To quote a saying, 'some you win and some you lose.' But at the moment, I'm more interested in what's happening with the Stokers."

"I'm afraid its good news and bad news from them," said BB. "They've managed to make contact with 'Connexion,' who after lots of haggling, are now happy to supply the drugs late tomorrow night. But Eazy is being a real pain in the butt, by insisting Elijah should be present at the warehouse when we do the deal."

"Why the hell would he want that lunatic there?"

"Because somewhere in his twisted mind, I don't think Eazy trusts us." Maxi stared at the TV screen and the frozen image of the ballerina holding the flower. "They say 'Serendipity' is an act of happy discovery BB and come tomorrow, this young ballet dancer should make me at least fourteen million pounds richer." He then snapped his fingers. "Yet I'd give it all away just like that, if I could make this nightmare disappear and have Kelly here with me today!"

BB gave a sympathetic smile. "If all goes well, it shouldn't take long to solve this Serbian problem and then we can all move on."

Maxi took a deep breath and focused on the ceiling. "Tell Eazy Stoker he can bring his crazy son to the meeting, just as long as he keeps his big stupid mouth shut!"

BB was about to leave the office when something else occurred to him. "What about Vinny the Gecko?"

"Hell man, I'd forgotten all about him," laughed Maxi. "I take it he's still in the warehouse?"

BB nodded. "Twixy Hartley is pissed off from babysitting him. He won't go anywhere near his room due to the stink of Pepperoni Pizzas and stale tobacco."

Maxi turned serious. "We can't let him go yet BB, we're much too close to risk that. Besides, there's always the chance Vinny might get brave and start blabbing to the wrong people."

"We could keep him for another twenty four hours. Once we've disposed of the bodies and the Transit van, I can get Twixy to drop him off at Highwater Estate."

"That should be more than enough to sort this out, but in the meantime, ask him to change Vinny's meals to Chinese takeaway. Everyone loves a beef curry!" grinned Maxi.

Part Thirteen

Caversham Cut Warehouse

Maxi watched the Chrysler Voyager crest the rise and ease into the vacant space beside the Range Rover. Eli as ever, went through the usual routine of opening the rear passenger door so his father might more easily exit the vehicle. Having watched this rigmarole on a couple of occasions, BB Benson was of the opinion that if Eazy Stoker had a licence, he couldn't drive a car.

"I bet the lazy so-and-so never took a test," he muttered.

"Who cares?" said Maxi. "I'm just glad he made it to the warehouse."

This sentiment, however, didn't apply to his unpredictable son, who hefted a large canvas holdall from the boot and took an AK47 assault rifle from inside.

"What the hell's that doing here?" asked an astonished Maxi.

Eazy smiled. "That, 'Mister Big time', is a souvenir from the war in Iraq and a little extra insurance on my part!"

"I thought we'd agreed on a single gun for each of us?"

"And so we did."

Maxi gestured to the menacing Eli. "Then how come 'Elliot Ness' here gets invited to the party?"

The Jamaican gave a rueful shake of his curly white head. "The thought of just two Glocks doesn't quite rock my boat man, especially when we're about to meet a couple of fuckin Nazi Storm-troopers!"

Maxi was close to losing his temper. "If we stick to the agreed plan, then there's no reason why it won't work. Yet this madness is bound to cause problems!"

"Not if they don't get to see our little piece of insurance."

Maxi shook his head in disbelief as BB whispered in his ear, "It's too late for arguments, they'll be here in a few minutes."

A further complication arose when Eazy asked a more than pertinent question. "Which one of these two Serbs am I supposed to kill?"

The thought of choosing a particular brother had never occurred to Maxi. "What does it matter? They're both going to die anyway."

"I ain't interested in personalities, man, I just wanna know where to stand when this shit kicks off."

Maxi gave a half shrug. "Do you have a preference?"

"I sure as hell do 'Mister Big Time', I prefer to pull the trigger first!" He then held out a hand. "And I'll take that their tasty piece of ironmongery if you please."

BB Benson passed him the Glock and smiled. "Make sure the safety catch is on, or you might end up with another hole in your arse!"

Ignoring the jibe, Eazy pointed the gun at Maxi's chest. "Must be nearly forty years since I wanted to use one of these."

BB casually stepped between them. "I think you'll find he's the wrong target."

The ageing Jamaican smiled and eased the gun out of sight. "Well now, that might not always be the case." He then pointed a finger in his son's direction. "Bring that there contraption over here, boy, it's time to show these two doubting fuckers how we gonna do this."

"Yes Papa," replied an obedient Eli, who shuffled his way towards the car.

BB Benson was close to shutting down the warehouse's CCTV system, when Vinny began complaining about his unlawful incarceration. "When are you bastards going to let me out of here?" he cried.

"Just a few more hours," BB assured him. "Then it'll all be over and you can go home."

"What will be over?" asked a concerned Vinny.

"Nothing for you to worry your shiny little head about," smiled BB, before going below to ensure all was ready to welcome their two 'special' guests. Outside in the real world, the alley was exactly how he'd expected it to be, cold, silent and deserted. Turning his collar up against a chill wind, he stood in the shadows of the entrance and awaited the arrival of the Serbians. At two minutes past midnight, the dipped headlights belonging to a Ford Transit turned the corner and slowed to a halt in front of the warehouse doors. There was no doubting it was them; the van ticked all the right boxes. Hoping to speed things up, BB set the gate in motion, but began to fume in frustration when they paused at the threshold and took in their surroundings.

"Move your arses!" he scowled.

Satisfied there was no obvious danger, the van edged into the warehouse, its rear end only just clearing the doors before BB pressed the close button. In the dim light, he could just about make out the two bearded males wearing identical Beanie hats. Remembering the ground rules, he opened his coat and turned full circle so they might see he was unarmed. "Evening boys, my name is *Popeye* and I'm expecting an urgent delivery of goods."

Recognising the agreed password, the Serbs were content to take part in this same infantile charade. "I'm *Tom*," grunted the beard in the driver's seat, before pointing to the beard in the passenger seat "and this is *Jerry*." His clipped English instantly identifying him as a foreigner, but more importantly, set the wheels in motion.

"Okay *Popeye,* where to next?"

BB pointed to the slope. "We're a bit cramped for space down here, but there's plenty of room up on the next level."

"You lead and we'll follow," advised *Tom.*

The sight of BB walking before the vehicle reminded Maxi of a funeral procession; all he was needed a black coat and top hat. Yet the satisfied look and wily wink, all but confirmed their search was over. Following behind in the Transit van were the two Serbians, where a different type of surprise lay in store as they reached the threshold.

"*Obo je hobo*," said Marko. "This is new."

As if in a car showroom, a line of expensive looking vehicles encircled the floor, the nearest being a classic red Studebaker saloon. "Looks like some kind of vintage motor museum," muttered Ziggy.

Marko pointed a finger. "Yeah, but not as ancient as him."

Over to their right sat a shiny black Range Rover, with its rear door hinged open to the concrete ceiling. Casually arraigned in the middle of its carpet-lined boot, sat a slim black man with a crop of curly white hair that stood out against his dark ebony skin. One hand was draped across a large briefcase, the other resting on a silver-topped cane. His tan chequered suit suggesting he was into bright flamboyant clothes. "I can remember Tino saying this mob were from the West Indies, yet don't recall him saying they dressed like clowns."

Ziggy shook his head. "*Veoma cudno.* Very strange."

A suspicious Marko turned his attention to the pockmarked youth leaning against the car's rear brake light. He wore a plain white tee shirt and had both thumbs hooked into the side pockets of his jeans. "He looks like trouble."

"Maybe," replied Ziggy. "Although from what I can see, he doesn't have a weapon."

"Do you think he's with the clown in the fancy suit?"

Marko focused on the white-haired Eazy. "Who knows, but as long as they have the code, we do business."

In an effort to keep things moving, BB Benson indicated for the driver to swing around to his left. "What do you think?" asked Ziggy.

Marko gave a shrug. "Not sure. The grey-haired guy in the Armani suit looks a little too old for this game, but judging by the hang of his clothes, I'd say he's clean of a weapon."

"Okay," grunted Ziggy. "Let's do it."

Maxi and the others watched with baited breath as the Transit completed the first part of the manoeuvre. Then gave a huge sigh of relief the second it started to edge backwards. "Just a few feet more baby," he whispered and when done, was amazed to watch the two near identical brothers clamber from the van and stand before them. Maxi smiled. Chalky Johnson had described them to an absolute tee! Their second-hand uniforms appeared to have been purchased from an army surplus store, their shiny soft-soled Doc Martin boots straight from a shop window. And if push came to shove, both might just about pass off as a couple of plumbers, but in reality, looked more like two heavies from some South American dictator's private army. Maxi was first to notice something different with the driver's outfit; the zips on the bottom of his fatigues were at least six inches longer than those of his brother. His suspicions were soon interrupted by the staccato sound of *Tom*'s voice.

"Where's the money?" He demanded.

Maxi pointed to where Eazy was holding court in the rear of the Range Rover.

"I suggest you speak with him," he said with an obliging smile.

The white haired Jamaican flipped open the lid of the leather case and pointed to its contents. "As agreed, half a million pounds in used notes."

In a well-practiced routine, Marko made straight for the cash and Ziggy stood guard on the van.

"Very professional," whispered Maxi.

"I wonder if they ever blink or scratch their arses?" muttered BB.

In order to check the cash, Marko needed to pass Eli, who suddenly straightened and adopted a more aggressive posture. Less than ten feet away, stood Maxi who was close to spitting fire; this macho shit was never meant to be part of the script. Ignoring his 'in your face' attitude, the Serb casually eased Eli to one side as if he were a child. "You're in my way, black-man, and I don't like that."

The loud snap of Eazy's fingers warned his son to back off. "No offence intended, mister white-man, my son's just bein' cautious, especially with all this here money lying around." Yet something inside had warned Marko to be careful, he was none too happy with the son's surly attitude. His next task was to check out the boot of the Range Rover, where to his annoyance, the old man had smiled and refused to move an inch.

Peering over his shoulder, he could see a leather coat hanging from a hook and large canvas holdall, which he assumed would be used to collect the drugs. Satisfied all was as it should be, he turned his attention to the briefcase and as normal, selected five wads of money from five different places. Having chosen one particular wedge, he took a £50 pound note from the middle and held it up so he might check it for watermark, iron strip and quality of print. A whole minute went by before he appeared to be satisfied and said, "Okay, we can do business!"

At first Maxi had assumed he was speaking to him and then realised it was actually meant for Ziggy, who without saying a word, unlocked the van. With the doors open wide, Maxi could only marvel at their barefaced cheek and ingenuity. The interior was exactly as Chalky had predicted it would be. The walls on either side were lined with shelves containing every type of object a plumber might need. Neatly suspended from the roof on Bungees was the solid metal device required for bending pipes.

Watching the routine, he'd completely forgotten why they needed to unload the heavy wooden toolbox out onto the concrete deck. That is, until Ziggy took a portable gun and began to unscrew different sections of the flooring. This in turn revealed the airtight compartments used to transport the drugs. In less than a minute, they'd completed the task and Marko pointed to the cocaine packages.

Another snap of Eazy's fingers sent Eli strolling in the direction of the van; sampling drugs for strength and quality was the one job he excelled in. On a whim, he'd decided to go through the same routine as the Serbian and chose a package two layers down. A small razor-sharp flick-knife appeared in his hand, which he used to make a small incision in one corner of the wrapping. Both parties waited in silent expectation as he placed a tiny sliver of white powder on the tip of his tongue. "This is good shit," he declared, the tension-filled air lifting like a winter fog.

Marko was next to speak. "Seeing as everyone is happy with the goods, I suggest we complete the deal and get the fuck out of here!"

Anticipating what might come next, Easy took the holdall from the boot and threw it to his son. "Fill this up, boy, and make sure you don't miss a fingernail of shit!" Without further hesitation, Eli began to transfer the drugs to the canvas bag. Anxious to keep things moving along, a watching Marko was less than happy with the black man's progress.

"Ziggy, give him a hand," he whispered. "I'll go and collect the money." Still perched in the rear of the Range rover, Easy lit a thin cheroot and relaxed.

"Looks like you've just won the jackpot boy," he smiled, indicating to the bulging briefcase.

Ignoring his puerile attempt at English humour, Marko began to close the lid and then found he had a problem; he was unable to fasten the locks. A swift look inside revealed the reason why; his earlier disruption of the money was making it near impossible to secure them in place. Further frustration arose, when he realised Ziggy and the black man were close to filling the canvas bag with cocaine. Cursing his luck and having no other choice, he wrapped one arm around the briefcase, tucked it under his arm and turned towards the van. He'd only gone three paces when a large wad of money slipped from one corner and tumbled towards the floor.

In that same instant and realising this might be his only chance, Maxi reached for the gun in his waistband, only to discover he was a fraction too late. In one lightning sweep, Ziggy had caught the wad of money inches before it hit the concrete floor and turned to face him. His moment of triumph however, had lasted no more than a few seconds before a snarling voice came from behind. "Okay, you two arseholes, drop the briefcase and move away!"

The stark warning threatened dire consequences should they contemplate disobeying it; a risk neither felt like taking. An even bigger surprise came when they turned to find Elijah standing beside the Range Rover with an AK 47 rifle pointed in their direction. As per his instructions, Marko quickly shuffled to his left; Ziggy to the right, leaving a clear uninterrupted view of the van's interior. Moving the gun barrel from side to side, Elijah issued another warning. "Remember to keep them hands wide apart boys, if I see you waggle even a finger, I'll cut you both in two!"

Thinking back, Marko vaguely recalled seeing a leather coat hanging in the rear of the Range Rover; the one he'd dismissed out of hand. Nonetheless, it meant the balance of power was firmly in favour of this strange group of weirdoes. Ziggy stared at the AK47. "What now?" he muttered.

"What do you think? We play for time and do whatever he asks!"

A smiling Eli was beginning to enjoy his new role. "The time for talking is over pilgrims. From now on, you speak only when I tell you to."

Still confused, *Tom* purposely ignored him. "Can someone tell me what the hell's going on around here?"

Eazy pulled the Glock from his waistband and gave a sermon-like reply. "*The time has come for all sinners to repent!*"

In desperation, he turned to Maxi. "Hey man, what's with this crazy nigger?"

"I'd be careful what you say Marko, insults like that can make him very trigger happy!"

It might have been casually said, yet the mere mention of his proper Christian name sent both brothers into a stunned silence; their true identities had always been a carefully kept secret.

For Maxi however, this was the moment he'd been waiting for. Armed with Tufty McClellan's inside information, he was now determined to make the two Serbians squirm!

"Nice to see you back in town Marko, sorry I missed your last trip."

Tom however, had decided to plead ignorance. "You've got the wrong person mister, I've never been here before."

"Well, isn't that strange," smiled Maxi. "I could have sworn it was you. Maybe I should ask your brother."

"There's no need; where I go, he goes."

Maxi looked doubtful. "Better check your diary, my friend. A transit van just like yours was spotted here last August Bank Holiday, probably on a drugs run. When he'd finished doing his business, the driver still had time to watch a football game and then stop for a piss in a nearby Park. Yet here is the most important part. According to a passing motorist, he was the absolute spitting image of your brother."

Marko shrugged. "So what? One bearded man looks much the same as another and there must be a thousand white vans roaming the streets. Come to think of it, I don't recall a law that says a man can't empty his bladder when needed."

"That I can agree with," conceded Maxi. "But there is a law that says you can't murder two innocent teenagers!"

This wasn't quite what Marko was expecting and in desperation, turned to BB Benson. "What the fuck's going on, *Popeye?* I thought we were here to supply drugs, not talk about some teenage murders!"

"And so we are, *Tom,* but seeing as you're here, we thought you might like to look at a couple of photographs."

Maxi reached to his pocket and showed him Kelly's holiday snap. "Recognise the girl in the middle?"

Marko gave a shake of the head.

"I thought not, but your brother will, isn't that right, Luka?"

As before, both men were open mouthed on hearing the casual use of their Christian names. Maxi meanwhile, had decided it was time to stop playing around and go for the jugular! "We know everything there is to know about you two. The place you were born, date of birth, even the high school you attended. And I think I'd be right in saying you had English lessons and you're both fanatical supporters of Red Star Belgrade football club." Marko and Ziggy could only listen in silent disbelief as the stranger spoke on. "We then come to 1991,

426

the year you joined Arkan's Tigers and of course November 1995. That was the month you became involved in the death of two Swedish Doctors, although I hear tell they never did discover who pulled the trigger."

Marko suddenly began to have deep misgivings; delivering drugs was always going to have a risk factor; as well as being well paid, but this was different and so were these lunatics waving their guns around!

On a whim Maxi thought he'd have a little more fun. "I suppose we have to thank your boss Colonel Petrovic for sending you here tonight, because without him we might never have met."

"Who the hell are you and what do you want?" screamed Marko.

Eazy pointed the Glock at his head, and answered the question. "We're here on a special mission pilgrim; we've been chosen to carry out the word of the Lord."

"What does that mean?"

"It means we're going to kill you both and in doing so, avenge the deaths of our grandchildren."

Marko and Ziggy looked at each other in open alarm. "This is madness and we don't know anything about your dead children!"

Eazy held Moses' autopsy photo in one hand and waved the Glock in the other. "This is my grandson and you two blaspheming sinners killed him!"

Marko began to make a last minute plea. "Will you crazy fucking people wait a minute? There's something I have to say."

"The time for talking is over, Pilgrim!"

Marko carried on regardless. "I swear to God I've never set foot in Liverpool, or watched a football match and come to think of it, never stopped to have a piss in a park!"

Maxi listened to these heartfelt words, but knew it didn't change the situation one bit. "I think you're telling the truth, Marko, and on reflection, believe you know nothing about Ziggy's past demeanours."

"What demeanours, what the hell are you talking about?"

"Your younger brother is a long-time serial killer!"

"That's bullshit!"

"If only that were true," whispered Maxi. "Because if that were so, my beautiful granddaughter and young Moses would still be alive today; but they're not Marko. Both are lying in deep cold graves and he's the one responsible for their deaths."

Eazy began to quote from the Bible, chapter and verse. "Romans 12 to 19. *Vengeance is mine sayeth the Lord, and I will repay those responsible!*"

A sweating Marko began to engage. "We never had Bible classes where I come from, but I do remember something that says forgiving keeps a man strong and lends him faith!"

Maxi smiled. "You're a little too late for that, my friend."

Eazy swung his gun from one brother to the other. "Lectivus 24: *If a man takes the life of an innocent, then he shall surely be put to a painful death!*"

Marko looked pleadingly to Maxi. "You people are insane and I still don't know who he's supposed to have killed!"

Maxi aimed the Glock dead centre of Luka's forehead.

"For reasons of his own, *Ziggy the Knife* has spent the last twenty years killing a host of innocent young blonde girls, the bulk of them spread across Eastern Europe. He begins by raping and torturing them and when done, likes to execute them in a variety of sadistic ways. From what we can gather, there's a victim for each of the years, the first being from your own home town of Erdivos in 1995."

"I don't believe that, who did he kill there?"

"A young blonde girl named Tatiana Mestovic."

Marko instanly remembered the sweat-filled night in the bathroom and the look on his face said it all.

"But of course!" exclaimed Maxi. "Tatiana was Ziggy's first girlfriend, so you must have known her personally!" As if to rub it in, he decided to give him a few details. "In 2006, they found her mutilated body hidden in the woods near the Hungarian border. Apparently, she'd been kidnapped from Erdivos ten years earlier. The Serbian police are convinced she was the first to die, but can't say how many more dead girls are lying buried out there."

Marko looked him in the eye. "These murders have nothing to do with me."

Maxi knew the Bible quote wasn't exact, but said it anyway. *"The sins of the father shall be visited on all of the family."*

"Them words comes from 'Exodus'," chortled Eazy. "And let's not forget. *An eye for an eye and a tooth for a tooth!"*

Maxi kept the gun pointed unerringly at Ziggy's head, but spoke only to Marko. "It's a pity your sadistic brother didn't die during the Bosnian War. If he had, all those young innocent people would still be alive and we wouldn't be here today."

Eli moved beside his father, the AK47 trained on the two brothers, as Eazy eased back the trigger on the Glock.

"Okay, now and together!" said Maxi.

The two shots were close, but not close enough to be classed as simultaneous: one bullet exiting the chamber fractionally ahead of the other.

The first ripped through Eazy's chequered suit and killed him instantly, the impact throwing his body backwards and into the boot of the Range Rover. The second wiped the smile off Eli's grinning face by removing his two front teeth, plus most of his brains, the wiry hair at the back of his head catching the bullet. Yet as he met his maker, the muscles in his arm constricted a fraction, thus causing his right index finger to tighten on the hair-trigger of the AK47.

The weapon burst into life with a chattering roar of gunfire that lasted but seconds, yet tore apart anything that lay in its deadly destructive path. Momentarily distracted by this ear-splitting fusillade, Maxi hesitated in firing his own gun; time enough for Ziggy to make his own move. Within the same heartbeat, he whipped the Berretta from his jacket and fired twice, both 9mm missiles hitting the tall grey haired stranger high in the chest and with devastating effect.

As a fatally wounded Maxi toppled to the floor, the giant beside him let out a roar of rage and leapt across the short space that divided them. In the blink of an eye and before Ziggy could move, this screaming crazy mad bear was on top of him, one hand clamped around his throat, the other wrestling for the Berretta. He'd responded in kind by grasping his opponent's windpipe; both men grunting and snarling like demons as they fought to gain control.

Their struggle, however, had lasted less than ten seconds, before Ziggy realised that this ageing *Popeye* was no walkover. In fact, he was one seriously tough bastard, who bit-by-bit was beginning to gain the upper hand. This became painfully obvious the moment he began to smash his wrist against the side of the wooden toolbox, the excruciating blows forcing him to let go of the Berretta; which clattered out of sight across the concrete floor. In another superhuman effort, *Popeye* had somehow managed to twist on top of him, grab his throat with both hands and whisper. "Time to die a painful death you Serbian piece of shit, just like our beautiful Kelly, who was worth so much more than you!"

With his own gun missing in the struggle, Ziggy began to rain a series of blows against the side of his opponent's head, all to no avail. As each solid thud hit the target, *Popeye* gave another grunt of satisfaction and steadily increased the pressure on his Adam's apple.

Realising his life-blood and oxygen was rapidly running out, Ziggy tried to reach the knife in his boot, but the giant pinning him to floor made it impossible for him to move his leg. In one last act of desperation, he began to scrabble around searching for anything he might use as weapon and in a moment of joy, felt the tip of a gun barrel. Realising it had to be the tall grey-haired man's Glock, he used a finger to spin it around so he might grab the weapon.

Without hesitation, he rammed it against his ribs and fired twice; naturally assuming this would kill him instantly, but to his amazement, instead of dying, the grip around his throat tightened and a hoarse voice whispered. "It's not my time, you Serbian bastard, I have to make sure that you meet the Devil first!"

With his head swimming and strength about to fail, Ziggy repositioned the gun against what he hoped was more flesh and pulled the trigger once again. The result this time was almost instantaneous; as he felt the giant stiffen, the pressure on his throat begin to ease and watched him topple sideways to the floor. Free from the clutches of this incredible hulk, he staggered unsteadily to his feet and took in huge gulps of lung-filling air. Yet was truly shocked when he saw the death and destruction all around.

The AK47 had stitched a neat line of 39mm slugs across the van's left rear door; Marko's body included. As a result, his bloodied torso lay sprawled across the piles of money, his vacant eyes staring emptily into space. Ziggy was able to see where the first bullet had entered his left thigh, the last finishing high in his chest, the air around still filled with the acrid smell of spent cordite.

Scrambling across the tool chest, he began to caress Marko's face. "No! No! No…" he cried. "This is not the way it was supposed to be!" He then remembered the whine of the bullets as they'd ricocheted off the metal bending machine, one making a hole in the roof, another through the windscreen. His suffering however wasn't quite over; more misery was yet to come. "Jan?" he whispered. "This is Ziggy, are you okay?"

The silence told its own tale, as he inched his way towards the cab; only to find his worst fears confirmed. Concealed between the rear of the driver's seat and the storage racks, lay Marko's now deceased brother-in-law. His head was slumped forward onto the dustsheet that covered his body, a trickle of blood seeping from the hole in the side of his skull. The still warm pistol he'd used to kill the two Jamaicans, hanging limply in his hand. For a moment Ziggy lost control of his senses and began to wail like a demented madman. "Noooooo…" he screamed, his hands splintering the wooden shelving either side of him.

He still couldn't say why, but the Jamaican's plea for a shipment of drugs had worried him from day one. So much so, he'd spent a whole morning badgering his brother into taking Jan along as a temporary backup, even offering to cut him a share of his fee as way of payment. But never in his wildest dreams did he imagine both of them would die in the process. It was only now and with hindsight, did he realise they'd made a major blunder in taking this strange welcoming committee at face value.

Yet who could have imagined that this meeting wasn't about drugs, but a clever plot to lure them to Liverpool. And what about the tall grey-haired one with the Armani suit? Ziggy was amazed to find he wasn't just an observer, but a main player. Especially when he'd waved a picture of the dead blonde girl and screamed it was his granddaughter.

And who'd have thought the wrinkled Jamaican was related to the black kid who'd kicked him in the face in the park? Some questions definitely needed answering. The first being, how did they know he and Marko worked for 'Connexion' and how could they possibly have gained access to their confidential background information? But more importantly, who were these dead fuckers, who'd been so eager to kill them and Ziggy knew just the person to ask!

Clambering from the van, he surveyed the carnage all around and pondered what to do next. For a moment he'd considered reloading the drugs and money, closing the van doors and try to make his way back to London. Sadly, the bullet holes in the roof and windscreen had put paid to that idea. Yet if he stayed, knew there was always the chance he might be killed by another gang member, or armed police.

Realising he had no other choice, he decided to leave everything as it was and take only what he could carry. Common sense said the holdall full of drugs was much too bulky a prospect and the briefcase would shine like a beacon in the dark. He then spotted a small sports bag sat amongst the copper fittings and quickly began to fill it with £50 notes. In next to no time, he'd managed to stuff it to the top and pull the zip closed. He was still searching for his Berretta when he saw the photograph held in the hand of his grey-haired accuser.

Out of curiosity, he prised it from between his fingers and took a closer look. The picture portrayed three people. In the middle was the smiling blonde girl, flanking her on either side was a young boy and a fair-haired woman; who had to be their mother. In Ziggy's eyes the holiday snap screamed of injustice, anger and deep resentment. Ten feet away lay his dead brother, whose blood was slowly beginning to bleach the money a deep crimson colour.

Taking deep breaths and desperately trying to keep control of his temper, he looked again at the smiling faces in the photo. "Why should they be so happy?" he cried.

"The girl was a preening slut who needed to be taught a lesson and if the truth be known, was no better than the rest of the sluts who had much in common. They were a hoard of blonde conniving bitches, who took the greatest of pleasure in humiliating innocent young men and my decision to inflict a painful death on them all is more than justified!" A feeling of righteous vindication surged through his body as he heard the truth in his words.

However, he wanted more than just speeches. He wanted others to suffer for the unpardonable passing of Marko and Jan. The Jamaican in the clown suit had been mighty loud in espousing the virtues of the Bible, thus giving Ziggy some food for thought. "Am I not wronged like them?" he whispered to the bodies lying on the floor. "And am I not deserving of some kind of vengeance?" His finger pointed accusingly at the tall grey-haired male lying covered in blood. "Is it not written that the sins of the father shall be visited upon all the family?" In the deathly silence, no reply was forthcoming.

He then remembered a much more important question, was he alone or might there be others hiding in the shadows? No matter the answer, he needed to leave this place of sin and put some distance between himself and Liverpool. Folding the photo in two, he slipped it in his shirt pocket and went looking for a way out. At first glance the concrete slope appeared to be the easiest means of escape, but being wide open, gave him no cover should someone open fire. Ever reluctant to expose himself to such dangers, he went in search of a better solution and found it almost immediately.

An unlit sign above a doorway said 'Exit'. Taking one last painful look at his brother's dead body, he headed in that direction and to his relief, found it was just a short stairway with an emergency door at the bottom. Adjusting the bag on his shoulder, he turned off the lights and plunged the place into darkness.

As he was about to step through the door, a faint rattling sound caught his attention. He froze for a moment, his senses on high alert as he tried to discover where it was coming from. But needed less than a second to realise it was on the same floor and somewhere nearby. He was also wondering whether he should just ignore it and head for the exit, when something inside urged him to have a look and with that, he turned the lights on again.

Liverpool City Centre
3.45 am

The car slowed to a halt at the junction of Vauxhall and Pall Mall. "Where to now, Guv?"

Carson pointed to his left. "Caversham Cut, I think, is somewhere down there."

An uncertain Jacko was about to follow his lead, when the high-pitched wailing of an ambulance passed them by and swerved to the right.

"You sure, Guv?"

A look of doubt crossed Carson's face. "There again, I could be wrong."

Jacko went in pursuit of the flashing lights and two streets further on, met a massive roadblock with lots of heavily armed police standing guard.

"I know they said it was a major incident Guv, but I wasn't expecting this."

"If they're dragging me out of bed in the middle of the night, Jacko, then it has to be something cuffing important."

"Wow, look at this, Guv, it seems as if this mob are taking no chances with security. I don't ever remember them checking an ambulance entering a crime scene."

An intrigued Carson watched a medic throw open the rear doors, so the armed guard might see his vehicle was empty. "Looks like we're next in line."

Jacko edged forward and flashed his warrant card. "DS Jackson and DSI Carson from M.S.C.U."

"Morning sir, sorry about the hassle," replied the uniform; "But we've been ordered to double check anything that comes and goes from the area."

"Expecting trouble?" asked Jacko. His eyes flicking to the guns pointed in their direction.

"I've no idea, Sir. Let's hope not."

"Talking of crime scenes," smiled Carson.

The uniform immediately took the hint. "Sorry Sir, it's straight across the road and down the side-street on your left, but I suggest you park here and walk the rest on foot. Caversham Cut is chock full of the emergency services." Taking the hint, they turned the corner where the flashing lights from a range of different vehicles helped illuminate the tall red brickwork of the nearby warehouses. Yet it would take more than a bright shaft of light, to enhance the ugly two-story edifice that was the Crime Scene.

"Funny thing Guv, but I can't ever remember coming down here before."

"That's because it's one-way and doesn't really go anywhere."

Crossing the narrow street, the detectives came upon a throng of white-suited people moving around inside the warehouse; plus more armed guards. They were about to produce their official IDs, when a familiar voice rang out. "That's okay, officer, I've been expecting these two gentlemen."

Carson gave a relieved grunt. "Sgt Fitzpatrick, I do believe."

The uniform smiled appreciatively, before handing them a set of protective clothes. "I think you're going to need these, Sir."

"Thanks, Sgt, but I'd appreciate it more if you can tell us what the hell's going on."

The officer pointed to the concrete slope. "There's been a major shooting incident on the floor above; bodies lying everywhere."

Jacko immediately focused on the taped off incline and the two forensics dusting the area for prints. "Dead bodies?"

"Yes Sir, it reminds me of an old Western movie I saw as a kid, it was called *Gunfight at the OK Corral.*"

Carson grinned at the memory and took in his surroundings. "Do we know who owns this place?"

"Not at the moment, Sir, but if you'd like to don your kit and follow me, I'll tell you what we do know." Once suited and booted, the two detectives padded behind, as he took them towards a doorway with an unlit exit sign above. This in turn led to a narrow staircase, where another forensic was dusting down a crash door that opened out onto the main road.

Throughout their short walk, Fitzpatrick had continued with his narrative. "A passing patrol car noticed this emergency exit hanging ajar at around 2.30 am and as routine, decided to investigate. The ground floor was in complete darkness, a fast check by the uniforms confirming nothing untoward had taken place, and so they decided to take a look upstairs."

Jacko and Carson followed Sgt Fitzpatrick's rear as he climbed the steps to the next level. "Like the ground floor, this was also in darkness, but when they switched on the lights, had the shock of their lives!"

A scene of loud noisy organised chaos met them, as they saw a group of auxiliaries setting up extra floodlights, and a team of medics pushing steel gurneys here and there. Fitzpatrick pointed to his left. "As you can see Sir, most of the action is centred around the Ford Transit van."

The mere mention of the name had both detectives wide-eyed and excited.

"Do we know who owns it?" asked Jacko.

"At the moment, I don't know much about anything, Sir, but this lady should be able to help."

"You are late," came a voice from behind.

The detectives turned to see a baggy, white-suited Simone walking towards them.

"We couldn't get parked," Jacko replied with a smile.

"Care to fill us in?" prompted Carson.

"It's more a case of where do you start," replied Simone.

The glare of the floodlights, plus the constant flash and whirr of the high-speed cameras always reminded Jacko of a photo-shoot. Except, there were no tasty models in fancy clothes on this particular set, just lots of dead bodies.

"Six males, all deceased and all as a result of gunfire," began Simone. "At first we thought this was some kind of drugs deal gone wrong. But didn't take us long to realise who most of these people are." She then pointed at the two bodies nearest to her. "We think the big one with two bullet holes in his chest is Maxi Hamilton."

Jacko blinked in amazement. "Jeez, I thought he looked familiar, but never imagined he would be involved in something like this!"

"Hang on," said Carson. "I want to check something." Taking a Biro pen from his pocket he used it to lift the middle finger on the left hand and nodded. "Oh yes, this is definitely Maxi Hamilton."

"How can you tell, Guv?"

"The fingertip is missing. I remember Archie Speed saying Hamilton lost it in the sixties and was the reason he ditched playing the guitar and began selling drugs."

Jacko pointed to the human hulk lying face down at his feet. "So who's he?"

Simone gave a negative shake of the head. "Not sure yet, has to be one of Hamilton's men. But talking of drug dealers," her finger pointing to the checker-suited body lying in the back of the Range Rover. "The one with the single hole in his chest is the notorious one-time drugs baron, Eazy Stoker."

It was now Carson's turn to be open-mouthed. "Stone the cuffin' crows! And I take it the one with the AK47 is his son Elijah?"

"Yes Inspector, he died as a result of being shot through the mouth."

"But still managed to pull the trigger first?"

"We assume so, but hopefully should have a better idea when ballistics have finished their investigation."

"Might take a while," said a perspiring Steve Delaney.

Carson nodded to the Transit van. "What about the bearded one spread-eagled across the money?"

Simone paused. "That we think is Marko Tomovic."

"You're not serious!" gasped a disbelieving Jacko.

"Absolutely," she replied.

"So where's his brother?"

"Sorry to say, but he's not here."

"Not here? Wait a minute, I thought you'd found six dead bodies?"

"We did, but Ziggy Tomovic isn't one of them."

"Cuffing hell!" spluttered Carson.

A confused Jacko came next. "I thought the brothers were near inseparable and always travelled together."

"So did we."

"Then where's Ziggy?"

"If he's not in the building, we can only assume he must have escaped."

"Oh great," groaned Jacko. "But you did say six bodies, so where's the other one?"

"Lying dead in the back of the van."

"Do we know who he is?"

Simone smiled. "In a word, no."

"Do we at least have a clue what side he was on?"

"Considering he used a revolver to shoot Eazy and Elijah dead, I'd say he was definitely with the Tomovic brothers. But this is not the only crime scene. There's another one that requires your expert attention." Shuffling behind in the wake of a shapeless Simone, their short walk took them back in the direction of the emergency staircase. On the way Jacko admired an original Phantom V. Rolls Royce, that shone like the star it was. "Oh to be rich," he sighed.

Carson gave a wry smile. "True, but only if you're alive to enjoy it."

"Amen to that, Guv!" he whispered with feeling.

Their ultimate destination appeared to be a couple of windowless rooms, each with a sturdy wooden door. The other feature being the constant bustle of forensics as they shuffled backwards and forwards between them.

Simone pointed to a door on the right. "In there, if you please gentlemen."

Inside, they could smell the stale tobacco smoke and see the empty Chinese takeaway boxes piled high on the table. Careful not to touch anything, the two detectives waited patiently at the rear, seeing as most of the attention was centred on someone lying on a camp bed. They could now understand why Sgt Fitzpatrick had compared it to a Wild West movie; there really were bodies everywhere. The cameraman took one last shot and spoke over his shoulder to the Medics. "Okay boys, this one's a bit of a mess, but he's all yours."

"S.C.U." interrupted Jacko. "Can we have a look first?"

The Forensic appeared surprised. "Sorry mate, I thought you were the people from the morgue."

Jacko gave a winning smile and moved closer to the bed so as to get a better view. "Holy shit!" he gasped.

Staring at the ceiling with his throat cut from ear to ear, lay the bloodied form of Vinny the Gecko!"

"Looks like Ziggy left his calling card," grunted Carson.

435

Ealing, West London

The morning dew helped deaden the crunch of tyres on gravel, as the van stopped alongside the row of garages. The dashboard clock said it was 4.45 am: a reminder it had taken nearly four hours of careful driving to get here. Sitting in the dark, Ziggy remembered when he'd first noticed the advert in the window of the grocer's shop. It said, '*Double garage for rent, plus electricity if needed.*' Further inquiry had revealed it belonged to an old lady whose husband had recently passed away.

According to the shopkeeper, the couple were avid cyclists, who'd never owned a motorcar in their life. So, with this tragic change of circumstances, she'd decided to empty the garage and rent it as a way of supplementing her now reduced income. For Ziggy however, it'd been a real godsend and the perfect place to park his pride and joy: a dark green VW California camper van.

Another plus point was the small sink that sat in one corner of the garage. Yet the real bonus came with news that because it was quiet and secluded, the burglary rate in this area was practically zero. Having come this far, Ziggy sat and waited. *Another few minutes won't hurt*, he whispered, the need for caution overcoming his urge to hurry, as well as giving him time to reflect on what took place four hours ago.

Only now did he realise the Jamaican's frantic plea for drugs had been a carefully orchestrated plan to kill him and Marko. But thankfully, his warning that something didn't feel right and his brother agreeing to let Jan follow behind in the Opel had saved at least one life: his own. Minutes before reaching the warehouse, they'd parked the Opel van in a side street, hid the keys under the bumper and waited for Jan to slip into the rear of the Transit.

As well as being just a precautionary measure, it meant he could earn some extra pocket money. But none of them had foreseen the treachery that lay ahead, or the shock of seeing the pock-faced Jamaican with the AK47. Sitting in the dark, he could remember him threatening to kill them both and wonder if Jan, who was less than 10 ft. away, would recognise the danger and help?

To his eternal credit, his soldierly instinct had come storming through and he'd fired his gun twice, killing both Jamaicans dead. But the eventual cost in life and limb had been truly staggering! And what of his own injuries? Notwithstanding some facial cuts and bruising, he'd escaped the mayhem more or less unscathed. It had also been a huge stroke of luck in him discovering the exit out onto the street, especially when he went in search of the Opel van. Not long after leaving the warehouse, he'd remembered the backstreet where the van was parked, found the keys and driven to the lock-up here in Ealing.

And yet in spite of all that had gone before, he knew this was not the time to be whinging and crying over spilt milk. "Stop fucking about and move!" he snarled. Switching on the single overhead light, he took an industrial-size black

436

plastic bag from a nearby box, opened it out on the floor and stripped off of his blood-stained clothes, underpants, boots and all. When finished, he secured the bag with a zip-tie and threw it in the rear of the Opel van; ready to be disposed of later. Making good use of the small sink, he'd then scrubbed as much of the dried blood from his face and hands as he could, and when done, donned a fresh set of clothes.

"Vengeance is mine!" whispered Ziggy as he switched off the light.

S.C.U.
4.50 am

The two detectives were enjoying an early morning cup of sludge in the quiet of the S.C.U., when Bastion pushed through the door wearing a tracksuit and trainers.

"Someone's in a hurry," muttered Jacko.

Carson nodded in agreement. "Maybe he jogged all the way here."

"Bit old for that, if you ask me."

Yet before he could comment any further, the Chief Superintendent was in his office. "Is it true?" he asked.

Carson nodded slowly. "Yes Sir, Maxi Hamilton is dead."

"How?"

"At the moment it's still open to conjecture, but from what we can gather, it would appear he and Eazy Stoker lured the Tomovic brothers to Caversham Cut and tried to kill them."

Bastion was still trying to take it all in. "Why?"

"Not really sure Sir, but it looks as if they were trying to exact some kind of revenge for the murder of their grandchildren. Then it all went pear-shaped."

"How?" he asked again.

Jacko answered for him. "We've just received a copy of the warehouse security video Sir, which I think might more easily answer any questions."

The Concorde-like nose took in some air before giving a single nod of approval. Jacko switched on the oversized TV and began to fill him in with the details. "It looks as if the security system was switched off in most areas, which is not surprising, considering what was meant to happen. But for some reason, be it accidental or otherwise, the camera situated in this one area was left running, which tells us frame by frame what actually took place."

Bastion was hanging on to every word as Jacko continued, "There's something else you have to remember, Sir. The CCTV has no sound and the camera in question is recording a somewhat limited view of events. Meaning, we don't actually get to see the gunman hiding in the back of the Transit van."

Bastion grunted in understanding, but having watched the video twice, Jacko was curious as to how he would react to what they'd jokingly termed *Gunfight at the OK Corral*. At first he appeared to be fascinated by the black and white silent movie-style action taking place. Then sat up straight and looked truly aghast at the startling sight of an AK47 being pointed at the two brothers. "Where did that come from?"

"Steve Delaney at Ballistics reckons it's a souvenir from the Iraqi war."

"How can he tell?"

"The black PVC insulation tape wrapped around the grip is only made in Baghdad."

Next came an animated Maxi Hamilton and Eazy Stoker, waving their guns around as though they were kids toys. Then out of nowhere came the bullet in Stoker's chest, Eli's head being thrown back in agony and the sub-machine gun's two-second burst of destructive gunfire. But it was only until he watched Ziggy Tomovic shoot dead the colossus that was Maxi Hamilton and later become embroiled in a desperate struggle for his own life, did Bastion understand the reality of what was taking place on screen.

"Gripping stuff, eh?" murmured Carson.

"More like savagery let loose," whispered a shaken Bastion.

"Vinny the Gecko is next to die, Sir," added Jacko.

"I think we can skip that one, Sergeant, I've seen enough for now."

Jacko stopped the recording and waited for the obvious questions.

"Do we know who owns the warehouse?"

"No Sir, but considering we found Vinny lying dead in one of the rooms with his throat cut and all those expensive cars stored there, one can only assume it belongs to Maxi Hamilton."

Bastion turned to Carson. "It's a pity there's no sound, Nathan, it would have been interesting to hear what was being said before the shooting started."

"Judging by the semantics, Sir, I'd say there was a ding-dong of an argument going on."

"Do you think Maxi Hamilton really was about to pull the trigger and shoot, or just trying to scare the hell out of them?"

"He looked pretty angry to me, Sir."

"What about the brothers? Considering he's been shot seven times, we're unlikely to get any answers from this Marko Tomovic chap, are we?"

"This is true," conceded Carson.

Bastion polished the tip of his nose before turning to Jacko. "What do we know about this mystery shooter hidden in the rear of the van?"

"Nothing at the moment, Sir. Although Ballistics have confirmed the weapon used is an ex-Polish police revolver."

"Any ID or serial numbers on the guns?"

Jacko shook his head. "Afraid not. Somebody's taken the trouble to file off any relevant information. It's the same with all the victims; there was no ID on any of them, not even a driving licence. But we did find two sets of magnetic plates hidden behind the driver's seat, which hopefully might give us a clue." He then passed him another photocopy. "This petrol receipt was also found lying on the dashboard."

Bastion scanned the sheet. "What's significant about this?"

"The Ford Transit has a diesel engine, whereas this is for a tank of unleaded petrol."

"Where and when?"

"An Esso station situated in Walthamstow, just before 8.30 pm last night."

"So?"

"If you remember Sir, the assistant working at the plumbing wholesalers said Pieter and Pauli, the two fake Poles, would often use Worthing's Transit van to collect their gear in. He then recalled a time when one of them arrived in a small grey Opel van driven by another, much younger Polish male."

Bastion waited for more.

"I was wondering if maybe he'd topped the van up in Walthamstow and travelled to Liverpool as some kind of back up."

"Thus giving Ziggy another means of escape should anything go wrong?"

Jacko shrugged. "Could be."

"I don't suppose there's any sign of him?"

Jacko shook his head. "The security video times him turning off the lights at 12.35 am, which we assume was just after he'd killed Vinny the Gecko."

Bastion looked at his watch. "Hell man, he could be anywhere by now."

"That being the case," interrupted Carson. "We've forwarded a copy of the dead shooter's DNA and fingerprints to Interpol. And assuming he did escape in the Opel van, we've asked Traffic for all CTTV movement in and around the City from 10 pm last night. Oh, and there was something else we think might be very important, Sir." He then nodded to Jacko. "Rewind the tape, Sergeant."

The TV footage scrolled back to the point where Ziggy was seen stumbling about and gesticulating to the dead bodies lying on the floor. He then hesitated, stooped down and reached for the gun lying beside Maxi Hamilton. Watching closely, Bastion's eyes narrowed when he saw Ziggy take something from the deceased millionaire's hand.

"What's that?" he asked.

"That, Sir, is a photograph of Maxi Hamilton's estranged family."

Walthamstow
5.25 am

The sun had just begun to rise in the sky, as he parked the campervan in the rear alley and used his key to gain access to the garage. Once inside, he went in search of something he was badly in need of, a mug of strong black coffee. For the last few years and due to the hours they'd been keeping, it had become normal practice to keep a pot of the stuff percolating away on the stove. A fingertip touch on the jug assured him it was still piping hot, but as he reached for a cup in the cupboard, heard a voice from behind. "Ziggy?"

Expecting to be alone at this time of day, he turned to find Katrina framed in the kitchen doorway still wearing her dressing gown. "I heard a noise," she began. Then her eyes opened wide in fright. "What happened to your face and hands?" His fingers instinctively felt for the puffy bruises on his cheeks and he saw the torn knuckles and fingernails.

"Liverpool was a trap," he stuttered uncertainly.

"What do you mean, trap? Where's Marko?"

Ziggy looked away in guilt. "He's dead, and so is Jan."

Katrina closed her eyes and gave an anguished cry. "Oh God no!" she whispered.

Ziggy turned to face her. "The whole thing was a setup. There was no money to do a deal and the so-called *meet* was just a ploy to kill us and steal the drugs."

"How did they die?" she asked in bewilderment.

Ziggy shook his head. "I'm not sure, but someone on their side opened fire, then all hell broke loose with bullets flying everywhere." He held up his bloodied hands as though they were evidence. "I was attacked by this huge murderous bastard and only just managed to survive!"

"Where are Marko and Jan now?" she mumbled with tear-filled eyes.

"Still in the Transit van in Liverpool," he stuttered.

"Why didn't you bring them back with you?" she cried in accusation.

"I couldn't!" he replied forcefully. "The windscreen had a bullet hole in it and there was no way it could be moved!"

"Then how did *you* get back?"

Ziggy hesitated before replying. "When it was over, everyone around was dead, but I was lucky enough to stay alive. I then remembered where Jan's Opel van was parked and used it to get home."

Katrina was still trying to understand what was happening when Ziggy saw his chance. "I think you should leave here straightaway."

"Leave, why?" she gasped in bewilderment.

"Because the Transit van and Marko are still in Liverpool and the police will have found them by now."

Katrina was still looking confused as he rammed home his argument. "It's only a matter of time before they search the van, find a connection and come knocking on our door!"

"Where can I go?" she cried out loud.

"Go back to Poland," he insisted.

Katrina's eyes opened wide again. "What about Grigor and his schooling?"

Ziggy's voice took on an edge. "You have to understand that your life here in the UK is over. Within a few short hours, there could be a hundred armed policemen surrounding this building and after that, nothing will ever be the same again!"

A look of realisation suddenly appeared in her eyes and the dreaded fear of what might follow. "How can I possibly get away?" she whispered.

Ziggy reached for the sports bag and zipped it open. "There's £50,000 in here, which should be more than enough to get you where you want. Nevertheless, you'll have to be quick and careful how you do it."

Her eyes pleaded for more information.

"Take your car and park it in the long-stay carpark situated close to the Eurostar Terminal. If you hurry, you should be able catch the early train to Paris. From there you can take another train south, and make for the east coast of Italy. It's important you don't use a credit card to pay for anything; use the money instead." He then had a thought. "Talking of credit cards, where are yours?"

"Upstairs in my handbag," she replied.

Ziggy fixed his eyes on hers. "You won't need them where you're going Katrina. Besides, they're an easy way of tracing your movements, so leave them on the table. I'll take care of them."

He then remembered something else. "Do you still have your original passport? The one in your maiden name?"

"Somewhere," she muttered in bemusement.

"Good. I suggest you use that for a few days. Although once you and the boy are in Europe, I don't think you'll need to show it again. I'd also advise you to travel with just one suitcase each; a small one for Grigor and medium size one for yourself."

Katrina appeared ready to shed more tears. "Why Italy?" she mumbled.

Ziggy's voice took on a softer tone. "Because it's full of holidaymakers who are constantly moving from place to place. The local hoteliers are reputed to prefer cash and ask no questions."

Her eyes still seemed unconvinced.

"I know how hard this is for you, but it's important the police don't discover where you're going. So I think you should disappear for a while, or until most of this has blown over. By then it shouldn't be a problem in catching a ferry to somewhere like Croatia and a train onwards to Poland. Once home, your father will be able to sort out new credit cards, or anything else you might need." He was waiting for this message to sink in when Marko's son, still dressed in his pyjamas, appeared in the doorway.

"He's been listening to everything we've said," a shocked Katrina whispered.

Ziggy, who'd always liked the boy, stooped down so they were eye to eye and placed both hands on his shoulders. "Your father is no longer with us, Grigor, which means that you are now head of the family. Do you understand?"

The boy nodded in silence.

"Good. It's important that you be brave and take care of your Mama. Right?"

The boy nodded again.

Ziggy looked into his eyes and paused before speaking, "There's something else you should remember, which I think is more important than anything that's gone before. Your father was a great man who didn't deserve to die like this and I personally intend to avenge his death. Understand?"

Grigor nodded again in perfect understanding.

"Good, now go and change your clothes, you have a long journey ahead of you."

As the boy disappeared through the door, Ziggy turned to his mother. "I think you should do the same, but when you go, wear a hat and sunglasses, it will make it so much harder for anyone to spot you."

"You seem to have thought of everything," Katrina whispered.

"Marko's not here anymore," he said with a shrug. "So I have to finish what needs to be done."

"What might that be?"

"Nothing for you to worry your head about," he smiled. "Just pack some clothes and take care of the boy. I'll do the rest."

Aftermath
S.C.U.
11.45 am

Jacko appeared in the doorway holding two Styrofoam cups. "Fancy a drop of warm sludge?"

Carson smiled. "Only if it's got three sugars in it."

"There might be four, but you'll probably need them."

"You look shagged."

Jacko stifled a yawn. "I feel as if I've been up all night."

Carson pointed to the chair opposite. "Take a pew and join the insomniacs club."

Jacko dropped into the seat and held up a sheaf of paper. "These are the latest updates from the warehouse in Caversham Cut."

"What have we got?"

"More snakes and ladders."

"Ladders first, as always Jacko."

"Drugs estimate the cocaine found in the Transit van is worth half a million pounds and a possible street value of more than double that. They're also convinced the money in the briefcase is well short of that amount."

"Which means some of it has gone missing?"

"Yes Guv, they reckon around fifty grand's worth."

"That would probably explain what Ziggy was doing in the van."

Jacko nodded. "Yeah, but with it being side on, the CCTV camera didn't show us exactly what was happening. Yet Ziggy was definitely carrying a bulging shoulder bag when he disappeared."

"I wonder if he's thinking of doing a runner? Especially now he has some money."

"Maybe Guv, but first we have climb another ladder and then slide down a few more slippery snakes."

Carson gave a wry smile and waited.

"The magnetic plates found on the Transit van are an exact duplicate of those spotted outside Liverpool football ground and Worthing's plumbing firm in London. But digging deeper, Forensics discovered another set hidden behind a wooden panel. According to Swansea Licencing, these are registered to one Makary Waslov, a Polish national who lives in Walthamstow."

Carson snapped his fingers. "The petrol receipt found in the van, didn't that come from somewhere around there?"

"Yes Guv. Which is why we asked the local police to visit this address and tell us if there was anything suspicious going on."

"And?"

"That was over an hour ago and minutes before someone spotted smoke pouring from the building. It was only after the Fire Brigade had managed to put out the blaze and douse the place down, did they get a chance to look inside. According to the Officer in charge, the ground floor reeked of petrol fumes; which all but confirms someone must have set fire to it."

"Arson?"

"Without a doubt."

"Anyone inside?"

"No."

"What else did they find?"

"A metal kitchen table piled high with still smoking paperwork, credit cards and photographs."

"So the fire was meant to dispose of anything that might help identify them?"

"It looks that way."

"Cuffin' hell," muttered Carson "Do we know who lives there?"

"According to the neighbours, a Polish family named Waslov have occupied the place for about two years."

"Any sign of them?"

Jacko shook his head, "Vanished into thin air."

"This family, do we know any of their Christian names?"

"Yes Guv, the father was called Makary, mother Katrina and the young son Grigor, but someone called Lukasz lived there as well. He was believed to be the brother."

"Can I have a look?"

Jacko passed him the sheet of paper.

Carson smiled. "Notice anything odd about these Christian names?"

"Yes Guv, they might be Polish, but they're very similar to Marko and Luka in Serbian."

"Which make it that much easy to remember, especially when you're chatting to one another or strangers."

"Plus, there's no need for Pieter or Pauli," added Jacko.

Carson shook his head. "What else did they find?"

"The Poles ran a small plumbing and heating business from a double garage situated at the rear of the building. The neighbours can recall seeing a white Transit van and a small grey Opel regularly parked inside. Oh yeah, a young Polish guy, who everyone assumed worked for the firm, would arrive at 8.00 am every morning and drive the smaller van away."

"What time did the neighbour first report the fire?"

"Just after 6.30 am."

"And I take it the double garage was empty at that time?"

Jacko consulted his notes briefly and nodded in the affirmative.

"So if it wasn't there then, where's the Opel van now and who set fire to the building?"

"Good question Guv, but I'd put my money on Ziggy being the culprit."

"I agree. Yet according to the warehouse CCTV, he was here in Liverpool literally slitting people's throats. So how did he manage to get back to London sometime before 6.00 am?"

"Maybe the Opel van did follow behind as back-up and he used it to journey home. It might also explain why the dead gunman was hiding in the back of the Transit."

"Do any of the neighbours remember the licence number of the grey van?"

"I doubt it Guv, most people can just about remember their own."

Carson gave a grunt of acknowledgment and moved on. "What about this mystery gunman, do we know anything about him?"

"Not at the moment. Other than a small dove tattooed on his right arm, we have very little to go on. But I'm convinced he was the one who visited the plumbing wholesalers with Marko Tomovic. The assistant behind the counter insisted he was a genuine Pole and drove a small compact grey van."

"What about the handgun that killed the Stokers?"

"According to Steve Delaney at Ballistics, the weapon is an old Polish GWARD .38 service revolver that was phased out years ago."

"Serial number?"

"No such luck."

Still in thought, Carson used a pencil to stir his cup of sludge. "Let's move on to the big guy lying next to Hamilton. Do we know who he is?"

"Not yet."

"No ID or mobile phone?"

Jacko shook his head.

"These people like to travel light, don't they? It's a wonder he was wearing a pair of cuffin' underpants."

"His face was so badly cut and bruised there's no way we'd show it on TV."

"Police files?"

"Nothing that matches."

"What now?"

"I was thinking of asking your mate Archie Speed to have a look. It could be this BB Benson punter, who as I understand it, was once Hamilton's right hand man."

Carson's face lit up. "Nice one Jacko, but I've got a better idea."

"What's that, Guv?"

"We'll ask someone who spent most of his life trying to put him behind bars."

"Oh shit," groaned Jacko. "You don't mean Hughie McClellan?"

"Why not," grinned Carson, "If anyone can recognise Benson, even after all these years, then it has to be Tufty."

"What about all the confidential information he's already leaked to Hamilton? I reckon it's him we should be investigating!"

Carson shrugged. "Maybe, although I'm not sure we're ever going to prove any of that, especially with Maxi being dead. But technically, I'd say Tufty's still connected to our case."

"And here's me thinking we'd finally got rid of the grumpy Jock pain in the arse!"

Hillside Lodge, Surrey

Ziggy parked the campervan a hundred yards away and set off in search of his first objective; a tall red brick wall that ran left and right. The night sky was a combination of dark cloud and bright moonlight, a brisk wind deciding how it might affect the ground below. Keeping to the shadows, Ziggy followed the wall until he came upon a twisted pine tree that grew alongside. With one eye on the sky above, he waited until a sizeable mass of cloud had begun to drift his way and when directly overhead, plunged everything into semi-darkness.

Seizing the moment, he clambered to the lower branches, vaulted over the wall and landed in the soft soil 10 ft. below. Crouching in the shadows, he froze for a second and listened for any sounds to suggest he might have been spotted. Once assured that all was as it should be, he gave a smile of satisfaction and had a quick look around. Beyond the bushes and momentarily illuminated in the moonlight, he could see a manicured lawn, whose tailored edges reached the elegant manor house it served. This tall imposing structure was bedecked with ivy and had a roofed boardwalk that no matter the season, would allow a person to stroll from front to back without getting wet.

Ziggy however, was more interested in the two heavies sat on wicker chairs with their heads close together. At first he'd been unsure as to what they were doing, until he saw the flickering light reflected on their faces and realised they were watching the screen of a mobile phone. Keeping the Berretta by his side, he edged his way towards them and when close enough heard one chuckle in Serbian, "*Pogledaj velicinu njegovog kurca*!" Look at the size of his dick!

Ziggy shook his head. It didn't take much imagination to understand what was keeping these two meatheads occupied. Stepping silently onto the porch, he crept up behind them and when a couple of feet away, pulled the trigger twice. Ironically, the only ray of sunshine in all this shit was that he'd never met these clowns. The other being their last thoughts would be one of raunchy pleasure as they departed this earth. A fast grab of their coat collars was enough to stop them from slipping off the chairs and staining the wooden terrace.

Having visited the Manor many times before, meant he knew the routine these meatheads used and how easy it would be to take them out. Confident all was well at the rear, he was about to move around to the front of the house when the sweet tang of burnt tobacco stopped him in his tracks. A quick peek around the corner had soon confirmed his suspicions. Where normally there'd be two cars parked in the courtyard there were now three: a Jaguar saloon for the two dead clowns, and a shiny BMW X5 belonging to the man who employed them. But who owned the third expensive-looking Mercedes Benz AMG, with its all-round tinted windows? And who the fuck was smoking what could only be Pall Mall?

Another quick look answered all his questions. Leaning against one of the pillars was a tall stranger. Yet this clown didn't look like someone who would spend time watching Porn on his phone and by his confident attitude, appeared to be very much on the ball. He was also holding a Glock in one hand and a smouldering cigarette in the other. *Has to be the driver of the Mercedes*, thought Ziggy.

His next problem however, was how to dispose of him without getting killed in the process. Then pleasantly surprised to see the professional solve the problem for him. On the terrace stood a large swing-seat that was mostly used in the summertime. Ziggy could remember the many times he himself had sat there waiting for Marko to finish inside and it looked as if 'danger man' was about to do the same.

Problem was, the seat was a cushioned low-slung affair and the driver like everybody else, had to look behind before they sat down. In that split second of distraction, Ziggy stepped around the corner and pulled the trigger. The look of surprise was there for all to see, as the bullet made a perfect circle in the middle of his forehead and the clown slumped sideways on the bed. *Couldn't have planned it better myself*, thought Ziggy, whilst neatly arranging a soft wool blanket over the body.

Now came the serious part. In the middle of the Georgian terrace, sat a large black wooden door with highly polished brass knocker. However, Ziggy had no intentions of making his presence known just yet; this after all, was meant to be a surprise visit. Quietly turning the handle, he inched it open a fraction and seeing it was all clear, stepped into a well-lit hallway that was exactly as he first remembered it. The floor was of a soft white and pink marbled tile. The wood-panelled walls, a rich deep mahogany colour, that perfectly reflected the glow from the crystal chandelier hanging from the ceiling. But what he loved most of all, was the superb polished staircase that grandly wound its way to the floor above.

Oh, to live in a place like this, he thought, as he admired the extravagances of another age. Yet he wasn't here to appreciate these lavish ornate surroundings, he was looking for answers. The hallway was of a semi-circular nature, with various doors leading to a variety of different rooms. But Ziggy was only interested in the one to the left of the staircase; the one where he and Marko had spent many hours playing cards. Keeping as quiet as a mouse, he placed one ear against the door, squinted an eye and listened.

At first he could hear nothing, then a second later, caught the faint sound of voices talking. Keeping the gun by his side, he opened the door and slipped into a dimly lit, but familiar looking book-lined study. Within a thick haze of cigarette smoke he could see two men having a quiet, yet meaningful conversation. The thinner of them was sat in an upright leather armchair and using a tall standard lamp as a means of illumination. The other perched behind an antique mahogany desk, with a matching decorative brass fitting, but neither had noticed him until he stepped into the light.

"Ziggy?" gasped Tino. "Is that you?"

"Who else?" he replied.

"Jesus man, you look like shit. What's going on and where's Marko?"

"Dead."

Tino looked a little pained, but unfazed at this decidedly bad news. "We had a hunch that might be the case and presumed you'd been killed as well."

"Close, but not quite," he said with a smile.

Tino looked to explain. "When we received no call saying it was a done deal, we'd naturally assumed something had gone wrong. Then the late-night news said there'd been a major shooting incident, with dead bodies lying everywhere."

Ziggy gave a lopsided grin. "Luckily, I wasn't one of them."

Tino was about to ask another question when he saw the silencer screwed to the Berretta. "Hey, what's with the gun?"

"This is to help me get some answers."

"About what?"

"About why you set me and Marko up."

Tino looked momentarily stunned and inched his hand towards the desk.

Ziggy shook his head. "I wouldn't bother with the alarm my friend, both the guards are dead." He then smiled at Petrovic. "And sad to say, so is yours."

The Colonel looked as if he were about to explode at the loss of his top man. "What is this lunacy, Tomovic, and what the fuck are you talking about?"

Ziggy waved the gun from side to side. "I'd like to know why you sent me and Marko to Liverpool, so a couple of vigilantes could blow our heads off!"

Tino could just about speak. "What?" he gasped in astonishment.

"You heard me," snarled Ziggy. "We thought we were delivering the usual van load of drugs and collecting £500,000 as payment, but I've since realised that the money was payment for your help in getting rid of us."

Petrovic's eyes hardened. "That's bullshit, the money was an agreed amount as payment for the heroin."

"That's not what they told us."

"Who's they?" asked a still confused Tino.

"The reception committee."

Petrovic watched the silencer waving in his direction and began to get nervous. "Take it easy, Ziggy, and tell us what really happened last night."

"Okay Colonel, but even though we knew there'd be West Indians involved, I'd still like to know who ordered the drugs and chose the meeting place?"

"That's confidential information and you know it!" snapped Tino. "The deal is, we never tell you a client's name in case anything goes wrong, especially if you get caught delivering the drugs."

"So who's Popeye?"

Tino looked at Petrovic, who was more concerned with the gun. "Tell him, for fuck's sake!"

"Okay, okay," he muttered. "He's a Jamaican drug dealer named Eazy Stoker. He's also the person who ordered the heroin and chose the meeting place."

"Well, isn't that strange," grinned Ziggy. "Because the fucker I met at the gate last night was some white guy aged around seventy and dressed in a flash Armani suit. And now I think of it, he didn't look anything like a Jamaican. But he did know that 'Popeye' was the password, and insisted the deal was taking place on the floor above. At the time I thought this move very unwise, but Marko had said it looked okay and so we followed him up to the next level."

"Why the next level?" asked Tino.

"Because that's where they intended to kill us."

Petrovic blinked twice and tried to understand. "You still haven't told us who would want to kill you, or why."

Keeping the gun purposefully pointed at the Colonel's head, Ziggy took a seat in the chair opposite. "The Reception Committee consisted of three others. One was a tall grey-haired guy, who looked to be the same age as 'Popeye' and used the same tailor. He'd also smiled a lot, and said he was there as part of the deal. The other two black guys, who I now assume had to be the Jamaicans, were in charge of the money. The older one who was dressed in a fancy check-suit liked to preach and quote from the Bible. But the younger pock-faced fucker, who I didn't like period, was a surly looking bastard badly in need of some manners." Ziggy paused, thinking of what happened next.

"A minute after Marko had said we could go ahead with the deal. The ugly one has pulled an AK47 rifle out of nowhere and took us both prisoner. Then to make things worse, the two flash punters pull a couple of Glocks from their waistbands and begin waving them around. At first we'd assumed it was some kind of double cross and warned there'd be serious repercussions if anything happened to us, but how wrong we were. One Armani suit began to brag that he wasn't worried about comebacks, because the money was payment for ensuring we'd be in Liverpool last night. He then began to ramble on about how this was payback time, seeing as how we'd supposedly killed two of their family members." Ziggy shook his head. "And then the strangest of things happened."

Tino couldn't help himself. "What?"

"This tall grey-haired guy called me by my first name."

"I don't understand," Tino spluttered in confusion.

Ziggy laughed at his own stupidity. "I'd been arguing like crazy that they had the wrong people. That is, until he pointed the Glock at my head and called me 'Luka'."

Petrovic's mouth dropped open in surprise. "What happened then?"

Ziggy swung the Beretta in his direction. "He started to tell me my life story."

"What?"

"Yes, Colonel. He began to talk about how he knew we were the Tomovic brothers and came from a place called Erdivos in Serbia. He also knew the school we went to and attended regular English lessons. In fact, he told me a whole heap of shit that I'd completely forgotten about!"

Tino asked the next question. "How could he know all that?"

Ziggy swung the gun back in his direction. "That's what I'm here to find out. My brother's dead and I want to know the reason why?"

"You don't seriously think we had anything to do with it."

Ziggy didn't reply.

"Jesus fuck, this is madness," cried Tino.

The Colonel began to take a more pragmatic approach. "Why would we want these people to kill you?"

"Half a million pounds is a good start," shrugged Ziggy.

"But we don't need money, we have plenty of the stuff in the safe."

Ziggy pointed his gun at the ceiling. "Tino has always complained about how much it costs to run this place."

"For Christ's sake, I was talking about paying the fucking gardener!" Petrovic tried changing the subject again. "Nevertheless, something must have gone badly wrong in Liverpool, because even though Marko's dead, you're still here to tell the tale."

Ziggy nodded silently.

"So, why didn't they kill you?"

"Because we took along some extra protection."

"What does that mean?"

"We hid another shooter in the van."

"Who?"

"Marko's brother-in-law."

Petrovic was stunned. "Why would you do that?"

"Marko was worried we might encounter some problems along the way and asked Jan to come along for the ride. As it turned out he was right, the whole thing was a well organised plan to kill us."

Petrovic saw a chink of light. "But that doesn't say we had anything to do with it!"

"True, yet doesn't explain how they knew so much about us, Colonel." Petrovic was stumped for a reply.

Tino interrupted with another question, "So when did the shooting start?"

Ziggy thought for a second. "This Stoker clown was about ready to shoot Marko dead and the one in the 'Armani' suit intent on sending me to heaven. Then Jan fired first and all hell broke loose. Within the blink of an eye bullets were flying everywhere and no one survived."

"Except you," whispered Tino.

"That's right, everyone was dead except little old me."

Petrovic saw a glimmer of hope. "So there's no one alive to say we were actually involved?"

Ziggy shook his head. "That's right, Colonel, but that doesn't quite get you off the hook. Because a few minutes before the guns started blazing, the smiling bastard in the Armani suit began to tell me about something that'd happened many years ago in Bosnia. He said it was all about a mystery attack on two Swedish doctors and how they'd tragically died. According to him, those responsible for the killings had never been found. But what really had me going was how he could have known me and Marko were there that day."

Petrovic's eyes narrowed. "Well, I didn't tell him," he snarled in defiance.

"And neither did I," stuttered Tino.

"So who did?" asked Ziggy. "But more importantly, why?"

"I've told you before, Tomovic, I don't know any of these people and I've never spoken to, or had any kind of communication with them!"

"Okay, I really would like to believe you, Colonel, but why did the man in the Armani suit tell me that without you, he would never have been able to do it?"

"Do what?"

"Make sure Marko and I were in Liverpool last night."

Petrovic began to panic. "I don't know what this is all about, but I swear to God I know nothing about anyone trying to kill you."

Ziggy smiled. "Then maybe I should tell you his exact words. He said, 'none of this tonight would have been possible without the Colonel's help?"

"So it *was* you all along!" cried an accusing Tino.

"Shut up, you stupid bastard," whispered Petrovic. "This is just some kind of crazy trick to keep the money and the drugs for himself."

Ziggy shook his head. "Sorry Colonel, I left it all behind in Liverpool, Marko's body included."

"So what are you going to do now?" asked an anxious Tino.

"Now?" smiled Ziggy. "Now I'm going to kill you both."

Tino nearly fainted. "Me? Why the hell are you going to kill me?"

"Because just like the Colonel here, I don't trust you."

"Jesus fuck, Ziggy, if it hadn't been for me, you and Marko would still be clearing blocked toilet drains."

"And I appreciate that, Tino, but if you'd been a little more circumspect in your dealings, then my brother would still be alive today."

"You won't get away with this," growled Petrovic.

Ziggy shrugged. "Maybe, but they do say The Lord works in mysterious ways, so I think now is a good time to move on and ask forgiveness for your sins."

"I haven't committed any sins," protested Tino.

"Little lies will get you three hail Marys every time," smiled Ziggy.

Petrovic was getting more worried by the minute. "Surely there must be some way of sorting this mess out?"

Ziggy shook his head. "Sorry boys, the time for talking is over and it's now time for you both to meet your maker." He then pointed the gun at Tino. "I think you should go first."

"Why me?" he bleated.

"Because you've always liked to be first in the queue; be it at the bar, or any place something's being handed out for free. So I think it only right that you say a prayer and die like a soldier."

Tino started to wave his hands about. "Wait! Wait!" he pleaded in desperation. "I've just remembered something that I think you should know." He then pointed a finger at the Colonel. "It concerns him and the way your parents died!"

Petrovic was halfway out of the leather chair, when Ziggy pulled the trigger and shot him through the shoulder, the impact enough to throw him back in his seat. He then pointed the gun in Tino's direction.

"Keep talking."

"It was back in '97 and around the time the authorities were looking to indict Arkan for war crimes. They'd been sifting and searching for anything that might tie him to these past incidents and as you'd imagine, the Tomovic brothers were a potential time bomb if discovered. Yet Arkan was loyal and had no intention of letting that happen, so he told the 'Fixer' to do whatever was needed to get you out of the country. But this wasn't easy, especially as your father and mother were still alive in Erdivos. So in 2001 and with the help of the local police, he organised for a couple of incendiary devices to be thrown through the ground floor windows, and report it as an accident. Sad to say, both your parents were asleep in the bedroom, and a few months later you'd moved to Poland."

A stunned Ziggy sat in silence as he tried to take this in.

Petrovic, however, was more intent on having the last word. "You stupid fool," he gasped through the pain. "This lunatic will kill us both, no matter what you say!"

Ziggy swung around and looked him in the eye. "True, Colonel. But it will give me the greatest of pleasure in killing you first." Petrovic was about ready to spit in his face, when a neat hole appeared in the middle of his forehead and made a terrible mess of the antique leather chair behind.

"Why didn't you mention this before?"

An ashen-faced Tino could just about speak. "He's not known as the 'Fixer' for nothing!"

"But if you'd have said something earlier, Marko might still be alive."

Tino looked guilty. "I know Ziggy, but I had no idea the bastard was planning on getting you both killed."

"The sins of the fathers," smiled Ziggy.

Tino's ears pricked up at once. "What does that mean?"

"Nothing, my friend, it's just a quote I've heard lately."

Tino was still nervous. "What are you going to do now?"

Ziggy shrugged. "I'm not sure yet. Maybe I'll take a break and go fishing."

Tino nodded. "Good move, we could all do with some time off from this mess."

Ziggy pointed to a wooden panel in the wall. "But first I'll need some cash from that large vault of yours."

Tino leapt out his chair and went to the metal safe. "No problem, no problem. How much do you need?"

Ziggy thought for a second, then smiled. "I think I'll take it all."

Tino balked. "Holy shit, as much as that?" He then saw the angry look and returned the smile. "No problem, Ziggy, just help yourself to what you want."

Ziggy stood and watched him twirl the dials. "And while you're at it, Tino, can I have one of those quality fake ID cards you keep in there?"

"Sure, sure," he mumbled. "You can have anything you want, just don't shoot!"

S.C.U., Liverpool

He'd been so busy reading the latest report Jacko hadn't noticed McClellan sat in Carson's office.

"Oops, sorry Guv, I didn't know you were busy."

"That's okay, Sergeant, and as it turns out, you're just in time to hear Hughie's latest news."

Jacko gave a half-hearted nod to the ex-Commander, who was making one of his rare, yet most unwelcome appearances. "Must be important Sir," he said through gritted teeth. "Especially if you had to tell us in person."

Tufty gave a half-smile in response and then ignored him. "As I was saying, Nathan, this whole business has come right out of the blue."

Jacko glanced at his boss and raised a questioning eyebrow.

Carson gave a shake of the head and decided to call a truce between the two warring factions. "Considering my No. 2 has yet to hear any of this, Hughie, I think it might be best if you start from the top."

Tufty gave a grunt of Scottish frustration and addressed Jacko directly. "Have you ever heard of someone called Bonaparte Bunifido?"

"Not to my knowledge, Sir."

"What about BB Benson?"

Jacko felt like telling McClellan to piss off, but knew he had to play the game.

"I think we're all aware of who he is, Sir."

"Well I'm here to say you could be wrong."

Jacko was even more confused. "Excuse me?"

"A few days ago I was taking part in a golf tournament being held down South. It was one of them inter-club type competitions, which is always a good excuse for the boys to have a piss up and get away for the weekend. Anyway, we'd won a few and lost a few games, and then decided it was time to head for the bar for a little refreshment."

Jacko could only imagine what that entailed as Hughie droned on.

"Which is when one of the members from the opposing team began to talk in length about his extensive golfing travels. According to him, he loved to fly around the world and play on some unusual golf courses, the last one being in Azerbaijan. He'd then prattled on about it having a fabulous layout, besides being one of the best he'd ever played on. He was also proud to say that he was one of the first people to play all 18 holes and recorded the event to prove it.

"At this point, I'd nearly lost the will to live, until he began showing us some live video shots on his mobile phone. Most were of the fairways and bunkers, but there was one in particular that caught my attention. It was a snapshot of the people who'd been behind the project and I'm not talking about the players. This was of those who'd actually designed and financed the whole thing."

Carson passed Jacko a copy of the photograph. "Recognise anyone?" There was no doubting the picture was an informal one and taken off the cuff. Yet it looked obvious one person in particular was trying to hide his face.

"Well, I'll be damned," said Jacko. "That looks like the late BB Benson."

"Correction," said Tufty McClellan. "That is, in fact, the late Bonaparte Bunifido, who when alive, spent most of his years domiciled in Monaco. Not only that, he ran a successful business called 'Napoleon Enterprises' that specialised in constructing high quality golf courses."

Jacko looked at Carson. "Can I ask how all this came to light?"

A smug-looking Tufty answered for him. "It's not as difficult as you think, Sergeant, especially if you move in all the right circles and know exactly who to ask."

Jacko was still stumped. "I admit that I only saw Benson dead at the crime scene, but are we still talking about the same man?"

"Oh aye laddie, that's him alright."

"So who exactly was this BB Benson?"

"A flash arrogant drug pusher who I met a long time ago here in Liverpool. Although that's not his real name; a check of 'Births and Deaths' has revealed no such person was registered at the home address given, or in the year he was born. However, in 1982 and around the time he went missing, a British passport was issued in the name of one Bonaparte Bunifido."

"Which we assume was BB Benson's real name and the same year Hamilton disappeared to Spain."

Jacko shook his head. "No wonder we couldn't find them, Guv. One was hiding under a sombrero and the other was playing roulette in the casinos. All the same, that can only mean Benson was prepared to sacrifice everything he'd achieved in life by helping Maxi Hamilton kill the two Tomovic brothers. And who can forget the images from the security camera when he and Ziggy fought to the death."

"Loyalty to the end," nodded Carson.

"Maybe," grinned McClellan. "But I've watched that same security video a few times and I think they're still peddling drugs just like they did forty years ago! Which means they'll both soon be 6 ft. under and all the money in China won't bring them back!"

Tufty's snide comment reminded Jacko of why he was there. "Talking of dead bodies, Sir. This latest report from the London Met makes for some very disturbing reading. It's regarding the gangland killing that took place a couple of days ago; the one they think might be Russian related."

Carson sipped on his cup of warm sludge. "Better start from the top Sergeant, just so we don't miss anything."

Jacko did as requested. "The shootings took place at an isolated property named Hillside Lodge, which I believe is somewhere in West Surrey. They're not sure who actually owns the place, but it has 10 ft. high walls and an automatic gate, meaning it's not easy to get in or out. According to the report, a local gardener goes there once a week to water the plants and generally make sure everything is in order.

He knows the entry code, which means he can make a visit even when there's no one at home. Two days ago, he arrives at the property and as usual starts mowing the grass. He's halfway down the rear lawn, when he notices two men watching him from the raised terrace that skirts the house. At first, he thinks nothing of it, seeing as there are some cars parked in the drive and as you do, tries to ignore them. But after he's been up and down a few times, begins to smell a rat." Jacko smiled. "That was how the gardener described it, Guv."

Carson kept a straight face. "I think we all know what he meant, Sergeant."

"A closer look revealed lots of dried bloodstains splattered around their upper body areas, which has him rapidly reaching for his phone and dialling 999. Within the hour, a van load of armed SO18 officers and team of Forensics have descended on the said property, looking for answers."

Jacko checked the report again. "The first surprise was the discovery of another body lying on a swing bed situated at the front of the house. He'd apparently been shot once in the forehead, a blanket used as a means of hiding him and the gun he was holding. The two stiffs in the wicker chairs had pretty much the same MO, but in their case, shot from behind at close range."

"Has to be drugs," growled McClellan.

Jacko ignored the Scot's interruption and moved on. "The next surprise came when they began exploring the ground floor areas and entered a book-lined study. An initial scan of the room had revealed one deceased male sat in a chair, with multiple gunshot wounds to his upper body. However, this was later revised down to just two, one in the shoulder the other in the forehead. A further search of the study discovered something very unusual; another male, crouched on his knees, with his head stuck in an open safe, which I might add was empty.

According to the autopsy and just like the two stiffs on the terrace, he'd been shot once in the back of the head. At first, the sight of an empty safe had the boys down south thinking that maybe it was just a case of armed robbery; and then the Ballistics report came in." Jacko turned a page looking for the relevant information. "According to this, the weapon is the same as the one used to kill Maxi Hamilton here in Liverpool."

"Cuffin' hell," groaned Carson. "This has to be Ziggy."

"I'm afraid so, Guv, although that's not the only bad news." He then read from a different sheet of paper. "We received this report from the Bedfordshire police less than an hour ago. It informs us of another incident that took place at around 8.00 am this morning. It would appear that a certain Alderman Troughton and his wife were about to take their Bentley Continental on a daytrip to London, when someone decided otherwise. According to Deng, their maid, the couple had said their usual goodbyes and left the house just after 8.00 am. She, in turn, thought no more about it and carried on clearing away the breakfast dishes.

"However, and not long after, a glance through the kitchen window has revealed the car was still parked in the courtyard with its engine running. Thinking that maybe they'd forgotten something important, Deng went to see if she could help in any way. Then had the shock of her life when she opened the driver's door. The Alderman and his wife looked as if they were asleep; he on the steering wheel and she on the dashboard; however, both had been shot in the back of the head."

Carson slumped back in his chair. "Something tells me there's more bad news."

"Afraid so Guv. It would appear their unknown assailant was hiding on the back seat and waiting for them to climb aboard. All it took were two quick pulls of the trigger and it was game over."

"Any witnesses?"

"No. But when they asked the maid if there'd been any domestic problems, or seen any strangers hanging about, she said everything appeared to be normal. Then remembered the two Polish plumbers who'd worked on the house around eighteen months ago."

"You must be cuffin joking," groaned Carson.

"I wish I was, Guv, but it seems the Tomovic brothers had spent a whole summer replacing the pipework at the Hall, only to be thrown off the job without being paid."

"Any clues why?"

"In her interview, the maid admitted the Alderman wasn't a very honourable man and would use any excuse to 'rip them off'. Be that as it may, she confirmed that the Poles were literally boiling mad at how they'd been treated."

"Mad enough to go back and kill them," grunted McClellan.

"And it goes without saying, Ballistics will confirm Ziggy pulled the trigger at both the killings, Guv."

"Whatever you do, Jacko, don't upset your cuffin' plumber," warned Carson.

"That wasn't all he left behind, Guv; have a look at these"

Carson studied the photographs taken from both crimes scenes and let out another groan. "Oh shit!"

"Can I see?" asked a curious McClellan.

"Be my guest," said Carson.

The subject was a single sheet of A4 paper covered in blue felt pen. One had been placed in the lap of the mystery male sat in the leather chair, the other pinned to the back of the Alderman's shirt, and both declared: *Vengeance is mine said the Lord!*

Tufty gave a smile. "If I remember my Bible lessons correctly Nathan, that comes from Romans 12:19-20, and says this Ziggy person has a score to settle."

"And here's me thinking Eazy Stoker was the only religious fanatic around here!"

"Maybe it's catching, Guv."

"Jacko?"

"I was thinking about the security video, but more importantly, the footage where Ziggy realises everybody's dead. I know there's no sound, but you can tell by the way he begins to stumble about just how badly it affected him."

"You mean when he finds his twin brother has been shot to pieces?"

"That's right Guv, but what's really worrying me, is when he kneels down and takes the photograph from a dead Maxi Hamilton's hand."

Carson had to think. "Are we talking about the one showing the Freeland family on holiday?"

"That's the one. Although I don't think he was admiring their suntans; something tells me he has much more in store for them."

Gone Fishing

'Anglers Paradise' was an exclusive, privately owned lake, whose many attractions included five acres of freshwater fishing, all of which was set in a lush leafy valley. In addition to the variety of different size fish available. There was the added bonus of twenty state of the art fixed 'statics', or luxury mobile homes that one might rent, plus a modern shower block and trendy cafe. The busy season was coming to an end and bookings had fallen off, which gave Albie Swan, who ran the place the opportunity to do some DIY. It also meant that after a long hot stretch, his small band of helpers could take a well-earned break and he might more easily assess the fish stocks.

It was quiet and he'd been on his way to hang the 'Closed for two weeks' sign on the gate, when a green VW campervan came up the drive and stopped beside him.

"Morning," chimed Albie, as the driver's window rolled down.

"Hi," replied the driver, who wore a bright 'Yankees' baseball cap, black leather gloves and wraparound sunglasses.

"How can I help?"

The driver peered through the windscreen. "I'd like to do some fishing if I can."

Even though the driver spoke half decent English, Albie couldn't quite place his accent. "Sorry mate, we're closed for maintenance."

The stranger glanced at the board, rubbed his clean-shaven chin and thought for a second. "This is a mighty big place, my friend, are you sure there's no way you could squeeze me in?"

Albie shook his head. "Not a chance."

The driver pondered for a second longer before replying, "That's a real shame, because in a couple of months' time, I intend to board a ferry to France and take part in a prize fishing contest at Lac de Madine. I've competed in it once before, but didn't even get near the scoreboard. So I was thinking that maybe I should try and get a little practice in beforehand and this looks like the perfect place to do it."

Albie's face took on a sympathetic look. "I've heard of that competition and know how hard it is to beat them 'Frogs', especially when it's on their territory. Unfortunately the restaurant's closed and the 'Statics' have all been cleaned and sealed until we open for business again."

"Statics?" asked the driver.

Albie pointed to where the two rows of luxury caravans lay. "They're what we call Statics."

"How much is it to rent one?"

"Normally £500 a week."

"And you're here on your own?"

Albie nodded. "Yes, there's only me, at the moment."

The driver rubbed his chin as if thinking. "What if I make you an offer?"

"Offer?" queried Albie.

"Yeah, I don't need a Static, but I'll gladly give you £1,000 in cash, with no questions asked, if you let me and my little campervan park out of the way somewhere."

This had completely thrown Albie, who hesitated before shaking his head. "Sorry mate, no can do."

The driver looked disappointed. "Who's going to know, man? I'm as quiet as a mouse, tidy as a housewife and promise never to piss in your lake."

Albie hesitated and thought about the so-called 'offer'. All the bookings these days were normally purchased online and paid for by credit card, so it was rare to see real money, never mind touch it. He then thought of the people who owned this place. They didn't exactly pay him a fortune in wages and were more than likely sunning their backsides at their villa in Barbados.

"What's your name, big man?"

"Pauli," came the reply.

"And what do you do for a living?"

"I work on the oil rigs out in the Far-East, one month on, one month off."

"And you're not from around here?"

"No, I'm originally from Georgia, which is near Russia."

Albie still looked doubtful, until Pauli smiled and passed him a well-worn ID card. "This is officially me."

The reduced photograph looked like him, just. The information on the card written in something he couldn't understand. "Do you drink?"

"Never touch the stuff."

"Not even vodka?"

"Not even vodka."

This snippet appeared to remove any misgivings he might have about the Georgian.

"Okay big man, beyond the last static is a nice shady spot where you can park and set up home. If needed, there's a power point you can use, but sorry to say there's no hot water in the shower block."

Pauli shrugged, "No problem, I'll just shiver a little."

Albie smiled and held out his hand. "You said something about an offer."

The two weeks had quickly gone by and come tomorrow morning, most of the staff would have returned from holiday. So with this in mind, Albie went in search of Pauli, only to have a pleasant surprise; the big man had already moved on. But when he thought about it, was more than relieved. The Georgian might have been as good as his word. In that he would always be up at the crack of dawn, make his way to his berth, a secluded spot by the waterside and spend the rest of the day hidden amongst the bushes. To give him his due, he'd always left the toilet and shower rooms spotless, but 'creepy' wasn't the word.

He could clearly remember the first night of Pauli's stay and how he'd literally frightened the shit out of him. He'd been doing his usual late-night rounds, when he heard the distant sound of a guitar strumming away in the dark. Recognising the tune as one of David Bowie's, he'd headed in its direction with the intention of trying to get a little closer. As he was halfway up the path, the music had abruptly stopped and Albie stopped with it.

Standing in the darkness, he'd cocked an ear and waited for it to start again; only to realise someone was standing behind him. The problem was, they were so close he could actually hear the sound of breathing in his ears. With the hairs on the back of his neck beginning to rise and fearful of what might happen next, he'd swiftly shuffled off in the direction of his cottage and what he hoped was safety.

From then on, he'd decided to give Pauli a wide berth and leave him to it. Yet as he observed the empty space where the VW was once parked, he realised the big man must have just upped sticks in the middle of the night and disappeared. "Hope he doesn't come back again," he muttered.

As the day went by, he'd put all thoughts of Pauli out of his mind, when the police car rumbled up the drive.

"Morning," said Albie.

"Morning, Sir," replied the driver, who clambered out and donned his hat.

"Is there a problem?"

His colleague joined him in looking around. "Not really Sir, just a routine enquiry."

"Oh that's good," smiled Albie. "How can I help?"

"Nice place Sir, exactly how big is it?" asked the driver.

"Five acres including the lake."

"Lots of good fishing?"

"You better believe it."

His colleague pointed to the Statics. "And you rent these caravans out?"

Albie was about to explain that these were the latest thing in luxury mobile homes, then thought better of it. "They're for hire when the complex is open, but we've been closed for a couple of weeks doing maintenance."

The two policemen looked surprised. "Oh, sorry Sir, we'd assumed you were open all year round."

"We are, but have to close now and then to do the odd repair job and check the fish stocks."

"So you haven't had any visitors for the past fourteen days?"

"No officer, today will be the first for paying guests."

"Well, that was a wasted journey," sighed the driver.

"To true," agreed his mate.

"Sorry to have bothered you," said the driver. "As I said, it's just a routine inquiry."

Albie was suddenly curious. "Exactly who, or what are you looking for, officer?"

"There's a dangerous killer on the loose. Who, we've been informed, likes to go fishing in his spare time. So, knowing just how big a place this is, we decided it might be worth checking out."

Albie was suddenly nervous. "Do you know what this person looks like?"

The driver nodded and passed him a sheet of paper. 'This is the latest 'Identikit' of the suspect, issued just a few days ago, or so we've been told."

Albie began to sweat: the image might portray someone with long dark hair and a stubbly chin, but deep inside he had a feeling it might be Pauli.

"Do you know this person's name?"

"Yes Sir, his real name is Luka Tomovic, but often known as Ziggy."

Albie couldn't help himself. "And do you know where he's from?"

The policeman looked confused "I couldn't say for sure, but I think he's originally from Serbia, or somewhere like that."

Albie was about to ask if that was anywhere near Georgia, when he remembered the £1,000 lying in his bedroom drawer, plus the fact he'd let the stranger in the VW campervan stay for two weeks. Christ, if his employers found out, he'd be out on his ear; even though he'd worked at Anglers Paradise since school.

"You okay, Sir?" asked the driver. "You look a little pale."

"Yes, of course," he replied. "I'm just trying to think if it looked like any of our past clients, they do come in all shapes and sizes."

"Any luck?"

Without thinking, Albie shook his head. "Sorry boys; never seen him before."

The policemen looked mildly disappointed, but unsurprised at the reply. "Well thanks for having a look Sir, but if you do see anyone matching the description, give us a call."

"No problem," said Albie. They were about to climb in the police car when he asked another impromptu question. "Has this Ziggy person actually been seen around here?"

The two policemen looked doubtful. "Not as far as we know Sir, this is just one of them nationwide alerts and if the truth be known, he's more than likely fishing in Scotland."

"So how does he get about?"

"Sorry Sir?"

"I mean does he have a vehicle of some kind?"

The driver nodded. "We've heard he's been driving a small grey Opel van."

Albie gave a sigh of relief. "Well, I certainly haven't seen one of those around here, officer."

Waytree Crescent

Compared to the lawless Highwater Housing Estate that dominated the nearby skyline, Waytree Crescent, was a virtual oasis of peace. The ten bungalows, supposedly built by Maxi Hamilton in the eighties, were hidden from view by a circular tree-lined drive and a narrow road that sloped gently downwards. Nevertheless, today would be Jacko's fourth visit since they'd discovered that Kelly Freeland lived just a few hundred yards up the road from the crime scene. Yet he and his Boss had still managed to differ, on how best to warn her mother of the potential dangers presented by Ziggy Tomovic.

"I think you should take Smithy along and make it official."

Jacko looked doubtful. "I'd rather do it alone Guv, the last thing we need is to be heavy-handed and frighten the life out her."

"Personally, I don't care how it's done, but if we don't move her soon, Tomovic might do it for us!"

On this, Jacko was in full agreement. More so, when recalling the latest round of murderous escapades perpetrated by Ziggy, or the fact he could just as easily find her address on the Internet. This was still foremost in his mind, as he slowed to a halt outside the Freeland's home only to find the lady herself waiting to greet him. "Morning Sergeant. To what do I owe this unexpected pleasure?"

"A couple of things," began Jacko. "I assume you've heard the coroner's office has agreed to release your father's body for burial in two weeks' time."

Steffi gave a thin smile. "Yes and I intend it to be just a small private family cremation, no cameras, no press, nothing special."

Jacko nodded in understanding. "Of course, but unfortunately there is a more delicate matter that we need to talk about."

Steffi smiled and waved a hand in apology. "Sorry to keep you out on the doorstep, Sergeant, if you'd like to come inside, I'd be happy to rustle up some fresh coffee."

"A half-decent cup of anything would be greatly appreciated," he grinned in return. Stepping through the door and into the hallway was enough to remind him of his surroundings. To his left lay the kitchen and patio area, the large comfortable lounge was straight ahead, on his right the three bedrooms; the one in the middle being Kelly's. He was just about to take a seat at the table, when Kristian and his friend Tommo came hurrying through the back door.

"Oh, hello boys," smiled Steffi. "Thought you'd gone to play football."

"Forgot my boots," replied Kristian, who immediately noted Jacko's presence.

Steffi nodded in his direction. "Do you remember Sergeant Jackson?"

"Yeah, of course I do. How are things Sergeant?

Jacko yo-yoed his head, "Bit stressed out, but getting there."

Kristian gave a shrug. "In the end I suppose that's what we're all trying to do."

Jacko was about to reply, when Steffi gave him a mug of coffee and asked, "So, what was it you wanted to talk about?"

Unsure of whether to proceed, Jacko nodded towards the two boys. "As I said, it's a rather delicate matter and I was hoping to discuss it with you in private."

Steffi gave a sigh. "It wouldn't matter if you told me the world was about to end tomorrow, Sgt. Because within minutes, I'd have told Kristian, who, I have no doubt would go running next-door and tell Tommo and although we're not exactly on neighbourhood watch, it is a close-knit group of people who've always looked out for one another, meaning they would know too."

It was now Jacko's turn to decide what to do next, but in the end opted to go with the flow. "Okay," he said. "Although what I'm about to tell you is confidential and might be upsetting." He was expecting some kind of reaction, but when none was forthcoming, decided to carry on. "It concerns the person responsible for the deaths of your daughter Kelly, and father Maxi Hamilton. Recent reports from the south of England, have indicated that although the suspect is now on the run, he's still managed to visit a number of old acquaintances and settle a few scores."

Steffi blinked once. "What does that mean?"

"They think he's killed at least six more people."

Steffi held his stare. "Does that mean I could be next on the list?"

Jacko shrugged. "No one can say for sure, but there's a chance he may come here."

"Why?"

Jacko thought of how best to explain. "They think this Tomovic has somehow lost the plot and is blaming everyone for the death of his brother."

"Does that 'everyone' include me?"

"Maybe."

"So what happens next?"

"We'd advise you to keep out sight for a while."

"You mean close the curtains?"

Jacko smiled. "Not exactly, we were thinking of maybe moving you and your son to a safe-house."

"No way!" Kristian declared forcefully.

"It would only be for a short while, or until we find him," added Jacko.

"I don't care. This is our home and I won't let some scumbag Serbian force us out!"

"And I agree," said Steffi. "From what you've told us, the police still have no idea where he is, meaning the search could take forever."

"There again, Mrs Freeland, he might appear on your doorstep tomorrow."

"But you don't know that."

Jacko shook his head. "No, the chances are he might never come here."

Steffi's attitude became one of defiance. "Which means, Sgt, that we are going nowhere."

Faced with such resistance, Jacko looked for a more acceptable alternative. "Okay, what if we keep an eye on you from a distance?"

"How exactly will that work?"

Jacko pointed beyond the wire fence. "We'll have a man patrol the Park at night and have an unmarked squad car sat outside your front door. With a bit of luck, that should scare him off."

"That's assuming he comes at all."

Jacko smiled. "Better to be safe than sorry."

Liverpool General Hospital

Jacko's mobile phone began to ring.

Simone nudged him in the back. "Sam, are you awake?"

"Yeah," he yawned, then realised it was 4.23 am.

"Who is it?"

"The hospital."

Simone sat up. "What's wrong?"

"According to lady on the phone, they've just had a DCI Nathan Carson admitted into A&E."

"Oh my God, is he okay?'

"I don't know, but I intend to find out."

"Give me a minute, I'm coming with you."

Notwithstanding the sun had yet to rise in the sky, Liverpool General Hospital was still a major hive of activity, none more so than the Main Reception Desk, where a frustrated Jacko and Simone met a real conundrum. "Yes Sergeant, I *can* confirm that DCI Nathan Carson has been transferred from A&E, but unfortunately can't say where."

Jacko listened to the receptionist's reply with some suspicion; how can you just lose a patient? Although in truth, was praying it wasn't the hospital morgue. Luckily all was revealed a moment later. "Ah yes, here he is," smiled the lady. "He's been sedated, and transferred to the new admissions ward; supposedly for observation."

"Observation?"

"Yes Sergeant, they think it might be gallstones."

"Well, that's a relief," sighed Simone. "I'm no medical doctor, but I know gallstones can be incredibly painful. I can also understand why they thought it might be cardiac-related. "

"Where the hell are your gallstones?" asked Jacko, as they caught the lift to the third floor.

"If you have any at all, Sam, they're usually hanging around in your gall bladder."

Jacko was thinking of asking some more questions, and then remembered Stretch Malone. If anyone knew the ins and outs of gallstones, he'd be the one to talk to. He was also surprised to discover his boss had been moved to a bed on the main ward; a situation he was less than happy with. "Excuse me, nurse, can you tell me why DCI Carson, who's a senior police officer, isn't in a private room?"

The freshly ironed blue uniform identified the lady as a busy 'Staff Nurse Jones', who looked to have other things on her mind. "I would imagine it's because the hospital is overcrowded," she said by way of explanation. "But I can assure you that we should be able to move him in the next two hours."

468

Jacko could fully understand her dilemma, yet was more concerned with the vulnerability of a defenceless Carson lying in an open ward. "That, of course, will help greatly, but in the mean time I intend to place an armed guard at the entrance, so we can more easily keep an eye on him."

"Are you expecting some kind of trouble, Sergeant?"

"Of course not," smiled Jacko. "Just a routine precaution."

The patient was halfway down the ward and propped up in bed with an array of drips attached to the back of his hand. "How we doing, Guv?'

Carson took in a lungful of air and grunted. "Okay."

"Painful?"

"Only when I laugh."

Jacko tapped his chest. "Well, at least it's not your ticker."

Carson gave a thin smile. "So they say."

"Any idea how long you're going to be in here?"

"Not sure yet, although one of the orderlies pushing the gurney reckons it could be at least a week."

Jacko indicated to the staff nurse. "She's assured me you'll have a room of your own soon. Meaning you don't have to argue about what's on the TV."

"Sod the TV, I'm more interested in how this might affect our investigation."

"I was thinking about that myself Guv. The last thing we need is another senior officer blundering about and making all the wrong decisions."

Carson winced in pain. "Which is why I'm recommending that you take over the day to day running of the S.C.U."

Jacko looked genuinely surprised. "You're not serious?"

"Of course I am. Nobody knows more about this Tomovic business than you do." He then smiled at Simone standing beside him. "What do you think, Professor?"

"Couldn't have chosen a better man myself, Nathan."

"What about Superintendent Bastion?" asked Jacko.

"Don't worry about him," grunted Carson. "I'll ring 'Fred Astaire' just before 6.00 am and tell him the good news. No doubt he'll call you a few minutes later confirming the situation."

"Talking of situations, Guv. I was hoping to present you with a long list of armed detectives who'd be willing to spend a few hours parked outside the Freeland's house. However, that looks highly unlikely at the moment."

"Short-staffed?"

Jacko nodded. "Some of the troops are away on holidays, the rest on sick leave."

"Meaning?"

"We'll have to ask Bastion if we can borrow a couple of his armed uniforms to act as temporary drivers. If he's willing to help, we can then use our own men to keep looking for Ziggy Tomovic."

"How long are we talking about?"

"I was hoping for maybe a few days, there again, it might just as easily take a couple of weeks."

"I can tell you right now, Jacko, that Bastion will swear blind he's short of men. The truth is, he'll be more concerned with the cost of overtime."

"Can't see any other solution, Guv."

"Welcome to the club," he winced again.

S.C.U.

'This should be interesting, thought Jacko as he stepped from the lift. He was also wondering how the troops would act when they discovered he'd become interim head of the S.C.U. *Let's hope they don't get the hump and make life awkward.*

But to his surprise, word of his temporary upgrade had proved to be no problem, as Stretch and Smithy stood to mock attention and saluted him.

"Glad to hear of your speedy promotion, Sir!" barked Malone.

"Same here," grinned Smithy.

"Give us a break," laughed Jacko, "Life's hard enough without you two lunatics!"

"So how is the Boss on a scale of one to ten?" asked Stretch.

"Racked with pain, which I'd say is about seven on the Richter Scale. But other than that, definitely getting there." He was about to mention gallstones, when Smithy gave him some disappointing news.

"Tufty McClellan arrived a few minutes before you did."

"Oh shit," groaned Jacko. "What does *he* want?"

"Didn't say, but as always headed straight for the Information Boards." It was obvious the jungle drums had started early and told everyone of Carson's unexpected incarceration at the General Hospital. Which if true, meant Jacko had no choice other than listen to McClellan's usual drivel. Yet that didn't necessarily mean he had to roll over like a poodle and let the nosey so-and-so inspect his Display Boards whenever he felt like!

"Can I help you, Sir?" He smiled through gritted teeth.

McClellan who'd been more interested in what was in front of his nose, rather than his immediate surroundings, turned to face him, "Aye Sergeant, I was just wondering how my good friend Nathan Carson is doing?"

Jacko gave a sarcastic smile. "The DCI is doing fine, Sir and tells me that thankfully, it's just a simple case of gallstones."

"Is that what you say?" growled Tufty. "Well let me tell you Sergeant, that I had the same problem a few years back. But with the help of the latest laser treatment, had my own billiard size ones blasted in situ. Only trouble was, it took more than a week to piss the debris down the toilet."

The thought of McClellan pissing bits of gallstone down the loo was something Jacko didn't need to think about. "Is that all, Sir?"

"Not quite," replied Tufty, who pointed to the last Display Board.

"Looking at this, Sergeant, I see you have a raft of new information regarding the late BB Benson, or Bonaparte Bunifido to give him his real name."

Damn, thought Jacko. This stuff had only just arrived by fax and even Carson was yet to see it. There again he had to admit, McClellan was first to discover the Monaco connection, so couldn't just be ignored or fobbed off. "Yes Sir," he growled in reply. "There have been a few new developments since our last chat and we've since managed to uncover some rather surprising facts about Benson's past life."

Tufty nodded to the Board. "I haven't had the chance to read it in any real detail Sergeant, but would I be right in saying the man was a bigamist?"

Jacko gave a sigh of exasperation and shook his head. "No Sir, I think that would be far from the truth."

"So, what have you discovered?"

Considering Smithy had done most of the legwork, Jacko resented the idea of having to explain it to the grumpy, short-tempered Scotsman. "It would seem BB Benson has knelt at the altar more than once," he began. "His first marriage was to an American model named Haley Lindholf, who he wed in 1984 and divorced in 1990. But within that, let's say fruitful period of time, still managed to produce two sons, Rufus and Saul. According to the reports, they left each other on good terms and were more than happy to go their own separate ways. Incidentally Sir, she still resides at their luxury family home in Palm Beach, Florida."

Tufty looked distinctly unimpressed as Jacko continued.

"His next was with a Brazilian lady, who hailed from the city of Sao Paolo. Her name was Jacinta Morales, who I'm led to believe, was famous for writing racy novels. They tied the knot in 1992, divorced in 1999 and as before managed to produce two offspring. This time, however, there was a difference in gender with her having a boy and a girl. And as with his first wife and offspring, Benson parted on more than satisfactory terms."

"How can you be so sure of this Sergeant?"

"Because we simply carried on where you left off and asked the French Police to make some discreet inquiries on our behalf. Sure enough, they discovered a Mademoiselle Anne-Marie Bunifido, residing in an exclusive penthouse apartment on the Monaco Waterfront. Apparently she was Benson's third, but this time 'common law' wife, who'd lived with him for many years. But here's a thing, when they'd asked about her late husband's supposed shady background. The Madame had literally blown her top and insisted he was a well-respected man of great integrity. She then went to great lengths in telling them about his extended family and the many times he'd invited his ex-wives and children to stay with them in Monaco.

"In conclusion, an irate Madame Bunifido is insisting we ship her missing husband's body back to France, so he can give him the burial he deserves. The French police have also decided that, should it open up a can of worms and cast a shadow on the Principality, they won't take this inquiry any further."

"Stupid frigging Frogs!" snapped McClellan.

"Nevertheless and as I've said before, it still makes me wonder why BB Benson was prepared to risk all he'd achieved in life, so as to help Maxi Hamilton kill the Tomovic brothers."

"The twisted loyalty of two thieves springs to mind, Sergeant."

"That maybe," said Jacko. "But just like you, I've watched the warehouse video a couple of times and I'm of the opinion that if it hadn't been for Ziggy finding Hamilton's gun lying by his leg, BB Benson would have done us all a favour and strangled the bastard to death with his bare hands."

"Are you trying to say he was some kind of hero, Sergeant?"

"No, Sir. I'm simply voicing an opinion."

"Well, I'm not sure everybody would agree with your so-called 'opinion'."

"I'm sure you're right, Sir," smiled Jacko.

A somewhat mollified Tufty changed the subject. "Talking of Ziggy, do you have any idea where he might be?"

Jacko shook his head. "Not at the moment Sir, although most of the country are on high alert and the public have been warned not to approach him under any circumstances."

"Are you still proposing to stakeout the Freeland's place?"

"Sir?"

Tufty smiled. "I've heard a whisper that Ziggy is holding some kind of grudge or vendetta against the Freelands. And that being the case, was wondering if you were thinking of placing the family under surveillance?"

Holy shit, thought Jacko, *this pain knows more about our operations than I do!* He was about to tell him that nothing had yet been decided, when Tufty hit him with another bombshell.

"It's also come to my attention that should this operation go ahead, there's a danger it might be compromised by a lack of manpower."

For a second Jacko was lost for words. "Sir?"

"You're short of men, Sergeant, that's why I'm offering you my services."

"Services? What kind of services?"

"The type that only many years of experience in the field can bring, and of course, one shouldn't forget the expertise that goes with it."

"Excuse me, Sir," stuttered Jacko. "But you've been retired from the force for close on fifteen years."

"A mere technicality," sneered Tufty, who waved his official pass in the air. "Besides, this should give me all the authority I need!"

Jacko wasn't sure whether to laugh or cry at the pantomime taking place before him. "I hope you do realise, Sir, that what you're holding isn't a warrant card of any kind, it's just a Visitor's Pass?"

"Aye Sergeant, but as I said, it'll do for now."

A still bemused Jacko asked, "Can I ask exactly how you intend to help us, Sir?"

Private Room, 32c

Taff the Mack had a secret; he was terrified of hospitals and the merest whiff of liniment would make him go weak at the knees. This fear was mostly due to his Uncle Ivor warning that although you went *in* whole, it didn't necessarily mean you came *out in* one piece; especially when the surgeon had mistakenly removed the wrong limb. So it was with some relief he'd discovered that Nathan Carson was in a private room and not on a ward full of people awaiting the Grim Reaper. Even so, his own fear levels nearly went through the roof, when he opened the door and heard a loud groaning sound from inside.

"Is he alright Jacko?"

"Yeah, he's okay Taff, it's just his reaction to the bad news."

"What bad news?"

"Tufty McClellan is looking to become part of the Park surveillance team."

"Jesus Mary and Joseph! Does he mean it, or was he just having a laugh?"

Jacko gave a sarcastic laugh of his own. "Didn't sound like it to me."

"Are you sure he was being serious?"

"He was when I spoke with him early this morning."

"Why?"

"God knows. But since he discovered that BB Benson was living a lavish life in Monaco, he's been hanging around the S.C.U. looking for anything that might inflate his ego. Where, we assume he must have heard about the shortage of men and offered to help."

"So how exactly is Tufty going to come to our aid?"

"Says he's going to endow us with the benefit of his vast experience and sit alongside the driver."

Taff looked even more perplexed. "Does he know this is going to be an armed and extremely dangerous operation?"

"Oh yeah, but that didn't seem to bother him one bit. In fact he was delighted. Said he'd learnt how to handle firearms back in the eighties."

Carson interrupted with a painful grimace. "He's right Taff and it all stems from when the IRA tried to kill Maggie Thatcher by blowing up her hotel in Brighton. In the massive investigation that followed, all senior police officers were ordered to undertake courses in self-protection. So it goes without saying that McClellan would have learnt how to use a handgun."

"Yeah, but we're not talking about a gang of Irish Republicans here Guv. This Ziggy is one vicious bastard, who's happy to slaughter anyone who gets in his way."

"What about Superintendent Bastion, does he know about this?"

"Yes Taff, I rang him the minute the Wee Jock had left the room."

"And?'

"He thought the whole thing was hilarious and couldn't stop laughing."

"So what the hell does that mean?"

"What it means Taff, is that we haven't quite gotten rid of him yet," groaned Carson. "And because Bastion was so impressed with his unearthing of the Monaco business, he's prepared to let Tufty hang around the S.C.U. for another week or so."

"Hang on, Nathan, as I understand it, McClellan's role is purely that of an advisor, which in my book means he's not even in the bloody Force!"

"I know that, Taff, but it would appear the Good Lord and Superintendent Bastion move in much more mysterious ways."

"I wonder if Cressida is behind all this?"

"Who's she Taff?"

"McClellan's wife and someone who needs to be avoided at all times."

"Cuffin' hell, you could be right Taff, and also explain why he's decided to haunt us at the S.C.U."

"Anyone want to tell me what this is all about?" asked Jacko.

"Cressida McClellan was, and probably still is, the driving force behind Tufty's rise to fame. But as everyone knows fame always comes with a price and unfortunately for Tufty, she was the one he had to pay."

Part Fourteen

'A Day in the Life'
Waytree Crescent

12.30 am

"You okay with country music?" asked the driver.

"Yeah, no problem," grunted his partner. "As long as it's not too loud." Ignoring his plea, the driver tweaked up the volume a fraction, hoping to hear Willy Nelson rather than the person sat next to him. "Looks like a quiet night," he added by way of pointless conversation.

"That's because everyone's asleep in bed," his partner scowled. But a second later noticed some unexpected movement in his wing mirror. "Hello, I didn't know they delivered drinks at this time of night?"

The driver was instantly awake. "What's that?"

"Looks like one of ours is bringing us some refreshments."

The driver had but a second to see a uniformed officer appear alongside the car carrying two steaming mugs of coffee. He was just about to warn there shouldn't be anyone else in the Crescent, when his partner pushed the 'open' button.

"Wait! Wait!" he screamed. But it was too late. The window was already halfway down and a face appeared in the gap.

"Morning boys," grinned Ziggy. "Brought you something to drink." But instead of hot coffee, found they were staring at a gun fitted with a silencer. Without saying another word, a smiling Ziggy pulled the trigger twice, killing both men instantly, the blood spurting out of their heads like two mini fountains. His next move was to pour the still warm coffee into the gutter and drop the empty mugs into the passenger footwell.

With a smile on his face and the pretence that all was well, he began a mini conversation with the two dead men and minutes later, waved them goodbye. Keeping to his plan, he turned towards the Freelands' house, strolled up the garden path and once within the shadows, went in search of a means of entry. First on the list was what looked to be the side entrance to the kitchen area. This he recalled, was an opaque glass-panelled door set back in a small recess, so as to allow room to store a couple of rubbish bins. It was also the perfect place for him to conceal his knapsack and pay a quick visit to the two now 'sleeping policemen'.

A quick flash of his torch indicated this might be the easiest way of gaining entry, but past experience warned that breaking glass was both noisy and messy. He was still running his fingers around the edge of the door when to his surprise, heard a solid *click* and watched it open a fraction. Suspicious of such good fortune, Ziggy took a step backwards and pointed the Berretta straight ahead. But instead of hostile gunfire, heard a 'meowing' sound and watched a large white cat skip past his ankle and squeeze its way inside.

An ambush? he wondered. *Well, if it was, the two dead suckers in the squad car didn't know about it.* But no matter the reason, his real concern was why the door had opened in the first place. A closer look said it wasn't exactly ancient, there again, hardly brand new. So, maybe someone had innocently forgotten to drop the catch. Whatever the reason, it meant he now had an easy entry, but still needed to be careful. Once inside, the faint aroma of fried onions made his stomach rumble and a fleeting (*should have eaten earlier*) moment crossed his mind.

On the other side of the kitchen he could see an open door, which he hoped would give him access to the rest of the house and as always, he was right. Beyond was a hallway that ran the length of the bungalow, the improved light helping to reveal six more rooms; all of which he intended to investigate. The nearest to him had disappointingly proved to be no more than a closet full of coats, his torch highlighting a mixture of summer and winter clothes. The one opposite however was much more interesting. In here was a large spacious lounge, filled with a range of comfortable furniture and an oversized TV. But his eyes were immediately drawn to the holiday snap taking pride of place on a nearby table.

It was an exact copy of the one in his shirt pocket.

Next was the house bathroom, whose still damp walls were clear evidence someone had recently taken a shower. Three paces across the hall and he found exactly what he was looking for, the master bedroom. Switching off his pencil-torch and keeping the gun out of sight, he turned the handle and stepped inside. The room was in darkness, the only illumination coming from the radio alarm clock sat on the bedside table, dim, yet still bright enough to outline someone sleeping beneath the covers.

A sudden movement to his right made him jump and point the gun in that direction, only to see his own reflection mirrored in the wardrobe doors. Amused at his own foolishness, he moved to the side of the bed and gave a smile. It was the blonde girl's mother. He then remembered, there were other places yet to be investigated and if necessary, loose ends to be taken care of. In short, he needed to ensure no one interrupted his forthcoming half hour of pleasure. Quietly retracing his steps, he slipped out into the hallway and moved to the next room along, which he discovered was that of the dead girl.

Panning the narrow beam torch back and forth in the dark, Ziggy was amazed to see the multitude of pictures and posters adorning the walls. It was as if the bedroom were now a loving shrine, with the girl's face portrayed in every photo. Then from the corner of his eye, saw the same holiday photo sat on a shelf above the bed. Looking closer, he recognised the smiling boy and recalled a news report saying the girl had a younger brother named Kristian: whom he had yet to find.

It was only then did he remember that there was one more room to search. Moving along the passage, he held the gun at the ready and slowly opened the door, but to his disappointment found it empty. The heavy metal posters pinned to the walls and the Spanish acoustic guitar hanging above the bed, reminded him of his own teenage room back home in Erdivos. A more detailed search however, had confirmed that the room was indeed unoccupied. *So where the fuck is he?* he hissed.

Judging by the smoothness of the covers, it was obvious the bed hadn't been slept in, suggesting the boy might have stayed over at one of his friends. Which meant this was an unexpected and unforeseen hitch. His plan had been to kill him first and then his mother, but only when he'd finished playing with her tits. Closing the door, Ziggy gave a smile, *the boy might not know it, but tonight was definitely his lucky one.*

Time was also of importance. The two dead policemen he assumed would have to call in regularly and confirm their status. Which he estimated should be on the hour and give him more than enough time to do what was needed and when done, vanish into the night. Meanwhile, back at the perfumed boudoir, everything appeared to be as before. The woman was still asleep, the only sound, her steady soft rhythmic breathing. Treading carefully so as not to disturb her, he moved to the side of the bed and began his routine. The gun he returned to its holster, thus making it much easier for him to unbuckle his belt and unzip his fly. Next came the knife hidden in his boot, its familiar feel bringing an even bigger smile to his face.

Whenever possible, he liked to have a certain amount of spontaneity, plus the ability to surprise his victims. Yet fear had also played a major part in these rituals and tonight would be no different. Taking hold of the bedclothes in one hand, he whipped them back in one sweeping move and exposed the woman lying face down on the bed. Instantly awake, but confused as to what was happening, she began to struggle and cry out. Having experienced this type of reaction many times before, Ziggy had the perfect answer.

Leaping on the bed, he landed astride her upper thighs, put his hands on her shoulders and held her down. Then in an act of pure malice, placed the blade against her left cheek and hissed. "Shhhhhh…" As predicted, the woman froze in fear as he leaned in and whispered, "Silence, or lots of pain!"

This more than anything had caused her to fall silent and give him the opportunity to do a little exploring of his own. Aware of the dangers DNA might bring, Ziggy had always taken measures to ensure he didn't leave anything behind. Yet at the moment, none of that seemed to matter. He was more interested in running his hands over the woman's silky soft skin and curious to see what she looked like in the flesh. His torch however, was less than adequate for such a task and remembering the bedside light, reached across and switched it on.

The result was both instantaneous and satisfying, as a warm even glow spread itself over the woman's body. In the soft light, he was able to see that other than a skimpy thong, she was completely naked and for reasons he couldn't quite fathom, began to feel some sexual arousal.

Yet if that was a surprise, then what happened next was equally mind blowing. For the first time in fuck knows how long, Ziggy's dick began to grow into a real *hard on*! But this didn't feel like the usual frustrating *Semi* that would require some extra encouragement by way of masturbation. This was the kind of erection his brother Marko had once described as a super *Humdinger!*

Excited at what might lie ahead, Ziggy dropped his shorts to his knees, thus ensuring there'd be plenty of room around his crotch when needed. Once free of its cotton constraints and as if it had a life of its own, Ziggy's erection continued to grow unabated. "Baby, baby, baby," he crowed and began to wave it from side to side like a weapon of war. He was just about to cut the skimpy thong in half and get down to business, when he heard an odd rustling sound from behind.

For a second he thought it was just his imagination, but when he turned to look, had the shock of his life. Without noticing, the wardrobe door closest to him had slid open 18 inches and an even bigger surprise lay in store. Less than six feet away and pointed straight at his head, was the barrel of a shotgun. "What the fuck?" Ziggy whispered in disbelief.

1.30 am

With sirens wailing and blue lights flashing, Jacko screeched around the bend, put his foot to the floor and raced up Park Drive.

"Take it easy, Sam," warned Simone, as they hurtled past Junkies Corner and sped in the direction of Waytree Crescent.

"Okay, okay," he muttered, but didn't ease off; he was more concerned in what was lighting up the night sky ahead. Yet something said he might be too late when he saw a couple of armed SO18 Specials guarding the entrance. *Oh shit*, he thought, *if this mob are here, then things really are bad.* Skidding to a halt, he clambered from the car and held his ID above his head. "I'm DS Jackson from the S.C.U. and the lady with me is Dr Simone le Roux, Head of Forensics."

The officer in charge quickly scanned both sets of credentials and once satisfied, lowered his gun and let them through. However, instead of the usual sleepy tree-lined enclave, the Crescent looked more like a mini-war zone. This mostly due to the Emergency Services running around like a horde of headless chickens.

"Something tells me I've been here before," grunted Jacko.

"Me too," agreed Simone, as they squeezed their way past a couple of squad cars parked at the bottom of the slope. She was about to make another observation, when she saw a familiar face in the crowd. "Sam, Sam," she cried. "Look who's there!"

Jacko followed to where her finger was pointed and gave a sigh of relief. "Oh yes," he whooped in delight, before crossing the road and tapping him on the shoulder. "Excuse me mate, but someone said you were dead."

A surprised look appeared on Smithy's face. "Sarge?"

"I had a call twenty minutes ago saying two of the surveillance team had been taken out and seeing as your shift began at 12.00 am, I'd naturally assumed you were one of them."

Smithy looked just as relieved. "I'm just glad the lorry broke down outside my apartment block."

"Lorry, what lorry?"

"The one delivering furniture to the top floor."

"What, at 11.00 pm at night?"

Smithy shrugged. "It's a strange world we live in, Sarge."

"So how did that affect you?"

"It was blocking the main entrance and I couldn't get my car out."

Jacko shook his head. "Meaning?"

"I was going to be late for work."

"What happened then?"

"I rang despatch, told them about the problem and said I might not get there until after midnight. They said okay, and we'll try to organise a temporary replacement."

Jacko had a sinking feeling in his stomach. "So who did they get?"

Smithy pointed across the street. "I think you'll find him in there."

As normal and in order to keep the crime scene intact, the unmarked squad car was enclosed within a large white Forensic tent. Yet when he saw who was in the passenger seat, his eyes nearly jumped out of their sockets.

"Holy Christ," he spluttered. "Tufty McClellan?"

Smithy nodded without answering.

"How the hell did he get there?"

"Good question, Sarge. But from what I hear, Hughie turned up at the Dispatch Desk, waved his visitors pass and said he was the stand in surveillance officer. The armed driver, who didn't know him from Adam, had no choice other than let him come on-board. I reached headquarters at around 12.30 am, went for a quick cup of coffee and then the place went crazy."

"Because of the shootings?"

Smithy nodded again. "That and the attack on the Freelands."

Jacko was immediately concerned. "Oh hell, I'd forgotten about them. Are they okay?"

"Yeah I think so. Badly shaken, but mostly unscathed."

Jacko pointed to McClellan. "Do we know who's responsible for this?"

"Not yet. I got here a few minutes before you did, but judging by the bullet in the head style shootings, I'd say it has to be Ziggy."

Jacko groaned. "I did warn the Freelands that Tomovic might come visiting, but they just wouldn't listen!"

"Well I'd say they're both lucky to be alive."

"Want to tell me what we do know?"

"Whoever killed McClellan and the driver, sneaked into Waytree Park and cut through the wire fence at the rear of the Freeland's place."

Jacko was genuinely surprised. "That fence, I'm told is 18 ft. high, has a 2 ft. thick hedge in front of it and supposed to be virtually impregnable."

Smithy lifted an eyebrow. "Not if you've got a pair of bolt cutters stowed in your haversack. They reckon Ziggy must have spent an hour nibbling his way through the bushes; made himself a regular king-size rabbit hole."

"Forensics found a small flask of coffee in the haversack and two empty mugs in the car. Seems Ziggy delivered two warm drinks and a couple of hot shots to go with it."

"How could he possibly do that? This place is supposed to be watertight."

"That's what I thought, but there's something else you should see, Sarge."

Jacko wasn't sure what could be so important, until a Forensic opened McClellan's jacket and revealed a hidden shoulder holster.

"Hughie has a gun?"

Smithy nodded. "My friend here tells me it's a classic Smith & Wesson .38 revolver."

"What the hell was he going to do with that?"

"No idea Sarge. Shoot Ziggy in the arse and hopefully play the triumphant hero?"

Jacko was still remembering Carson's story of the Brighton Bombing, when Simone appeared in the tent. "Sam, Smithy? You're both needed in the house, now." Next stop was a pair of overshoes and sterile gloves, but once inside the bungalow, knew he was on much more familiar ground. To his left lay the warm friendly kitchen where he'd only recently drank coffee. Straight ahead the lounge and to his right the bedrooms; each illuminated by an array of Forensic lighting.

Simone however, was interested in the Master Bedroom only. "This, I've been told is where all the action is."

"Action?"

"Yes Sam, there's another dead body in there."

"Anyone we know?"

"I'm not sure."

"Who's running the show?"

"Steve Delaney."

Relieved to discover it was his favourite Ballistics expert, Jacko stepped through the door and found the man himself standing in front of a mirrored wardrobe.

"Morning Sarge, how are we doing?"

Jacko stretched his neck muscles and grunted. "Still trying to wake up."

Steve grinned. "Should be like us, always on duty."

Jacko gave him a friendly finger. "Yeah?"

"Yeah! But I have to warn you, gentlemen, that this is not for the faint-hearted."

"That's okay, mate, we're like elephants, very thick-skinned," retorted Smithy.

Steve smiled again and pointed to the blood-stained bed. "According to the lady of the house, she awoke in the dark to find a someone sitting on her back. The man, she said, was heavy, had a long thin knife and was threatening to kill her if she made a sound. Unable to see his face, and thinking he was about to slit her throat, she was more than grateful to hear two loud bangs and feel him disappear into thin air."

Jacko paused before asking. "Is it Ziggy?"

"We think so."

"What does *think* mean?"

"We're sure, and we're not sure."

"When will we know?"

"When we've finished doing our investigation."

"Okay, is he dead?"

"As a doornail."

"Well, thank Christ for that, but my other question is, how did he die?"

"Someone shot him, twice."

Jacko was stunned. "You're kidding me?"

Steve shook his head.

"When?"

"About an hour ago."

"Where is he now?"

"Right behind you, straddled between the bed and the wall."

Damn, thought Jacko. In the noisy crowded room, he'd been more interested in the wardrobes, rather than the Forensic taking photographs a few feet away. Yet was still heartened to see pair of black leather *Doc Martins* boots protruding from the between gap. (Ziggy wore them all the time.) Although what came next wasn't quite what he was expecting; the boots were attached to a bald-headed, clean-shaven policeman, who didn't remotely look like the bearded Serbian killer. More disappointment lay ahead, when he saw most of the dead man's lower body was covered in blood and half his face was missing.

"Holy shit, what a mess!"

"You said it, Sergeant, and judging by his bogus uniform, it's easy to see why McClellan thought 'PC Plod' was delivering free coffees."

Jacko agreed that in the dark, it would be near impossible to say if the policeman was the real thing. Yet at the same time was ready to pose another question. "Are you sure this is our man?"

"Everything points to it being him. We have the gun he used to kill McClellan and the driver. Plus a bucketload of his DNA and a snapshot of the girl and her family hidden in his shirt pocket."

Jacko nodded. "Okay, so any idea who killed him?"

"At first, we assumed they came through the door and shot him from behind."

"What? Do you mean like a stalker, or assassin?"

Steve nodded. "Yes, something like that. I would imagine he had plenty of enemies in his time."

"I know a few dead Serbian ones," murmured Jacko.

"But we've since discovered his killer was actually hiding in the wardrobe."

Jacko was intrigued. "Any idea who?"

"Not yet."

"Okay, are you sure that's why he was there?"

"I didn't say it was a he."

"You mean it might have been a she?"

"I didn't say that either. At the moment, we're not sure who it was."

"So why were they there?"

"To kill him, of course."

Jacko sighed and pointed to the body. "You'd need more than a pea-shooter to do that kind of damage."

"A .410 shotgun would fit the bill. Although something tells me this wasn't one of those quick, 'bang, bang, you're dead' situations. I'm of the opinion this was a carefully planned operation designed to kill him."

Jacko was all ears. "Want to tell us how?"

Steve moved back to the wardrobe, stepped inside and turned to face them. "Whoever killed Ziggy must have known about the interconnecting door from the girl's bedroom and used it to gain access to this wardrobe." He then held an imaginary gun to his shoulder and pointed it at the bed. "I'm guessing they were standing right here, when he or she slid open the door and found Ziggy bare-arsed and ready to rape the woman. Although we've since discovered that Ziggy, or whoever killed him, must have had some kind of confrontation, or Mexican Standoff."

"In what way?"

"According to Mrs Freeland, the man sat on top of her was facing the window with his back to the wardrobe. Yet something must have made him turn, see the gun and realise he was now in a life and death situation. Having no other options, I think he threw the knife and tried to kill whoever was hiding in the wardrobe. Which he did and missed."

"How can you be so sure?"

"Because Simone, the knife is right here next to my head."

It was only when he moved his shoulder to one side, did they see the dagger impaled in the side of the melamine wall.

"Wow, it must have missed them by a bloody whisker."

Steve shrugged. "It doesn't matter, he still missed."

"So what happened next?"

The gunman fired once, but kept the trajectory shoulder high, so they wouldn't hit Mrs Freeland in the process."

"How can you tell?" asked Smithy.

"By the size of the gun and height of the lead pellets embedded in the wall. They'd hoped the impact would be enough to either kill, or seriously injure the guy attacking Mrs Freeland."

"What about the stomach wound, Steve?"

"Ah, that's a different story and you're right about the gunman taking no chances with him surviving. Which is why they reloaded the gun and moved to where Ziggy was lying beside the bed."

The room suddenly came to a standstill, as Steve re-enacted the scene by stepping from the wardrobe and walking to where the bloodied body lay. He then pointed his imaginary shotgun at Ziggy's crotch and said, "Boom!"

"Jesus," gasped Smithy. "Do you mean he blew his balls off?"

Steve nodded. "Every last shred and within minutes, our serial killer has bled to death."

Simone glanced to the heavens and whispered, "Amen to that."

Jacko shook his head in disbelief. "And here's me thinking he'd been shot in the stomach."

"I wouldn't worry too much, Sergeant, after all it's not that far away."

Jacko changed the subject. "Tell me about the gun, Steve."

Happy to be back on safer ground, the Ballistics expert pointed to the pebbled-dashed wall. "Looking at the size of the 'spread', I'd say the weapon was a single barrel .410 shotgun, which would normally be used in shooting birds or rabbits."

"Are we talking about a Ladies Gun?"

"Yes Sergeant, that's exactly what I mean. Because as you know, a .12 bore shotgun has a real kick when you pull the trigger. Whereas, the .410 is both lightweight and much easier to handle."

"What about cartridges? As I remember it, when you unload a shotgun, the empty shell cases usually end up on the floor."

Steve shook his head. "That would depend on the gun. Some eject the shells automatically, but some don't. So if they did fire twice, which we assume they must have, they might just as easily picked up the shells and put them in their pocket."

Jacko pointed to the bloodied body. "Do you think a woman could have done this? And don't tell me that I'm the Detective."

Steve gave a shrug. "At the moment I couldn't say who did it. The only thing I do know; is that they took the gun with them."

"How do you know?"

"Because Mrs Freeland's son said so in his statement."

Jacko had completely forgotten about them. "Kristian saw something?"

"As I understand it."

"What exactly did he say?"

"Near enough the same as his mother's statement. Says he was fast asleep in bed and awoken by two loud bangs. Fearing the worst, he got dressed and left his bedroom. As he stepped out into the hall, he spotted a shadowy figure hurrying into the kitchen and then, supposedly out into the garden."

"He didn't think of running after them?"

"Not according to his statement. Said he was more interested in making sure his mother was safe. Which is understandable under the circumstances."

"What else did he say?"

"He was convinced the person was carrying a gun."

"Are you sure?"

"That's what he said."

Jacko was thoughtful. "What happened next?"

"He ran into the bedroom, grabbed a dressing gown for his mother, who he insists was in a bad way and once assured the way was clear, raced for the safety of the Crescent."

Jacko turned to Smithy. "Where are the Freelands now?"

"They've taken them down to Headquarters for their own safety. The mother was terrified the gunman might come back and kill them later."

"Okay, get on the blower Smithy and ask Central for more men. Tell them it's urgent and explain how an armed and dangerous fugitive might still be on the loose. In the meantime, let's start checking the Crescent, as well as the Park, there's always a chance he or she could be hiding in the bushes somewhere."

3.30 am

Jacko dropped Simone outside her flat and gave a wink. "Try and get some sleep Professor; I'll see you later."

"Aren't you coming with me?"

"No. I need to head back to the office and check a few things out."

"Won't it wait?"

"Sorry. It could be important."

"Want to tell me?"

"Not yet. But if true, you'll be first to know."

A frustrated Simone watched as Jacko disappeared in the direction of police headquarters, where, other than a bolshie drunk hoping for a free night in the cells, the reception area was deserted. Jacko, however, didn't want company, all he needed was some information from the man behind the desk. "Morning Wayne, I'd like to talk with the woman and her son, who arrived here about two hours ago."

The uniform scanned the screen. "What's her name again Sarge? "

"Steffi Freeland."

"Oh yes, I remember her. She was the tasty blonde bird wearing the silk dressing gown. We were told to keep them somewhere safe. So put I them in room 402 on the fourth floor."

It was no secret that most offenders, be it drunks or otherwise, would be processed through the ground floor areas and if charged banged-up in the cells below. Whereas, special guests like Steffi and Kristian, were kept in a more secure environment, thus ensuring no mad gunman could get near them. Jacko was just about to press the button for the fourth floor, when he saw Smithy waving for him to hold the lift.

"Jeez mate, you look done in, how are you?"

"Rubbed out Sarge, but improving by the minute."

Jacko sensed some good news. "Heard anything from the search teams?"

Smithy grinned. "As expected, the Waytree mob drew a blank. Then two sharp-eyed patrolmen noticed a green VW campervan parked badly in a private lane. At first they'd thought nothing of it, until a fast licence check revealed the vehicle is registered to a Polish National called Jan Lizinski."

"I've heard that name before."

"And so you should Sarge. Lizinski just happens to live in Walthamstow and we assume shot both the Jamaicans dead in Maxi Hamilton's warehouse."

"You mean the gunman lying dead in the back of the Transit van?"

"That's him."

Jacko began to get excited. "This has to be the same Jan who visited the plumbing centre with Marko Tomovic."

"You've got it."

Jacko closed his eyes as if in mock prayer. "Tell me it's Christmas already, Smithy."

"There's more, Sarge. Ziggy's camper van had blackout curtains all around, but a torch beam revealed a couple of fishing rods lying on the rear shelf."

"And we all know he loves to go fishing, don't we?"

Smithy's grin widened. "From what I've heard, it was his favourite pastime."

"What else did they find?"

"Nothing at the moment. They're worried the van might be booby-trapped, so asked the Bomb Disposal Squad to check it out."

"Damn, how long that's going to take?"

"Not sure, but I would imagine they'll need to blow the doors off."

Jacko knew he should be grateful, but was more worried they might do a 'Butch Cassidy' and blow the campervan to pieces, thus destroying lots of vital evidence in the process.

Smithy meantime, was curious. "Where are we going now Sarge?"

"To have a word with the Freelands about tonight's break-in."

"Something wrong?"

"Not really. I just need to ask them a few questions whilst everything is still fresh in their minds."

"It's nearly 4.00 am Sarge, do you think they'll be awake?"

Jacko nodded slowly, "Yeah, I'm not sure why, but something tells me they won't be asleep just yet."

The same couldn't be said for the young uniform nodding off in the chair outside room 402. Who was instantly awake when he saw the two Detectives exiting the lift, "Morning Sir," he muttered, whilst straightening his tie. Smithy instantly recognised him as a member of the opposing quiz team, who regularly thrashed his own in the Grosvenor Bar.

"Swotty Swinton, isn't it?"

"Yes Sir," he replied in embarrassment.

"How are things?"

"Okay Sir, everything's fine, nothing to report."

"Any sign of our guests?"

"How do you mean, Sir?"

"Are they up and about?"

"Yes I think so. In fact they ordered some tea and sandwiches from the Canteen about ten minutes ago."

Jacko rubbed his stomach. "I could murder a full English breakfast; what about you, Smithy?"

"I can smell the sausage and black pudding from here."

A confused Swotty didn't know what to think, as Jacko tapped on the door and waited. A few moments of silence went by before a familiar face appeared in the doorway.

"Hi Kristian, how are you?"

"Sergeant Jackson," he said with a surprised look. "I wasn't expecting to see you."

Jacko returned the smile. "Thought I might drop by and make sure you're both comfortable."

Kristian shrugged. "It's a little cramped, but other than that, we're fine."

Jacko decided to add to the overcrowding. "Can we come in?"

"Yes, of course," he said apologetically. "My mother's fixing her hair and stuff in the washroom; should be out in a minute."

Having used room 402 many times in the past, Jacko was well acquainted with its layout. He'd often sat on one of the two sofas that doubled as temporary beds and gone for a pee in the small washroom, but luxury hotel it certainly wasn't. That said, it did have a fair-sized coffee table where one might spread out some paperwork if needed. He was about to take a seat, when the washroom door opened, and Steffi Freeland stepped into the room.

"Oh, hello Sergeant Jackson, how nice to see you."

Under the circumstances and for someone who'd been just inches from death, the lady with the classic features looked to be keeping it all together. It was easy to see why Wayne at the front desk had been so impressed with the silk dressing gown; it definitely didn't hide much in the way of female shape. Although at the moment, Jacko wasn't interested in such fanciful thoughts: only the here and now.

"How are you, Mrs Freeland?"

She closed her eyes briefly before replying. "I'm okay. Just trying to get over what happened tonight."

Remembering the manner of Kelly's brutal death and their first tearful meeting at the hospital, Jacko was happy to give her some less painful news. "I'm not sure if anyone has told you, but Ziggy Tomovic is dead."

"Oh, thank God," she whispered.

Kristian was more enthusiastic. "Get in, you beauty!" he whooped.

Steffi however wanted more answers. "How can you be so sure Sergeant?"

"Because somebody shot him twice. Once in the head and once in, let's call them his unmentionables. Which means he won't be back to terrorise anyone again."

"I know it's wrong, Sergeant and I know I shouldn't say this, but I'm just glad the bastard got what he deserved!"

"And I imagine that whoever pulled the trigger was thinking the exact same thing," added Jacko. "But we're still looking to discover who that person might be. Which is why I'd like to ask you a couple of questions."

"We did give a statement to the police lady," interrupted Kristian.

"I'm aware of that," smiled Jacko. "But I just want to double check a couple of things, if that's okay?"

Steffi smiled back. "Yes, of course Sergeant, how can we help?"

"I'd like you to cast your mind back and tell me about the attack itself. Other than Ziggy, did you see or hear anyone else in the room?"

Steffi shook her head. "No, I don't think so."

Jacko looked sympathetic. "I can imagine how hard this is for you, but these questions are important."

Steffi waited patiently for the next one.

"Can you remember him turning to look behind?"

"Sorry? I'm not sure I understand?"

"At the moment, all the evidence points to a gunman hiding in the wardrobe and we think Tomovic turned his head to see whoever that was."

The blue eyes looked near to tears. "I don't know if he did or didn't Sergeant. All I do remember is a loud explosive bang, followed by smoke everywhere. At that point, I thought I was going to be next, until I heard another loud bang and someone running out of the room."

"Excuse me? Are you saying someone actually left the room?"

Steffi hesitated. "I think so, but I was frightened and confused with what was going on around me."

Jacko nodded sympathetically and waited for more.

"I was lying face down on the bed desperately trying not to move, when Kristian ran in and gave me my dressing gown. He said it was too dangerous to stay and we had to get out as soon as possible."

"Kristian?"

"That's just the way it happened, Sergeant."

"Want to tell me in your own words, just for the record?"

"Sure. I was awoken by a strange muffled bang and thought I'd been dreaming. But a few seconds later, heard another one and realised it was coming from somewhere in the house."

"You say you were asleep?"

"Yeah, it took me a few seconds to climb out of bed, throw on some kit and cross the room."

"What happened next?"

"I ran out into the hallway and caught a fleeting glimpse of a shadowy figure heading into the kitchen."

"Could you see their face, or maybe what they looked like?"

"Nah, it was too dark."

Jacko thought for a second. "Can you at least say whether they were male or female?"

Kristian shrugged. "Not really, but now that I think about it, I suppose there's nothing to say it couldn't have been a woman."

"What makes you say that?"

"I don't know, maybe it was the way they moved."

"What else did you see?"

"As I said it was dark, but I think either he or she might have been carrying a gun."

Jacko and Smithy exchanged glances. "Are you absolutely sure?"

Kristian shrugged again. "I did hear two bangs and could see smoke hanging in the air; so what else could it have been?"

Jacko was about to ask another question, when the door suddenly opened and a familiar sounding voice filled the air. "Good morning, Sergeant Jackson. I hope I'm not interrupting anything important? Especially as these two people are my clients and nobody talks to them unless I say so!"

"Oh shit," whispered Smithy. "It's Hamilton's solicitor and the tasty-looking bird from SEL."

Aware their impromptu interview was over, Jacko thought it best to explain their presence in the room. "Good morning, Mr Levi. When we heard there might be another hitman on the loose, we moved Mrs Freeland and her son here for their own safety. We were also hoping to ascertain any more information that might help us solve the case."

Clinton looked unimpressed. "I'm sure you were, Sergeant, but I don't need to tell you that Mrs Freeland and her son have already given their statements, which as far as I'm concerned, should be the end of the matter. It's plain to see that both are traumatised and exhausted by tonight's events. So if you don't mind, it would be greatly appreciated if you might give us some time so I can speak with my clients and, when ready, leave."

4.10 am

Outside room 402, Smithy posed a question, "What time does your shift finish, Swotty?"

"6.00 am," he'd replied.

"I don't suppose you know who came second at the Battle of Hastings?"

"Sorry?" he'd asked in confusion.

Smithy smiled sympathetically and patted him on the head. "It's alright mate, no one's perfect."

It was only when they'd reached the hi-speed lifts, did he ask a more important question. "Where to now Sarge, up or down?"

Jacko hesitated. 'Up' meant the S.C.U. and more work, whereas 'Down' would take them both in the direction of home and a few hours' sleep. But at the moment, he didn't have much choice. "I need to check some things out Smithy. Look for somewhere to grab a few hours' kip and meet me in the S.C.U. around 7.00 am."

Smithy gave a grateful nod. "Okay Sarge, will do."

4.43 am

Other than the night cleaner emptying the wastepaper baskets, the S.C.U. was deserted. In the quiet of Carson's office, Jacko was so engrossed in the report he was reading, he hadn't noticed someone standing in the doorway.

"Oh, hello Sir, I didn't hear you come in."

Bastion pointed to his leather moccasins. "That's because these don't have steel tips, Sergeant."

Jacko smiled. Judging by the rest of his clothes, casual jacket, denim jeans and crumpled tee shirt, the Superintendent must have forgone his usual tracksuit and trainers. It was also rare for a senior officer to be so self-deprecating, especially when it came to his beloved *Fred Astaire* shoes. Still, judging by the look on his face he wasn't here just to make jokes.

"What's going on, Sergeant? My mobile is in near meltdown from the people screaming in my ear!"

Jacko rubbed his chin. "I'm not sure how to tell you this Sir, but ex-Commander Hughie McClellan was shot dead tonight."

Bastion's face turned grey. "Shot dead? How? Where?"

"On a surveillance operation."

"Surveillance operation? What bloody surveillance operation?"

Jacko chose his words carefully. "Because of the threat to the Freeland family, we've had a couple of teams working around the clock at 'Waytree Crescent'. For reasons I'm just beginning to understand, it would appear McClellan and his driver were gunned down just after midnight."

"Good God," whispered Bastion. "By whom?"

"Ziggy Tomovic."

"Hang on! Isn't he this serial killer you're supposed to be searching for?"

"Yes Sir."

"Then how in God's name was he able to shoot McClellan right under your bloody noses, and how could Hughie be part of this surveillance operation?"

"He replaced another member of my Team without having the proper authorisation and Tomovic supposedly took them both by surprise."

"What?"

"Yes, Sir. One of my men was unexpectedly delayed, which meant he couldn't make it to HQ on time. So he called in and advised despatch they would need to find someone else to take his place. That's when the ex-Commander has decided to take himself down to the lower operations area and inform the Duty Officer he was the new relief."

"Good grief, you're not serious?"

Jacko shrugged. "I'm afraid so, Sir."

"What time was this?"

"11.30 pm."

"And Hughie McClellan was still here in the S.C.U.?"

"Oh yes. No matter the time of day, you could always find him hanging about either reading the latest reports, or eyeing up the Information Boards. I can remember one time when he strolled in wearing a dinner suit and bow tie. At first, I thought he was going to a function, then discovered he'd already been there and was on his way home."

"What did he want, Sergeant?"

"Nothing in particular Sir, he just couldn't resist the chance to stop and look around. Which was exactly what happened when Smithy called in saying he'd been delayed. From what I've heard the driver wasn't exactly overjoyed with the situation, but we all know how stroppy the ex-Commander could be, especially when he couldn't get his own way."

Bastion closed his eyes and rubbed his temples. "Bloody damn fool!"

"There is something else you should know Sir. McClellan was in full possession of a handgun, which I've since discovered was licenced in his name."

Bastion's eyes narrowed. "Was the gun used in any way?"

"Not that I'm aware of Sir."

"So why did he have it on him?"

Jacko shook his head. "I've no idea. Maybe he was hoping to shoot Tomovic and relive some of his former glories."

"But the gun was still in its shoulder holster?"

"According to Forensics."

"Did they find anything hidden in his clothes, a note of some kind?"

"Not in his clothes, but they did find a folded piece of paper in the palm of one hand."

"Was there anything written on it?"

"Yes Sir. Just four words scribbled in pencil."

"What did they say?"

"*Flower of Scotland please.*"

"Oh hell," groaned Bastion.

"Do you know what it means Sir?"

Bastion shook his head in despair. "Yes Sergeant. It's a famous Scottish song and McClellan wants it played at his funeral."

Jacko was stunned. "I don't understand, why would he want that?"

"Because, Sergeant Jackson, Hughie McClellan's past life has come back to haunt him and he intended to get himself killed tonight."

"Killed? Why?"

"He was about to be arrested for crimes whilst in high office."

"Are you saying this was some kind of suicide note, Sir?"

Bastion nodded. "Almost certainly. Which means Hughie must have heard the bad news and decided to take the 'Kamikaze' way out!"

"Why would he do that?"

Bastion grimaced. "Before I tell you the reason, Sergeant, I think it only right I should apologise to Nathan Carson and yourself."

Jacko was becoming more confused. "For what, Sir?"

"Two reasons, the first being that for the last few months, we've been actively investigating Hughie McClellan, secondly, for not telling you."

Jacko ran his hands through his hair in exasperation. "I'd appreciate it more if you did tell us why, Sir?"

"It's taken a while, Sergeant, but we're now convinced that the ex-Commander has, or was leaking information to Maxi Hamilton."

Jacko couldn't believe his ears. "Excuse me Sir, but I've saying that for weeks!"

"I know Sergeant, but without any real evidence and considering who we were talking about, it was near impossible to prove." He then sighed resignedly. "But seeing as Hughie is now dead, I'm more than happy to bring you up to speed."

"I'd appreciate it, Sir."

"Not long after this case began, I had an unexpected phone call from ex-Commander McClellan. Having only met him and his wife on the odd official occasion, I was surprised to discover he was in possession of my personal mobile number and offering to let me know anything about Maxi Hamilton's past, no matter the time of day. It took a few minutes, but when he'd finished babbling on about how he could help, I asked him how he knew the millionaire was related to Kelly Freeland, considering that information was classified.

"To which he'd muttered something about meeting Mitch Brennan the day before and her murder popping up during their conversation. Yet, when I rang Mitch a few minutes later, he assured me that although he'd chatted with his former Boss, he wouldn't dream of talking about an on-going murder case, especially with someone who was no longer in the police force.

"My suspicions were further aroused when later that same morning, your report concerning the death of Hamilton's wife in America and Archie Speed's recollections of the Liverpool drug scene landed on my desk. It was only then did I realise McClellan was looking to be part of the Waytree Park murder case."

"A question, Sir. Is that why you gave Hughie McClellan a pass to the S.C.U.?"

"Yes Sergeant. I was wondering why he would go to such measures just to become part of your investigating team."

Jacko's eyes hardened. "But you never thought of telling us?"

Bastion smiled. "Trust me Sergeant, it was nothing personal and I know there's none better than Nathan Carson at running a tight ship. But McClellan was no fool and I couldn't take the chance of someone saying the wrong thing and him smelling a rat."

"So what exactly you did find, Sir?"

"For the first few weeks? Nothing."

"But you must have known about The Baltimore Switch and the missing file on Maxi Hamilton?"

"Yes, of course Sergeant, but after weeks of searching through reams of dusty old paperwork, we could find nothing to say he, or McClellan were in any way responsible, or connected to these events."

"What about Archie Speed's story of Hamilton selling drugs in the sixties?"

"Again, very informative and entertaining reading Sergeant, but as before, nothing we could actually prove in a Court of Law."

"Then, something must have made him want to commit suicide, Sir?"

"Yes Sergeant, although the breakthrough we needed, didn't come from the ex-Commander, it came from Marilyn Pinkerton."

"Who's she?"

"The late Tufty McClellan's wife."

Jacko's eyes narrowed. "Excuse me Sir, I thought her name was Cressida. Are we still talking about the same woman?"

Bastion nodded. "That's the name written on her official birth certificate."

"So if Pinkerton is her maiden name and Marilyn her Christian name, where does Cressida McClellan fit into all this?"

"From what we can gather, Pinky Pinkerton, as her father was known, was a bit of a 'fly by night' and obsessed with the screen idol Marilyn Monroe. So when his only daughter was born, decided to call her Marilyn in homage to the late star. However, his young offspring, who I agree, doesn't look anything like the Blonde Bombshell, utterly detested the name and in a fit of pique, decided to call herself Cressida. Who, we've since discovered, was a famous Greek heroine in the Trojan Wars."

Jacko shook his head. "Can I ask how all this came to light, Sir?"

"We came across it by accident."

"Who is *we* Sir?"

Bastion smiled. "Sorry Sergeant, he's this super whizz-kid computer expert named Mike Robin who specialises in finding hidden secrets. We were doing due diligence on McClellan's past affairs—you know, looking for anything dodgy in his bank accounts and stuff like that—when we discovered that although the ex-Commander and his wife shared a mutual bank account, she'd always had one of her own. However, this particular account was in the name of Marilyn Pinkerton."

"Not Cressida?"

"No Sergeant, 'Cressida', or 'Cressie', was the fictitious name she preferred to be known by."

"Is it that important, Sir?"

"Not at first, but it was when we went in search of more information. As luck would have it, we discovered that the bank still kept a detailed record of Ms Pinkerton's statements. Most of it going back to when she'd first opened the account in the early 60s."

"Which is long before she met Tufty."

"Yes, by at least twenty years. Although a closer look at the statements confirmed she'd rarely used the account for her own means. Yet, there was this one occasion in 1984 when £11,000 had been deposited and then moved on less than twenty four hours later."

"Do we have any idea where it went Sir?"

"Yes Sergeant, 'HMRC'."

"The Taxman?" queried Jacko.

"Assumedly to pay off Marilyn Cressida Pinkerton's outstanding tax debts."

"Are you saying Tufty's wife had money problems?"

"More than that Sergeant, according to my super-duper whizz-kid, she was on the verge of bankruptcy and about to lose everything."

"Where did he get this from?"

"Most of it comes from the files of HMRC and the three letters she sent begging for more time to sort out her problems. The first arrived in the year 1980 and told how her father had recently passed away, thus leaving her with lots of unforeseen debt. Two more followed, one in '81, the other in '82, both containing the same plea; more time please. Then in August 1983, a more up-beat kind of missive arrived at HMRC. This had purported good news and told of how one of Cressida's uncles had recently passed away, leaving her with a small inheritance. It'd further declared that she was now in a position to settle all her debts and move forward with her life. As expected, HMRC didn't give a hoot what she might do next, they were only interested in the money."

"Did she have a rich uncle, Sir?"

Bastion shrugged. "If she did, we couldn't find him."

"So where did the money come from?"

"It was wired from an offshore bank account in the Channel Islands." Jacko's eyebrows lifted. "And the sender?"

"According to bank records, the account holder was a Scotsman from Dumfries, named Angus Mackie. They then gave us his date of birth and passport number, which we later discovered was false. Well, only in that the original Angus Mackie was born here in Liverpool and drowned when he was just eight years old."

"Oh wow," laughed Jacko. "Whoever set this up, definitely knew what they were doing."

"With that I can agree Sergeant. But unfortunately for him, it would appear our fictitious Mr Mackie made one fatal mistake."

"Mistake? What kind Sir?"

"The Bank, whom I have to say are completely innocent in all this, especially as half the politicians in the UK hide their money in off-shore accounts, couldn't have been more helpful. They informed us that throughout the months of 2002, Mr Angus Mackie had systematically emptied his bank account."

"What exactly does emptied mean Sir?"

"What it means Sergeant, is that he closed his off-shore account and transferred all the funds back to the UK, or to be more specific, a London bank."

Jacko's heart began to beat faster. "Do we know which one?"

"Oh yes, Sergeant and the name of the recipient."

Jacko couldn't stand the suspense. "Who is it Sir?"

"The Right Honourable Hughie McClellan, MBE."

"Holy shit!" cried Jacko. "I'd always thought he was dodgy, but not like this."

"The bank have since confirmed, that the total amount transferred to London was close to £650,000 pounds,"

"Wow, not bad for a Police Inspector."

"Yes Sergeant. Although we have to remember that Hughie became a politician in 1996, which would normally signal a substantial increase in income. Yet I'd have liked to hear him explain how in 1982, £5,000 was deposited in his account on three separate occasions and another for £102,000 in 1983."

"Do we know where the money originally came from, Sir?"

Bastion shook his head. "Only that it was from a bank in Zurich, Switzerland."

"Has to be some kind of pay-off."

"It looks that way, but if true, confirms he was guilty of Bribery and Corruption."

"The Baltimore Switch?"

"Possibly, but now that both he and Maxi Hamilton are dead, I can't see us ever proving either of them were involved."

"I wonder why he moved his money back to the UK, Sir?"

"Good question Sergeant, I don't see him getting better interest rates on this side of the Channel."

"I'm still curious as to how he got caught with his wife's tax bill, Sir."

Bastion smiled. "From what we can gather, most of Hughie's friends had assumed he'd hit the jackpot and married some rich spinster. When in truth, although he had pots of money hidden in Jersey, it was Cressie who was on the verge of bankruptcy. Yet it must have suited them both to let people think that way, more so when he'd settled her tax debts, meaning she could keep her house, as well as her reputation. He on the other hand was now free to live the life of a gentlemen, even though he was paying through the nose in order to do so."

"What about the offshore account, Sir? Do you think his wife knew of it?"

"I doubt it. Hughie was much too shrewd for that and is probably the reason why he sent the money to Marilyn Pinkerton's personal account. Who I might add, didn't ask any awkward questions and was just glad to settle her debts."

"So how did he take it, Sir? Especially when you told him about his secret bank account in Jersey."

"Well, that's the strangest thing Sergeant, I never had the opportunity to confront the ex-Commander with the evidence we'd found."

Jacko was surprised. "Why was that, Sir?"

"Because there was no way I could accuse him of a crime without first presenting the evidence to a panel of senior officers, and we're talking about lots of 'gold braid' here, Sergeant. Who, having pontificated for hours over the file, decided it was much too serious a matter for them to pass judgment on and recommended it be forwarded to the Public Prosecutors Office."

"So when did Hughie find out, Sir?"

"Sometime last night."

"How?"

"Has to be The Old Boys Network."

"You're not serious?"

"Oh yes Sergeant, even in this age of super technology, things like the grapevine still exist. I can just imagine how many calls went whistling across the airwaves, as they heard of Hughie's imminent downfall."

"Were these charges enough to send Hughie down the suicide route?" Bastion nodded. "Absolutely. Once the story hit the headlines saying Drug Buster McClellan was being prosecuted for offences committed in office, his reputation and life was over. I remember one 'gold braid' whispering to a colleague, 'McClellan is fucking done for'!"

"And you're convinced suicide was his only way out?"

Bastion nodded. "A bullet in the brain is not the best way to go, Sergeant, but it's preferable to doing a ten-year stretch and exercising with a crowd of angry inmates."

Jacko was still shaking his head in disbelief. "So what do we do now, Sir?"

"As in?"

"How do we explain his death at Waytree Crescent?"

Bastion shrugged. "Tell the truth."

"Excuse me, Sir?"

"I see no reason why we should lie about what happened tonight, just be a little more frugal with the truth. Especially when we tell the world Hughie McClellan died in an operational accident."

"Frugal, in what way?"

"We forget to mention Hughie was an interfering old fool, who wasn't supposed to be there in the first place!"

"What about his wife Sir? I can recall DCI Carson saying she was a bit of a battle-axe and the real reason the ex-Commander spent so much time in the S.C.U.; he didn't want to go home."

"That's putting it mildly Sergeant. In my experience, an angry Cressida McClellan can be worse than a grizzly bear with a sore arse and definitely not for the faint hearted."

Jacko was relieved he didn't have to meet her, but suddenly discovered he had problems of his own. Bastion was desperate for a cup of coffee and a trip to the machine in the hallway was the only answer.

"A question Sergeant. Considering this Waytree Park business was supposed to be a relatively risk free operation. How was this Tomovic person able to kill McClellan and one of my driver with such ease?"

Jacko waited for the plastic cup to fill before answering. "Sometime after 1.30 am, one of our search patrols came across a green camper van parked not far from the crime scene."

"Camper van? Is that like a motorhome?"

"Not quite Sir, this is what you might call a smaller version but has pretty much everything you'd need to be self-sufficient. Which meant Ziggy could use the motorway services to do his ablutions and visit the local supermarkets to buy food. But here's the real surprise. The van is officially registered in the name of

Jan Lizinski, who just happens to be Marko Tomovic's brother-in-law and also employed in their plumbing business."

"Am I right in saying there was a young Pole killed in Hamilton's warehouse?"

Jacko nodded. "Yes Sir, his body was found lying in the back of the Transit van."

"Damn, no wonder we couldn't find this Ziggy person. He's driving a vehicle registered in someone else's name and moving around whenever he feels like it."

"There's more Sir. When the team eventually forced their way inside, they found a fake Russian ID inside the glove compartment and what looks to be a recent photo of Ziggy with a shaven head. Next to it was a brochure for 'Angler's Paradise,' a fishing resort somewhere in Bedfordshire, which we intend to look into. But here's the real find, hidden in another compartment, was a large holdall containing 75,000 Euros and £50,000 in used notes."

Bastion's eyebrows lifted. "My, that's an awful lot of money, Sergeant."

"Not exactly spare change is it, Sir? I reckon it must have come from Hillside Lodge, the place where Ziggy reputedly murdered five of his fellow gangland members."

"Ah yes, I remember it now. The dead bodies were strewn all over the place."

"Yes Sir, and The Met have since confirmed the gun used in the shootings, is the one responsible for the death of Maxi Hamilton at the warehouse."

"Not to mention Alderman Troughton and his wife?"

"That's right, but there was one other thing. The Serbian police are now able to identify the man lying head first in the open safe. His name is Tino Karavak, a well-known mobster, who similar to Alderman Troughton and his wife, was despatched with a single bullet to the back of the head."

"And I take it that anything else of value, has long since disappeared with whoever pulled the trigger?"

"Yes Sir, other than some useless paperwork, the safe was empty."

"Okay Sergeant, let's get back to the business in hand and bring me up to date with what's happened so far."

"We've since discovered that Ziggy slipped into Waytree Park under the cover of darkness and cut his way through the fence at the rear of the Freeland's property. Once inside, he was then able to approach the surveillance car dressed as a policeman carrying two cups of coffee."

"Policeman? Coffee?"

"Yes Sir, it would appear he'd taken the trouble to ensure his little charade would fool most people, especially McClellan and the driver. "

"In what way?"

"The fake police uniform we think was rented from a fancy dress shop, and the gun adapted to look like part of his kit."

"Is this the same gun that's been doing all of the killing?"

"Yes Sir."

"Tell me more about this coffee business."

"It was a clever ruse designed to fool everybody and makes me think Ziggy had been planning this for days. Forensics came across a still warm flask of coffee hidden nearby in the Freelands kitchen doorway."

"When you say 'fool everybody', Sergeant. Do I assume you mean my courageous driver and the fool sat in the passenger seat?"

"Err, yes Sir," grunted Jacko.

"Okay, let's move on."

"Not long after he'd killed them both, Ziggy broke into the bungalow and went in search of Mrs Freelands' bedroom."

"Supposedly with the intentions of raping and cutting her throat?"

"That would appear to be his normal MO, Sir."

"And I take it something major happened to interrupt his killing spree?"

"I wouldn't say interrupt, more like terminate it full stop."

"In what way?"

"As I understand it, Ziggy was about to go through his usual attack routine, when someone came from behind and shot him twice."

"Was it one of our men?"

"I'm afraid not Sir. Whoever killed him, was hiding in the wardrobe and used a .410 shotgun to finish him off. But they weren't exactly worried how he died; one cartridge was used on his face, the other on his Wang."

"Wang, Sergeant?"

"Sorry Sir, I meant his penis."

"Ouch! That must have hurt. Although it is unusual to hear of a .410 being used as murder weapon and I'm not talking about on his Wang."

Jacko smiled and took a couple of close-ups from the folder he'd brought with him. "This is true Sir, but I think these photos, which have just arrived from Forensics should explain exactly what happened."

Bastion studied the pictures in silence, his eyes flicking from one to the other. "The face appears to be a bloody mess Sergeant, but at the same time confirms this policeman is both clean shaven and bald headed."

"We think Ziggy removed most of his facial hair as part of his disguise."

Bastion pointed to the next picture. "And considering his Wang is missing, along with everything else, would you not agree this attack is looking more like some kind of revenge job?"

"Without a doubt Sir, but not I might add, before Ziggy had attempted to kill whoever was hiding in the wardrobe."

"Kill, in what way?"

"Delaney from Forensics thinks Tomovic must have spotted the gun and threw his dagger at whoever was standing behind him. But luckily for them it missed by a hair's breadth and here's the proof Sir."

The photo showed a smiling Steve holding his ear against the razor sharp knife embedded in the wood.

"Very droll," commented Bastion. "But considering how many enemies this Ziggy must have made in the past, might this attack not have come from one of them?"

"We did consider the idea Sir, but in the end could find no evidence to support that theory."

"So Sergeant, do you have a theory as to who might have done it?"

"Yes Sir. I think Ziggy Tomovic was killed by Kristian Freeland."

Bastion eyebrows went skyward.

"Are we talking about Mrs Freelands son?"

"Yes Sir."

"And you're convinced he killed Ziggy Tomovic?"

"Absolutely."

"Well I'd certainly be interested to know how Sergeant."

Jacko jumped in at the deep end. "I realise this might sound a little far-fetched Sir. But I'm convinced the boy heard a noise outside the house and fearing the worst, took the shotgun and hid in the wardrobe. But it was only when this mystery person had begun to attack his mother, did he realise it was Ziggy."

"How could he be sure it was him?"

"The foot long blade would help."

Bastion nodded. "Makes sense I suppose."

"This was all the proof Kristian needed, before he slid open the wardrobe door and shot him twice. Although in the boy's defence, I think his original intention had been to shoot him just once in the head. But when he saw Ziggy's trousers hanging down around his knees, decided to reload the gun and blow his balls off."

"A lesson not to do it again Sergeant?"

"Something like that Sir."

"Where did he get the gun from?"

"I'm not sure yet."

Bastion nodded. "Okay, where is it now?"

"I'm convinced it's still hidden in his friend's house."

"How can you be so sure?"

"It's the only way he could have disposed of it."

Bastion massaged the tip of his nose. "Okay, tell me more Sergeant."

"I estimate it would have taken Kristian less than a minute to leave the bedroom, run through the kitchen and out into the back garden. Waiting on the other side of the hedge was his friend Tom Hart, who grabbed the gun and hid it nearby."

"Do you think Kristian's mother would have been aware of this?"

"I doubt it Sir, she'd been so petrified by the noise and smoke, she didn't dare move a muscle until her son had said it was safe for them to leave the house."

"Sounds convincing so far Sergeant, but where's the proof?"

Jacko mentally checked his facts before continuing. "I found quite a few anomalies in Kristian's story. The first being that when I interviewed him in room 402, he insisted he'd been fast asleep and woken by two loud bangs. However, when I checked his bedroom just after the incident, it was obvious the bed hadn't been slept in and the sheets only slightly disturbed. In my opinion, it was as if someone had been lying on top of them, Sir."

Bastion smiled. "There's no law to say you can't sleep on top of a bed, Sergeant."

An unconvinced Jacko moved on. "Next came the mystery of the back door, where Forensics have since confirmed there was no forced entry of any kind. However, they did find the catch in the 'up' position, meaning the kitchen door was unlocked throughout this whole incident."

"How did Kristian explain that away?"

"Said he let the cat out earlier that evening and must have forgotten to drop the catch behind him."

"I take it you think there was an alternative reason for him to leave it open?"

"Yes Sir. I think he intentionally left it unlocked so Ziggy could gain easy access to the house."

"Why?"

"So he could kill him."

"You're not serious?"

"Yes Sir."

"Anything else?"

"The interconnecting wardrobes."

"I assume they're also important?"

"Very Sir."

"Why?"

"Because to my knowledge, less than five people knew of them, me included."

"How did you become one of the chosen few Sergeant?"

"I came across it by accident while investigating Kelly Freelands murder. I'd been searching through her clothes looking for any clues, and noticed that if I pushed a wooden panel to the right, I could actually step into the wardrobe beyond. Which of course was in Mrs Freelands bedroom."

"And the only other person who knew about this arrangement was Kristian?"

"Yes Sir. He was aware that before the fitted wardrobes, there'd been a doorway between the two rooms."

Bastion's left earlobe was next in line for the massage treatment. "Lots of bits and pieces here Sergeant, but nothing you can really get your teeth into. So maybe it's time we went back to the missing shotgun. Because without this crucial piece of evidence, much of what you say could be classed as speculation, or hearsay."

"I'm aware of that Sir, but something very important has since come to light."

"What was that?"

"I've been reading through the reports from the door to door inquiries, the ones carried out by the uniforms not long after the main event. One old lady, who lives directly opposite the Freelands, said she saw someone in a white van delivering a parcel there earlier this evening."

"What time was this Sergeant?"

"Around 7.30 pm."

"Did anyone else see this?"

"No Sir. Mrs Freeland had already left in her car ten minutes earlier, and the surveillance team had naturally followed behind, as per their instructions."

"Did this white van have a name and address on it?"

"Not according to the lady."

"What about the parcel Sergeant, did she see that?"

"Yes Sir. She described it as being a pale blue narrow box, approximately 3 ft. long and 10" wide. In addition, it had a pink ribbon with a bow and she thought it might contain flowers."

"So it wasn't a paper package type of delivery?"

"No Sir, it was a slim oblong box."

"Who signed for it?"

"Kristian Freeland."

"Any thoughts of what it might contain, Sergeant?"

Jacko smiled. "A shotgun maybe?"

Bastion returned the smile. "You could be right, Sergeant, but I'm more interested in what else came to light."

"I decided to do a check on Kristian Freeland's mobile phone for the last twenty-four hours. And as you'd expect, most of the incoming calls were identifiable as being from his friends. However, at exactly 7.32 pm, he received a text from an ex-directory number that said. 'It could be tonight, hope this keeps you safe. Good luck.'"

"Was this mystery number traceable, Sergeant?"

"No Sir, and I have a feeling we'll still be searching for it in weeks to come."

"But you think it had something to do with the delivery?"

"I'm certain of it."

"Well in my book, Sergeant, one text of encouragement, identifiable or otherwise, doesn't really prove intent to supply a weapon."

"I understand that, Sir. However, five minutes after the parcel arrived, Kristian sent a text to Tom Hart's phone asking him to come next door to his place."

"Which would have been at 7.37 pm."

"Yes Sir. But more importantly, he sent another message to the same phone at 12.15 am precisely."

"What did it say?"

"Just four words, 'Get ready, he's here.'"

"Bastion began checking for wax on the end of his finger. "Mm, yes Sergeant, I see what you mean, very interesting."

"That's what I thought, Sir."

"So, what do you intend to do now?"

"Look for the gun."

"Where?"

"Tom Hart's house."

"I thought you'd already searched there."

"We have, but only in the gardens."

"So where do you think the gun is now?"

"Has to be hidden somewhere in the garage."

"Notwithstanding the garden has been searched once already Sergeant, I imagine you might need a warrant to gain entry to the rest of the house, or garage for that matter."

"I'm aware of that Sir, but I can't see them getting rid of the gun in such a short space of time. Not with the uniforms checking anything moving in or out of the Crescent."

"What if it's not there?"

Jacko shrugged. "I doubt it will matter too much."

"Why?"

"Because we're not talking about two hardened criminals here. And once Forensics have discovered some gunpowder residue, of which there should be plenty. I reckon they'll both crack, especially Kristian's friend Tom Hart."

"What happens then?"

"Sir?"

"What do you intend to do next?"

Jacko looked surprised. "We'll arrest both teenagers and charge them with the premeditated murder of Luka Tomovic."

Bastion nodded whilst stirring his coffee. "Such a shame," he said at last.

"What is Sir?"

"The thought of making criminals out these two brave young men."

A surprised Jacko was about to make another comment, when Bastion looked into his eyes. "Can I ask you a question Sergeant? And I'd like a truthful answer please."

"Sir?"

"What would your reaction be, if you walked into the bedroom and found Ziggy Tomovic just about to rape your mother and once done, slit her throat from ear to ear?"

Jacko was silent before answering. "The truth Sir?"

The Superintendent nodded once.

"I'd tear the bastard to pieces, or die trying."

Bastion's eyes turned a flinty grey as he listened to Jacko's reply. "And believe me Sergeant, so would I!"

The silence in the hallway was broken only by the sound of a vacuum cleaner whirring away in the distance, as both men grasped the enormity of their mutual resolve. A stunned Jacko spoke next. "I can remember the DCI arguing that most men would kill to save their own, and under the circumstances, I assume this has to be a perfect example."

Bastion smiled grimly. "Yes Sergeant and as I too have a wife and daughter; who I would gladly give my life for, you can include me that in that particular club."

Jacko threw his empty cup in the bin. "So what happens now?"

"That, I'm afraid, is for you to decide."

"Me?"

"Yes Sergeant Jackson. As I understand it, you are now in sole charge of the S.C.U. and therefore have the final word."

Jacko took a deep breath and spoke his mind. "I'm convinced that Ziggy Tomovic was shot twice by Kristian Freeland and Tom Hart helped him get rid of the gun. Are you suggesting otherwise, Sir?"

Bastion's face relaxed. "No Sergeant, I'm not suggesting anything of the sort, only that you take a more objective view of what happened tonight. But first, are we both agreed that with death of Ziggy Tomovic, the world is a much safer place?"

"Absolutely."

"And all these years of murder and mayhem will become a forgotten nightmare?"

Jacko nodded.

"Well at least that's something. So let's move on to our two young suspects. Do they have a criminal record of any kind?"

"No Sir."

"Are they of good character?"

"Oh yes, I've met them a few times and thought they were just your normal everyday teenagers. I've since heard that young Hart is a brilliant footballer, who might one day play in the Premier League."

"Kristian?"

"Much the same. Although he's still trying to come to terms with the deaths of his sister and grandfather."

"And let's not forget Sergeant, how Tomovic broke into their house tonight, looking to rape and murder his mother."

"True. But can we just overlook the fact that Kristian Freeland purposely left the back door open and blew Ziggy to pieces with a shotgun."

"Allegedly, Sergeant Jackson, only allegedly."

"Okay Sir. I'll admit that at the moment, we can't really say if he was the one who pulled the trigger."

"Not without the gun and cartridges to prove it Sergeant. We should also remember that the boy ran into the bedroom to rescue his mother and in doing so, would almost certainly have become contaminated with gun residue."

Jacko sighed reluctantly. "I am aware of that Sir."

"Another thing Sergeant, a good lawyer could always argue that it was self-defence, especially as the intruder in question had tried to pin the boy's head to the wardrobe with a foot long knife."

"If that was the case Sir, why didn't Kristian just admit to killing Ziggy?"

Bastion waved a hand dismissively. "I can think of a few good reasons why he'd be reluctant to take that road Sergeant. The obvious one being he didn't want to go to jail, even if it might be for a short period of time."

"What about justice, Sir?"

"What about it?"

Jacko shrugged. "Well, we are police officers who've sworn to uphold the Law, no matter the consequences."

Bastion held his stare again. "I've been in this business long enough to know about the Law and its consequences Sergeant. Although there were times, especially in Northern Ireland, when I'd wondered what the word justice stood for. And no matter how hard I tried, I could never understand why some crazy lunatic bomber, would try to kill the young and old, all in the name of their so called 'justice'!"

"So what would you advise Sir?"

Bastion's eyes narrowed in thought. "Who else knows about tonight?"

"No one."

"What about the text messages?"

Jacko shrugged again. "I only read them myself an hour ago."

"And you haven't written up your report yet?"

"No Sir."

Bastion smiled. "Then my advice Sergeant is to do nothing."

"Sir?"

"In my opinion, it would be an absolute travesty of justice if these two boys were ever charged with the death of Ziggy Tomovic. And I very much doubt that the good people of this City would be out there in the car park, waving their banners and congratulating us both for doing so. In fact Sergeant, if I had the choice, I'd give them both a medal for bravery!"

"What about the investigation?

"Save it for a rainy day."

Jacko's mouth opened. "Sorry Sir?"

"Look at it this way Sergeant, should they step out of line, or blot their copybooks in the future. Then there's nothing to say we might take a fresh look at the evidence from tonight and arrest them both forthwith."

"Sounds like probation to me."

"More like Parole Sergeant."

"So how do we explain away the brutal death of Ziggy Tomovic?"

"Revenge Sergeant, plain old revenge by person or persons unknown."

"Do you think the world's Press would believe that's what really happened?"

"Why not? Ziggy's camper van was found two minutes' walk away with a huge amount of money hidden inside. So who's to say that one of his many enemies hadn't followed him to Liverpool looking to recover the missing loot? And who could possibly deny that one of them might have crawled through the fence and shot him twice, like all vengeful gangsters are liable to do?"

Jacko was still undecided. "I'm not sure what to do Sir, it's a big ask."

Bastion took a sip of his coffee and smiled in sympathy. "I know that, Sergeant. But sometimes you just have to take the bull by the horns and make a choice, be it good or bad. My own secret was to do whatever I felt was best, no matter the outcome."

"Not much fun being in charge is it Sir?"

"It all depends on how you look at it Sergeant, unbearably tough job, or a challenge to be relished? In the end, it's your decision to make."

Jacko chewed his lip and mulled it over in silence, then realised there could be only one answer. "Okay Sir, Parole it is."

"Excellent," smiled Bastion. "Couldn't have made a better choice myself. But can I give you one last piece of advice."

"What's that Sir?"

"Share the load."

"Sir?"

"Have a confidential chat with someone you can trust."

"Any thoughts?"

"Yes Sergeant, there's a senior police officer lying in a hospital bed who's probably waiting for your call. I imagine he would fit the bill splendidly!"

Jacko grinned. "It's still early, do you think he'll be awake?"

Bastion threw his Styrofoam cup in the bin and nodded. "Yes Sergeant, and just like me, Nathan Carson is a very light sleeper. See you at 10.00 am for the usual Press Briefing."

"Yes Sir."

"Oh, and there is one other thing Sergeant."

"Yes Sir?"

"Get that damn coffee machine sorted. I've never tasted anything as bad in all my bloody life!"

Waytree Crescent
6.30 am

In the early morning quiet, Tommo had been listening to the sound of the police beavering away at the Freeland's place, when something caught his eye. Mr Greenhaulgh, who lived opposite and always left for work at 6.30 am, suddenly found he had a problem. He was about to depart the Crescent in his flash new Kia saloon, when he encountered one of the two the Forensic vans blocking the circular driveway. This had entailed him taking a sharp left, instead of his usual right turn in order to reach the exit slope.

Next was the squad car containing a couple of armed policemen parked at the bottom of the same incline, thus ensuring only authorised people could enter or leave. Tommo edged a little further down the garden path, so he might better watch the Kia pull alongside and listen to Mr Greenhaulgh chatting with the two officers inside. A second later and the uniform in the passenger seat stepped from the vehicle, peered through the Kia's windows and following another brief exchange, tapped it on the roof, thus giving it the all clear.

Tommo was about to go indoors and take a shower, when he heard a different, but just as familiar sound. Headed in the same direction was Mrs Morley, who religiously took her two Pekinese dogs for a walk every morning in Waytree Park. Curious as to what might happen next, Tommo watched the excited dogs yap their way towards the slope and seconds later saw the policeman's hand appear through the open window and nonchalantly wave them on.

Within minutes of observing this everyday activity by his fellow neighbours, he went hurrying in the direction of the house garage. An industrious half hour later and he reappeared via the side door, astride his pushbike and toting a large sports bag on his shoulder. Taking a deep breath and trying to act as normal as possible, he cycled towards the police car.

"Excuse me, officer," he said through the open window. "Is it okay for me to leave the Crescent? I have to do some early morning football training."

The uniform in the passenger side was suspicious. "Who are you again?"

"Tom Hart and I live next door to the Freeland's."

His colleague in the driver's seat sounded a little more sympathetic. "I take it you must have known the dead girl?"

Tommo, who looked about ready to cry, nodded slowly.

"What's in the bag?' asked the suspicious one.

"My football kit."

"Can I take a look?"

"Yeah, sure," said Tommo, who zipped open the bag to reveal a mixture of neatly ironed football tops and shorts.

"What's underneath?"

"Just my towel and scruffy boots."

The driver gave his mate a nudge. "Leave the kid alone, Jake, he's probably gone through enough turmoil already without you giving him a hard time."

Jake, who was only doing his job, looked skywards and shook his head. "Okay, okay Fred, I'm just making sure that anything going in or out has been checked, as per orders."

"I know that, mate, but this kid doesn't look like a mass murderer to me."

"Hang on a minute, I thought this mass killer was already dead in the bedroom?"

"He is, which is why I don't think he's a problem."

Jake gave a shrug and pressed the button on his chest intercom. "Calling Zero 37?"

"*Zero 37 receiving you.*"

"There's a young kid who's about to leave the Crescent, don't worry about checking him out though, we've already done so."

"*Okay Jake, no problem.*"

Tommo cycled up the slope and met the SO18 uniform waiting at the top.

He was dressed all in black, menacingly tall, and carried a lethal array of weapons, the most obvious one being his Heckler and Koch sub-machine gun.

"You must be Tom Hart," he smiled.

"And you must be Zero 37," he replied.

The policeman grinned at his cheek. "Football training?"

"Yeah."

"Bit early, isn't it?"

"Trying to get into the first team."

The man in black smiled again. "Okay son, let's hope you make it."

"I'll do my best," he replied. He then adjusted the sports bag so that it sat more comfortably over his shoulder and sidestepped the few press reporters still hanging around. Rather than head towards Highwater and the main roundabout, he instead turned left and began pedalling in the opposite direction. A mile further down the lane and he came upon a place he hadn't visited in years; the Municipal Tip. In an odd way, the chain-mail fence enclosing the dump, had always reminded him of Waytree Park, its sole purpose being to keep intruders out.

But like most of the kids from around here, he knew how to gain easy entry by pulling back a corner of the fence that had been hanging loose for years. When through to the other side, he listened for any sound or movement, but other than the squabbling seagulls that used it as a daily diner, the place was silent and deserted. This was exactly as it should be, seeing as the Tip was Council owned and restricted to its employees only. Who in their infinite wisdom, wouldn't dream of stepping through the gates until it was 8.00 am on the dot.

With this in mind, Tommo expertly skirted around the piles of rubbish and went in search of one object in particular; the giant Caterpillar tractor they used to move the mountains of shit from A to B. A short trudge later and he saw a bright yellow one parked exactly where the driver had left it the day before, slap bang in the middle of two sky high heaps of garbage. He was also delighted to see the flattened pathway created in its wake, which would help in keeping his new trainers clean. Yet Tommo had no intention of climbing aboard and starting the engine, he just needed somewhere safe to stand. Adjusting the sports bag on his shoulder, he used the short metal ladder to reach the tracks, shimmied along past the driver's cab and climbed the last few feet, thus enabling him to reach his true destination; the tractor's bright yellow engine cover. Staring at the mountains of rubbish towering over his head, he was just about ready to complete his task when he remembered how he'd come to be here.

Twelve Hours Earlier

The text message said; 'Come to my place ASAP.'

Intrigued as to what might be so important, Tommo finished his burger and headed for his friend's house next door. Where to his surprise, he saw Kristian waiting for him in the doorway. "My mother's gone out and there's no else at home, but I reckon it'll still be safer if we talk in my bedroom."

Mystified at what might be so hush-hush, he followed him along the hall and took his usual seat at the computer desk. "I see the police car has gone missing from outside your front door."

Kristian shook his head. "That's because they follow my mother everywhere, even when she goes the loo!"

"So what's going down?"

"This is no joke, Tommo, but I've heard a whisper that Ziggy Tomovic is going to try and kill us both."

"Who, you and me?"

"No, you dickhead, me and my mother!"

"Oh sorry Kris, I'd forgotten all about the policeman's warning."

"This has nothing to do with Sgt Jackson."

"Then who?"

"Sorry mate, I can't tell you that."

"Why?"

"Because the less you know, then the safer it will be. But more importantly, it means you can act the innocent when it's all over."

"When what's all over?"

"When I've managed to kill him."

"Who?"

"Ziggy Tomovic!"

"Shit man, how the hell are you going to do that?"

Without saying another word, Kristian reached under the bed and produced a long black silk bag, its top end tied with a twisted gold thread.

"Is that a gun in there?" gulped Tommo.

Kristian gave a nod, sat back on the bed and placed the bag across his knees. His friend could only watch in wide-eyed amazement as he untied the knot and produced a gleaming, highly polished single-barrel shotgun from within its silky interior.

"Wow!" gasped Tommo in genuine awe. "Where did you get that from?"

Kristian pointed to a pale blue oblong box lying on the floor. "It came in that."

"Do you know who sent it?"

Kristian shrugged. "Haven't got a clue."

"Is it loaded?"

"Not yet."

"Can I have a look?"

Kristian passed him the gun.

Tommo lovingly ran his fingertips over the delicate engraving surrounding the breech and trigger areas. "Whooo," he whispered. "This really is something else."

Kristian nodded in agreement. "I'm not really sure how old it is, but assume it's fully functioning. Which means that if you pull the trigger and stand in the way, it will blow your head off."

"Does it have any cartridges?"

Kristian took four narrow cylindrical shells from his pocket.

"Not very big ones for a shotgun are they?"

"That's because this is a .410 shotgun and sometimes known as a 'Ladies' gun."

"How do you know that?"

"I checked it on the Internet."

Tommo shook his head. "Well it still looks deadly to me!"

"I'm just hoping the damn thing works when needed."

"Can I ask a question, Kristian?"

"Yeah, of course."

"Considering half of Merseyside's armed police are keeping tabs outside your door, all of whom I might add, could blow this Ziggy to pieces. Why are you trying to do their job for them?"

"Because I don't trust them."

Tommo looked exasperated. "But they're professionals!"

"And so is he. But that's not the only thing he has going for him. From what I've heard, he's one ruthless bastard whose managed to survive shit knows how many attempts to kill him. Which is why I'm taking no chances should he come calling here."

"So you seriously intend to kill him?"

Kristian nodded twice.

"How exactly?"

"As I said before, Tommo, I don't want to give you any exact details, but admit that I might need your help."

"Help? What kind of help?"

"Once it's all over, I want you to hide the gun for a few days."

Tommo looked both surprised and confused. "Say that again?"

Kristian tried to explain. "Even though I want to get rid of this Serbian lunatic, I don't necessarily want to spend five years in jail just for the pleasure of doing it; which I hear is now the mandatory term for manslaughter. But if the police can't find the weapon used to kill him, then it becomes near impossible to prove exactly who did."

"That's assuming you survive this encounter with Ziggy."

Kristian shrugged. "Well if that happens, no one will give a shit either way."

"So how am I supposed to help?"

"As I see it, I should have just over a minute to do the business, put the folded gun in a small holdall and race for the rear garden. If all goes to plan, I would then throw the bag over the hedge; where I hope you will be waiting to take it inside."

"What happens next?"

"Nothing Tommo, all I would need you to do is hide the gun somewhere in your garage roof space and watch the fireworks take place later."

"What happens in a few days' time?"

"Hopefully, I'll be back here again and take it off your hands."

"What will you do with it?"

"Destroy it I suppose."

"How?

"I'm not sure yet, probably try and cut it into small pieces."

"It's a nice gun."

Kristian nodded and turned the gleaming weapon over in his hands. "I've discovered that because it's hinged here next to the trigger, you can split it in two." He then demonstrated the manoeuvre by separating the barrel from the stock. "Which should make it easier for me to cut it up."

"What will he or she say?"

"Sorry?"

"Whoever it was that gave you the gun."

Kristian gave a shrug. "I've no idea. I didn't think of asking them."

"It's such a nice gun, it seems a shame to destroy it."

Kristian was confused. "You're not thinking of keeping it are you?'

"No, no!" declared Tommo. "It seems such a shame to cut such a beautiful thing like that into pieces."

Kristian sensed something was wrong. "Are you okay?"

"Yeah, I'm alright."

"You sure?"

"Of course," he mumbled uncertainly.

"Want to tell me the truth?"

Tommo looked at the floor before answering, "I'm sorry Kristian, but I don't think I'm cut out for this."

"Can you tell me why?"

"I'm just worried of what might happen if it all goes wrong, and I get caught with the gun."

"You could be a hero."

"This is true, or I could lose everything, especially my football career."

Kristian shrugged. "I know it's a lot to ask, Tommo, but there's a lot at stake."

"Sorry mate."

"Is there no way I can convince you to help?"

Tommo kept looking at the floor and shook his head.

Kristian could feel for his long-time friend, but realised he had no choice. "If you won't do it for me, will you at least do it for her?"

Using both hands, Tommo took his neatly ironed football kit from inside the bag, and placed it on the engine cover. Next came his towel and scruffy football boots. Then came the most important piece of kit; a small blue Nike sports bag hidden below. Taking his time, he opened the zip and saw the reason why he was here. Wrapped inside an old oily jumper, were the remains of what was once a beautiful single barrel shotgun. Their original plan had been for him to hide the gun until Kristian could come and retrieve it.

But as he'd watched the ease with which the other neighbours had been able to leave the Crescent, he'd swiftly decided otherwise. With him being a proficient part-time handyman, and so he might do his thing uninterrupted, his father had long ago constructed a small workshop at the rear of their double garage. His mother, however, who hated loud banging noises period, had insisted he make it as soundproof as possible and when done, had to admit it was quite impressive. The studwork walls were packed solid with sound deadening material, the resulting finish meaning he could make as much noise as he wanted.

His father had also kitted it out with a workbench and vice, plus some shelves for his many tools. Although Tommo was only interested in one particular piece of equipment; the battery powered portable grinder, with the super-sharp hi-speed diamond blade. In the past he'd watched his father cut through virtually anything, even high tensile steel.

Checking the family were still asleep, he donned a pair of his father's rubber work gloves, took the blue Nike bag from its hiding place in the garage roof and set to work. Before he could move on, his first task was to clean the weapon from end to end so as to remove any traces of DNA. Disassembling the gun hadn't been as difficult as he'd first imagined either. Many parts, like the wooden shoulder stock and trigger guard were simply screwed on.

He'd also remembered Kristian showing him how to split the gun in two, and the bench vice was all that was needed to hold the barrel firmly in place. In next to no time, he'd cut it into 15 pieces, each of which had fallen neatly into the blue Nike bag below. However, there were some parts that Kristian had warned would need special attention. One was the trigger mechanism, the other being the two spent shotgun cartridges. The first proved to be no real problem, as he'd simply wrapped a piece of cloth around the firing pin, and tapped it hard with a hammer.

To his surprise, it had broken in two with a sharp snap, allowing him to drop the pieces into the bag with the other bits of metal. The cartridges were just as easy; a good hard squeeze with the bench vice crushing both their brass casings almost flat. He'd been wondering how best to dispense with the debris, when an old favourite caught his eye. Poking out of a cardboard box up in the garage roof-space was a large catapult he'd bought whilst holidaying in Turkey a few years ago. At the time it had been just a novel idea, but when back home in Liverpool, had been the perfect weapon to scare away the birds. This, he knew would be perfect in sending the smaller sections of gun barrel flying to all parts of the dump. The larger pieces, like the Stock and Fore-end he'd shove under the tracks, and imagine the crushing sound when the tractor moved backwards and forwards.

Still, it wasn't just masculine bravado which brought him here today, or a desire to help Kristian hide the gun, it was the photograph of his beautiful sister lying dead in the Morgue. The image of her pale ashen face and the sudden realisation that she was gone forever had literally stunned him into tears. But the real reason for his grief lay not in sympathy of a vengeful brother, but because Tommo had been in love with Kelly Freeland for as long as he could remember. His infatuation with the blonde ethereal beauty from next door had begun more than ten years ago, when he and his family had first moved to Waytree Crescent. Where instead of joy, there'd been much disappointment, and many mountains to climb, especially when he'd discovered that Kelly was two years older than he was. So instead of being a playmate, he'd always been regarded as much too young to take part in the more 'grown up' games, and relegated to playing alone. This situation had changed little over the years, as they'd both grown older, and sadly, drifted further apart, she becoming a tall statuesque young lady, he the hulking admirer from next door.

That is until this one occasion not so long ago, when something wonderful had happened. It had taken place early one evening when he'd been having a cold drink in the Freelands' kitchen. He and Kristian had been discussing the latest football scores, when Kelly breezed into the room wearing a white clingy dress that literally took his breath away.

"Gosh, you look good, going anywhere special?"

"Yes Mum, I'm off to the Echo Arena to see a concert, and something to eat later."

"How are you getting into town, bus?"

"No way, someone's giving me a lift."

"Anyone we know?"

Kelly smiled wickedly. "Now that would be telling."

Next came Kristian's voice. "Guess what Kell? It's Tommo's 17th birthday today."

His sister's eyes opened wide in genuine delight. "Oh wow, how fantastic is that!"

Tommo felt as though he was going to shrivel up and die of embarrassment, as she and her mother had casually discussed his age while he'd listened in silence. Then came the moment he would never forget. When the chatty conversation had ended, Kelly walked to where he was sat at the table, took his face in her hands and said, "If I'd known it was your birthday Tommo, I would have sent you a card, but hopefully this will do instead."

Then to his dumbstruck amazement, she'd closed her eyes and kissed him on the lips. Having never kissed a girl before, Tommo was at a complete loss of what to do next, but his masculine instincts had soon taken over, and he'd closed his too.

The exquisite touch of her lips had lasted for no more than a few seconds, yet it was one he would remember for the rest of his life. However, Kelly wasn't quite finished. Gently caressing his face with one hand, she used the other to run it through his hair. "My brother tells me that you're about to become a famous football star, is that true?"

Tommo shrugged and mumbled. "I don't know, maybe."

Kelly smiled, kissed the tip of his nose and whispered. "A wise old friend once told me that there are no 'maybes' in this life. If you have a dream to fulfil, then go and grab it with both hands, just like he did. Okay?"

Tommo nodded in wide-eyed agreement, as she collected her things, pecked Steffi on the cheek and swept out the room with a "Bye, bye boys!" ringing in their ears.

Placing the last piece of gun barrel inside the leather thong, Tommo drew back on the elasticated rubber and watched it whistle off into the distance, never to be seen again. Yet in his own mind knew that, if given the choice, he would have been first in the queue to pull the trigger and kill Ziggy Tomovic!

Merseyside Police Headquarters
7.30 am

Levi Clinton was first out of the lift as the doors opened onto a now busy ground floor reception area. Next came Kristian, Michaela and last of all Steffi, who saw Jacko standing alone by the main desk. Leaving them to chat amongst themselves, she strolled towards him, smiled and held out her hand. "Hello Sergeant Jackson."

Jacko took the proffered hand and went through the usual formalities. "Mrs Freeland, how are you this morning?"

"I'm good. What about you?"

"Hungry."

"Maybe I should buy you breakfast as a reward? Considering all you've done for us Sergeant, it's the least I can do."

Jacko grinned. "Sounds tempting, but I have tons of paperwork to get through before I can even think about filling an empty stomach."

"Perhaps another time."

"Why not." It was only then did he notice she was still holding his hand.

"There is one other thing Sergeant and it's something we should never forget."

"What's that Mrs Freeland?"

"Always be grateful when an avenging angel, no matter how young or innocent they may be, appears from nowhere and saves your life."

At first Jacko was a little puzzled, until he saw she was staring intently into his eyes and realised she was talking about her son Kristian. But before he could reply, Mother Hen's voice, in the rotund shape of Levi Clinton, came booming across the room. "Are we ready to leave, Steffi? The car is waiting for us outside."

"On my way," she called over her shoulder. Then to Jacko's surprise, kissed him on the cheek and whispered, "Thank you for all you've done Sergeant, we'll be forever in your debt."

Maxi's Range Rover was parked outside the main entrance with the distinctive shape of Twixy Bannerman sat behind the wheel.

"Best not hang around too long," clucked Clinton Levi, "or they're bound to give us a parking ticket!"

Kristian was about to climb aboard, when he saw a vintage green sports car turning into the courtyard.

"Late as always," chided Clinton.

"Who is it?" Asked Steffi.

"Looks like Hawksworth Jones," said Twixy. "But I'm not sure he can leave his car there."

All eyes were focused on the large yellow square painted on the tarmac that said: *NO PARKING AT ANY TIME.*

"Someone had better tell him to move, or they'll tow it away," advised Michaela.

"I'll do it," said Kristian.

Walking towards the open-top car, he could see the famous 'Lotus' badge fixed to the radiator and the ubiquitous leather belt strapped around its sleek bonnet.

"Morning Mr Jones."

"Hello Kristian, how are you?"

"I'm okay Sir."

"And your mother?"

Kristian nodded. "Yes, she's fine."

"Thank God for that. Clinton rang me an hour ago and said you'd been attacked by this crazy serial killer."

"We were, but luckily, we've managed to stay alive and he's dead. Oh and before I forget, Twixy's advising you should move your car before you get booked."

Hawksworth Jones suddenly looked flustered. "Yes, I suppose I better had, don't want to upset the local Bobbies do we."

Starting the engine, he was about to put the Lotus into reverse, when Kristian moved closer.

"Thanks for the gun and the warning," he whispered.

The old man's face took on a pained expression. "Sorry?"

"The gun and the warning you sent to me two days ago."

Hawksworth Jones continued to look confused. "Excuse me, I don't understand…"

Kristian smiled. "A blue oblong box was delivered to my house marked as special delivery. There was no name or address of the sender, but wrapped inside a black silk bag was a .410 shotgun and a note warning Ziggy Tomovic was about to kill me and my mother."

The old man's face became even more aghast. "And you think that I sent you this so-called 'present'?"

"Yes Sir."

"Why?"

Kristian reached into the pocket of his jeans and took out a small brass oval plate. He then held it up so he might see. "Because I found this screwed to the butt of the shotgun."

The plate was brightly polished and had the initials LHJ engraved on it. "Now I don't know what the L stands for Sir, but I didn't have to be a genius to work out what HJ meant."

For a second the old man looked as if he were about to explode, then his face began to soften and turned into a wan smile. "Ah, the identity plate. Yes I have to admit, Kristian, I'd completely overlooked that."

"Can I ask who 'L' is?"

Hawksworth Jones nodded. "The gun belonged to my late wife, Linda."

"Why would she own a shotgun, Sir?"

"Because we've always lived in the countryside and even though she was the most beautiful and gentlest lady in the world. She was also a member of the local gun club and liked to roam the land blasting some poor unfortunate out of the sky. But the damn thing's been lying around the house for ages and I didn't know what to do with it. Then I thought of you and wondered if it might help in some way. Although I must admit, my idea was for you to point the gun at Ziggy and scare him off, not actually kill him."

"Well, I'm just glad you did, Sir, otherwise we might not be here today."

The old man nodded. "Was it difficult, Kristian? You know…to shoot him?"

"I didn't really think about it at the time. All I was concerned with was trying to stop him from murdering my mother."

"Nonetheless, having to make that life or death decision must have been hard for you?"

Kristian shrugged. "Yes, I suppose so. Although I wasn't really sure what would happen if we met face to face."

"Was he scared?"

Kristian shook his head. "No Sir, not at all. In fact, at one point, I'm sure he was daring me to kill him."

Hawksworth Jones was amazed at what came next.

"My original plan was to try and confront him in the hallway, but he'd already sneaked into my mother's bedroom. So my only other choice was to pass through Kelly's wardrobe and try to get behind him."

"Good Lord, I'd forgotten all about the secret panel."

"Yes Sir and luckily for us, he didn't know about it either. Which meant when I slid the door open, he was kneeling on the bed with a knife in his hand. Even though he was less than six feet away and had his back turned, I wasn't sure whether I could shoot him. Then I had an idea and decided to attract his attention by making a kind of whooshing sound. I could tell from his reaction that it'd worked and he knew someone was standing behind him. Although what happened next was completely unexpected."

"In what way?"

"The room was lit only by the bedside lamp, making it difficult for me to see properly. Then literally out of nowhere, this huge knife passed within inches of my face and slammed into the wardrobe wall. It was only then did I realise Ziggy had somehow managed to twist his body around and throw it at my throat."

"Lucky for you he missed."

"Yes Sir, but then came the really crazy bit. Even though he was weapon-less, it still didn't stop him from daring me to kill him."

"Why would he do that?"

"I don't know. Maybe he was hoping I'd just drop the gun and run, but when I didn't, he started to get really nasty."

"In what way?"

"He laughed in my face and began pointing down towards his crotch. At first, I wasn't sure what he meant, then realised he was holding something in his hand: it was his dick Sir and he had a real hard-on. And as if that wasn't bad enough, he pointed towards my mother and said, 'This is for the bitch behind me.' That's when I pulled the trigger."

Hawksworth Jones closed his eyes and shook his head. "Well, at least he's dead."

Kristian smiled. "Yes Sir, Ziggy Tomovic has gone forever, but I was wondering how you knew he was going to attack us?"

"I had a quiet word with a friend from my club. He's an ex-police chief who still has plenty of contacts in the force."

"And they knew about Ziggy?"

"Fortunately, yes, and the surveillance operation."

"Sending me the gun had to be risky move."

The old man nodded. "Yes, I suppose it was."

"Can I ask why?"

Hawksworth Jones stared ahead for a moment. "I suppose it was because I owed your grandfather so much."

"He did tell me you were very close, Sir."

"Ah, but did he tell you how he'd literally saved my life?"

"Not that I remember."

The old man's eyes glazed over a little as he recalled the past. "I'm originally from London and my family being bankers, were very wealthy. Then sometime in the late 70s I was at Cambridge studying Economics, when I met this beautiful young student called Linda. She'd been studying History at the time and within weeks of our meeting, was convinced she was the girl I wanted to marry.

"However, when I informed my toffee-nosed father that I wanted to wed a girl from up north—Linda was originally from the Wirral—he absolutely blew his top and threatened to disown me forever. Which of course, he eventually did. Luckily, I was made of much sterner stuff and coming from good banking stock, had a fair idea of how to make money. So, casting all worries aside, we decided to tie the knot and head north. Yet Liverpool at this time had proved to be no cakewalk.

"There was a lot of poverty around as well as social unrest, the riots in '81 being a perfect example. Despite this, I'd been pleasantly surprised to discover that if you looked carefully, there were still lots of wealthy people looking to make an investment. Having been encouraged by all of this positivity, I began a business consultancy in Dale Street. The word soon spread and the clients came rolling in, bringing lots of money with them. We later bought a house close to Linda's parents in the Wirral and life at the time was pretty good.

"Then one day in '82, I had a call from a cousin of mine. He asked if I might be interested in a free trip to Kenya and while there, take a look at a private Safari

Park some South Africans were about to develop. I, of course, had jumped at the offer and a week later we left Gatwick on the Thursday evening and arrived at our hotel in Mombasa early Friday morning. However, what the South African promoters had forgot to mention, was the project was a near six-hour car journey out into the bush and the same coming back. At the time, we'd just laughed off the long dusty day and looked forward to having a cold beer at the hotel bar.

"What I didn't expect to see was an excited manager waiting outside on the steps and insisting I should ring home straight away. It seemed there'd been some kind of emergency and my wife Linda had left eight messages saying she desperately needed to speak to me. Naturally, I'd thought something might be wrong with one of the children and began to panic. However, when we'd finally managed to talk to each other and have a real conversation, she said the kids were fine, but we were practically broke. At first I'd assumed she was just exaggerating, until she'd explained that something had spooked the world stock markets, and share prices had been plummeting all day."

Hawksworth Jones smiled at the thought. "You see Kristian, under normal circumstances, I'd have been watching the Markets, and if anything looked suspect, sold it in a flash. But on this occasion I wasn't at the helm. I was in Kenya, where the telephone lines were so bad; it took a lifetime just to get a taxi. So it wasn't until I'd made it home did I realise the extent of the damage and see we'd lost everything; our clients' money included. From then on, things slowly began to get worse, as people started to close their accounts and demand their money back. In less than a month, the house was up for sale and Linda and the kids had gone to live with her parents."

"What about you, Sir?"

"Me?" he smiled. "I'd struggled along as best I could, while hoping for some divine intervention and strangely, it came in the form of this." Kristian peered into the car as Hawksworth Jones, pulled back his coat sleeve.

"A wrist watch?"

"Yes, Kristian, but not any old watch. This is a solid gold Rolex Oyster Perpetual, which my father gave me on my 21st birthday. It's also very valuable."

"So how did that help Sir?"

"A year before we went under, some friends had asked me if I'd like to visit a gambling club called Goodman's Casino. At the time, I said that I'd never had a bet in my life, let alone go gambling. They convinced me it was just a bit of fun and said I'd enjoy it. And so it turned out to be. We'd had a go at all the different tables and I won some money playing Roulette. Yet when I sat down to play Poker, I just knew this was my lucky table. It's essentially a game of chance and bluff, which I have to say, I was damn good at. Come the end of the night and I'd more or less doubled my stake."

Hawksworth Jones smiled again. "I was so happy, you think I'd just won the 'Pools'. Which is why in desperation, I thought I'd return to the casino and try again. At the time, I'd been down to my last three hundred pounds and was hoping that maybe I could double it at the poker table. I mentioned to the manager that I'd visited the place once before and they let me in no problem. For the first hour I'd been having the odd bet and holding my own. Then I had a sudden streak of luck and every turn of the cards was a winner. So much so, that I was up nearly two 'grand' on my original stake. I knew there and then that it was time to cash my chips in, but like a greedy fool, couldn't resist having one more go." His wrinkled eyes narrowed as he remembered the moment.

"At first there'd been six of us around the table. But as the stakes grew higher, they'd dropped off one by one, until there were only two of us left. I can remember thinking that my three Queens and pair of Tens, would be very hard to beat and so increased the stake at every call. But my opponent was thinking along the same lines and matched it each time.

"Within minutes a crowd had gathered around the table, as news of our 'Battle Royale' spread. However, the rules of the game are strict and dictate that you either 'call' or raise the stakes, which were £100 a time. In the blink of an eye, there was nearly £5000 in chips lying on the table and I sensed my small nondescript opponent was getting a little nervous. So with a flourish I called his bluff and raised the stakes another £200, thinking he'd fold. But instead of collapsing like a pile of cards, he said. 'I'll take that bet and raise you another £400'.

"This meant I needed another £600 to stay in the game, or walk away without seeing his cards. But I didn't have that amount of money to play with. So, taking a deep breath, I left the table, walked to the cashier's desk and asked for £600 worth of chips. Yet because I had no cash, used my gold Rolex watch as security, to which the manager had readily agreed.

"A half hour later and I staggered out into the street, threw up in the gutter and headed for my office in Dale Street, where a half bottle of whisky awaited me. Minutes before I fell into a drunken stupor, I remembered seeing the three kings and two aces my opponent had laid on the table. This had me wondering if I should accidently step out in front of a passing bus and end it all. At least Linda and the children would be able to claim on my insurance policy.

"Come the next morning, I was still fast asleep at my desk, when a tall blonde-haired man entered the office looking to speak with a certain RHJ. When I mumbled that they were my initials, he took a seat opposite, laid my Rolex watch on the desk and said. 'I think this is yours.' What came next was simply amazing. He said his name was Maxi Hamilton and had recently heard of my misfortunes. But he wasn't there to give advice, or free handouts.

"He was looking for someone with the know-how and skill to help him create a new company. It was also important this new entity be legitimate, and completely above board. He'd then casually inquired if I knew anything about offshore banking. When I said 'yes, of course,' he'd smiled and said. 'Excellent! I don't mind paying my share of taxes, just as long as I'm not being ripped off.' It was at this our first meeting that he'd talked about moving to Spain and developing some property. Yet during all our discussions, I don't ever recall a fee or wage of any kind being mentioned. But such trivialities didn't matter. In the end, it was your grandfather's ability to spot the perfect business opportunity and my skill as his financial advisor, which helped create a global empire that spans the world. And now, it's yours."

"Mine?"

"Yes Kristian, SEL belongs to you."

"How?"

"From the day you were born, your grandfather had always hoped that either you or Kelly would succeed him at SEL. Then soon realised your sister was never meant to spend her life behind a desk. Maxi compared it to putting a beautiful songbird in a gilded cage. So we then focused our attention on you, seeing as you were next in line."

"Did I pass the interview?"

"With flying colours! In fact your grandfather was so impressed with your attitude, he flew us all down to Monaco for a celebratory dinner with BB Benson."

"I really miss them both," he whispered.

Clinton nodded. "I know son, we all do. But now it's time for you to stand tall and make a decision; yes or no."

"I don't know much about business, Sir."

"I'm aware of that, Kristian, but in the bigger picture that's the least of our worries."

"What happens if I agree?"

"It means you can stop saying 'Sir' and call me Hawkeye, like all my friends do."

"And then?"

"We kit you out in a wardrobe of new clothes."

"What kind of clothes?"

Hawkeye smiled. "Your grandfather was confident enough to make you his sole heir and with luck, my new personal assistant. So I think he would fully expect you to dress like one."

"Savile Row?"

Hawkeye smiled. "If that's what you prefer."

Kristian grinned. "I think John Lewis will do for now."

"Excellent choice, but before you re-join your mother, can I make a couple of suggestions?"

An expectant silence awaited Kristian as he returned to the Range Rover.

"Everything Okay?" asked an anxious Clinton.

"Yes, I think so."

"What about Hawkeye? Did he explain the situation so as you could understand it all?"

"Oh yes, he went through everything in great detail."

"And have you made a decision?"

"Yep."

"And?"

"I've agreed to join SEL."

"Fantastic!" declared Clinton, his hands clapping together like a circus Seal.

"Welcome aboard skipper," added a delighted Michaela.

"This is unbelievable," whispered Steffi."

"No my dear," smiled Clinton. "This is what your father had always hoped for."

"So what happens now?"

"That is for our new CEO to decide."

Kristian was thoughtful for a second. "Can I make a suggestion Clinton?"

"Yes, of course."

"I would imagine Waytree Crescent is in a real mess at the moment, and my mother's never been to El Rondo Penthouse. So can we go there please?"

"Yes Sir!"

Obituary
Liverpool Echo Ten Days Later

The funeral of the 'Right Honourable Hughie McClellan', took place yesterday in the splendour of the Anglican Cathedral. In a well-attended service, hundreds of friends and admirers were gathered to say a last farewell, to the ex-Commander, who many still regard as one of Liverpool's finest. Those with long memories will recall Hughie arriving from over the border forty years ago, with the intention of 'cleaning up the city' as he used to say, and he took no prisoners in his war against crime.

    His family however, will remember him as being a jovial and humble person, who was always willing to help others. His decision to retire from the police force and become an MP in the early nineties was regarded as a huge blow at the time. And yet despite his age, Hughie was still prepared to heed the call and give his fellow officers the benefit of his experience. Sadly, it was whilst advising them on a dangerous surveillance operation he was caught in the crossfire and later succumbed to his wounds. Our sincere condolences go out to his wife, Cressida and family, in their time of need. All were agreed, that the most poignant moment came when with a rousing choir leading the way, the congregation stood and sang 'Flower of Scotland', Hughie's favourite song.

The Grosvenor Bar
Two Days Later

Hooky Wilson shuffled towards the booth carrying two drinks. "Here you go, gentlemen, a pint of lager for the Sergeant and a Lime and Soda for the DCI. Who I must admit is looking better by the day."

Carson took a sip of his drink and spluttered. "Cuffin' hell Hooky, I can't believe you actually charge for this rhubarb!"

"They do say it's good for cleaning your kidneys, Guv."

"I don't care what they say, Jacko, I'd rather have a bit of pain than drink this stuff."

"Talking of pains, gentlemen. I read about Tufty McClellan's funeral this morning, seems they gave him real good send-off."

Carson nodded. "The only thing missing was a twenty-one gun salute and a lowering of the Scottish flag."

Hooky grinned. "According to the obituary, he was supposed to be a jovial and humble sort of chap, but I don't ever remember him being like that. Do you?"

"Maybe he had a twin brother, who told jokes for a living."

"Well if he did Jacko, he didn't tell them in here."

The two Detectives waited for Hooky to disappear behind the bar, before continuing with their conversation. "So what do you think Jacko, can we close the file on the 'Park Murders'?"

"Yeah, I think so Guv. With Tomovic dead and everyone satisfied with the result, I'd say we can class it as done and dusted."

"What about you? Any sleepless nights?"

"No, not really."

"Happy with the two youngsters walking free?"

Jacko nodded. "Absolutely. I'd have been upset to see them go to prison."

"I agree. It makes my blood run cold every time I think of all those girls Ziggy murdered."

"Well thankfully he's gone and won't be doing it anymore."

Carson sipped his drink and nodded. "Heard from Bastion lately?"

"Not a dickybird."

"Devious so-and-so. Who'd have thought he'd been investigating McClellan right under our noses?"

"He did apologise in the end Guv."

"Bit late for that Jacko, especially as Tufty was already dead."

"I must admit I was absolutely gobsmacked when he told me about the secret off-shore account in Jersey."

"And I find it hard to believe that after all this time, he really was involved with Maxi Hamilton."

"When you think about it, Guv, it must have taken some bottle for him to sit in the car and wait for Ziggy to shoot him dead."

"True, although you have to remember that Hughie was old school and if necessary, would do anything to save his reputation."

"Even go as far as committing hari-kari?"

"Yes Jacko, even suicide. But he was no fool and knew what might lie ahead if he went jail. So in the end thought it best to fall on his sword."

"Or one of Ziggy's bullets in the head?"

"No matter which way he went, dying on duty has more or less guaranteed his reputation and we can all breathe a sigh of relief."

"His wife didn't look too troubled either Guv. In fact there was one time when I saw her laughing with some friends at the funeral."

"I wouldn't worry about Cressida. She'll have inherited all his money, plus a fat pension to go with it."

"They say everything comes to those who wait Guv."

"They do indeed, Jacko."

"So are you agreed that we've finally put this case to bed?"

"Yes Jacko, I think we've definitely 'squared the circle'."

"I haven't heard that before Guv, what does it mean?"

Carson smiled. "Basically, it means doing the impossible."

Jacko was still waiting for more.

Carson sipped on his soft drink and tried to explain. "For hundreds of years, geometers and mathematicians have theorised whether it was possible to create a square, by using the same area as a circle. Which I might add was no easy thing at the time. But my old man, who'd worked all his life as a Building Inspector, would come home from some site meeting, shake his head and mutter, 'I reckon they'll need to square the circle before that will work.' And it was only years later did I ask him what it meant."

"Sounds to me as if they're trying to put a square peg into a round hole, Guv."

Carson nodded. "Nice one, Jacko, I never thought of it like that."

Sharecropper Heights
Three Weeks Later

Steffi parked in the shadow of the high-rise known as Sharecropper Heights. She was still wondering what to do next, when a tap on the glass made her jump. Standing beside the Range Rover was a young black kid, whose rotating finger suggested she lower the window.

"You Mrs Freeland?" he asked.

"Yes, that's me," she replied nervously.

The boy suddenly became officious. "Leave your car here, lady, but remember to lock all the doors and windows."

"Will it be safe?"

The boy nodded once and pointed over her shoulder. Another four boys had magically appeared from nowhere and took up station around the car. "Don't worry, they're here to guarantee nobody goes near it."

She was still unsure of her next move, until the boy motioned skywards and said, "Someone's waiting to meet you up there."

Steffi followed his finger and saw Sarah waving a hand on the 10th floor high above them. "Through the doors," he instructed, his hand pointing toward the tower block entrance. In the foyer, another boy was using an arm to hold the lift doors open and a finger poised to press the button. "This way, lady."

The lift reeked of dried urine and stale disinfectant, the journey taking less than a minute to complete. Yet still gave her time to remember why she was here. To everyone's relief, the Coroner had at last agreed to release the bodies of Kelly and Moses for burial. Desperate to get away from the public glare, Steffi had decided on a private ceremony for her own daughter.

Whereas Estelle, who was of a more passionate and religious nature, had chosen to let her friends and relations say their last farewells in a church service. Having gone through the same heart-breaking grief, Steffi thought it only right she should attend the ceremony and pass on her own heartfelt sympathies. However, and due to the throng of people hoping to do the same, suddenly found she was being pushed further to the rear. Then heard a familiar voice from the side. "Mrs Freeland?"

Steffi turned to see a young black girl wearing a dark grey hat and veil. "Yes."

"Do you remember me? I was at the Inquest."

Steffi took her hand. "Oh yes, of course, I do. You're Sarah Sweetman, Moses' older sister."

The girl nodded and smiled. "That's right, but I didn't expect to see you here today."

Steffi pointed to the crowds. "I was hoping to speak with your mother and tell her how sorry I am."

A tear formed in Sarah's eye. "Oh, thank you Mrs Freeland. I can't tell you how much that will mean to her." She was about to continue the conversation, when a loud voice began calling her name. "I'm so sorry, but I have to go. The cars are waiting to take us to the cemetery." She then paused for a second and said, "Do you have a pen I could use?"

"Yes," replied Steffi, rummaging through her bag.

Sarah took an 'Order of Service' sheet from her pocket, and began scribbling on the back. "This is the number for my mobile phone, give me a call and maybe we can organise a get-together."

Both funerals had taken place weeks ago, but at the moment Steffi was rumbling upwards in a disinfected lift, wondering if it had been worth the trouble. Thankfully, the friendly face waiting to greet her was enough to banish all such fears.

"Hi Mrs Freeland," smiled the girl.

"Hello Sarah, how are you?"

"I'm good and so glad to see you made it."

"Is your Momma okay?"

"Yes, she's just fine and waiting for you inside."

Steffi followed Sarah along the hallway, but could only stop and stare through an open door, where a young black boy, clad only in a pair of red skimpy briefs was admiring himself in a full-length mirror. "You'll have to ignore my brother, Mrs Freeland, he's just discovered girls."

Steffi smiled, remembering Kristian's own first nervous foray into the world of the opposite sex. "He'll be okay once he's had a kiss and cuddle."

Sarah grinned. "Benny's gone way beyond that, Mrs Freeland, and one whiff of his new deodorant would knock any girlfriend out cold!"

A fit of the giggles consumed them both, as they left the hallway and entered the kitchen. Unsure of what may lie ahead, Steffi was surprised to find a plastic table and four chairs sat in the middle of the room. Another was the sight of Estelle peeling potatoes at the sink, whilst humming along to a Reggae tune playing on the radio.

"Hi Momma," called Sarah. "Look who's come to visit?'

The half peeled 'King Edward' hit the water with a splash, as an excited Estelle began wiping her hands on her apron. "Well now, what we got here," she cried in delight. "And doesn't she look super-dooper?"

Steffi was wondering what the fuss was all about, until Sarah added, "We just love those smart clothes you're wearing, Mrs Freeland."

It was only then did Steffi remember just how much her life had changed in the past few months. Due to the generosity of Kristian, she'd been transformed from an everyday hard working nurse, into one of the richest women in the world. But in retrospect, it'd taken the devastating death of her daughter Kelly to achieve it. A still excited Estelle interrupted her thoughts by ushering her to the table.

"Have a seat, honey, and I'll make us a nice cup of tea."

This gave Steffi the opportunity to take a closer look at her surroundings and what a surprise. If being the mother of a major drug dealer meant Estelle having lots of money, it was in no way reflected in this sparsely furnished room. From what she could see, the only piece of decoration was a faded poster of Jamaica that was beginning to curl where it hung on the wall. Another was the portable TV sat on the worktop that had no sound, just picture only. A smiling Estelle returned with the two cups and took a seat opposite.

"How's you doin' Honey?"

Steffi sighed. "I have riches beyond my wildest dreams and yet I'd give it all away if I could only turn the clock back six months."

"Ain't dat the truth," whispered Estelle. "Every time I hear a noise in the hallway, I'm expecting a grinnin young Moses to cum walkin' thru the door."

"Well Benny looks to have changed his ways."

"Maybe honey, but I reckon it's only since he's heard how Eazy and Elijah got themselves shot dead in the warehouse. Made him tink about stayin' alive a bit longer and help keep those shiny front teeth of his all in one place."

"I read in the news about Noah being arrested. Is he still in police custody?"

"Yup," nodded Estelle.

"Was it drugs related?"

Estelle held her gaze before answering. "Sure was Honey. Damn fool boy got caught with a whole load of that Heroin shit. Appears he was just about to load it into the lock-up he uses, when some law-abiding citizen has rung the police and told them all about it."

Looking across the table Steffi was in no doubt *whom* that person might be, but desperate to ask another question. "If convicted, how long will he get?"

"Hopefully seven years, but with time off for good behaviour? Probably five."

"Will he come back here?"

Estelle's brow furrowed. "You mean Sharecropper Heights?"

Steffi nodded.

"No way. I heard a rumour he's already lookin' to take over Papa Eazy's operation in the south of the City, which I imagin will still be waitin for him when he's done his time in prison."

"Are you glad he's gone?"

"Oh yes Honey, him and Eazy both. But especially Elijah Stoker. I pray the good Lord is making that evil son of a bitch pay for his sins!"

"What about you? Will you be alright?"

Estelle smiled and reached for Steffi's hand. "Now don't you go worrying yourself about me Honey. I'll be just fine."

"What about money?"

"What about it?"

"I could help…. if you needed me too."

Estelle began to chuckle out loud. "Well now, ain't you the good-natured one?"

She then rose from the table, moved to the kitchen sink and beckoned for Steffi to join her. "I never did ask for much in this life honey, but ain't that view just somethin' to die for?"

One Month Later
Liverpool John Lennon Airport

"How long before they call the flight, Professor?"

"We have another thirty minutes."

"Excellent," smiled Jacko. "Time enough for us to squeeze in a quick coffee."

"I'll have my usual frothy cappuccino without chocolate please."

Jacko returned with the two drinks and found Simone chatting animatedly on her mobile phone.

"Who is it?" he mouthed across the table.

"Zelda," she replied. "Who sends her love."

Jacko gave a thumbs-up and grinned like a Cheshire cat. He liked *The Bird from Bosnia,* she was definitely one of his favourite people. In between loud gasps of *Oh no…* their two-way conversation was interspersed with the odd giggle and plenty of gobbledygook he would never understand.

"How is she?" he asked, when they'd eventually finished saying their goodbyes.

"Pregnant," smiled Simone.

"No way!" laughed Jacko.

"Hm, hm," she nodded. "Did the test yesterday and found it was positive."

"Wow, was it intended?"

Simone nodded again. "Yes, I think so."

"Who's the hubby again?"

"A Bosnian politician named Linus Samarova."

"Ah yes, I remember him. Isn't he the one going for the Presidency?"

"That's him and Zelda reckons he's got a good chance of winning the election."

"Exciting times," said Jacko. "Although when you're married to a dish like Zelda, I'm not sure whether to be green with envy, or worried for his long-term sanity."

"He'll be okay, Sam. From what I've heard, Linus is pretty strong willed and has plenty of savvy to go with it."

Jacko was still thinking about her reply when she asked him a question. "How's Nathan doing?"

"Fantastic. When I spoke to him last night, he said he was having the time of his life down in sunny Devon."

"Oh that's great news. And his daughter is happy to have him stay there?"

"Oh yes. Karen says that now he's taken early retirement, he's welcome to stay as long as he likes. They live in this big old ramshackle house and Nathan has his own place on the side. But what he loves more than anything is playing with his two grandchildren Wade and Chloe."

Simone grinned. "I'd always suspected he was a big softy at heart, yet never imagined him as being the doting grandfather."

"They do say stranger things happen at sea."

Simone smiled. "Maybe, but what about you Sam, are you ready to do the Inspectors Examination?"

Jacko thought for a second and then nodded. "Yes I think so, especially as Bastion has fast-tracked it to take place next month."

"Confident?"

"As much as I can be. According to my mentor *Fred Astaire,* I should pass it with my eyes closed."

"And I agree Sam, no-one could have asked for a better teacher than Nathan Carson."

Jacko smiled. "They say great minds think alike and Bastion has been telling me the same thing for weeks."

She was about to agree with him, when her phone gave a loud ping. "Yikes, the plane's started boarding already, better get a move on."

Jacko instinctively reached for the walk-on suitcase and then heard Simone say, "No Sam. Remember our agreement? We part here."

It was only then did he notice how she'd moved in front of him and was blocking the way to the escalator and ultimately the Departures Lounge on the second floor.

Jacko shrugged. "Yeah, but that *was* last week Professor."

"It doesn't matter when it was Sam and this would be hard enough under any circumstances. But I don't intend to leave here with soggy wet mascara running down my cheeks."

Jacko could see the determination written on her face. "Okay Professor, but do I at least get a hug?"

Simone fell into his arms and they kissed long and hard, neither of them sure of when they might meet again.

"I think two weeks' notice is definitely pushing it," he whispered in her ear.

"I know Sam, but it was always coming."

"I hate cuffin' Americans."

"No, you don't."

"Okay. I don't exactly hate them, but I wish you weren't going to live with them."

"It's only for two years."

"That's a whole lifetime to some people."

"But you're not anyone Sam and it'll pass by sooner than you think."

"Can I come and visit?"

Simone took her walk-on case from his hand, kissed him on the lips and whispered in his ear. "Anytime you like."

As the crowds at the check-in parted momentarily, Jacko could only watch as the tall graceful shape of Simone le Roux walked out of his life. Moving to better position, he was still watching her every move, as she strolled towards the escalator pulling her case behind. For a moment his heart leapt, as she paused and began searching for something in her bag. Yet the minor halt was only to give the 'Cudecar Cancer' lady a small donation towards the cause. He was also wondering whether to call out and stop her before she reached the point of no return, but something inside said no. At the last second, Simone turned, smiled that smile, blew him a kiss and was gone.

Eighteen Months later
Marbella, Spain

The two limousines made their way along what was once a dusty dirt track. But with the help of a layer of tarmac and a row of palm trees, had since been transformed into a modern driveway. "I can remember a time when this road was so bumpy, it was near impossible for me to ride my tricycle," smiled Steffi.

Kristian watched the fronds gently swaying in the breeze. "It looks as if grandad has made lots of changes since then."

"Yes, but not there," said Steffi, her finger pointing straight ahead.

From the comfort of the air-conditioned Mercedes, neither of them had noticed the car beginning to slow, until they'd entered the blossomed filled courtyard of Finca Bougainvillea. First from the car was Pepe the driver, who opened the rear passenger door and helped her out. "Gracias," said Steffi, as she stepped into the warm Spanish sunshine, and even though she was wearing sunglasses, needed to shade her eyes from the glare. Unlike her visit to the fabulous El Rondo penthouse in Liverpool, this was the one journey she'd been dreading the most. It had taken many months of deliberation, but in the end she had to admit that her life had changed forever and there was no going back. "I can't believe that after all these years, it would still be so beautiful," she whispered.

Kristian, who was admiring the multi-coloured display, gestured towards the Main entrance and smiled. "Look Ma, I think someone is waiting to greet you."

It was only then did she notice one of the huge wooden doors was half open and see the slim figure standing in the shadows.

"Go and say hello," he whispered.

At first Steffi was hesitant, until Kristian gave the gentlest of nudges and said, "It's okay Ma, she won't bite."

From where she stood, the lady appeared to be middle-aged, wore a white silk blouse, dark skirt and had classical greying, bouffant styled hair.

Moving closer, she was still unsure of who it might be and then heard a voice from the past.

"*Hola princesa, bienveneda de la Casa.* Hello princess welcome home."

"Carlota?" gasped Steffi.

The lady held out her arms. "Si," she replied. "It is me Carlota del Reye, and I am so happy to see you again."

Steffi let out a cry of joy and fell into the embrace of the lady from so long ago. This was the same lady, whom when she was child, had shared many a wonderful night on the terrace with her mother and father.

Carlotta gently took Steffi's face in her hands. "You look so much like your mother, it is almost uncanny."

"I had no idea this was about to happen," she said in wide-eyed amazement.

Carlota looked across at Kristian. "You have your son to thank for this, he is so much older than his years."

Steffi shook her fist at the smirking faces of Hawkeye, Michaela, and Clinton, who all knew about the surprise meeting. "I'm not finished with you lot yet," she threatened in mock anger.

"*Venga.* Come," said Carlota. "There is much we have to see."

To her delight, Steffi discovered that nothing had changed. The large open lounge, with its high wooden beams and whitewashed walls were as before. The dark oak doors and polished staircase had suffered little over the years and as on the first day, Carlota had lit a fire in the fireplace. Yet, what still took pride of place was her mother's beautiful antique four-piece leather suite. Steffi closed her eyes and ran a fingertip over the soft luxurious texture of the settee. "I used to sit here as a child and colour in my books. And after all these years, I can still hear my mother warning me not to get any paint or crayon on it."

"Si, Señora Sandra was very passionate about Casa Bougainvillea and would do anything to keep it that way."

"I know Carlota and I intend to be just like her."

"Perfecto Señora Steffi," she said with a smile, then pointed to the staircase. "If you would like to come this way, por favour?"

At first Steffi was a little hesitant then saw the door to her bedroom above was open.

"It's okay," smiled Kristian. "I'm coming too."

The familiar sound of her son's voice and the firm feel of his hand were enough to embolden Steffi as they followed Carlota up the stairs. As before, nothing had changed. The bedroom windows were open wide and the sweet smell of wild flowers filled the air. "Oh, look at this," whispered Steffi. "I feel as though I've been transported back in time," as she wandered around the room, touching and looking at things that brought back so many memories. Her favourite hairbrush lying on the dressing table, the pure white sheets on her comfortable big girl's bed and the gossamer like mosquito net enclosing it. Next was the tall delicately carved oak wardrobe that took up most of one wall. "Now this," she smiled. "Used to frighten the life out me at first, when I was a child, but I soon came to love it."

"Why don't you look inside, Señora Steffi?"

A puzzled look appeared on her face. "Is there something I should see?"

"There's only one way to find out, Ma."

"Okay," laughed Steffi, "I don't mind playing games." Yet when she opened the door, saw nothing other than a black silk dress hanging on the rail.

"Oh gosh," she said in amazement. "I can remember my mother wearing this on special occasions."

"That is correct, Señora."

"Then why is it here?"

"Because your father left it for you."

"Me, why?"

"He'd always hoped that one day you would return to Finca Bougainvillea and wear the dress, just like your mother all those years ago."

"Did he tell you that?"

"Si Señora."

"When?"

"Just before he died."

With tears forming in her eyes, Steffi reached for the dress and held it against her face. "It's been more than thirty years and yet I can still smell her perfume." She was about to hold it in front of the mirror when something made her stop. "Can you give me a minute please?"

"What's wrong Ma?"

"I'm not sure, but I hope it's not what I think it is."

Kristian and Carlota could only watch as Steffi went to the bed and parted the mosquito net. "Oh no…" she cried, the tears beginning to fall down her cheeks.

"Ma, are you okay?" asked Kristian.

Steffi however, wasn't listening; she was staring at the tattered woollen object lying on the pillow.

"Do you know what it is Carlota?" whispered Kristian.

"Si Señor, it's your mother's favourite doll *Emilia*, and the last time she saw it, was the morning your Aunt Charlotte spirited her away."

The sight of the black cocktail dress and her long-lost doll was all too much for Steffi, who sat on the bed and began to sob uncontrollably. A mystified Kristian was ready to see if he could help, when Carlota's voice held him back. "No Señor. I think it best we leave her for now. She has lots to think about and much to cry over. But hopefully she will sleep and all will be well."

Yet Steffi hadn't slept; she'd cried the bitter tears of a life lost and what might have been. She could clearly remember the days of uncertainty, a time when she'd been unable to speak to her mother on the phone. The fateful morning her Aunty Charlotte had rushed into the room, said they must leave immediately and begun to pack a small suitcase. (In the mad dash, Steffi had completely forgotten to take *Emilia* with her.)

"Where are we going?" she'd asked.

"Liverpool."

"Why?"

"Because your mother's dead."

Steffi could remember bursting into tears when she heard these devastating words. "How did she die?" she sobbed.

"Your father killed her."

This had made her cry even more. "But why would he kill her?"

Such an awkward question had completely thrown Aunt Charlotte, who hastily replied. "Your father didn't exactly kill your mother, but he's still a bad man who sells drugs and took her to a dangerous place, where another drug dealer shot her dead." She'd then warned that if she stayed in Spain, she too would become a drug addict. To the traumatised ears of a frantic seven year old, this had been a devastating piece of news, but at the time very believable. So much so, she'd willingly sacrificed her life in sunny Marbella, for a new and supposedly safer one in Liverpool.

However, Aunty Charlotte wasn't quite finished in spinning her web of deceit. Especially when she'd say her father was an evil devil who should be in jail. In the years that followed, she would become panic stricken, when her Aunty said they would be meeting him and the doctors at the Psychiatric Clinic. Yet in the same breath whisper that everything would be okay if she acted dumb and so it had proved to be.

Luckily, Kristian had warned her long ago that Charlotte's stories were just a sordid mixture of half-truths and lies. All perpetrated by a twisted vindictive woman, who'd had a long-standing hatred of her father. And what of him? In truth he'd been a loving family man, who'd been devastated at the death of his wife and the rejection of his only daughter. He'd lost his own life in trying to bring Ziggy Tomovic to justice and in one last wonderful gesture, entrusted his fortune to Kristian. Steffi sat on the side of the bed and let her tears dry, but knew what she must do next.

Clinton and Hawkeye were having a quiet conversation with one another, when they saw Carlota bless herself three times and whisper, "Madre de Dios, Senora Sandra…?"

Looking up, they saw a beautiful blonde apparition dressed in a simple, yet classic black dress standing alone at the top of the stairs.

Kristian was first to move and took the stairs two at a time. Once there, he held out a hand, bowed formerly and said, "*Encantado de conocerte Señora.* I'm so pleased to meet you, madam."

"Spanish lessons?" asked a surprised Steffi.

"Si, with lots of help from Carlota," grinned Kristian.

Steffi was amazed at her son's formal use of the Spanish language. "*El placer es todo mio Señor.* The pleasure is all mine, Sir," she half stuttered in reply.

To laughter and loud applause from those below, the two of them descended the stairs holding hands, as if they were part of some regal ostentatious ball.

"Wonderful," cried Clinton Levi.

"Beautiful," mumbled an equally awestruck Hawkeye Jones, who was never normally lost for words. "If I didn't know it was you, Steffi, I swear it was your mother come back to life."

"I agree Señor, the resemblance is incredible," added Carlota.

"If your father were here today Steffi, he would have been overjoyed to see you wearing this dress," enthused Michaela.

"Stupendous, stupendous," chortled Clinton, who was close to tears.

Kristian held his hands up. "Okay everyone and although we appreciate your enthusiasm, it's time for us to move on." With the small entourage following behind, a smiling Carlota opened the doors to the terrace.

"Mmm…" sighed Michaela, as the heat flooded in and a warm breeze caressed her face. "That definitely feels like Spain!"

"Oh yes, doesn't it just," agreed Hawkeye. "I once read that the sun and olive oil can help you live to a ripe old age."

"I'll definitely have some of that," grunted Clinton, even though he would never contemplate taking off his clothes and sunbathing.

Steffi however, was only interested in what lay ahead. Beyond was the huge wooden dining table, where in the past she'd enjoyed so many delicious meals. Then came the padded wicker sunbeds, where she and her father had spent so many hours gazing out to sea, or searching the night sky for shooting stars. But, of course, nothing could beat *Miguel Delgado's* superb swimming pool, whose sparkling waters forever glistened like diamonds in the afternoon sun. Steffi scooped up a handful of the cool liquid and slowly let it trickle through her fingers. "I can't remember how many hours I spent splashing about in here, but they were probably the best years of my life."

"Si, Señora Steffi. I have many fond memories of you and the Van Arnson family swimming here."

"Gosh, I wonder where they are now, Carlota?"

"I met Kliff and Brigitte not so long ago in Marbella, they said their son Roland is now a well-respected lawyer."

"Oh wow, I can remember being madly in love with him when I was young!"

"Then perhaps you should meet him sometime Señora Steffi. I'm told he is still very handsome and recently divorced."

"Are you trying to play matchmaker, Carlota?"

A puzzled look came over her face. "What is this 'matchmaker', Señora Steffi?"

"You know exactly what I mean," she grinned.

The two of them were still enjoying a private giggle, when Clinton's stentorian voice came booming out from the other side of the pool. "Hey you two ladies; come and have a look at this fine *object d'art*."

Curious as to what was so interesting, Steffi and Carlota crossed the terrace to where the small group had gathered. "Okay gentlemen, what's so important?" she asked. A smiling Hawkeye stepped to one side so she could see. Steffi's hand instantly flew to her mouth in amazement. "Oh my god, I know what this is, it's Paco's outdoor barbeque."

"Si Señora," smiled Carlota. "And as we all know, it was his great pride and joy."

"It looks to be in perfect working order," added Steffi.

"That's because when Paco died, your father insisted it should be kept clean and never left to deteriorate, or gather rust."

"I can still remember the day he went to the market to buy a fish and came back with Moby Dick strapped to his back!"

"Si Señora Steffi," laughed Carlota. "But can you remember the suckling pig?"

"How could I forget? The smell and taste were absolutely fantastic."

"Paco could create many tasty things on his simple barbeque."

"Is it true he died Carlota?"

"Si Señora Steffi. He passed away more than ten years ago."

"So where is he now?"

The elegantly dressed Spanish lady pointed a finger. "If you will be so good as to come this way por favor."

Steffi was first to follow, the rest keeping in step as Carlota led them back towards the house. They'd gone no more than five paces, when she slowed and pointed to a gap between the trees that lined the terrace. "Through here please," she smiled.

I know this, thought Steffi. *It's the pathway leading to the stone cottage.* But to her surprise, found the winding dirt track of her infancy, had since been paved over and planted with flowers on either side.

Well, well," she thought. *It would appear some things never change, whilst others do.* Yet when she turned the first corner, became wide-eyed with astonishment. "Oh my goodness," she gasped. "This is just unbelievable."

Where there'd once been a thicket of twisted vines and deep under growth, was now a carefully cultivated semi-circular garden. It measured approximately twenty metres in length, the depth reaching ten metres into the bush. But what really stunned Steffi, were the four immaculately kept, flower-bedecked graves. Kristian had said her mother was buried here, but she'd never expected anything like this.

Carlota stopped at the nearest grave and smiled. "I think this is who you might be looking for Señora."

Steffi stared down at the simple polished marble headstone that represented one of the graves. "Hernandez?" she asked.

"Si Señora, that was Paco's surname, although not many people know this."

"Neither did I. But I do recognise the hat. He used to wear one like it all the time."

"Fabulous piece of carving," commented Hawkeye, as he and the others admired a near perfect replica of the 'Captain's Cap' some local artisan had created from a single piece of stone. "The only thing missing," smiled Steffi, "is a carving of his smelly cigar. Paco didn't smoke it, he just loved to chew it throughout the day."

If the gardener's grave was impressive in its simplicity, then the one ten feet away was truly breath taking. In a circular bed of roses stood a tall decorative column, with a huge winged angel atop and was no ordinary statue. This masterpiece had been carved in pure white marble and was so beautiful the great Leonardo de Vinci himself might have sculpted it. The wings alone measured 6 feet from tip to tip, their width and size casting shadows over the angel kneeling beneath them. However, it was the pleading eyes and beautifully sculpted arm pointing downwards that really took one's breath away. "Here, Señora Steffi, is your mother's last resting place," said Carlota.

Awestruck and with tears filling her eyes, Steffi could only stare at the words carved in the column below:

Here lies my darling wife Sandra, who was my love, my life and my soul. And I know that someday soon we shall meet again in the distant depths of eternity. Forever yours Maxi.

Beneath the carved inscription were her name, date of birth, and when she died. *Sandra Hamilton, 1947-1982*

"It looks like her Guardian Angel," she said in wonder.

"This was how your father wanted it to be Senora. He designed the statue himself and had it specially commissioned by a famous French sculptor."

"It's just so beautiful."

"Magnificent," agreed Clinton Levi.

"I think that every time I come here," smiled Hawkeye.

Through her tears, Steffi noticed one other small detail. "Look," she whispered. "There's a photograph." Covered with glass and expertly recessed in the stone pedestal, was the picture of a blonde smiling woman in a black dress.

"You and your mother are so alike, you could be looking into the mirror Senora Steffi."

"Remarkable," agreed Hawkeye.

"Could be two peas in a pod," declared Clinton.

Kristian placed an arm around his mother's trembling shoulders. "I would have loved to have met her."

Steffi closed her eyes and nodded. "She was so wonderful and I can't believe I was fooled for all these years."

Kristian gently squeezed her shoulder. "It's not your fault, you didn't know any different. Kelly and I had always thought Charlotte was our real grandmother."

"Was it jealousy, or hate that made her do it?"

Kristian shook his head. "I don't know, maybe a bit of both. But it's just water under the bridge and time for us to move on."

Steffi gave a sad smile and allowed him to lead her to the next grave where a different kind of surprise awaited her. If Sandra's memorial was intended to be the last word in ostentation, this was of much poorer fare, yet at the same, very familiar to those who knew Maxi. "I know what this is," smiled Steffi.

"I thought you might," laughed Kristian.

In the middle of a two-tiered platform, stood an 8 ft tall pillar made of black polished marble, but its crowning glory was the huge circle sat on top.

"It's the SEL building and the disc has to be the El Rondo penthouse."

"Got it first time Ma."

"But why this of all things?" she asked, her hand pointing to the imposing edifice.

Kristian nodded to Clinton and Hawkeye who were listening to the conversation. "We'd been racking our brains for months on what to do for the best; do we build another 'Arc de Triomphe,' or maybe the 'Hanging Gardens of Babylon'? Nobody could really say, and then Michaela suggested we have this made, seeing it sort of represents all of his achievements."

Steffi read the words carved in the column. *Maxi Hamilton, devoted husband of Sandra, and loving father of Steffi, his only daughter.*

"Simple, but in truth says everything," grunted Clinton.

"Tells the story of his life," chuckled Hawkeye.

"I think grandad would have loved it," smiled Kristian.

They were still gathered around and admiring the tall edifice, when a strange wailing sound came from behind.

"What's this?" asked Clinton, who turned to look.

"A most special and surprise visitor Señor," said Carlota.

Everyone was wondering who it might be. When a nurse in a white uniform appeared on the path pushing an old wheelchair.

"Someone has come to pay their respects Señora Steffi."

"Who is it?" she asked, then saw whoever was sat in the wheelchair had hair as white as the nurses uniform and wore a dress as black as the tall marble column.

"Magdalena?" she gasped.

"Si Señora," whispered Carlota. "The lady who loved you as though you were her own has come to say hello."

Steffi shook her head in confusion. "With Paco being dead, I assumed she'd died too."

"Not yet Señora, although she is nearly ninety-four years old."

"Where does she live?"

"When Paco passed away, your father insisted on moving her out of the cottage and into a private nursing home, where she now spends her days."

"She knows you're here Ma and is desperate to see you."

"Although it is important she doesn't get too excited Señorita Steffi, her heart is not as strong as it was and her sight is beginning to fail."

Yet nobody had told Magdalena, who as she came closer, held her hands out as though in prayer and began to wail like a banshee.

"What's wrong?" asked a startled Steffi.

A concerned Carlota went to speak with the disturbed old lady. A few moments of urgent whispering passed back and forth, before she turned, smiled and indicated for Steffi to step forward.

"What's wrong; is there a problem?"

"No Señorita, everything is fine. Magdalena thinks you are your mother."

Steffi was open mouthed in amazement. "Why…?"

"The dress, Señorita, and because you look so much like her. She thinks the Angel has spoken and you've somehow returned from the grave."

"But what shall I do now?"

"Speak to her."

Steffi was stunned. "Does she speak any English?"

"No, only Española."

"Then how do we communicate?"

"There was a time, Señorita Steffi, when you could always make yourself understood."

"But I was only a child then," she groaned.

"I know, but perhaps when Magdalena hears your voice, she will recognise it and realise who you are."

Steffi turned to Kristian, who shrugged and said, "Just go for it,"

"I'm not sure how," she whispered.

"You will only know if you try, Señora Steffi."

Throughout this terse sounding exchange, Magdalena had watched and listened in frightened silence, her eyes flicking between them as if trying to comprehend what was being said. Then Steffi knelt beside the wheelchair and whispered, "Hola Magdalena, recuerdas a tu princesa bombonita?" *Hello Magdalena, do you remember your princess bombonita?*

The reaction was almost immediate. "Princesa, eres tu?" *Princess, is it you?*

Steffi smiled at Carlota. "I'm not sure how, but I think she understands me."

"It's your voice she recognises, Steffi, keep talking."

"Si Magdalena soy yo princesa bombonita." *Yes Magdalena, it's me princess bombonita.'*

As if relieved, the old lady began to cry and lavish kisses on Steffi's hands and face.

"Ella esta aqui, mi princesa Steffi ha vuelta a casa." *She is here, my princess Steffi has come home.*

Kristian, who was trying to keep up with what was being said, asked the obvious question. "What's going on?"

Carlota shook her head. "It's all my fault Señor and I should have remembered."

"Remembered what?"

"When your mother was a young, we all called her princess, or princesa in Spanish. But not Magdalena, she'd always preferred to call her 'princesa Steffi', or 'bombonita,' which is an affectionate way of addressing young children."

"And she recognised that?"

"Si Señor, Magdalena didn't have children of her own and therefore would never have forgotten it."

A delighted Kristian looked at his three companions and began to laugh. "How do we follow that?"

"I suggest we finish what we really came here for," said Clinton.

"Superb idea," smiled Hawkeye.

"I'm all for that." nodded Michaela.

Clinton turned to Carlota. "Is Magdalena okay now?"

"Si Señor."

"Excellent!" He then indicated to the limousine driver. "Pepe, this way please."

A now curious Steffi, watched as the driver stepped forward holding a large box in both hands.

"What's this?" she asked.

"One last surprise, my dear."

"What kind of surprise?"

Clinton nodded to Hawkeye, who lifted a gold clasp and opened the doors to a felt-lined casket. Inside was a large stone urn with two crossed golf clubs carved on the front.

"This my dear is BB Benson. "

Steffi was stunned. "Uncle BB?" she gasped.

"Yes my child, these are the remains of your favourite uncle."

"How did he get here?" she stuttered.

"I think your son can best answer that," smiled Hawkeye.

"It would appear Uncle BB had three wives, two ex and one common-law," began Kristian. "In addition, he'd sired four children, all of whom are fully grown, miss him greatly and are desperate to have his last remains. Problem is, they reside on three different continents and live thousands of miles apart. So in order to alleviate this tricky conundrum, we flew them to Acapulco for a long weekend. Then over a meal one night, we told them of the close bond between BB and grandad and suggested this might be his final resting place."

Steffi followed his hand to where an empty column stood next to Maxi's. "As you can see, we have yet to decide on the exact words."

"But how will they visit his grave?"

"Easy, we will fly them here for free, anytime they want."

They were all still discussing the problem facing them, when a frail voice came from behind. "BB Benson?" it whispered.

Steffi was first to turn and see Magdalena's outstretched hand pointing towards her. "BB Benson?" she whispered once again.

"What does she want?" asked Clinton.

"I'm not sure," she replied, then realised the old lady wasn't actually pointing at her. "It's the Urn!" she cried. "Magdalena wants to touch the Urn."

"Why?" asked Michaela.

Carlota spoke next. "Because it's BB Benson."

Michaela was still confused. "Sorry?"

"What you have to understand Señora, is that even though we all loved BB Benson, Magdalena worshipped the very ground he walked on. She'd been devastated at the news of Señor Maxi's death, but inconsolable when she heard BB had gone too. Simply because it meant he would no longer visit her at the Nursing home."

"Did he come here often?" asked Kristian.

"Si Señor, four or five times a year."

"And you think Magdalena saw the Urn and heard BB's name being mentioned?"

"Si, Senora Steffi, almost certainly."

"So what happens now?" asked Clinton.

"We let her touch it," declared Steffi.

"Why not?" said Kristian, who motioned to the driver holding the box. "Can you bring it a little closer, *por favor*?"

"Si Senor," replied Pepe. A few seconds later and he was on his haunches holding the heavy casket in front of him. He then whispered, "Mira mama, aqui esta BB Benson." *Look mama, here is BB Benson.*

Magdalena held out a shaking hand. "Mas cerca por favour." *Closer please.*

Pepe did as asked and watched her run the tip of a finger over the Urn. She then closed her eyes, kissed it once and said, "Ahora puedo morir feliz." *Now I can die happy.*

Epilogue
Latest news from T.A.B.
The Anfield Blogger

Sources at Liverpool F.C. have confirmed that Tom Hart, the talented young footballer, who many say has the mercurial speed of Michael Owen and the goal-scoring prowess of Robbie Fowler, has signed for the club. Although, it has yet to be officially announced, they're all agreed that one of the most gifted strikers in Europe will be a welcome addition to their ever-growing ranks. As stated earlier, a whole host of clubs, some as far away as Germany and Spain have reportedly been offering huge sums of money in order to secure his signature. Tommo however, who was born and bred in Liverpool, never had any doubts as to where his future lay.

A close friend of mine said we only live once and if you have a dream, then you should go out and get it. My one ambition in life was to play for Liverpool Football Club and thanks to her wise words, have now fulfilled that dream.

Wise words from one so young, **T.A.B.**